'If Hindu Raj does become a fact,

it will, no doubt, be the greatest calamity for this country. . . .

Hindu Raj must be prevented at any cost.'

Dr. B.R. Ambedkar

[*Pakistan or the Partition of India*, 1946, pp. 354-5]

The RSS

The RSS

A Menace to India

A.G. Noorani

Offset edition first published in March 2019.
Reprinted May 2019.
First paperback edition September 2019.
Digital print edition, January 2020.

LeftWord Books
2254/2A Shadi Khampur
New Ranjit Nagar
New Delhi 110008
INDIA

LeftWord Books is the publishing division of
Naya Rasta Publishers Pvt. Ltd.

leftword.com

ISBN 978-81-940778-7-9

To

Jawaharlal Nehru

Abul Kalam Azad

C. Rajagopalachari, and

M.A. Ansari

Who believed in and dedicated themselves to the India which the poet Raghupati Sahay 'Firaq' Gorakhpuri described in this immortal couplet:

Sar zamin-e-Hind par aqwam-e-aalam ke, Firaq,
Kafile aate rahe aur Hindustan banta gaya

(On the soil of Hindustan, O Firaq
Caravans from all over the world kept coming,
And so was Hindustan made)

Contents

Preface 11
Introduction 13
1. Why Was the RSS Set Up? 52
2. The RSS's 19th-century Heritage 64
3. Commitments of Indian Nationalism 73
4. Collaboration with the British 80
5. The RSS Woos Europe's Fascists 86
6. Savarkar Captures the Mahasabha 93
7. The RSS Acquires a Bible 100
8. The RSS at Independence 108
9. The RSS and Gandhi's Assassination 116
10. The Ban on the RSS 124
11. Golwalkar and Mookerjee's Pact on the Jana Sangh 131
12. Mookerjee, RSS and Jana Sangh 138
13. The RSS After Mookerjee 149
14. The RSS, the Emergency and the Janata Party 172
15. The BJP's Birth and the RSS's Problem 203
16. Power in the Name of Ram 223
17. How Modi Profited by a Pogrom 268
18. The Advani Episode 282
19. The RSS in Triumph 300
20. RSS Selects India's Prime Minister 311
21. RSS Raj Under Modi 328
22. Endgame in 2018 365
23. RSS & Violence 379
24. RSS's Progeny: ABVP, VHP & Bajrang Dal 405
25. RSS's Self-Revelation to Tax and Charity Authorities 416
Bibliography 425

CONTENTS

Appendices

Appendix 1. RSS Prayer and Oath 430

Appendix 2. Constitution of the RSS 431

Appendix 3. RSS Declared Unlawful 439

Appendix 4. Golwalkar's Interaction With Home Minister Sardar Patel 440

Appendix 5. Justice On Trial 441

Appendix 6. 'Guruji-Indiraji Correspondence' 486

Appendix 7. Deoras's Correspondence during the Emergency with Indira Gandhi, S.B. Chavan and Vinoba Bhave 488

Appendix 8. In the Court of the District Judge, Nagpur 499

Appendix 9. 'Limaye for consensus on RSS, other affiliates' 513

Appendix 10. 'All responsible for Janata crisis' 515

Appendix 11. 'Modern Hate' 519

Appendix 12. 'The Sangh is my soul' 525

Appendix 13. A Four-point Appeal to Muslims of India' 528

Appendix 14. 'Nanavati or not, the state apparatus in Gujarat cannot be absolved' 530

Appendix 15. Interview with BJP leader Narendra Modi 531

Appendix 16. 'Chaining 1,200 Years' 534

Index of Names of People and Organisations 536

Preface

This book has long been in the making, but only in the author's mind. I could never sit down to write it out. The slim volume I wrote, *The RSS and the BJP: A Division of Labour*, published by LeftWord was launched by Jyoti Basu on 6 December 2000 at the Banga Bhawan in New Delhi. None knew then that on the same day, perhaps at the same time, Prime Minister Atal Bihari Vajpayee was waxing eloquent on Ayodhya in the Lok Sabha.

The book was well received. But the sub-title, I later realised, was wrong. A 'division' implies parity of status. The RSS disabused the minds of the BJP's leaders of any notion of parity. It was the Master. The BJP was its Political Department.

It is not easy to write of the RSS. As Prime Minister Jawaharlal Nehru wrote to the RSS chief, M.S. Golwalkar, on 10 November 1948:

> It would appear that the declared objectives have little to do with the real ones and with the activities carried on in various forms and ways by people associated with the RSS. These real objectives appear to be completely opposed to the decisions of the Indian Parliament and the provisions of the proposed Constitution of India. The activities, according to our information, are anti-national and often subversive and violent.

This was confirmed by the RSS's prevarications and downright falsehood, thirty years later. To evade income tax it claimed to be a charitable organisation before the Income Tax Officer. It said the opposite to the Charity Commissioner to escape registration as a charitable trust. More, it claimed a right to attribute to well-known terms meanings which it chose to assign to them, rather like Humpty Dumpty's scornful retort to Alice in *Through the Looking-Glass*: 'When I use a word, it means just what I choose it to mean – neither more nor less.' In one breath the RSS says that all Indians are Hindus, only to assert, in the next breath, that Hindus constitute the majority. Reasoned debate is impossible.

This book shows that the RSS is much more than a threat to communal amity. It poses a wider challenge. It is a threat to democratic governance and, even worse, a menace to India, the India which the nation strove to establish. It poses a threat to its values. In the last few years India has been battling for its very soul.

The debts I have incurred are many. I wish sincerely to thank Asaduddin Owaisi, M.P., for providing me, among other documents, English translations of documents in Hindi and prodding me continuously to write. In this his secretary Syed Mushtaq Ahmed was a big help; so were these friends: S. Iftikhar Gilani,

Chief of National Bureau, *DNA*, Qurban Ali, veteran journalist and a committed socialist, and Ravi Nair, Executive Director, South Asia Centre for Human Rights. Prakash Kumar Sinha worked tirelessly on my scribblings to produce a typescript. My loyal Jeeves, Javed Alam of Faizabad, proved to be indispensable – fetching books from shelves, taking manuscripts to Prakash Kumar Sinha and bringing the typescript back to me, and other chores. To all of them I am most grateful.

I advisedly mention these friends last. My friend Sudhanva Deshpande, Managing Editor, LeftWord Books. This is my fourth book he has published, taking enormous pains over the manuscript. His colleague Nazeef Mollah did the same patiently, tirelessly. LeftWord itself deserves my deep gratitude.

For flaws in argument or even of fact I bear sole responsibility.

I did no 'field work', as such. I relied on the excellent works of Christophe Jaffrelot, Pralay Kanungo, Chetan Bhatt, Shamsul Islam and some others, which is fairly acknowledged in the book with full references.

To the reader, I have but one plea in the words of Bacon in his essay *Of Studies*: 'Read not to contradict and confute; nor to believe and take for granted; nor to find talk and discourse; but to weigh and consider.'

A.G. Noorani
Mumbai, 26 January 2019

Introduction

Jab Gulistan ko lahoo ki zaroorat parhi, sub se pahle hamari hi gardan kati/ Phir bhi kahte hain hum se yeh ahle chaman, yeh chaman hai hamara, tumhara nahin.

(When the Garden needed blood, it was our necks that were first slit/ Yet the ones in the Garden tell us, this Garden is ours, not yours.)

This couplet accurately sums up Muslim sentiment in India today. Muslims suffered most in the Great Indian Mutiny in 1857. They fought the British together with their Hindu compatriots. But by the end of the 19th century cries rent the air that the Muslims were later arrivals, invaders in fact; the land belonged to Hindus and they alone will lay down the law for all its peoples to follow.

In this early part of the 21st century the cries have not subsided. They have become louder, shriller and more menacing. The forces who raise the cry not only threaten all the minorities, they deny the very concept of a minority within a State, the concept of Indian nationalism. How has this come to pass?

After the Mutiny's collapse, the last Mughal Emperor Bahadur Shah Zafar was tried for waging war against the British Crown, by a British Military Commission in the Diwan-e-Khas of the Red Fort at Delhi. The farce lasted for 21 days. For the prosecution the Judge-Advocate said:

> I, of course, allude to the cause, either remote or immediate, which gave rise to a revolt unparalleled in the annals of history, either for the savagery which has been its distinctive feature, or for the suddenness with which elements, hitherto deemed utterly discordant on the score of religion, have united themselves in a common crusade against a faith which, as regards the inhabitants of this country, whether Muhammadan or Hindu, was certainly a most unaggressive one. I fear, however, the subject is still but imperfectly elucidated; and I may perhaps be in error in attributing to a religious influence a movement which, after all, may prove to have been merely a political one – *a struggle of the natives for power and place, by the expulsion from the country of a people alien in religion, in blood, in colour, in habits, in feelings and in everything.* (Italics mine, throughout the book)

Bahadur Shah Zafar was the one around whom both communities rallied as a symbol of revolt and unity.

Insignificant and contemptible as to any outward show of power, it would appear that this possessor of mere nominal royalty has even been looked upon by Muhammadan fanaticism as the head and culminating star of its faith. In him have still been centred the hopes and aspirations of millions. They have looked up to him as the source of honour, and, more than this, he has proved the rallying point not only to Muhammadans, but to thousands of others with whom it was supposed no bond of fanatical union could possibly be established.[1]

Asoka Mehta went deeper.

When the rebellion began Hindus and Muslims participated in it in large numbers. It was not a rebellion of one community. But the Mussalmans, for historical and ideological reasons, were more violently anti-British than the Hindus. To many of them, inspired by the philosophy of Shah Waliulla, India under British rule was *Dar-ul-Harb*, and a jehad against the alien ruler was not only a national necessity but a religious duty. The British, therefore, feared the fiery and excitable Muslim more than the proverbially mild Hindu.

The hand of repression fell heavily on the Muslims – they were as it were tattooed with terror. Many of their leading men – such as the Nawabs of Jhajjar, Ballabgarh, Faruknagar and Furukabad – were hanged or exiled . . . Muslim property was widely confiscated. After the reoccupation of Delhi, Hindus were allowed to return within a few months, but the Mohammedan population was altogether excluded and the attachment on their houses was lifted only in 1859. In the Delhi Division every Muslim was mulcted of a quarter of his real property while the fine levied on the Hindus was just ten per cent.

The wrath of the rulers was mainly directed against the Muslims. 'Show these rascally Mussulmans,' wrote Capt. Roberts (the future Field-Marshal Lord Roberts), 'that with God's help, Englishmen will still be masters of India.' The suffering of the Muslims were great, innocent and guilty alike perished in the flaming vengeance of the victors. The family of even staunch loyalists like Syed Ahmed Khan paid a heavy toll in hardship and death. The terror and dismay of the time are caught in the letters of Ghalib, 'Shaher sahra ho gaya' ('The city has become a howling wilderness'). Urdubazar is gone, what then of Urdu? Delhi is no more a city, it is a camp – the fort, the town, the bazaars, and the canals, all are gone! . . .

The Muslims not only braved more and suffered more in the Mutiny, but they refused to accept defeat and remained unreconciled for a long time. They kept up resistance in different forms. . . . They rejected English education and

[1] *The Trial of Muhammad Bahadur Shah*, edited with an Introduction by H.L.O. Garrett, Lahore: Punjab Government Records Office Publication, 1933.

> thereby steadily lost ground in professions and in the government services. While the Hindus were absorbing western ideas and adjusting themselves to the new circumstances, the Muslims remained aloof, estranged, wrapped up in their traditional beliefs. The Muslim renaissance that had been growing in Delhi wilted with the Mutiny.[2]

Savarkar also wrote a book on the Revolt of 1857: *The Indian War of Independence of 1857*. He excelled Asoka Mehta in praising the Muslims for their role in 1857.

> What were they that Moulvies preached them, learned Brahmins blessed them, that for their success prayers went up to Heaven from the mosques of Delhi and the temples of Benares? The great principles were Swadharma and Swaraj. In the thundering roar of 'Din, Din', which rose to protect religion, when there were evident signs of a cunning, dangerous and destructive attack on religion dearer than life, and in the terrific blows dealt at the chain of slavery with the holy desire of acquiring Swaraj . . . [T]he principles of Swadharma and Swaraj will be embedded in the bone and marrow of all the sons of Hindusthan![3]

Here, 'Hindustan' is used very much in the same sense as was used by the great Muhammad Iqbal in his famous poem: '*Saare jahan se accha Hindustan hamara*' ('Our Hindustan is the best among all the countries of the world').

There was generous praise for the last Mughal Emperor Bahadur Shah Zafar and, most of all, for 'that patriot Moulvie Ahmad Shah, whose sacred name has cast a halo round Hindusthan . . . As soon as the news of his death reached England, the relieved Englishmen felt that the most formidable enemy of the British in Northern India was no more'. In support of this assertion he cited Holmes's *History of the Indian Mutiny* (p. 539). Savarkar spared himself no pains.

Claims to greatness of Hyder Ali and Tipu Sultan were not overlooked, either. 'The danger to the Independence of India was first perceived by Nana Farnavis of Poona and Hyder Sahib of Mysore. . . . The Gadi of Tanjore, the Masnad of Mysore, the Rajgarh of Sahyadri, the Dewan-i-Khas of Delhi were among the select actors' in the drama that was unfolding in India.[4]

The feeling is unmistakable: *The Indian War of Independence* was written by a man proud of his religious and cultural heritage, proud of Maharashtra's past and yet someone who sought to blend regional and religious loyalties together in an overarching loyalty to the Indian nation. Interestingly, there is an entire chapter devoted to Ayodhya (Chapter IV). This chapter, however, contains none of the

[2] Asoka Mehta, *1857: The Great Rebellion*, Bombay: Hind Kitabs, 1946, pp. 1, 7, 68-70.

[3] V.D. Savarkar, *The Indian War of Independence of 1857*, pp. 7-8.

[4] Ibid., pp. 14-5.

falsehoods retailed by his political heirs of today. The message, throughout, is one of national unity, of *Indian* nationalism.

Nana Sahib, son of Baji Rao, had the brilliant Azimullah Khan as his trusted emissary, the author noted. One gets a good idea of Savarkar's outlook at the time from this passage:

> Nana's programme was first to fight a united fight, to make India free and, by removing internecine warfare, to establish the rule of the United States of India which would, thus, take its rightful place in the council of the free nations of the earth. He, also, felt that the meaning of 'Hindusthan' was thereafter the united nation of the adherents of Islam as well as Hinduism. As long as the Mahomedans lived in India in the capacity of the alien rulers, so long, to be willing to live with them like brothers was to acknowledge national weakness. Hence, it was, upto then, necessary for the Hindus to consider the Mahomedans as foreigners. And moreover this rulership of the Mahomedans, Guru Govind in the Panjab, Rana Pratap in Rajputana, Chhatrasal in Bundelkhand, and the Mahrattas, by even sitting upon the throne at Delhi, had destroyed; and, after a struggle of centuries, Hindu sovereignty had defeated the rulership of the Mahomedans and had come to its own all over India. It was no national shame to join hands with Mahomedans then, but it would, on the contrary, be an act of generosity.
>
> *So, now, the antagonism between the Hindus and the Mahomedans might be consigned to the past.* Their present relation was one not of rulers and ruled, foreigner and native, but simply that of brothers, with the one difference between them of religion alone. For, they were both children of the soil of Hindusthan. Their names were different, but they were all children of the same Mother. India, therefore, being the common mother of these two, they were brothers by blood.
>
> Nana Sahib, Bahadur Shah of Delhi, Moulvie Ahmad Shah, Khan Bahadur Khan, and other leaders of 1857 felt this relationship to some extent and, so, gathered round the flag of Swadesh leaving aside their enmity, now so unreasonable and stupid. In short, the broad features of the policy of Nana Sahib and Azimullah were that the Hindus and the Mahomedans should unite and fight shoulder to shoulder for the independence of their country and that, when freedom was gained, the United States of India should be formed under the Indian rulers and princes.[5]

He keeps returning to this theme of unity between Hindus and Muslims and keeps emphasising that in the struggle for independence, the two must act as brothers.

5 Ibid., pp. 62-3.

> These five days [in Delhi] will be ever memorable in the history of Hindusthan [for yet another reason]! Because these five days proclaimed by beat of drum the end [for the time being at any rate] of the continuous fight between the Hindus and Mahomedans dating from the invasion of Mahmud of Ghazni. . . . [I]t was proclaimed first that the Hindus and the Mahomedans are not rivals, not conquerors and conquered, but brethren! Bharatmata (Mother India) who was, in times past, freed from Mahomedan [sic] yoke by Shivaji, Pratap Singh, Chhatrasal, Pratapaditya, Guru Govind Singh, and Mahadaji Scindia – that Bharatmata gave the sacred mandate that day. 'Henceforward you are equal and brothers; I am equally the mother of you both!' The five days during which Hindus and Mahomedans proclaimed that India was their country and that they were all brethren, the days when Hindus and Mahomedans unanimously raised the flag of national freedom at Delhi, these days are for ever memorable in the history of Hindusthan![6]

There was praise for 'the Crescent of the Islamites' as much as for 'the spears of the Maharattas'.[7] The Mughals had come and ruled as foreign conquerors. 1857 consigned that to the past. Bahadur Shah was acclaimed as the King by all Indians.

> So, in the truer sense, we said that the raising of Bahadur Shah to the throne of India was no restoration at all. But rather it was the declaration that the longstanding war between the Hindu and the Mahomedan had ended, that tyranny had ceased . . . Let, then, Hindus and Mahomedans send forth their hearty, conscientious, and most loyal homage to this elected or freely accepted Emperor of their native soil on the 11th of May, 1857![8]

Not only Muslim personalities but Muslim masses, indeed even 'the mullahs', receive high praise: 'Also, among the vast Mussalman population of the town, the Mullahs were very busy. Thousands of Mussalmans were only awaiting the signal with a firm determination to offer their blood on the battle-field in the cause of country and religion.'

Savarkar was writing of the past. But his admonitions were clearly meant for the future.

> The Englishmen will try, now also, their old work of deception; they will try to incite the Hindus to rise against Mussalmans, and the Mahomedans to rise against the Hindus. But, Hindu Brethren! Do not fall into their nets. It is hardly necessary to tell our clever Hindu brethren that the English never keep their promises. . . .

6 Ibid., p. 105.
7 Ibid., p. 80.
8 Ibid., p. 234.

> Mussalmans, if you revere the Koran, and Hindus, if you revere the cow-mother, forget now your minor differences and unite together in this sacred war! Jump into the battlefield fighting under one banner, and wash away the name of the English from India in streams of blood! If the Hindus will join hands with the Mahomedans in this war, if they will also take the field for the freedom of our country, then, as a reward for their patriotism, the killing of cows will be put a stop to.[9]

Savarkar was brought to the Cellular Jail in the Andamans on 4 July 1911. In that very year he pleaded for clemency. His whole outlook began to change.[10] Savarkar wrote his *Hindutva*, the Bible of the RSS, while in prison. It was smuggled out for limited circulation and was first published in 1923 after his release from prison. The *volte face* remains unexplained.

By then two streams competed for political allegiance, the Indian National Congress and Hindu militant revivalism.[11] Lala Lajpat Rai was not a militant but by far the ablest of the group; erudite, articulate and cultured. He was most unlike Savarkar and the RSS chiefs from 1925 to 2019.

He was the first to propound the two-nation theory and also the first to suggest partition of India. In 1899 he wrote, 'Hindus are a nation in themselves, because they represent a civilisation all their own.' This line occurred, ironically in an article he wrote in *Hindustan Review* for the Indian National Congress. Some of his ideas went into Savarkar's *Hindutva*.[12] In his presidential address to the Hindu Mahasabha on 11 April 1923 he said, 'It is no use concealing the fact than the Indian National Congress is predominantly a Hindu organisation.'[13]

But, he was far removed from the champions of Hindutva in, both, approach and language. He attacked Pan-Islamism but only to add:

> But in their own way, Hindu revivalists have left nothing undone to create a strictly exclusive and aggressive communal feeling. Early in the eighties of the last century some of the Hindu religious leaders came to the conclusion that Hinduism was doomed unless it adopted the aggressive features of militant Islam and militant Christianity. The Arya Samaj is a kind of militant Hinduism. But the idea was by no means confined to the Arya Samaj. Swami Vivekanand and his gifted disciple Sister Nivedita, among others, were of the same mind. The articles which she wrote on aggressive Hinduism are the clearest evidence

[9] Ibid., p. 145.

[10] Vide A.G. Noorani, *Savarkar and Hindutva*, New Delhi: LeftWord Books, 2002.

[11] Vide Chapters 2 and 3.

[12] Chetan Bhatt, *Hindu Nationalism: Origins, Ideologies and Modern Myths*, Oxford, New York: Berg Publishers, 2001, p. 50.

[13] O.P. Ralhan (ed.), *Hindu Mahasabha*, Delhi: Anmol Publications, 1997, p. 125.

> of that mentality. It must be remembered in this connection that Western knowledge, Western thought and Western mentality took hold of the Hindu mind at a very early period during British rule.[14]

His proposal for partition of India in 1924 closely resembles the Mountbatten Plan of 1947:

> I would suggest that a remedy should be sought by which the Muslims might get a decisive majority without trampling on the sensitiveness of the Hindus and the Sikhs. My suggestion is that the Punjab should be partitioned into two provinces, the Western Punjab with a large Muslim majority, to be a Muslim-governed Province; and the Eastern Punjab, with a large Hindu-Sikh majority, to be a non-Muslim governed Province. . . . Under my scheme the Muslims will have four Muslim States: (1) The Pathan province or the North-West Frontier, (2) Western Punjab, (3) Sindh, and (4) Eastern Bengal. If there are compact Muslim communities in any other part of India, sufficiently large to form a Province, they should be similarly constituted. But it should be distinctly understood that this is not a united India. It means a clear partition of India into a Muslim India and a non-Muslim India.[15]

But can you imagine Savarkar or any of the leaders of the RSS, Jana Sangh or the BJP speaking in these terms? To continue:

> Let us live and struggle for freedom as brothers whose interests are one and indivisible. Let us live and die for each other, so that India may live and prosper as a Nation. India is neither Hindu nor Muslim. It is not even both. It is one. It is India. To the Hindus, I will say, 'If there are any among you who still dream of a Hindu Raj in this country; who think they can crush the Mussalmans and be the supreme power in this land, tell them that they are fools, or to be more accurate, that they are insane, and that their insanity will ruin their Hinduism along with their country. For God's sake don't listen to them and don't be guilty of patricide.'[16] . . .

Lajpat Rai respected India's diversities as Dr. Vanya Vaidehi Bhargav points out. Her dissertation at Oxford University was on his nationalist thought. In an article in *Indian Express* of 29 January 2019 she wrote:

[14] 'The Hindu-Muslim Problem', in *Writings and Speeches*, vol. 2, comprising articles he wrote for *The Tribune* and other newspapers, ed. Vijaya Chandra Joshi, Jullundur: University Publishers, 1966, p. 203.

[15] Ibid, pp. 212-3.

[16] Ibid, p. 221.

In his 1918 book, *The Problem of National Education*, Lajpat Rai insisted that 'we modern Indians can be as well proud of a Hali, an Iqbal, a Mohani as of Tagore, Roy and Harishchandra. We are proud of Sir Syed Ahmed Khan as of Ram Mohan Roy and Dayanand'. Similarly, he insisted that 'the educated Mussulman does not withhold his admiration from the religious, philosophic, and epic literature of India, just as the educated Hindu reckons the Taj and Fatehpur Sikri among the glories, not of Muslim but of Indian architecture'. For the Lajpat Rai of these years, Akbar was a role model whose memory ought to inspire Hindus and Muslims 'in building the future national edifice in such a way as to combine not just the best of the two cultures, but also the best of the new one, that has since been born in the West, from which India is drawing copiously'.

Lajpat Rai's embrace of diversity as a crucial ingredient of national culture was evident in his strong aversion to the imposition of a homogeneous culture on the Indian nation. He declared: 'To require India to coalesce into a nation with one religion and one tongue . . . would revive the medieval idea of one empire, one people, one church.' Even after Lajpat Rai turned to the Hindu Mahasabha for numerous complicated reasons, he never renounced his commitment to India's religio-cultural diversity. Lajpat Rai shows that a politics sensitive to the interests of Hindus can be free of a 'tyrannical' desire to impose religio-cultural homogeneity on the nation.

Around the same time a Muslim leader said:

I emphatically refuse – to say that, the English people should have the monopoly of power here. It is said that we are going on at a tremendous speed, that we are in a minority and the Government of his country might afterwards become a Hindu Government. I want to give an answer to this. I particularly wish to address my Mahomedan friends on this point. Do you think, in the first instance, as to whether it is possible that the government of this country could become a Hindu Government? Do you think that that Government could be conducted by ballot boxes? Do you think that because the Hindus are in the majority, therefore they could carry on a measure, in the Legislative Assembly, and there is an end of it? If seventy millions of Mussalmans do not approve of a measure, which is carried by a ballot box, do you think that it could be enforced and administered in this country? (Cries of 'No, No'.) Do you think that the Hindu statesmen, with their intellect, with their past history, would ever think of – when they get self-government – enforcing a measure by ballot box? (Cries of 'No, No'.) Then what is there to fear? (Cries of 'Nothing'.) Therefore, I say to my Moslem friends not to fear. This is a bogey, which is put before you by your enemies (Cries of 'Hear', 'Hear') to frighten you, to scare

> you away from the co-operation with the Hindus which is essential for the establishment of self-government. (Cries of 'Hear', 'Hear'.) If this country is not to be governed by the Hindus, let me tell you in the same spirit, it was not to be governed by the Mahomedans either and certainly not by the English. (Cries of 'Certainly not'.) It is to be governed by the people (Cries of 'Hear', 'Hear') and the sons of this country (Cries of 'Hear', 'Hear'), and I, standing here – I believe that I am voicing the feeling of the whole of India – say that what we demand is the immediate transfer of the substantial power of Government of *this country* (Cries of 'Hear', 'Hear') and that is the principal demand of our scheme of reform.[17]

The significance of this speech lies in the fact that it was delivered at the session of the Muslim League at Calcutta in December 1917 by Lajpat Rai's friend, Mohammed Ali Jinnah. The 'scheme of reform' he referred to was the Lucknow Pact of 1916 between the Congress and the League. Lajpat Rai's biographer Feroz Chand noted that they would freely walk into each other's room in the Central Assembly and at times go together to Malaviya.[18]

This is hardly surprising. Maulana Hasrat Mohani, a socialist to the core was devoted to Tilak, wrote a praise of the soil of Mathura. Professor C.M. Naim, Professor Emeritus in the Department of South Asian Languages and Civilizations in the University of Chicago wrote an erudite paper on Maulana Hasrat Mohani, master of the Urdu ghazal.[19] The Sufi in the Maulana made him immune to bigotry. The RSS will never able to destroy that heritage of India.

Lajpat Rai's colleague Pandit Madan Mohan Malaviya would not have spoken thus. The Italian scholar Marzia Casolari wrote:

> Benares became one of the centres, if not the main centre, for the construction of a politicised Hindu identity. The life of the town was involved at several levels. One of the key figures of this process was certainly Madan Mohan Malaviya. He was associated to the 'Bharat Dharm Mahamandal' right from its foundation at Haridwar in 1887.

He led the moves for the foundation of the Hindu University by 1916, and was its vice-chancellor from 1919 to 1939.

17 R.K. Prabhu (ed.), *An Anthology of Modern Indian Eloquence*, Bharatiya Vidya Bhavan, 1965, p. 132.

18 Feroz Chand, *Lajpat Rai: Life and Work*, New Delhi: Publications Division, Ministry of Information and Broadcasting, 1978, p. 497.

19 'The Maulana Who Loved Krishna', *Economic & Political Weekly*, vol. 48, no. 17, 27 April 2013, pp. 37-44.

> Under Malaviya's discretion the BHU became a workshop in the construction of political Hinduism, not only at a local level. . . . The foundation of the BHU was the accomplishment of Malaviya's efforts to strengthen the Hindu sense of identity and cohesiveness. The BHU thus became the public platform from which Malaviya propagandised his political ideas.

She amplified:

> The BHU was the result of the increasing sense of militancy in the Hindu segment of Indian society. . . . Certainly, Malaviya's project had a great deal in common with the RSS programme of building up the Hindu national character. Physical education and military training of BHU students took place under Malaviya's exhortations. Indeed, the BHU had a most vigorous University Training Corps (UTC). Malaviya had never been a member, but he encouraged students to take part in the activities of the RSS and authorised an RSS building within the campus. The BHU branch of the RSS became very active from 1928, thanks to Malaviya's sanction and the activity of a number of volunteers. The BHU was thus finally absorbed in the milieu of militant Hinduism.[20]

The soil was prepared for decades, since the 19th century, for the RSS to sow its seeds of hate and strife after its establishment in 1925. It did not formally adopt Savarkar's *Hindutva* for sometime; but it did so fully in substance. Its core doctrine is that the Hindus are the original inhabitants of India; the Muslims came as invaders who converted Hindus to Islam.

Not for the first time in history was history deliberately distorted to secure a political goal. Mohammed Ali Jinnah referred to the Muslim majority Provinces in the north-west as 'our homelands'. He had no explanation for Bengal. That apart, Islam first came to India in the South. Traces of the early arrival are still to be found there in Kerala.

The distinguished historian Romila Thapar has torn such theories to the shreds; beginning with James Mill's division of Indian history into Hindu civilisation, Muslim civilisation and British civilisation; 'interestingly enough, not Christian civilisation'.

She notes that:

> It is assumed that the period from about 1000 B.C. to A.D. 1200 can be called Hindu because the ruling dynasties of the subcontinent subscribed to the Hindu religion. However, even on the basis of dynastic history alone, this

20 Marzia Casolari, 'Role of Benares in Constructing Political Hindu Identity', *Economic & Political Weekly*, vol. 37, no. 15, 13 April 2002, pp. 1410 and 1417.

period cannot correctly be described as Hindu since there were a number of major dynasties which cannot be fitted into this description – the Mauryas, the Indo-Greeks, the Shakas and the Kushanas. Many of their kings were Buddhists and although not antagonistic to the Hindus, they consciously identified themselves as Buddhists. Should there then be another period called the Buddhist period, the duration of which could be from about 500 B.C. to A.D. 300?

The same is true of the 'Muslim invader'. He was not mentioned by religion but by ethnic origin.

It is significant that today when we write about this period of history we bracket together the Arabs, the Turks and the Persians and describe them all by the single term, 'the Muslims'. Yet until the thirteenth century, the word Muslim is rarely used in the sources to describe these various peoples. The sources of this period do not use a religious terminology but refer to them in a purely political manner. Thus the Turks are described as Turushkas, and the Arabs as Yavanas. The word Yavana was used traditionally for all persons coming from west Asia and the Mediterranean irrespective of whether they were Greek, Roman or Arab. The word itself, Yavana in Sanskrit is a back-formation of the Prakrit Yona and derives ultimately from Ionia, the Ionian Greeks who had the earliest and closest contacts with western Asia.

Another term used for the Turks, Persians and Arabs was mleccha. This word again has an ancient ancestry, first occurring in the Rig Veda. The term was used primarily for those people who spoke a non-Aryan language and therefore were unfamiliar with Aryan culture. The earliest mlecchas were therefore various tribes living mainly in parts of northern and central India and speaking a non-Aryan language. Later and by extension the term was used for foreigners.

'Muslim rule' was established in India at different times and at difference places. 'And Mahmud of Ghazni existed in the bosom of Hindu despoilers of temples also; for example, Harsha, an 11th century ruler of Kashmir "for whom the despoiling of temples was an organised, institutionalised activity".' He had a special officer, the Devotpatanayaka 'whose special job it was to plunder the temple' as Kalhana recorded in *Rajatarangini*.

Romila Thapar concludes her brilliant essay with this warning:

Historians cannot allow the discipline of history to degenerate to the extent that false history becomes instrumental in the promotion of political mythology. Since historians can, consciously or unconsciously, become the intellectual

> progenitors of political beliefs, the analysis of history thereby becomes particularly crucial to political ideologies.[21]

Romila Thapar elaborated her analysis in the 4th Kappen Memorial Lecture in 1999. She emphasised that India's past, if read with sensitivity, can be seen to be conducive to creating a secular society. There were no two rival monoliths, Hindu and Muslim, until the last few centuries.

'For almost a thousand years, Buddhism was a major Indian religion.' Buddhists were attacked ferociously.

> The use of 'Hindu' as an identity by those whom we today call Hindus, does not gain currency until about the fifteenth century. Prior to that religious identity was based on sect and caste and an all-inclusive term was not thought necessary. . . . Equally interesting is the fact that the Hindus did not initially refer to those who arrived in India as followers of Islam, as Muslims. There were diverse forms of identity which have their own historical interest. The Arabs conquered Sind, but came more frequently as traders from west Asia.
>
> They were employed in high administrative positions in the territory of the Rashtrakuta rulers, and are frequently referred to as Tajikas. The Turks who came from central Asia and Afghanistan are described by the ethnic term, Turushka. Some were also referred to as Shakas and Yavanas, the former being the old name for the Scythians of central Asia and the latter, for the Greeks. The use of the term mleccha, is a marker of social distance, used for those viewed as being outside caste society. Since a variety of people from tribals to local kings are variously called mleccha, it cannot be assumed that it always carried a sense of contempt. . . .
>
> What is interesting is that even the Turks and the Arabs do not seem to see themselves as part of a single Islamic expedition. In the Turko-Persian chronicles, conquests in India and the establishing of Islamic rule through the Delhi Sultanate is attributed entirely to Mahmud of Ghazni. The Arabs are generally ignored, even though their contacts and conquests preceded those of Mahmud.

Temples were destroyed not only out of religious bigotry but also because of their wealth. There was, however, another reason. 'The temple was not just a place of worship. Like the church and the mosque it was also an institution. The destruction of temples therefore cannot be explained away simplistically as invariably an expression of religious bigotry.'[22]

[21] *Communalism and the Writing of Indian History*, Delhi: People's Publishing House, 1969; pp. 6, 7, 8 and 15.

[22] Romila Thapar, *Historical Interpretations and the Secularising of Indian Society*, Bangalore:

An important, indeed crucial, question is seldom asked: What has the RSS to show apart from false history, divisive politics, and cultural themes far removed from the noble traditions of Hinduism. What it calls 'culture' is a euphemism for that ideology. The proponent of 'cultural nationalism' Savarkar himself made that emphatically clear. He, in his essay *Hindutva*. Its publisher S.S. Savarkar, who knew him closely, explained in the Preface.

> Savarkar had to *coin some new words* such as 'Hindutva', 'Hinduness', 'Hindudom' in order to express totality of the cultural, historical, and above all the national aspects along with the religious one, which mark out the Hindu People as a whole. The definition is not consequently meant to be a definition of Hindu Dharma, or Hindu religion. It is a definition of 'Hinduness'. It is essentially national in its outlook and comprehends the Hindu People as a Hindu-Rashtra.

It is a political not a religious concept. It was formulated anew by Savarkar.

Savarkar confirms that 'here it is enough to point out that Hindutva is not identical with what is vaguely indicated by the term Hinduism'.[23] He said: 'We have tried already to draw a clear line of demarcation between the two conceptions and protested against *the wrong use of the word Hinduism to denote the Sanatan Dharma alone. Hindutva is not identical with Hindu Dharma*.'[24] Savarkar was an atheist.

Religion and religious values are beyond the reckoning of the RSS and its BJP's leaders. They did not hesitate to exploit for their political ends the name of Shri Ramachandra, revered by millions, for the aims of their sordid politics. Sushma Swaraj admitted at Bhopal on 14 April 2000 that the temple movement was '*purely political in nature and had nothing to do with religion*'. This exposes the sheer hypocrisy of their cries of 'national honour' and 'nationalist feelings' neither of which moved devout Hindus like Gandhi, Rajaji, Lajpat Rai, Malaviya and Tilak to demand possession of the Babri Masjid at Ayodhya. L.K. Advani revealed his motives on 11 June 1989, immediately after he got the BJP to adopt a resolution on the Masjid at its Palampur session. 'I am sure it would translate into votes' – and make him prime minister. He expressed this hope repeatedly. 'Had I not played the Ram factor effectively I would have definitely lost from the New Delhi constituency,' he said on 18 June 1991. He yielded the palm reluctantly to Atal Bihari Vajpayee in 1995 after it became evident that, despite his sordid plans which entailed bloodshed and bad blood among Indians, the country would not accept him as prime minister. Nearly a quarter century of rancorous politics had to elapse

Visthar, 1999, pp. 6-8, 18-20, 25-6.

23 Savarkar, *Hindutva: Who is a Hindu?*, Mumbai: S.S. Savarkar, Veer Savarkar Prakashan, 1969, p. 4.

24 Ibid., p. 121.

before he was told that the office belonged to his protégé, Narendra Modi, not to him.

The RSS's doctrines admit of no compromise. They demand surrender of the minorities. Murli Manohar Joshi said on 12 January 1991:

> I say that all Indian Muslims are Mohammadiya Hindus; all Indian Christians are Christi Hindus. They are Hindus who have adopted Christianity and Islam as their religion. Thus neither Muslims nor Christians are acceptable with distinct identities of their own. They must be 'Hinduised'.[25]

For the last 40 years, ever since the Janata Party government set up the Minorities Commission, the RSS and, later, the Jana Sangh and the BJP rejected the very concept of minorities. Muslims, Christians and Sikhs are not minorities although Articles 29 and 30 of India's Constitution use the word and protect minorities against denial of their rights by the majority community.

In this, as on very many other concepts, it acts against the trends of modern times; against modernity itself and, what is more, against India's history. The Indian National Congress offered protection to the minorities at the outset,[26] as did the Lucknow Pact of 1916 between the Congress and the Muslim League, co-authored by Bal Gangadhar Tilak and M.A. Jinnah. On 28 December 1927 the Congress adopted, at its 42nd Session in Madras, a comprehensive Resolution on Minorities.[27] There exists an active Minority Rights Group in London and a U.N. Sub-Commission on the Prevention of Discrimination and the Protection of Minorities.

Internationally, the term began with the Treaty between the Allied and Associated Powers and Poland on the Protection of Minorities on 28 June 1919 after the First World War. The U.N. General Assembly passed Resolution 47/135 on 18 December 1992 embodying in its Annex a Declaration of the Rights of Persons Belonging to National or Ethnic, Religious and Linguistic Minorities. In 1994 the Council of Europe adopted a Framework Convention for the Protection of National Minorities. It runs into 32 Articles and is a binding legal document.[28]

The RSS-BJP outlook is opposed to well-settled international and national trends. The Sangh parivar (family) seeks to accomplish its ends by the force of a brute majority; politically, by marginalising minority votes though motivated

[25] *Sunday Observer*, 13 January 1991.

[26] Vide A.G. Noorani, *Badruddin Tyabji*, New Delhi: Publications Division, Government of India, 1969.

[27] Vide Iqbal A. Ansari, *Readings on Minorities: Perspectives and Documents*, 2 volumes, New Delhi: Institute of Objective Studies, 1996; vol. 2, p. 95 for the text. These volumes contain full texts of Indian and international texts on protection of minorities.

[28] Ibid., vol. 2, pp. 357-69.

delimitation of constituencies, ignoring Muslim members in awarding party tickets and the like.

The religious majority becomes a political majority in Parliament and acquires State power to wield power unchecked. The Constitution and judicial checks help – but a little. The Supreme Court has retreated from its first liberal ruling on the autonomy of minority educational institutions. In the Ayodhya case it split along religious lines. Justice J.S. Verma went out of his way to make observations which he knew were one-sided and helpful to the Hindus which quoted him enthusiastically in the High Court.

Crucially, his judgment in the Hindutva case was shocking. The governing text, surely, is Savarkar's essay *Hindutva*. A student who cites instead a work by an obscure Muslim cleric will be rapped on his knuckles. A journalist who commits that offence will be accused of intellectual dishonesty. But that is just what Justice Verma did. He not only quoted, instead, an obscure Muslim cleric, but quoted him misleadingly.[29]

The BJP's 1999 Manifesto dishonestly claimed that 'the Supreme Court, had, finally, endorsed the true meaning and content of Hindutva as being consistent with the true meaning and definition of secularism'. This is utterly false. The Court's final ruling is yet to be given. The BJP knows this very well. On 16 April 1996 a three-member Bench of the Court, comprising Justices K. Ramaswamy, S.P. Bharucha and K.S. Paripoornan referred to a larger Bench of five judges the highly unsatisfactory judgment given by Justice J.S. Verma, on 11 December 1995, on behalf of himself and Justice N.P. Singh and K. Venkataswami. It was, therefore, not a final ruling on Hindutva.

In 2017 the Court refused to correct a palpable error. Twenty years later, the Supreme Court had the opportunity and duty to settle the conflict between the rulings. The judgments given by a five-member Bench of the Supreme Court on 2 January 2017, *consciously avoided ruling on the issue whether advocacy of Hindutva vitiates an election*.[30] It thus did a grave disservice to the nation. By choosing in advance to rule on a much more limited issue, it shirked its responsibility. Pending before the Court were two references to a larger Bench of five judges. One was on the issue of Hindutva which was 20 years old. The other was on the limited issue of appeals to voters on the grounds of religion, caste, etc. The Court refused to touch the first. It struck off the Hindutva issue and gave a narrowly divided ruling (4-3) on the limited issue.

V.D. Savarkar himself was at great pains to emphasise that Hindutva must not be 'confounded with the other cognate term Hinduism';[31] that 'Hindutva is not

[29] *Dr. Ramesh Prabhoo vs. Prabhakar K. Kunte*, (1996) 1 Supreme Court Cases [hereafter SCC] 130; and *Manohar Joshi vs Nitin Bhaurao Patil*, (1996) 1 SCC 169.

[30] *Abhiram Singh vs. C.D. Commachen*, (2017) 2 SCC 692.

[31] Savarkar, *Hindutva*, p. 3.

identical with what is vaguely indicated by the term Hinduism'. 'Hindutva is not identical with Hindu Dharma; nor is Hindu Dharma identical with Hinduism.'[32] The Supreme Court could have nipped the mischief in the bud.

Hinduism may be hard to define. Not so Hindutva, unless, of course, one identifies it with Hinduism. Justice Verma did just that: 'Ordinarily, Hindutva is understood as a way of life or a state of mind and it is not to be equated with, or understood as, religious Hindu fundamentalism.' Has the BJP extended time, effort, and money all these years to espouse 'a way of life'? That certainly is not how Hindutva is 'ordinarily' understood.

Justice Verma proceeded to quote an obscure book. The quotation and his inference deserve to be set out in full:

> In '*Indian Muslims – the Need for a Positive Outlook*' by Maulana Wahiduddin Khan (1994) it is said: 'The strategy worked out to solve the minorities problem was, although differently worded, that of Hindutva or Indianisation. This strategy, briefly stated, aims at developing a uniform culture by obliterating the differences between all of the cultures coexisting in the country. This was felt to be the way to communal harmony and national unity. It was thought that this would put an end once and for all to the minorities problem.'

From this Justice Verma concluded: 'The above opinion indicates that the word "Hindutva" is used and understood as a synonym of "Indianisation".' But if the Maulana was to be quoted, he should have been quoted fairly and understood properly.

Far from supporting the Judge's conclusion, the quote refutes it thoroughly. It was not in praise of Hindutva or its euphemism 'Indianisation' but in their censure. The paragraph preceding it lamented that Hindus did not treat the partition as 'just an incident in past history'. The subsequent strategy 'to solve the minorities problem', through Hindutva or Indianisation, sought to impose 'a uniform culture by obliterating the differences between all of the cultures co-existing in the country'. Unlike Justice Verma, who quotes this to imply approval of this process, the Maulana disapproved of it.

This becomes all too clear from the very next sentence after his comment that it was thought that the obliteration would end the minorities problem. That sentence reads: 'However beautiful this suggestion may appear to be, it is certainly impracticable.' *Justice Verma did not note this sentence at all.*[33] The Maulana's book is no authority on Hindutva. Its Bible is Savarkar's book *Hindutva* which Justice Verma ignored, studiously. He ignored all the standard works on Hindutva also. Why?

[32] Ibid., p. 121.

[33] *Dr. Ramesh Prabhoo vs. Prabhakar K. Kunte*, p. 81.

A powerful plea was made for reversal of Justice Verma's judgments on Hindutva. He rejected it brusquely on 22 March 1996.[34]

> A careful and dispassionate reading of the decision would show that the apprehensions and misgivings expressed in the writ petition, are imaginary and baseless. . . . We may add that the deficiency, if any, in the statutory prohibition enacting the corrupt practice in Section 123 of the Representation of the People Act, has to be cured by legislation.

All this proved too much for other Judges of the Supreme Court. A few days later, on 16 April 1996, came a ruling by a different Bench comprising Justices K. Ramaswamy, S.P. Bharucha, and K.S. Paripoornan in *Abhiram Singh vs. C.D. Commachen & Ors.*[35] *All* the previous cases were referred to. The Court said:

> As stated earlier, when and under what circumstances, speeches of the leaders of the political party or the appeal of any other person with the consent by a candidate or his election agent to vote or refrain from voting on the ground of religion, race, caste or community or language, etc. or promotion or an attempt to promote feelings of enmity or hatred between different classes of citizens of India on the ground of religion, race, caste, community or language with the consent of the candidate or his election agent for the furtherance of the prospects of the election of the candidate or for prejudicially affecting the election of any candidate constitutes corrupt practice under sub-sections (3) or (3A) of Section 123. *Its content and scope also require to be clearly laid down authoritatively lest miscarriage of justice* in interpretation of 'corrupt practice' involved in every election petition would ensue. *The purity of election process gets fouled* and be [sic] fraught with deleterious effect in a democratic polity.
>
> Thus, without expressing any opinion on these questions, we are of the view that *the entire* case requires to be heard and decided by a larger Bench of five Judges since the decision thereon impinges upon the purity of election process and requires to be decided authoritatively.
>
> We, therefore, direct the Registry to place the case before our learned brother, the Chief Justice, for constituting a larger Bench of five Judges, and, if possible, *at an early date* so that all the questions arising in the present appeal could be decided authoritatively and expeditiously.

Thus two issues were to be referred to a larger bench. One was responsibility for the speeches of the party earlier. The other was Hindutva, 'the content and scope' of the speeches. To leave no room for doubt the Judges stressed its bearing

[34] *Mohammad Aslam vs. Union of India & Ors.*, (1996) 2 SCC 749.

[35] (1996) 3 SCC 665.

on the 'purity of the electoral process' and the deleterious effect in a democratic polity. Two decades rolled by without any Chief Justice constituting the Bench. Meanwhile, the Lok Sabha went to the polls in 1998, 1999, 2004, 2009 and 2014 without any check on the BJP's propaganda.

The references by a larger Bench in two cases were heard on the limited issue. In *Narayan Singh vs. Sunderlal Patwa*,[36] a Constitution Bench of the Court observed, in its order dated 28 August 2002, that the High Court in that case had construed Section 123(3) of the Representation of the People Act, 1951 'to mean that it will not be a corrupt practice when the voters belonging to some other religion are appealed, *other than the religion of the candidate*'.

In a judgment delivered on 2 January 2017 (*Abhiram Singh vs. C.D. Commachen*, (2017) 2 SCC 692) it was said:

> The present civil appeal was initially referred by a Bench of three judges to a Constitution Bench *on 16 April 1996* [(1996) 3 SCC 665]. When the civil appeal came up before a Constitution Bench [(2014) 14 SCC 382], one of the questions which fell for consideration was the interpretation of Section 123(3). Following the reference to seven Judges made in Narayan Singh, the present civil appeal was also referred on the question of the interpretation of Section 123(3). The order of reference dated *30 January 2014* [not of 16 April 1996] explains the limited nature of the reference, thus:
>
> 'Be that as it may, since one of the questions involved in the present appeal is already referred to a larger Bench of seven Judges, we think it appropriate to refer this appeal *to a limited extent* regarding interpretation of sub-section (3) of Section 123 of the 1951 Act to a larger Bench of seven Judges.'
>
> The reference to seven Judges is limited to the interpretation of Section 123(3).

Why is the emphasis on the 'limited nature'? The 1996 reference covered the wider issue of Hindutva also. It was whittled down to *exclude* Hindutva and confine the reference to the issue raised in Narayan Singh's case. The reference to 'the content and scope' of speech was ignored.

The Reference Order in 1996 was truncated in advance. When the case came up for hearing on 25 October 2016 the Chief Justice of India, T.S. Thakur said, '*We will not reconsider the 1995 judgment and also not examine Hindutva or religion at this stage*' – which the Order of Reference on 16 April 1996 clearly required a larger Bench to do. 'At this stage, we will confine ourselves to the issue *raised before us in the reference*.' He might, and ought to have, added 'as truncated by us'. He added wrongly, 'In this reference there is no mention of the word Hindutva.' Indeed not; for the words in the Order of 16 April 1996 directed a reference of an omnibus

[36] (2003) 9 SCC 300.

nature which *included* J.S. Verma's judgment. His conclusion was emphatic: 'We will not go into Hindutva at this stage.'[37] At what stage, then, pray?

The seven-judge Bench gave a divided verdict on 2 January 2017 (*Abhiram Singh vs. C.D. Commachen & Ors.*). In issue was interpretation of Section 123(3) of the Representation of the People Act, 1951 which forbids

> The appeal by a candidate or his agent or by any other person with the consent of a candidate or his election agent to vote or refrain from voting for any person on the ground of *his* religion, race, caste, community or language or the use of, or appeal to, religious symbols or the use of, or appeal to, national symbols, such as the national flag or the national emblem, for the furtherance of the prospects of the election of that candidate or for prejudicially affecting the election of any candidate.

Section 123(3A) reads:

> The promotion of, or attempt to promote, feelings of enmity or hatred between different classes of the citizens of India on grounds of religion, race, caste, community, or language, by a candidate or his agent or any other person with the consent of a candidate or his election agent for the furtherance of the prospects of that candidate or for prejudicially affecting the election of any candidate.

Around the same time Section 153A of the Penal Code was also amended in a 'package deal', as the Judges remarked Hindutva surely violates both Section 123(3) as well as (3A).

Justices B.N. Lokur and L. Nageswara Rao held that Section 123 'must be given a broad and purposive interpretation so as to cover not only a plea to the voters by the candidate or his agent or some one on the ground of *his* religion or caste – as all earlier cases had said – but also on grounds *of the voter's* religion, caste etc.' This was the result of a 'purposive' interpretation which gives free rein to the Judges' subjective inclinations.

Justice S.A. Bobde concurred: 'The word "his" occurring in the Section refers not only to the candidate or his agent but is also intended to refer to the voter i.e. the elector.' This was a quantum jump in which Chief Justice T.S. Thakur joined enthusiastically. He quoted revealingly this passage in an earlier case [(2015) 8 SCC 1] in which the Supreme Court said: 'In the background of the constitutional mandate, the question is not what the statute does say *but what the statute must say*. If the Act or the Rules or the bye-laws do not say what they should say in terms of the Constitution, *it is the duty of the court to read the constitutional spirit and*

[37] *The Asian Age*, 26 October 2016.

concept into the Acts.' This is a naked usurpation of legislative power by the Court.

Against this background, the powerful dissent by Justice Dr. D.Y. Chandrachud, in which Justices Adarsh Kumar Goel and Uday Umesh Lalit concurred, comes as a relief. It has been established for centuries that a penal provision must be construed strictly. There is no room for stretching it in the name of 'purposive' interpretation. Justice Chandrachud said:

> The vote is solicited for a candidate or there is an appeal not to vote for a candidate. Each of these expressions is in the singular. They are followed by expression 'on the ground of his religion . . .' The expression 'his religion . . .' must necessarily qualify what precedes; namely, the religion of the candidate in whose favour a vote is sought or that of another candidate against whom there is an appeal to refrain from voting. 'His' religion (and the same principle would apply to 'his' race, 'his' caste, 'his' community, or 'his' language) must hence refer to the religion of the person in whose favour votes are solicited or the person against whom there is an appeal for refraining from casting a ballot.

The majority view spelt a majoritarian not a secular polity. Consider just two facts. On 10 August 2013 the NCP leader Sharad Pawar referred to police bias against Muslims. 'How will they see this country as their own country?'[38]

All hell broke loose in Mumbai's press the day after Asaduddin Owaisi, president of the Majlis-e-Ittehadul Muslimeen, said in the city on 1 January 2017 that Muslims must get Rs. 7,000 crores in the Mumbai Municipal Corporation's budget of Rs. 37,000 crores.

However, as far back as on 2 July 1980, the United States Supreme Court upheld a law which set aside 10 per cent of the public works contracts for businesses owned by members of racial minorities. H. Earl Fullilove, a white New York contractor, challenged the law on the ground that it discriminated against whites.

Chief Justice Warren Burger said that affirmative action programmes by Congress may 'deprive some people who may themselves be innocent', but that a limited 'sharing of the burden by innocent parties is not impermissible' under the Constitution:

> The Congress has not sought to give select minority groups a preferred standing in the construction industry, but has embarked on a remedial program to place them on a more equitable footing with respect to public contracting opportunities. There has been no showing in this case that Congress has inadvertently effected an invidious discrimination by excluding from coverage an identifiable minority group that has been the victim of a degree of

[38] Vide the writer's article 'Muslims & Police', *Frontline*, 12 and 26 December 2014.

> disadvantage and discrimination equal to or greater than that suffered by the groups encompassed by the minority business enterprise program.[39]

Would an elected legislator be unseated if he had made such a demand during his election campaign? It is woefully clear that it is not politicians alone who need to be educated about the rights of the minorities. Chief Justice T.S. Thakur, of course, knew the consequences of his ruling.

One of the greatest judges of the U.S. Supreme Court Benjamin N. Cardozo wisely observed:

> The great tides and currents which engulf the rest of men do not turn aside in their course and pass the judges by. We like to figure to ourselves the processes of justice as coldly objective and impersonal. The law, conceived of as a real existence, dwelling apart and alone, speaks, through the voices of priests and ministers, the words which they have no choice except to utter.[40]

Thus, it is not necessary for the regime of the day to promote a constitutional amendment to proclaim India as a Hindu State in the certain knowledge that it would be struck down. It has simply to govern as if it was governing a Hindu state. This is just what Narendra Modi did in Gujarat and has done in India since 2014.

Dr. B.R. Ambedkar was a wise and far-sighted man. He warned the Constituent Assembly, on 4 November 1948, while moving for the adoption of the Draft Constitution.

> While everybody recognises the necessity of the diffusion of Constitutional morality for the peaceful working of a democratic Constitution, there are two things interconnected with it which are not, unfortunately, generally recognised. One is that the form of administration has a close connection with the form of the Constitution. The form of the administration must be appropriate to and in the same sense as the form of the Constitution. The other is that *it is perfectly possible to pervert the Constitution, without changing its form by merely changing the form of the administration and to make it inconsistent and opposed to the spirit of the Constitution.* It follows that it is only where people are saturated with Constitutional morality, such as the one described by Grote the historian, that one can take the risk of omitting from the Constitution details of administration and leaving it for the Legislature to prescribe them. The question is, can we presume such a diffusion of Constitutional morality? Constitutional morality is not a natural sentiment. It has to be cultivated. We

[39] *Fullilove vs. Klutznick*, 448 U.S. 448 (1980).

[40] Benjamin N. Cardozo, *The Nature of the Judicial Process*, New Haven: Yale University Press, 1921, p. 168.

> must realise that our people have yet to learn it. Democracy in India is only a top dressing on an Indian soil, which is essentially undemocratic.[41]

The Modi strategy is clear to all. Pack institutions with Hindutva men, impose Yogis as chief ministers, cripple the cabinet system, suborn the civil service and try to influence the judiciary.

The RSS is at war with India's past and not with the Mughals alone. It belittles three of the greatest builders of the Indian State – Ashoka, the Buddhist, Akbar, the Muslim and Nehru, a civilised Enlightened Hindu. It would wipe out centuries of achievement for which the world has acclaimed India and replace that with its own narrow, divisive ideology; derided and despised by most in India and by all outside. The question brooks no evasion: What kind of India does it promise Indians it would create?

Its own credentials and intellectual capacity for anything constructive and enlightening are severely constricted. Professor Donald Eugene Smith wrote as far back as in 1963 in his acclaimed work *India as a Secular State*:

> Nehru once remarked that Hindu communalism was the Indian version of fascism, and, in the case of the RSS, it is not difficult to perceive certain similarities. The leader principle, the stress on militarism, the doctrine of racial-cultural superiority, ultra-nationalism infused with religious idealism, the use of symbols of past greatness, the emphasis on national solidarity, the exclusion of religious or ethnic minorities from the nation-concept – all of these features of the RSS are highly reminiscent of fascist movements in Europe. Fascism, however, is associated with a concept of state-worship; the state as the all-absorbing reality in which the individual loses himself and in so doing finds ultimate meaning.
>
> This conception has no counterpart in RSS ideology; in fact, the Sangh explicitly rejects the notion that its objectives could be attained through the power of the state. Its aim is the regeneration of Hindu society, which must come from within. However, it is impossible to say how the RSS would respond if political power ever came within reach, either directly or through the Jana Sangh. The implementation of certain aspects of its ideology (the policy toward Muslims and other minorities, for example) presupposes extensive use of the machinery of the state.[42]

Read this bit in Golwalkar's statement on 2 November 1948.

[41] *Constituent Assembly Debates*, vol. 7, p. 38.

[42] *India as a Secular State*, Princeton University Press, 1963, p. 468.

> We are a Hindu body. To a Hindu, the State is and has always been a secular fact. It was only a departure from the Hindu way of life that brought about, for the first time, a non-secular theocratic concept of State under Ashoka.[43]

One wonders if the uneducated, uneducable men in the RSS read anything. Hindu and Muslim scholars have always tried to understand each other's faith. Pandit Sunderlal's book *The Gita and the Quran* was translated into English by Syed Asadullah and was published in 1957 by the Institute of Indo-Middle East Cultural Studies, Hyderabad with a Foreword by its president Syed Abdul Latif. The author concluded with these words:

> The Quran lays its special emphasis on two things. One is faith: the other is good deeds or righteous activity. In respect of the former, one should believe in One God and in all the scriptures inspired by him and all the prophets raised among all the peoples and in the good forces of life and finally in the life after death. In respect of the other, one should keep his desires under proper control and do good to others.
>
> The truth is that the basic principles of the Quran, even as of other great scriptures, constitute a universal message for all mankind and point clearly to every earnest mind the way to religious and spiritual progress. If we approach the Quran with sincerity and love, we are bound to realise that it offers to us that universal humanism which is the essence of all religions, called by the Hindu Sants 'Prem Dharam' and by the Muslim Sufis 'Madhhabi-i-Ishq', the Religion of Love.[44]

Who was a true Hindu pray, Pandit Sunderlal or Hedgewar or his successors to this day?

The Asian Age published on 28 February, 1 March and 2 March 1995 a learned article by Swami Ranganathananda on Prophet Muhammad's love for mankind.

This writer may be forgiven for lapsing into a personal experience. My father Abdul Majeed Noorani was a devotee of certain peer (saint). One of his peerbhais and a friend became a family friend. Saleh Muhammad Chicha introduced me to Islam, Prophet Muhammad's life, Sufism, the *Meditations* of Marcus Aurelius, the Ethics of Seneca and of Epictetus. Above all, he introduced me to the Bhagwad Gita. I was around 16. What made my studies easier was a discovery I myself made in a small library in a Muslim locality in Mumbai. It had the lectures of Swami Rama Tirth. Since he made laudatory comments on Prophet Muhammad, the bridge-building became easier. Even now, 73 years later, I remember Saleh Muhammad

[43] *Justice on Trial*, p. 80.

[44] *The Gita and the Quran*, p. 146.

Chicha's words: 'Hindu philosophy teaches the technique of Self-Realisation.'

I reproduce here a poem in praise of Swami Rama Tirth in Urdu with an English translation.

Hum-baghal darya se hai ai qatra-e-betaab tu,
Pahle gohar tha, bana ab gohar-e-nayaab tu.

Ah! khola kis ada se tu ne raaz-e-rang-o-boo,
Main abhi tak hoon aseer-e-imtiaz-e-rang-o-boo.

Mit ke ghogha zindagi ka shorish-e-mahshar bana,
Yeh sharara bujh ke aatish khana-e-Azar bana.

Nafi-e-hasti ik karishma hai dil-e-agah ka,
La ke darya mein nihan moti hai illallah ka.

Chashm-e-nabeena se makhfi ma'ani-e-anjam hai,
Tham gayi jis dam tarap, seemab seem-e-kham hai.

Tor deta hai but-e-hasti ko Ibrahim-e-ishq,
Hosh ka daaru hai goya masti-e-tasneem-e-ishq.

(You have merged into the river, O restless water-drop,
A pearl before, you have become a pearl of rarer sort.

In lucid terms you have unveiled the secret of the scent and shade,
While I am still engaged in the maze of form and face.

The noise of life has ended in the roar of the doomsday,
The extinguished spark has re-emerged as eternal blaze.

Denial of self is the task of a well-enlightened mind,
The pearl of truth lies concealed in the illusory waves of time.

The meaning of the goal of life is hidden from the blinkered eye,
The mercury robbed of restless urge is a scrap of metal white.

The knight of love can break the self, falsely idolised as God,
Intoxicating wine of love is a sense-awakening draught.)[45]

45 K.C. Kanda, *Allama Iqbal: Selected Poetry*, New Delhi: New Dawn Press, an imprint of Sterling Publishers, 2006, p. 139. Dr. Kanda is yet to receive the acknowledgement that is

The author of the poem was Iqbal – who had made a deep study of Hinduism.

March 1940 heard two pronouncements by two Muslim leaders on the future of Muslims. One was by Mohammed Ali Jinnah on the Pakistan Resolution which the Muslim League adopted on 23 March 1940. A few days earlier, on 2 March 1940, Abul Kalam Azad delivered his presidential address to a session of the Indian National Congress at Ramgarh. This neglected classic echoes Firaq's words and provides a comprehensive manifesto which is strikingly relevant even now, nearly eighty years later.

Azad said:

> I am a Musalman and am proud of the fact. Islam's splendid traditions of thirteen hundred years are my inheritance. I am unwilling to lose even the smallest part of this inheritance. The teaching and history of Islam, its arts and letters and civilisation are my wealth and my fortune. It is my duty to protect them.
>
> As a Musalman I have a special interest in Islamic religion and culture and I cannot tolerate any interference with them. But in addition to these sentiments, I have others also which the realities and conditions of my life have forced upon me. The spirit of Islam does not come in the way of these sentiments; it guides and helps me forward. I am proud of being an Indian. I am a part of the indivisible unity that is Indian nationality. *I am indispensable to this noble edifice and without me this splendid structure of India is incomplete.* I am an essential element which has gone to build India, I can never surrender this claim.
>
> It was India's historic destiny that many human races and cultures and religions should flow to her, finding a home in her hospitable soil, and that many a caravan should find rest here. Even before the dawn of history, these caravans trekked into India and wave after wave of new-comers followed. This vast and fertile land gave welcome to all and took them to her bosom. One of the last three caravans, following the footsteps of its predecessors, was that of the followers of Islam. This came here and settled here for good. *This led to a meeting of the culture-currents of two different races. Like the Ganga and the Yamuna, they flowed for a while through separate courses, but nature's immutable law brought them together and joined them in a sangam.*
>
> This fusion was a notable event in history. Since then, destiny, in her own hidden way, began to fashion a new India in place of the old. We brought our treasures with us, and India too was full of the riches of her own precious heritage. We gave our wealth to her and she unlocked the doors of her own treasures to us. We gave her what she needed most, the most precious of gifts from Islam's treasury, the message of democracy and human equality. . . .

due to him for his many excellent works on Urdu poets.

> Full eleven centuries have passed by since then. *Islam has now as great a claim on the soil of India as Hinduism.* If Hinduism has been the religion of the people here for several thousands of years, Islam also has been their religion for a thousand years. Just as a Hindu can say with pride that he is an Indian and follows Hinduism, so also we can say with equal pride that we are Indians and follow Islam. I shall enlarge this orbit still further. The Indian Christian is equally entitled to say with pride that he is an Indian and is following a religion of India, namely Christianity.
>
> Eleven hundred years of common history have enriched India with our common achievements. Our languages, our poetry, our literature, our culture, our art, our dress, our manners and customs, the innumerable happenings of our daily life, everything bears the stamp of our joint endeavour. There is indeed no aspect of our life which has escaped this stamp. Our languages were different, but we grew to use a common language; our manners and customs were dissimilar, but they acted and reacted on each other and thus produced a new synthesis. Our old dress may be seen only in ancient pictures, of by-gone days; no one wears it today. This joint wealth is the heritage of our common nationality and we do not want to leave it and go back to the times when this joint life had not begun.[46]

Azad used the same metaphor as Firaq did; the Caravans that arrived to build India and make it what it is today. Very few Urdu poets were as steeped in English literature as Firaq was. He taught at the Allahabad University.

We have a very thought-provoking analysis by Firaq in interviews to a friend Sumat Prakash Shauq.[47] Firaq said:

> As India became independent, numerous obstacles were placed in the path of the growth and development of Urdu. During the last 50 years, many Hindi poets have begun to blindly push in Sanskrit words in droves into Hindi but they have not succeeded in producing good literature. About 96 to 97 per cent of Sanskrit words cannot be implanted into Hindi phonology and lexicon. The poetry of Surdas, Tulsidas and other great Hindi poets bears testimony to this. Yet thousands of Sanskrit words can, with benefit, be assimilated in Urdu literature and this will happen if Urdu is permitted to have a future.
>
> Hindu culture does not depend upon Sanskrit words alone even though certain specific Sanskrit words have a special meaning and relevance for expressing this culture. Hindu thought, customs, habits, sentiments and sensibility can in substantial measure be given an expression in Urdu literature. Some of it has already been done. The times are changing. Western styles are having a deep impact on Hindu life and society. Krishan Chander, Khwaja

[46] Arsh Malsiani, *Abul Kalam Azad*, New Delhi: Publications Division, 1976, pp. 154-5.

[47] Sumat Prakash Shauq, *Thus Spoke Firaq*, New Delhi: Allied Publishers, 1992.

Ahmad Abbas, Ismat Chughtai, Rajinder Singh Bedi, Qurrat-ul-Ain Haidar and other Hindu and Muslim writers in India and in Pakistan are producing great literature which reflects the Hindu way of life and the composite Hindu-Muslim culture. It gives glimpses of the influence exercised on them by western culture and the modern times. This literature cannot be branded as 'foreign' or Islamic.

Shauq: You have said that if Urdu survives it promises a great future. What do you think about the future of Urdu in India?

Firaq: Fanatical supporters of Hindi are under the illusion [sic] due to which the traditions of Hindu culture and literary excellence could not find place in Urdu literature. But people forget that Urdu is a much wider reality than Muslim Urdu. As Asghar says:

Ay Sheikh woh basit haqiqat thi kufr ki
Kuch quaid-o-band ne jise iman bana diya

(O Sheikh, heresy is that vast reality
Which subjected to constraints turns into faith)

If iman (faith) be taken to symbolise the Muslim style of Urdu, it will mean that our Muslim countrymen have so far remained deprived of many rich facets of Hindu life. Without causing any damage to Urdu, Prem Chand, Durga Sahai Suroor, Chakbast and I have so changed Urdu from within as was not possible in the beginning for any Muslim, or even for a Hindu with an imitative attitude and devotion towards the Urdu written by Muslims. Without using Sanskrit words and using Arabic-Persian words, without narrow-mindedness and fanaticism, the temperament of Urdu can be harmonised with that of Kalidas and such other Sanskrit writers. . . .

The Hindu writers just mentioned have not been able to represent Hindu literary temper, traditions and culture. The most sensitive and live face of *Khadi Boli* is Urdu, not that Urdu alone which has been written by Muslims, but the Urdu which has deeper and wider possibilities. We have now reached a stage when Muslim Urdu writers of India and Pakistan would have gladly followed in the footsteps of Hindu writers just as many Muslim fiction writers followed Prem Chand and produced beautiful fiction representing the Hindu temperament. But the powers that be did not let Urdu become such a running stream of the land of the Ganga and Yamuna. This is a great tragedy of our culture.[48] . . .

Firaq added:

[48] Ibid., p. 58.

> It was the sun of New India that Ghalib had seen rising. It was not a Hindu or a Muslim India, but an India where Hindus and Muslims lived together. Hakim Ajmal Khan, Shibli, Maulana Hussain Ahmad Madni, Maulana Abul Kalam Azad, Mahatma Gandhi, Pandit Jawaharlal Nehru and millions of their followers represented this India.

This is the India which the RSS seeks to destroy. Firaq sensed that and warned against it.

> Besides, we have to guard our people against the venomous propaganda of the Rashtriya Swayamsevak Sangh (RSS), the Hindu Mahasabha, and the Jan Sangh. We have to give the Indian Muslim a personality and a character which is different from the pattern set by Iqbal, Jinnah and the communalist Muslim League and some Muslim countries. We have also to liberate 40 crore Hindus from the shackles of narrow-minded orthodox Hindustan.[49]

The judiciary has proved to be a frail reed to rely on. The legislature and the executive it supports are bent on following their majoritarian course. The Sangh Parivar rejects the national flag and prefers its own saffron flag, the Bhagwa dhwaj. It rejects India's Constitution as well. It published its 'White Paper' denouncing the Constitution as 'anti-Hindu' and outlining the kind of polity it wishes to establish in the country, on 1 January 1993. Its front cover posed two questions: 'Who is the destroyer of India's integrity, brotherhood and communal amity?' and 'Who has spread starvation, unemployment, corruption and irreligion?' The answer is provided in the title of the White Paper – '*Vartaman* Indian *Samvidhan*'.

The word 'Indian' has been used in the Hindi title with a purpose. The implication is that it is an Indian rather than a Hindu Constitution. That is its central theme. In the foreword, Swami Hiranand writes: 'The present Constitution is contrary to the country's culture, character, circumstances, situation, etc. It is foreign-oriented.' Commending his document to the reader, he concludes: 'We will have to think afresh about our economic policy, judicial and administrative structure and other national institutions only after nullifying the present Constitution.' It has to be discarded completely as a matter of high priority: 'The damage done by two hundred years long rule of the British is negligible as compared to the harm done by our Constitution. The conspiracy to convert Bharat into India continues.' He laments that 'we are known as Indians the world over' and reminds the reader that 'the freedom struggle was fought in the name of Hinduism. Vande Mataram was our national song . . . in post-Independence India, Hindustan and Vande Mataram have been exterminated. Jana Gana Mana, a song to welcome George V, has become our national anthem'.

[49] Ibid., pp. 95-6.

The pamphlet was not a sudden outburst. It was a calculated move, made after full deliberation. On 25 December 1992, soon after the demolition of the Babri Masjid, its author Swami Muktanand held a press conference in New Delhi, at the residence of a BJP member of parliament, jointly with Swami Vamdeo Maharaj. They gave a call to the nation to reject the 'anti-Hindu Constitution': 'We have no faith in the country's laws' and 'the sadhus are above the law of the land'. India's citizenship law which considers all born in the country as its natural citizens is 'humbug'. A week later, Muktanand's pamphlet was published.

Fittingly enough, the mother of the *parivar*, the RSS, was the first to express its views on the White Paper. In January 1993 the then *de facto* RSS supremo, Rajendra Singh wrote:

> The present conflict can be partially attributed to the inadequacies of our system in responding to the needs of the essential India, its tradition, values and ethos . . . Certain specialities of this country should be reflected in the Constitution. In place of 'India that is Bharat', we should have said 'Bharat that is Hindustan'. Official documents refer to the 'composite culture', but ours is certainly not a composite culture. Culture is not wearing of clothes or speaking languages. In a very fundamental sense, this country has a unique cultural oneness. No country, if it has to survive, can have compartments. All this shows that changes are needed in the Constitution. A Constitution more suited to the ethos and genius of this country should be adopted in the future.[50]

On 24 January 1993 at Anantpur, Andhra Pradesh, M.M. Joshi, then BJP president, 'reiterated the demand for a fresh look at the Constitution'. Thus, far from being disowned, Muktanand's pamphlet has been confirmed in the *parivar*'s distinctive style – creep stealthily, make ambiguous formulations, follow them by explicit assertions – and strike.

The pamphlet complains: 'Westernised people unfamiliar with the culture and history of India are the creators of our Constitution.' K.M. Munshi, was one of them. He was also one of the founders of the VHP. It condemns reservations for the Scheduled Castes, Scheduled Tribes and Backward Classes. The minorities fare worse. The Constitution is denounced in intemperate language. 'This Constitution can be called a pile of garbage . . . the Constitution of India is an enemy of the nation's unity and integrity.'

The RSS proceeds unchecked and not against Muslims alone. Christians and Sikhs come within its net. It began during the rule of the Vajpayee government and became worse under Modi. The attacks mounted steeply after the BJP-led government assumed office at the Centre in March 1998. The then Archbishop of Delhi, Alan de Lastic, said: 'What I have noticed is that ever since this Government

[50] *The Indian Express*, 14 January 1993.

came to power at the Centre, the attacks on Christians and Christian missionaries have increased.'[51] The government refused to condemn them. Union Home Minister L.K. Advani was false to his oath of office ('do right to all manner of people in accordance with the Constitution and the law without fear or favour, affection or ill-will'). He said in Baroda: 'There is no law and order problem in Gujarat.'[52] Three days later the D.G.P. said: 'The VHP and the Bajrang Dal were taking the law into their own hands.'[53] He also said that 'incidents of communal violence had increased manifold over the last few months; recently the crime rate in the State had increased by as much as 9.6 per cent. On an average, 39 crimes of serious nature like murder, rape and dacoity were reported in the State every day.' A member of the investigation team sent by the Minorities Commission revealed: 'After initial reluctance, the officials named VHP and Bajrang Dal allegedly involved in the mob attacks on Christians and Muslims.'[54]

Christians did not rush to register their protest, as they did on 4 December, but for long keep pleading for succour. On 4 December 1998, nearly 23 million Christians across the country observed a protest day demanding that the governments at the Centre and in the states check the growing violence against members of the community. A letter of protest, drawn up by the United Christians' Forum for Human Rights (UCFHR), said: 'Since January 1998 there has been more violence against the Christian community than in all the 50 years of the country's Independence. Nuns have been raped, priests executed, Bibles burnt, churches demolished, educational institutions destroyed and religious people harassed.'

This is persecution in the strict dictionary meaning of the word 'pursue with enmity and ill-treatment'. Mabel Rebello of the Congress (I) told the Rajya Sabha that day that '50 per cent of these [incidents] have occurred in Gujarat where the BJP is in power'.

The Bajrang Dal threatened Christian-run educational institutions in Karnataka with dire consequences if they did not 'Hinduise' them. Rajendra Singh declared at an RSS camp in Meerut on 22 November 1998: 'Muslims and Christians will have to accept Hindu culture as their own if Hindus are to treat them as Indians.'[55] The UCFHR bitterly complained in an open letter published on 19 November:

> The state has failed to do its duty to protect the life, dignity and property of the victims. At many places, it seemed as if the Centre and the State governments tacitly supported the communal groups. How is it otherwise that the State

[51] *Sunday*, 22 November 1998.
[52] *The Hindu*, 3 August 1998.
[53] *Hindustan Times*, 6 August 1998.
[54] *The Indian Express*, 12 August 1998.
[55] *The Asian Age*, 23 November 1998.

governments have not taken any action against the virulent and anti-national statements of the VHP, RSS, Jagran Manch and Bajrang Dal?

While the Sangh *parivar*'s animosity towards Muslims is well-known, its attitude towards Christians took many people by surprise. But, Vishwa Hindu Parishad general secretary Giriraj Kishore said in Chandigarh on 25 November: 'Today the Christians constitute a greater threat than the collective threat from separatist Muslim elements.' Describing G.S. Tohra, president of the Shiromani Gurdwara Prabandhak Committee, as a 'separatists', he said, 'all minorities including Muslims and Christians must accept that their ancestors were Hindus'. They must all return to the Hindu fold.

Donald Eugene Smith recalled in his work the desecration of a church in Bihar in 1955 and the almost total destruction in 1957 of the Gass Memorial Centre at Raipur.

They are not the only offenders: 'Look at the Jews; neither centuries of prosperity nor sense of gratitude for the shelter they found can make them more attached or even equally attached to the several countries they inhabit,' Savarkar wrote.

Golwalkar's book, *Bunch of Thoughts*, praised the book *Hindutva* and amplified its ideology. The BJP has used it as a political weapon with dangerous consequences. Chapter XII of *Bunch of Thoughts* is devoted to three 'Internal Threats' – Muslims, Christians and the Communists. Of the first two he wrote: 'Together with the change in their faith, gone are the spirit of love and devotion for the nation. Nor does it end there. They have also developed a feeling of identification with the enemies of this land. They look to some foreign lands as their holy places.' They are asked to return to the Hindu fold.

Not that it will be of much help. 'For a Hindu, he gets the first *sanskar* when he is still in his mother's womb. . . . We are, therefore, born as Hindus. About the others, they are born to this world as simple unnamed human beings and later on, either circumcised or baptised, they become Muslims or Christians.' There is, thus, no room for compromise.

Ram Swarup's tract *Hinduism vis-à-vis Christianity and Islam* contained his views about 'native' faiths. 'What is happening in India is also happening elsewhere. In America even the vestiges of once [sic], a rich spiritual culture of the Indians, is no more.' He developed the theme in its sequel *Hindu View of Christianity and Islam* (1992). 'The two ideologies have been active and systematic persecutors of pagan nations, cultures and religions.' He goes on to quote approvingly: 'Gore Vidal says that from a "barbaric Bronze Age text known as Old Testament, three anti-human religions have evolved – Judaism, Christianity and Islam"; he also calls them "sky-god religions".'

Ram Swarup damns all three religions as 'great persecutors'. The Hindu response of old was wrong. He writes:

> First, they tried to 'reform' themselves and be like their rulers. . . . One God, a revealed Book and prophets. . . . The Brahmo Samaj, the Arya Samaj, and the Akalis also claimed monotheism and iconoclasm . . . in the case of the Akalis, the new look has also become the basis of a new separatist-militant politics. . . .
>
> The second way the Hindus adopted was that of 'synthesis'. The synthesisers claimed that all religions preach the same thing. They found in the Bible and the Quran all the truths of the Upanishads and *vice-versa.*

The wrath wells up as he proceeds to deliver a message which explains why the country has had to undergo what it has all these years, especially since 1990:

> India became politically free in 1947, but it is ruled by anti-Hindu Hindus. The old mental slavery continues and it has yet to win its cultural and intellectual independence. India is entering into the second phase of its freedom struggle; the struggle for regaining its Hindu identity. The new struggle is as difficult as the old one. Hindus are disorganised, self-alienated, morally and ideologically disarmed. They lack leadership; the Hindu elites have become illiterate about their spiritual heritage and history and indifferent and even hostile towards their religion. . . . India's higher education, its academia and media are in the hands of Hindu-hating elite.

Note what Ram Swarup has to say of the caste system:

> Once when Hinduism was strong, castes represented a *natural* and healthy diversity, but now in its present state of weakness these are used for its dismemberment. Old vested interests joined by new ones have come together to make use of the caste factor in a big way in order to keep Hindus down.

Ram Swarup adopts a dual approach in *Hindu-Sikh Relationship* (1985). He woos them as 'the members of Hindu society' but denounces them for thinking that 'they were different'. Base motives are freely attributed:

> Thanks to the Green Revolution and various other factors, the Sikhs have become relatively more rich and prosperous. No wonder, they have begun to find that the Hindu bond is not good enough for them and they seek a new identity readily available to them in their names and outer symbols. This is an understandable human frailty.

He defends the storming of the Golden Temple. It 'became an arsenal, a fort, sanctuary for criminals. This grave situation called for necessary action which caused some *unavoidable* damage to the building'. There followed 'protest meetings, resolutions', which he deprecates. 'The whole thing created widespread resentment all over India which burst into a most unwholesome violence when Mrs. Indira Gandhi was assassinated. A growing resentment at the arrogant Akali politics is the main cause of this fearful happening.'

This is of a piece with the *Organiser*'s defence of Gandhi's assassination in its editorial (11 January 1970) – 'turned the people's wrath on himself'.

Sita Ram Goel's ardour is reflected in his three books *Catholic Ashrams* (1988), *Papacy, Its Doctrine and History* (1986) and *History of Hindu-Christian Encounters* (1989). His preface to the second edition (1996) of the book on Hindu-Christian encounters explains a lot:

> The Sangh parivar, which had turned cold towards Hindu causes over the years, *was startled by the rout of the Bharatiya Janata Party in the 1984 elections, and decided to renew its Hindu character. The Ramajanmabhoomi Movement was the result.* The Movement was aimed at arresting Islamic aggression. Christianity or its missions were hardly mentioned. Nevertheless, it was Christianity which showed the greatest concern at this new Hindu stir, and started crying 'wolf'. Its media power in the West raised a storm, saying that Hindus were out to destroy the minorities in India and impose a Nazi regime. The storm is still raging and no one knows when it will subside, if at all.

Thus, 'the storm' was unleashed for reasons of power through election victories.

It is with some hesitation that one turns to Goel's book *Jesus Christ: An Artifice for Aggression*, so wantonly offensive it is. The focus now is not on the missionaries, or politics, or history. The target is the faith itself; Christianity as a religion. Why? Because hitherto

> We Hindus have remained occupied with the behaviour patterns of Muslims and Christians and not with the belief systems which create those behaviour patterns. We object to Christian missions, but refuse to discuss Christianity and its God, Jesus. We object to Islamic terrorisms, but refuse to have a look at Islam and its prophet, Muhammad. I see no sense or logic in this Hindu habit.

Is there any other country in the world where such theses are written for such a purpose? One wonders. 'Now, I could see why the history of Christianity had been what it had been. The source of the poison was in the Jesus of the gospels.'

The Immaculate Conception of Virgin Mary is attacked wantonly. There are chapters on the Jesus of history, of fiction and of faith. The thesis? He did not exist in history.

> The quantum of crimes committed by Muhammad's Islam was only slightly smaller than that of the crimes committed by the Christianity of the Jesus Christ.... The parallel between Jesus and Hitler was seen as still more striking. The Nazi creed, as laid down by Hitler, did not sound much different from the Christian creed as preached by Jesus in the gospels.

Goel is dismayed to find that Jesus Christ 'should continue to retain his hallow [sic]' in India. 'Christianity is accepted as a religion not only by the westernised Hindu elite but also by Hindu saints, scholars, and political platforms.'

Jesus Christ has been 'praised to the skies, particularly by Mahatma Gandhi'. But,

> It is high time for Hindus to learn that Jesus Christ symbolises no spiritual power, or moral uprightness. He is no more than an artifice for legitimising wanton imperialist aggression. The aggressors have found him to be highly profitable so far. By the same token, Hindus should know that Jesus means nothing but mischief for their country and culture. The West where he flourished for long has discarded him as junk. There is no reason why Hindus should buy him. He is the type of junk that cannot be re-cycled. He can only poison the environment.

The virulence of the language reveals the depths of the hatred. This is what Indians are up against – a powerful hate group, enjoying the patronage of politicians in power and in the administration, which is out to wipe out all traces not only of secularism and democracy but of religious tolerance, religious and cultural diversity and, indeed, of decency itself from India.

A publishing house in Old Delhi churns out such vitriol unchecked. The RSS's war on history very much covers Christendom. Sita Ram Goel wrote a 530 page tome entitled *History of Hindu-Christian Encounters, A.D. 304 to 1996*. He also wrote *Jesus Christ: An Artifice for Aggression* (1994). With soul mates Major T.R. Vedantham and Ram Swarup he wrote *Christianity: An Imperialist Ideology*.

Ram Swarup competed enthusiastically. He wrote: *Hindu View of Christianity and Islam*, and *Hinduism vis-à-vis Christianity and Islam*. Special mention is merited by two other literary products of Ram Swarup. *Buddhism vis-à-vis Hinduism* seeks to assimilate Buddhism into Hinduism and denounces Buddhists who reject that.

He made a similar effort with Sikhism in his pamphlet *Hindu-Sikh Relationship*. It was published in February 1985. These extracts reveal its thesis and political purpose.

Hindus were Sikhs and Sikhs were Hindus. The distinction between them was functional, not fundamental. A Sikh was a Hindu in a particular role. When under the changed circumstances, he could not play that role, he reverted to his original status.

As early as 1872, the loyal Sikhs supported the cruel suppression of the Namdhari Sikhs who had started a Swadeshi movement. They were described as a 'wicked and misguided sect'. The same forces described the Ghadarites in 1914 as 'rebels' who should be dealt with mercilessly.

These organisations also spearheaded the movement for the de-Hinduisation of the Sikhs and preached that the Sikhs were distinct from the Hindus. Anticipating the Muslims, they represented to the British Government as far back as 1888 that they be recognised as a separate community. They expelled the Brahmins from the Har Mandir, where the latter had worked as priests. They also threw out the idols of 'Hindu' Gods from this temple, which were installed there.

Surprisingly enough, the game continues to be played even after the British left. The minorities are encouraged to feel insecure and aggrieved. The minority stick is found handy to beat the majority. Hindu-baiting is politically profitable and intellectually fashionable. Constantly under attack, a Hindu tries to save himself by self-accusation; he behaves as if he is making amends for being a Hindu.

The atmosphere provided hot-house conditions for the growth of divisive politics. Our Sikh brethren too remembered the old lesson (never really forgotten), taught to them by the British, that they were different. . . . Under the pressure of this psychology, grievances were manufactured; extreme slogans were put forward with which even moderate elements had to keep pace. In the last few years, even the politics of murder was introduced. Finding no check, it knew not where to stop; it became a law unto itself; it began to dictate, to bully. Camps came up in India as well as across the border, where young men were taught killing, sabotage and guerrilla warfare. The temple at Amritsar became an arsenal, a fort, a sanctuary for criminals. This grave situation *called for necessary action* which caused some *unavoidable* damage to the building. When this happened, the same people who looked at the previous drama, either helplessly or with an indulgent eye, felt outraged. There were protest meetings, resolutions, desertions from the army, aid committees for the suspects apprehended, and even calls and vows to take revenge. The extremists were forgotten. There were two standards at work; there was a complete lack of self-reflection even among the more moderate and responsible Sikh leaders.

The whole thing created wide-spread resentment all over India which burst into a most unwholesome violence when Mrs. Indira Gandhi was assassinated. The befoggers have again got busy and they explain the whole

> tragedy in terms of collusion between the politicians and the police. But this conspiracy theory cannot explain the range and the virulence of the tragedy. A growing resentment at the arrogant Akali politics is the main cause of this fearful happening.[56]

Comment is superfluous on the exertions by these writers and their factory of hate. But as two devoted friends of India the scholars Susanne Hoeber Rudolph and Lloyd I. Rudolph pointed out in a brilliant essay published by *The New Republic* on 22 March 1993 entitled 'Modern Hate', the hate is very modern. History is drummed up to support imagined wrongs and bolster aggression inspired by hate.

Modern hate is a manufactured product to suit the ends of political warfare. As Rudolf said:

> 'Ancient hatreds' function like the 'evil empire'. That term too was a projection on a scrim, obscuring the motives and practice that lay behind it. The doctrine of ancient hatreds may become the post-cold war's most robust mystification, a way of having an enemy and knowing evil that deceives as it satisfies. The hatred is modern and may be closer than we think.

The intensification of Hindutva has acted, as intended by its followers, to divert attention from the fact that almost half the population of India is at or below the poverty line and is denied even the most basic rights and amenities. Instead of working towards providing these rights and amenities to the tribals and the Dalits, the focus has been shifted to the irrelevant question of the right to convert. The hype surrounding the issue of which Indians are indigenous and which are foreign, basing this identity on the false premise of whether they follow a religion which is indigenous to the subcontinent or is west Asian in origin, has led to the most inhuman and unethical behaviour on the part of groups claiming to defend Hinduism and is directed towards those labelled as Muslims and Christians.

This is all that Sangh Parivar has to offer. When one reads the resolutions of the RSS, the BJP and the VHP and the utterances of their leaders one is appalled by their antediluvian outlook, their rejection of Muslims, Christians, Sikhs and Buddhists, disdain for national heroes from Ashoka, Akbar to Jawaharlal Nehru, their contempt for Western intellectual tradition and, indeed, for any intellectual approach at all. Sweeping rejection of 'Western' civilisation is puerile; if juxtaposed with the controversy on revivalism, it reflects an infantile malady. No one now identifies Westernisation with modernisation. The crucial test is rationalism. In a lecture on *Modernisation of a Traditional Society*, one of the most incisive writers on religion and reason Wilfred Cantwell Smith said:

[56] Ram Swarup, *Hindu-Sikh Relationship*, New Delhi: Voice of India, 1985, pp. 11, 14-5, 18-24.

> The fact is that the West has begun in only extremely incipient fashion to understand any civilisation other than its own. Perforce, it has tended to approach others in the terms that it has worked out for itself; and these are often inappropriate. The structure of a western Faculty of Arts, for instance, is in my considered judgment and experience in need of serious re-thinking and modification for this new period of western history, in which its intellectual horizon has been suddenly broadened to transcend its own civilisation, within whose boundaries it had thought until yesterday. Now that it is attempting to include the whole world in its purview, there is a serious question whether departments like history, economics, art, literature, and the like and more recent ones like religion are the most intelligent and serviceable way to slice up human experience, other people's as well as one's own.
>
> To reconstruct our thinking here, we in the West shall need the help of intellectuals from the non-western world, who understand enough of modern western culture and thought to talk to us, and yet are intellectually strong and honest and creative enough to talk back to us, or rather to talk forward with us – not in repudiation or hostile debate, but in colloquium, towards the construction of new categories of thinking adequate to our new multi-cultural world.[57]

Are the RSS and its political department, the BJP, equal to the challenges of modernity? They obviously are not. We must not stop at that. We must proceed to ask ourselves whatever happened in our history that led to the rise of such vile forces in our public life. Why do Hindus, including some modernists, support them? It would be wrong to ignore their concerns. Clearly our polity needs intellectual exertions which touch the roots of the problem.

The BJP's obeisance is understandable. The RSS's arm provides muscle men during and between elections and its ideology promises comforts of certitude. One awaits a rigorous effort to get at the roots of our malaise of today.

One man foresaw it all before and after independence – Jawaharlal Nehru. Yezdi Gundevia, was noted for his independence, integrity and a touch of irreverence. As foreign secretary he began convening on Fridays meetings of officers, from under-secretaries upwards, where they talked with no holds barred. Let Gundevia describe their encounter with the Prime Minister.

> Friday morning, 11 o'clock, I walked the Prime Minister to the jam-packed Conference Room. He sat down, smiled all round and said, 'Well, what's your agenda today?'

[57] The lectures were delivered at Sapru House, New Delhi on 23, 24 and 25 March 1984 under the auspices of the Indian Council of World Affairs. They were published in a slim volume by that name – *Modernisation of a Traditional Society* – by Asia Publishing House, 1965.

'We have no agenda, sir, but maybe some of them would like to ask you some questions,' I said.

'Not very difficult questions, I hope,' he said, and everybody laughed.

There was silence. I heard one pin drop. Then I heard another pin drop. Was that Muthu's hairpin? She was religiously looking at the ceiling. Had someone told my favourite female firebrand deputy to keep mum that morning? Not I. Was everybody scared of the fire-eating Nehru, I wondered. Then I ventured: 'Well, sir, if these people don't want to ask you any questions, maybe I could suggest one of my themes. The Indian National Congress has been the only political party in power from the point of Independence, unlike so many countries where there is a change of government after one or another election. The Civil Servant in India is, as a result, tuned only to the Congress policies. You lay down the policy and we carry out your policies . . .'

'You carry out the policies, do you!' interrupted the Prime Minister with obvious sarcasm.

'Of course, we do,' I said with emphasis. 'If we don't, then who does?' I asked pertinently.

'All right, all right, carry on,' said Nehru.

'Well, sir, this being the case, what happens if tomorrow, shall we say, the communists come into power? We have had a communist government in Kerala. But what happens to the Services if the communists are elected to power, tomorrow, at the Centre, here in New Delhi?'

He pondered over my long drawn out question and then said, looking across the room, 'Communists, communists, communists! Why are all of you so obsessed with communists and communism: What is it that communists can do that we cannot do and have not done for the country: Why do you imagine the communists will ever be voted into power at the Centre!' There was a long pause after this and then he said, spelling it out slowly and very deliberately. 'The danger to India, mark you, is not communism. It is Hindu right-wing communalism.'

There was some discussion after this. Someone said something about the communist government in Kerala. Someone said something about the RSS and the Hindu Mahasabha. The Prime Minister answered the questions, seriously sometimes and quite jovially, here and there. The questions and the discussion are not important. Towards the end he repeated his thesis. 'The danger to India is not communism. It is Hindu right-wing communalism.'

The meeting was over and as I took the Prime Minister back to his room, I could hear the hum of excited voices that he had left behind in the Conference Room. Call it *obiter dicta*, call it famous last words. I have always looked upon what Jawaharlal said at this officers' meeting that day as not only his famous last words, but one of the most prophetic pronouncements that he ever made.

That was fifty-five years ago.[58]

The poison has spread alarmingly since. But the forces that spread it are not invincible. They *can* be defeated provided that those who oppose it are ready and equipped to meet the challenge at all levels; not least at the ideological level which sadly few care to meet. But 'if the trumpet give an uncertain sound, who shall prepare himself to the battle?'

What is at stake is not only the Indian Dream. What is at stake is the soul of India.

58 Y.D. Gundevia, *Outside the Archives*, Sangam Books, 1984, pp. 209-10.

1. Why Was the RSS Set Up?

Beyond a doubt, the Rashtriya Swayamsevak Sangh (RSS) is the most powerful organisation in India today; complete with a private army of its own, unquestionably obeying its leader who functions on fascist lines on the Fuehrer principle.

Its *pracharak* (active preacher) Narendra Modi is now prime minister of India. Its stamp is evident in very many fields of national life. In 1951 it set up a political front, the Bharatiya Jana Sangh, which merged into the Janata Party in 1977 only to walk out of it in 1980. In issue was its superior loyalty to its parent and mentor, the RSS; not the Janata Party. Within months of its defection, the Jana Sangh re-emerged in 1980; not under the name under which it had functioned for nearly three decades but as the Bharatiya Janata Party deceptively to claim a respectable lineage. On 6 November 1977, when he was minister for external affairs in the Janata Party government headed by Morarji Desai, Atal Bihari Vajpayee gave this assurance, 'When we joined the Janata Party we had given up old beliefs and facts and there was no question of going back'; a tacit admission of the incompatibility between the party's ideology and that of the Jana Sangh. In 1980 he asked, '[W]hen did we get away from the Jana Sangh?' Very revealing was his candid disclosure on 22 July 1985, 'we wanted to assert our views in the (Janata Party) Government but the Government broke up too soon. Had we been in power for some more time, we would have imparted a new thinking to India's politics' – the lament of a failed Trojan horse.

Deceptive double talk marks the RSS utterances; to wit, that it is a 'cultural' organisation, not a political one; it is a 'nationalist' not a communal body; all who live in India are Hindus, while defining the term to exclude those who are not Hindu by faith; it neither controls the BJP nor interferes in its internal affairs. It is another matter that it sent two presidents of the Jana Sangh (Mauli Chandra Sharma and Balraj Madhok) and one of the BJP (Lal Krishna Advani) packing.

In 2018, no one in his right mind entertains the notions of old which some Indian and Western writers fondly entertained; namely that the BJP would cut loose from the RSS and emerge as India's moderate conservative party offering lip sympathy to Hindutva. Thirty years ago, in 1987 two scholars accurately described their relationship.

> The BJP for its part will try to develop into a national political force, but it is questionable whether it can do so with a cadre drawn largely from the RSS. Within the party's organisational structure, the cadre has been reluctant to share power with politically prominent figures from non-RSS backgrounds

> who could mobilise mass support for the party. The RSS training, emphasising the sacrifice of self for the larger good, and the apolitical orientation of the RSS ideology, make it unlikely that politically charismatic figures will emerge from within its own ranks. On the other hand, it is questionable if the BJP could survive politically without the RSS cadre, and the cadre will not stay unless the leadership of the party stays firmly in the hands of the 'brotherhood'.[1]

The last two decades, particularly, have demonstrated the soundness of their analysis. The BJP depends precariously on the RSS's cadres. Himachal Pradesh is a small state but 'an army of 30,000 RSS workers descended on the State to ensure the BJP's victory in the November 9 Assembly elections'. There are 700 RSS shakhas (units) and 25 'sister organisations' in the state.[2] Imagine the size of the RSS's armies that will go on a rampage all over the country for the Lok Sabha election due in 2019.

The RSS's supremo Mohan Bhagwat gets more strident by the day. Addressing a gathering of RSS volunteers at Indore on 27 October 2017, he said, 'Whose country is Germany? It is a country of Germans, Britain is a country of Britishers, America is a country of Americans, and in the same way Hindustan is a country of Hindus. It does not mean that Hindustan is not the country of other people . . . The term "Hindu" covers all those who are the sons of Bharat Mata (Mother India), descendants of Indian ancestors and *who live in accordance with the Indian culture*.'[3] The catch lies in the italicised proviso. A Hindu is one who practises 'Indian' (i.e. Hindu culture). This is the RSS-BJP family (the Sangh Parivar's) concept of 'cultural nationalism' which every election manifesto of the BJP in the last quarter century espouses.

The RSS's uniqueness and prominence obscure a question which goes to the very roots of the matter – *Why was it set up at all?* What role did it aspire to play in India's national life? The All-India Hindu Mahasabha was set up in 1915. The five who joined hands to establish the RSS on Dussehra Day, September 1925 were all members of the Mahasabha. What contribution did it aspire to make to India's movement for freedom from British rule?

In 1925 that movement was at its peak. The Mahasabha was a powerful party led by leaders like Pandit Madan Mohan Malaviya and Lala Lajpat Rai. Where, then, was the need for yet another body with similar aims? As Dr. B.R. Ambedkar explained, British rule in India passed through three stages. In the first,

[1] Walter K. Andersen and Shridhar D. Damle, *The Brotherhood in Saffron: The Rashtriya Swayamsevak Sangh and Hindu Revivalism*, New Delhi: Vistaar Publications, 1987, pp. 238-9.

[2] Lalit Mohan, 'RSS' invisible machinery wooing HP voters', *The Tribune*, 6 November 2017.

[3] 'Like Germany of Germans, Hindustan of Hindus: RSS', *The Tribune*, 29 November 2017.

> the British Government held the view which was a complete negation of India's claim for freedom. It was proclaimed by Lawrence whose statue in Calcutta has the motto: 'The British conquered India by the sword and they will hold it by the sword.' This attitude is dead and buried and it is no exaggeration to say that every Englishman today is ashamed of it. This stage was followed by another in which the argument of the British Government against India's freedom was the alleged incapacity of Indians for Parliamentary institutions. It began with Lord Ripon's regime which was followed by an attempt to give political training to Indians, first in the field of Local Self-Government, and then under the Montagu-Chelmsford reforms in the field of provincial Government. We have now entered the third or the present stage. The British Government is now ashamed to say that they will hold India by the sword. It no longer says that Indians have no capacity to run Parliamentary institutions. The British Government admits India's right to freedom, even to independence, if Indians so desire. The British Government admits the right of Indians to frame their own constitution. There can be no greater proof of this new angle of vision than the Cripps proposals. The condition precedent laid down by the British Government for India's freedom is that Indians must produce a constitution which has the concurrence of the important elements in the national life of the country. Such is the stage we have reached in 1946.[4]

But neither the RSS nor the Hindu Mahasabha, or their 19th-century ideological ancestors in Hindu revivalism, had any desire to put their shoulder to the wheel and help in the freedom movement. They obstructed it and thought nothing of collaborating with the British.

The RSS and the Mahasabha were torn apart by ego clashes and zeal for organisational independence. They shared the ideology of Hindutva propounded by Vinayak Damodar Savarkar in his essay *Hindutva* published in 1925. They also shared the membership and loyalty of Gandhi's assassin Nathuram Vinayak Godse. The RSS's founder was Keshav Baliram Hedgewar. His political guru was B.S. Moonje. In later years the RSS reversed the roles to establish Hedgewar's primacy.

In an excellent study *RSS's Tryst with Politics: From Hedgewar to Sudarshan*, the scholar Pralay Kanungo notes that while the Mahasabha was content to assert the 'legitimate rights of the Hindus as a majority community' Hedgewar made a significant shift from the Mahasabha's *Hindu Raj* (Hindu Rule) to *Hindu Rashtra* (Hindu Nation).[5] This was coupled with aggressive spread of hate as Hedgewar denounced Muslims as 'Yavana Snakes' and a determined programme for building

4 B.R. Ambedkar, *What Congress and Gandhi Have Done to the Untouchables*, Bombay: Thacker & Co. Ltd., 1946, p. 177.

5 Pralay Kanungo, *RSS's Tryst with Politics: From Hedgewar to Sudarshan*, Manohar Publishers, 2002, p. 43.

a private army of 'volunteers'. They played an important role in communal riots, as several Commissions of Inquiry found.

It is useful to consult C.P. Bhishikar's hagiographic essay *Sangh-Vriksh Ke Beej: Dr. Keshavrao Hedgewar* (Delhi: Suruchi Prakashan, 1994). He was chief editor *Tarun Bharat*, a swayamsevak, and wrote studies on Deen Dayal Upadhyaya and Hedgewar. He acquired the Hindi translation of the Marathi text from K.S. Sudarshan, the RSS chief. The author is indebted to a friend for the English translation.

The importance of his contribution of 1994 lies not in its being an accurate account, but as a revelatory exposition of the RSS's reflections on its past, its assessment of the situation in 1994, and its vision for future.

> Sangh means organised power of Hindus. The reason for this is Hindus are the only fate makers of this nation. They are its natural masters. This country is theirs and uplift and fall of the nation is dependent on them. History offers the conclusion that this is a Hindu nation. The present [i.e. 1994] situation also indicates the same.
>
> The first feature of the Sangh system was everyday Shakha, through which the swayamsevaks are gathered on a daily basis. With the physical and mental programmes of the Shakha interest on training and sacraments can be cast to work in discipline. Masculine [sic] developing sticks, arrow, spear, crook, javelin, etc. and fun Kabaddi like sports. . . .
>
> Doctor sahib, while explaining the meaning of autonomy used to say that, from the ancient times, India was the country of Hindus, therefore the national life here shall be made rich by them only, and nobody shall have the courage to attack or shock it. In his view the imagination of 'Empire of Hindus' is that, the cultural effect of India shall be outside also and the people of the world will follow the best living values of Hindus [Jagadguru; a world teacher].
>
> Doctor sahib made it clear that, the policy of Sangh is to keep away from politics and organise Hindus, any member from any party who wants to be part of Hindu organisation work can come into Sangh. . . . The principle of 'Hindutva is Nationality' of Sangh was not acceptable to Congress. They have taken the imagination of the Bhanmati family Nationality. Their opinion was whoever lives within the geographical borders of India, this is their Nation. Hence, in the view of Congress the Sangh which works for Hindu organisation was communal.

Bhishikar cites instances of Hedgewar instilling in Hindus the idea of revenge. 'With the blows of lathis their heads were broken and there was a situation of crying "Touba-Touba". Hindus were cautious and there was nothing left for Muslims but to put their legs on their heads and run away. *The total community was ready for revenge.*' Hedgewar rejected Syama Prasad Mookerjee's proposal that the RSS should enter politics. 'India is the only nation which was born with the blessing of immortality.'

Importantly, Bhishikar traces the RSS's roots to the revivalists of the 19th century.

> In the second half of nineteenth century and in the first half of twentieth century the Sage Dayanand, Ramkrishna Paramahamsa, Swami Vivekanand, Swami Ramteerth, Mahayogi Arvind and Raman Maharshi like spiritual people have said this is the fate of the Nation. Consciousness has awakened in the nation and the independence movement has started, and *Vande Mataram has become Mahamantra of that movement. . . .*
>
> In the second half of the nineteenth century and in the first half of twentieth century there were many intellectuals in this country. The series of great intellectuals of spirituality, religion, culture, training, social improvement, politics, administration, and science in different fields may surprise us. Doctor sahib was born in this national atmosphere.

The RSS fostered a siege mentality.

> Where there was authority of Hindus not only in Hindustan but in nearby nations for thousand-five hundred years, today the situation is that even in Hindustan the Hindus cannot call this nation as Hindustan. Today Hindu society is surrounded by many difficulties. The defect is ours, we are weak and asleep. On one side is the foreign administrators' political dominance and on other hand the social torture of Muslims on us. We are stuck in between the blades of a scissor. If I speak on the attacks made on Hindus to make them Muslims, while raping our daughters and daughters-in-law, I cannot control my emotions. Hence, I will not speak more on that; also Christians were injuring us. If we want to protect our society from these attacks, we have to organise ourselves. With this one intention in the year 1925 the Rashtriya Swayamsevak Sangh was established.

The 'ghar wapsi' programme of conversions to Hinduism was conceived then. For all its cultivated ambiguities, a stern consistency marks the RSS's policies since its very inception. It was born to oppose the Congress's secular creed and continues to do this for nearly a century. '"Secularism" always adopts the ways of anti-Hindu . . . The Sangh has kept the holy Sanatan Hindu religion, our Ancient Hindu culture and our Hindu Nation and the Saffron flag of ancient times in its present form.' This explicit formulation exposes the double-speak. 'Culture' is inextricably intertwined with 'religion'.

In 1994 Bhishikar was emboldened to rejoice, 'Hindu society is moving on the path of the Sangh organisation.' He emphasised that 'Doctor sahib (Hedgewar) used to insist on *one* thing as a Hindu. His belief was that "Hindutva is Rashtriyata"'. The nation belongs to Hindus; the rest must conform. Hindustan does not signify the inclusive and proud Hindustan in Iqbal's famous poem. It signifies the land of Hindus as the RSS supremo Mohan Bhagwat made clear on 27 October 2017.

Every institution that represents a different outlook or ideology must be obliterated. The RSS and the BJP reject the very concept of a 'minority'. This at a time when the United Nations and Europe began moving in the opposite direction with multiple treaties and conventions on minority rights.

Bhishikar wrote:

> To achieve national unity and the protection of integrity, Sangh repeatedly pressed for ending the Minorities Commission; instead, we shall make a Human Rights Commission. Article 370 on Kashmir shall be abrogated, foreign Christian missionaries shall be thrown out and all foreign contributions in crores of rupees to Christian and Muslim institutions for change of religion shall be banned completely. The Sangh has given a clear warning to the citizens that whenever the Hindu is in a minority that Pradesh is cut from the Nation, hence it should be banned wherever by fraud or by force conversions are done. As regards Punjab, the role of the Sangh is totally national. It has said that, the Sikhs are the part of Hindu society.

A neglected aspect of the RSS's *raison d'être* is its ambition for global leadership – Jagadguru. A 'World Mission'.

Bhishikar's hagiography is not history. We have accurate historical accounts from scholars of repute. The decision to set up the RSS was triggered off by communal riots in Nagpur which affected Hedgewar's mind. It was highly receptive to their impact. He deplored the fact that 'Out of 1.5 lakh (150,000) population of Nagpur, Muslims are only 20 thousand. But still we feel insecure. Muslims were never afraid of 1 lakh 30 thousand Hindus. So this question should be regarded hereafter as the question of the Hindus. The Muslims themselves have taught us to behave as Hindus while in the Congress, and as Hindus outside the Congress.' During this period of escalating Hindu-Muslim animosity in Nagpur, Hedgewar began to develop the intellectual foundations of the RSS. A major influence on his thinking was a handwritten manuscript of Vinayak Damodar Savarkar's *Hindutva* which advanced the thesis that the Hindus were a nation.[6]

Chetan Bhatt also notes this recurring theme. The 'nineteenth century linearism paradigm of Hindu glory, *degradation* and invigoration'. Imagined degradation provokes aggressive invigoration. Lajpat Rai wrote:

[6] Anderson and Damle, *The Brotherhood in Saffron*, p. 33.

> A question has often haunted us, asleep or awake, as to why is it that notwithstanding the presence among us of great, vigorous and elevating truths, and of the very highest conception of morality, we [Hindus] have been a subject race, held down for so many centuries by sets of people who were neither physically nor spiritually nor even intellectually so superior to us as *a fortiori* to demand our subjection. ('The one pressing need of India.')[7]

The myths prevail to this day and so does the haunting spectre.

The RSS was founded on Vijaya Dashami Day at Hedgewar's residence. Present were B.S. Moonje, Babarao Savarkar, elder brother of V.D. Savarkar, L.V. Paranjpe and B.B. Thakkar. 'This group consisted entirely of Hindu Mahasabha activists. . . . Hedgewar was delegated the task of recruiting teenage boys.'[8] D.R. Goyal, a former swayamsevak, mentions the same names in his book *Rashtriya Swayamsewak Sangh*.[9] However, the RSS's organ *Organiser* mentions different names for the 'Founding Fathers': Pandharinath Balkrishna; Gopal Mukund; Prabhakar Balwant, L.V. Paranjpe, Govind Sitaram, Anant Ganesh, Vitthal Govind and Krishnaji Neelkanth Mofreel. Besides them, the following were present at the first meeting. Narayan Yashwant, Raghunath Bande, Anna Vaidya, Narhar Palekar, Annaji Gaikwad, Devghar, Bapurao Telang, Balasaheb Athalye and Advocate Vishwanath. Vinayak Kelkar and Baburao Sonarkar's names are omitted.[10]

It took the RSS a year to acquire its name in 1926. Bhatt recalls what followed.

> From May of that year, the RSS instituted a daily routine of physical exercise, military drills and marches, weapons training, ideological inculcation, and Hindu nationalist prayers to 'the motherland and Holyland' and to the RSS's new saffron flag (*bhagwa dhwaj*). The RSS's *shakhas included danda* (weapons training with lathi or a wooden staff), *khadga* (sword training), *vetracharma* (fighting with canes), precision drill marching and *yogchap* (callisthenic exercises such as with a lezim – metal plates wound together around a wooden bar and played with the hands). Its training today extends to non-Indian martial arts. Its distinctive salute (pranam) to the saffron flag, although also common among other youth groups in the 1920s and 1930s (including those of Congress), today cannot but evoke the period of 1930s Europe.
>
> The RSS's prayer was initially in Marathi and Hindi, but was changed at the end of 1939 into a 'new-Sanskrit' version. The prayer (composed by N.N. Bhide, a schoolteacher) glorified 'Hindubhumi' and 'Hindu Rashtra' while eliciting a declaration of Hindu 'heroism', and was to be later supplemented by

7 Quoted in Chetan Bhatt, *Hindu Nationalism*, p. 52.

8 Ibid., p. 119.

9 D.R. Goyal, *Rashtriya Swayamsewak Sangh*, Radha Krishna Prakashan, 2000, p. 69.

10 'RSS' 90 Transformative Years', *Organiser*, 11 December 2016.

> the RSS's Ekata Mantra and its Ekatmata Strota, among a range of distinctive Hindu nationalist 'unity' hymns and songs. The swayamsevaks – RSS members working in the service of the Hindu Nation – were obliged to wear the RSS's uniform from 1926. The next year the RSS's annual Officer Training Camp (OTC) was started and in 1928, the RSS undertook its first mass initiation of swayamsevaks, the latter swearing a lifelong oath of service and sacrifice that involved 'offering himself entirely – body, mind and wealth – for the preservation and progress of the Hindu Nation'. From this point, swayamsevaks were also to view the RSS flag as their only 'guru' or 'true preceptor', and offer monetary donations to it (in the manner of guru dakshina). The RSS transformed some Hindu traditions in which a disciple selects and follows a guru, ideally for life, into one in which the 'guru' is the Hindu nationalist flag.
>
> From 1930, the RSS began to institute the pracharak (full-time organiser) system whereby trained swayamsevak cadres were sent to other provinces to initiate branches (shakhas) and undertake the propagation of its ideology; it had trained about a hundred active pracharaks by the early 1940s. The RSS shakha network expanded and one shakha was started at Madan Mohan Malaviya's Banaras Hindu University at which Madhav Sadashiv Golwalkar was teaching. The latter became first the RSS sarkaryavah (General Secretary) and in 1940 the sarsanghchalak.
>
> In November 1929, the RSS inaugurated the office of sarsanghchalak (Supreme Leader or the 'Guide and Philosopher' of the RSS), the practice of pranam (a gesture of prayer) to the leader and the overriding organisational principle of eka chalak anuvartitva or subservience to the one 'Supreme Leader'. Also of importance was the characterisation of the sarsanghchalak as parampoojaniya – the principal one who is to be venerated.[11]

The one chosen to indoctrinate the young was a 'boudhik'; an 'intellectual' in residence, as it were. N.V. Godse was one such boudhik.

The original oath written by Hedgewar was given to 99 swayamsevaks at Nagpur in March 1928. It read:

> I, hereby remembering the Almighty and my ancestors, take a pledge that, I have become a member of the Rashtriya Swayamsevak Sangh to protect the sacred Hindu Dharma, Hindu Sanskriti and Hindu Society, and to make this Hindu Rashtra Independent. I will carry on the Sangh work honestly, selflessly and with all my physical, mental and monitory strength, and will stick to this resolve throughout my life.[12]

[11] Bhatt, *Hindu Nationalism*, pp. 119-20.

[12] From RSS Archives: The pledge that was given to 99 selected swayamsevaks at Nagpur in March 1928; *Organiser*, 11 December 2016.

After 1939 the oath (Pratigya) which new members have to be read was:

Before the All-Powerful God and my ancestors, I most solemnly take this oath, that I have become a member of the Rashtriya Swayamsevak Sangh in order to achieve all-round greatness of Bharatvarsh by fostering the growth of my sacred Hindu religion, Hindu society and Hindu culture. I shall perform the work of the Sangh honestly, disinterestedly, with my heart and soul, and I shall adhere to this oath all my life. Bharat Mata ki Jai.

Before 1939, the slogan in the oath was 'Jai Bajrang-Bali Balbhim-ki-Jai'.[13]

A Hindi-Marathi prayer which was sung in the RSS's shakha till 1939 when the present Sanskrit prayer was introduced read:

Salutations to you, O Motherland where I am born;
Salutations to you, O the Land of Aryas where I have grown;
Salutation to you, O Sacred Land where I have worked;
My body will ever and again bow to you in salutation;
O Guru, the messenger of Rama, grant us good character;

Give us soon all the virtues to become full Hindus;
Induct us to your grace and make us followers of Rama:
May we become celibate, defenders of faith and men of brave determination.
Victory to Samarth Shri Ramdas, the Guru of the Nation
Victory to Mother India.

The English version of the above Sanskrit prayer which is sung in the RSS shakhas these days is given below:

O Affectionate Motherland, I eternally bow to you.
O Land of Hindus, you have reared me in comfort.
O Sacred Land, the Great Creator of Good, may this body of mine be dedicated to you.
I again and again bow before you.

O God Almighty, we the integral parts of Hindu Rashtra salute you in reverence;
For your cause have we girded up our loins,
Give us your blessings for its accomplishment;
Give us also the invincible power, the purity of character which may win the respect of entire world and the wisdom which may facilitate the thorny path that we have consciously adopted.

[13] Goyal, *Rashtriya Swayamsewak Sangh*, pp. 248-9.

> Let our hearts be inspired by the bold determination to achieve salvation along with prosperity which alone is the outstanding means;
> Let undying and intense devotion to the goal be ever alive in our minds;
> With your blessings let our all-conquering organised force meet with eminent success in taking this Nation of ours to the highest pinnacle of glory while defending our dharma.
> Victory to Mother India![14]

At the November 1929 meeting Hedgewar put his stamp on the RSS by imposing the Fuehrer principle, the principle of *eka chalak anuvartitva* (to follow one leader). Appaji Joshi proposed Hedgewar's name as sarsanghchalak, the supreme director, on a life-time basis. It was quite clear that the sarsanghchalak would exercise absolute power in the organisation. Hedgewar categorically stated that a swayamsevak had to obey the orders of the sarsanghchalak at any stage, under any circumstances and without any hesitation.

The RSS's fortunes rose. A Central Intelligence Bureau report said that

> In one confidential report, the celebration of the Dussehra festival by the RSS at Nagpur in 1932 has been characterised as 'the most important political feature' in the south of C.P. & Berar. On this occasion 1,000 uniformed volunteers headed by Moonje marched past. The important personalities present included the Bhonsla king, G.D. Savarkar, Hedgewar and others. In 'an objectionable and provocative address', Hedgewar mentioned that 'the settlement of the political future of India was for the Hindus alone to decide. No interference either by foreigners or by non-Hindu residents of Hindia should be brooked'.[15]

Hedgewar started the RSS with only five persons in 1925 at Nagpur. By 1931, the RSS started moving beyond Nagpur and Wardha to Vidarbha region and the Hindi-speaking areas of Central Provinces. 'The Sangh could muster the active sympathy and support of numerous prominent Hindus of these provinces including Raja Laxmanrao Bhonsle of Nagpur, Raja Raghoji Rao Bhonsle, Sir Chitnivis, Hon. Tambe (former Governor of C.P. & Berar), Sir Morpant Joshi, Rao Bahadur Kelkar (former Minister of C.P. & Berar). With the patronage of these notables, the RSS increased its membership to 30,000 by 1937 in C.P. & Berar alone.'

In the nature of things there was bound to be some tension amidst collaboration

[14] Ibid., pp. 246-7. Vide Appendices 1 and 2 for the prayer and pledge, and the text of the RSS Constitution respectively.

[15] Kanungo, *RSS's Tryst with Politics*, p. 46, citing Memorandum of Government of India, Home Department Intelligence Bureau, No. 60-D, G-42, dated New Delhi, the 18th May 1942. Also see Partha Sarathi Gupta (ed.), *Towards Freedom: Documents on the Movement for Independence in India 1943-1944*, Part III, Delhi: Oxford University Press, 1997, p. 3047.

with the Mahasabha. Hedgewar was deeply influenced by V.D. Savarkar's *Hindutva*. He sought Savarkar's advice when he stayed with him for two days in March 1925, six months before he set up the RSS. The Mahasabha leader B.S. Moonje was Hedgewar's mentor. Hedgewar would not share the RSS's leadership with the Mahasabha while freely cooperating with it. He provided volunteers for the Mahasabha's sessions but they remained under his command. But they remained friends.

> The 1932 Delhi session of Mahasabha passed a resolution commending the activities of the RSS and expressed the urgent need to spread its network all over the country. In the same year, Bhai Parmanand extended a special invitation to Hedgewar to attend the Karachi session of Hind Yuvak Parishad. Hedgewar utilised his visit in establishing contacts with prominent Hindu leaders in Sindh and Punjab, who not only opened the door for the RSS but worked zealously to promote it in their areas. Babarao Savarkar brought the RSS in touch with Mahasabha activists in Delhi and Benaras, the areas of future expansion. Thus the RSS was able to penetrate the north-west and northern areas with the help of the Hindu Mahasabha. Organisationally, however, the RSS was independent of the Hindu Mahasabha. In fact the Mahasabha leadership was unhappy because RSS refused to become a subsidiary of their organisation.[16]

Babarao Savarkar remained Hedgewar's firm ally. In 1931 he merged his Tarun Hindu Sabha with the RSS. It expanded, targeting university campuses, particularly. Its pracharaks were active in Punjab, United Provinces (Uttar Pradesh now) and Bihar and entered the South in 1939.

> The expansion was steady and impressive. There were only 60 shakhas in 1931. In 1936, the RSS claimed to have 200 branches and 25,000 members. By 1939, there were 500 branches and 40,000 members; in 1940, the RSS had 700 branches and 80,000 members. Hedgewar also made his organisation financially sound. The income of the Sangh came from subscriptions and donations from volunteers, supporters and well-wishers, usually collected at the annual Guru purnima festival as Guru Dakshina. A 1939 report stated that Rs. 20,000 was kept as a fixed deposit with two Nagpur money-lenders, Chitnavis and Ghatate. Strict control was maintained over the finances of the Sangh and each branch was normally permitted to retain only a Rs. 200 deposit.

Along with the expansion and a sound financial position, its character also

16 Kanungo, *RSS's Tryst with Politics*, p. 47.

underwent a transformation from being a regional to an all-India organisation. Hedgewar was quite pragmatic; he decided to dilute the Maharashtrian emphasis of the RSS to make it acceptable to other regional Hindu traditions. Initially, it did not find an easy acceptance in northern India because of the opposition of the Arya Samaj to the idolatrous rituals and practices of the RSS. Therefore, the worship of Hanuman was given up and insistence on Hindu rituals was less emphasised. The prayer was changed to Sanskrit to break the regional barrier.

'Thus, Hedgewar's innovative organisational skill, missionary zeal and perseverance helped the RSS to grow considerably in a short time. By 1940, when Hedgewar died, the RSS had a nationwide presence except Assam, Orissa, and Kashmir.'[17]

Hedgewar rejoiced in his last speech to the Officers' Training Camp (OTC) in 1940: 'I see before my eyes today a miniature Hindu Rashtra.' He died on 21 June 1940. The OTC deserves note. It was set up in 1927. There were about 500 shakhas and 100,000 swayamsevaks when his chosen successor M.S. Golwalkar took over. When he died in 1973, there were over 10,000 shakhas with a total membership of about a million. The rise, however impressive, raises questions. What and who contributed to it? The RSS spread poison; but not without help.

On 2 December 1926 Motilal Nehru bitterly wrote his son, Jawaharlal Nehru, after a hotly contested election.

> Communal hatred and heavy bribing of the voters was the order of the day. I am thoroughly disgusted and am now seriously thinking of retiring from public life. What is worrying me is how to occupy my time. I am waiting for the Congress Session at Gauhati and keeping mum in the meanwhile. The Malaviya-Lala gang aided by Birla's money are making frantic efforts to capture the Congress.

It is unlikely that the munificence was Birla's alone; still less that it excluded the RSS.

The letter of 1926 foreshadowed a lot that marred Indian politics in the decades preceding 2018 – rabid communal propaganda which did not spare even Motilal Nehru; Big Business' help to communal politics; election malpractices and the secular forces' weaknesses. The RSS gained by tapping on its 19th-century lineage and its cooperation with British rulers.

17 Ibid., p. 50.

2. The RSS's 19th-century Heritage

'Hindu nationalism was constructed as an ideology between the 1870s and the 1920s . . . it is important to trace its antecedents especially since a similar pattern is observable from the late nineteenth century onwards.'[1]

Another scholar Chetan Bhatt highlights an important aspect.

> Various thinkers from the Arya Samaj, the Indian National Congress, the Hindu Sangathan movement, the early Hindu Sabhas and the pre-Savarkar Hindu Mahasabha, and the variety of revolutionary nationalist groups and Hindu 'proto-ecclesiastical' institutions can be accurately described as Hindu nationalists in the strong sense, rather than as Indian nationalists with Hindu leanings.[2] . . .

Dayanand Saraswati (1824-1883) began as the Hindu Luther, out to rid the faith of what he considered deviations from the Four Vedas such as idol worship, abuses of priesthood and untouchability. He established the Arya Samaj in 1875. It has 'since reflected the militant character of its founder and, from its stronghold in the Punjab, has contributed to the militancy of Hindu nationalism'.[3] He set up the Dayanand Anglo-Vedic (DAV) College in Lahore in 1886.

He launched also two movements of baleful consequences. *Sangathan* (organisation) and *shuddhi* (purification of non-Hindus by conversion to Hinduism), the basis of *ghar wapsi* of today. He expressed his political views in Chapter VI of his book *Satyartha Prakash*.

Initiated to awaken the Hindus, his programme was confined to them. The result was that 'his ideas paved the way for the emergence of the ideology of the Hindu Nation and Hindu Nationalism . . . Dayananda injected an element of militancy and zealotry in Hinduism. The chief beneficiaries of this spirit in the country were the revivalists of the twenties'.[4]

An All-India Shuddhi Sabha was set up in 1923 under the auspices of the Arya Samaj. The proselytising programme had come to stay. Its twin was *sangathan* (Hindu consolidation). Bankim Chandra Chatterjee (1838-1894) was no less

[1] Christophe Jaffrelot, *The Hindu Nationalist Movement and Indian Politics*, Viking, 1996, p. 11.

[2] Bhatt, *Hindu Nationalism*, p. 440.

[3] Stephen Hay (ed.), *Sources of Indian Tradition*, vol. 2, Columbia University Press, 1988, pp. 53-4.

[4] B.R. Purohit, *Hindu Revivalism and Indian Nationalism*, Bhopal: Madhupriya, 1990, p. 50; a neglected work.

influential. His poem 'Bande Mataram' still arouses fierce controversy as 'a virtual anthem for the contemporary movement'. It was composed as a song in 1875 and inserted in his novel *Anandamath* first published in 1882, on its completion. It begins in Sanskrit, turns into Bengali and returns to Sanskrit. The Motherland was identified with Hindu religious deities; first with Durga, the demon-slaying goddess, only to be transformed into the image of Kali, an angry and destructive force.

Who is this Mother whom the country was fighting? The song, read in context, in the novel, provides the answer. It reads thus:

BANDE MATARAM
MOTHER, I bow to thee!
Rich with thy hurrying streams,
Bright with thy orchard gleams,
Cool with the winds of delight,
Dark fields waving, Mother of might,
Mother free.

Glory of moonlight dreams,
Over thy branches and lordly streams,
Clad in thy blossoming trees,
Mother, giver of ease,
Laughing low and sweet,
Mother, I kiss thy feet,
Speaker sweet and low,
Mother, to thee I bow.

Who hath said thou art weak in thy lands,
When the swords flash out in seventy million hands,
And seventy million voices roar
Thy dreadful name from shore to shore?
With many strengths who art mighty and strong.
To thee I call, Mother and Lord![5]

Thou who savest, arise and save!
To her I cry who ever her foemen drave
Back from plain and sea
And shook herself free.

Thou art wisdom, thou art law,

[5] Bankim Chandra Chatterjee, *Anandamath*. English translation by Aurobindo Ghose.

Thou art heart, our soul, our breath,
Thou the love divine, the awe
In our hearts that conquers death.
Thine the strength that nerves the arm,
Thine the beauty, thine the charm,
Every image divine,
In our temples is but shine.
Thou art Durga, Lady and Queen,
With her hands that strike and her swords of sheen.
Thou art Lakshmi lotus-throned
And the Muse, a hundred-toned.
Pure and perfect without peer
Mother, lend thine ear.

Rich with thy hurrying streams,
Bright with thy orchard gleams,
Dark of hue, O candid fair,
In thy soul, with jewelled hair
And thy glorious smile divine,
Loveliest of all Earthly lands,
Showering wealth from well-stored hands
Mother, Mother mine!
Mother sweet, I bow to thee
Mother great and free![6]

The context of this extract is that Satyananda, the leader of a band of sanyasis, had just won a victory over Muslim forces and their British officers. To him came a figure who spoke with the voice of God, instructing him to cease from fighting.

Satyananda: Come; I am ready. But, my lord, clear up this doubt in my mind. Why at the very moment in which I have removed all barriers from before our eternal Faith, do you order me to cease?

He: Your task is accomplished. *The Muslim power is destroyed. There is nothing else for you to do. No good can come of needless slaughter.*

S: The Muslim power has indeed been destroyed, but the dominion of the Hindus has not yet been established. The British still hold Calcutta.

He: Hindu dominion will not be established now. If you remain at your work, men will be killed to no purpose. Therefore come.

S: (greatly pained) My Lord, if Hindu dominion is not going to be established, who will rule? Will the Muslim kings return?

[6] *Anandamath*, Part IV, ch. 8. English translation by T.W. Clark.

He: No. The English will rule. . . .

He: Your vow is fulfilled. You have brought fortune to your mother. You have set up a British government. Give up your fighting. Let the people take to their ploughs. Let the earth be rich with harvest and the people rich with wealth.

S: (weeping hot tears) I will make my mother rich with harvest in the blood of her foes.

He: Who is the foe? There are no foes now. The English are friends as well as rulers. And no one can defeat them in battle.[7]

It is hard to see how such a song as this can be imposed on non-Hindus as a national anthem. In 1937 the Congress Working Committee adopted a rather woolly resolution on the song. It recommended that 'at national gatherings only the first two stanzas should be sung'. A song that requires a surgical operation was rightly rejected as a national anthem and cannot be imposed on all as the BJP-ruled governments in some states seek to do.

In an erudite essay entitled 'Imagining Hindu Rashtra: The Hindu and the Muslim in Bankim Chandra's Writings', Tanika Sarkar concluded:

> Bankim bequeathed a set of historical judgments on the nature and consequences of Muslim rule in Bengal: 'How does our Muslim ruler protect us? We have lost our religion, our caste, our honour and family name, and now we are about to lose our very lives. . . . How can Hinduism survive unless we drive out these dissolute swine?' (*Anandamath*, Bankim, p. 727.) These ideological moves do not need proper historical authentication since they are posed in a fictional space; the pseudo-historical comments, however, carry an immense weight of conviction, nonetheless, particularly since Bankim was known for a highly historicist thrust in his discursive prose. They are, therefore, insidiously authenticated, and then they justify political rallying cries of extreme virulence: 'Kill the low Muslims' is the refrain that is repetitively raised in *Anandamath*. (Bankim, p. 784.) Even though Bankim never made use of the recent theories of the colonial drain of wealth, he used the same motif to describe the flight of money from Bengal to Delhi in the form of a heavy revenue burden in Mughal times. ('Bangalar Itihasa', *Vividha Prabandha*, *Bankimchandra Rachanabali*, II, p. 332.)
>
> Perhaps the most significant way in which Bankim served as a bridge between nineteenth-century Hindu revivalism and the later, anti-Muslim, violent politics was *by providing an immensely powerful visual image of*

[7] C.H. Philips with the cooperation of H.L. Singh and B.N. Pandey, *The Evolution of India and Pakistan, 1858 to 1947: Select Documents*, London: Oxford University Press, 1962, pp. 117-20.

communal violence and by giving it the status of an apocalyptic holy war. He stamped the image indelibly on the imagination of communal politics by fusing the impulse of community violence and revenge into the spectacle of a female body.

In his last novel, *Sitaram*, Gangaram, the brother of the heroine Shree, is unjustly charged and sentenced to execution by a tyrannical Muslim faqir (holy man) and a qazi (judge). Unable to stop this mockery of justice, Shree goes to the place of execution, where a big crowd, including many Hindus, has gathered to watch the event. In despair, Shree tries to rally them to save a fellow Hindu, to instil a sense of brotherhood and mutual responsibility by evoking the fact that a man of their community is being killed by another community. Shree does not invoke the theme of justice, nor does she try to rally subjects against tyranny and misrule. Quite spontaneously the words that rise to her mouth are words of community solidarity and violence.

Then Gangaram saw a goddess like figure among the green leaves of the huge tree. Her feet resting on two branches, the right hand clutching a tender branch, the left hand swirling her sari, she was calling out: 'Kill, kill. . . .' Her long, unbound tresses were dancing in the wind, her proud feet were swinging the branches up and down, up and down, as if Durga herself was dancing on the lion on the battlefield. Shree had no more shame left, no consciousness, no fear, no rest. She kept calling out – 'Kill, kill the enemy . . . The enemy of the country, the enemy of Hindus, my enemy . . . kill, kill the enemy.' (*Sitaram*, Bankim, I, p. 881.)[8]

By any test, Lala Lajpat Rai (1865-1928) was a towering figure. A man of learning, he was the first to propound the two-nation theory as well as propose the partition of India. In 1899 he wrote, 'Hindus are a nation in themselves because they represent a civilisation all their own.'[9]

The damage had been done. In a series of articles for *The Tribune* (Lahore) of 14 December 1924 he wrote:

My suggestion is that the Punjab should be partitioned into two provinces, the Western Punjab with a large Muslim majority, to be a Muslim-governed province; and the Eastern Punjab, with a large Hindu-Sikh majority, to be a non-Muslim governed Province. I do not discuss Bengal. To me it is unimaginable that the rich and highly progressive and alive Hindus of Bengal will ever work out the Pact agreed to by Mr. C.R. Das. I will make the same

8 Tanika Sarkar, 'Imagining Hindu Rashtra', in *Making India Hindu: Religion, Community, and the Politics of Democracy in India*, ed. David E. Ludden, New Delhi: Oxford University Press, 1996, p. 180.

9 Bhatt, *Hindu Nationalism*, p. 41.

> suggestion in their case, but if Bengal is prepared to accept Mr. Das's Pact, I have nothing to say. It is its own look-out.
>
> Maulana Hasrat Mohani has recently said that the Muslims will never agree to India's having Dominion status under the British. What they aim at are separate Muslim States in India, united with Hindu States under a National Federal Government. He is also in favour of smaller States containing compact Hindu and Muslim populations. If communal representation with separate electorates is to be the rule, then Maulana Hasrat's scheme as to smaller provinces seems to be the only workable proposition. Under my scheme the Muslims will have four Muslim States: (1) The Pathan province or the North-West Frontier, (2) Western Punjab, (3) Sindh, and (4) Eastern Bengal. If there are compact Muslim communities in any other part of India, sufficiently large to form a Province, they should be similarly constituted. But it should be distinctly understood that this is not a united India. It means a clear partition of India into a Muslim India and a non-Muslim India.

This is not a comprehensive survey of the RSS's ideological ancestry. The contributions of the Hindu Mahasabha and V.D. Savarkar merit a separate discussion. But enough is set out to trace the march of Hindutva in history. Lala Har Dayal's effusion in 1925 reveals that outlook even in a 'revolutionary'. He wrote his political testament in the *Pratap* (Lahore).

> I declare that the future of the Hindu race, of Hindustan and of the Punjab, rests on these four pillars: (1) Hindu Sangathan, (2) Hindu Raj, (3) Shuddhi of Moslems, and (4) Conquest and Shuddhi of Afghanistan and the Frontiers. So long as the Hindu nation does not accomplish these four things, the safety of our children and great-grand-children will be ever in danger, and the safety of the Hindu race will be impossible. The Hindu race has but one history, and its institutions are homogeneous. But the Musalmans and Christians are far removed from the confines of Hinduism, for their religions are alien and they love Persian, Arab and European institutions. . . . If Hindus want to protect themselves, they must conquer Afghanistan and the frontiers and convert all the mountain tribes.[10]

The pre-1925 Hindu Mahasabha is relevant to the question as to why the RSS was established when there existed a strong political party patronised by powerful figures like Lajpat Rai and Madan Mohan Malaviya who stridently espoused Hindu claims. A Note by G.V. Ketkar, editor of *Mahratta* and secretary, All-India Hindu Mahasabha authoritatively traced its history, 'aims and present policy'.[11]

[10] Quoted in B.R. Ambedkar, *Pakistan or the Partition of India*, 1946, p. 117.

[11] N.N. Mitra (ed.), *The Indian Annual Register*, vol. 1, 1941, pp. 276-81.

The first Hindu Sabha was established in the Punjab in 1907. Its object *inter alia* was to 'protect, promote and represent the interests of the Hindu community'. A conference was held in Lahore in 1909 which Lala Lajpat Rai attended. The first Akhil Bharatiya Hindu Mahasabha was held in 1914 at Haridwar. Till 1928 Pandit Madan Mohan Malaviya and Lala Lajpat Rai led the Hindu Mahasabha. Both were also active in the Indian National Congress. In 1937 V.D. Savarkar took over and propounded the two nation theory which Lajpat Rai had advocated at the 1909 Conference, 'Hindus are a nation in themselves, because they represent a type of civilisation all their own.'[12] Within India he would be 'a Hindu first and an Indian afterwards', vis-à-vis non-Indians he would be an Indian first and a Hindu afterwards. The Hindu movement... does not contemplate the exclusion of anyone who is prepared to sail under the Hindu flag.[13]

In the 1921 session the Sabha was renamed as the All-India Hindu Mahasabha. Chetan Bhatt narrates its progress.

> From 1925, the Mahasabha, which was committed to a strategy of co-operation, allowed its provincial Sabhas to contest provincial elections and its elected officers to take up government posts. Under Malaviya, the Mahasabha had made significant inroads into the political machinery of Congress, opposing both the Gandhian and Swarajist factions and their (divergent) strategies of non-cooperation. By 1926, the Mahasabha had not only claimed the right, within Congress, of its local Sabha to nominate their own candidates for local elections but had attempted to get Congress to abstain from provincial elections where the Mahasabha proffered an alternative candidate representing 'Hindu interests'.

From the early 1920s, the attention of the All-India Hindu Mahasabha turned towards the issues of religious conversions and *shuddhi*, and the formation of the All-India Shuddhi Sabha in 1923 under the aegis of the Arya Samaj. This had two aspects; campaigns to 'reclaim' 'neo-Christians' and 'neo-Muslims', and eventually any Muslims, into Hinduism.

In 1909, Lt. Colonel U.N. Mukerji of the Indian Military Service published an influential pamphlet, *Hindus – A dying race*, based on his articles to *The Bengalee*. The pamphlet hugely influenced an Arya Samajist, Munshi Ram (1857-1926), who had become a *sanyasi*, Swami Shraddhanand, and was a key founder of the Hindu Sangathan movement that emerged from the revitalised Hindu Mahasabha of the early 1920s.

Shraddhanand urged that Brahmins abolish intra-caste differences, and that the Rajputs, Khatris, Jats, Gujjars and others' conduct should become the

[12] Ibid., p. 277.

[13] Ibid.

determining factors in fixing the Varna of a Hindu. But inter-dining among all the castes should be commenced at once – not promiscuous eating out of the same cup and dish like Muhammadans, but partaking of food in separate cups and dishes served by decent Shudras.

Shraddhanand urged the adoption of Hindi and the Devanagari script throughout India, and, as the first step towards Hindu national solidarity and unity (sangathan), building of a Hindu Rashtra mandir (Hindu Nation temple) in every town and major city, which would hold at least as many people as the major mosques in northern India. The Hindu Rashtra mandir would be based on the 'worship of the cow as mother, the goddess of knowledge, and the motherland'.[14]

Thus, in 1925 there existed a powerful Hindu Mahasabha led by men like Malaviya and Lajpat Rai who very much shared the same worldview as that of the RSS. Why, then, was the RSS set up? There were two obvious differences between the two. The leaders of the Mahasabha were politicians, who fought elections. Malaviya and Lajpat Rai were members of the Central Legislative Assembly. Secondly, they abhorred violence. The stalwarts of Hindu resurgence since the 19th century and leaders who sympathised with them were men of culture, erudition and dignity – Dayanand Saraswati, Bankim Chandra Chatterjee, Vivekananda, Aurobindo Ghose, Lajpat Rai, Bal Gangadhar Tilak and Malaviya. The RSS's leaders from Hedgewar, Golwalkar to this day provide a study in contrast. They are coarse, uneducated and authoritarian. They spew hate and extol violence. Malaviya's contribution to the rise of the RSS deserves greater notice than it has received.

The RSS abjured electoral politics and embraced organised use of violence. Conceived in the aftermath of the communal riots in Nagpur, its avowed aim was to 'overpower the enemy'. The lathi was no ornament. It was an integral part of the RSS programme. It was adopted at the instance of Moonje, Hedgewar's mentor.[15] On Dussehra festivals 'a set of weapons is worshipped'; martial music is played and 'en masse the Swayamsevaks demonstrate their skill with the lathi, sword and various exercises'.[16]

The RSS's present chief Mohan Bhagwat candidly stated its significance at a meeting 'with the intellectuals of Delhi' on 20 December 2007. He said:

> If you see the training manual of the Police you will find that the weapon training is only 25%. The remaining 75% of training is the same, which is imparted to the swayamsevak in the third year training camp. So when the Police and Army personnel meet us, they say that it would take 4-5 months for ordinary people to learn use of weapons, if required. But if we get the swayamsevaks, they can be prepared for sending them to the border within 3-4

[14] Bhatt, *Hindu Nationalism*, pp. 61-8.

[15] Kanungo, *RSS's Tryst with Politics*, p. 44.

[16] Andersen and Damle, *The Brotherhood in Saffron*, p. 93.

> days. Therefore, the importance of lathi is very much there. Bankim Chandra Chatterjee has said 'O stick, your days are over, but if the trained hands come forward to wield you, there would be no action beyond you to accomplish'. So training to wield the stick would continue to stay in the RSS.[17]

The text reflects the sub-text.

The conclusion is irresistible and obvious. The *RSS was established as an armed, militant wing of Hindu Nationalism in order to overpower and wipe out Indian Nationalism from the country.*

[17] Mohan Bhagwat, *The Hindu Renaissance*, trans. S.D. Mohan, New Delhi: Suruchi Prakashan, 2008, pp. 20-1.

3. Commitments of Indian Nationalism

No praise can be too high for Jawaharlal Nehru's moral courage in asserting the nation's commitment to the ideal of secularism in the dark days after the partition of India. He is its most articulate and consistent opponent. His detractors would do well, however, to reflect on the record of Indian Nationalism since its birth in 1885. Nehru did not coin the word 'secular'. It was part of the Congress's discourse. So was concern for the rights of the minorities. So, also, was the State's neutrality between the country's diverse faiths. There was a firm, total rejection of the concept of a Hindu State.

W.C. Bonnerjee, the Congress's first president, laid down its objects at the very first session held in Mumbai on 28 December 1885. One of them was 'the eradication . . . of all possible race, creed or provincial prejudices . . . and the fuller development and consolidation of . . . sentiments of national unity'; in short, an inclusive nationalism.[1] The second Congress president was Dadabhai Naoroji. The third was Badruddin Tyabji.

We owe to G.A. Ganesan of the erstwhile Madras for publishing the texts of the *Congress' Resolutions and Presidential Addresses* in 2 volumes from 1855 to 1934: To read them is to realise the depth of the nation's commitment to secularism from the very inception of the Congress. The Report of the Second Congress (1886) made it clear that religious community was irrelevant to membership in the nationalist organisation. 'The Congress is a community of temporal interests and not of spiritual convictions that qualify men to represent each other in the discussion of political questions; we hold their general interests in this country being identical, Hindus, Christians, Muslims and Parsis may fitly as members of their respective communities represent each other in the discussion of public secular affairs.'[2]

Under Article XXVII of its constitution no subject shall be discussed if a majority of three-quarters of Hindus or Muslims objected to it. This seems wrong now. In the 19th century the Congress was out to win the confidence of all sections of Indian society.

This is what the great Surendranath Banerjea said in his presidential address to the Congress in 1895: 'It is the Congress of united India, of Hindus and Mahomedans, of Christians, of Parsees and of Sikhs; here we stand upon a common platform – here we have all agreed to bring our own social and religious differences . . . we have common rights and common grievances . . . you have infused a new

[1] Pattabhi Sitaramayya, *The History of the Indian National Congress, Vol. 1 (1885-1935)*, Bombay: Padma Publications, 1946, p. 18.

[2] *Report and Proceedings of the Second Indian National Congress.*

enthusiasm into your countrymen . . . you have made them vibrate with the new born sentiment of an awakened nationality . . .' It was *Indian* nationalism to which the *Indian National* Congress was committed.

In 1896, R.M. Sayani, a Muslim from Mumbai, spoke in his address of a 'United India' based on Indian nationalism. Presidential addresses of the time were long and scholarly. A fine tradition was set. In 1909, Malaviya expressed the hope that 'feelings of patriotism and brotherliness will continue to increase among Hindus, Mahomedans, Christians and Parsis, until they shall flow like a smooth but mighty river welding the people of all communities into a great and united nation'.

Babu Amvica Charan Mazumdar discussed the communal question in 1916 and said 'neither the Parsis nor the Mahomedans of India owe any temporal allegiance either to the Shah of Persia or the Sultan of Turkey. They are now Indians as much as Hindus'. He lauded the Lucknow Pact between the Congress and the Muslim League which was hammered out by Bal Gangadhar Tilak and Mohammed Ali Jinnah in 1916 when the Congress and the Muslim League met in that city around the same time to ratify the Pact.

In 1923 Maulana Mohammed Ali said, 'I have dreamed of the dream of a federation, grander, nobler and infinitely more spiritual than the United States of America.' To S. Srinivasa Aiyangar goes the credit for a masterly exposition of India's secular nationalism in his address in 1926. It bears quotation *in extenso* because of its relevance to our times, nearly a century later. He referred to the Congress ideals of nationalism, unity and justice and said that communalism was a negation of nationalism and is an obstacle to Swaraj.

> I am confident that wherever intensive propaganda, sincere and persuasive, clearly analyses the fallacies underlying it, communalism will go to the wall. . . . The differences between Hindus and Mussalmans or between Brahmins and non-Brahmins are by no means such as to prevent them from being one nation. There is no conflict of interests between them in respect of all those matters which tend to their common welfare or make for a national advance or relate to the establishment and development of self-governing institutions.
>
> Religious doctrines and institutions and such social usages and personal laws as have historically been due to a distinctive culture are alone peculiar to any religious community. There should therefore be a fundamental law of Swaraj to guard against the making of laws by any legislature in India that may affect liberty of conscience, freedom of religious observance or association, the right to religious education and, at the option of the community concerned, the right to personal laws.
>
> Moreover, no community can, in these days, really progress in secular affairs unless the nation as a whole advances; unless, in other words, the other communities either acquiesce in the rise of one community or make

equal progress. The best way of advancing politically one's own community is, therefore, to raise the status of all the communities as a whole. For, if you seek to advance your own community, all the other communities bind themselves together against yours. Communalism is not so much a positive idea of benefiting one's community as a destructive desire to obtain advantages at the expense of the other communities.

The intrusion into politics of religion, and very often of dogmatic religion, must be resisted as a primitive or mediaeval idea, born of theocracies, and disastrous alike to religion and to politics. Hinduism and Islam will gain immeasurably in strength and purity if they are not mixed up with secular politics. Lastly, let us clearly grasp the truth that neither Hinduism nor Islam stands in danger of being destroyed by the other. Both are great religions, aged old; and both have an abiding hold on vast populations.

Hindus and Mussalmans have lived in the past and will live in the future as patriotic fellow citizens and firm and loyal friends. In the transaction of public affairs, in all matters of secular advancement, in all aspects of the administration and on all public, political and national questions, they easily can and should think and feel and act as Indians. I fervently appeal to Hindu and Mussalman leaders with all the strength of my feeble voice to consider the need for concerted action in a calm and dispassionate spirit and to unite indissolubly for their common deliverance.

Dr. M.A. Ansari spoke in 1927 in the context of a certain deterioration in the communal atmosphere.

While attempting to solve the Hindu-Muslim question we should not, however, mistake the symptom for the disease. The political and religious differences which are straining the relations between the two communities are but outward manifestations of a deeper conflict, not peculiar to India or unknown to history. It is essentially a problem of two different cultures, each with its own outlook on life, coming in close contact with one another. The best remedy lies in a recognition of the right of each culture to exist, in a development of a spirit of tolerance and respect and in the encouragement and cultivation of cultural affinity by the establishment of national institutions where young people of both the communities will come into touch with each other and get opportunities to study and understand the ideals underlying the civilisation of both. . . .

The All-India Congress Committee issued invitations to prominent Hindu and Muslim leaders to give the Committee the benefit of their advice and help him and the Committee to complete the good work begun at Mumbai. The result of these efforts is summed up in the two resolutions passed at the Unity Conference and adopted by the All-India Congress Committee.

> Hindus are at liberty to take processions and play music before any mosque at any time for religious or other purposes but there should be no stoppage of the processions nor special demonstrations in front of a mosque nor shall the songs or music sung or played in front of a mosque be such as is calculated to cause annoyance or special disturbance to the worshippers in the mosque.
>
> Muslims are at liberty to sacrifice cows or, subject to existing municipal laws regulating the slaughter of animals for purposes of food, to slaughter cows, in any town or village, in any place not being a thoroughfare nor one in the vicinity of a temple or a mandir nor one exposed to the gaze of Hindus.
>
> Cows should not be led in procession or in demonstration for sacrifice or slaughter.
>
> Having regard to the deep-rooted sentiment of the Hindu community in the matter of cow-killing, the Muslim community is earnestly appealed to, so to conduct the cow sacrifice or slaughter as not to cause annoyance to the Hindus of the town or village concerned.

The tragic divide that overcame the country should not obscure what the stalwarts said earlier. After paying rich tributes to Maulana Mohammed Ali's patriotism, what Vallabhbhai Patel said in his presidential address to the historic Karachi Congress in 1931 is strikingly relevant. He referred to 'the continued exploitation of India for close on two centuries' – unlike Narendra Modi or the RSS's 1,000 years[3] – and said,

> The Congress can be no party to any constitution which does not contain a solution of the communal question that is not designed to satisfy the respective parties. As a Hindu I would adopt my predecessor's formula and present the minorities with a Swadeshi fountain-pen and paper and let them write out their demands. And I should endorse them. I know that it is the quickest method. But it requires courage on the part of the Hindus. What we want is a heart-unity, not patched up paper-unity that will break under the slightest strain. That unity can only come when the majority takes courage in both the hands and is prepared to change places with the minority. This would be the highest wisdom.[4]

By the time Maulana Azad delivered his presidential address at the Ramgarh

[3] Vide Appendix 16.

[4] Vide *Congress Presidential Addresses: Second Series, 1911-1934*, Madras: G.A. Natesan & Co., 1934.

session on 20 March 1940, three days before the Muslim League passed the Pakistan Resolution at Lahore, a lot had changed. He said:

> I am a Musalman and am proud of that fact. Islam's splendid traditions of thirteen hundred years are my inheritance. I am unwilling to lose even the smallest part of this inheritance. The teaching and history of Islam, its arts and letters and civilisation are my wealth and my fortune. It is my duty to protect them.
>
> As a Musalman I have a special interest in Islamic religion and culture and I cannot tolerate any interference with them. But in addition to these sentiments, I have others also which the realities and conditions of my life have forced upon me. The spirit of Islam does not come in the way of these sentiments; it guides and helps me forward. I am proud of being an Indian; I am a part of the indivisible unity that is Indian nationality. I am indispensable to this noble edifice and without me this splendid structure of India is incomplete. I am an essential element which has gone to build India, I can never surrender this claim.
>
> It was India's historic destiny that many human races and cultures and religions should flow to her, finding a home in her hospitable soil, and that many a caravan should find rest here. Even before the dawn of history, these caravans trekked into India and wave after wave of new-comers followed. This vast and fertile land gave welcome to all and took them to her bosom. One of last three caravans, following the footsteps of its predecessors, was that of the followers of Islam. This came here and settled here for good. This led to a meeting of the culture-currents of two different races. Like the Ganga and the Yamuna, they flowed for a while through separate courses, but nature's immutable law brought them together and joined them in a *sangam*. This fusion was a notable event in history. Since then, destiny, in her own hidden way, began to fashion a new India in place of the old. We brought our treasures with us, and India too was full of the riches of her own precious heritage. We gave our wealth to her and she unlocked the doors of her own treasures to us. We gave her, what she needed most, the most precious of gifts from Islam's treasury, the message of democracy and human equality. Full eleven centuries have passed by since then. Islam has now as great a claim on the soil of India as Hinduism.[5]

By the mid-thirties, the communal climate had deteriorated. Rather late in the day the Congress decided to debar members of communal parties from its membership of its elected bodies. Article V(c) of the Congress constitution stated: 'No person who is a member of any elected Congress committee can be a member

[5] Malsiani, *Abul Kalam Azad*, p. 154.

of a communal organisation, the object or programme of which involves political activities which in the opinion of the working committee are anti-national and in conflict with those of the Congress.' It was only in 1938 that the Working Committee declared that for the purposes of this article, the Hindu Mahasabha and the Muslim League were to be regarded as communal organisations.

Its implementation was another matter. The general secretary J.B. Kripalani ruled that Article V(c) 'refers not to primary members of any communal organisation but to members of elected committees'. There was nothing 'to prevent ordinary members of such organisations from being office holder in the Congress organisation'.[6]

The partition of India did not affect the Congress leaders' resolve. Members of the Constituent Assembly of India took it for granted that India would be a secular State. The Constituent Assembly Debates show that its members simply took secularism for granted and saw no need for its explicit mention. The Supreme Court has held that secularism is part of the unamendable 'basic structure' of the Constitution. The judges explicitly referred to the 42nd Amendment of 1976 and said that it only made explicit what was implied in the Constitution.

On 3 December 1948, Professor K.T. Shah moved this amendment. 'The State in India being secular shall have no concern with any religion, creed or profession of faith; and shall observe an attitude of absolute neutrality in all matters relating to the religion of any class of its citizens or other persons in the Union.' He acknowledged that 'We have proclaimed it time and again that the State in India is secular'. Members agreed with that. There was no need to state the obvious. The amendment got nowhere.[7]

On the same day, Lokanath Misra also said: 'We have declared the State to be a secular state.'[8] On 6 December, H.V. Kamath said: 'We have certainly declared that India would be a secular State.'[9] He was followed by Pandit Lakshmi Kanta Maitra, who said:

> By secular state, as I understand it, is meant that the state is not going to make any discrimination whatsoever on the ground of religion or community against any person professing any particular form of religious faith. This means in essence that no particular religion in the state will receive any state patronage whatsoever. The state is not going to establish, patronise or endow any particular religion to the exclusion of or in preference to others and that no

[6] James E. Dillard, 'The Fortune of Nehru's Mass Contacts Campaign and the Rise of Muslim Separatism', *Journal of South Asian and Middle Eastern Studies*, vol. XXXI, no. 2, Winter 2008, pp. 43-65.

[7] *Constituent Assembly of India Debates (Proceedings)*, vol. 7, p. 815.

[8] Ibid.

[9] Ibid., p. 825.

> citizen in the state will have any preferential treatment or will be discriminated against simply on the ground that he professed a particular form of religion. In other words in the affairs of the state the possessing of any particular religion will not be taken into consideration at all.[10]

On 7 December 1948, M. Ananthasayanam Ayyangar, later Speaker of the Lok Sabha, acknowledged: 'We are pledged to make the state a secular one.'[11]

In 1994 the Supreme Court ruled that secularism is part of the unamendable basic structure of the Constitution.[12]

But no law can effectively deter a government from flouting this by administrative measures. The historical record establishes four facts. First, the nation embraced the ideal of secularism as far back as in 1885. Secondly, what it establishes as clearly is that Hindu revivalism reared its head precisely at that very moment and it gave birth to the Hindu Mahasabha and the RSS. Thirdly, these bodies were at war with India's secular nationalism from their very inception. *Lastly, they were no part of the freedom movement. They chose, instead, to collaborate with British imperialism in order to marginalise, if not eliminate, the Congress.*

[10] Ibid., p. 831.

[11] Ibid, p. 881.

[12] *S.R. Bommai vs. Union of India*, (1994) 3 SCC 1.

4. Collaboration with the British

Andersen and Damle record:

> Golwalkar was not a revolutionary in the conventional sense of the term. The British understood this. In an official report on RSS activity, prepared in 1943, the Home Department concluded that, 'it would be difficult to argue that the RSS constitutes an immediate menace to law and order. . . . ' Commenting on the violence that accompanied the 1942 Quit-India Movement, the Bombay Home Department observed: 'the Sangh has scrupulously kept itself within the law, and in particular, has refrained from taking part in the disturbances that broke out in August, 1942' . . .

On the outbreak of the Second World War on 3 September 1939, Congress ministries in the Provinces resigned. Savarkar met the Viceroy Lord Linlithgow on 3 October 1939 and pledged his enthusiastic cooperation to the British which Linlithgow reported to the Secretary of State for India, Lord Zetland.

> The situation, [Savarkar] said, was that His Majesty's Government must now turn to the Hindus and work with their support. After all, though we and the Hindus have had a good deal of difficulty with one another in the past that was equally true of the relations between Great Britain and the French and, as recent events had shown, of relations between Russia and Germany. Our interests were now the same and we must therefore work together. Even though now the most moderate of men, he had himself been in the past an adherent of a revolutionary party, as possibly, I might be aware. (I confirmed that I was.) But now that our interests were so closely bound together the essential thing was for Hinduism and Great Britain to be friends, and the old antagonism was no longer necessary.[1]

This was of a piece with his entire record since his arrival in the Andamans on 4 July 1911. We shall consider it in greater detail in Chapter 6. The RSS as well as his acolyte Syama Prasad Mookerjee followed the same line – opposition to the Congress and collaboration with the British rulers of the day. The record was unearthed by scholars only after the country's independence.

Not surprisingly, as Minister for Human Resources Development in the Vajpayee government, Murli Manohar Joshi actively prevented publication of the

[1] Vide Noorani, *Savarkar and Hindutva*, p. 3.

series of collections of hitherto unpublished documents from the archives. Partha Sarathi Gupta's *Towards Freedom: Documents on the Movement for Independence in India 1943-1944*, Part III (Oxford University Press, 1997) blazed the trail.

Scholars like Professor Bipan Chandra did the rest (see, e.g., *Communalism in Modern India* [Vikas, 1987]). The cow protection movement which began in the 1880s was directed against Muslims. The British cantonments 'were left relatively free to carry on cow slaughter on a large scale'.

The Jana Sangh's founder Syama Prasad Mookerjee did not lag behind his hero Savarkar. He was a member of Maulvi A.K. Fazlul Haq's ministry in Bengal though in 1940 he had moved the Pakistan Resolution; not to forget the Mahasabha's membership of the Sindh ministry despite its Assembly's adoption of a resolution in support of the partition.

The Mahasabha and the RSS opposed the Congress's Quit India Resolution of 8 August 1942. What few know is that S.P. Mookerjee wrote to the Governor of Bengal Sir John Herbert on 26 July *advising him to crush the revolt which had begun to brew*. These extracts speak for themselves.

> I have been thinking over the questions which we discussed at some length at the last Cabinet Meeting, specially arising out of the threatened Congress movement. It is of utmost importance that there should be complete understanding between you, as Governor, and your colleagues during the present critical period.
>
> Let me now refer to the situation that may be created in the province as a result of any widespread movement launched by the Congress. Anybody, who during the war, plans to stir up mass feelings, resulting in internal disturbances or insecurity, must be resisted by any Government that may function for the time being.
>
> Today we do not wish either party to rake up past differences. Today the issue is: do we regard the new aggression from Japan or Germany as a menace to the cause of human liberty including that of India? . . . I shall say that the ideal for which they fought so long has been achieved. It is recognised today by Britain and her representatives in India that so far as Britain and India go, India's right of independence is acknowledged. Therefore, there is no further quarrel between them and us as regards our past relationship.
>
> *The question is how to combat this movement in Bengal?* The administration of the province should be carried on in such a manner that *in spite of the best efforts of the Congress, this movement will fail to take root in the province.* It should be possible for us, especially responsible ministers, to be able to tell the public that the freedom for which the Congress has started the movement, already belongs to the representatives of the people. In some spheres it might be limited during the emergency. Indians have to trust the British. . . .

> It is for this reason that I ask you with all the emphasis at my command that you should take immediate steps for raising a Bengali army in land, sea and air, and ask them to defend their own freedom.
>
> I hope you will appreciate the spirit which has prompted me to write this letter to you. No one knows what the future has in store for us. As one of your ministers, I am willing to offer you my whole-hearted co-operation and serve my province and country at this hour of crisis.[2]

He met Jinnah in Mumbai. They spoke for three hours.

Mookerjee had a clear concept of Hindu Raj, regardless of what the Constitution says. 'As seventy five percent of the population were Hindus, and if India was to adopt a democratic form of government, the Hindus would automatically play a major role in it. We were just not willing to entertain any proposal to partition India.'[3] This would be a majoritarian State in which the major community would lay down the law; the minorities would not share power as in a secular democracy. Mookerjee's logic came in handy to advocates of partition.

'I wanted to immerse myself in some constructive work to help the Hindus regain their lost glory.'[4] Politics would be its extended play. In Bengal the Muslim majority was a mere 54.7 per cent of the total population; far inferior to the Hindus economically, educationally and in some other respects. But he sought for Hindus 'protection as a minority community . . . victims of communal aggression'. In 1939 Savarkar came to Bengal; Mookerjee joined the Mahasabha and succeeded him as its president in 1943.

Mookerjee's speeches revealed an outlook he had not exposed openly earlier.[5] Seven years later he founded the Bharatiya Jana Sangh to promote the same ideology.

These extracts trace the source of the rhetoric we now read and hear from the BJP, particularly since Narendra Modi became prime minister.

> Hindus must develop their *race*-consciousness, not with any narrow end in view but with a full determination to throw their lot in any world movement for the elevation of mankind. Centuries of political subjugation have destroyed our spirit of resistance and we dare not think ourselves as the inheritors of a free and proud race, who once ruled the destinies of this country and influenced the thought and culture of many peoples abroad.[6]

[2] S.P. Mookerjee, *Leaves from a Diary*, Oxford University Press, pp. 175, 179, 183.

[3] Ibid., p. 106.

[4] Ibid., p. 146.

[5] S.P. Mookerjee, *Awake Hindusthan*, Calcutta: Ramesh Chandra Banerjee, 1944.

[6] Ibid., p. 27; 14 April 1940.

Communalism is combined with racism, a fact often overlooked.

> One of the tasks of the Hindu Mahasabha will be to build up a national militia. . . . In times of emergency they should also be available for such work as they may be called upon to do for the protection of the honour and liberty of the oppressed.
>
> Non-violence
>
> is not the creed of the Hindu Mahasabha. Centuries of political subjection have almost blotted out the memory of Hindu valour and strength and broken the backbone of the people.[7]

He wanted the 'maths and temples' to take up the cause.

The policy of collaboration with the British was pursued profitably. On 29 November 1941, he said,

> The Mahasabha has called upon all Hindus to join the Army, the Navy and the Air Force in as large numbers as possible and take the fullest advantage of the facilities that the British Government is offering us under force of circumstances and primarily in its own interests. We shall commit a grave blunder if we allow the Indian Forces to fall short of Hindu elements at least in proportion to our strength of population.[8]

His logic was plain, 'Why should Hindus feel shy to stand up for their rights which are identical with those of the country itself?'[9] Facts meant nothing to him. 'Gandhiji declared that India would be independent by 31 December 1921.' This was false. That year Gandhi opposed Hasrat Mohani's motion in the Congress for complete independence as being premature.[10]

While all this was afoot, Mookerjee also 'established contacts with the RSS'. He met Hedgewar in 1940.[11]

The RSS's strategy paid off. Golwalkar claimed, on 25 October 1942, that the Sangh had 1,500 branches and 2 lakh members all over India. Its members had infiltrated 'in all key services, both civil and military'. It had enrolled 'reliable

[7] Ibid., p. 48; 7 December 1940.

[8] Ibid., p. 102.

[9] Ibid., p. 190.

[10] Ambedkar, *Pakistan or the Partition of India*, p. 270.

[11] B.D. Graham, 'Syama Prasad Mookerjee and the Communalist Alternative', in *Soundings in Modern South Asian History*, ed. D.A Low, Berkeley: University of California Press, 1968, p. 335. He has also authored *Hindu Nationalism and Indian Politics: The Origin and Development of the Bharatiya Jana Sangh*, New York: Cambridge University Press, 1990.

government servants, teachers and clerks' and set up shakhas in the Gun Carriage Factory, Jabalpur and the Ordnance Factory, Khamaria 'to attract military personnel'.[12]

The authorities were not ignorant.

> The Rashtriya Swayamsevak Sangh maintained 'a very rigid secrecy' and took pains 'to avoid the attention of the authorities'. Its 'ultimate aim is an India ruled over by the Hindus and its [sic] has been quietly preparing for this for years'. The Government of Punjab warned New Delhi on 21 January 1944 that the RSS 'is communal in character and is becoming increasingly popular among Hindus. Its leaders feel that it is necessary to exercise the greatest caution in working for the Hindu domination of India and the activities of the organisation are conducted with great secrecy.' The reports from other provinces were not different. The British responded with promulgating the Camps and Parades (Control) Order, 1944 to deal alike with the RSS, the Khaksars and the Muslim League's National Guard.[13]

Partha Sarathi Gupta's volume has an official Note on the RSS's training camps in 1944 with official comment.[14]

The RSS got actively involved in riots in 1946-47. Rising communal tension helped it in its campaign. Collaboration with the British and opposition to the Congress were two prongs of the same strategy. The British were going to quit; prepare to deal with Muslims. This was said in so many words. An official summary of District Reports concluded:

> In the perception of the government, the RSS did not pose an immediate menace to law and order. Thus positioning itself outside the scrutiny of the British, the RSS expanded quite considerably during these years. In a speech on 25 October 1942, Golwalkar claimed that the Sangh all over India had 1,500 branches and 2,00,000 members. However, as per the government estimate, by 1943, the membership of the Sangh in British India reached 76,000 (excluding the figures of the Indian states).
>
> Golwalkar adopted the method of infiltration of the RSS members in all the key services, both civil and military. The RSS not only enrolled reliable government servants, teachers and clerks, it also set up new branches in the Gun Carriage Factory, Jubbulpore and the Ordnance Factory, Khamaria to attract military personnel.[15] . . .

[12] Kanungo, *RSS's Tryst with Politics*, p. 53.

[13] Ibid., p. 54.

[14] Gupta, *Towards Freedom*, p. 3219.

[15] Kanungo, *RSS's Tryst with Politics*, p. 53.

Golwalkar's outward compliance with government orders was 'no more than a smoke-screen behind which to carry on secretly or in a modified form the very activities that he has renounced'. The government of Central Provinces at Nagpur printed a confidential pamphlet containing detailed information regarding the strength, organisation and activities of the RSS from all the districts of the province. A summary of the District Reports concluded: 'Their policy is to wait until they themselves are better prepared and the state of the country offers better opportunities for intervention . . . the Sangh, though not now dangerous, might become a menace later in times of serious communal disturbances, etc.'[16]

This strategy reveals S.P. Mookerjee's outlook. He hated Muslims as 'a set of converts from the dregs of Hindu society'.[17]

[16] Gupta, *Towards Freedom*, pp. 3038, 3211 and 3219.

[17] Joya Chatterji, *Bengal Divided: Hindu Communalism and Partition, 1932-1947*, Cambridge: Cambridge University Press, 1994, p. 189.

5. The RSS Woos Europe's Fascists

The Fuehrer principle was embedded in the RSS's structure ever since its birth. Article 12 of its constitution makes that clear.

> Late Dr. Keshav Baliram Hedgewar, the Founder of the Sangh, was the Adya (First) Sar Sangh chalak. Shri Madhav Sadashiv Golwalkar was nominated Sar Sangh chalak by him in consultation with the then Kendriya Karyakari Mandal. He is the Sar Sangh chalak since then. The Sar Sangh chalak will nominate his successor, as and when the necessity arises, with the consent of the then Kendriya Karyakari Mandal.
>
> The Sar Sangh chalak is the guide and philosopher of the Rashtriya Swayamsevak Sangh. He may attend, summon or address any assembly of the swayamsevaks, pratinidhi sabhas, and karyakari mandals, severally or jointly.

Article 13 says:

> (a) The elected members of the Akhil Bharatiya Pratinidhi Sabha [vide Art. 15] shall elect the Sar Karyavaha. (b) The Sar Karyavaha shall act in consultation with the Sar Sangh chalak.

Article 14 amplifies:

> (a) The Sar Karyavaha shall form the Kendriya Karyakari Mandal. The Mandal shall consist of the following office bearers: (i) Sar Karyavaha (he will preside) (ii) One or more Sah-Sar Karyavahas (iii) Akhil Bharatiya Sharirik Shikshan Pramukh (iv) Akhil Bharatiya Baudhik Shikshan Pramukh (v) Akhil Bharatiya Prachar Pramukh (vi) Akhil Bharatiya Nidhi Pramukh.
>
> (b) The Kendriya Karyakari Mandal shall have in addition not less than five members who shall be chosen from among the Karyakari Mandal of the provinces.

The Fuehrer runs the show through his hand-picked gauleiters. In 1942, a leading member, P.C. Sahasrabudhe, praised dictatorships, the Fuehrer principle of Germany and the leader principle of Mussolini.[1]

The Italian scholar Marzia Casolari's essay[2] created a stir. It was based on

1 Bipan Chandra, *Communalism in Modern India*, Delhi: Vikas, 1987, p. 117, fn. 76.

2 Marzia Casolari, 'Hindutva's Foreign Tie-up in the 1930s', *Economic & Political Weekly*, vol.

painstaking research in the National Archives of India as well as in Rome. It was strikingly original and broke new ground. Its title was 'Hindutva's Foreign Tie-up in 1930s: Archival Evidence'.

In 2011 was published the fruits of Marzia Casolari's stupendous research in a book *In the Shade of the Swastika: The Ambiguous Relationship between Indian Nationalism and Nazi-Fascism.*

The RSS's approach to the fascists in Europe was not merely tactical. It sprang naturally from the very nature of Hindu nationalism. Which is why fascism and Nazism were so attractive. 'Some features of the organisation of the Hindu right, their social structure, their ideology, their racial discourse derives largely from these influences.' Admiration for Benito Mussolini gave way to hero-worship of Adolph Hitler especially with Savarkar. Bengal and the Province of Bombay proved a fertile field. B.S. Moonje's trip to Italy in 1931 and his meeting with Mussolini was a turning point. Militarism and racialism provided the cement. 'Muslims became the main target of Hindu policy, and Muslims started to be perceived and described as more threatening than the British rulers.'[3] If British imperialism was acceptable as an ally, why not Italian fascism or German Nazism as well?

Italian consulates in Kolkata and Mumbai enlisted collaborators. 'Relations with politically minded intellectuals in Bengal had developed considerably, also involving leading figures such as Syama Prasad Mookerjee (1901-1953). Mookerjee, a leading Hindu Nationalist and founder of the Jana Sangh, was also chancellor of the University of Calcutta from 1934 to 1938. In a letter to Gentile, Tucci described Mookerjee as "our most important collaborator" in Calcutta, together with Das Gupta.'[4]

Giuseppe Tucci was a disciple of Carlo Formichi, an India-scholar. Both knew Rabindranath Tagore. Giovanni Gentile was a fascist philosopher. Surendra Nath Das Gupta, a distinguished professor at the University of Calcutta, was 'a collaborator of the fascist regime on the cultural front'.[5] Pran Nath Roy was one of Tucci's pupils. He taught Italian literature at Banaras and Calcutta Universities. He received a hefty 700 liras from the Foreign Officer in Rome every month for his work at universities and for fascist propaganda in Indian journals. It was a close net network. Syama Prasad Mookerjee was a valued asset.

> The RSS method of recruitment was practically identical to that of the Balilla youth organisation in Italy. Shakha members, for instance, were grouped according to their age (6-7 to 10; 10 to 14; 14 to 28; 28 and older). This is

35, no. 4, 22-28 January 2000.

3 Marzia Casolari, *In the Shade of the Swastika: The Ambiguous Relationship Between Indian Nationalism and Nazi-Fascism*, Bologna: I Libri di Emil, 2011, p. 17.

4 Ibid., p. 47.

5 Ibid., p. 42.

amazingly similar to the age bands of the hierarchical organisation of the fascist youth organisations, with its subdivision of boys and young men in Figli della Lupa, Balilla, Avanguardisti, and Camicie Nere (Sons of the She-Wolf, Balilla, Avant-gardists and Black-shirts). The hierarchical ordering of RSS members, however, came after the organisation was founded and may well have been derived from fascism, as we shall see.

Initially, the RSS must have been very closely modelled on the akharas, the Bengali gymnasiums where martial arts and paramilitary training were performed – and the secret societies founded in Maharashtra by young militants close to Tilak, including the Savarkar brothers.[6]

At the end of the Round Table Conference in London in 1931, Moonje visited Germany and Italy and found the concept of fascism very attractive, as he recorded in his diary.

> The idea of Fascism vividly brings out the conception of unity amongst people. India and particularly Hindu India need some such Institution for the military regeneration of the Hindus: so that the artificial distinction so much emphasised by the British of martial and non-martial classes amongst the Hindus may disappear. Our Institution of Rashtriya Swayamsevak Sangh of Nagpur under Dr. Hedgewar is of this kind, though quite independently conceived. I will spend the rest of my life in developing and extending this institution of Dr. Hedgewar all through out [sic] the Maharashtra and other provinces.

What attracted him besides the ideology was its military organisation.

> The Balilla Institutions and the conception of the whole organisation have appealed to me most, though there is still not discipline and organisation of high order. The whole idea is conceived by Mussolini for the military regeneration of Italy. Italians, by nature, appear to be ease-loving and non-martial like the Indians generally. They have cultivated, like Indians, the works of peace and neglected the cultivation of the art of war. Mussolini saw the essential weakness of his country and conceived the idea of the Balilla organisation.[7]

Moonje met Mussolini on 19 March 1931. Moonje told him,

> I have already started an organisation of my own, conceived independently

[6] Ibid., p. 57.
[7] Ibid., p. 69.

> with similar objectives. I shall have no hesitation to raise my voice from the public platform both in India and England whenever occasion may arise in praise of your Balilla and Fascist organisations. I wish them good luck and every success.[8]

The RSS was conceived as a military wing of Hindu nationalism. To Moonje, Mussolini was 'one of the great men of the European world'.

On his return to India, Moonje founded a military school connected to the RSS and strengthened the RSS organisation. He was the bond between the RSS and the Hindu Mahasabha. Hedgewar was his protégé, a fact which the RSS downplays. He became president of the Mahasabha in 1927 and invited the RSS to attend its annual session at Ahmedabad. Hedgewar was able to meet with Mahasabha leaders. He was secretary of the Mahasabha between 1926 and 1931. At a meeting with Hedgewar and Laloo Gokhale on 31 March 1934, Moonje said,

> I have thought out a scheme based on Hindu Dharm Shastra which provides for standardisation of Hinduism throughout India . . . But the point is that this ideal can not be brought to effect unless we have our own swaraj with a Hindu as a Dictator like Shivaji of old or Mussolini or Hitler of the present day in Italy and Germany. But this does not mean that we have to sit with folded hands until [sic] some such dictator arises in India. We should formulate a scientific scheme and carry on propaganda for it.[9]

In 1934 was founded the Bhonsala Military School as well as the Central Hindu Military Education Society whose aim was 'to bring about military regeneration of the Hindus and fit Hindu youths for undertaking the *entire* responsibility for the defence of their motherland'. Others – Muslims, Sikhs, Christians, Parsis and the rest – were excluded.

Moonje tapped the Maharajas of Kashmir, Indore, Travancore, Bikaner, Udaipur, Jaipur and some others. The Intelligence Bureau's Note on the RSS warned 'it is perhaps no exaggeration to assert that the Sangh hopes to be in future India what the "Fascist" are Italy and the "Nazis" in Germany'. This was written in 1933.

V.D. Savarkar pursued the same line. He said on 1 August 1938,

> [T]he Hindu Sanghatanists in India hold that Germany was perfectly justified in uniting the Austrian and Sudeten Germans under the German Flag. Democracy itself demanded that the will of the people must prevail in choosing their own Government. Germany demanded plebiscite, the Germans under the Czechs wanted to join their kith and kin in Germany.

[8] Ibid., p. 73.

[9] Ibid., p. 785.

In 1937 he said also that India should follow the German example to solve the 'Muslim problem'. On 29 July 1939 he said:

> Nationality did not depend so much on a common geographical area as on unity of thought, religion, language and culture. For this reason the Germans and the Jews could not be regarded as a nation.

Germans are 'the nation in Germany', 'Jews are a community'. Savarkar liaised with the consulates of Germany, Italy and Japan. He had good relations with Jugal Kishore Birla, elder brother of G.D. Birla, a 'follower' of Gandhi, and sympathiser of the Mahasabha.

Casolari writes:

> While there is no archival evidence of any contacts between Savarkar and the Italian Consulate or Consulate officials, plenty of records are available, showing Savarkar's connections with German agents. From November 1938 on, Savarkar had been writing to two German agents, G.L. Lesczczynski – representative of the German News Agencies – and a certain P. Pazze. The latter was fronting as a manager of a company based in Bombay, but he was involved in propaganda activities orchestrated by the German Consulate. These two fellows arranged the publication of Savarkar's speech in the *Völkischer Beobachter*. However, before going ahead with the publication, Lesczczynski wanted to know how big was the party headed by Savarkar, in order to know 'exactly what amount of influence the Hindu Maha Sabha wields in the country, the strength of its membership etc.' On 22nd November, the party headquarters promptly informed Lesczczynski that 'So far as the Hindu Mahasabha is concerned it is an All India organisation representing Hindus just as the Moslem League represents the Moslems. Its membership runs [sic] several thousands'.
>
> Over the next few months, relations between Germany and the Hindus increased. In early December, Malekar sent Lesczczynski a copy of an article published in an unspecified 'Marathi leading Daily', in which Germany's conduct over the Jewish question was described in favourable terms. Two days later, Lesczczynski sent Savarkar a complimentary copy of Mein Kampf.

As Germany's fortunes in Europe rose, thanks to Britain's appeasement policy, so did Savarkar's esteem for its ideology and its affinity with Hindutva. On the eve of the War, a Mahasabha spokesman said on 25 March 1939,

> Germany's solemn idea of the revival of the Aryan culture, the glorification of the Swastika, her patronage of Vedic learning and the ardent championship of the tradition of the Indo-Germanic civilisation are welcomed by the religious

> and sensible Hindus of India with a jubilant hope. Only a few socialists headed by Pandit J. Nehru have created a bubble of resentment against the present Government of Germany, but their activities are far from having any significance in India. The vain imprecations of Mahatma Gandhi against Germany's indispensable [sic] vigour in matters of internal policy obtain but little regard in so far as they are uttered by a man who has always betrayed and confused the country with an affected mysticism. I think that Germany's crusade against the enemies of Aryan culture will bring all the Aryan nations of the World to their senses and awaken the Indian Hindus for the restoration of their lost glory.[10]

After the War broke out Savarkar pledged his cooperation to the Viceroy Lord Linlithgow while Moonje began mobilising a military with 'an anti-Muslim character' while the 'RSS was to play a leading role in its organisation'.

On 19 August 1940

> Savarkar provided Lord Linlithgow with a list of Hindu Mahasabha members for inclusion in the prospected Executive Council. The list included Moonje and Syama Prasad Mookerjee. In a letter of 26 September to the Viceroy, Moonje remarked that the Hindus 'will be in a position to give immensely large help both in men, material and intellect than the Muslim League can hope to do, in organising the defence of India, on modern scientific lines . . . Thus Hindustan and Britain are allied together in unshakable bond of union for long long years to come'.

He would not have written this without Mookerjee's approval. Complicit in the quest for militarisation was one who also professed to being a liberal – M.R. Jayakar, once president of the Mahasabha, a leading light of the liberals in partnership with Tej Bahadur Sapru and a member of the Judicial Committee of the Privy Council in London.

The RSS-Mahasabha combine had no qualms about supporting dictators as a report on the Officers' Training Camp of the RSS held in April-May 1942 in Pune revealed:

> Dr. P.C. Sahasrabudhe addressed the volunteers on three occasions. On 4.5.1942 he announced that the Sangh followed the principle of dictatorship. Denouncing democratic Government as an unsatisfactory form of Government, he quoted France as a typical example and, praising dictatorship, he pointed to Japan, Russia and Germany. He particularly praised the Fuehrer principle of Germany. On 21.5.1942 he drew attention to the value of propaganda, quoting

[10] Ibid., pp. 156-7.

> Russia and Germany as examples, and again extolled the virtues of the Leader principle, citing Mussolini's success as a further example.[11]

Marzia Casolari has rendered great service to the truth by bringing to light documents which she found in her painstaking research. Her exposure is thorough and her conclusions are pre-eminently sound.

> Considering the strength and the extension of the RSS from the early 1940s on, two aspects emerge which require particular attention. The first aspect is represented by the progressive growth of the RSS, right from its foundation. This was probably due to the adoption of a systematic work at the grass-root level. As already pointed out, between 1936 and 1941 the RSS had grown almost four-fold in terms of branches and, in terms of membership, six-fold. The second aspect is represented by a couple of questions that arise spontaneously: who was the enemy? Has this militia been used against any one? Unfortunately, this militia became effective during the partition, when the Sangh Parivar forces massacred the Indian citizens belonging to the 'enemy' community. This concept of 'enemy' made the whole difference between Indian nationalism and Hindu nationalism.[12]

The battle is still on with yet greater fury.

[11] Ibid., pp. 186-7.

[12] Ibid., p. 187.

6. Savarkar Captures the Mahasabha

V.D. Savarkar became president of the Hindu Mahasabha in 1937 and held the office for seven terms. He yielded it to his disciple Syama Prasad Mookerjee. Savarkar brought along his theory of Hindutva and cemented the Mahasabha's relations with the RSS. Above all, he imparted to it a new tone and direction. Presidents like Lajpat Rai were men of character, scholarship and personal grace. Savarkar was devoid of all three. He was worse than coarse. He was venomous. Deceitful, he was a man with a past.

He had instigated and encouraged three murders. But was convicted only for the murder of A.T.M. Jackson, Collector of Nashik District, a known sympathiser of Indian aspirations, in 1909. He got away with the murder of Curzon Wylie of the India Office in the same year and also with the attempted murder of the Acting Governor of Bombay Ernest Hotson in 1931. (He was saved by his bullet-proof vest.) He was privy to Gandhi's assassination on 30 January 1948. In each case the trigger was pulled by someone else; the assassination was directed by him. He was close to Gandhi's assassin Nathuram Godse whose brother Gopal said in an interview to Arvind Rajagopal, 'All the brothers were in the RSS. Nathuram, Dattatreya, myself and Govind. You can say we grew up in the RSS rather than in our homes.'[1]

This gruesome record is matched by a record of abject apologies and assurances of good behaviour towards the British rulers. Here is a record of both.

1. Savarkar was brought to the Cellular Jail in the Andamans on 4 July 1911. Within six months he was on his knees with a 'petition for clemency'. Savarkar referred to it in his next petition sent on 14 November 1913 which read:

> In the end, may I remind your honour to be so good as to go through the petition for clemency, that I had sent in 1911, and to sanction it for being forwarded to the Indian Government? The latest development of the Indian Politics and the conciliating policy of the Government have thrown open the constitutional line once more. Now no man having the good of India and Humanity at Heart will blindly step on the thorny paths which, in the excited and hopeless situation of India in 1906-1907, beguiled us from the path of peace and progress. Therefore, if the Government in their manifold beneficence and mercy release me, I for one cannot but be the staunchest

1 Arvind Rajagopal, '"He did not leave the RSS": Interview with Gopal Godse', *Frontline*, 28 January 1994, pp. 93-4.

> advocate of constitutional progress *and loyalty to the English Government* which is the foremost condition of that progress.

2. In October 1913, the Home Minister of the Viceroy's Executive Council, Sir Reginald Craddock, visited the Jail and met Savarkar. His note of 23 November 1913, recorded Savarkar's pleas for mercy. Savarkar had submitted his second mercy petition on 14 November 1913: '*I am ready to serve the Government in any capacity they like. . . .* Where else can the prodigal son return but to the parental doors of the Government?'

3. On 22 March 1920 Home Minister Sir William Vincent said:

> Two petitions were received from Vinayak Damodar Savarkar – one in 1914 and another in 1917, through the Superintendent, Port Blair. In the former he offered his services to Government during the war in any capacity and prayed that a general amnesty be granted to all political prisoners. The second petition was confined to the latter proposal.

There was one in 1917 besides that of 1913 which perhaps is the one Vincent referred to as one of 1914.

On 30 March 1920, he begged for 'a last chance to submit his case before it is too late'. He demeaned himself by citing cases of fellow prisoners, Aurobindo Ghose's brother Barin and others. 'They had even in Port Blair been suspected of a serious plot.' *He* was the loyalist.

> So far from believing in the militant school of the type, I do not contribute even to the peaceful and philosophical anarchism of a Kuropatkin [sic] or a Tolstoy. And as to my revolutionary tendencies in the past:– it is not only now for the object of sharing the clemency but years before this have I informed of and written to the Government in my petitions (1918, 1914) about my firm intention to abide by the constitution and stand by it as soon as a beginning was made to frame it by Mr. Montagu. Since that the Reforms and then the Proclamation have only confirmed me in my views and recently I have publicly avowed my faith in and readiness to stand by the side of orderly and constitutional development.

For good measure he added: 'I am sincere in expressing my earnest intention of treading the constitutional path and trying my humble best to render the hands of the British dominion a bond of love and respect and a mutual help. *Such an Empire as is foreshadowed in the Proclamation, wins my hearty adherence.*' So much for his nationalism.

Savarkar concluded:

> I and my brother are perfectly willing to give a pledge of not participating in politics for a definite and reasonable period that the Government would indicate . . . This or any pledge, e.g., of remaining in a particular province or reporting our movements to the police for a definite period after our release – any such reasonable conditions meant genuinely to ensure the safety of the State would be gladly accepted by me and my brother.

4. On 22 February 1948, to the Commissioner of Police, Bombay, in order to avert prosecution for Gandhi's murder: 'I shall refrain from taking part in any communal or political public activity for any period the Government may require.'

5. On 13 July 1950, he gave an undertaking to Chief Justice M.C. Chagla and Justice P.B. Gajendragadkar of the Bombay High Court: '. . . would not take any part whatever in political activity and would remain in my house in Bombay' for a year. He resigned as president of the Hindu Mahasabha.

In 1924 he had accepted two conditions which the government imposed for his release: (a) he would reside in the Ratnagiri District and not go out without permission; (b)

> That the said Vinayak Damodar Savarkar will reside within the territories administered by the Governor of Bombay in Council and within the Ratnagiri District within the said territories, and will not go beyond the limits of that district without the permission of the Government, or in case of urgency of the District Magistrate; and (c) That he will not engage Publicly or privately in any manner of political activities without the consent of the Government for a period of five years, *such restriction being renewable at the discretion of Government at the expiry of the said term.*
>
> Mr. Savarkar has already indicated his acceptance of these terms. He has also, though it was explained to him that it was in no way made condition of his release, submitted the following statement:- 'I hereby acknowledge that I had a fair trial and just sentence. I heartily abhor – methods of violence resorted to in days gone by, and I feel myself duty bound to uphold Law and the constitution in the best of my powers and am willing to make the Reform a success in so far as I may be allowed to do in future.'

There were no depths to which he would not stoop.

This record is unsurpassed in its infamy in all the annals preceding and following Savarkar's tenure in politics.[2] No true patriot would forgive such a person.

[2] Vide Noorani, *Savarkar and Hindutva.*

Savarkar is not only forgiven, he is idolised and his portrait was hung in the Central Hall of Parliament facing that of the man he conspired to kill, Gandhi. The reason is that Savarkar expounded Hindu nationalism in a manner which would appeal to the surging group of Hindu nationalists.

It was because of his essay *Hindutva: Who is a Hindu?*, published in 1923 under the pseudonym 'A Maratha' because he was in prison. Its thesis was summed up crisply by Dr. B.R. Ambedkar. His definition of a Hindu – which forms the basis of Hindutva – 'has been framed with great care and caution'. A Hindu is one who regards India as both his Fatherland (pitribhoomi) as well as his Holyland (punyabhoomi). 'It is designed to serve two purposes which Mr. Savarkar has in view. First, to exclude from it Muslims, Christians, Parsis and Jews by prescribing the recognition of India as Holy Land as a qualification of being a Hindu. Secondly, to include Buddhists, Jains, Sikhs, etc., by not insisting upon belief in the sanctity of the Vedas as an element in the qualifications.'[3]

Savarkar died a political failure. He and his Hindu Mahasabha had ceased to be players in Indian politics since the early forties. But his ideology took a new life once it was adopted by the RSS in its entirety. It is writ large in Golwalkar's book *We or Our Nationhood Defined* (1938). Vajpayee was wrong in saying in the Rajya Sabha on 6 May 2002 that the book represented Golwalkar's personal views. It was cited in a formal legal document filed in 1978 before the District Judge, Nagpur by the RSS, as an organisation. Dhananjay Keer records that in a speech in Mumbai on 15 May 1963 Golwalkar said that 'he found the principles of nationalism scientifically explained in Savarkar's great work Hindutva. To him it was a text-book, a scientific book'. It was on this occasion also that Golwalkar publicly acknowledged his debt to the book *Rashtra Meemansa* by Savarkar's elder brother Babarao (G.D.) Savarkar. Golwalkar's own *Bunch of Thoughts* reflects a deep impress of Hindutva. It has a whole chapter denouncing 'Territorial Nationalism'. It was also relied on by the RSS in the 1978 document. Golwalkar himself acknowledged that 'Veer Savarkarji wrote a beautiful book "*Hindutva*" and *Hindu Mahasabha* based itself on that pure philosophy of Hindu Nationalism'.[4]

Savarkar was at pains at the very outset to emphasise that Hindutva is different from Hinduism.

> Here it is enough to point out that Hindutva is not identical with what is vaguely indicated by the term Hinduism. By an 'ism' it is generally meant a theory or a code more or less based on spiritual or religious dogma or system. But when we attempt to investigate into the essential significance of Hindutva

[3] Ambedkar, *Pakistan or the Partition of India*, p. 139.

[4] Dhananjay Keer, *Veer Savarkar*, Popular Prakashan, 1966, p. 527. References to Savarkar's book are from *Hindutva: Who is a Hindu?*

we do not primarily – and certainly not mainly – concern ourselves with any particular theocratic or religious dogma or creed.

He explained:

> We have tried already to draw a clear line of demarcation between the two conceptions and protested against the wrong use of the word Hinduism to denote the Sanatan Dharma alone. Hindutva is not identical with Hindu Dharma; nor is Hindu Dharma identical with Hinduism.

Hinduism is an ancient religion. Hindutva is a modern construct; a short term for what came to be called 'cultural nationalism'. Emphasis on this distinction is writ large all over the writing. 'Although the root-meaning of the word Hindu like the sister epithet Hindi may mean only an Indian, yet as it is we would be straining the usage of words too much – we fear, to the point of breaking – if we call a Mohammedan a Hindu because of his being a resident of India.' Hinduism is noble. Hindutva is the ideology of hate.

The two-nation theory propounded by Lajpat Rai was strongly affirmed. 'The Hindus are not merely the citizens of Indian state because they are united not only by the bonds of the love they bear to a common motherland but also by the bonds of a common blood. They are not only a Nation but also a race-jati.' This is racialism in its grossest form.

The test is explicitly set on.

> To every Hindu, from the Santal to the Sadhu this Bharat bhumi this Sindhusthan is at once a Pitribhu and a Punyabhu – fatherland and a holy land. That is why . . . some of our Mohammedan or Christian countrymen who had originally been forcibly converted to a non-Hindu religion and who consequently have inherited along with Hindus, a common Fatherland and a greater part of the wealth of a common culture – language, law, customs, folklore and history – are not and cannot be recognised as Hindus. For though Hindusthan to them is Fatherland as to any other Hindu yet it is not to them a Holyland too. Their holy land is far off in Arabia or Palestine.

They are invited to 'return' to the fold.

> Ye, who by race, by blood, by culture, by nationality, possess almost all the essentials of Hindutva and had been forcibly snatched out of our ancestral home by the hand of violence – ye, have only to render wholehearted love to our common Mother and recognise her not only as Fatherland (Pitribhu) but

> even as a Holyland (Punyabhu); and ye would be most welcome to the Hindu fold.

These twin inextricably related themes recur in the RSS's themes to this day. Muslims do not belong to the fold and they should return to it. Since they are outside the fold they are not full citizens of India merely because they were born on its territory. 'Territorial nationalism' is categorically rejected. The only solution is conversion to Hinduism – *ghar wapsi*.

> These are the essentials of Hindutva – a common nation (Rashtra), *a common race (Jati)*, and a common civilisation (Sanskriti). All these essentials could best be summed up by stating in brief that he is a Hindu to whom Sindhusthan is not only a Pitribhu but also a Punyabhu. For the first two essentials of Hindutva – nation and Jati – are clearly denoted and connoted by the word Pitribhu while the third essential of Sanskriti is pre-eminently implied by the word Punyabhu, as it is precisely Sanskriti including sanskaras i.e. rites and rituals, ceremonies and sacraments, that makes a land a Holyland.

Christians and Jews fare no better than Muslims.

> Look at the Jews; neither centuries of prosperity nor sense of gratitude for the shelter they found can make them more attached or even equally attached to the several countries they inhabit . . . they, like the Mohammedans would naturally set the interests of their Holyland above those of their Motherland.

No room was left for any compromise. The concept of a 'composite culture' was rejected. This credo Savarkar affirmed in ringing terms in his first presidential address to the Mahasabha at Ahmedabad in 1937. He went on to preside over seven annual sessions.[5]

He proudly recalled that he 'had coined the word "Hindutva". The test precisely is a common Holyland'. Accordingly 'the Indian Mohammedans, Jews, Christians, Parsees, etc. are excluded from claiming themselves as Hindus which in reality also they do not, – in spite of their recognising Hindusthan as their fatherland'. Also excluded are 'the Japanese, the Chinese and others from the Hindu fold' though they regard India as their 'Holyland'. Such idiosyncrasies should not obscure the fact that the core of Savarkar's Hindutva is adopted by the RSS and the BJP.

It was in 1937 that Savarkar said:

> Let us bravely face unpleasant facts as they are. India cannot be assumed today

5 V.D. Savarkar, *Hindu Rashtra Darshan: A Collection of his Presidential Speeches*, Bombay, 1949.

to be a Unitarian and homogeneous nation, but on the contrary there are two nations in the main: the Hindus and the Moslems, in India.

The theme was amplified the next year at the Nagpur session.

> Yes, we Hindus are a Nation by ourselves. Because religious, *racial*, cultural and historical affinities bind us intimately into a homogeneous nation and added to it we are most pre-eminently gifted with a territorial unity as well. *Our racial being is identified with India* – our beloved Fatherland and our Holyland, above all and irrespective of it all we Hindus will to be a Nation and, therefore, we are a Nation . . . the Hindus are a nation in India – in Hindusthan, and the Muslim minority, a community.

This was repeated in 1939 at the Kolkata session.

In a statement on 19 December 1947 Savarkar lauded the U.N. General Assembly's resolution on the partition of Palestine, with the establishment of the State of Israel. Indeed 'the whole of Palestine ought to have been restored to the Jews'.[6]

Reckless slander is in the Sangh Parivar's DNA. In late 1947 Savarkar said:

> Had not Gandhiji himself conspired with the Ali Brothers to invite an invasion by the Pathans and to enthrone the Amir of Afghanistan as the Emperor of India? Had he not declared again in the year 1940 in writing and repeated it now and then that if the Nizam, subduing the Hindu Princes and with the support of Frontier tribes, took Delhi and became the ruler of India that would be a perfect Home Rule, a cent percent Swaraj? Thus a Pathani or a Nizami Moslem Raj is to Gandhiji a cent per cent Swaraj. But Hindu Raj? Oh no!

Savarkar supported closer links with the RSS as Marzia Casolari documented. He need not have worried. The RSS was not idle. It was on the rise, replacing the Mahasabha and leaving Savarkar high and dry. Organisationally it had made huge saffron hay while the sun of British rule shone at high noon. It was ready to play its role. The partition riots and the massacres provided ample opportunity. Golwalkar had acquired complete control over the RSS.

[6] *Historic Statements by Veer Savarkar*, p. 220.

7. The RSS Acquires a Bible

Madhav Sadashiv Golwalkar was general secretary of the RSS under the sarsanghchalak (the head) Hedgewar. He was formally anointed as sarsanghchalak on 3 July 1940 after Hedgewar's death on 21 June 1940. He held that post till Madhukar Dattatraya Deoras took over in 1973 on Golwalkar's death. Deoras had been general secretary since 1965. Golwalkar was the longest serving supremo of the RSS. His mark on it endures.

Even before he took over in 1940 Golwalkar had nailed his colours to the mast. On 22 March 1939 he wrote the preface to his book aptly entitled 'We or Our Nationhood Defined'. It was published by Bharat Publications at Nagpur. He acknowledged his debt to V.D. Savarkar's elder brother Ganesh D. (Babarao) Savarkar. 'His work *Rashtra Meemansa* in Marathi has been one of my chief sources of inspiration and help.'

There was no mistaking the fact that the author sought to provide a manual of the RSS. Like Savarkar, Golwalkar sought to define the Hindu Nation.

> I have throughout the work scrupulously stuck to one idea 'Nation' and except where it was unavoidable have given no consideration to the allied concept, the 'State'. 'Nation' being a cultural unit, and 'State' a political one, the two concepts are clearly distinguishable, although there is certainly a good deal of mutual overlapping. Considerations about the 'Hindu State' or as people now please to call it, the 'Indian State', have been reserved. If it is possible, the question may form the subject matter of another book.

The emphasis was on Hindu Rashtra, the nation. Once it was duly mobilised, Hindu Raj the State would follow, as Mookerjee pointed out. 'In this country, our "Nation" means and . . . always must mean the Hindu Nation and naught else.'[1] The book was dedicated to 'the Divine Mother – the Hindu Nation'. In his foreword, M.S. Aney declared, 'The democratic State shall be under the sovereignty of the Nationality to which the majority of the people in the State belongs.'[2] It was to be uncontrolled majoritarianism. *The Hindu Rashtra would sustain Hindu Raj.*

To read this book is to realise its significance. It elaborates Savarkar's doctrine in simple and explicit words and puts on it the imprimatur of the RSS's approval. Its explicit language drove Vajpayee to disown it, unsuccessfully though. Golwalkar elaborated on this very doctrine in 1966 in his book *Bunch of Thoughts* which is

[1] M.S. Golwalkar, *We or Our Nationhood Defined*, p. 2.

[2] Ibid., p. xx.

no less candid (Vikrama Prakashan, Bengaluru). These two books comprise an integral whole with Savarkar's *Hindutva* blending them together.

We or Our Nationhood Defined shared Savarkar's views on Palestine.

> The recent attempt at rehabilitating Palestine with its ancient population of the Jews is nothing more than an effort to reconstruct the broken edifice and revitalise the practically dead Hebrew National life.

He comes to the main thesis.

> Now we shall proceed to understand our Nationhood in the light of this scientific concept. Here is our vast country, Hindusthan, the land of the Hindus, their home country, hereditary territory, a definite geographical unity, delimited naturally by the sublime Himalayas on the North and the limitless ocean on the other three sides, an ideal piece of land, deserving in every respect to be called a country, fulfilling all that the word should imply in the Nation idea. Living in this country since pre-historic times, is the ancient Race – the Hindu Race, united together by common traditions, by memories of common glory and disaster, by similar historical, political, social, religious and other experiences, living and evolving, under the same influences, a common culture, a common mother language, common customs, common aspirations. This great Hindu Race professes its illustrious Hindu Religion, the only Religion in the world worthy of being so denominated, which in its variety is still an organic whole, capable of feeding the noble aspirations of all men, of all stages, of all grades, aptitudes and capacities, enriched by the noblest philosophy of life in all its functions, and hallowed by an unbroken, interminable succession of divine spiritual geniuses, a religion of which any sane man may be justly proud.

The RSS's racial outlook has been ignored.

> Guided by this Religion in all walks of life, individual, social, political, the Race evolved a culture, which despite the degenerating contact with the debased 'civilisations' of the Mussalmans and the Europeans, for the last ten centuries, is still the noblest in the world. . . . The spirit of broad Catholicism, generosity, toleration, truth, sacrifice and love for all life, which characterises the average Hindu mind, not wholly vitiated by Western influence, bears eloquent testimony to the greatness of Hindu culture. And even those, spoiled by contamination with foreign influences, do not but compare favourably with the best in the rest of the world.
>
> Not only has this culture been most markedly offensive in moulding man

> after the picture of God, but in the field of learning (we distinguish learning and knowledge) also, it has produced, to the immortal glory of the Race, intellectual giants, outstanding the great savants of the modern scientific world. Great mathematicians like Bhaskaracharya, great chemists and physicians like the authors of the Charak Samhita, Bhavaprakash and Sushruta, great artists and sculptors, whose works like the Taj, the Ajanta paintings, the Werool (Ellora) Caves, and numerous others well known to the world still delight and charm the people of the world.

It is this author who inspired Modi's famous speech in Mumbai at the Reliance Hurkisondas Hospital on plastic surgery in ancient India. Golwalkar lists heroes galore. Not one Muslim figure in the list.

There comes this famous passage which explains Vajpayee's disclaimer.

> We repeat; in Hindusthan, the land of the Hindus, lives and should live the Hindu Nation – satisfying all the five essential requirements of the scientific nation concept of the modern world. Consequently only those movements are truly 'National' as aim at re-building, re-vitalising and emancipating from its present stupor, the Hindu Nation. Those only are nationalist patriots, who, with the aspiration to glorify the Hindu race and Nation next to their heart, are prompted into activity and strive to achieve that goal. All others are either traitors and enemies to the National cause, or, to take a charitable view, idiots.

Mark the affinities. Like Savarkar, Golwalkar also offers a choice.

> There are only two courses open to the foreign elements, either to merge themselves in the national race and adopt its culture, or to live at its mercy so long as the national race may allow them to do so and to quit the country at the sweet will of the national race. That is the only sound view on the minorities problem. That is the only logical and correct solution. That alone keeps the national life healthy and undisturbed. That alone keeps the Nation safe from the danger of a cancer developing into its body politic of the creation of a state within the state.
>
> From this standpoint, sanctioned by the experience of shrewd old nations, the foreign races in Hindusthan must either adopt Hindu culture and language, must learn to respect and hold in reverence Hindu religion, must entertain no idea but those of the glorification of the Hindu race and culture, i.e., of the Hindu nation and must lose their separate existence to merge in the Hindu race, or may stay in the country, wholly subordinated to the Hindu Nation, claiming nothing, deserving no privileges, far less any preferential treatment – not even citizen's rights. There is, at least should be, no other course for them

> to adopt. We are an old nation; let us deal, as old nations ought to and do deal, with the foreign races, who have chosen to live in our country.

Logically enough, 'territorial nationalism' is categorically rejected. When the Indian National Congress was founded

> [T]he amazing theory was propounded that the Nation is composed of all those who, for one reason or the other happen to live at the time in the country. The absurd result of such a view is that European adventurers, who for their private, selfish ends came to the land but yesterday, have earned a place in the National polity and under our present constitution have their representatives in the 'National' Legislatures of the country. Indeed they have made our country a veritable serai.

The reference to Europeans is far-fetched. The real aim is the Muslim 'outsider'.

Golwalkar knew that the vast majority of Hindus rejected his regressive theory. He attacks them.

> This 'Educated' class of Hindus became in truth slaves of the English, as the late Dr. S.V. Ketkar has aptly described them. They had cut their traces, lost their footing in the National past, and become deculturised, denationalised people. But they also formed the bulk of the 'Congress' and found no difficulty in eagerly gulping down the extra-ordinary absurdity, that their country was not theirs, but belonged to the strangers and enemies of their Race equally with them. . . . But as we have seen we Hindus have been living, thousands of years, a full National life in Hindusthan. How can we be 'communal' having as we do, no other interests but those relating our Country, our Nation?

This explains why, both the RSS and the BJP assert that they are not 'communal'. As believers in Hindu nationalism, they are 'nationalists'.

Bunch of Thoughts, a much longer book of 439 pages, puts the seal of finality on the doctrine. It cannot be disowned. The RSS has a global outlook and a global mission as it is a Jagadguru (universal teacher).

> Our arms stretched as far as America on the one side – that was long long before Columbus 'discovered' America! – and on the other to China, Japan, Cambodia, Malaya, Siam, Indonesia and all the South-East Asian countries and right up to Mongolia and Siberia in the North. Our powerful political empire too spread over these South-East areas and continued for 1,400 years, the Shailendra empire alone flourishing for over 700 years – standing as a powerful bulwark against Chinese expansion.

> During all those centuries, there were neither uprisings by the local people nor their exterminations which would have been the inevitable result if there had been the slightest sign of domination or exploitation by a foreign people and a foreign culture. On the contrary, those people were grateful to us. They adored our nation and longed to give up their mortal coils on the banks of Ganga. That stands in glowing contrast to the bloodstained pages of the history of expansion of Islam and Christianity and now Communism.

Democracy is 'a myth'. There is scorn for 'the high-sounding principle of "individual freedom"'. It is not the minorities alone whom the RSS targets. It is democracy itself. Chauvinism pervades throughout. 'The average man of this country was at one time incomparably superior to the average man of other lands.' Revivalism, based on myths, supports chauvinism.

'*If partition is a settled fact we are here to unsettle it.*' The two-nation theory is reiterated.

> All the requisites for making a full-fledged nation are thus fulfilled in the life of this great Hindu People. Therefore we say that in this land of ours, Bharat, the national life is of the Hindu People. In short, this is the Hindu Nation. . . .
>
> He cannot be a Hindu at all who is intolerant of other faiths. But the question before us now is, what is the attitude of those people who have been converted to Islam or Christianity? They are born in this land, no doubt. But are they true to its salt? Are they grateful towards this land which has brought them up? Do they feel that they are the children of this land and its tradition, and that to serve it is their great good fortune? Do they feel it a duty to serve her? No! Together with the change in their faith, gone are the spirit of love and devotion for the nation. Nor does it end there. They have also developed a feeling of identification with the enemies of this land. They look to some foreign lands as their holy places.

The Savarkar text of 1923 is affirmed 45 years later. So is his offer of return to the Hindu fold.

> Everybody knows that only a handful of Muslims came here as enemies and invaders. So also only a few foreign Christian missionaries came here. Now the Muslims and Christians have enormously grown in number. They did not grow just by multiplication as in the case of fishes. They converted the local population. We can trace our ancestry to a common source, from where one portion was taken away from the Hindu fold and became Muslim and another became Christian. The rest could not be converted and they have remained as Hindus.

> . . . It is our duty to call these our forlorn brothers, suffering under religious slavery for centuries, back to their ancestral home. As honest freedom-loving men, let them overthrow all signs of slavery and domination and follow the ancestral ways of devotion and national life. All types of slavery are repugnant to our nature and should be given up. This is a call for all those brothers to take their original place in our national life. . . .
>
> There are some people who claim that they have achieved unity of Hindus, Muslims, Christians and all others on the political and economic plane. But why limit the oneness only there? Why not make it more wide and more comprehensive so as to fuse them all in the Hindu way of life, in our dharma and take them back as lost brothers? To those who speak of unity on the political and economic plane, we say that we stand not only for political and economic unity but also for cultural and religious unity.

It is *religious* unity which the RSS seeks in the name of 'cultural unity'. It is an impossible goal.

Chapter X and XI on 'Territorial Nationalism' are capped by Chapter XII on 'Internal Threats'. They are the Muslims, the Christians and the Communists. Nothing had changed since 1923 or has changed since 1966. The RSS and the BJP are stuck in the same groove.

> They forget that here was already a full-fledged ancient nation of the Hindus and the various communities which were living in the country were here either as guests, the Jews and Parsis, or as invaders, the Muslims and Christians. They never faced the question how all such heterogeneous groups could be called as children of the soil merely because, by an accident, they happened to reside in a common territory under the rule of a common enemy.[3] . . .
>
> The theories of territorial nationalism and of common danger, which formed the basis for our concept of nation, had deprived us of the positive and inspiring content of our real Hindu Nationhood and made many of the 'freedom movements' virtually anti-British movements. Anti-Britishism was equated with patriotism and nationalism. This reactionary view has had disastrous effects upon the entire course of the freedom struggle.

But, India's freedom movement was based entirely on 'territorial nationalism'. We were all Indians, regardless of caste or creed. Muslims are denounced in these terms.

> History has recorded that their antagonism was not merely political. Had it been so, they could have been won over in a very short time. But it was so deep-

[3] M.S. Golwalkar, *Bunch of Thoughts*, Bangalore: Sahitya Sindhu, 1968, p. 142.

> rooted that whatever we believe in, the Muslim was wholly hostile to it. If we worship in the temple, he would desecrate it. If we carry on *bhajans* and car [sic] festivals, that would irritate him. If we worship cow, he would like to eat it. If we glorify woman as a symbol of sacred motherhood, he would like to molest her. He was tooth and nail opposed to our way of life in all aspects – religious, cultural, social etc. He had imbibed that hostility to the very core.[4]

Elaborating the theme Golwalkar wrote:

> The Hindu was told that he was imbecile, that he had no spirit, no stamina to stand on his own legs and fight for the independence of his motherland and that all this had to be injected into him in the form of Muslim blood. What a shame, what a misfortune that our own leaders should have come forward to knock out the ancient and indomitable faith in ourselves and destroy our spirit of self-confidence and self-reliance, which is the very life-breath of a people! Those who declared 'No *swaraj* without Hindu-Muslim unity' have thus perpetrated the greatest treason on our society. They have committed the most heinous sin of killing the life-spirit of a great and ancient people. . . .
>
> Here we had leaders who were, as if, pledged to sap all manliness from their own people. However, this is not a mere accident of history. This leadership only came as a bitter climax of the despicable tribe of so many of our ancestors who during the past twelve hundred years sold their national honour and freedom to foreigners, and joined hands with the inveterate enemies of our country and our religion in cutting the throats of their own kith and kin to gratify their personal egoism, selfishness and rivalry. No wonder nemesis overtook such a people in the form of such a self-destructive leadership.[5]

This was a clear allusion to Gandhi. Even as late as in 1966 Golwalkar expressed hate for Gandhi in the same terms that Savarkar did. A red thread of continuity runs through the Hindu revivalism of the 19th century, Lala Lajpat Rai and Madan Mohan Malaviya's utterances, Savarkar's Hindutva and Golwalkar's writings to this day in the present RSS supremo's utterances.

These propositions form the basis of the BJP's election manifestoes since the nineties with their espousal of 'cultural nationalism'. They can be summed up thus: (1) The Hindus form a nation by themselves; India belongs to them. Not only the territory but the ideology of Hindutva or 'cultural nationalism' binds them together. (2) The minorities, especially the Muslims and the Christians, do not form part of this nation. They do not and cannot stand on the same footing as the Hindus. They must conform to the Hindu way of life. (3) They can, however, accept

[4] Ibid., p. 148.

[5] Ibid., pp. 132-3.

the Hindu faith and merge with the majority. (4) Until that is done, the Hindus will rule as they please.

As L.K. Advani proudly declared at Ayodhya on 19 November 1990: 'Henceforth only those who fight for Hindu interests would rule India.' Shortly before this, he had complained on 2 October 1990 that 'secular policy is putting unreasonable restrictions on Hindu aspirations'. This reveals the kind of polity he wishes to build in place of the Constitution.

Narendra Modi will not disagree with this, of course. Golwalkar's exertions were not confined to 'literary' pursuits. He was in the main a man of action.

8. The RSS at Independence

The nation enthusiastically celebrated the dawn of independence. Differences of the past were forgotten. Dr. B.R. Ambedkar was made a member of the Union Cabinet, a decision lauded by all. He proved himself worthy of the honour. The same cannot be said of another surprise; the Hindu Mahasabha's leader Syama Prasad's inclusion in the Nehru Cabinet. Mystery still surrounds the reasons for this action. He behaved as a representative of the Mahasabha and a champion of the RSS in the Cabinet. In doing so, he created differences between Prime Minister Nehru and his deputy Vallabhbhai Patel which were reflected in the rifts in the Cabinet between their respective supporters.

Unlike the RSS, Patel was no supporter of a Hindu State. He flatly rejected a suggestion by B.M. Birla in these categorical terms in a letter of 10 June 1947, on the eve of independence, after the Partition Plan of 3 June was announced.

> I do not think it will be possible to consider Hindustan as a Hindu State with Hinduism as the State religion. We must not forget that there are other minorities *whose protection is our primary responsibility*. The State must exist for all, irrespective of Caste or creed.[1]

The Nehru-Patel differences arose over other issues of policy which were as consequential.[2]

The principal opposition party then was the Communist Party of India which itself was in the throes of an upheaval. On its part, the RSS lost no time in unfurling its banner of total rejection of the secular polity the nation had in mind. Its rantings were ascribed to the bitterness over the partition of India on religious lines. Neglected were its mainsprings, which had roots in the 19th century. The RSS began espousing its ideology stridently immediately on independence and began intervening actively in the bloodbath that followed.

It published a weekly, *Organiser*, as its organ. Its first issue dated 3 July 1947 actually hit the stands on 14 August 1947. It received strong support from Big Business. Later, Charat Ram of Delhi Cloth Mills 'was also a great support in

1 Durga Das (ed.), *Sardar Patel's Correspondence 1945-50*, vol. IV, Ahmedabad: Navajivan Publishing House, 1972, pp. 56-7; hereafter cited as *SPC*.

2 Vide Neerja Singh (ed.), *Nehru-Patel: Agreement within Differences (Select Documents and Correspondences 1933-1950)*, National Book Trust, 2010 and P.N. Chopra (ed.), *Sardar Patel: Muslims and Refugees*, Konark Publishers, 2004.

this endeavour', the 70 years' commemoration issue of 28 January 2018 gratefully acknowledged.

Its first editorial entitled 'Glorious Hindu Nation' was ominous. It was a challenge to the new India which was ignored to great detriment. It said:

> We have no reason to be afraid of our future. We have no cause to despond. All we have to do to remount our throne is to respond to the awakened *race*-spirit and re-rouse our national consciousness, and victory is in our grasp. The undying voices of our sages call; let us gird up our loins and follow them. The spirit of the race beckons to us and has lighted for its benighted children the path to their cherished ideal, with beacons of undying spiritual splendour. Let us rouse ourselves to our true nationality, let us follow the lead of our race-spirit and fill the heavens with the clarion call of the Vedic seers 'from sea to sea over all the land – One Nation', one glorious, splendorous Hindu Nation benignly shedding peace and plenty over the whole world.

There was no reference to the partition. It was a stark avowal of an ideology enunciated since the 19th century. Indian nationalism was based on race and religion. Its ambitions were global.

Its attacks on Muslims were widespread and brutal. In a letter to Home Minister Patel on 30 September 1947, Nehru mentioned 'well organised bands' operating in Delhi, Shimla, Kalka and other places.

> The Hindu bands seemed to owe allegiance to the RSS. It seems to me clear that the RSS have had a great deal to do with the present disturbances not only in Delhi but elsewhere. In Amritsar their activities have been very obvious . . . [S]till noted members of the RSS were appointed as special magistrates and special police officers.[3]

He complained to Patel again on 30 December 1947; this time on the misconduct of the Maharaja of Jammu & Kashmir, Hari Singh, and his Premier Meher Chand Mahajan. '[T]he arms we have sent for them [the state government] have been kept back and distributed to the RSS people . . . I am inclined to think that Mahajan sympathises with these activities and perhaps helps them.'[4]

Nehru felt so intensely that he shot off another letter to Patel on the same day. 'The RSS is accused with reason of having organised killing of the Muslims

[3] S. Gopal (ed.), *Selected Works of Jawaharlal Nehru. Second Series*, vol. 4, Jawaharlal Nehru Memorial Fund, 1986, p. 113; cited hereinafter as *SWJN*.

[4] Ibid., p. 413.

in Jammu.'[5] The then prime minister of Kashmir Sheikh Muhammad Abdullah confirms this in his autobiography. Referring to Jammu he wrote 'the entire Muslim population there was at the mercy of the Rashtriya Swayam Sevak Sangh [sic]. Sometimes under their vigilance [sic], Muslim women would be spirited away from their camps'.[6]

The RSS had gone into action immediately on Kashmir's accession to India on 26 October 1947. Four days later Nehru wrote to Patel, 'Information has reached me that the RSS volunteers have been organised in East Punjab to be sent to Jammu for a campaign against the Muslims. . . . The whole Kashmir position will crack up if in Jammu Province an anti-Muslim drive takes place now.'[7] Nehru regarded the RSS as a 'dangerous organisation and fascist in the strictly technical sense of the word'.[8]

Nehru asked the premier of Uttar Pradesh, Govind Ballabh Pant, 'You told me that you are going to take action against the RSS. When is this going to happen?'[9] This was on 29 December 1947. By then Pant had warded off Home Secretary Rajeshwar Dayal's advice to arrest Golwalkar, after the police had seized a truck-load of papers baring his plans to put Muslims to the sword. Well before that, on 17 December, Nehru had written to Pant:

> You mentioned to me when we saw each other last about the steps you intended to take against the RSS. Lal Bahadur gave me some further details of the information you possess. He told me that probably you will take some action within a fortnight and *the first step you intended taking was to inform the leader of the RSS of the evidence you possess.* I am glad you are moving in this matter as it is becoming very evident that the RSS is a most objectionable and dangerous organisation and it has been responsible for a great deal of the trouble we have had. In Ajmer recently it was the RSS that functioned. I am sure we must not allow this mischief to continue.[10]

Nehru alerted the premiers of the Provinces in one of his circular letters to them dated 7 December 1947:

> We have a great deal of evidence to show that the RSS is an organisation which is in the nature of a private army and which is definitely proceeding on the strictest Nazi lines, even following the technique of organisation. It is not our

5 Ibid., p. 414.
6 Sheikh Abdullah, *The Blazing Chinar*, Srinagar: Gulshan Books, 1995, p. 302.
7 *SWJN*, vol. 4, pp. 290-1.
8 Ibid., p. 330.
9 Ibid., p. 222.
10 Ibid., p. 476.

desire to interfere with civil liberties. But training in arms of large numbers of persons with the obvious intention of using them is not something that can be encouraged.

> . . . I have some knowledge of the way the Nazi movement developed in Germany. It attracted by its superficial trappings and strict discipline considerable numbers of lower middle class young men and women who are normally not too intelligent and for whom life appeared to offer little to attract them. And so they drifted towards the Nazi party because its policy and programme, such as they were, were simple, negative and did not require an active effort of the mind. The Nazi party brought Germany to ruin and I have little doubt that if these tendencies are allowed to spread and increase in India, they would do enormous injury to India. No doubt India would survive. But she would be grievously wounded and would take a long time to recover.[11]

What of the elephant in the Cabinet room – Syama Prasad Mookerjee? Nehru brought to his notice, in a letter on 28 September 1947, shortly after independence, an Associated Press message which read thus:

> Mr. L.B. Bhopatkar, President of the All-India Hindu Mahasabha, addressing a press conference here this morning said that Dr. Syama Prasad Mookerjee was in the Indian Cabinet as a representative of the Hindu Mahasabha and would stay there as long as the Mahasabha asked him to remain. His allegiance was to the Hindu Mahasabha and *Bhagwa Jhanda*. That had been made clear even before his joining the Cabinet. It was the *Bhagwa Jhanda* which was flying over Dr. Mookerjee's house in Delhi and not the Tri-colour.

Nehru had agreed to his retention of membership of the Mahasabha. But

> [S]o far as I remember there was no mention of your joining the Cabinet as a representative of the Hindu Mahasabha owing allegiance to that Sabha's mandate. Certainly this was not made clear to me in any way and if this had been mentioned, it would have created difficulties. I did not even know that the Bhagwa Jhanda was flying over your house instead of the National Flag. It seems to me very odd that a Minister should fly any flag but the National Flag.

Mookerjee replied on 30 September 1947 that though a member of the Hindu Mahasabha, he had not joined the Cabinet 'as a nominee of any organisation' nor had any question been raised at any time about his being 'bound to accept any mandate from the Hindu Mahasabha'. He added that while the national flag flew over his house from 15 August 1947, '*the Bhagwa Jhanda also flew from time to*

[11] Ibid., p. 461.

time'. A disingenuous evasion of an impropriety. Bhopatkar's evidence was to the contrary.

Significantly, two days later Nehru made a point of telling him,

> According to reliable information, reaching us from intelligence reports and other sources, the RSS has played an important part in the Delhi disturbances and is even now a very disturbing element. I am informing you of this as you spoke to me once about the RSS.[12]

Nehru and Mookerjee were very uncomfortable with each other. On 28 January 1948 just two days before Gandhi's assassination Nehru shot off two letters. To Patel he wrote:

> Lal Bahadur Shastri, Minister, U.P. Government, tells me that they have received information to the effect that RSS men are being trained in Bharatpur with arms. Many of these people go from the U.P. for training in camps or otherwise and then return with arms. We had heard previously of such training camps being run in Bharatpur State. Apparently this kind of thing is still going on to some extent and the U.P. Government are rather worried about it.

The editor's footnote added: 'RSS camps and rallies had been arranged in May-June 1947 in the State of Bharatpur and Alwar and military training was also given to RSS volunteers in these States.'

Mookerjee was informed.

> For some time past I have been greatly distressed by the activities of the Hindu Mahasabha. At the present moment it is functioning not only as the main opposition to the Government and to the Congress in India but as an organisation continually inciting to violence. The RSS has behaved in an even worse way and we have collected a mass of information about its very objectionable activities and its close association with riots and disorder.
>
> Apart from what I have written above, what pains me most is the extreme vulgarity and indecency of speeches being made from Hindu Mahasabha platforms. 'Gandhi Murdabad' is one of their special slogans. Recently a prominent leader of the Hindu Mahasabha stated that an objective to be aimed at was the hanging of Nehru, Sardar Patel and Maulana Azad. . . . I wrote to you specially because of your own close association with the Hindu Mahasabha. We are continually being asked in our party, in the Constituent Assembly as well as elsewhere as to your position in this matter. I should be grateful to you

12 Ibid., p. 507.

> if you will let me know how you propose to deal with this situation which must be as embarrassing to you as it is to me.[13]

Gandhi's assassination prompted Nehru to take up with Mookerjee the issue of the Mahasabha's stand. Reminding him of his earlier letter, Nehru said:

> Since then a great tragedy has taken place and the situation has infinitely worsened. The Hindu Mahasabha is associated in people's minds in some ways with the tragedy and, as you know, there is a great deal of excitement in the country. Whatever our attitude to the Hindu Mahasabha might be, the question I raised in my last letter to you faces us still and with greater intensity. Already members of our party in the Assembly are asking me this question and insist on an answer. It is very probable that they might raise it at the party meeting this afternoon.
>
> I myself am convinced that the day for communal organisations in politics is past and we should not encourage them in any way. In particular it is difficult and embarrassing for all concerned for a Minister of the Central Government to be personally associated with a communal organisation like Hindu Mahasabha which, even on the political plane, is opposed to our general policy and indeed to the Government as a whole. . . . I think that the time has come for you to raise your voice against communal organisations including the Mahasabha and, in any event, to sever your connection with the Hindu Mahasabha.[14]

Mookerjee did not. On the contrary, he kept up a steady flow of letters to Patel pleading on behalf of the Mahasabha and Savarkar.

Nehru was as unrelenting in a letter on 24 August 1948:

> A few days ago it was announced in the press that the Hindu Mahasabha had decided to return to the political field. This piece of news obviously has considerable significance and it has been treated as such by the press. In view of our resolution on communalism we cannot approve of any such activity of an organisation which has been and is strictly communal. Even if some minor change in its rules is made enabling others to join it, the organisation must necessarily, in the circumstances, continue to be communal and the Government will treat it in accordance with the directions of that resolution.
>
> The position is made worse by the fact that Savarkar is being tried in the conspiracy to murder Gandhi. Whatever the result of the trial, Savarkar does

13 *SWJN*, vol. 5, 1987, pp. 30-1.

14 Ibid., pp. 46-7.

not come out well from it. Meanwhile, reports come to us about renewed activities of the RSS in various provinces. These activities, though outwardly peaceful, are reported to be of a subversive nature and designed to challenge the Government again as was done in the past.

In view of all this, I feel that you should remove any misapprehension from the public mind about your continued connection with the Hindu Mahasabha. That there is this misapprehension has been clear from numerous comments in the newspapers. It is far better to take the public, not to mention the members of the Congress Party in the legislature, into our confidence. Or else rumours spread and create mischief. Apart from the public, I should like to know myself if you are still connected with the Hindu Mahasabha.

Mookerjee replied:

I have not the least desire to embarrass you in any way. Should you at any time feel that my connection with Government should cease, you have only to mention this to me and I shall readily comply with your desire.

He threw the ball back in Nehru's court knowing full well that the Prime Minister would not create a bigger rift in his Cabinet.[15] Nehru's remarks on a communal party ostensibly open to all apply to the Jana Sangh which Mookerjee founded in 1951 and to its successor, the BJP.

By 1947, 'the RSS was probably the best organised of the para-military groups'.[16] It had a record of unchecked activity since 1925. Men in high places in administration and business supported it. 'The Delhi police has apparently a goodly number of sympathisers with it' and also in the Central Provinces (Madhya Pradesh), Nehru complained.[17]

Premiers of Provinces were alerted as early as on 5 January 1948.

The RSS has played an important part in recent developments and evidence has been collected to implicate it in certain very horrible happenings. It is openly stated by their leaders that the RSS is not a political body but there can be no doubt that their policy and programmes are political, intensely communal and based on violent activities. They have to be kept in check and we must not be misled by their pious professions which are completely at variance with their policy.[18]

15 *SWJN*, vol. 7, 1988, pp. 12-3.
16 Andersen and Damle, *The Brotherhood in Saffron*, p. 48.
17 *SWJN*, vol. 5, pp. 67 and 69.
18 Ibid., p. 305.

The RSS's progress was interrupted by two events. Gandhi's assassination and, in consequence, the Government of India's ban on the RSS. For two reasons it did not take it long for it to recover. One was its strong organisational structure. The other was its infiltration in many spheres of life and the support it had acquired, not least from some in the administration.

9. The RSS and Gandhi's Assassination

But for the culpable inaction of two senior Congress leaders in office, the assassination of Gandhi, on 30 January 1948, by Nathuram Godse would have been averted and the conspiracy to assassinate him would have been exposed. Savarkar's complicity in it would have become known to the nation. The RSS's chief Golwalkar's personal complicity in the murders in North India would also have stood exposed. Its effect on this body would have been enormous. The two Congress leaders were Govind Ballabh Pant, Premier of Uttar Pradesh and Morarji Desai, Home Minister of Bombay Province.

Golwalkar's recorded role in the communal riots was authoritatively laid bare in 1998 by none other than the then home secretary of Uttar Pradesh, Rajeshwar Dayal, I.C.S. He rose to be foreign secretary. His memoirs created a stir.

He revealed:

> I must record an episode of a very grave nature when the procrastination and indecision of the U.P. Cabinet led to dire consequences. When communal tension was still at fever-pitch, the Deputy Inspector-General of Police of Western Range, a very seasoned and capable officer, B.B.L. Jaitley, arrived at my house in great secrecy. He was accompanied by two of his officers who brought with them two large steel trunks securely locked. When the trunks were opened, they revealed incontrovertible evidence of a dastardly conspiracy to create a communal holocaust throughout the western districts of the province. The trunks were crammed with blueprints of great accuracy and professionalism of every town and village in that vast area, prominently marking out the Muslim localities and habitations. There were also detailed instructions regarding access to the various locations, and other matters which amply revealed their sinister purport.
>
> Greatly alarmed by those revelations, I immediately took the police party to the Premier's house. There, in a closed room, Jaitley gave a full report of his discovery, backed by all the evidence contained in the steel trunks. Timely raids conducted on the premises of the RSS (Rashtriya Swayam Sevak Sangh) had brought the massive conspiracy to light. *The whole plot had been concerted under the direction and supervision of the Supremo of the organisation himself.* Both Jaitley and I pressed for the immediate arrest of the prime accused, Shri Golwalkar, who was still in the area.
>
> Pantji could not but accept the evidence of his eyes and ears and expressed

deep concern. But instead of agreeing to the immediate arrest of the ring leader as we had hoped, and as (Rafi Ahmad) Kidwai would have done, he asked for the matter to be placed for consideration by the Cabinet at its next meeting. It was no doubt a matter of political delicacy as the roots of the RSS had gone deep into the body politic. There were also other political compulsions as RSS sympathisers, both covert and overt, were to be found in the Congress party itself and even in the Cabinet. It was no secret that the presiding officer of the Upper House, Atma Govind Kher, was himself an adherent and his sons were openly members of the RSS.

At the Cabinet meeting there was the usual procrastination and much irrelevant talk. The fact that the police had unearthed a conspiracy which would have set the whole province in flames and that the officers concerned deserved warm commendation hardly seemed to figure in the discussion. What ultimately emerged was that a letter should be issued to Shri Golwalkar pointing out the contents and nature of the evidence which had been gathered and demanding an explanation thereof. At my insistence, such a letter if it were to be sent, should be issued by the Premier himself to carry greater weight. Pantji asked me to prepare a draft, which I did in imitation of his own characteristic style. The letter was to be delivered forthwith and two police officers were assigned for the purpose.

Golwalkar, however, had been tipped off and he was nowhere to be found in the area. He was tracked down southwards but he managed to elude the couriers in pursuit. This infructuous chase continued from place to place and weeks passed. Came 30 January 1948 when the Mahatma, that supreme apostle of peace, fell to a bullet fired by an RSS fanatic. The whole tragic episode left me sick at heart.[1]

The RSS would have been dealt a deadly, if not fatal, blow if its chief had been caught with a smoking gun.

The RSS went to town screaming that the assassin Nathuram Vinayak Godse did not belong to it and it was not responsible for the crime. That is raising an Aunt Sally for the pleasure of knocking her down. No one ever alleged that the RSS's central unit, Kendriya Karyakari Mandal, passed a resolution at its cavern in Nagpur to direct or authorise the crime. An organisation, be it a body corporate or a registered society, acts only through its members. Its reputation would be affected even if a member acted on his own or if the crime was inspired by the body's own outlook; e.g. a corrupt company's official cheating someone even if it be in a personal capacity. The RSS's denial of Godse's membership received short shrift from his brother Gopal Godse: 'All the brothers were in the RSS. Nathuram,

[1] Rajeshwar Dayal, *A Life of Our Times*, Orient Longman, 1998, pp. 93-4.

Dattatreya, myself and Govind. You can say we grew up in the RSS rather than in our homes.'[2]

Both, the RSS and the Mahasabha, voiced freely their hatred for Gandhi. Vallabhbhai Patel, Union Home Minister, an accomplished criminal lawyer, had access to intelligence reports. Three letters which he wrote accurately summed up the situation.

In a letter to Prime Minister Jawaharlal Nehru, on 27 January 1948 Patel said,

> I have kept myself almost in daily touch with the progress of the investigation regarding Bapu's assassination case. I devote a large part of my evening to discussing with Sanjevi [D.J. Sanjevi was Director of Intelligence Bureau] the day's progress and giving instructions to him on any points that arise. All the main accused have given long and detailed statements of their activities. In one case, the statement extends to ninety typed pages. From their statements, it is quite clear that no part of the conspiracy took place in Delhi. The centres of activity were Poona, Bombay, Ahmednagar and Gwalior. Delhi was, of course, the terminating point of their activity, but by no means its centre; nor do they seem to have spent more than a day or two at a time, and that too only twice between 19 and 30 January. It also clearly emerges from these statements that the RSS was not involved in it at all. It was a fanatical wing of the Hindu Mahasabha directly under Savarkar that [hatched] the conspiracy and saw it through. . . .
>
> Of course, his assassination was welcomed by those of the RSS and the Mahasabha who were strongly opposed to his way of thinking and to his policy. But beyond this, I do not think it is possible, on the evidence which has come before us, to implicate any other members of the RSS or the Hindu Mahasabha.[3]

His Cabinet colleague, S.P. Mookerjee was not in the least interested in bringing the culprits to book. His concern was to protect the prime mover in the conspiracy. Significantly, on the very day the Special Court was set up, 4 May 1948, he tried to throw his weight around to get Savarkar off the hook. He wrote to Patel, 'I understand Savarkar's name is being mentioned in this connection. I do not know what evidence has been found against him.' The ignorance was poorly feigned. He cited his age, 'sacrifices and suffering'. Patel's reply on 6 May was prompt and revealing. The Advocate-General of Bombay C.K. Daphtary was in-charge of the case with other lawyers.

> I have also told them that, if they come to the view that Savarkar should be

[2] Arvind Rajagopal, 'He did not leave the RSS'.

[3] *SPC*, vol. VI, 1973, pp. 56-7.

> included, the papers should be placed before me before action is taken. This is, of course, in so far as the question of guilt is concerned from the point of view of law and justice. Morally, it is possible that one's conviction may be the other way about.
>
> I quite agree with you that the Hindu Mahasabha, as an organisation, was not concerned in the conspiracy that led to Gandhiji's murder; but at the same time, we cannot shut our eyes to the fact that an appreciable number of the members of the Mahasabha gloated over the tragedy and distributed sweets. On this matter, reliable reports have come to us from all parts of the country. Further, militant communalism, which was preached until only a few months ago by many spokesmen of the Mahasabha, including men like Mahant Digbijoy Nath, Prof. Ram Singh and Deshpande, could not but be regarded as a danger to public security. The same would apply *to the RSS, with the additional danger inherent in an organisation run in secret on military or semi-military lines.*[4]

If Savarkar was cited as an accused it was because Patel was convinced of his complicity in the crime. Even if the evidence was inadequate to prove Savarkar's guilt in a court of law, 'morally, it is possible that one's conviction may be the other way about', Patel warned Mookerjee.

But Mookerjee kept on pestering Patel who wrote back to him in these terms on 18 July 1948:

> As regards the RSS and the Hindu Mahasabha, the case relating to Gandhiji's murder is sub judice and I should not like to say anything about the participation of the two organisations, but our reports do confirm that, as a result of the activities of these two bodies, *particularly the former, an atmosphere was created in the country in which such a ghastly tragedy became possible.* There is no doubt in my mind that the extreme section of the Hindu Mahasabha was involved in this conspiracy. The activities of the RSS constituted a clear threat to the existence of Government and the State.
>
> Our reports show that those activities, despite the ban, have not died down. Indeed, as time has marched on, the RSS circles are becoming more defiant and are indulging in their subversive activities in an increasing measure.[5]

It is unthinkable that Patel was not informed by the Intelligence Bureau of Golwalkar's escape in Lucknow. The trial proceedings are set out in the writer's book *Savarkar and Hindutva*.[6]

4 Ibid., pp. 65-6.

5 Ibid., p. 323.

6 Noorani, *Savarkar and Hindutva*, pp. 109-30.

Morarji Desai's culpable obstruction of Nagarvala's attempt to arrest Savarkar before the assassination was compounded with his astonishing conduct in the trial court. On 1 September 1948 *The Times of India* carried the text of the leading prosecuting counsel, the Advocate-General of Bombay, C.K. Daphtary's application to Judge Atma Charan the day before.

> In cross-examination of the Honourable Mr. Morarji Desai, Counsel for accused number seven [V.D. Savarkar] asked the following question, 'Did you have any other information about Savarkar, besides Professor Jain's statement for directing steps to be taken as regards him?'
>
> The witness answered the question as follows: 'Shall I give the full facts? I am prepared to answer. It is for him [Savarkar] to decide.' Counsel for accused number seven thereafter stated that he dropped the question. The prosecution submitted that the question, answer and the statement of counsel should be recorded but Your Honour declined to do so. It is submitted that the question, the answer and the statement of counsel for accused number seven should have gone on the record.

There is not one good reason for a judge to justify the refusal. Swapan Das Gupta, a journalist, disclosed on TV on 12 July 2012 that L.K. Advani had told him that according to Morarji Desai, Savarkar was complicit in Gandhi's murder but got away with it. The need for independent evidence is a rule of prudence. The Judge accepted the approver's evidence as being truthful. He was entitled to acquit Savarkar; but given the evidence on record he had no right to give him this clean chit: 'There is thus no reason to suppose that Vinayak D. Savarkar had *any* hand in what took place in Delhi on 20 January 1948 and 30 January 1948.' Why did he stretch his conclusion to that extent?

A later disclosure explains the Judge's softness towards Savarkar. P.L. Inamdar, an advocate at Gwalior, was a committed Hindu Mahasabhaite. He defended Dr. P.S. Parchure and Gopal Godse at the trial and won an acquittal for the former on appeal in the High Court. His memoirs reveal a lot.[7]

Savarkar 'was very nervous and was getting more and more agitated as the trial proceeded'. He sought a meeting with Inamdar.

> He repeatedly asked me if he would be acquitted and wanted me to assure him sincerely. What I noted was that he did not ask me a single question about the case against my clients, Dr. Parchure and Gopal Godse, or about any of the other accused including Nathuram, nor any question about me personally. I spent nearly three hours with him. He thanked me when I took his leave, again bowing low and touching his feet.

[7] P.L. Inamdar, *The Story of the Red Fort Trial, 1948-49*, Popular Prakashan, 1979.

Inamdar suggests that Savarkar's statement in court was false.

Judgment was delivered by Judge Atma Charan on 10 February 1949. Inamdar was shocked at Savarkar's acquittal.

> Surprisingly, I do not remember even today, when and how Atma Charan read out the operative portion of the order of acquittal of Savarkar! All I remember even today is that I had tried to look hard at Atma Charan, asking myself if he was the same Atma Charan who had one day said to me: 'Believe me, I shall do full justice to the case which you have so ably put up!' I angrily told myself, 'Yes, this is Atma Charan's answer to the last paragraph of the summing up of the case!'[8]

He has praise for Atma Charan's good manners. But read this:

> I was an eye-witness to his listening to Nathuram's argument with rapt polite attention, at one stage even with tearful eyes.[9]

One has not heard of a judge sitting 'with tearful eyes' while listening to a political tirade by a murderer. He had heard a mass of evidence against Godse.

Rulings of the Privy Council and of the Supreme Court built up a body of case law which established that independent corroboration of the approver's evidence in respect of material particulars is necessary, albeit not every material particular. Were it not for the tapes, Richard Nixon would have gone scot-free. King Henry II of England could not have been charged with instigating the murder of Becket even though the instigation was clear: 'Who will free me from this turbulent priest?' and, more provocatively, 'What a parcel of fools and dastards have I nourished in my house, that not one of them will avenge me of this one upstart clerk?'

In his judgment dated 10 February 1949, Judge Atma Charan acquitted Savarkar. He found the approver Badge to be a truthful witness but held that the corroborative evidence was vague and inadequate. A conviction, in the circumstance, would be 'unsafe', he ruled. Twenty years later, on 30 September 1969, Justice Jeevan Lal Kapur, of the Supreme Court sitting as Commission of Inquiry, concluded emphatically in his Report, after a rigorous analysis of evidence, that 'all these facts taken together were destructive of any theory other than the conspiracy to murder by Savarkar and his group'.

The Commission had before it evidence which was not tendered before the trial court. It included the testimony of Savarkar's aides given after his death. They deposed to the visits of Godse and Narayan Apte on which the Court had found the evidence in corroboration to be weak and vague. If these aides had deposed in

[8] Ibid., p. 147.

[9] Ibid., p. 151.

court, Savarkar could not have escaped conviction for the crime.

Even in 1948, two incontrovertible facts sufficed to damn Savarkar in the eyes of all right thinking persons. In any case of conspiracy, the relationship between the accused is a fact of crucial importance. So is the conduct of the accused.

A mass of evidence surfaced to show that Godse and Apte had unrestricted access to Savarkar. Godse added that in 1947 'we felt in our heart of hearts that time had come when we should bid goodbye to Veer Savarkar's lead and cease to consult him in our future plans'. This protective lie was repeated for emphasis:

> We resolved not to confide any of our new plans to any of them including Veer Savarkar. . . . I re-assert that it is not true that Veer Savarkar had any knowledge of my activities which ultimately led me to fire shots at Gandhiji.

Only a year or two after Savarkar's death, his aides spoke up before the Kapur Commission and provided ample corroboration of Badge's evidence. The Commission's Report notes:

> The statement of Appa Ramchandra Kasar, Bodyguard of V.D. Savarkar, which was recorded by the Bombay Police on 4th March, 1948 shows that even in 1946 Apte and Godse were frequent visitors of Savarkar and Karkare also sometimes visited him. . . . In August, 1947, when Savarkar went to Poona in connection with a meeting Godse and Apte were always with Savarkar and were discussing with him the future policy of the Hindu Mahasabha and he told them that he himself was getting old and they would have to carry on the work. . . .
>
> Gajanan Vishnu Damle, Secretary of Savarkar, was also examined on 4th March, 1948 by the Bombay Police. . . . Apte was a frequent visitor to Savarkar's house and sometimes came with Godse. Savarkar had lent Rs. 15000 to Apte and Godse for the newspaper when security was demanded from the Agrani. That paper was stopped and the newspaper called the Hindu Rashtra was started. Savarkar was one of its Directors and Apte and Godse were the Managing agents.
>
> In the first week of January 1948, Karkare and a Punjabi refugee boy came to see Savarkar and they both had an interview with Savarkar for about half an hour or 45 minutes. Neither of them came to see Savarkar again. Apte and Godse came to see Savarkar about the middle of January 1948, late at night. The statement of both these witnesses show that both Apte and Godse were frequent visitors of Savarkar at Bombay and at Conferences and at every meeting they are shown to have been with Savarkar. . . . This evidence also shows that Karkare was also well known to Savarkar and was also a frequent visitor. Badge also used to visit Savarkar. Dr. Parchure also visited him. All this

> shows that people who were subsequently involved in the murder of Mahatma Gandhi were all congregating sometime or the other at Savarkar Sadan and sometimes had long interviews with Savarkar: It is significant that Karkare and Madanlal visited Savarkar before they left for Delhi and Apte and Godse visited him both before the bomb was thrown and also before the murder was committed and on each occasion they had a long interview.

Why were Savarkar's two aides not produced as witnesses in the trial court is a mystery. Had they testified, Savarkar would have been convicted. There was none of the ambiguity surrounding Godse and Apte's visits to Savarkar on 14 and 17 January 1948. A.R. Kasar, Savarkar's bodyguard, told the Kapur Commission that they visited him on or about the 23rd or 24th January which was when they returned from Delhi after the bomb incident. G.V. Damle, Savarkar's secretary, deposed that Godse and Apte saw Savarkar 'in the middle of January and sat with him [Savarkar] in his garden'.

Justice Kapur's findings, however, are all too clear. After listing the information available to Nagarvala he concluded: 'All these facts taken together were destructive of any theory other than the conspiracy to murder by Savarkar and his group.'

In his Crime Report No. 1, Nagarvala had stated that 'Savarkar was at the back of the conspiracy and that he was feigning illness'. Nagarvala's letter of 31 January 1948, the day after the assassination, mentioned that Savarkar, Godse and Apte met for 40 minutes 'on the eve of their departure to Delhi' on the strength of what Kasar and Damle disclosed to him. 'These two had access to the house of Savarkar without any restriction.' In short, Godse and Apte met Savarkar again, in the absence of Badge and in addition to their meetings on 14 and 17 January.

Justice Kapur also found that 'many RSS members were members of the Hindu Mahasabha'. One of his conclusions read, '(4) (a) The RSS was the best organised and militant Hindu organisation in India and although it was not affiliated to the Hindu Mahasabha, its prominent organisers and workers were members or sponsors of the Hindu Mahasabha ideology.'

Savarkar died in 1966; a broken man and a miserable political failure in ignominy after the last of his abject undertakings on 20 July 1950. He had moved close to the RSS which was on the rise. The Mahasabha had gone into decline even before he became its president in 1937. He could not revive it. But he left behind a poisonous legacy which possessed the RSS and its political outfit, the BJP. In a speech on Savarkar's 80th birthday on 15 May 1963, Golwalkar acknowledged his debt to *Hindutva*.[10]

[10] Keer, *Veer Savarkar*, p. 527.

10. The Ban on the RSS

Golwalkar was arrested on 1 February 1948, immediately after Gandhi's assassination on 30 January. Three days later, the RSS was banned as an 'unlawful association'. He was released from prison on 6 August 1948. The ban was lifted on 11 July 1949. The RSS published the correspondence between Golwalkar on the one hand and Nehru and Patel on the other. It falsifies its claim that the ban was lifted unconditionally. The ruse was repeated in 1976 during the Emergency when O.P. Mathur assured Charan Singh that after the Emergency the RSS would be dissolved. The correspondence is of more than historic interest. *It bears on its present status.*

The government did lift the ban as a gesture of clemency or mercy. The RSS had begged for it persistently. *It was granted conditionally.* Once the ban was lifted the RSS broke the conditions and proceeded on its course as if nothing had happened. The relevant documents are available in an RSS publication *Justice on Trial* which was published in December 1958 (Prakashan Vibhag, RSS, Karnataka). They belie the claims in the foreword that the ban was lifted 'unconditionally' without any 'humiliating commitments by Sri Guruji (M.S. Golwalkar) on behalf of the RSS'. Gandhi was assassinated on 30 January 1948 by Nathuram Godse, a Mahasabhaite who was no less loyal to the RSS. His brother Gopal testified to that. Golwalkar was arrested on 3 February. The Government of India issued a communiqué on 4 February declaring the RSS unlawful 'in the Chief Commissioners' Provinces. Similar action is also being taken in the Governors' Provinces'. They acted in tandem with the Centre; but each Province could put its own spin on lifting of the ban.

The communiqué noted a consistent feature of the RSS conduct; namely that its conduct did not conform to its claims and professions.

> Government have, however, noticed with regret that in practice members of the Rashtriya Swayamsevak Sangh have not adhered to their professed ideals. Undesirable and even dangerous activities have been carried on by members of the Sangh. It has been carried on by members of the Sangh. It has been found that in several parts of the country individual members of Rashtriya Swayamsevak Sangh have indulged in acts of violence involving arson, robbery, dacoity, and murder and have collected illicit arms and ammunitions.
>
> They have been found circulating leaflets exhorting people to resort to terrorist methods, to collect fire arms, to create disaffection against the Government and suborn the Police and the Military. These activities

> have been carried on under a cloak of secrecy, and the Government have considered from time to time how far these activities rendered it incumbent on them to deal with the Sangh in its corporate capacity. The last occasion when the Government defined this attitude was when the Premiers and the Home Ministers of Provinces met in Delhi in conference towards the end of November.
>
> It was then unanimously agreed that the stage when the Sangh should be dealt with as an association had not yet arrived and that individuals should continue to be dealt with sternly as hitherto. The objectionable and harmful activities of Sangh have, however, continued unabated and the cult of violence sponsored and inspired by the activities of the Sangh has claimed many victims. The latest and the most precious to fall was Gandhiji himself.
>
> It was, therefore, decided to declare the Sangh as an unlawful association.[1]

Golwalkar issued a statement on 8 February announcing his decision 'to disband the RSS till the time the ban is there'. Four conditions were imposed on Golwalkar: (1) not to leave Nagpur except with the previous consent of the district magistrate in writing; (2) not to address any public meeting; (3) not to publish 'any matter' in any newspaper, journal or magazine without the previous approval of the district magistrate; and (4) 'not to engage himself or associate with any person engaged in any activity tending directly or indirectly to excite disaffection against or to embarrass the Provincial or Central Government or to promote a feeling of hatred or enmity between different classes and subjects of the Indian Dominion or to disturb public peace'.

Golwalkar did not flout these humiliating conditions. He began a correspondence with Nehru and Patel who, in turn, were in intense correspondence with each other on the subject. Golwalkar wrote to both on 11 August 1948 soon after his release from prison on 6 August. To a reminder to Nehru on 24 September, Nehru's private secretary, A.V. Pai replied, on 27 September, reiterating the charges. Golwalkar even called on Patel in Mumbai on 15 August and again on 17 October in New Delhi of which Patel informed Nehru.

> I have made my views quite clear to Golwalkar, viz. that the Sangh will have to change its entire outlook and its programme before Provincial Governments could be satisfied that these activities would cease to be a menace to the peace and tranquillity of India. I also drew his attention to the reports which we are receiving regarding the secret activities of RSS men.[2]

He was satisfied with the assurances he had received from Golwalkar before

[1] Vide Appendix 3 for the text.

[2] *SPC*, vol. VII, p. 261.

lifting the ban. He told Nehru, 'It was only after I had made him agree to a satisfactory constitution for the RSS and got some assurance and undertakings in regard to the Sangh policy for the future that I thought it safe to release him.'[3]

The correspondence supports Patel's claim and belies the RSS's claim that the ban was lifted 'unconditionally'. Mediators had intervened, including G.D. Birla.[4] The correspondence was conducted simultaneously with their efforts and those of the RSS's point man, Eknath Ranade.

Nehru was unmoved.

> It would appear that the declared objectives have little to do with the real ones and with the activities carried on in various forms and ways by people associated with the RSS. These real objectives appear to be completely opposed to the decisions of the Indian Parliament and the provision for the proposed Constitution. The activities . . . are anti-national and often subversive and violent.[5]

Nehru was referring to the Constituent Assembly's resolution on 3 April 1948 which reads thus:

> Whereas it is essential for the proper functioning of democracy and the growth of national unity and solidarity that communalism should be eliminated from Indian life, this Assembly is of the opinion that no communal organisation which by its constitution or by the exercise of discretionary power vested in any of its officers or organs, admits to or excludes from its membership persons on grounds of religion, race and caste, or any of them, should be permitted to engage in any activities other than those essential for the bona fide religious, cultural, social and educational needs of the community, and that all steps, legislative and administrative, necessary to prevent such activities should be taken.[6]

Mookerjee was privy to this. On 8 August the Mahasabha decided to resume its political activities.

After the initial sparring Patel and Golwalkar settled down to business. It began with Patel's letter addressed to 'Brother Golwalkar' on 11 September. 'I am thoroughly convinced that the RSS men can carry on their patriotic endeavour only by joining the Congress and not by keeping separate or by opposing.' Golwalkar's response was clear.

[3] *SPC*, vol. IX, p. 146.

[4] Andersen and Damle, *The Brotherhood in Saffron*, p. 53.

[5] *SWJN*, vol. 8, 1989, p. 122.

[6] Smith, *India as a Secular State*, pp. 473-4 for the text.

> I tried my utmost to see that between the Congress, which is capable of delivering goods in the political field and is at present the ruling party, and the Rashtriya Swayamsevak Sangh in the cultural field, which has achieved success in creating a matchless spirit of patriotism, brotherhood and selflessness among the people, there be no bad blood, there is only everlasting mutual love, one supplementing and complementing the other, both meeting in a sacred confluence.

A draft constitution of the RSS was prepared by Eknath Ranade, P.B. Dani and M.D. Deoras, later the RSS's chief. It was rejected by the government.

> A specific declaration, under Article 4, of allegiance to the Constitution of India as established by law and an explicit acceptance in Article 5 of the National Flag (with the Bhagwa Dhwaja as organisational flag of the Sangh) would be necessary for satisfying the country that there are no reservations in regard to allegiance to the State.[7]

In November 1948 the talks collapsed; mediators revived them. Chief among them was T.R.V. Sastry, a lawyer in Chennai. In a statement published in *The Hindu* on 13 July 1949, he gave the RSS's version of the negotiations. He had drafted a constitution which Golwalkar approved in prison after his re-arrest, following his decision to flout the ban. The government rejected any mediation and insisted on direct contacts.

Sastry claimed,

> The National Flag has been accepted in the Constitution and Mr. M.S. Golwalkar's acceptance is repeated by him according to A.P.I. I do not think any serious objection remains under this head.
>
> There is then the charge of communalism in spirit if not in letter. The organisation admits Hindus of all sorts and denomination. Boys of all communities meet in its many activities without discrimination. The objects and nature of this association do not admit of non-Hindus being members. The spirit of their work is bound to change in the changed conditions of the times under a self-governing India.[8]

This was in reply to the government's communiqué of 11 July announcing the lifting of the ban.

In March this year, the RSS leader wrote to the Government forwarding

7 H.V.R. Iyengar, Home Secretary's note to Golwalkar on 3 May 1949.

8 *Justice on Trial*, p. 96.

> a draft Constitution, the terms of which were examined by Government in consultation with the Provinces. The Government of India conveyed to the RSS leader their reactions on the draft and he has now generally accepted the suggestions made by the Government of India and the clarifications made by him indicate that the relevant provisions of the Constitution are intended to be worked in the spirit contemplated by the Government.
>
> The RSS leader has undertaken to make the loyalty to the Union Constitution and respect for the National Flag more explicit in the Constitution of the RSS and to provide clearly that persons believing or resorting to violent and secret methods will have no place in the Sangh. The RSS leader has also clarified that the Constitution will be worked on a democratic basis. In particular, the office of the Sarsanghchalak would, in effect, be elective in that the successor would be nominated with the consent of the then Karyakari Mandal. It would be open to any member of the Sangh to leave it at any time without breaking the pledge and the admission of minors will be subject to the option of the guardian to withdraw his ward under a written request sent to the Sangh authorities.
>
> In the light of the modifications made and clarifications given by the RSS leader, the Government of India have come to the conclusion that the RSS organisation should be *given an opportunity* to function as a democratic, cultural organisation owing loyalty to the Indian Constitution and recognising the National Flag eschewing secrecy and abjuring violence.

It was on these explicit conditions that the ban was lifted. Golwalkar's claim belatedly on 31 July, that it was unconditional was false. On 7 October 1949, while Nehru was abroad, the Congress party's Working Committee voted that RSS members could join the Congress as primary members. The decision immediately set off a controversy within the ruling party, with Patel's supporters generally supporting the action and Nehru's supporters opposed to it. A.G. Kher, Minister for Local Self-Government in the United Provinces, and a staunch supporter of Patel, responded to the critics of the 7 October decision by predicting that an adverse decision regarding the participation of RSS members in the Congress might force the RSS into politics.

The *Mahratta* of Pune wrote on 18 November 1949:

> The members of the organisation [RSS] cannot take part in politics unless they join some political organisation. The main political parties are the Congress, the Socialists, the Communists, the Hindu Mahasabha, the Muslim League, and the RSPI. Do we desire that RSS youths should join other groups which are opposed to Congress, or should we desire they should join us? Let those who desire that RSS should not be admitted even as primary members of Congress

understand the implications of their attitude. They are compelling RSS men to join the opponents of Congress if they have to take part in politics.[9]

Kher's warning to the Congress proved prophetic, as RSS leaders began to consider seriously the question of political involvement. On 17 November 1949 after Nehru's return from the United States, the Congress Working Committee rescinded its earlier decision. It ruled that RSS members could join the Congress as primary members, but only if they first gave up their RSS membership. The RSS would assume some role in the political process.[10]

By then Mookerjee could see his clout diminish by the day and began looking around for other options. Since the old guard rejected his proposals, he resigned from the Mahasabha on 23 November 1949. His proposals were that it should 'limit itself to social, cultural and religious problems' or 'abandon its communalist composition and open its doors to every citizen, regardless of religion who was ready to accept its economic and political programme'.[11] The latter option is what he implemented for the Jana Sangh which he set up in 1951.

The RSS had its own plans. It was not idle during the ban. It evaded it. Activists opened a new front. Students were mobilised. The first group was formed at Delhi University. Others followed.

> In July 1948, Madhok – a teacher who argued that the infiltration of student organisations was a vital task – founded in Delhi, with approval from Nagpur, the Akhil Bharatiya Vidyarthi Parishad (ABVP). In conformity to RSS philosophy, the task of this organisation was to bring about collaboration between all those involved in university education, since the teachers and the taught are both wheels of the same car. It would be a rival to the All India Students' Federation, which was described as being dominated by 'Communist agitators'.[12]

A highly respected journal *The Caravan* published a detailed exposé of the activities of these storm troopers of the RSS in its issue of October 2017 (pp. 36-55), entitled 'Student Days: The Age of ABVP' by Priyanka Dubey. It was founded on 9 July 1949. She wrote:

> [K.N. Govindacharya's] telling began with the death of Mohandas Gandhi. 'In the aftermath of Gandhi-ji's assassination, the RSS was banned, starting in February 1948,' he said. The majority of the organisation's cadre at the time

9 *Mahratta*, 18 November 1949.

10 Andersen and Damle, *The Brotherhood in Saffron*, pp. 55-6.

11 Jaffrelot, *The Hindu Nationalist Movement and Indian Politics*, p. 91.

12 Ibid., p. 27.

was young, and 'the Sangh wanted to find a way to organise and continue its meetings normally. So it started meeting under the name of the Akhil Bharatiya Vidhyarthi [sic]Parishad'.

The ABVP was officially registered in July the following year. Just days after that, on 11 July 1949, the ban on the RSS was lifted. Suddenly 'there was no immediate need for the ABVP,' Govindacharya said, and it was sidelined.

11. Golwalkar and Mookerjee's Pact on the Jana Sangh

It was a Faustian pact under which Mookerjee accepted Golwalkar's terms on the establishment of a new political party the Bharatiya Jana Sangh. Each had its own compulsions. Young activists were urging Golwalkar to float a political party. He refused. The King reigns but under the guidance of the Raj Guru who can even dethrone him. In August 1949 pressmen asked him, 'Is it a fact that the Sangh plans to capture power?' Golwalkar's answer is revealing. 'We have kept before ourselves the idea of Bhagwan Shri Krishna who held a big empire under his thumb, but refused to become the emperor himself.'[1]

The RSS sent two presidents of the Jana Sangh – Mauli Chandra Sharma and Balraj Madhok – packing home in 1954 and 1973 respectively as also a president of its successor the Bharatiya Janata Party, L.K. Advani in 2005.

Golwalkar's calculations, expounded at length in his *Bunch of Thoughts* (1966), are as relevant now in 2018 as they were in 1951. They led him to reject Savarkar's overtures. The RSS aspired to be a dominant force. This is what he wrote:

> The political rulers were never the standard-bearers of our society. They were never taken as the props of our national life. Saints and sages, who had risen above the mundane temptations of self and power and had dedicated themselves wholly for establishing a happy, virtuous and integrated state of society were its constant torch-bearers. They represented the dharmashala [religious authority]. The king was only an ardent follower of that higher moral authority. . . .
>
> *We aspire to become the radiating centre of all the age-old cherished ideals of our society – just as the indescribable power which radiates through the sun.* Then the political power which draws its life from that source of society, will have no other [goal] but to reflect the same radiance.[2]

Mookerjee did not resign from the Nehru Cabinet on the Nehru-Liaquat pact on the minorities. He resigned on 1 April 1950 while it was under intense debate in the Cabinet. It was signed on 8 April after diluting the draft. He began talking aimlessly of refugees from East Pakistan and 'appeasement' of Pakistan. The truth was that Nehru had gained ascendancy in the Cabinet and Mookerjee felt stifled.

Mookerjee met Golwalkar in 1940, the year in which he clashed with Subhas

[1] *Spotlights: Guruji Answers*, Bangalore: Sahitya Sindhu, 1974, p. 158.

[2] Golwalkar, *Bunch of Thoughts*, pp. 93 and 103.

Chandra Bose. He had come into contact with the founder of the RSS, Hedgewar, in the mid-thirties and praised the RSS at a rally in Lahore in 1940 as 'the only silver lining in the cloudy sky of India'.[3]

The initiative for a pact was taken by Vasant Rao Oak, a leading RSS member. In 1949, even while Mookerjee was a member of Nehru's Cabinet, he was in parleys with Oak on the formation of a new political party. Oak told Myron Weiner, an erudite scholar, that he had assured Mookerjee that 'if he left the Government the RSS would support him and start a new party'.[4]

Weiner's appraisal of Mookerjee was sound. 'His political record showed an ability to shift from one organisation to another and, when necessary, to be a freelance independent.'[5] Mookerjee was in the Congress in the late '20s; a member of the Bengal Cabinet of Maulvi Fazlul Haq, who had moved the Pakistan Resolution of the Muslim League in 1940; joined the Mahasabha under Savarkar's leadership and the Union Cabinet under Nehru.

The idea of a new party took shape in late 1949. Mookerjee went to Nagpur several times between November 1949 and the spring of 1950 to meet Golwalkar. It is unlikely that the Intelligence Bureau did not inform Nehru and Patel what their colleague was up to.

In the *Organiser* of 25 June 1956 Golwalkar revealed the talks.

> One of my old colleagues who had developed a liking for political work to a degree uncommon and undesirable for a Swayamsevak of the RSS, Sri Vasant Rao Oak, was in close contact with him for a long time and his association seems to have prompted Dr. Mookerjee to seek my cooperation and help in the matter. . . . Naturally I had to warn him that the RSS could not be drawn into politics, that it could not play second fiddle to any political or other party since no organisation devoted to the wholesale regeneration of the real i.e. cultural life of the Nation could ever function successfully if it was tried to be used as a hand maid of political parties.

Jaffrelot writes:

> By the end of 1950, when Tandon was at loggerheads with Nehru, Mookerjee had gathered in Delhi a group consisting not only of swayamsevaks (V.R. Oak, B. Madhok, Bhai Mahavir), but also of Hindu traditionalist politicians such as M.C. Sharma and various Arya Samajists (Lala Yodh Raj, President of the Punjab National Bank, his brother Balraj Bhalla, and Mahashe Krishnan,

3 Balraj Madhok, *Portrait of a Martyr: Biography of Dr. Shyama Prasad Mookerji*, Jaico Pub. House, 1969, p. 96.

4 Myron Weiner, *Party Politics in India*, Princeton University Press, 1957, p. 186.

5 Ibid., p. 187.

editor-in-chief of *Pratap*). This team, with the addition of Hans Raj Gupta and Dharmavir, met on 16 January 1951 to discuss the setting-up of a party in the Delhi region and in Punjab to prepare one constitution for a pan-Indian party. The draft constitution of this All India people's party (Bharatiya Jana Sangh) was circulated to potential sympathisers. [Oak is Oke in Jaffrelot's book.]

Faced with the unresponsiveness of the RSS leaders, Mookerjee showed his determination by setting up a 'People's Party' in West Bengal on 23 April 1951. On 27 May, a meeting was held at Jullundur, at the instigation of Madhok, to found a Jana Sangh which would represent Punjab and Delhi.[6]

The pact was sealed. Each side, the RSS and Mookerjee, rejoiced that it had acquired a political party; the RSS, to project its ideology and Mookerjee, to serve as a platform from which to further his ambitions and fight the 1952 general elections. But Mookerjee forgot one cardinal reality. It was the RSS which would provide not only the muscle, its cadres, and leaders but also the money.

We have an authoritative statement of the accord from Madhok who participated in the talks.

> They [RSS men] had, therefore, begun to feel the urgent need of a political organisation which could reflect the ideology and ideas of the RSS in the political sphere and should, therefore, be able to command the willing allegiance of the RSS workers and supporters. This need, it was felt, would become more pressing after the introduction of adult franchise in the country. . . .
>
> Dr. Mookerji was aware of this trend of thought in the RSS circles. He knew that the attitude of the RSS which drew its main strength and sustenance from the lower middle and working classes, towards social and economic problems of the country could not be anything but reactionary. The RSS approach to the problems of culture, nationalism, and partition had his fullest approval. He, therefore, instinctively felt that any political organisation sponsored by, or enjoying the confidence of the RSS could surely and speedily become such a force in the political life of the country as may command his fullest allegiance and also succeed in mobilising and consolidating the non-Congress and non-Communist nationalist public opinion into an effective opposition. But the RSS leadership was not yet clear in its mind about the shape and character of the political party to which it could lend its support and the role it would have to play in bringing it into existence.

There was no disagreement on ideology. 'The Muslim problem, he was convinced, could be solved in free India, once for all, if their outlook on cultural,

[6] Jaffrelot, *The Hindu Nationalist Movement and Indian Politics*, pp. 117-8. Vide also Bruce Graham, *Hindu Nationalism and Indian Politics*, p. 27.

social and political problems of the country was Hinduised or nationalised while leaving them free, in keeping with the Hindu tradition of absolute tolerance, to carry on their religion and way of worship as they pleased.'[7] On the name, Mookerjee adopted a subterfuge. He disapproved of 'Hindu Rashtriya' for tactical reasons.

Madhok revealed that,

> In the discussion of the day the approach of the proposed political party to the term 'Hindu Rashtra' and its political, social and cultural implications figured prominently. Some of the persons present argued that though they were in full agreement with the concept of 'Hindu Rashtra', yet they would not like it to be incorporated or used in the objectives of the proposed party because that might create misunderstanding in the minds of some people. That provoked Dr. Mookerji who gave a convincing exposition of the concept of 'Hindu Rashtra' as he understood it. He explained that the British had deliberately given a narrow sectarian connotation to the word Hindu for their imperialistic ends and the Congress leaders had played their game in denouncing everything Hindu as communal.
>
> It should be the duty of the new organisation, he pleaded, to dispel these misconceptions and make the world familiar with the broad national import of the word Hindu, the geographical and historical name of the people of Hindustan. 'Hindu Rashtra', he argued, was a noble concept. It brought out the basic oneness and the common tradition of all the different sects and creeds of India. It did not denote any particular religion but a commonwealth of all the religions and sects of the country because, whatever be the way of worship of any particular individual, he could not, if he was to be a national of India, cut himself as under from the common cultural and historical traditions of the country. As such it is not, and never was, a communal or narrow concept. Those, he argued, who were scared away by the very word Hindu could not be depended upon for safeguarding the cultural and territorial heritage of the country.

Mookerjee, as an astute tactician, resorted to a subterfuge.

> But he was opposed to the word being imposed on those who were not, for the time being, prepared to accept it. He, therefore, suggested that the word Bharatiya and Indian, which are synonyms of the word Hindu but are more acceptable to those under the influence of West, as also to those who lack courage of conviction, should also be used along with the word Hindu till

[7] Jaffrelot, *Hindu Nationalist Movement and Indian Politics*, p. 93.

> such people shed their inferiority complex and learn to take pride in their own name and traditions.[8]

Bruce Graham's characterisation was apt. 'The Jana Sangh was, to a very real extent, a projection of the RSS into constitutional politics.'

In November 1954 Mauli Chandra Sharma, one of the founders of the Jana Sangh and its national president resigned from the party accusing the RSS of interference in the party's affairs. Another founder Madhok was expelled.

Dr. B.D. Graham's meticulous description of the immediate aftermath of the Golwalkar-Mookerjee pact shows that it was the RSS which had triumphed.

> It was the young workers of the RSS who built the party up in 1951 and who carried it through the 1951-2 elections. Their price was organisational control; rather than adapt themselves to the democratic requirements of the formal constitution, they aimed deliberately at taking over the focal executive positions of secretary, organiser and treasurer in the State and All-India Working Committees, and from these they set out to control the day-to-day functioning of the party. A measure of their success was provided in November 1954, when Mauli Chandra Sharma, one of the organisation's founders and at that time its national president, resigned his office and charged the RSS with exercising undue influence within the party. Within a few days, Guru Dutt, another founding member and President of the Delhi State Jana Sangh, resigned on the same grounds.
>
> From the statements of these two men, it would appear that the RSS had tried to influence the choice of election of candidates and party officers to the extent of antagonising the 'liberal' party members, many of whom belonged to the RSS but felt that the Jana Sangh should be run on democratic lines. The implications of RSS control had been discussed at the Jana Sangh's All-India Committee in August 1954 but the matter had been referred to a subsequent meeting which the General Secretary, Din Dayal Upadhyaya (a former RSS man), had refused to convene. Sharma had submitted his resignation as President in the belief that this would oblige Upadhyaya to call the All-India Committee together, but Upadhyaya (who is said to have consulted Golwalkar) referred the matter instead to the Working Committee, dominated by an RSS majority, which accepted the resignation, and appointed an interim president. Sharma claimed that trouble with the RSS was not a new thing.
>
> The late Dr. Mookerjee was often seriously perturbed by the demands of RSS leaders for a decisive role in matters like the appointment of office-bearers, nomination of candidates for elections and matters of policy. He

[8] Ibid., pp. 99-100.

however hoped that the rank and file of the RSS would be drawn out into the arena of democratic public life through their association with the Jana Sangh.

A vigorous and calculated drive was launched to turn the Jana Sangh into a convenient handle of the RSS. Orders were issued from their headquarters through their emissaries and the Jana Sangh was expected to carry them out. Many workers and groups all over the country resented this and the Delhi State Jana Sangh as a body refused to comply.

When another group of 'liberals' left the Jana Sangh in July 1961, they told similar stories. They claimed that the initial decision to found the party had been taken by the RSS Working Committee shortly after the lifting of the official ban on 12 July 1949, that Golwalkar had delegated RSS organisers to hold key posts in the newly formed party, that the RSS always took an active interest in the choice of Jana Sangh office-bearers, and that Golwalkar and his lieutenants were consulted before the selection of top leadership and the making of policy decisions.

In truth the ban had led Golwalkar to think of a political front. Graham held that

> the Jana Sangh was, to a very real extent, a projection of the RSS into constitutional politics. Most of Mookerjee's key organisers had come from the RSS and their experience in the hard work of establishing and sustaining local committees made them indispensable; Din Dayal Upadhyaya, who was chosen as the party's General Secretary, was an RSS cadre who had worked amongst the villagers of Uttar Pradesh and had impressed Mookerjee with his ability as Secretary of the Uttar Pradesh Jana Sangh; Atul Behari Vajpayee, one of the party's All-India Secretaries, had joined the RSS during his student days and had later worked as editor on several nationalist Hindi journals, including the Delhi *Vir Arjun*; professor Mahavir, a member of the Central Executive and Professor of History at New Delhi's Camp College, had been an RSS worker for almost twenty years; Balraj Madhok, founder of the Punjab Jana Sangh, had been during the war a full-time RSS organiser in Jammu and Kashmir; and Bapu Saheb Sohni had been appointed RSS organiser in Berar in 1936 and later became one of the most influential members of the Jana Sangh's All-India Working Committee.[9]

From the very beginning Sharma had to submit to the RSS's wishes on the composition of his Working Committee. They were the ones who could stand up to him at the RSS's behest. He resisted and had to quit. This was, and still is, Mookerjee's heritage. Not he, but the RSS had acquired a political party. He was not

[9] Graham, 'Syama Prasad Mookerjee and the Communalist Alternative', pp. 353-4.

a force for the good of the country. 'He appealed powerfully to the darker strain in the political life of his countrymen.'[10] Sixty-five years after his death in 1953, the strain has become darker and bids fair to become worse. History has vindicated Nehru's censure: the Jana Sangh was the 'illegitimate child of the RSS'.[11]

[10] Ibid., p. 366.

[11] *The Hindu*, 6 January 1952.

12. Mookerjee, RSS and Jana Sangh

It is easier to form a political party; vastly more difficult to run it. Syama Prasad Mookerjee realised that the RSS very much intended to have a hold over the Jana Sangh which was set up under a pact between them. Mookerjee chafed at this; but he could do nothing. The RSS had not provided muscle and the wherewithal to the Jana Sangh to promote Mookerjee as a leader. He was to be Hindenburg; Golwalkar was Hitler, the wielder of real power. The RSS needed a political front; he needed a political platform.

Myron Weiner, doyen of American political scientists who specialised on Indian politics, noted in his classic *Party Politics in India*, 'RSS members played a key role in organising the new party . . . [and] among the top leadership of the party, RSS leaders were in major positions.'[1] As for Mookerjee, Weiner aptly remarked: 'His record showed an ability to shift from one organisation to another and, when necessary to be a freelance independent.' In the late '20s he was a Congress member of the Bengal Legislative Council. In 1937 he was elected to the Council as an independent but soon fell under the influence of Savarkar. In 1939 joined the Hindu Mahasabha.[2]

In 1941 he joined the Bengal Cabinet headed by Fazlul Haq, who had moved the Pakistan Resolution at the Muslim League's session at Lahore on 23 March 1940. In 1942 he was advising the Governor on how to crush the Congress's Quit India Movement. In 1947 he joined the ministry at the Centre led by Jawaharlal Nehru; resigning in April 1950 to form the Jana Sangh.

Mohammed Ali Jinnah was not overlooked. As its vice-chancellor, Mookerjee invited him to address students of the Calcutta University at the Ashutosh Hall on 21 August 1936 and paid rich tributes to him as 'an Indian nationalist . . . one of those fighters who know how to fight stubbornly for the attainment of the ideal which they have made their own.'[3] He met Jinnah again a few years later at his house for three hours, after Jinnah had unfurled the Pakistan flag.

The Jana Sangh's manifesto was published on 29 October 1951. It was patterned on the RSS. It said:

> The object of the Bharatiya Jana Sangh is the rebuilding of Bharat on the basis of Bharatiya *Sanskriti* and *Maryada* as a political, social and economic

1 Myron Weiner, *Party Politics in India*, p. 194.

2 Ibid., p. 187.

3 Waheed Ahmad (ed.), *The Nation's Voice: Speeches and Statements*, vol. 1, Karachi: Quaid-i-Azam Academy, 1992, p. 79.

democracy granting equality of opportunity and liberty to individuals so as to make her a prosperous, powerful and united nation, progressive, modern and enlightened, able to withstand the aggressive designs of others and to pull her weight in the council of nations for the establishment of world peace.[4]

Compare this with the BJP's election manifestoes and one is struck by a remarkable consistency in the themes which change in the terminology does not conceal. That consistency was ensured by the RSS. Mookerjee placed Mauli Chandra Sharma, son of a Mahasabha leader Din Dayal Sharma in charge of the party organisation. A non-RSS man, he soon came to grief. On 4 November 1954, he was obliged to resign not only as president but also from the party. He issued a statement on 3 November 1954 which resonates even now, sixty years later. He said:

> Acute differences of opinion on the question of interference by the RSS in the affairs of the Jana Sangh have been growing for over a year. Many RSS workers have entered the party since its inception. They were welcomed, as RSS leaders had publically declared that it was a purely cultural body having nothing to do with politics and that its members were perfectly free to join any political party. In practice, however, it did not prove to be so.
>
> The late Dr. Mookerjee was often seriously perturbed by the demands of RSS leaders for a decisive role in matters like the appointment of office-bearers, nomination of candidates for elections and matters of policy. We however hoped that the rank and file of the RSS would be drawn out into the arena of democratic public life through their association with the Jana Sangh.
>
> A vigorous and calculated drive was launched to turn the Jana Sangh into a convenient handle of the RSS. Orders were issued from their headquarters through their emissaries and the Jana Sangh was expected to carry them out. Many workers and groups all over the country resented this and the Delhi State Jana Sangh as a body refused to comply.[5]

The president of the party's Delhi unit, Guru Dutt Vaidya, also offered to resign. He alleged that a special emissary from the RSS high command had tried to secure the executive of the unit and have it replaced by another consisting of 'persons nominated by the RSS authorities'.[6]

Mookerjee's presidential address at the opening convention of the Jana Sangh

[4] Craig Baxter, *The Jana Sangh: A Biography of an Indian Political Party*, London: Oxford University Press, 1969, p. 84.

[5] *The Statesman*, 4 November 1954; quoted in Graham, *Hindu Nationalism and Indian Politics*, p. 64.

[6] Ibid.

in Delhi on 21 October 1951, is noteworthy for its emphases and omissions.[7] It ran into 11 closely printed pages. A mere nine lines were devoted to Kashmir to demand withdrawal of the case from the United Nations; rule out a plebiscite, and recover the areas administered by Pakistan. There was no reference to Jammu.

There was a tirade against Nehru in his coarse idiom.

> Having repeatedly sacrificed Bharatiya nationalism at the altar of Muslim communalism and even after partition having surrendered to the whims and howls of Pakistan Government, it does not lie in the mouth of Mr. Nehru to accuse others of communalism. There is no communalism in Bharat today except the new policy of Muslim appeasement which has been started by Mr. Nehru and his friends for the purpose of winning their votes at the forthcoming elections. . . . Mr. Nehru, the Arch-Fascist of India, accuses others of fascism.

Pandit Prem Nath Dogra, president of the Jammu-based Praja Parishad and formerly head of the RSS's Jammu unit, met Mookerjee in Western Court in New Delhi early in May 1952. It was called 'momentous' by Madhok; for good reason. Mookerjee acquired a 'cause' on which to whip up communal and chauvinistic feelings. 'For Dr. Mookerjee it was a challenge and an opportunity to galvanise' the Jana Sangh.[8]

Dogra's exertions had a two point agenda; to dislodge from power the prime minister of the state of Jammu and Kashmir Sheikh Muhammad Abdullah, as he then was. He promoted a strong leftist programme. It included confiscation of lands without compensation as part of the 'land to the tiller programme'.

Graham points out that:

> The economic power of the Dogra landlords had been seriously undermined in 1951 by the Big Landed Estates Abolition Act, which had provided for the confiscation of large holdings without compensation and for the transfer of land to the tillers. The Praja Parishad was further disturbed when Sheikh Abdullah, with the approval of the Government of India, began preparations for the framing of a State Constitution intended to provide a firmer legal basis for the special status of Jammu and Kashmir within the Indian Union. To this end, a Constituent Assembly had been elected at the end of 1951 and, having adopted a provisional Constitution, it had begun work on a definite document.
>
> The Jana Sangh did not have its own party units in Jammu and Kashmir but it was in sympathy with the Praja Parishad and with its vigorous leader, Prem Nath Dogra, a Brahman, formerly a civil servant in the princely state, who had at one stage headed the RSS groups in Jammu city.

[7] *Why Bharatiya Jana Sangh*, Daryaganj, Delhi: Bharat Mudranalaya.

[8] Madhok, *Portrait of a Martyr*, p. 194.

At its Kanpur session, on 31 December 1952, the Jana Sangh took up the Dogras' cause. It asked for a Round Table Conference of the 'recognised leaders of India' (read: including Mookerjee) of the Praja Parishad and of the Government of Jammu & Kashmir. Dogra was arrested on 26 December 1952. Three months later, the Jana Sangh entered the fray in right earnest. It joined the Ram Rajya Parishad and the Hindu Mahasabha in a full-scale satyagraha. Mookerjee calculated that the initiative was his and his nemesis, Nehru, would be thrown on the defensive. The RSS supported him. The agitation fizzled out but not before exacting a terrible price – Mookerjee's death and a trail of bitterness which exacerbated the Jammu-Kashmir divide.

Mookerjee returned to Kolkata from where he hit up on a time honoured tactic – initiate a correspondence to keep up his morale and that of his party in a battle he knew he could not win, so impossible were his demands. The entire correspondence was published by the Jana Sangh's general secretary Deen Dayal Upadhyaya.[9]

Mookerjee began with a letter to Nehru on 9 January 1953 with a copy to Sheikh Abdullah. His concern was 'the situation in Jammu' and he hinted at a trifurcation of the state into Jammu, Kashmir and Ladakh. Each 'represented different types of people; their languages, their outlook, their environments, their habits and modes of life'. If there is 'a general plebiscite what will be the fate of Jammu in case the majority of the people, consisting of Moslems [sic] vote against India?' Communalism was blended with regionalism.

The areas under Pakistan's administration must be regained; by war, he hinted. Pakistan will not surrender it. 'How, then, it is asked are we going to get this back? . . . It will be nothing short of national disgrace and humiliation, if we fail to regain this lost portion of our own territory.' Meanwhile, Article 370 or the state's autonomy must go, at least in relation to Jammu; a breakup of the state. He proposed tripartite talks; implying a parity of status for himself.

Nehru replied promptly on 10 January. He was anxious 'to settle finally the whole Jammu and Kashmir issue'. But 'there is no magic way of solving it by decree or Act of Parliament as some people seem to imagine'.

Mookerjee replied on 3 February accusing Nehru of 'your failure to stand against Moslem communalism in India'. He asked 'when and how will the accession of the State of Jammu and Kashmir to India be finally settled'. He raked up again the issue of the Pakistan administered part of Kashmir.

Sheikh Abdullah, who had met Mookerjee in Srinagar in 1952, replied to him on 4 February 1953 by a devastating letter, drafted obviously by his colleague Mirza Mohammed Afzal Beg, an outstandingly able lawyer. He quoted from Mookerjee's followers' vicious speeches:

[9] *Integrate Kashmir: Mukherjee, Nehru & Abdullah Correspondence*, Delhi: Publicity Department, Bharatiya Jana Sangh; cited hereinafter.

There is conclusive evidence to show that the Praja Parishad is determined to force a solution of the entire Kashmir issue on communal lines. Its leaders have expressed their views publicly to this effect and I give below a few extracts from their speeches. . . . 'Our way is not with Kashmir. Sheikh is not acceptable to us. We cannot tolerate Jammu and Ladakh going to the winds. We want the people to have blind faith in Praja Parishad and get ready by putting shrouds to attain our goal.' (Shree Madan Lal, Secy., City Praja Parishad, at Samba on 20-10-52.)

'We would put an end to Sh. Abdullah and other workers of the National Conference. We will suck their blood. We will root out this Government and send them to Kashmir. We do not like this Raj.' (Rishi Kumar Kaushal, Member, Praja Parishad Working Committee, at Reasi on 23-11-52.)

What is really intended has been given out in a recent publication of the Praja Parishad. It says: '. . . The present Constituent Assembly consists of 75 members. Its detail is as follows:

Province	*General*	*Muslim*	*Buddhist*	*Total*
Kashmir	3	41	..	44
Jammu	21	8	..	29
Ladakh	..	1	1	2
Total	24	50	1	75

'These figures clearly show that Sheikh Abdullah's Muslim dominance cannot and should not be forced upon Hindu Buddhists of Jammu and Ladakh. . . .' (Page 12 of the pamphlet entitled 'Jammu rejects a separate Constitution for Jammu and Kashmir State' issued by the Publicity Secretary, All Jammu and Kashmir Praja Parishad, Jammu.)

The Sheikh continued:

You cannot be unaware of the possible repercussions in Kashmir as a result of this agitation which is led by a militant Hindu leadership and which in the past has made its attitude towards the Muslims amply clear. If the agitation grows unforeseen forces may be released which would seriously threaten the foundations of the State. I cannot persuade myself to think that you want to solve the Kashmir problem through disintegration and chaos.

He was alluding to the masses of Muslims in Jammu in 1947.

On Article 370, Sheikh Abdullah took a deadly aim, 'This arrangement has not been arrived at now but as early as in 1949 when you happened to be a part of the Government.' He added:

> So far as we are concerned, we have maintained that the special position accorded to the State can alone be the source of a growing unity and closer association between the State and India. The Constituent Assembly of India took note of the special circumstances obtaining in the State and made provisions accordingly. But, if the basis of this relationship is sought to be altered, certain consequences are bound to follow for which all of us must be prepared.

The Praja Parishad (read: the RSS) was against the Constitution of India itself.

> Some of them have openly demanded that it should conform to Hindu ideals. . . . The Praja Parishad leaders have made it clear that they will not rest till they have rid Jammu Hindus of what they call the haunting fear of Muslim domination of Kashmir. To such an attitude, what answer can I give?

This moving passage in the Sheikh's letter reveals a lot.

> The people of Jammu and Kashmir State, made their choice for the secular ideal long before the partition of India took place. They successfully withstood the onslaughts of Pakistan leadership, their temptations and coercion and finally their wanton aggression in 1947. When Pakistan raiders were knocking at the very door of Srinagar, the Muslims of Kashmir offered their bravest sons as a sacrifice to protect their cherished ideals of secularism and human brotherhood. It happened at a time when they had nobody round about to render them assistance, when darkness surrounded them all round, when their co-religionists were being brutally massacred at the hands of those very leaders of Praja Parishad who now claim their loyalty to the secular ideals of India. Since then the bonds of kinship between India and Kashmir have been greatly strengthened.

Six months later the man who expressed these heartfelt sentiments was removed from the office of Prime Minister of the State of Jammu & Kashmir; dismissed from his office, and put in prison for eleven years. The RSS and its political front had fouled the atmosphere. He concluded, 'Let me assure you and the people of India that the Muslims in Kashmir will not falter from their ideals even if they are left alone in this great battle for secularism and human brotherhood.'

A question which Mookerjee posed to Nehru, on 8 February 1952, has contemporary relevance. 'Does democracy mean the imposition by brute force of the will of the majority on the minority?' This is the RSS's basic approach ever since its birth in 1925. Like the RSS, Mookerjee was frozen in times of old. 'The Dogras were the rulers of the State *for generations* and the position had suddenly been reversed when you came into power.' This is a patent falsehood. Gulab Singh, the Dogra chieftain of Jammu acquired Kashmir in 1846 from the East India Company for Rs. 75 lakh under the Treaty of Amritsar of 16 March 1846 and by betraying his masters, the Sikh Darbar at Lahore. He called himself their slave; the Governor-General's 'Zurkharid' (bought with gold).[10]

Mookerjee's lament, which he shared with the RSS's Jammuites, explains a lot that is happening today. Mookerjee's rude badgerings provoked the Sheikh to shed his initial hesitation and write of the RSS with brutal candour.

> While referring to the Bhagwa flag, you suggest that there would be nothing wrong in its adoption if the country so chooses. I do not know whether you consider that this could happen only when militant Hindu communalism triumphs in India. In that unfortunate event where can Kashmir stand? Let me repeat that even then its people will continue their fight for Gandhiji's ideology to the bitter end. The father of the Nation did not give his life in vain. This noble sacrifice will always inspire and sustain us as it did in the critical days of 1947.
>
> You do not mention its connection with RSS. Everyone is familiar with the role played by the leaders of RSS in Jammu in 1947, precisely at the same time when we were resisting Muslim communalism in Kashmir.

He then proceeded to attack the main culprit.

> The RSS leaders singularly failed to appreciate the spirit of this gesture. When following Gandhiji's assassination, the organisation was banned, it emerged under the garb of the Praja Parishad with the same programme and leadership. . . . So long as this organisation continues to be an instrument in the hands of the RSS leaders, I regret it will not be possible for us to recognise this organisation.

Abdullah went further to remind him of the Maharaja's treachery:

> An invasion was launched on Kashmir from Pakistan. The Maharaja, instead of facing bravely the onslaught of the invaders along with the people, deserted them, moved down to a safer place in Jammu, where he aligned himself with militant Hindu communalism, further aggravating the already critical situation. This is the unpatriotic and anti-national record of the Maharaja for whom you show so much concern.

10 Vide Amarinder Singh, *The Last Sunset: The Rise and Fall of the Lahore Durbar*, Roli Books, 2009.

His son and heir Karan Singh shares that outlook to this day. Since Sheikh Abdullah was known to be pro-left, Mookerjee accused him of having the state's flag as 'a camouflage for using the Communist flag'.

The correspondence ended in February 1953. It was conducted in an atmosphere fouled by the RSS. After Mookerjee's resignation from the Nehru Cabinet in April 1950, the RSS shed all restraint in its communal activities. On 10 April 1952, Abdullah delivered his famous Ranbirsinghpura speech in which he declared 'Kashmir's accession to India will have to be of a restricted nature so long as communalism has a foothold on the soil of India. Many Kashmiris fear what will happen to them and their position if, for instance, something happens to Pandit Nehru'.

Nehru voiced his fears on the impact of the RSS's campaigns on the people of Kashmir at a public meeting in Kolkata on New Year's Day 1952.

> Now these Hindu communal parties like the Jana Sangh and Rashtriya Swayamsevak Sangh and another party called the Praja Parishad in Jammu have launched an agitation against the Shaikh Abdullah Government. They abuse him and want the old Maharaja to come back. Now you can imagine what this means. At the moment, it is Shaikh Abdullah who is completely opposed to Pakistan. There is no doubt about it that he is the leader of the people of Kashmir, a very great leader. If tomorrow Shaikh Abdullah wanted Kashmir to join Pakistan, neither I nor all the forces of India would be able to stop it because if the leader decides, it will happen. So what the Jana Sangh and the Swayamsevak Sangh are doing is to play into the hands of Pakistan. Pakistan too wants to topple the Shaikh Abdullah Government and the Jana Sangh wants to do the same. . . . There can be no greater vindication than this of our secular policies, our Constitution, that we have drawn the people of Kashmir towards us. But just imagine what would have happened in Kashmir if the Jana Sangh or any other communal party had been at the helm of affairs. The people of Kashmir say that they are fed up with this communalism. Why should they live in a country where the Jana Sangh and the Rashtriya Swayamsevak Sangh are constantly beleaguering them? They will go elsewhere and they will not stay with us.[11]

In a statement in Parliament on 25 March 1953 Nehru said:

> Then again it has been proposed – nothing has been said about it at this moment – 'Well, if not Kashmir, let Jammu become completely inter-related with India'. That obviously means that the Jammu and Kashmir State is disrupted. And we support this famous process of integration by disruption and by throwing

[11] *SWJN*, vol. 17, pp. 76 and 78.

> away inevitably the rest of the State into somebody's lap. But a little logic will show that all these things lead to something which is entirely opposed to the so-called demands of the Praja Parishad or Jana Sangh. Every step that they are taking or have taken leads them away from India, away from the very things that they demand.[12]

Mookerjee gave a call to observe 10 March 1953 as Jammu & Kashmir Day. The die was cast. He entered the state, was served with an order banning his entry into the state on 10 May at Madhopora and was taken to Srinagar where he was detained in a small bungalow. He died of a heart attack on 23 June.

Nehru confided to his close friend B.C. Roy, Chief Minister of West Bengal, twice in confidence. On 29 June he wrote:

> It is difficult to speak openly about the injurious results of this movement. It has made the Kashmir problem far more difficult than it ever was. Before this movement was started, I had little doubt in my mind that the final decision about Kashmir would be in our favour, however long it might take. But this movement has upset all my calculations and weakened our position in Kashmir terribly. I am for the moment talking about the Kashmir Valley only. As you know, the people in the Valley are over ninety per cent Muslim. The reaction of the Jammu Praja Parishad movement on them has been very great. They have become frightened of the communal elements in Jammu and in India and their previous wish to be attached to India has weakened. Indeed, at the moment, all the hostile forces against us are dominant in Kashmir. The Pakistanis in Kashmir have taken full advantage of this and have even come out in the open for the first time. If Hindu communalists could organise a movement in Jammu, why should not Muslim communalists function in Kashmir? The position now is that if there was a plebiscite, a great majority of Muslims in Kashmir would go against us.
>
> So, this movement of the Praja Parishad, which aims at a closer integration of Kashmir State with India, has had the opposite effect. It is true that so far as Jammu Province is concerned, it has demonstrated that a majority of Hindus there want closer integration. Nobody ever doubted that and, whatever happens, Jammu cannot leave India. There need be no apprehension about that. The whole difficulty has been about the Valley of Kashmir and we are on the point of losing it because of the Praja Parishad movement. Psychologically we have lost it and it would be difficult to get back to the older position. . . .
>
> In the ultimate analysis, we gain Kashmir if we gain the goodwill of the people there. We cannot keep it at the point of the bayonet if it is clear that the people do not want us. For the first time public cries are raised in Kashmir

12 Ibid., vol. 21, p. 222.

> that the Indian Army should get out. If I feel strongly on this subject, you will understand me. Nothing more harmful to our cause in the State could have been done even by our enemies.

There was a huge outcry over the death; with predictable consequences. Nehru wrote to B.C. Roy, Chief Minister of West Bengal, again on 29 July:

> Undoubtedly, a major reason for this has been the Praja Parishad and Jana Sangh agitation and its reactions in the Valley of Kashmir. Whatever its justification might have been in Jammu itself, the reactions in the Valley of that agitation in Jammu and various parts of India had the most harmful results. The inhabitants of Kashmir, and they are 90% Muslims, saw the communal face of India and were frightened by it. Their desire for remaining with India weakened and in fact many thought that they would be suppressed in many ways if they were completely merged with India. . . .
>
> It is clear that we cannot, in the ultimate analysis, hold Kashmir or the Valley by force of arms alone. If it is patent that the people there do not want us to remain, then we have no case left and we cannot continue for long.[13]

Mookerjee's adventure did not bring Kashmir closer to India. Forgotten in the grief over the death was a somersault similar to the ones Mookerjee had taken all his political career. He was a member of Nehru's Cabinet from 15 August 1947 to 1 April 1950. It was during this period that the most momentous decisions concerning Kashmir were taken. Mookerjee was privy to all of them. They were:

1. The pledge to hold a plebiscite in Kashmir made in Governor-General Mountbatten's letter of 26 October 1947 to the ruler Hari Singh while accepting his offer of accession to India. This was repeated in several letters by Nehru to the Government of Pakistan. They were known to Mookerjee and were published in a White Paper in 1948.

2. India's reference of the matter to the U.N. Security Council on 1 January 1948 (S/628). The rest followed since the complaint was made under Article 35 in Chapter VI of the U.N. Charter, which deals with 'Pacific Settlement of Disputes' and not under Chapter VII which deals with 'acts of aggression'.

3. In his statement to the Security Council on 6 February 1948, N. Gopalaswamy Ayyangar said that Kashmir 'will be free, by means of a plebiscite, either to ratify her accession to India or to change her mind and accede to Pakistan or remain independent'.

4. On 1 January 1949 India proposed and Pakistan accepted a ceasefire in the state leaving a big chunk of territory in Pakistan.

5. India accepted the two Resolutions on plebiscite proposed by the U.N.

[13] *SWJN*, vol. 23, pp. 296-7.

Commission for India and Pakistan on 13 August 1948 and 6 January 1949. The UNCIP was established by the Security Council.

6. On 27 July 1949 both States drew up a ceasefire line in the state (S/AC. 12/ TC.4). It was partitioned *de facto*.

7. There followed well-publicised mediatory efforts by the president of the Security Council General A.G. McNaughton of Canada.

8. The Government of India was publicly pledged to holding a plebiscite in Kashmir under U.N. auspices till Mookerjee's resignation in 1950. Repeated pledges were made. Mookerjee did not resign. He took a U-turn in 1951 after his resignation; this time to demand withdrawal of the Kashmir dispute from the U.N. and steps forcibly to recover from Pakistan the areas it administers.

9. Article 370 records a compact between the State of Jammu & Kashmir and the Union of India. It was negotiated for five long months from May to October 1949 by Nehru, Vallabhbhai Patel, Sheikh Abdullah and Mirza Afzal Beg. Mookerjee was well aware of these long drawn talks. Article 370 was sponsored in the Constituent Assembly by the Government of India and was adopted on 17 October 1949. Mookerjee was a party to this as he was, indeed, to the government's decisions from August 1947 to April 1950. What a violent somersault did Mookerjee perform.

He went back on all this in 1951 when he embarked on his adventurist course to garner support for the Jana Sangh. 'Your blind guides, which strain at a grant, and swallow a camel' (Saint Mathew, 23:24).

Mookerjee died a political failure, but the damage he inflicted on the nation has had lasting consequences. The RSS sponsored agitation culminated eventually in a Resolution adopted by its Akhil Bharatiya Karyakari Mandal at Kurukshetra on 29 June 2002 when plebiscite was as dead as dodo. It demanded a 'separate statehood for the Jammu region', a Union Territory status for Ladakh, and Kashmir's 'full integration with Bharat'.[14]

[14] *Reorganisation of Jammu & Kashmir State: Problem and the Solution*, Delhi: Indraprastha Vishwa Samvad Kendra.

13. The RSS After Mookerjee

There was no danger of the Jana Sangh withering away after Mookerjee's death. The RSS was there to hold it together. Myron Weiner noticed after his extensive interviews, 'There was a feeling on the part of RSS leaders and rank and file that they needed a party of their own which would be a tightly knit organisation of RSS members.'

There was little scope for non-RSS members. They lacked the devotion and discipline of RSS members. 'They believed that in the final analysis Jana Sangh depended upon the work and contribution of its RSS members. *It was this lack of reliance upon non-RSS members and leaders which enabled the party to survive* and grow even after the death of Syama Prasad Mookerjee in 1953.'[1]

Between the RSS on the one side and the Congress on the other, lay a fundamental, unbridgeable divide; a chasm which the Janata Party discovered in 1978-79 and persists even now in 2018, with yet greater virulence. It cannot be bridged. Gandhi, Nehru and Patel held that the Congress had to acquiesce in the partition of India because the people of some of its territories – Sindh, West Punjab, Balochistan, the North-West Frontier Province and East Bengal – had registered their resolve, in the general elections of 1945-46, to secede from India and form a separate State, Pakistan. It was a *territorial* split. There was no adult suffrage then. The franchise was a restricted one.

In 1947, under Nehru's far-sighted leadership, India won its case at the United Nations that it was, in international law, a successor State to the erstwhile United India. The Union of India retained its membership of the United Nations. Pakistan had to apply anew for it. From this flowed a clear ideological consequence. The India of 1947 was the secular democratic polity which the founders of the Indian National Congress had envisioned.

The RSS had as sharp an alternative vision which its ideological ancestors had enunciated in the 19th century. Its founders and leaders amplified it ever since its formulation in 1925. Much before the partition of India. Savarkar propounded the two-nation theory in 1924; Jinnah did so in 1939. The RSS wanted a Hindu Rashtra to sustain Hindu Raj. Partition of India gave it an opportunity.

On 21 January 1950 at Nagpur the RSS Kendriya Karyakari Mandal categorically declared 'That the theory that the partition of the motherland was on a territorial basis is untrue and fraught with disastrous consequences and needs to be abandoned'.[2]

1 Weiner, *Party Politics in India*, pp. 197-8.

2 *RSS Resolves: 1950-2007: Resolutions passed by ABPS and ABKM of the RSS from 1950-2007,*

The real target was secularism. While urging that the concept be abandoned, the RSS's resolution did not spell out precisely what its alternative was. It did not have to. The writings of Golwalkar and Savarkar were clear enough. The RSS did not conceal its reservations on the national flag or the Constitution.

It had adopted a flag as its own which was conferred formal recognition in Article 3 of its revised constitution in 1949. The language reflects its reservations on the national flag. 'While recognising the duty of every citizen to be loyal to and to respect the State, i.e. not national flag, the Sangh has its flag, the 'Bhagwa Dhwaj' – the age-old symbol of Hindu Culture.' The emphasis is on the latter, as the language shows. It is to the RSS's flag that its members bow in obeisance; to it they donate offerings. As we shall see later this has great advantage in paying the tax on its income. That the State has yielded to this reveals a lot.

Golwalkar's attitude did not change one bit. He had said on 14 July 1946 in Nagpur: 'It was the saffron flag which in totality represented *Bhartiya* [Indian] culture. It was the embodiment of God. We firmly believe that in the end the whole nation will bow before this saffron flag.'[3]

When India's Constituent Assembly adopted the tricolour as the National Flag, the *Organiser*, in its issue dated 14 August 1947, denigrated the choice in the following words:

> The people who have come to power by the kick of fate may give in our hands the Tricolour but it will never be respected and owned by Hindus. The word three is in itself an evil, and a flag having three colours will certainly produce a very bad psychological effect and is injurious to a country.

Even after independence the RSS refused to accept the tricolour as the National Flag. Golwalkar wrote in the book *Bunch of Thoughts*:

> Our leaders have set up a new flag for our country. Why did they do so? It is just a case of drifting and imitating. . . . Ours is an ancient and great nation with a glorious past. Then, had we no flag of our own? Had we no national emblem at all these thousands of years? Undoubtedly we had. Then why this utter void, this utter vacuum in our minds?[4]

This was published in 1968 after the Constitution had been enacted.

New Delhi: Suruchi Prakashan, p. 2.

3 M.S. Golwalkar, *Shri Guruji Samagr Darshan* [Collected works of Golwalkar in Hindi], vol. I, Nagpur: Bhartiya Vichar Sadhna, p. 98.

4 Golwalkar, *Bunch of Thoughts*, pp. 237-8; vide Shamsul Islam, *RSS Primer*, Pharos, 2014, pp. 11-2.

Whatever restraint Syama Prasad Mookerjee's presence imposed on the Jana Sangh vanished after his death. But he left behind an administrative legacy of unacceptably mild ideological commitment; Mauli Chandra Sharma, a non-RSS man, was made one of the two general secretaries. The Jana Sangh's General Council met at Allahabad in August 1953 and asked Sharma to serve as an interim president until a new president was elected at the next annual session in Mumbai. It was held in January 1954.

However, the real executive authority was vested in an RSS faithful Deen Dayal Upadhyaya. A conflict between him and Sharma could not long be averted. He enjoyed the loyalty of the RSS cadres and had a firm grip on the levers of power in the party organisation. Upadhyaya emerged as the prime ideologue of the parivar. Sharma rejected Upadhyaya's list of names for the working committee and selected his own nominees. He was entitled to do so under the party constitution. Sharma tried to buy time by a compromise. Among the RSS men he accepted in his 29-member executive were men who emerged as top leaders: Deen Dayal Upadhyaya, Atal Bihari Vajpayee, Balraj Madhok, Nana Deshmukh, Bhairon Singh Shekhawat, Sunder Singh Bhandari and Jagannath Rao Joshi.

If Sharma thought that while he had lost in Mumbai in January 1954 he would be retrieved at the All India General Council meeting at Indore in August 1954, he was sadly mistaken. His assertiveness irked the RSS. He questioned the role of the organising secretary Upadhyaya; that is, the RSS itself. He was obliged to resign in November 1954, bitterly complaining of the RSS's interference. Bapusaheb Soni was made interim president until the next session at Jodhpur in December 1954. Prem Nath Dogra, the RSS's chief at Jammu and of its front, the Praja Parishad, was appointed president of the Jana Sangh.

Jaffrelot's conclusion is fair:

> The main conclusion to be drawn from this episode is that, although the RSS leaders were willing to become involved in the work of setting up a political party because they were persuaded to agree with certain of their own 'activists' that party politics could not be ignored, they were not prepared to allow the Jana Sangh to be taken over by politicians who would ignore their organisation and make policy compromises in order to attract support rapidly. In order to prevent such an outcome, they virtually converted the Jana Sangh into a front organisation and thus kept it within the framework of the other groups affiliated to the RSS. . . .
>
> From 1954 onwards, leaders of the Jana Sangh with an RSS background reshaped the political programme and organisation of the party in conformity with those of the mother organisation. The main architect of this transformation was D. Upadhyaya, who was to remain the party's General Secretary till 1967

> with the full support of Golwalkar. In the eyes of his peers and of those in charge in Nagpur, he represented the '*ideal swayamsevak*'.[5]

His thesis *Integral Humanism* (1965) was lauded to the skies. The RSS was in search of an 'intellectual' who would appeal to the rising educated class. It plumped for this essay.

Pralay Kanungo explains why he appealed to the RSS and won its superiors' approval. He did not seek to replace any of its holy books – Savarkar's *Hindutva* or Golwalkar's *We or Our Nationhood Defined. Bunch of Thoughts* came later in 1968. Upadhyaya simply amplified what Golwalkar wrote.

> Deendayal Upadhyaya supplements Golwalkar's cultural nationalism with his theory of integral humanism (*Ekatma Manavavad*). This new theory adds some sophistication to the RSS concept of *Hindu Rashtra* and enriches its ideological underpinnings. Upadhyaya avoids the crude, aggressive, and offensive formulations of Golwalkar's *We or Our Nationhood Defined* and offers a refined version of nation and culture.
>
> Though essentially he shares Golwalkar's formulations, Deendayal adds some innovative dimensions to it. Despite Golwalkar's talk of India's spiritual mission in the world, he very rarely went beyond the confines of nation. Upadhyaya, on the contrary, talked of integration of the nation with the rest of humanity, universe and the Almighty (*Parameshi*). But this integration is more emotional and philosophical rather than political. . . .
>
> He concludes that the soul of Bharat could be properly understood only from a cultural point of view. To him the nation is not a political but a cultural concept. Elaborating further, he writes, *the basis of our nationalism is not simply Bharat but Bharat Mata; Bharat would remain just a piece of land if the word Mata is taken away*. The first characteristic of a Bharatiya culture is that it looks upon life as an integrated whole. However, to him there can be only one culture in India. The slogans of many cultures can break this country into pieces and destroy it. This very much reflects Golwalkar's ideas.[6]

Intellectuals there were in the Congress, the CPI and the Socialist Party. The Jana Sangh could now boast it had acquired one. The RSS maintained its control of the Jana Sangh through its cadres and through the general secretary. Upadhyaya held this post from 1954 to 1967, wielding executive power in the party.

In 1967 the Congress suffered a rout in the Assembly election in the north of the country from Punjab to West Bengal. The opposition parties formed United Front coalitions called the Samyukta Vidhayak Dal. The Jana Sangh participated

[5] Jaffrelot, *The Hindu Nationalist Movement and Indian Politics*, p. 123.

[6] Kanungo, *RSS's Tryst with Politics*, pp. 118-9.

the coalitions in Bihar, Haryana, Uttar Pradesh, Punjab, and Madhya Pradesh. It accepted the Akali Dal as a major force in Punjab; elsewhere the Sangh accepted the Communist Party of India as a coalition partner. There was sharp criticism over this with Madhok pitted against Vajpayee. The latter won. The RSS sought acceptance and respectability.

In his presidential address to the party in 1967 Upadhyaya advocated precisely this line:

> We should also be cautious about people who see in every popular agitation the hidden hand of communism and [who] suggest that agitation must be crushed. In the changing situation at present, public agitations are natural and even essential. In fact, they are the medium of expression of social awakening. It is of course necessary that these agitations should be made instruments of constructive revolution and not allowed to become violent and adventurist. Therefore, we must actively participate in popular movements and try to guide them.[7]

Upadhyaya evidently aspired to replicate this experiment at the Centre.

Tragedy struck the party with almost paralytic force. On 11 February 1968 Upadhyaya's dead body was found lying 748 feet from the end of the Mughalsarai railway station at which the train had halted. He had boarded the Sealdah Express in the evening on 10 February for Lucknow. He was clutching a five-rupee note in his hand. The last time anyone saw him alive was at Jaunpur, shortly after midnight. One M.P. Singh, who travelled in the adjoining cabin of the same coach, saw someone enter Upadhyaya's cabin at Mughalsarai and walk off with his file and bedding. This man he identified in Court as Bharat Lal. Together with Ram Awadh, Bharat Lal was charged with murder and theft. Both were acquitted of the capital charge. Bharat Lal alone was convicted of the theft of the belongings of the deceased. He appealed to the Allahabad High Court. The Sessions Judge remarked in his judgment that 'the offence of murder not having been proved against the accused, the problem of truth about the murder still remains'. The Government of India appointed Justice Y.V. Chandrachud of Bombay High Court as the Commission of Inquiry.

That Upadhyaya was murdered was not contested by anybody. The CBI said that the murder was committed by common thieves for small gain, and was conceived and executed on the spur of the moment. The Jana Sangh put the CBI on the mat, as it were, by making a frontal attack on it. But little did it realise that the specific accusation it made and the mass of evidence it adduced put the credibility of the party itself on trial.

[7] Andersen and Damle, *The Brotherhood in Saffron*, p. 124.

The Jana Sangh's treasurer, Nana Deshmukh, was chairman of a committee appointed by the Sangh's president to collect data relating to the murder. He filed his statement of the case and figured as one of the 51 witnesses examined by the Jana Sangh before the Commission.

Justice Chandrachud's Report analysed in meticulous detail the evidence and the arguments advanced. He held: 'That Shri Upadhyaya was pushed out of the running train when he was standing near the door of the I Class compartment of the F.C.T. bogie; that he dashed against the tractions pole and died an instantaneous death; and the injuries on his person were caused in a single transaction and they were such as could not have been caused inside the compartment.' He also held that the murder 'was accompanied by an immediate theft, which shows that the two are part and parcel of the same transaction'.

Finally, the Judge observed: 'I can say with a certain amount of confidence that nothing that has come before me can support the accusation that there was any politics in Shri Upadhyaya's murder. Undoubtedly, he had political rivals but his death is the rash and extempore handiwork of mere thieves. Neither the Communists nor the 'communalists' (Muslims, no doubt) accused by the Jana Sangh, nor Dr. A.J. Faridi of the Muslim Majlis, are connected directly or indirectly, with the murder,' as alleged by the Jana Sangh.

Its case was that certain Muslim organisations had held Upadhyaya responsible for the communal riots at Meerut. It was openly declared that Jana Sangh leaders had to be eliminated. Some communists, it said, were willing to lend a helping hand to the communalists. Ever since the Kozhikode session, which was held in December 1967, Upadhyaya was being shadowed by suspicious characters. Ultimately, the communists and communalists joined hands, and took the help of Major Surendra Mohan Sharma for perpetrating the murder of Upadhyaya. Major Sharma was the son-in-law of V.N. Sharma, who in turn was said to be closely connected with Dr. Faridi, the president of 'Majlis Mushawarat'.

Major Sharma travelled in the Ist Class compartment of the FCT bogie from Lucknow so that he could wait for an opportune moment to execute the conspiracy. At the other end, namely, at Mughalsarai, the communists had taken the necessary steps to further the object of the conspiracy. Accordingly, Upadhyaya was murdered in the running train after it had left Zafarabad at 12.41 a.m. He must have been struck on the right side of his head while entering the 'B' cabin with the right side towards the corridor. Thereafter he must have been thrown on the berth, with someone sitting on his chest and someone on his legs. The dead body was subsequently placed near the traction pole to simulate an accident.

Clearly, central to this thesis are the roles of Major Sharma and Dr. Faridi, and the links between them. Major S.M. Sharma was married just three weeks before the murder. He left Lucknow by the same train as Upadhyaya. The Major gave irrefutable evidence that he travelled as far as Gamoh and reached his regiment late on 11 February.

Dr. A.J. Faridi, a heart specialist practising at Lucknow, was the founder-president of the Muslim Majlis. The Jana Sangh examined three witnesses in support of its case that not only communists but Muslims like Dr. Faridi had conspired to murder Upadhyaya. The evidence of the first witness did not even connect Dr. Faridi by name with the public meeting of which he deposed. The second did, but his version of Dr. Faridi's speech was not borne out by the very journal in which he said it was reported. The Jana Sangh's counsel conceded as much.

The last witness came to depose to cordial relations between V.N. Sharma, the Major's father-in-law, and Dr. Faridi. Unfortunately for him, the Judge had before him a certified copy of a criminal complaint filed by Sharma against Dr. Faridi, alleging trespass in respect of a part of the premises let out by Dr. Faridi to 'Cipla' company of which Sharma was the branch manager. Another record showed the company to be in arrears of rent from November 1966 to January 1970.

The Judge said: 'In my opinion, the charge against Dr. Faridi that he is connected with the murder of Upadhyaya is baseless. It is significant that in the report of the Committee appointed by Shri Vajpayee, of which Shri Nanaji Deshmukh was the Chairman, there is no reference to Dr. Faridi whatsoever.'

The Jana Sangh's case was that the murder was committed in the compartment; the CBI's, that it was done by pushing Upadhyaya out of the moving train. The Commission's observations on some of the circumstantial factors are noteworthy.

> I am unable to agree that the bloodstains in the compartment and the toilet, which should have been found if the murder was committed in the compartment, might have got wiped out or washed in the normal process when the bogie was cleaned. It is clear from the evidence of S.R. Kandu, the train examiner at Howrah, that it was not washed before it was sealed. . . . It is significant that the clothes on the person of Shri Upadhyaya and the article in the bedding showed no signs of struggle. There was no tear on any part of the clothing. There was no injury on the face and indeed there was no defensive injury on any part of Shri Upadhyaya's person.

The nature of the injuries also went against the Sangh's theory. It produced two witnesses travelling in the adjoining IIIrd Class compartment who said they heard a shriek and a thud, something which M.P. Singh, Upadhyaya's next-door neighbour in the same coach, did not. Rejections abound in the Report.

Ramacharya Pandya, a party worker, said he heard of the death on 11 February in the morning and passed on the information, among others, to Nana Deshmukh, who asked him to proceed to Mughalsarai and collect information regarding the death. Pandya did so and made jottings in his diary. *The Judge found the diary to be a got-up document.* Deshmukh gave Upadhyaya's itinerary to D.I.G. Lobo on 2 March. The diary noted it in advance on 17 February. What was claimed to be a personal diary of a poet-politician turned out to be a got-up investigation diary with large blanks.

The Judge remarked: 'If there was no political event worth noting in the diary during those days, his Muse at least could not have so cruelly deserted him. . . . I must express my disapproval that anyone should have been a party to the fabrication of a document for the purpose of producing it as evidence.'

Deshmukh himself did not escape unscathed.

> I cannot accept Shri Nanaji Deshmukh's statement that he had told Ramacharya on the 11th morning on phone that he should collect the relevant information. Nanaji was then in Bombay and knew nothing about the murder. In fact, there is a good basis for doubting that Ramacharya at all telephoned Nanaji from Lucknow on the 11th morning. Om Prakash Chatwal of the Lucknow Telephone Exchange, who was examined before me by the CBI, has stated that no trunk call was made from telephone number 23509 (Lucknow) to Bombay on the 11th February, 1968. 23509 is the telephone number of the Jana Sangh Karyalaya, Lucknow, where Ramacharya says he received the information about Shri Upadhyaya's death.

Nana Deshmukh had produced a false document before Justice Chandrachud and also testified falsely on oath.

Barely was the Report published when *Organiser* came out with the indictment: 'Chandrachud Follows in Shah Nawaz's Footsteps'. This sordid episode reflects the Sangh Parivar's McCarthyite technique of slander. Involved in it was a leading figure, Nana Deshmukh, an RSS favourite. Slandered falsely was a man of high repute, Dr. A.J. Faridi.

Another upheaval which had been in the making for sometime erupted five years later with the expulsion of Balraj Madhok in 1973. As one of the founders of the Jana Sangh, he had begun to take himself very seriously slighting all others. Elected president in March 1966, he lost no time in attempting to acquire control of the party machine. Upadhyaya's role as guide and spokesman was curtailed. By the time Upadhyaya replaced him in December 1967 he had done a lot to ruffle feathers all round. Madhok opposed joining coalitions which had communists among its members. He had deep sympathy with the Swatantra Party and had close relations with its leader M.R. Masani. He began publicly to question the party's stand on various issues; for example, nationalisation of banks. The crux of the matter was that he was never as close to the RSS as Upadhyaya and Advani were. It fell to Advani's lot to administer the *coup de grace* when he succeeded Vajpayee as president in 1973. Madhok was asking for trouble by demanding that the party's internal workings be made more democratic by the abolition of the *Sangathan mantris* (organisation secretaries).[8]

An acrimonious exchange of letters followed in which Advani accused Madhok, not without cause, of having an 'inflated ego'. This is the second principle of the RSS's policy, besides its control over the BJP. No leader should foster a personality cult. Beyond a point, the offender would be shown the door. As early as on 10 June 1972 Madhok ventilated his grievances in public. The Jana Sangh was 'a Hindu party'. Vajpayee had 'spoiled' its image by his 'leftist' postures. He criticised the RSS dominance.[9]

Ironically, in 2005, it was Advani's turn to criticise the RSS interference in the internal workings of the BJP. Mauli Chandra Sharma's experience in 1954, Madhok's in 1973 and Advani's in 2005 have a common link – the RSS's control over the party it had set up.

In a letter to Advani on 7 March 1973 Madhok asserted,

> The organising secretaries who happen to be the real power in the Jana Sangh, having been conversant only with the working system of the RSS want to run Jana Sangh on the same lines. They have nothing but contempt for democratic forms, norms, and conventions. Dissent of any kind is anathema to them. They want to suppress all dissidents in the name of discipline. They are interested more in control than in growth of the party. That is the real problem and dilemma of Jana Sangh which will have to be resolved one day. The sooner it is resolved the better it would be for the RSS, the Jana Sangh and the country.[10]

A decade later Madhok claimed that he had been approached to serve as president in mid-1965 but had declined. He revealed:

> I explained that the organising secretaries had become accustomed to dummy Presidents and I could not be a dummy. This would lead to friction and tension. The suggestion was repeated a few months later with the plea that party needed a President during the election year who could write and speak in both Hindi and English so that the party could make a show in South India as well. I was, therefore, required to accept the responsibility as a matter of duty. I agreed, but made it clear that I would have to be given a free hand if I was to show results in the general elections which were due in February 1967.[11]

8 Jaffrelot, *The Hindu Nationalist Movement and Indian Politics*, p. 236.
9 *The Statesman*, 11 June 1972.
10 B.D. Graham, *Hindu Nationalism and Indian Politics*, p. 77.
11 Ibid., p. 89.

Madhok's tendency to air differences in public did not endear him to his colleagues. He lacked the collegial spirit.

Advani could not have expelled Madhok without the prior approval of Golwalkar. Hence his refusal to submit the case to Golwalkar, as Madhok had suggested. He took his case to the party cadre and eventually to the public.

> He wrote that the Jana Sangh had developed into an RSS front organisation and, while not personally opposed to the RSS, he was against its 'dominating' influence in the party. He wrote that the Jana Sangh was not able to mobilise additional support because of RSS influence. He identified Vajpayee as the leader of the forces which were subverting the party's traditional ideological orientation.[12]

Madhok was being opportunistic. He knew the terms of the Golwalkar-Mookerjee pact as also the fact that the majority of the Jana Sangh's cadre came from the RSS; as high as 90 per cent of them.[13] Their loyalties, personal and ideological, to the RSS were strong.

In a study of the RSS the upheavals in its political front are relevant in so far as they reveal the RSS's exertions. These were supplemented by a systematic propaganda barrage by both; the RSS's *Organiser* leading the chorus with the same refrain. Unity in diversity is fine; but 'all the creeds that form the commonwealth of the Bharatiya Rashtra have their share in the stream of Bharatiya Culture, which has flowed down from the Vedas, in the contribution made by different peoples, creeds and cultures that came in touch with it in the course of history, in such a way as to make them indistinguishable part and parcel of the main current'.[14]

The grievance against Muslims and Christians was that they did not embrace 'Bharatiya Culture which has flowed down from the Vedas'. That this cry is still heard in 2018, nearly seventy years later, with greater force with State support should alert the country to the menace it faces. Nothing has changed in that group's thinking since 1925.

On 7 January 1957 *Organiser* published the text of a revealing resolution of the Jana Sangh on 'Indian Culture'. It reads:

> The Bharatiya Jana Sangh resolves that for the development of nationalism one culture should be imbibed in all the nationals of the country. For the implementation of this task the society and the Government should take the following steps: 1. Education should be based on national culture. 2. The birth-

12 Andersen and Damle, *The Brotherhood in Saffron*, p. 187, citing *The Indian Express*, 30 March 1973.

13 Ibid., p. 189.

14 *Organiser*, 24 March 1952.

days of national heroes and similar other occasions be celebrated as national days. 3. The major festivals of Bharat be solemnised and celebrated as national festivals. 4. Efforts be made on the part of the Government and the society so that Indian society may develop on the basis of national traditions. 5. The study of Sanskrit be revived as an essential ingredient of scholarship. 6. That Indian History be re-written so that it may be the History of the Indian People and not that of their oppressors and invaders. 7. (a) The Jana Sangh exhorts the Hindu Samaj to remove the inherent social evils and weaknesses especially the inequality arising out of caste-difference. (b) It is the duty of the Hindu society to Indianise those sections of India's national being which were shaken out of their national moorings and made to look outside the country for inspiration. Hindu society should assimilate them completely. Only in this way communalism can be rooted out and the unity and solidarity of the nation established.

This is the very agenda which Narendra Modi is following at the Centre and in the states, through the BJP chief ministers. Fundamentally the BJP, like its predecessor the Jana Sangh and its mentor, the RSS, rejects the very concept of a minority; despite its recognition in the Constitution of India in Articles 26, 29 and 30 and international conventions galore.

This is what Vajpayee said in 1956:

> The concept of majority-minority is itself incorrect. Those who think in these terms are ignorant of the real form of Bharatiya Nationalism, and its evolution. All foreigners who came to Bharat, like the Shakas and the Huns, were so completely merged in the current of Bharatiya life that now they are unrecognisable as a separate entity. As long as we retain this wonderful capacity of assimilation our nation progressed and will continue to progress. . . . We would welcome a Muslim or a Christian who wants to leave a religion forced upon his fore-fathers, and return to the ancestral fold. But anyone genuinely believing in Islam or Christianity as the way of salvation here and hereafter, will be given full freedom of conscience. . . .
>
> Difference in religion does not mean difference in culture. Culture belongs to the land and the culture that has sprung from the land of Bharat is one and indivisible. It has been a meeting place for different and differing sects and theologies since Vedic times. The talk of a separate or composite culture is not only illogical but dangerous, for it undermines national solidarity and fosters fissiparous tendencies.

In 1979, as members of the Janata Party, Vajpayee and Advani accepted the concept of India's 'composite culture'; albeit only to discard it shortly thereafter.

The post-Mookerjee Jana Sangh was shaped by Golwalkar and able lieutenants like Vajpayee, Advani, and Nana Deshmukh. Upadhyaya died an untimely death in 1968 but left his mark as an ideologue respected by those leaders. Madhok and Nana Deshmukh were more extremist than the rest. The irascible Madhok was always a difficult colleague. Deshmukh was an organisation man; a go-getter with access to businessmen, industrialists and a newspaper baron. By the mid-eighties he began to feel stifled by the others, left active politics and retired to do 'social work' at Gonda.

Those two decades, from 1953 to 1973 saw a lot – Jawaharlal Nehru's death in May 1964, his successor Lal Bahadur Shastri's death at Tashkent in January 1966, after the war which Pakistan launched in September 1965, the founding of the Vishwa Hindu Parishad and the Bangladesh War in December 1971. It saw Indira Gandhi's rise to total power by 1972. Golwalkar was never averse to a pact with her or her party the Indian National Congress, then, in 1976, or in 1980. The Jana Sangh was his tool.

The Jana Sangh's launching of a movement for Indianisation was a significant event. Little recalled now, this was a trailer for the BJP's Hindutva movement in 1990. The other significant event was the eruption of the first major political riot in Jabalpur in February 1951. A leading journalist, Inder Malhotra, wrote in 1969: 'The strength and influence of the avowedly communal and objectionably militant Hindu parties have grown alarmingly. This cannot be utterly unconnected with the distressing rise in the number of communal incidents and riots. It would, of course, be unfair to believe or even allege that the entire or even the bulk of the majority community is under the influence of communalists. . . .'[15]

On New Year's Day 1970, *The Indian Express* carried a detailed report on the RSS which noted that the growth of the RSS has coincided with the recent wave of communal riots in the country.

That the riots spread at an alarming pace after a period of quiet after the partition destroys a good many hypotheses. A Union Home Ministry review recorded:

> From 1954 to 1960 there was a clear and consistent *downward trend*, 1960 being a remarkably good year with only 26 communal incidents in the whole country. This trend was sharply reversed in 1961. The increase was, however, largely in Bihar, Madhya Pradesh, Uttar Pradesh, and West Bengal. There was a substantial fall during the next two years indicating stabilisation of the situation. 1964 was an abnormal year when largely as a repercussion of serious communal riots in East Pakistan there was large scale communal violence in West Bengal, Bihar, and Orissa. There was no marked rise in communal

[15] *The Statesman*, 6 October 1969.

> incidents in other parts of the country. Because of the two conflicts with Pakistan, there was serious apprehension of communal trouble in 1965, but most parts of the country remained on the whole peaceful; it was only in Maharashtra and particularly in and around Poona that there was a very large number of incidents mostly involving loss of property; the incidents followed a case of sacrilege and had no connection with the Indo-Pak conflict. In 1966 the number of incidents fell, but it was still relatively high and therefore a matter of concern.
>
> The special feature of incidents in 1966 was that Andhra Pradesh and Maharashtra [which] had earlier been relatively free from communal trouble (except the Poona incidents of 1965), indicated persistent tension. The deterioration in communal relations noticed in 1966 continued in 1967, the most serious outbreak of violence being in Ranchi where 155 lives were lost in week-long disturbances. There was a marked rise in incidents in Andhra Pradesh, Bihar, and Uttar Pradesh as compared to 1966. A disturbing development of 1967 was extension of communal tension to Jammu & Kashmir.[16] . . .

Smith recorded in his book *India as a Secular State* that 'the Muslims are generally the relative losers in terms of lives lost and property destroyed. The serious communal riots in Jabalpur and other cities and towns of Madhya Pradesh in February 1961 resulted in the loss of fifty-five lives, mostly Muslims'.[17] Jabalpur set a trend which was not reversed. In this, the RSS played a major role.

The RSS went on to stoke many other fires thereafter. The relatively calm atmosphere of the Nehru era was shattered. With the deaths of the founder Mookerjee and the ideologue Upadhyaya, it fell to the other leaders to spell out the Jana Sangh's policy and programme. Publication of Golwalkar's *Bunch of Thoughts* helped them to keep in line.

A document adopted in January 1965 contains a comprehensive enunciation of the Jana Sangh's credo ('Bharatiya Jana Sangh: Principles and Policy'; adopted by the Bharatiya Pratinidhi Sabha on 25-26 January 1965). Expositions of the concept of 'cultural nationalism' in the BJP's recent manifestoes and other documents are a rehash of what this document said.

> With this country as its home, the Indian people have developed and lived a culture which is one and the same from the Himalayas to the seas. For a vast land like ours it was but natural that somewhat different patterns of life should have grown in different areas and sections. But all of them stand integrally

[16] Mimeographed copy, Union Home Ministry, June 1968, prepared for the National Integration Council.

[17] Smith, *India as a Secular State*, p. 454.

> united in Bharatiya *Samskriti* which has never been tied to the strings of any particular dogma or creed. All the creeds that form the commonwealth of Bharatiya Rashtra have their share in the stream of Bharatiya culture which has flown down since the Vedas in unbroken continuity, absorbing and assimilating contributions made by different peoples, creeds and cultures that came in contact with it in the course of history, in such a way as to make them indistinguishable part and parcel of the main current. The Bharatiya culture is thus, like Bharatvarsh, one and indivisible. Any talk of composite culture, therefore, is not only untrue but also dangerous, for it tends to weaken national unity and encourage fissiparous tendencies.
>
> India is an ancient nation. The advent of freedom has meant only unfolding of a new chapter in its history. It is not the birth of any new nation. Naturally the basis of Indian nationalism is loyalty to the whole of Bharat and its eternal and distinctive culture. . . .
>
> So long as Pakistan subsists as a separate Islamic state, hostile to India, the position of Indian Muslims will remain delicate. . . . Christian and other missionaries in India will have to be freed from foreign influence and control. They should not be allowed to act as agents of foreign powers. Only a unitary form of government can effectively contribute to the invigoration of one nationhood based on One Country, One People and One Culture. The concept of a federal state hampers national integration.[18]

The Sangh parivar is a late and reluctant, perhaps insincere, convert to federalism.

Golwalkar did not spare Buddhists and Jains:

> So far as Jainism and Buddhism are concerned, they have never made any contribution to social and political thought as such; we have not inherited any arthashastras (knowledge of economics and politics) or dharmashastras (social law) from them. All we have from them are the various miksha-shastras pertaining to the supreme salvation of the individual soul.[19]

Nazi Germany inspired the RSS. Golwalkar wrote with unconcealed admiration in *We or Our Nationhood Defined*: 'The national pride of the German is the talk of the whole world. The Germans drove out of their country the Jews only in order to maintain their racial and cultural purity. Germany has also shown that it is very difficult for fundamentally different races to (live) together.'

This outlook shaped its views on foreign policy. The logical corollary of *ghar*

18 *Bharatiya Jana Sangh: Principles and Policy*, Delhi: Bharatiya Jana Sangh, Arjun Press, 1965, pp. 16-8.

19 *Organiser*, 10 June 1963.

wapsi was recovery of the lands which once belonged to Bharat. The RSS advocated a Hindu foreign policy. *Organiser* of 2 July 1967, explained:

> For purposes of an active diplomacy the world map should be recast to indicate an order of priorities in relation to areas of influence. Since Hindu culture extended to areas beyond our present political frontiers, we should strive towards a closer and a more abiding understanding with Asian countries, especially in Southeast Asia and the Far East. Our diplomacy may succeed in some African countries too on the same ground. Nepal being the only Hindu state, it can be India's best friend.

It favoured an alliance with the United States.

The RSS supported the aggressive Zionist militarism of Israel against the Arabs and showed complete unconcern for the cause of the dispossessed Palestinians. It tried to bolster this stand by discovering affinities between Zionism and Vedic culture. Soon after the Six-day War, the *Organiser* of 18 June 1967 said: 'In the unexpected success of Israeli arms I see a faint spark of what Vedic culture can do to revive and restore us to our rightful place in the world. The origins of Judaism hark back to the essential truths of the Vedas and their code of laws and social customs is based largely on the tenets of Hindu dharmashastras.'

In a speech to an RSS camp near Delhi on 8-10 November 1968 Golwalkar shed all restraint.

> The society that has lived on this land since thousands of years as sons of the soil is the Hindu society. This is an historical fact, and a matter of actual experience also. In whose heart indeed do we find a feeling of reverence, respect and affection for the motherland? Whose heart quivers with anguish when any injury is inflicted on the motherland? If the answer to this question were to be boldly given, it is plain – the Hindu's. It is the Hindu society which cherishes in its bosom a feeling of deep filial devotion to this land. It is this society which regards every particle of this motherland as sacred, *which regards it its religion to worship everything associated with this soil.* The rivers and lakes of this country are for it places of holy pilgrimage. The peaks of mountains are the abodes of Divinity itself. I do not think any other nation in the world cherishes so intense and sublime a feeling in respect of its country as does the Hindu society, which sees God and Godliness in every particle of this soil.

His views on the minorities, expressed in 1968, still govern the RSS's outlook on them fifty years later in 2018.

> Firstly, there are the followers of the Christian faith. In the Naga Hills, and in

> the hill regions of Assam they have already taken to the path of open revolt, while in the Jharkhand and other regions they are preparing for one. Next, there are the followers of the Islamic faith, to whose aggression this country has been subjected to for the last one thousand years. Although most of the Muslims in the country today belong originally to the Hindu society and their forefathers embraced Islam simply because of force, temptation, self-interest or deceit. There has not been much change in that regard. . . .
>
> The one fact that emerges clearly from all this is that the Hindu Samaj has been living on this land as its devoted son, and that it has a common *dharma* and *sanskriti*, a common history, a community of mutual interests, a common sharing of joys and sorrows, a common appraisal of enemies and friends and a common aspiration for the future. Then, there is its glorious lineage of noble ancestors, the great men and seers who have protected and enriched the nation. This Hindu society cherishes a natural desire to make the nation strong, prosperous and great in all respects, to attain such cultural heights that each individual member of it becomes a model for all mankind in character and righteous conduct. Unlike other nations, this society would like to use its national strength not for the destruction of other people but for the service of the world because that in fact has been the mandate of our forefathers. . . . It is the Hindu society which constitutes the nation in this country. It thus stands proved by history, science and experience, that this is the Hindu Rashtra.
>
> Hindu Rashtra is not a doctrine or dogma. It is the truth, and should be acknowledged as such.[20]

This forms the core of the view that Bharat is Jagadguru – teacher of the world. This claim reveals a lot; but it has escaped close study.

The RSS was out to erase the word 'minority' from India's political lexicon. In March 1969 it published a pamphlet entitled 'Hindu Rashtra and Minorities'. The minorities are free to worship as they wish; but they must embrace Bharatiya culture, a euphemism for the Hindu faith.

> If, however, the Muslims and Christians feel that they are habituated to pray God in the manner of Islam or Christianity for a long time, and that those ways of worship strike a sympathetic chord in their hearts, then certainly they are welcome to continue in those paths. But for the rest, they must be one with the national current.
>
> The answer to the so-called problem of 'religious minorities' can be found only in this historically correct, rational and positive approach of Hindu Rashtra. Otherwise, the so-called minorities are bound to become more and

[20] M.S. Golwalkar, *The Answer to All Questions*, New Delhi: Rashtriya Swayamsevak Sangh, 1968.

more hardened in their separate shells of religion and turn into a dreadful source of disruption of our body politic.

So, all that is expected of our Muslim and Christian co-citizens is the shedding of the notions of their being 'religious minorities' as also their foreign mental complexion and merging themselves in the common national stream of this soil.

Mookerjee had rejected the concept of 'territorial nationalism' at the very outset. At its Kanpur session held in December 1952 under his chairmanship a resolution was adopted declaring:

> It is the considered view of the Jana Sangh which is borne out by the history of other countries as well that geographical unity alone cannot sustain nationalism. So long as the people of India shared a common national outlook and owned a common culture, its unity and nationalism were preserved in spite of its being divided into a number of states.

At its Patna session on 30 December 1969, the BJS nailed its colours to the mast with a resolution on Indianisation.

> Bharatiya Jana Sangh being the champion of Indian nationalism and committed to preservation and strengthening of Indian unity feels particularly concerned over this state of affairs, and demands that:–
>
> 1. Every effort should be made to revive and strengthen the sense of nationalism which is the sum total of cohesive forces in any country. This requires a clear understanding of the concept of nationalism and its mainsprings.
>
> 2. Indianisation – by which we mean the subordination of all narrow loyalties like those of religion, caste, region, language or dogma to the overriding loyalty to the nation of all fissiparous elements, especially of those with extra-territorial loyalties or allegiance, overt or covert, to the two-nation theory.

A witch-hunt was to be launched. 'With the lapse of Preventive Detention Act, the need for enacting a law of treason has become an imperative necessity. This law should define treason and treasonable activities and lay down deterrent punishment for all persons and parties indulging in such activities.'[21] More candid was his pamphlet *Indian Nationalism* (New Delhi: Bharati Sahitya Sadan, 1969).

It was clearly modelled on Savarkar's *Hindutva*.

[21] Balraj Madhok, *Indianisation?: What, Why and How*, New Delhi: S. Chand & Co., 1970, pp. 102-3.

> This comprehension of India as the common motherland (Matri Bhoomi) and holy land (Punya Bhoomi) of the Indian people as a whole, irrespective of caste or creed, has grown with the evolution of Indian history. The early Vedic literature is full of hymns in propitiation of the land on which the Rigvedic Aryans lived. There is one full chapter in Rigveda – Prithvi Sukta – in which mother earth as the land of the Aryan people is praised. The word Rashtra in the sense of country or nation is also first used in Rigveda.
>
> Bharatiya Rashtra, the Indian Nation or the Hindu Rashtra thus stand for the same thing and should convey exactly the same sense. Those who feel shy of the term Hindu but take pride in being called Indians either betray pitiable ignorance about their own past or have not yet been able to shed their mental slavery of the West, particularly of the English, which makes them prefer the names given by them to their own original names.

This even flow of the national life was disturbed with the advent of Islam in Bharat.[22] He added:

> The new invaders showed their dragon's teeth, started destruction of the symbols of national life and employed all and every means to subvert the loyalty of the Hindus to their motherland and her age-old cultural ideals. By their conversion to Islam, the leaders of Hindu society began giving serious thought to the new and unprecedented situation.
>
> Thus began the struggle between Indian nationalism, the will to exist and maintain its distinct personality by the Hindu Rashtra and the alien Islam and its denationalised or de-Hinduised Indian allies, which has continued with varying vicissitudes to this day. It was not merely a struggle between two religions or two social orders. It was a struggle between the Indian nation, the national society of India and the aliens who wanted to submerge her.[23]

He was more candid than others, though they thought alike.

The Indian National Congress he held to be a British creation. So was Indian nationalism. 'Anglicised Indians' fell for it. Incredibly, their stand 'was to strengthen the foundations of British rule in India'; a libel on Indian nationalists like Dadabhai Naoroji, Tilak, Gokhale, Pherozeshah Mehta, Gandhi, the Nehrus and Vallabhbhai Patel; indeed all outside the ranks of the RSS and its many outfits.

> Thus began the efforts to weld the people of India into a new nation without reference to any of the basic unities which form the basis of nationalism and which existed in India to an ample degree. Instead, common habitation of

[22] Balraj Madhok, *Indian Nationalism*, Bharati Sahitya Sadan, 1969, p. 42.

[23] Ibid., p. 45.

the people in India, their common economic interests and their common aspiration for self-rule and consequent opposition to British rule, were put forth as the new basis of the Indian nationalism.

There came Madhok's Arya Samaj to retrieve the situation. He cited the Sangh parivar's heroes.

They presented India to the Indian masses as Bharat Mata, the common mother of all true Bharatiyas whose life she had sustained through thick and thin. Bankim presented her as Durga, the destroyer of enemies in his eternal song, Vande Mataram, while Lokmanya Tilak brought the people in touch with their culture and heritage through *Shivaji Utsav* and *Ganesh Utsav*.

Gandhi is fiercely attacked; Nehru, even more so.

It began to be asserted that since India was a secular state, it was common property of all people living in it including those Muslims who had voted for Pakistan and had made no secret of their emotional and physical attachment with that state. To make this acceptable to the people new cliches and catchwords like secular, composite nationalism and secular democracy were given currency and the entire propaganda machinery at the command of the government was pressed into service to force these new fangled notions down the throats of gullible and simple hearted people of India. Pt. Jawaharlal Nehru who himself, being part individualist and part internationalist, was mortally afraid of Indian nationalism, put his full weight behind this new approach. As a clever politician in passionate love with power, he used it to win the bloc votes of the Muslims for the Congress. This approach suited the communists also in their bid to further disrupt India. They now developed the theory that residual India was a multi-cultural and multi-national composite state. They too looked upon Pt. Nehru as their patron saint and used him well for forcing this disruptive ideology down the throats of Anglicised Indian intelligentsia which was almost hypnotised by Pt. Nehru.[24]

In the concluding chapter Madhok declared:

It is the Hinduness or Hindutva of a man which makes him a national of India. Hinduism is not a very happy expression because it creates confusion in the people's mind about the word Hindu. It creates the impression of its being a creed or religion, a particular dogma and form of worship, which it is not. It comprehends within itself all the forms of worship prevalent in India which do

[24] Ibid., p. 85.

not interfere with the worshipper's loyalty to India, her culture and tradition, history and great men.

All Indians are therefore Hindus as they are all Bharatiyas. These three words are synonymous. They all refer to the nationals of India. It is therefore really strange that people who take pride in calling themselves Indians – the Greek form of Hindu – feel ashamed of being called Hindus. It is like an Englishman feeling ashamed of being called English while taking pride in being called 'Farangi' or 'Angrez', the names used by Indians for them. It betrays the mental slavery of Anglicised Indians which they must shed. . . .

Christians and Muslims living in India are also Hindus if India and Indian culture command their first and foremost allegiance. They all form part of Hindu Rashtra or the Indian Nation. This consciousness is today lacking in most Muslims and some Christians of India. The most urgent problem of Indian nationalism today, therefore, is to Indianise or Hinduise such people. . . .

A precise recipe is provided:

India existed long before the birth of Islam or Christianity. Indian heroes like Rama and Krishna and epics like Ramayana and Mahabharata have not ceased to be their heroes and epics respectively simply because they, or their forefathers, changed their religion under some pressure, political or economic. They must learn to take pride in India's past which is their past as well. They must adopt Indian names just as the Indonesian or Chinese Muslims have Indonesian or Chinese names. In short they must adopt the Indian attitude – the national attitude – towards their religion which must cease to colour their loyalties towards the main-springs of Indian nationalism. All talk of separate Muslim or Christian or for that matter of Sikh or Jain culture must stop. India is one country and it has but one culture.[25]

Madhok's views were not repudiated by the Jana Sangh. They reflected its views and the RSS's views. It was his attacks on Vajpayee and Advani and his attempts to loosen the RSS's grip which led to his grief.

Madhok himself spelt out his differences clearly enough.

My differences with the Jana Sangh and its RSS *bosses* have been mainly on two counts. I have been opposed to the Sangh being run as a front organisation of the RSS. I wanted it to function as an independent political party and therefore wanted the posts of organising secretaries to be abolished. Secondly, I was opposed to the Leftist stance adopted by the Sangh in pursuit of its policy

[25] Ibid., p. 97.

> of befriending Mrs. Gandhi. . . . I made both these things clear in my note submitted to the Working Committee at Kanpur.[26]

When he helped in the Golwalkar-Mookerjee pact in 1951, he surely knew who then would be the boss; the two decades since confirmed its terms in practice. The note sealed his fate. He went nowhere.

India's pride, its rich cultural diversity, is given short shrift. Madhok was shown the door; but the ideology which he expounded in such detail was expounded by Savarkar in his *Hindutva* in 1924. He was inspired by the Hindu revivalists of the 19th century. Madhok's exposition is relevant now because it did no more than express the RSS's ideology expounded in its three holy books – Savarkar's *Hindutva* and Golwalkar's *We or Our Nationhood Defined* and *Bunch of Thoughts*. The 'moderate' Vajpayee *accepted it in parliament and in his presidential address at the Jana Sangh's 16th All India Session on 28 December 1969.*

Prime Minister Indira Gandhi tore into pieces his defence of Indianisation. Vajpayee ardently supported the doctrine in parliament. Indira Gandhi said that 'his theory is not quite so innocent. Mr. Vajpayee would not waste his energy in stating something which is so obvious. He and those of his way of thinking have a very definite purpose'. Vajpayee proudly declared he is a member of the RSS. According to the chief of the RSS, Mr. M.S. Golwalkar (22 February 1970), 'The one hope of redemption is nationalism which, in the case of Hindusthan, is Hinduism.'

Clearly, then what the Jana Sangh was up against was the spirit of Indian liberalism, the whole ethos of a democratic secular Indian State. The opponents of Indianisation, Madhok threatened (5 April 1970), would either be converted or cowed down.

Hate and intolerance divided the country and led to unspeakable crimes. Over half a century has elapsed since the partition but hate and intolerance are still at large. It bespeaks the true character of the Indianisation which the Jana Sangh had in mind that *Organiser* should, in an editorial (17 January 1970) entitled 'Indianisation', write this of Gandhi's assassination: 'It was in support of Nehru's pro-Pakistan stand that Gandhiji went on fast and, in the process, turned the people's wrath on himself.' It is a strange outlook which regards Godse's foul crime as an expression of 'the people's wrath'. It is this outlook which seeks to identify a particular culture as the national culture and impose it on the entire nation. This explains the paradox of people who hate the word Indian pleading for Indianisation.

The RSS injected communal poison in the country – by establishing the Vishwa Hindu Parishad in 1966. Preliminary discussions had begun on 28 August 1964 at Mumbai.[27] The VHP spearheaded the RSS's drive to demolish the Babri Masjid.

[26] A letter to *The Statesman*, 5 July 1973.

[27] Vide Manjari Katju's able works *Vishwa Hindu Parishad and Indian Politics*, Orient Longman, 2003, and *Hinduising Democracy: The Vishwa Hindu Parishad in Contemporary*

One of its declared objectives was 'liberation' of the Masjid, and the mosques at Mathura and Kashi [Varanasi]. The VHP in turn set up the Bajrang Dal in mid-1984.

The Indianisation movement fell into this pattern. More so, the communal riots, which also call for a fuller study. Like his mentor Hedgewar, Golwalkar did not rule out use of violence. On 11 June 1970 he met some editors of newspapers. Among them were Girilal Jain, Kuldip Nayar and D.R. Mankekar. This excerpt from a transcript of his talk published in *Organiser* (20 June 1970) records his frank avowals.

Q. Who will teach the Muslims to identify themselves completely with this country and its culture?
A. You and I, all of us.
Q. And how do we do it, by beating them?
A. Beating is of two kinds. A mother beating her child, and an enemy striking a man. We have not done any beating. But if and when we do teach by beating, it will be like the mother's, out of love and solicitude for the child's welfare.
Q. But it was a Hindu who killed Mahatma Gandhi.
A. Yes. But as you must be knowing, in the autumn of 1947, the Government had reports of certain Muslim groups wanting to kill him. Some Muslims had been threatening the Mahatma in his Bhangi Colony residence at Delhi. The Congress leaders asked us to help and we organised a round-the-clock vigil till the Mahatma moved to Birla House.
Q. Is there any place for violence in the life of a society?
A. Yes, but it should be used as a surgeon's knife. Even as a surgeon uses his knife to perform an operation to get rid of an infected portion to save the patient, so also violence in certain extraordinary circumstances can be used to cure the society of any malady that needs such a surgical intervention.
Q. Is not non-violence a virtue par excellence?
A. But, sometimes to protect non-violence itself violence becomes necessary!

Golwalkar travelled extensively to spread his gospel. He said: 'Once Muslims rationalise Islam there will be no difficulty.' His notions of Islam were perverse. 'The Koran lays down that if a divorced woman marries and begets a child within two years of the divorce, her child must be presumed to be born of her first husband.'[28] There is, of course, no such verse in the Quran. On this as on much else, Golwalkar and his successors and followers freely invented facts.

In view of recent assertions by an American scholar, it is important to recall what Deoras said on the admission of non-Hindus to the RSS at New Delhi on 11

India, New Text, 2017.

[28] *Organiser*, 23 June 1973.

November 1973 when he addressed a distinguished gathering at the Constitution Club. Asked pointedly 'Why does RSS not admit non-Hindus?' he replied, 'We will certainly consider the matter when we feel the Hindus are strong enough for that.' He went on falsely to invent an episode which had never happened. 'We do not want the sort of situation in which the Congress enters into a coalition with the Muslim League – and then has to withdraw the biography of Nehru under the League pressures.'

Both statements are false. The Congress rejected a coalition with the League in 1937. The League joined the Governor-General's Executive Council in 1946 independently of the Congress; both parties joined it at the invitation of the Viceroy Lord Wavell. Nehru's biography was *never* withdrawn. This is typical of the RSS's mendacious rhetoric.

Q. Why does not the RSS admit girls?

A. Even men in modern dress do not always have a modern mind. There is social resistance to men and women working together.[29]

Deoras's definition of a Hindu was precise: 'anyone who believes in a religious creed which has sprung from the soil of Hindustan is a Hindu as compared to those who believe in other religious thoughts' – i.e. Muslims, Christians, Jews and Parsis.[30] Deoras had reservations about their entry into the armed forces. He said at Bengaluru on 19 December 1973 that while he would not say that non-Hindus should not be admitted to the services, the government should take due care to avoid risks.[31]

Eager to keep his options open, Golwalkar wrote an unduly long letter to Indira Gandhi on 22 December 1971 congratulating her for her victory in the Bangladesh War. Her reply of 13 January 1972 was brevity itself. He rejoined with yet another letter on 18 January 1973.[32]

The events that followed were to plunge the nation in turmoil. All lost, India's democracy suffered. The RSS alone gained. It reached one step closer to the respectability it had long coveted.

29 *Hindustan Times*, 12 November 1973.

30 *The Indian Express*, 14 January 1974.

31 *The Indian Express*, 20 December 1973.

32 Vide *Organiser*, 16 June 1973, for the text of the letters.

14. The RSS, the Emergency and the Janata Party

The tumultuous events between 1974 and the end of 1979 saw the end of the RSS's isolation from the mainstream of Indian politics and, at one remove, that of its front, the Jana Sangh, as well. It provides instruction to those who would like the two to emerge as conservative but secular parties. Never before or after did the RSS meet such a propitiatious time for that radical change. It could have jumped at the opportunities, repeatedly offered, during this phase in its career; not only without loss of face but with great credit. The RSS and the Jana Sangh would have won plaudits all around. They spurned those opportunities, deviously and arrogantly.

On the one hand, the RSS joined the movement launched by Jayaprakash Narayan in 1974. Once the prime minister, Indira Gandhi, imposed her dictatorship – imprisoning leaders of opposition parties, imposing censorship on the press, and banning public meetings – the RSS chief M.D. (Balasaheb) Deoras, began a clandestine correspondence with her only to secure his release from prison and the lifting of the ban on the RSS. There was not a word about an end to the Emergency or the release of other detainees from prison.

Once the Emergency was over in 1977, the RSS kept JP and the party he helped to establish, the Janata Party, in suspense on opening its doors to non-Hindus. At the end of long drawn negotiations, it refused to countenance any change whatever. JP was rebuffed; his reputation impaired. The RSS went through those traumatic times determined not to change its ways. In the end, it broke up the Janata Party. But it did not revive the Jana Sangh which had merged with it. Instead it set up a new party, the Bharatiya Janata Party (BJP), to pose as a successor to the Janata Party and to JP and Gandhi's legacies. Not long thereafter, these pretences were shed and the BJP candidly admitted that it was the Jana Sangh revived. The RSS has not looked back since. It is extremely important to trace this phase of the RSS-JS's career; alike for their unwavering commitment to their vaunted ideology and for the tactics they would readily stoop to adopt.

JP's admiring biographers Allan and Wendy Scarfe tell us that 'by December 1973 he believed the situation was ripe for revolution as it had been in 1942, and he "felt an inner urge to give a call to youth" to enter the political arena.'[1] Since 1972, he had begun to take keen interest in electoral reforms; eradication of corruption and the establishment of an Ombudsman, the Lokpal. 'By December 1974 some of the worst of the Congress Party scandals were surfacing.'[2] As his agitation for 'Total Revolution' picked up speed, JP took a fateful step. He took the

[1] Allan and Wendy Scarfe, *J.P.: His Biography*, New Delhi: Orient Longman, 1997, p. 237.

[2] Ibid., p. 246.

support of the very organisation which he had criticised consistently, repeatedly.

The wall had been breached earlier when Ram Manohar Lohia issued a joint statement with Deen Dayal Upadhyaya on 12 April 1964, an India-Pakistan Confederation. But Lohia was not known for integrity. JP was. He had a stellar record on secularism; all the more remarkable for the fact that he was a devout Hindu, proud of the faith and culture.

JP's presidential address at the 11th National Convention against Communalism at New Delhi on 28 December 1968 still holds relevance to this day. He said:

> India being a country of many religions, almost every religious community has its own brand of communalism. They are all pernicious, but Hindu communalism is more pernicious than the others. One reason is that because the Hindus constitute a great majority of the population of India, Hindu communalism can easily masquerade as Indian nationalism, and denounce all opposition to it as being anti-national.
>
> Some, like the RSS, might do it openly by identifying the Indian Nation with the Hindu Rashtra, others might do it more subtly. But in every case, such identification is pregnant with national disintegration, because members of the other communities can never accept the position of second class citizens. Such a situation, therefore, has in it the seeds of perpetual conflict and ultimate disruption.

The RSS lay low after Gandhi's assassination in 1948.

> When, following Gandhiji's murder the Sangh was under a shadow, there were many protestations made about its being entirely a cultural organisation. But apparently emboldened by the timidity of the secular forces, it has now thrown its veil away and has emerged as the real power behind, and controller of the Bharatiya Jana Sangh. The secular protestations of the Jana Sangh will never be taken seriously unless it cuts the bonds that tie it so firmly to the RSS machine. Nor can the RSS be treated as a cultural organisation as long as it remains the mentor and effective manipulator of a political party.[3]

This makes it all the more tragic that JP accepted the RSS's help in the movement he launched in Bihar in 1974. For, in doing so, he sinned against the light and invested a destructive force with respectability. He acknowledged on 11 November 1974 that

> the RSS has, of course, been active in Bihar movement, not directly, but

[3] Bimal Prasad (ed.), *Jayaprakash Narayan: Selected Works*, vol. 9, New Delhi: Manohar, 2008, pp. 329-30.

> through its members in the Jana Sangh and the Vidyarthi Parishad. . . . Then, there are not only the Jana Sangh and the Vidyarthi Parishad, but the Socialist Party, the SSP the Cong (O) and their youth wings, the BSP and the Marxist Coordination Committee are all fully involved and active in the movement. The CPM has not joined the coordination committee of political parties, but has extended full support to the movement. So has the Forward Bloc.[4]

Set on a tragic course, he found its reversal very difficult. He was betrayed by the RSS in 1979 when he tried to bring matters to a head. Having acquired strength from him, it saw no reason to bow to his wishes. JP moved from one apology to another. He opined in a letter to the people of Bihar on 28 August 1976:

> So far as the RSS is concerned, it is true that I had been opposed to, and even a bitter critic of this organisation in the past. But nothing is static in this ever-changing world. Even the forms and principles of an organisation change and I believe that RSS too has changed and is changing in the light of experiences it has undergone.
>
> This organisation today is not what it was in the years past. The list of great men whom the Sangh volunteers remember every morning includes also the name of Mahatma Gandhi. The RSS and Jana Sangh are often dubbed as communalist. They are. I have therefore tried [sic] Rashtriya Swayamsevak Sangh to decommunalise them by allowing them to join our movement for total revolution. The young activists of these two organisations have worked in close cooperation with our Muslim students and youths, and this working together has removed misunderstandings and generated mutual faith. Any impartial observer would agree that this has been a significant contribution of this movement to the ideal of religious tolerance or secularism as it is called. I have thus tried to strengthen the foundation of secularism by bringing Jana Sangh and the RSS into the secular fold of total revolution. This is something different from the efforts made so far to eradicate communalism, and this effort of mine, I believe, is more constructive than what has been done so far.[5]

Little did he know that at the very moment the RSS chief was on his knees begging the Prime Minister, the chief minister of Maharashtra, S.B. Chavan, and Vinoba Bhave to secure his release from prison and lift the ban on the RSS. He had no other concerns; neither JP's release or that of other prisoners; least of all the lifting of the Emergency.

In later years the RSS and its followers touted JP's certificates of good conduct after they broke up the party he had founded. The Jana Sangh's newly elected

[4] Prasad (ed.), *Jayaprakash Narayan*, vol. 10, p. 386.

[5] Ibid., pp. 512-3.

president L.K. Advani invited JP to attend its 'national session in Delhi as a special guest of honour'. JP readily agreed and said in his speech on 7 March 1975, 'If the Jana Sangh is fascist, then Jayaprakash Narayan is also a fascist.'[6] Each side had its calculations; the Jana Sangh and the RSS were more realistic than JP.

Advani's account reveals:

> One day, he called Atalji and me and said 'I need your cooperation. You should join me in my movement'. I convened a special meeting of senior leaders of the party in Hyderabad to consider Jayaprakashji's proposal. In fact *I saw an opportunity in the JP movement to significantly expand the Jana Sangh's mass appeal and support base across the country.*[7]

At that time Deoras claimed to have 10,000 branches in the country and membership of a million. It had spread to Kerala where it set up 1,000 branches with 100 full-time workers. Uttar Pradesh had 2,500 branches.[8]

In the late evening of 25 June 1975 the President issued a Proclamation under Article 352(1) of India's Constitution declaring an emergency throughout India. Opposition leaders, JP included, were put in prison; press censorship was imposed and public meetings were banned. The fundamental rights were suspended.

On 4 July 1975, 26 organisations were proscribed, under the Defence of India Rules, 1971 which were made on the eve of the Bangladesh War. The RSS was among them. Some of its leaders were put in prison. Deoras was arrested at Nagpur on 30 June 1975. A definitive account of the course followed by the leaders of the opposition parties was written by Madhu Limaye.[9] Limaye was a voracious reader with a scholarly bent of mind; impassioned and intemperate in speech. None accused him of lack of integrity. His book provides invaluable texts on the opposition leaders' efforts to set up a united political party under JP's aegis. The RSS's position in it was discussed at the very inception in 1976. Limaye records also the RSS's attempts, in tandem, to placate Indira Gandhi. The entire correspondence was placed on the table of the Maharashtra Legislative Assembly by the Minister of State for Home R.P. Dalvi on 18 October 1977.[10]

The letters betray panic and desperation. On 22 August 1975 Deoras shot off a letter to Prime Minister Indira Gandhi claiming that her speech on Independence Day, 15 August, had 'prompted me to write this letter to you. . . . The Sangh has never indulged in any activity which could be dangerous for the internal security

[6] L.K. Advani, *My Country, My Life*, New Delhi: Rupa, p. 192.

[7] Ibid., p. 189.

[8] *The Times of India*, 25 February 1975.

[9] Madhu Limaye, *Janata Party Experiment: An Insider's Account of Opposition Politics, 1975-1977*, vol. 1, Delhi: B.R. Publishing Corporation, 1994.

[10] Vide Appendix 7 for the full text of Deoras's letters to Indira Gandhi, S.B. Chavan and Vinoba Bhave.

of the country or for the law and order situation. The aim of the RSS is to unify, and organise Hindu society. . . . I beseech you to rescind the ban imposed upon the RSS. I would be pleased to meet you if you so desire'. This letter, by MISA prisoner No. 308, Class 1, Andheri Yard, Yerwada Central Jail, Pune elicited no response.

On 16 July 1976 Deoras wrote again to 'Respected Mrs. Indira Gandhi'. He asserted that in none of the court judgments or in the report of any commission appointed by the government had it been said that the volunteers of the Sangh were involved 'in acts of violence in communal riots'. This was untrue. The Jaganmohan Reddy Commission of Inquiry into the Ahmedabad riots in 1969 and the Madon Commission on the Bhiwandi riots of 1970 had censured the RSS. 'There are people who allege that RSS is a communal organisation. This is a baseless charge.' He pleaded that the ban on the RSS be lifted. Eager to please, he praised her foreign policy. Specifically, 'your efforts to improve the [sic] relations with Pakistan and China are also praiseworthy'. Such sentiments have not been heard since.

At his bidding, evidently, one V.N. Bhide, a lawyer also lodged in Yerwada Central Prison, had written to the chief minister of Maharashtra, S.B. Chavan, earlier on 15 July 1975. He was 'the organiser of the RSS in Maharashtra'. Its central office-bearers in Delhi had 'issued a circular stating that it will remain defunct for the duration of the ban'. He offered to meet S.B. Chavan at any time. 'The Sangh has done nothing *against the Government or the Society* even remotely. There is no place for such things in the Sangh's programme.' He asked that the Sangh's workers held in detention be released.

Bhide's words could not possibly have been more widely worded. He was a lawyer. Implicit in the denial of past conduct was a pledge of future behaviour. If the government had jumped at the bait, the RSS would have cooperated with the government during the Emergency. Evidently, parleys were afoot between the RSS and the government. For, in a letter of 24 January 1976, Bhide referred to Chavan's demand for 'an undertaking . . . relating to politics and emergency' which he found difficult to accept. Deoras wrote to the Prime Minister again on 10 November 1975. On 16 June 1976 he asked Chavan to release him on parole 'with a view to clarifying certain issues'. He was moving towards a rapprochement by proposing 'it will not be proper to use the expression "good behaviour"' in the proposed undertaking. The principle of an undertaking by the detainees was accepted; only the terms had to be settled.

'On 6 July 1975, Rule No. 33, under the Defence of India Act, was applied to the RSS. Following this the office-bearers of the Sangh have notified suspension of all activities of the Sangh. Therefore there is no need to make non-participation in RSS activities a condition for the release.' Deoras and his lawyer Bhide were acting in concert with each other. This the chronology of the correspondence makes clear:

1. 15 July 1975: Advocate V.N. Bhide's letter to Chief Minister, S.B. Chavan, Maharashtra from Yerwada Jail.
2. 22 August 1975: Deoras's letter to Indira Gandhi from Yerwada Jail.
3. 10 November 1975: Deoras's second letter to Indira Gandhi.
4. 24 November 1975: RSS's Chief Organiser's letter to Chavan.
5. 22 December 1975: Deoras's letter to Chavan.
6. 24 January 1976: Bhide's letter to Chavan.
7. 12 July 1976: Bhide's letter to Chavan.
8. 16 July 1976: Deoras's letter to Indira Gandhi.
9. Deoras's two letters to Vinoba Bhave:
   - 12 January 1976: Deoras's letter to Vinoba Bhave.
   - Deoras's second letter to Bhave (undated).

A total of ten letters in six months.

The most damning letter in this abjectly grovelling series is Deoras's letter to Indira Gandhi on 10 November 1975. He began thus, 'Let me congratulate you as five judges of the Supreme Court have declared the validity of your election.' He knew, of course, that it was a sordid victory. She had got parliament to amend in her favour the Constitution and those provisions of the Representation of the People Act, 1951 which she had violated. Justice Jagmohan Lal Sinha of the Allahabad High Court found, on 12 June 1975, that she was guilty of using the services of a government employee and State help during her election campaign. The Supreme Court did not reverse those findings. The amended law rendered such an exercise futile. The deed warranted censure; not congratulations.

Deoras claimed that 'the thinking process of the Sangh is mainly based on Hindu spiritualism'. From 'cultural' pursuits to matters spiritual was quite a leap. Next came this brazen lie. 'The Sangh has been referred to in connection with the movement of Jaya Prakash Narayan. The name of the Sangh has been linked with the Bihar and the Gujarat movements again and again and without any cause. . . . *The Sangh has no connection with these movements*.' RSS members prided themselves for participating in the 'JP Movement'. In the Lok Sangharsh Committee, the RSS's students' wing, the Akhil Bharatiya Vidyarthi Parishad, virtually led the Chhatra Sangharsh Samiti. The RSS ideologue K.N. Govindacharya 'was one of the instigators of the Chhatra Sangharsh Samiti'. Nana Deshmukh of the RSS and the Jana Sangh acted as 'aide-de-camp' to JP.[11] On his arrest, JP entrusted Nana Deshmukh with the organisation of the movement. Once the Emergency was over the RSS and the Jana Sangh sought fame and reward for their role in the movement. Deoras's lies had a purpose. Once absolved of culpability for associating with JP, the RSS cadres could serve as foot-soldiers of what they had once called the Prime Minister's 'fascist' set up; a charge they repeated on release. Deoras's offer

[11] Jaffrelot, *The Hindu Nationalist Movement and Indian Politics*, pp. 258 and 268.

of collaboration in this letter was explicit; it left no room for retreat. It was offered on 10 November 1975 at an early stage of the installation of a set up which robbed Indians of their rights as free citizens: 'set free thousands of RSS workers and remove the restrictions on the Sangh. If done so, *power of selfless work on the part of lakhs of RSS volunteers will be utilised for national upliftment* (government as well as non-government) and as we all wish, our country will be prosperous. Awaiting the reply to my letter.'[12] Brahm Dutt's *Five Headed Monster* also contains Deoras's letters to Vinoba Bhave on 12 January 1976 and one later which is undated. In the first he flatly contradicted his false disavowal, made two months earlier in his letter to Indira Gandhi. In the second he repeated the offer he had made to her; hoping that Vinoba would transmit it to her with his endorsement.

> It has been published in the newspapers that the Hon'ble Prime Minister is going to meet you at the Pavnar Ashram on the 24th. Discussion relating to the present-day situation of our country will be held. This is my prayer to you that you kindly try to remove the wrong notion of the Prime Minister about the Sangh, and as a result of which the RSS volunteers will be set free, the ban on the Sangh will be lifted and such a condition will prevail *as to enable the volunteers of the Sangh to participate in the planned programme* of action relating to country's progress and prosperity *under the leadership of the Prime Minister.*[13]

Acceptance of Indira Gandhi's 'leadership' was explicit.

The RSS network ensured that Deoras's fiats reached all. He could not have disapproved of the letters of apology RSS men offered in jail. Three witnesses testified to this. Dr. G.G. Parikh, a Socialist detained at the Yerwada Jail in Pune, Madhu Limaye who was in Raipur, and Baba Adhav who was also in Yerwada Jail; as, indeed, was Deoras.

Deoras's first letter provided a signal for the followers to act on. The RSS's record during this period was exposed by Baba Adhav after the Emergency. He was disgusted at Deoras's campaign of self-glorification.

> Demonstration of self-eulogisation is all-pervading. But are the claims made by the RSS true? Though among the detenus under MISA the number of RSS men was large, many Sanghites proclaimed that they were detained though they had no connection either with the anti-emergency agitation of JP's movement.
>
> In fact, many of them upheld the emergency rule. 'JP has instigated the armed forces', they used to tell in their jail 'boudhik'. There was in effect no

12 Vide Brahm Dutt, *Five Headed Monster: A Factual Narrative of the Genesis of Janata Party*, New Delhi: Surge Publications, 1978, pp. 138-48.

13 Ibid., p. 148.

opposition to Indira-Sanjay politics, certainly not from their side. In fact, Sanjay Gandhi's anti-communist, laissez-faire and authoritarian views were hailed by them.

The pro-Sangh daily of Poona, *Tarun Bharat*, had made consistent efforts to hail Sanjay Gandhi. Their only regret was that, instead of accepting the cooperation of the RSS to implement the 20-point programme, the organisation was banned. There were severe attacks by Indira Gandhi not only on the RSS but also the educational institutions run by them. Poor Sanghites were feeling restless over this, and their 'ideological' doldrums was indeed pathetic.

Baba Adhav angrily remarked:

It is surprising that Deoras should say that Sangh workers had not surrendered. I do not know about the prisons elsewhere, but at Yervada and other jails in Maharashtra I know what happened. There used to be several meetings, debates and discussions. Also there was a lot of correspondence. The chief Deoras had good deal of correspondence with the former Prime Minister, Indira Gandhi, former Maharashtra Chief Minister Shankarrao Chavan, Vinoba Bhave and close associates of Sanjay Gandhi. In a press conference at Delhi he confessed about the two letters sent to Indira Gandhi. Journalists might have seen the copies of those letters. Balasaheb has sent one letter to Indira Gandhi on her birthday and another congratulating her on her exoneration by the Supreme Court.

For felicitating her on birthday one should not berate Deoras, but what about the sin of congratulating her for arbitrarily amending the Constitution and 'managing success at the Supreme Court'? Throughout the period of his detention Deoras was desperate to have a dialogue and an interview with Indira Gandhi. As far as I know, he contacted many people including the then Chief Minister of Maharashtra for this.

In February 1976, Indira Gandhi visited Bombay and in order to meet her, he got himself moved to St. George Hospital (Bombay), pretending illness. Through Shankarrao Chavan, an effort was made to see her, failing which a meeting with Shankarrao Chavan was sought by one Jana Sangh MLA outside the jail. However, if these efforts were not successful, it was not for want of will. To convince Shankarrao Chavan, he was approached repeatedly.

That signing an undertaking was a part of this effort is known to all the prisoners in Yervada jail. The following pro-forma of the written undertaking signed by these 'freedom fighters' brings into sharp relief their cowardice;

PRO-FORMA OF UNDERTAKING

Shri .... Detenu Class I .... prisoner agrees on affidavit that in case of my release I shall not do anything which is detrimental to internal security and public peace. Similarly, I shall not do anything which would hamper the distribution of essential goods. So also I shall not participate in any illegal activities. I shall not indulge in any activities which is prejudicial to the present emergency.

The Maharashtra government demanded written undertakings for conditional release of the detenus. The RSS and Sangh detenus decided independently to sign such undertakings. This caused a stir in the jail and socialist leaders like Bagaitkar, Babu Rao Samant and Dasrath Patil went to meet the Jana Sangh leader Mhalgi to dissuade his party people from signing this undertaking. *Mr. Mhalgi pleaded that the decision to sign the undertaking was taken by the top leaders of the RSS and Jana Sangh not confined to jail.* The pro-forma of this undertaking was agreed upon by those outsiders after conferring with the CM (the irony is that even among those who had signed the undertaking very few were released). By contrast freedom fighters like Shribhau Limaye and Dasrath Patil unequivocally refused to sign. Moreover, in their letter they rebuked the then CM that it was an insult to demand such an undertaking from freedom-fighters.

The directive of the 'struggle committee' outside jails was that the RSS and Jana Sangh people should not sign such an undertaking. This was conveyed to them by S.M. Joshi. However, the directive was ignored. Ultimately, the letter of JP was sent in. At Nasik jail the socialists decided that this undertaking should not be given. There was division between the RSS and Jana Sangh on the one hand and the socialists on the other. A senior leader of the RSS, Baba Bhide, used to address boudhik (ideological training camp) in which he always supported the emergency and emphasised that he had nothing to do with the anti-emergency struggle. Balasaheb Deoras himself said that 'had the government not banned the RSS, its volunteers would not have gone to jail in such large numbers by resorting to satyagraha'.

During this period there were several moves at Delhi level. It is quite likely that appeals were made to Indira Gandhi and Sanjay to intervene. Indeed, Deoras has admitted to have done so through Vinoba Bhave. Moving a step further they convened a meeting in Kashmir in which they even decided to make a change in the organisation and *modus operandi* of the RSS. Instead of Sar Sangh Chalak (the chief), a President was to be elected and admission to non-Hindus was decided upon and conveyed to Sanjay Gandhi. In this connection a Jana Sangh leader of Delhi, Hans Raj Gupta, is mentioned. The information on what exactly transpired between the two is buried in silence.

The reason for writing at such length about the RSS is that Deoras is masquerading that the RSS alone was the front-rank fighter in the anti-emergency struggle. The issue of undertaking was consigned to oblivion. To make their task easier, the government brought forward a 'memorandum'. This was no different from securing conditional release:

Sir,

Your case for detention has been reviewed by this government and it has been decided that the detention should be revoked subject to the condition that, you shall not participate in activities prejudicial to the present emergency and subject to good behaviour. You are requested to please note it.

Yours faithfully,
Sd/-
Section Officer Home Dept.
Govt. Of Maharashtra[14]

In another article, Baba Adhav elaborated:

Written queries were circulated in the Yervada Central Jail in Maharashtra three or four times, asking detenus if they would be prepared to sign an undertaking or a memorandum. I have seen with my own eyes a majority of the RSS detenus signing their assent to do so. During the emergency RSS supporters and workers outside the jails printed and circulated free dozens of booklets outlining the RSS stand vis-a-vis funds, national integrity, fascism, politics, violence, jingoism, ban on the RSS, progress and science, national policy, and also letters sent by Shri Deoras to Smt. Gandhi and Vinoba. A common foreword to these booklets stated that restraints on expression following proclamation of emergency on the one hand and the anti-RSS propaganda carried on by Government through audio-visual and other media on the other make it essential to place the RSS views on vital issues before the people so that they may get an insight into reality and may evaluate the situation fairly.

The booklet 'Justice Demands' brings out how Shri Deoras was anxious to reach a settlement with Smt. Gandhi. In a letter to Vinobaji, he writes: 'I request you to do your best to remove wrong impressions the P.M. is carrying about the Sangh and [to ensure that] the Sangh Swayamsevaks are released from the jails, the ban imposed on the Sangh is lifted and such conditions as will enable the Sangh and Swayamsevaks to actively participate in the development programmes in various fields under the leadership of P.M. are created.

'Praying for your blessings,
'Yours sincerely,

[14] Baba Adhav, *Secular Democracy*, Independence Number, August 1977, pp. 40-1; vide also Goyal, *Rashtriya Swayamsewak Sangh*, pp. 139-43.

'Madhukar Dattatraya Deoras
'Rashtriya Swayamsevak Sangh'[15]

D.R. Goyal who was in the know records:

> A separate call for controlling the MPs and centrally directing the political moves was created with headquarters at the New Delhi residence of Sundar Singh Bhandari. Consisting of Bhandari, Nanaji, Advani, Vajpayee and J.P. Mathur. It began to function under direct supervision of Bhaurao Deoras, the younger brother of the RSS chief. Bhaurao who had been the chief organiser of the eastern zone with headquarters at Kanpur was shifted to New Delhi as a sort of political commissar.[16]

Meanwhile another track was begun by the opposition leaders which Madhu Limaye traced with pertinent documents. JP was released on parole for health reasons. On 12 November 1975 he was afflicted with life threatening illness. Deoras could not have been ignorant of this when he repeated to Vinoba Bhave his offer of cooperation to the government on 12 January 1976. The offer was, however, kept secret from the opposition leaders when the Jana Sangh participated in meetings with them. Its great advantage was its underground network.

Jaffrelot provides a good account of this excursion.

> The movement went underground to organise itself for a long-drawn-out campaign. Of 1,336 pracharaks, only 186 had been arrested and most of the others continued their activities secretly. By the beginning of July, the national leaders who had gone underground had reconstituted the movement's network while seeking new local cadres to replace those in custody. During July a meeting of the principal pracharaks who were still at liberty was held in Bombay. The programme agreed upon considered the restoration of democracy and the lifting of the ban on the RSS as two indivisible objectives. The fact that the RSS fought against the Emergency above all to regain its legal status reflected the organisation's ambiguous attitude towards *democracy*, as suggested by Thengadi's subsequent analysis:
>
> It is accepted on all hands that the present democratic process in India is not a growth of the soil and it is neither adequate nor favourable nor capable from the point of view of conditions in and requirements of the country. But its protection can save the country from dictatorship.[17]

15 *Janata*, 16 September 1977.

16 Goyal, *Rashtriya Swayamsewak Sangh*, p. 145.

17 Jaffrelot, *The Hindu Nationalist Movement and Indian Politics*, p. 274.

Demand for restoration of democracy was linked to survival of the RSS. So were worries for collaboration with a prime minister who had all but destroyed democracy. Leaders of the opposition parties came around to accepting the idea of unity; opinion was divided on its forms: a merger or a federal party. The presence of the elephant in the room was noted at the very outset. On 8 February 1976 representatives of Charan Singh's Bharatiya Lok Dal, the Socialist Party, represented by Surendra Mohan, and the Jana Sangh met in Tihar jail. Surendra Mohan's note recorded:

> I have suggested to the leaders of the BLD and Jana Sangh that unification of our parties must lead to the mergers of our front organisations and the character of the RSS must undergo a fundamental change so that it can truly become an allied organisation of the new party. The continuance of RSS in its present form, controlling the activities of Jana Sangh, Vidyarthi Parishad and BMS workers even after the dissolution of these bodies will be injurious to the democratic and united functioning of the unified party.[18]

Charan Singh's release on 7 March 1976 gave an impetus to the moves. JP convened a meeting in Mumbai of nearly a score of leaders, including Acharya Kripalani, Charan Singh, H.M. Patel, S.M. Joshi, S. Nijalingappa, for Congress (O). The Jana Sangh was represented by its acting president O.P. Tyagi and Uttamrao Pandit. A Steering Committee of four was set up each representing his political party: the BLD, Congress (O), the Socialists, and the Jana Sangh. They drew up an Approach Paper. The new party was to be called the Janata Party.

Events had induced rethinking in the minds of some in the RSS. Dattopant Thengadi was tasked with infiltrating trade unions. He failed and set up another RSS front the Bharatiya Mazdoor Sangh in 1955. His letter to the Jana Sangh's general secretary Madhav Muley on 17 September 1976 is significant. He argued:

> Though our constitution unequivocally states the RSS is a cultural, a strictly non-political organisation, there is a misapprehension in certain quarters that the RSS is interfering in politics or the working of the political parties. It is absolutely baseless; but it is nevertheless prevailing in some political circles. It is, therefore, advisable to categorically restate our non-political character. This will be helpful in allaying such misapprehensions.[19]

At long last JP announced at a press conference on 25 May 1976 the formation of a new party, comprising of the Congress (O), the Socialist Party, the Lok Dal and the Jana Sangh. Charan Singh was adamant on their dissolution and merger. By the

[18] Limaye, *Janata Party Experiment*, p. 118.

[19] Vide Limaye, *Janata Party Experiment*, pp. 139-41 for the text.

time the four parties met in Delhi on 8 July 1976, *Charan Singh had read Deoras's incriminating letters*. This extract from the minutes of that acrimonious meeting is highly significant.

> 4. (a) Ch. Charan Singh raised the question of the RSS. He stated his firm belief that no RSS volunteer can join the New Party and no member of the New Party can join the RSS. It was a question of dual membership which could not be allowed and there should be no scope in the New Party for surreptitious work. (b) Shri Tyagi said that the New Party can lay down whatever conditions it sees fit. *Currently the RSS was banned and it stood dissolved.*

Limaye wrote:

> There were heated exchanges between the JS and the BLD. The Chaudhary pointed out that on 15 June 1976 *The Pioneer* of Lucknow had published the following news item: Lucknow, 14 June – The UP Jana Sangh has directed its units to refrain from taking part in activities subversive to law and order according to the acting General Secretary of the State Jana Sangh, Mr. Satya Prakash Agarwal.
>
> Mr. Agarwal in a statement said he had sent a circular letter to all party units saying that the Jana Sangh members should not participate in any unlawful activity. He said the party would extend its full cooperation to the Government in constructive programmes and social welfare activities.

Tyagi shifted his position. 'It was not right for a political party to prohibit its members' association with cultural or social organisations. . . .' He then specifically mentioned the Arya Samaj, and said that he would not permit any party to tell him what his relations with the Arya Samaj should be. 'To allow this would give rise to totalitarianism. . . .' The RSS and the Arya Samaj were not really comparable entities. The Arya Samaj was a social reform body and was for years engaged in educational work. The RSS was essentially a political body and its purpose was political.

Encouraged, Limaye lent his support to Charan Singh.

> If what I have heard is true, I think you did the right thing in raising that issue. The RSS is very much in politics no matter how vehemently they might deny the fact. The RSS will have to refashion itself in conformity with the principles of the new party. It will have to accept the principles of destruction of caste system and feudalism, of social equality and other progressive concepts. It will have to admit Muslims, Christians, Parsis and so on. The RSS may preserve

their autonomy while affiliating themselves ideologically with the new party.[20]

Tyagi lost his job. On 26 September he was made acting general secretary with U.L. Patil as acting president. The Jana Sangh appealed to all parties unconditionally to merge their separate entities in a single political party. It knew then what all the others felt about the RSS. Charan Singh made his position clear in a letter to Asoka Mehta of the Congress (O) on 8 October: 'I would like to suggest that we should make our position regarding the RSS and other Communal Organisations clear in the very first announcement that is made on behalf of the New Party. All the communal organisations we have in view have to be specified here and now.'[21]

Indira Gandhi announced her decision to hold elections to the Lok Sabha on 18 January 1977. The Janata Party's triumph in the elections reflected the mood in the country. People from all shades of opinion had met in jails, joined at meals and discussed the country's future. Communalism suffered a terrible blow. Pressures mounted on Deoras to lift the bar in the RSS on membership of non-Hindus. How he rode out the storm makes a fascinating study. It reveals the true nature of the RSS and the utter unrealism of the ones who asserted that it was about to change or, worse, it had changed as a result of its cadres' experience in the jail. Deoras's prison letters alone should have injected realism.

However, the experience did not mellow Deoras. It emboldened him. For the RSS had ceased to be a pariah. He declared his stand as early as on 25 February 1977 at a press meeting in Mumbai. The RSS 'wanted to set the Hindu house right first only thereafter could the question of others be taken up'.[22] He had never mentioned either the problems that beset it or the solution he had in mind. It was an excuse to bide his time; and in this he succeeded. Forty years have elapsed since; but reform is nowhere in sight. On his successor Mohan Bhagwat's oratorical performance in New Delhi in September 2018, more later.

Deoras also explained why the Jana Sangh was set up. In doing so he confirmed the RSS's paternity. None spoke in the RSS's defence when it was banned in 1948. 'The RSS was isolated. Not a single question about the RSS had been raised in Parliament or in any State Assembly. In those circumstances, some RSS members felt the need for a political party to serve the cause of the organisation.'[23] True to form he asserted that while 'some RSS members joined the Jana Sangh there was no other connection between the two organisations'. They had different flags, programmes, constitutions, cadres and office-bearers.[24]

Deoras gave an interview to Harish Bhanot of the *Hindustan Times*. In it

[20] Ibid., pp. 158-62.

[21] Ibid., p. 169.

[22] *The Indian Express*, 26 February 1977.

[23] Ibid.

[24] Ibid.

> He explained that the RSS had, since its inception in October 1925, devoted itself exclusively to the task of uniting Hindus for positive life. He added, it should be understood that Buddhists, Jains and Sikhs are all Hindus. The RSS, however, fully realised that the non-Hindus are also part of the nation 'and we have a common culture'. The suspicion sown in the minds of the people has disappeared to a large extent.
>
> Mr. Deoras said that the RSS executive committee and the general house would meet soon to take stock of recent historical developments. The executive which would meet at Nagpur on April 1 and 2 is expected to consider the question of throwing open the doors of the organisation to non-Hindus. Mr. Deoras explained that they would work on the basis of 'realism and magnanimity' and there would be no attempt to 'appease anybody' . . .
>
> The RSS chief asserted that his organisation was engaged in purely 'non-political, constructive and lawful activities', and none, except those who 'looked through imported goggles' could be unhappy with it. . . .
>
> 'There is no place for hatred in our mission and we have no ill-will towards those who frown at us'. . . .
>
> He said, the RSS branches are held in the open. It works silently, and not secretly. It is not a para-military organisation. In fact, it had virtually adopted the Congress Seva Dal pattern, which had been established by Dr. Hardikar before the birth of the RSS.[25]

All the more reason, one would think, why the RSS should have opened its door to all.

Deoras said the RSS was willing to consider the question of admitting Muslims in it 'but it would have been better if such a demand came from the Muslim brothers'.[26] He went to Delhi on 8 April to meet the acting president B.D. Jatti, Prime Minister Morarji Desai and others and was received among others by the RSS's northern region chief Hans Raj Gupta, who did not mince words. Non-Hindus were welcome to join the RSS; but they would have to accept its basic principles and programme and share its concept of the nation and patriotism (deshbhakti) as visualised by the RSS. They would be free to profess their faith. This is just what Savarkar and Golwalkar envisaged. They had no quarrel with 'forms of worship' but Hindu 'culture' must be accepted. Gupta said that there was no change in the RSS's views on Akhand Bharat.[27]

Gupta, obviously privy to the Executive Committee's discussions, had a point. How can one ask an organisation to accept membership of those who did not share its outlook, principles and programme? JP and others blurred over this. Their tacit

25 *The Times of India*, 11 April 1977; reproduced in Limaye, *Janata Party Experiment*, pp. 290-1.

26 *Free Press Journal*, 25 March 1977.

27 *Hindustan Times*, 9 April 1977.

assumption was that the opening of the doors would coincide was basic changes within the RSS but RSS had no desire to do that and without a radical change within it the outsiders would not join. The RSS equivocated and spoke in two voices.

Deoras met Morarji Desai on 10 April and offered his cooperation to the government in the social, economic and cultural fields. Elaborating on the offer at a press conference the next day *Hindustan Times* reported that he held out the promise of a structural change in the organisation and policies of the RSS,

> [B]ut such a change could only be brought about democratically, on the basis of discussions and consultations with the RSS cadres. He hoped to complete this by the first week of June. . . . While there had been a sea change in the attitude of RSS workers, because of their sharing the jails with the Jamaat-e-Islami workers during the emergency, there should be eagerness on the part of Muslim friends too to join the RSS. Deoras had no hesitation in declaring that his is a pro-Hindu organisation. Muslims are citizens of this country and, therefore, they should be in the mainstream. The doors of the RSS will be thrown open for them but a decision is yet to be taken. He had reminded Morarji Desai that 'Hinduism should not be forgotten'.[28]

Mohan Bhagwat's speech in September 2018 adhered to this line.

The refrain was kept up amidst contradictory tunes. At Kanpur on 18 April Deoras was slightly more precise. The concept of Hinduism had undergone radical changes and there was need to redefine it in the present context. The earlier definition was limited to putting the house in order but its present form would have to be made comprehensive to include every community in India. The RSS had two lakh active workers attending 10,000 shakhas.[29] The plan of reform awaits fulfilment.

At Kolkata, on 24 April, Deoras extended his offer of cooperation to Marxists and Muslims. The climate was favourable for opening negotiations with Muslims. The RSS was a social and cultural organisation.[30] The RSS's attitude towards the Congress and Indira Gandhi in particular has not received the notice it deserves. It has time and again made it plain to the Jana Sangh, and later to the BJP, that it was free to cooperate with others as well. Deoras was against prosecuting the former Prime Minister for her wrongs during the Emergency. He preferred a 'forget and forgive' attitude.[31]

The RSS's Akhil Bharatiya Pratinidhi Sabha met at Nagpur on 24-25 June and passed a resolution which put off a decision.

[28] *Hindustan Times*, 12 April 1977.

[29] *Hindustan Times*, 19 April 1977.

[30] *The Statesman*, 25 April 1977.

[31] *The Indian Express*, 8 May 1977.

> The atmosphere of amity and goodwill generated inside the jails and outside in the country during the struggle against the Emergency for restoration of democratic values has not only helped project the true image of the RSS, but has further enthused many well wishers of the country and of our organisation to urge that the RSS should initiate measures to remove the sense of alienation, caused by certain historical and political circumstances between the Hindus on the one hand and the Muslims, Christians and others on the other, for strengthening the cause of national integration.
>
> The Akhil Bharatiya Pratinidhi Sabha feels that this psychological and highly sensitive problem has to be tackled with care and caution, keeping it aloof from the pulls of politics, and requires sustained and perseverant efforts. For this purpose a free and frank dialogue with all the concerned sections in the country has to be initiated with a view to understanding all aspects of the problem and finding a solution to it, so that the erstwhile atmosphere of distrust and suspicion can be dispelled.
>
> The A.B.P.S. appeals to all those who feel the urgent need for national integration *to help the RSS in creating a non-political platform*, as a first step, where people can meet one another, exchange views and clear their doubts and thereby create love and confidence amongst the various sections and devise common programmes which would help us to move forward in the direction of our cherished goal.[32]

Talks between the Janata Party leaders and Deoras and the RSS general secretary Madhav Rao Muley failed to achieve any result. Deoras and Muley met JP in Mumbai on 11 June 1977 to assure him that it would take time for all sections of society to understand the RSS.[33]

At JP's instance Limaye met Deoras when Muley was also present. Limaye raised five issues:

> (1) Whether the RSS was a cultural-cum-volunteer organisation or a 'super-party'; (2) Whether the RSS would change its concept of 'nation' as Hindu Rashtra and treat all Indians, irrespective of their religion, as members of Indian or Bharatiya nation; (3) Whether the RSS was going to admit non-Hindus, as Deoras's own statements, soon after his release, indicated; (4) Whether the RSS would consider amalgamation with Rashtra Seva Dal, Congress Seva Dal and other volunteer organisations on the basis of a common outlook; and of the ABVP and BMS with the corresponding organisations of other Janata constituents; and (5) Whether, the Jana Sangh having accepted the Janata creed of democracy, secularism and decentralised socialism based on

32 *Organiser*, 4 July 1977.

33 *Hindustan Times*, 13 June 1977.

Gandhian values, the RSS would, without compromising its autonomous and independent character and continuing to devote itself to character building, have friendly relations with the Janata Party on the basis of a shared outlook?

He recorded this in an aide-memoire of 8 May 1977.[34]

The talks were reported in the press in August. Muley flatly denied that Limaye had held any discussions with him on the question of the integration of volunteer-cum-cultural organisations of the RSS. Limaye responded by publishing a Note he had drawn up after the talks.[35] In issue was the mergers of the ABVP and the Bharatiya Mazdoor Sangh in the Janata Party's counterparts.

The RSS's renewed confidence was due to the Jana Sanghis' successes in the Assembly polls in June 1977. In Madhya Pradesh, Rajasthan, Himachal Pradesh and Delhi former Jana Sangh men were at the head of the Janata Party governments. In the Centre they controlled the important portfolios like Information and Broadcasting – which gave them access to the press and enabled them to place their loyal men in key positions in the leading newspapers and news agencies – External Affairs and Industries. Besides, in the appointment of Ministers of State at the Centre, the Jana Sangh people had won the largest share. In the states ruled by BLD men such as Haryana, UP and Bihar the Jana Sangh activists had won control of a number of important ministries. Even in Odisha where they had no influence they had won a foothold in the government. In the new Lok Sabha there were anything between 85-90 M.P.s who accepted the direction of the Jana Sangh leadership.

'With this accession of strength it was no wonder that the RSS leadership determined that there was no need for them to change their outlook or structure or methodology. Many of them thought that it was a matter of time before the entire government of the country fell into their hands.'[36] Nana Deshmukh went to the press on 31 August, to announce that the issue of the RSS should be treated as closed.[37]

JP could no longer keep silent. In an interview to *Samyukta Varta*, a Hindi weekly, on 13 September he advised the Rashtriya Swayamsevak Sangh either to 'disband itself and merge with the youth and cultural organisations of the Janata Party', or at least 'to open its door to members of all the communities, including Muslims and Christians, and make it possible for members of all castes and communities, to hold the highest office in the organisation'.

JP said that organisations like the Vidyarthi Parishad, Bharatiya Mazdoor Sangh and RSS, which participated in the movement led by him, should now also

[34] Limaye, *Janata Party Experiment*, pp. 412-3.

[35] Vide Appendix 9 for the text.

[36] Limaye, *Janata Party Experiment*, pp. 425-6.

[37] *The Indian Express*, 1 September 1977.

join the front organisations being formed by the Janata Party. 'If this is not done, there will be great potential for discord and conflict in the future.'

When questioned that in March 1976, at a meeting of leaders of constituent units of the Janata Party he had admonished the Jana Sangh representatives for holding separate 'shakhas' in jails, he said he held the same view today and did not consider RSS to be purely a cultural body. Emphasising that there was no justification now for RSS to continue as a separate organisation 'in the changed circumstances', Narayan, however, appreciated their decommunalisation.

> In course of my contact with RSS leaders as well as cadres, I have noticed a change in their outlook. They no longer have a feeling of animosity towards other communities. But in their heart of hearts, they still believe in the concept of Hindu Rashtra.
>
> They remain preoccupied with organisation of the Hindus on the assumption that other communities like Muslims and Christians are already organised, while the Hindus continue to remain divided. This attitude of RSS leaders must change.

He hoped that 'they will give up the concept of Hindu Rashtra and adopt in its place that of Indian nationhood, which is a secular concept and embraces all communities living in India'.

The RSS general secretary, Madhav Rao Muley responded by writing a letter to JP on 23 September 1977. It read thus:

> Respected Shri Jayaprakash Ji, Sadar Namaskars. As I have great regard for you I was surprised to go through your statement on RSS dated 13.9.77. I was, therefore, sorry to read the statement which was obviously based upon inadequate information about our Organisation. In view of our intimate relations I always expected that you would take us into confidence and would discuss the matter with us (RSS) instead of utilising the press media for that purpose.
>
> Your statement dated 13.9.77, read together with on 20.9.77, gave me an impression that we have failed to understand precisely your views on different subjects. For example on 13th September you emphasised that there was no justification now for RSS to continue as a separate organisation in the changed circumstances and therefore it should join the front organisations of the Janata Party.
>
> On 20th September, you are reported to have said 'the Chhatra Yuva Vahini, a non-political organisation, could become an ideal instrument for creating an atmosphere for ridding Hindu society of social evils, like the caste system and untouchability'. Perhaps it could take on the task of inducing a

change in thinking and pave the way for reconstruction of society better than the youth wings of the political parties whose outlook was possibly confined to party interest. You have rightly observed that the youth had to be organised on a non-party basis, as involvement of political parties blurs the issue.

As you are aware the RSS is not an organisation of youths only. In its ranks it includes all age groups of the society. Though Swayamsevaks of RSS helped you in your movement against corruption in Bihar and were in the forefront of struggle against dictatorship during emergency, Sangh has a distinct mission of its own from its very inception. The RSS while remaining away from power politics has been continuously striving to inculcate in its members faith in the Bharatiya ideals and values of life and on that basis building up character, idealism, discipline and other national virtues. You have also always differentiated 'Jan Shakti' (People's Power) from 'Raj Shakti' and assigned the former a role much more important than that of the latter.

Against this background you will appreciate our bewilderment at your statement that there was no justification now for the continuance of RSS as a separate organisation in the changed circumstances, and that it should join the front organisation being formed by the ruling party.

With full regard for you, I may humbly state that it is less than fair to say that RSS is recently de-communalised. In this respect RSS is today what it has always been projected by interested parties. It is true that it was only when our Swayamsevaks worked in the Bihar Famine under your leadership that you could realise for the first time the non-communal character of RSS.

We have taken up the problem of national integration in our own modest way. We celebrated 'Rakshabandhan' festival throughout the country in which Muslims and Christians participated in several places. On Id-day in many places Swayamsevaks offered 'Id-Mubarak' to Muslim brethren.

The problem is a delicate one and you are also aware of the complexity of the problem. Explaining the absence of Muslims in the Chhatra Sangharsha Vahini you have rightly identified the malady, i.e. 'their hesitant attitude to happenings in the country'. As you remarked, 'Very few Muslims participated in the Bhoodan or Bihar movements.' We request you to consider seriously whether it is not worthwhile to give a trial to a more patient social process, instead of rushing through the traditional politically oriented moves.

You have referred to our 'Hindu Rashtra' concept. It is a cultural concept and not a political one. It only means faith in Bharatiya ideals and values of life and an attempt to restructure different aspects of our national life in accordance with the same, keeping in mind the needs of modern times. I do not think there is any reason to decry it, as yourself like Mahatmaji and Pujaya Vinobaji have been the votaries of Bharatiya culture. The allergy of the politicians for the term Hindu is understandable for their main concern for immediate popular vote and not the ultimate basic truth. I hope you will take an objective and dispassionate view of the things and not give undue weight to the biased propaganda of those who are against RSS because of their ulterior political motives.

Of course, these fundamentals cannot be thrashed out through correspondence or press statements. It would be appropriate to sit together and discuss these issues in details.

I hope you are maintaining progress in your health and pray the Almighty to bestow upon you a long and healthier life.

This was obviously written with Deoras's full approval.

JP retorted angrily to say that if necessary there should be a law to deal with the RSS. 'I am against any legal action, but if necessary that should be done.' The RSS should either open its doors to other communities or wind up its activities. 'I am clear that the RSS has no justification to exist now.' The RSS chief and some others were coming to meet him and he would make his views clear to them.[38]

JP and Deoras met twice at JP's residence in Patna; on 30 October and 1 November. After the first meeting Deoras disclosed that the main topic of their talks that day was admission of Muslims into the RSS. They had moved closer. He had had talks with Muslim leaders also. 'But admission of Muslims into the RSS cannot take place in haste.' He did not conceal his reservations. JP's demand, he explained, required the RSS to be attuned to new values. As this was a time-consuming process, quick results were not easy to produce. Deoras proceeded to go to the root of the problem which time could not possibly have solved. He had drawn JP's attention to 'the mode of prayers'. They would have to be altered to suit the new entrants without hurting the feelings of those accustomed to old ways for years. The problem was to condition the minds of the old timers to the new concepts. This would require time, he repeatedly stressed.[39]

It was for the first time that Deoras candidly stated his real problem. But the candour halted just as his exposition touched the heart of the problem. The RSS could not possibly agree to cease to be what it had been for 52 years. A body committed to the 'concept' of Hindutva, propagated by Savarkar, Golwalkar & Co. could not shed that ideology and become something radically new. Besides, there was no incentive for such a change. The RSS had survived two bans and ostracism. Its men were now in power at the Centre and in the states. JP's leverage was limited. The RSS had only to avoid a confrontation to avert a break. Krishna Kant, a Janata Party leader showed pressmen a copy of *Navjeevan*, a Hindi daily of Lucknow, which reported Deoras as assuring RSS members that the day was not far off when

38 *The Indian Express*, 30 October 1977.

39 *The Indian Express*, 31 October 1977.

power would come into their hands. Morarji Desai and Charan Singh were old men.[40]

Deoras had gone to JP with a powerful delegation determined to brazen out the mess. Accompanying him were his younger brother Bhaurao, Rajendra Singh, his successor to be, and a couple of others. JP's secretary Sachidanand briefed the press on the next day's meeting. Deoras had explained to JP that while the RSS considered Muslims and Christians as part and parcel of Indian life, it was of the opinion that the terms 'Hindu' and 'Bharatiya' were synonymous and that 'Hinduism was not associated with any particular form of worship'.[41] The RSS was 'seriously considering the admission of Muslims, Christians and others into its fold but affirmed at the same time that undue haste would not help'.

This contradiction, like many others, recurs constantly in the RSS's discourse. It would assert that all who lived in India are Bharatiya, a term 'synonymous' with 'Hindus'. On other occasions the term Hindu would be defined to mean the majority community. On Vijaya Dashami Day at Nagpur on 21 October, Deoras said that it was no secret that the RSS had been established to mobilise the Hindus in the country. In fact way back in 1925 this was the purpose of Dr. Hedgewar, the RSS's founder. 'What is wrong in mobilising the Hindus? 85 per cent of the people in the country are Hindus and unless they are organised and mobilised, healthy growth of society and the country cannot be achieved.'[42]

Clearly, the word Hindu was not synonymous with Indians or even Bharatiya as the RSS would claim at times. The RSS was set up in 1925 to mobilise the majority community. It lived to accomplish the goal it had set before it, namely a Hindu Rashtra or nation on which to build a Hindu State, Hindu Raj. All this was declared only a few days before Deoras met JP. After the meeting he reverted to the deceptive tune on 6 November. Every Indian was part of the national cultural mainstream. He needed time; non-Hindus could raise objections to the party flag, prayer and many such things.[43]

Given the basic character of the RSS no parleys could have persuaded it to shed its character and repudiate its commitment of half a century. JP had landed himself in a bind; in this he was not alone though. The RSS support was accepted in 1974. In 1976 it promised to cease its work, as O.P. Tyagi said. In 1977 the RSS backed out. JP, who had ever loathed the RSS, was keen to arrive at a compromise. The RSS refused to oblige. This conflict was inherent in the politics of 1974-75 and was inherently insoluble and inevitable. So was the break-up of the Janata Party. The RSS was fighting for its survival. Acceptance of JP's terms in 1977 or those of the Janata Party in 1979-80 spelt its divide.

[40] *Hindustan Times*, 28 October 1977.

[41] *The Indian Express*, 2 November 1977.

[42] *The Times of India*, 22 October 1977.

[43] *Hindustan Times*, 7 November 1977.

After JP's meetings with Deoras there was a lull for some time. The debate was revived in 1978. The newly-elected general secretary Rajendra Singh rejected any bar on RSS men joining the Janata Party. The RSS could not be divorced from politics. Its National Council had adopted resolutions on Centre-State relations, Nagaland and Kashmir.[44] Curiously on 4 April 1978 Deoras claimed some progress on admission of non-Hindus.[45]

This was untrue. Difference kept simmering not far below the surface. The RSS made itself comfortable, meanwhile. The situation was accurately summed up on 4 December 1978 in an editorial in *The Statesman*:

> The claim on the RSS's behalf that it had no part in the Aligarh clashes or in the organised attacks on Muslim minorities in Varanasi, Hyderabad and other cities, some as far afield as Tellicherry in Kerala, has yet to be convincingly established. On the other hand, the Union Home Ministry's reported proposal to ban RSS shakhas holding parades and weapons drills in as many as 14 cities prone to communal disturbances tells a different story.
>
> The RSS, which was somewhat diffidently casting about for a new role 20 months ago, has gained in confidence. Its cadres are active is schools and colleges all over the country, and as Mr. Limaye has said in his letter to the Prime Minister, the RSS volunteers made themselves 'useful' to the ruling party in Ujjain during Janata's conclave last month. Apparently some Janata leaders have veered round to the view that the RSS is a necessary evil and that it would eventually mellow and settle down to being the party's boy scouts' organisation although the late Madhav Rao Muley had unambiguously declared that it would be nobody's boy scouts. Mr. Limaye's concern over Central and State Ministers attending RSS functions is widely shared. Although he does not say so specifically, he was obviously referring to the Shishu Sangam, a massive three-day jamboree of 15,000 children from over 700 schools in the country. It was inaugurated by the President, Mr. Sanjiva Reddy, on 10 November. The festivities, at which Mr. Jagjivan Ram was one of the chief-guests, is generally believed to have been organised by the RSS. This may not be so, despite Mr. Balasaheb Deoras's conspicuous involvement. But it has created an unfortunate impression and there has been no attempt to allay the minorities' anxieties. Janata's standing as a secular political party is in some danger of being compromised by its association, direct or indirect, with the RSS and the fact that the number of RSS shakhas has increased from 9,000 to 12,000 in the past 20 months has reinforced the belief that, it enjoys official patronage.

Limaye opened a Pandora's box on 29 December 1978. That the RSS had

[44] *The Statesman*, 13 March 1978.

[45] *The Times of India*, 6 April 1978.

submitted contradictory affidavits on oath to the Charity Commissioner and to the income tax authorities was no secret. The tax authorities were told that the RSS was a political, not cultural body. The Charity Commissioner was given a different story. The episode merits a closer analysis in a separate chapter. On 12 March 1979 Deoras publicly admitted that the RSS had filed an affidavit in a Nagpur Court in which it admitted to being an organisation 'akin to politics'.[46] The documents tell their own tale.[47]

Atal Bihari Vajpayee was torn between his membership of the RSS and his fears of a split in the Janata Party. He said at Kolkata on 15 March 1979 that the RSS should be reformist in character and devote itself wholeheartedly to remove social ills like untouchability. He added, 'The RSS has no political ambitions. It is a cultural organisation.' Attacks on it were 'politically motivated'.[48] He kept in line with Deoras's claim on 4 March. 'We are not interested in politics.'[49]

Opinion within the country was building up against the RSS. On 24 April 1979 all, bar the Jana Sangh, attacked the details of the incriminating document trickled out in the press. Desai was prompted to write to Deoras asking him to clarify whether the RSS was a political body.[50] He had in mind minor curbs on ministers – no participation in RSS drills or rallies, no appearance in its uniform at its functions and the like.[51] At the same time he dismissed the controversy as irrelevant.

George Fernandes, a close colleague of Limaye, and Jagjivan Ram were neutral when the party's parliamentary board discussed the issue on 6 May. Desai supported Vajpayee on fears of a Jana Sangh take-over. Vajpayee replied that the solution was to stop enrolment of members and run the party on the basis of a consensus among the constituent parties.[52] That was the only way to save the party. An enrolment drive was underway in which the RSS cadres worked actively. Hence the fears of a take-over. The Jana Sangh members also mooted a national convention of the party in which they would muster a majority.

Vajpayee tried a lot to save the sinking boat. The RSS should open its doors to all citizens of the country.[53] Any attempt by the RSS to 'meddle with the Janata Party politics will not be tolerated. I am loyal only to the Janata Party'.[54]

In what appeared to be a breakthrough, the parliamentary board unanimously authorised Desai to evolve a solution to the 'dual membership' issue. The prospects

[46] *Hindustan Times*, 13 March 1979.

[47] Vide Chapter 25 and Appendix 8 for the texts of the sworn affidavits.

[48] *The Statesman*, 16 March 1979; UNI report.

[49] *Hindustan Times*, 5 March 1979.

[50] *The Statesman*, 30 April 1979.

[51] *The Hindu*, 1 May 1979.

[52] *The Statesman*, 7 May 1979.

[53] *The Indian Express*, 14 May 1979.

[54] Ibid.

of a solution were, however, bleak. Rajendra Singh indicated on 18 June that the RSS would only accept those who would acknowledge that their culture was 'rooted' in Indian soil. The RSS shakhas had even begun lessons on 'the Indian version of karate'.[55] Karate is of foreign origin. A clear understanding of the RSS's concept of 'culture' emerged in Deoras's interview to Saeed Naqvi, a veteran journalist. 'It is important that Muslims identify with Ram as an Indian Symbol.'[56]

As expected, Desai dithered. By the end of June 1979 moves were afoot to force a solution; if need be, by removing the Jana Sangh ministers. Limaye having resigned as the general secretary, demanded a decision on 'organisational elections'.[57] The RSS agreed to a suggestion that the Janata Party members be barred from participating in the day-to-day activities of the RSS, just as no office-bearer of a political party could hold office in the RSS. Rajendra Singh insisted that this would not cover participation in the shakhas which was every member's right.[58]

By now the Janata Party had lost power. Charan Singh forged a pact with Indira Gandhi which led to Desai's resignation as prime minister. On 2 August 1979 *The Indian Express* published Vajpayee's famous article which astonished everybody. He wrote:

> It is possible that some people genuinely feel apprehensive about the RSS. A certain onus accordingly devolved on the RSS, an onus that has not been discharged effectively by the RSS. Its repudiation of the theocratic form of the state was welcome, yet the question could legitimately be asked – why does it not open its doors to non-Hindus? Recent statements of the RSS Chief Mr. Deoras indicate that non-Hindus are being encouraged to join the organisation. A national corollary of this process would be clear enunciation by the RSS that by 'Hindu Rashtra' it means the Indian nation which includes non-Hindus as equal members.
>
> The other course of action open to the RSS could be to function only as a Hindu religious-cum-social-cultural organisation wedded to the task of eradicating the evils prevailing in Hindu society and revitalising it to face the challenges of modern times. The kind of selfless service that the RSS had rendered in times of natural calamities has endeared it even to its critics and has established beyond doubt its capacity for constructive work for ameliorating the suffering of those who are in need of help. Such an organisation will draw support and sustenance from members of various political parties as has been the case with institutions like the Arya Samaj.
>
> The Indian polity cannot survive, unless it is rooted in certain ideals.

55 *Hindustan Times*, 19 June 1979.

56 Saeed Naqvi, *Reflections of an Indian Muslim*, New Delhi: Har-Anand, 1993, p. 139.

57 *Hindustan Times*, 30 June 1979.

58 *Hindustan Times*, 2 August 1979.

> Among these are commitment to democracy, secularism, the equal participation of all communities and religions in national life, the upliftment of Harijans, Adivasis and the millions of the desperately poor. The country must develop on modern, scientific lines, ensuring at the same time social and distributive justice.
>
> Today we face a crisis of a magnitude which nations face only once in several centuries. The pursuit of personal ambition, factional interest and self-aggrandisement, so blatantly displayed by some politicians recently has not only made politicians as a class the object of ridicule but also undermined faith in our political system. Let all politicians search their souls, acknowledge their failings and mend their ways. What is now at stake is not the fortune of a handful of individuals or parties. At stake is the survival of our nation.

Rajendra Singh edged a bit further on. He recalled that 'in 1977, its volunteers participated in the Lok Sabha elections in the national interest under extraordinary political compulsions'. About the dual membership controversy in the Janata Party, he said,

> This is not an issue before us as the Sangh is not a political organisation. There is already a provision in our constitution for debarring the office-bearers of any political party from holding any key posts in the organisational network. Now we have decided to include MPs and MLAs as well in the category of such persons at the request of Janata Chief Chandra Shekhar and other well-meaning friends.

He indicated that the general body of the Sangh would meet sometime in March next, to make the necessary changes in its constitution. At present the Sangh was running 13,000 centres and 20,000 shakhas in the country. It was now a strong organisation. In Bihar, the number of its shakhas had increased from 1,000 to 1,400 during the last two years.[59] He had publicly expressed his disagreement with Vajpayee who, however, went on to claim that the RSS had been doing some rethinking on the line he had suggested in his article.[60]

Deoras threw a bombshell at a closed door meeting at Bhopal on 16 September. The tirade against the RSS was due to its increased popularity since the Emergency. In 10 years it would gain the popularity needed to form a government at the Centre. 'Nobody can grudge such an eventuality in a democratic set-up.'

He refused to play the tape which had recorded his remarks. 'The tapes would be played in due course.'[61] To shed light on the debate, the RSS organising secretary

59 *Hindustan Times*, 28 August 1979.

60 *Hindustan Times*, 14 September 1979.

61 *The Times of India*, 21 September 1979.

Yadava Rao Joshi explained the relationship between the RSS and the Jana Sangh. It was 'that of the father and the son but with independent views and thinking'.[62]

Vajpayee stuck to his stand. In an interview published in the Diwali issue of the Jana Sangh weekly, *Sadhana*, he said it would be impossible to preserve secularism in India if the Hindus became communal.[63] As before, some one or the other contradicted him; this time it was Deoras, no less. 'The Sangh believes in Hindu Rashtra', the invite to his rally in Mumbai said. 'Hindu society living here since time immemorial has given rise to a great and comprehensive life society [sic].' Reference to 'time immemorial' excludes non-Hindus; a principle avowed by Savarkar from which the RSS never budged. The theme was repeated at the rally on 27 October while the debate on dual membership was nearing closure.[64]

Vajpayee continued to plough his lonely furrow with none in the Jana Sangh to support him. On 18 December 1979 he called on the RSS to change its 'methodology, ideology, programme and activities'. This was a tall order. In an interview to an Urdu weekly he made no bones about his association in the past with the pro-CPI All India Students' Federation and his 'obligation' to Marx for providing an explanation of poverty. The CPI's support to the partition of India disillusioned him. Had he not joined the RSS he would have become a communist.[65] Deoras was unmoved. Organising the Hindus was a 'national necessity'. For Hindus constituted 85 per cent of the population of this country.[66]

When Indira Gandhi returned to power in the general election held in December 1979, Deoras pledged his cooperation with her. One and all must allow the Congress (I) to carry out its mandate.[67]

The dual membership issue was revived. This time Jagjivan Ram was in the forefront of the agitation. Within the RSS a section complained that the coalition had not helped it. L.K. Advani stridently put forth his view which was diametrically opposed to Vajpayee's. Meanwhile Deoras began seriously to explore avenues of cooperation with Indira Gandhi. She had 'changed' he said.[68] He went so far as to declare that the RSS had no differences with the Congress (I). The RSS had not worked for any of the parties in the election since the June 1977 Assembly election.[69] The *volte face* was immediately and sharply criticised by the Chief Minister of Gujarat Babubhai Patel.[70]

[62] *The Indian Express*, 24 September 1979.
[63] *Hindustan Times*, 25 October 1979.
[64] *The Indian Express*, 28 October 1979.
[65] *The Statesman*, 19 December 1979.
[66] *The Hindu*, January 1980.
[67] *The Indian Express*, 29 January 1980.
[68] *The Times of India*, 13 February 1980.
[69] *The Times of India*, 13 February 1980.
[70] *The Times of India*, 14 February 1980.

The Janata Party president, Chandra Shekhar worked out a formula which he took to Deoras at Nagpur who said, 'If this is standing in the way of the integration of the Janata Party there should be no objection to the acceptance of the formula. But this could be done only at the next Pratinidhi Sabha which was due to meet on 31 March.'[71]

The formula read:

> (1) No member of the Janata Party shall join or remain in a public organisation whose aims and objectives are not in harmony with the party. (2) The Janata Party office-bearers and legislators shall be prohibited from taking part in the day to day activities of the RSS.

The Jana Sangh's leaders in the Janata Party acted in concert with the RSS chief; Nana Deshmukh coordinating. The Janata Party had made a pact with the Devil. Its parleys, three years after its formation, centred on cosmetics; persuading the Devil to retract his hoofs and horns. They did not touch the evil within him. The formula was adopted, with inconsequential verbal charges by the Parliamentary Board on 26 February, and ratified by the National Executive the next day. It was reiterated by the parliamentary board on 18 March.[72] Vajpayee, Advani and Deshmukh agreed with the part concerning front organisations; but rejected the one on the RSS connection. The issue was remitted to the National Executive which was due to meet on 3 April.

The RSS's general secretary Rajendra Singh contemplated an amendment to the RSS constitution to exempt Janata Party legislators from the obligation to attend meetings of the Sangh's branches. M.G. Vaidya asked the RSS Marathi daily *Tarun Bharat*, 'Would any shop-keeper ask his customers not to patronise his shop?'[73]

The RSS refused to enlarge the disqualification clause. On 23 March its Pratinidhi Sabha passed this brief resolution.

> The Sarkaryavaha Prof. Rajendra Singh apprised the Akhil Bharatiya Karyakari Mandal (National Executive) of the circumstances and spirit in which his statement of 24 July 1979 was made. After due consideration, the ABKM felt that nothing need be done in this matter. The matter was later placed before the Akhil Bharatiya Pratinidhi Sabha and it endorsed the decision of the ABKM unanimously.

In his statement Rajendra Singh had promised the Janata Party chief Chandra Shekhar to put before the RSS Pratinidhi Sabha a suggestion to bar office-bearers

[71] *The Statesman*, 1 March 1980.

[72] *The Statesman* and *The Times of India*, 20 March 1980.

[73] *The Times of India*, 23 March 1980.

of political parties, members of parliament and state legislators from participation in the RSS activities.

The RSS constitution says that 'a swayamsevak (volunteer-member) who is an office-bearer of a political party shall not be eligible for election or be an appointee to any post so long as he is such an office-bearer'.

The Janata Party's efforts to resolve the crisis in its ranks in July 1978 got nowhere. It suggested to the RSS to widen this provision in its constitution to disqualify M.P.s and M.L.A.s along with the office-bearers of political parties from any elected post to which Deoras had agreed.[74] Deoras had assured Chandra Shekhar of this on 22 March.

> In the broader national interest, which is the need of the hour, I shall put before the Pratinidhi Sabha a proposal that no party office-bearer, MP or legislator of any political party should participate in the daily activities of the RSS.

Satisfied with the meeting, Mr. Chandra Shekhar returned to Delhi and urged the Janata Party parliamentary board to shelve the RSS issue for the time as he had found a solution to the problem. The solution was Mr. Deoras and the Pratinidhi Sabha would be barring politicians from participating in the daily activities of the RSS in March.[75]

In December 1977 they had objected to an amendment to Clause V of the Janata constitution which would have denied membership to anyone who was a member of any other organisation whose aims, objectives and activities were inconsistent with those of the Janata Party. At Morarji Desai's instance a decision was put off.

After the Janata government's fall in July 1979, the party amended Clause V to declare that the concept of a religious state was against the creed of the Janata Party. Chandra Shekhar negotiated a formula with Deoras whereby, like office-bearers of the parties, legislators would also be debarred from taking part in day-to-day RSS activities. It was to be confirmed by the RSS Pratinidhi Sabha in March 1980. Chandra Shekhar and Rajendra Singh announced the accord separately on 24 July 1979.

Yet, when the RSS Executive met on 23 March 1980, Singh apprised it of the circumstances and spirit in which his statement of 24 July 1979 was made. After due consideration, the ABKM (the Executive) felt that nothing need be done in the matter. The Pratinidhi Sabha endorsed the decision unanimously. In February 1980 the Janata Party Executive had adopted the agreed formula as a basis for discussion with the Jana Sangh faction. It said: 'No legislator or office-bearer of the Janata Party shall participate in the day-to-day activities of the RSS. No member of the

[74] *The Hindu*, 24 March 1980.

[75] *The Indian Express*, 23 March 1979.

Janata Party shall work in any front organisation which functions in competition to one sponsored by the Janata Party.'

On 18 March, the Janata parliamentary board adopted this formulation. The Jana Sangh accepted its second part, but not the first. The issue was remitted to the National Executive which was to meet on 3 April. But, on 26 March the Jana Sangh members called a convention of their supporters on 5 April 1980.

On 4 April, the National Executive adopted the parliamentary board's formulation by 17 votes as against 14 for Morarji's formula which the Jana Sangh had accepted. It read:

> Every member of the Janata Party shall unconditionally accept and strive to preserve the composite culture and secular state established in our country and nation not based on religion. He shall not allow his membership of any other organisation to derogate from this obligation. The National Executive further decided that: 1. No member of the Janata Party shall work in any front organisations which function in competition to any organisation sponsored by the Janata Party. 2. No member of what are described as constituent parties of the Janata Party should hold exclusive meetings of their own or take any action calculated to capture the elected organs of the party.

The next day the Jana Sangh decided to form a new party, the Bharatiya Janata Party (BJP). A futile effort to paper the cracks had ended.

JP lived to see his dreams shattered; his hopes betrayed. The leading Hindi weekly *Dinman* published, in its issue of 8-14 April 1979, the draft of a letter containing his views on the RSS which he had proposed to send to Morarji Desai before he fell ill and was removed to Jaslok Hospital on 18 March. The special representative of the weekly, Anand Kumar interviewed JP and met his principal colleagues in his Ashram at Kadam Kuan, Patna. The text of the letter is as follows:

> Some friends have repeatedly complained that the Rashtriya Swayam Sewak Sangh is making efforts to grab the leadership in the Government. Like other political parties the RSS is free to influence politics and it is doing so. But my only objection is that the RSS people are trying to influence politics under the garb of a cultural organisation. I have advised the leaders of the RSS to merge themselves with organisations sympathetic to them or get affiliated with the Janata Party. But, they declined my advice on the plea that they have their own distinct cultural identity and that they have nothing to do with politics. I absolutely do not agree with this logic of the RSS. I still feel that the RSS should merge itself with the pro-Janata organisations. But if it is bent upon retaining its own distinct identity I would then repeat that it should include in it, non-Hindus – Muslims, Christians, etc. I have always condemned Hindu

> nationalism of the RSS. For it is a dangerous doctrine and is against the ideal of composite Indian nationalism.
>
> In democracy every organisation has a right to propagate its philosophy or ideology – this is essence of democracy. But when it aspires to dominate politics, we would have to be careful to see whether such philosophy or ideology threatens the basic philosophy of Indian nationalism. I have no quarrel with the association of the RSS with the Janata Party. But it will have to give up its Hindu image and become completely secular. If it does not do so, it should keep its hands off politics and snap its ties with every faction of the Janata Party.
>
> But as Prime Minister of India, it is your duty to make efforts to improve the RSS or make it a secular force. Its efforts to upset the secular basis of Indian nationalism and the government should be opposed by all thinking individuals.

The *Dinman* correspondent also quoted JP as having told him, 'Every time the RSS people assure me that they would internally improve. But I do not know what do they do after going from here. It is continuing like this for the last four years. After all there is a limit to everything.'[76]

JP died in October 1979, disappointed with Morarji's performance ('a flop'), let down by the Janata Party leaders and betrayed by the RSS leaders like Nana Deshmukh and Deoras. He believed that the RSS could be reformed. The RSS demonstrated that it had no wish to be 'reformed' into a secular conservative party. It was determined to serve as Hindutva's spearhead come what may. To accomplish this, it was prepared to lie, cheat and deceive.

[76] *Janata*, 13 May 1979. *Janata* is a Mumbai weekly founded by JP. It is now edited by his devoted follower Dr. G.G. Parikh.

15. The BJP's Birth and the RSS's Problem

The BJP's birth in 1980, after the Jana Sangh's split with the Janata Party, ensured the RSS with yet greater control. It is important to note that while the BJP is ambiguous about the relationship, the RSS is explicit and open. Advani was vague. 'The RSS has a kind of moral authority which I believe is health-giving for the BJP.'[1] This is untrue. Acceptance of moral authority is a matter of choice. An organic relationship between a parent outfit and its special wing is not. The degree of control may vary. In the case of the BJP it has increased.

Years later the veteran RSS leader M.G. Vaidya was asked pointedly: 'What is the role of the RSS appointees who work inside the BJP as Organising Secretaries?' He was brutally frank in his reply. '*Isliye ki party theek dhang se chaley* (So that the party is run properly). The first in this role was Deendayal Upadhyaya with the Bharatiya Jana Sangh. We have sent people like Sunder Singh Bhandari and Kushabhau Thakre to the BJP in this role. The last person was Sanjay Joshi. Now it is Ram Lal. They work very closely with the RSS.'[2] Which political party in a democracy has controllers sent from outside? And what does it say of a 'cultural' body that it sends its commissars to ensure that its political front 'is run properly' ('*theek dhang se chaley*').

In 2005, Ram Madhav, then the RSS spokesman and now the BJP's general secretary, brushed aside Advani's call for a debate on the BJP's equation with the RSS after the RSS had sacked him as BJP president, that 'till now the BJP's relationship with the RSS was described as an umbilical cord'; an organic relationship.[3]

Like the Jana Sangh, the BJP was in reality the RSS performing in politics. It faced a problem as Vajpayee and Advani acquired a mass following. But their need for the RSS's cadres inhibited any attempt at autonomy.

The RSS is the mother. The BJP is its child tied to it by an umbilical cord. The cord is broken at birth to give the newborn child an independent existence. The RSS has flatly refused to break the cord and deny the Jana Sangh and, later, the BJP an independent existence. It gives them a good rope but retains the last word, ideologically and organisationally. The record since the birth of the Jana Sangh from 1951 till its formal dissolution and merger into the Janata Party in 1977 shows how unreal were the hopes and expectations that it would emerge as a secular conservative party and discard Savarkar's Hindutva and Golwalkar's teachings; in short, its ideology and *raison d'ètre*.

1 *Outlook*, 6 August 1997.
2 *Tehelka*, 12 September 2009.
3 *Outlook*, 3 October 2005.

Its break from the Janata Party in 1980 and subsequent performance to this day confirms that there was no way that the Jana Sangh members of the Janata Party would or could break the umbilical cord. JP's efforts in that direction as also those of the Janata Party he founded were unrealistic in the extreme. Pursuits of a compromise formula were, in reality, attempts to cover the cracks with paper. Had they succeeded, would Vajpayee and Advani have abandoned the RSS or would the RSS cease to be what it was for over half a century?

The RSS rushed to force a break. On 18 March 1980 the Janata Party's parliamentary board adopted a formulation which the Jana Sangh members could accept though only in part. The issue was remitted to the National Executive which was due to meet on 3 April. Before it could meet the Jana Sangh called a convention of its supporters on 5 April to set up a new party that day. The RSS's peremptory order forced the move. That was not the Jana Sangh revived. It was the Bharatiya Janata Party.

The new party faced an identity crisis at its very birth. The natural and honest course was revival of the Jana Sangh but the leaders decided, instead, to revive it under a new and deceptive name. The Jana Sangh had proved to be a 'banjar zamin' on which nothing can grow, Vajpayee told the writer in April 1979. Advani's claim that they were 'determined to chart a new course' was belied by his own conduct and that of the party.[4] Use of the name 'Janata' was designed to convey that 'we considered ourselves to be the true inheritance of the legacy of the Janata Party' and that of Jayaprakash Narayan.

On the dais at the inaugural convention at the Ferozeshah Kotla grounds three portraits were displayed, namely those of S.P. Mookerjee, founder of the Jana Sangh, Deen Dayal Upadhyaya, its 'ideological guide' and Jayaprakash Narayan, who was soon to be dropped as a guide. Upadhyaya's 'Integral Humanism' continued to be the guiding philosophy of the BJP, the party also affirmed its commitment, for the first time ever by an RSS front to 'Gandhian socialism'.[5] This innovation was also dropped later. Before the decade was out, this party openly advocated Hindutva. While in 1980 BJP leaders claimed to be the real heirs to the Janata Party of Jayaprakash Narayan, rather than to the Jana Sangh, today they claim to be closer to the RSS than the Jana Sangh was. Speaking to an RSS gathering in Coimbatore in 1990, Advani said, 'While in the case of the BJS the linkage [with the RSS] was only ideological, in the case of the BJP the linkage is both ideological and historical.' He asked his audience to realise that 'the BJP which you described as a good party is good only because of its association with the RSS'.[6]

On 26 February 1980, Advani himself had written to the Janata Party's president,

[4] Advani, *My Country, My Life*, p. 311.

[5] Ibid., p. 112.

[6] *The Telegraph*, 17 May 1990.

Chandra Shekhar: 'Our commitment to the party's principles and programmes, the concepts of Gandhian socialism and secularism, has been total and unequivocal.' This, of course, was to secularism as understood by the Janata Party – something which Advani subsequently dubbed as pseudo-secularism.

Whether as Jana Sangh or BJP it was the RSS in action through its political front. The new party did not act as if it was heir to the Janata Party at all. On 31 August 1980, Vajpayee, then BJP president, defended the RSS and accused the government of appeasing the minorities. At the party's first plenary convention in Mumbai on 28 December 1980, Vajpayee significantly recalled the history of the Jana Sangh. 'Gandhian socialism' was affirmed as one of the five commitments. The others were nationalism and national integration, democracy, 'positive secularism'. It did not gel. For the cadres yearned still for the Jana Sangh.

All the top leaders performed a *volte face*. On 6 November 1977 Vajpayee declared: 'When we joined the Janata Party we had given up our old beliefs and faiths and there was no question of going back.' Once in the BJP he asked, 'When did we get away from the Jana Sangh?' No less revealing was his remark on 22 July 1985: 'We wanted to assert our views in the (Janata Party) Government, but the Government broke up too soon. Had we been in power for some more time, we would have imparted a new thinking to India's politics.'

The RSS chief now felt himself freed from the restraints imposed by JP. He repeated the stereotype of the marauding Muslim, 'History says Muslim conversion was by force all over the world.'[7]

The true face of the BJP emerged later in the year at its convention in December 1980. But not before overtures to Indira Gandhi. Deoras declared 'we can cooperate with anyone for the welfare of the party'. This was his answer to a specific question on cooperating with Indira Gandhi.[8] On 16 August 1980 Vajpayee and Advani called on her to allege that Muslims were being pitted against 'the law and order machinery' by some. There was foreign hand 'behind the gory Moradabad riots'. The meeting was held at their request.[9] The veteran G.K. Reddy of *The Hindu*, however, reported, on 18 August, that 'for the first time since the Jallianwala massacre as many as 130 Muslims have died in a day'. It was at the Idgah. The overture failed.

Indira Gandhi was not one to be impressed by the two leaders. On 27 September at Kolkata, she accused the RSS and the BJP of responsibility for the communal riots in north India. They had acquired some 'respectability' during the three years of Janata Party rule.[10] Rebuffed by his emissaries' failure, Deoras revived his themes. 'In India Hinduism and nationalism are one.' He called upon

[7] 4 April 1980.

[8] *Organiser*, 9 March 1980.

[9] *Hindustan Times*, 17 August 1980.

[10] *The Statesman*, 28 September 1980.

Hindus to declare themselves as 'Hindus' in the census, mentioning their caste or 'panth' only in brackets.[11]

As the first three-day convention of the BJP began in Mumbai on 28 December 1980 the RSS element came to the fore. Deoras spoke of 'the imperative need for the unification of Hindus' as 'the need of the nation'.[12] Some members at the convention objected to the expression 'Gandhian socialism' and urged its replacement by 'Gandhian Ramrajya'. Sikandar Bakht, formerly of the Congress (O), rejected brusquely a suggestion by Mehboob Ali, former Janata Party minister in Rajasthan, that the minorities' interests must be protected. He said that they had same rights as the majority community. Use of the terms 'majority and minority' must be avoided.[13]

Bhaurao Deoras spoke at the concluding session, on 30 December, to express his satisfaction at the proceedings. Younger brother of the RSS chief, he was joint secretary of the RSS. The BJP's convention was preceded by the RSS's winter camp in the city.[14]

As luck would have it, issues arose to give the fledgling party something to exploit. There were reports that Harijan families in the entire village of Meenakshipuram in the Tirunelveli district in Tamil Nadu, had converted to Islam in February 1981. Gulf money and the usual suspects, Muslim leaders, became targets for attack. The Report of the Regional Director for SC/ST Welfare, Government of India, Madras exposed the charges to be false.[15]

Since 1978 there was an outbreak of communal riots in the country; especially in Uttar Pradesh and Bihar. The Aligarh Muslim University campus was affected by violence since the students and members of the faculties agitated for the restoration of its character as an educational institution established by Muslims which was entitled to autonomy as a fundamental right guaranteed by Article 30(1) of the Constitution of India.

In May 1972 was enacted an amendment to the Aligarh Muslim University Act, 1921 which sanctified denial of autonomy as a grossly erroneous ruling the Supreme Court had laid down.[16] Finally, on 31 December 1981 Indira Gandhi secured enactment of the AMU (Amendment) Act, 1981 restoring the University's autonomy.

All this was grist to the mill run by the RSS and the BJP. More poisonous grist followed. On 23 April 1985 came the Supreme Court's judgment in the famous

[11] 19 October; reported in *Organiser*, 26 October 1980.

[12] *The Indian Express*, 29 December 1980.

[13] *The Statesman*, 30 December 1980.

[14] *The Indian Express*, 31 December 1980.

[15] Vide A.G. Noorani, *The Muslims of India: A Documentary Record*, Oxford University Press, 2003, pp. 186-91 for the text. Vide also *The Hindu*, 15 June 1981 for a detailed report.

[16] *S. Aziz Basha vs. Union of India*, AIR 1968 S.C. 662. H.M. Seervai's withering critique of the judgment exposed its flaws; vide *Constitutional Law of India*, vol. 1, 1975, pp. 610-8.

Shah Bano case.[17] A myth was fostered sedulously and with considerable success that nullification of the Court's ruling by the Muslim Women (Protection of Rights on Divorce) Act, 1986 prompted Prime Minister Rajiv Gandhi to secure the opening of the locks of the Masjid and, thus, revive an issue that was to blight relations between the communities and undermine secular values in the country.

Neerja Chowdhury's reports in *The Statesman* on 20 April and 1 May 1986 revealed, on the basis of authoritative sources, that, in fact the sequence was the very opposite of the one in political mythology. There was a prior understanding between Indira Gandhi and later Rajiv Gandhi and VHP on the opening of the locks.

A decision to open the lock was taken by Indira Gandhi. It was carried out by Rajiv Gandhi and Arun Nehru after her death. It is Muslims who were given the sop of the Bill. It was moved in the Lok Sabha on 19 February 1986. The lock was opened on 1 February.

On 8 April 1984, the Vishwa Hindu Parishad (VHP) gave a clarion call for the removal of the Babri Masjid. A rath yatra began on 25 September. Indira Gandhi's assassination led to its suspension. It was revived from 25 places on 23 October 1985. A deadline was fixed for Shivaratri on 8 March 1986. The entire episode was reported in detail by Neerja Chowdhury, on the basis of an authoritative disclosure by 'a senior Vishwa Hindu Parishad leader', in two articles in *The Statesman* on 20 April and 1 May 1986.

Rajiv Gandhi took over her policy, Neerja Chowdhury reported:

> Mr. Rajiv Gandhi had indicated in no uncertain terms that the gates of the Ram Janmabhoomi must open to devotees before Shivaratri on 8 March 1986. The Ram Janmabhoomi Mukti Samiti was planning to break open the temple lock that day and a sadhu had vowed to immolate himself if the temple doors were not flung open. A senior Vishwa Hindu Parishad leader revealed this information confidentially.
>
> The local administration had been prepared in advance. The court verdict was announced at 4.40 p.m. on 1 February and the rusty lock was actually being broken at 5.19 p.m. A Doordarshan team was posted on the spot to capture for posterity surging crowds entering the shrine.

Neerja Chowdhury added:

> There is evidence of a connection between the opening of the doors of the disputed Ram Janmabhoomi in Ayodhya and the introduction of the Muslim [Bill] in Parliament, both of which have heightened communal tension in the country. This is evident from the way the Bill came to be framed according to

[17] *Mohammed Ahmed Khan vs. Shah Bano Begum*, (1985) 2 SCC 556.

information contained in the report of the general secretary of the All India Muslim Personal Law Board which was presented to the Board at its meeting on 23 February 1986.

Deoki Nandan Agarwal, a former judge of the Allahabad High Court and one of the leading figures in the Ramjanmabhoomi movement has recorded the background. The Vishwa Hindu Parishad (VHP) owed its existence to the Rashtriya Swayamsevak Sangh (RSS) chief M.S. Golwalkar and Swami Chinmayananda's deliberations in Mumbai on 19 August 1964. Its first session was held at the 1966 Kumbh Mela in Allahabad. Agarwal recalled:

> At its session held at Vigyan Bhavan, New Delhi, on 7 and 8 April 1984 the Dharma Sansad of the Vishwa Hindu Parishad gave a call for the removal of the three mosque-like structures raised by Muslim marauders after destroying the ancient Hindu temples, at Sri Rama Janma Bhumi, Ayodhya, Sri Krishna Janmasthan, Mathura, and of Kashi Vishwanath at Gyanvapi, Varanasi. The so-called Babari Masjid at Ayodhya was taken up first. Sri Rama Janma Bhumi Mukti Yagna Samiti was formed with Sri Dau Dayal Khanna as its convenor and Gorak Shapeethadishwar Mahant Sri Aveda Nathji as its President. In order to create national awareness and arouse public opinion in support of the cause of liberation of Sri Rama Janma Bhumi, the Vishwa Hindu Parishad organised a Rath-Yatra of Sri Rama Janaki Virajman on motorised chariot, which started from Sitamarhi in Bihar on 25 September 1984. The Ratha passed through important towns of Bihar and reached Ayodhya on 6 October 1984.
>
> Indira Gandhi's assassination on 31 October 1984 led to the suspension of the rath-yatra. But it was revived from twenty-five places on 23 October 1985. The VHP spearheaded the move. The D-day was fixed as 9 March 1986. Its leaders met the Chief Minister of Uttar Pradesh, Vir Bahadur Singh and the district magistrate.

Agarwal admitted: 'On 19 December 1985 Sri Vir Bahadur Singh, the Chief Minister of Uttar Pradesh visited Ayodhya on the occasion of the Ramayana Mela sponsored by government agencies. A few of us headed by our President Justice Shiva Nath Katju, had assembled at Ayodhya.' They met V.B. Singh.

A twenty-eight-year old local lawyer, Umesh Chandra Pandey, filed an application on 25 January 1986 in the court of the munsif seeking removal of the restrictions on the puja, in the case to which he was not a party. Nor did he implead the Muslims who were parties to the suit. The munsif declined, judiciously enough, to pass the order since the file in the main case of 1961 was in the High Court and orders could be made only in that suit. An appeal was filed on 31 January and heard on 1 February 1986. An application by Mohammad Hashim, a plaintiff in the case who came to know of the proceedings, for being impleaded, was rejected. K.M. Pandey, the district judge of Faizabad, recorded the statements of the district magistrate and the superintendent of police on the issue of law and order and in forty minutes ordered the opening of the locks. The locks were opened instantly. A TV crew was at hand.

The fate of the Babri mosque had sealed well before Rajiv Gandhi began his parleys with Muslim leaders on the Supreme Court's ruling. . . .

The locks were opened *first* on 1 February 1986. Parleys between Rajiv Gandhi and Muslim leaders picked up speed thereafter. As a sop the Muslims were given the Muslim Women's Bill.

These events must be viewed in the context of the RSS-BJP attempts to set the new party, the BJP, afloat. However, it was revival of the Jana Sangh not the establishment of a new party, which the cadres wanted at its New Delhi convention in April 1980. A correspondent who painstakingly took the soundings reported their mood. His report does more than capture the mood of the party then. It explains why the BJP had shed the false plumage it had put on to win popular acceptance. It deserves quotation *in extenso.*

> If the mood of the 4,000-odd delegates at the two-day convention called by Mr. L.K. Advani, is any indication, revival of the Jana Sangh after the Assembly elections is a distinct possibility.
>
> An overwhelming number of delegates most of them block, district and State-level office bearers and active workers of the erstwhile Jana Sangh, were in fact disappointed with the leadership's decision to name the new party as the Bharatiya Janata Party. . . .
>
> Many of them were, therefore, disappointed that the convention did not decide to opt for Jana Sangh. Defence of the Jana Sangh Central Ministers, Chief Ministers, praise of the RSS, its discipline, its patriotism and its high moral and social service record by all those who spoke, was as much the striking feature of the convention and the public rally as the strong criticism of the non-Jana Sangh faction leaders of the party.
>
> Many of those who sent in their suggestions for the party's name, symbol and flag, suggested 'Bhartiya Jana Sangh', lamp, and saffron flag, respectively. The delegate response to speeches from the dais was a very clear indication of their mood. Every time a delegate welcomed the Jana Sangh faction's decisions to walk out of the Janata Party, he or she was greeted with loud and prolonged applause and slogans of 'Bharat Mata Ki Jai'. When a woman delegate from Maharashtra said she was feeling free after 'suffering three years of continued suffocation in the Janata Party', she was wildly cheered.[18]

[18] *The Indian Express*, 7 April 1980.

But the RSS was set on developing the new party as a 'national alternative'. Advani knew that the BJP faced a dilemma. Why would people vote for a BJP seen as an RSS stooge? In an interview to the RSS weekly *Panchajanya* (Deepavali 1980), Advani disagreed with the view that the Janata Party would die because it had no ideology:

> Advani: No. I do not agree with it for in India a party based on ideology can at the most come to power in a small area. It cannot win the confidence of the entire country – neither the Communist Party nor the Jana Sangh in its original form.
>
> *Panchajanya*: But by ignoring the ideological appeal will you be able to keep together the cadres on the basis of these ideals?
>
> Advani: Effort is being made to make them understand. That is why I want the debate to go on. In this context, some people have criticised me although even during the Jana Sangh days I used to advocate these ideas. I have already said that the Jana Sangh was initially built as a party based on ideology but slowly it departed from that course.
>
> *Panchajanya*: However, despite its ideological anchorage, the Jana Sangh's appeal was steadily increasing.
>
> Advani: The appeal increased to the extent the ideology got diluted. Wherever the ideology was strong, its appeal diminished.

This strategy failed.

Indira Gandhi had stolen the BJP's clothes while its leaders were basking in the glow of popular applause. The communal poison had spread gradually to foul the atmosphere. In 1981, Karan Singh, a former health minister in Indira Gandhi's government, having deposed against her in the Shah Commission, left the Congress. All extremist Hindutvaites founded the Virat Hindu Samaj. He explained his decision as follows:

> The Virat Hindu Samaj, basically, was envisaged as a social reform organisation. The real, proximate cause was the conversions of Meenakshipuram. . . . I tried to put the emphasis on looking inwards. Why is it that people convert? Is it that the Harijans still feel discriminated against? The Hindu opinion was divided, even before independence into two streams, one is the RSS parivar [family], the other may be called the Congress parivar. The latter never call themselves Hindus but they are also good Hindus as anybody else. In a way the Virat Hindu Samaj was a sort of an attempt to bridge. I, having been in the Congress all my life, felt that there were people who may be turned off, who may not go to the RSS parivar but who would come here.

Karan Singh became president of the Virat Hindu Samaj. Its officers were staunch Hindutvaites, not secularists, Hans Raj Gupta and O.P. Tyagi (vice presidents), V.H. Dalmia (treasurer) and Ashok Singhal (general secretary).[19]

Vajpayee did what he could to make the BJP a success but the cadre's mood was different. In an interview to James M. Markham of *The New York Times* published on 14 June 1984 Vajpayee sharply criticised Indira Gandhi.

> Mrs. Gandhi is playing a very dangerous game. The long-term interests of the country are being sacrificed to short-term gains. But encouraging Hindu chauvinism is not going to pay. As the majority community, the Hindus must be above parochial politics.

Indira Gandhi's assassination on 31 October 1984 upset everyone's plans. Deoras admired her as well as her son Sanjay. The RSS support to the Jana Sangh in the 1984 general election to the Lok Sabha was the lowest ever as Neerja Chowdhury described the scene later. The RSS had been 'alienated from the BJP' and was

> known to have worked for the Congress (I) in the last elections. Even within the BJP, the RSS lobby is reportedly reasserting. The RSS too is in a state of ferment, say its middle-level workers. Despite the signals from their leadership to work for the BJP in the 1984 elections – Nanaji Deshmukh was an exception – the rank and file campaigned for the Congress (I) in many areas. This was not due to a secret understanding the RSS had reached with the Congress (I) as is widely believed, an RSS worker said. It was due to a crisis within the RSS. There is a growing disillusionment in the RSS cadre towards their leadership whose instructions on political matters they are not obeying. The leaders would prefer to let people go on believing that it was some kind of an agreement.

After the Janata experiment, many RSS workers began to feel that there was little to differentiate the BJP from the Congress (I). This impression got strengthened as Mrs. Gandhi made Hindu noises and the BJP resorted to secular rhetoric. The RSS worker felt that if he strengthened Mr. Rajiv Gandhi's hands, Hindu interest would be served.[20]

The RSS chief was far more alert to the mood in the rank and file of his outfit and its branch the BJP. He began a campaign to explain precisely who constituted the Hindus to enlist their support. In this he was utterly heedless of the contradiction. He was out to exploit the new situation. Men who were closet RSS supporters came out in the open as the RSS's ambitions had increased. It wanted to

[19] Jaffrelot, *The Hindu Nationalist Movement and Indian Politics*, pp. 364-5. Karan Singh's remarks were made in his interview with Jaffrelot on 9 February 1994.

[20] *The Statesman*, 20 April 1986.

form a national alternative to the Congress. At times Deoras talked of Hindus as the majority community which constituted 85 per cent of the country's population; at others he asserted that all in the country were Hindus. In some speeches he made the two points in one and the same speech. On 8 October 1981 he said that if Hindus are reduced to a minority in India, it will change the face of the country and its culture. Deoras referred to the mass conversion of Harijans to Islam in the south and said that if this continued, it would endanger the integrity of the country. He said Hindu culture was the 'backbone of democratic and secular values'.[21]

In Bengaluru he said on 4 January 1982: 'Hindus formed 85 per cent of the population of the country and the nation was identified as "Hindustan", the land of Hindus. Anyone who believed in the principles of democracy, socialism and secularism should realise that India could become democratic, socialist and secular only if it became a "Hindu Rashtra".'

He said there was no need for the minorities to fear the integration of Hindu society and the concept of Hindu Rashtra, as the Hindus looked upon those belonging to other communities as their brothers. Swami Vishwesha Teerth of Udupi Pejawara Math, who spoke on the occasion, said the activities of the RSS were a symbol of the awakening of the Hindu society from its deep slumber.[22]

There was no ambiguity in Deoras's assertion on 14 January 1984 that 'all Indians except Muslims and Christians can be considered Hindus, which would include Buddhists, Jains and Sikhs'.

The RSS readily associated religious leaders with its propaganda campaign. As the movement to demolish the Babri Masjid picked up speed in the late eighties the presence of religious leaders and sadhus increased.

RSS chiefs reserve their major pronouncements for the annual Vijaya Dashami Day at Nagpur. Deoras's speech on this occasion on 4 October 1984 did not suffer from lack of candour. He lamented that 'Gandharwa that is now called Afghanistan, we lost way back in the past and 37 years ago we lost those regions when Hindus had become a minority'.

This was a recurring theme. Hindus who were 85 per cent of the country's people, must not allow themselves to be reduced to a minority. Instilling such a fear was central to the RSS propaganda. It justified *ghar wapsi*, conversion to Hinduism. Nationalism was defined in a strange manner.

> It is a feeling of belonging on the basis of certain basic principles and widely-accepted norms. The first of these is an unquestioning devotion for the Motherland and ungrudging willingness to sacrifice everything at its altar, the second is a sense of respect for our ancestors and the third is to be a part and parcel of the culture of this country which consists in 'Unity in Diversity'.

21 *The Indian Express*, 9 October 1981.

22 *The Times of India*, 6 January 1982.

Deoras asserted that

> the fate of this country is linked – irrevocably linked – with the Hindus in this country. Whenever the Hindus were well-organised, were inspired by great ideals, the Hindu culture travelled far and wide in distant lands. The great thinkers of our ancient land have travelled in Brahmadesh, Syam, Anam, Java and other countries and tried to bring about an all-round reform in the life of the people there.[23]

For all the twists and turns, certain themes recur consistently in all the RSS pronouncements and, at one remove, in the BJP's as well. One of them is flat rejection of territorial or geographical nationalism. Every one born in India is not a member of the Indian nation. Deoras said in Pune on 15 January 1983, '[W]e reject geographical nationalism. Nationalism has its roots in people's minds; in their way, of thinking, their sentiments. That is why we stick to the word "Hindu". It reflects both our national and cultural aspirations.'[24] He added 'life here revolves around the Hindu society'.

The BJP had drifted away from the RSS, a little while. The RSS soon conveyed a message that it was none too pleased with the new set up of and the new ideas in the BJP. A special representative of *The Statesman* reported at length on the rumblings on 11 August 1983. It bears quotation *in extenso*:

> Is the RSS, of late, keeping itself away from its political ally, the BJP? Mr. Rajendra Singh did, however, admit that the RSS had been busy with its own cultural and social activity. . . . He, however, looked around to discuss this reporter's suggestion that the RSS leaders and workers are rumoured to be responding more to Mrs. Gandhi than the BJP as she is emerging as the champion of the Hindus. . . .
>
> Mr. Advani said he had noticed that Congress (I) leaders have been carrying 'a systematic whispering' campaign that the RSS was going away from the BJP since Mrs. Gandhi had now started going to temples and other Hindu places of worship whereas the BJP leaders did not do so.
>
> Mr. Advani said that the 'motivation seemed to cause a confusion in the minds of RSS cadres against the BJP' as a political party as well as among BJP sympathisers in the members of the public. The BJP general secretary also said that he would talk to the RSS leadership on the 'vicious designs' of vested interests to separate the RSS from the BJP.

[23] *Organiser*, 14 October 1984.

[24] *Organiser*.

Evidently the cadre's mood had not changed in the three years since *The Indian Express* reported it.

On the same day the correspondent reported also that in the five years between 1977 and 1982 the growth of the RSS had been 'phenomenal'. Its shakhas had increased from 6,000 to 19,000; 35,000 if the sub-branches were included. There were over 70,000 committed swayamsevaks, its general secretary Rajendra Singh revealed. Since its birth, the RSS attached great importance to the three-year annual camps at the headquarters in Nagpur. All in all, the RSS had expanded in new field.

Apparently oblivious to the RSS's renewed strength and confidence the BJP's president Vajpayee asked it to clarify that 'it does not stand for a Hindu Rashtra'.[25] Vajpayee himself preferred Bharatiya Rashtra to Hindu Rashtra.

Deoras replied on 19 September. The RSS was determined to organise all Hindus as one in the interest of the nation's progress.[26] Speaking at the Dussehra Utsav in Nagpur, Deoras further clarified that the real problem was not Muslims or Christians but rifts in Hindu society in which he included Jains and Sikhs. They were 'all Hindus'. He was more explicit at the Dasara Day rally on 16 October 1983. Hindus were the inheritors of the country's ancient past and culture. The problems would 'vanish' the moment the population was limited.

Meanwhile the Vishwa Hindu Parishad set up by the RSS in Mumbai in August 1964 was bestirring itself. It decided to organise on 16 November 1983 a month-long Ekatmata (soul union) Yojna, involving a hundred million.[27] Its secretary-general Harmohan Lal complained that 'only the Hindus call this land Bharat Mata. The others do not accept this as Mata'.

Financially, the RSS was more prosperous than any other body. In a seven-page note the Union Home Ministry recorded:

> The Rashtriya Swayamsevak Sangh (RSS) has streamlined the functioning of its front organisations to broaden its popular base and has deputed additional preachers to its labour, student, tribal, kisan and other fronts.
>
> This is the assessment of the Home Ministry contained in a seven page note, which discusses the strength of the RSS, factors for its growth, funds and its new policy formulations.
>
> Following the lifting of the ban in 1977, the note says, the RSS has made rapid strides in expanding its shakhas (branches) and its membership. It has been able to revive most of its defunct shakhas. In 1980, which was observed as shakha varsha, the shakhas rose to about 17,800. The Sangh claims a daily attendance of nearly 10 lakh at its shakhas.

25 *Hindustan Times*, 11 August 1983.

26 *The Indian Express*, 20 September 1983.

27 *The Times of India*, 10 November 1983.

> The growth of Hindu fronts at various places, formation of temple protection committees, especially in Kerala, celebrations of Hindu festivals and functions and rescue and rehabilitation work have also contributed to the strength of the RSS in some states. According to the note, the annual Gurudakshina collections of the RSS crossed the Rs. 1-crore mark in 1980. The collections have been held to be not liable for income tax on the principle of mutuality. . . .
>
> According to the Home Ministry, the RSS swayamsevaks and sympathisers are spread over many countries, organising their activities under various names like Bharatiya Swayamsevak Sangh, Friends of India Society International, Hindu Swayamsevak Sangh, etc. The main centres of activities abroad are the UK, the US, Mauritius and Kenya. Regular shakhas are reportedly organised in about 32 countries.
>
> The RSS fronts, according to the note, include Akhil Bharatiya Vidyarthi Parishad, Vishwa Hindu Parishad, Bharatiya Mazdoor Sangh, Vanvasi Kalyan Kendra, Vivekananda Kendra, Seva Bharti, Sanskar Bharti and Sahakar Bharti.
>
> The Vanvasi Kalyan Kendra is said to be concentrating on its organisational activities in the north-east, Bihar, Madhya Pradesh and Orissa 'to contain the activities of foreign Christian missionaries', the note says.[28]

Vajpayee would protest once in a while but only to conform. He did so eloquently at the BJP's National Council meeting in Indore. The RSS, he acknowledged, was the 'very inherent part of the BJP's structure'. The BJP leadership would never compromise on its 'unbreakable relationship' with the RSS on electoral understanding or alliance with non-communist parties. He said that he wanted to remove the dissatisfaction in the rank and file of the RSS that 'the BJP Central leadership was going away from the RSS'. The correspondent, M.H. Jadhav opined, 'Mr. Vajpayee is actually conscious it is the RSS cadre alone that is going to work for the BJP in the next election.'[29]

Deoras was not appeased. He issued a stiff reprimand two days later to ask the BJP to 'build up its own cadre and not depend on the RSS if it wants to survive in politics'; adding menacingly that a member of the RSS 'is free to vote and work for any political party he chooses' (read: the Congress). Referring to Indira Gandhi, he said 'if she does something good we should support her' but criticise if she 'does something bad'.

Deoras repeated his well-worn theme – all Indians except Muslims and Christians can be considered Hindus. This would include Buddhists, Jains and Sikhs.[30] It is not difficult to understand why these communities were singled out.

[28] Kuldip Nayar, *The Indian Express*, 28 November 1983.

[29] *The Statesman*, 12 January 1984.

[30] *The Indian Express*, 15 January 1984.

The RSS's Bible, Golwalkar's *Bunch of Thoughts*, had a chapter on 'Internal Threats' (Chapter XII). It singled them out in company with communists for posing a 'threat' to the nation. That this contradicts its assertion that all Indians in the country are Hindus is a matter of supreme indifference. Its strength lies in its indoctrinated cadres and its many outfits and others willing to accept its credentials if only the RSS would deliver soothing words. This technique was in display in the present RSS chief Mohan Bhagwat's staged performance at Vigyan Bhawan in New Delhi for three days, on 18, 19 and 20 September 2018. On this, more later.

Contradiction also marks the RSS's stand on conversions. Since it regards Muslims and Christians as converts from Hinduism, its drive to make them Hindus is *ghar wapsi* (return home) which became organised and assumed violent forms after Narendra Modi became prime minister in 2014.

Indifference to the RSS's pronouncements, as so much nonsense, is dangerous. There is a solid, core of consistency which is poisonous. In the light of the *ghar wapsi* campaign since 2014, it bears recalling that as far back as on 29 January 1984 Deoras told a camp of RSS workers at Thoothukudi that it was a national necessity to stop conversion of Hindus to other religions, and it was 'a necessity for the security of the nation'. He said that if the Hindus were reduced to a minority in any area, they were wiped out from that place and the territory was permanently lost to India. He cited in this connection Afghanistan, Balochistan, North-West Frontier Province and Bangladesh.

He regretted that the critics of RSS dubbed it a communal organisation for calling the country a 'Hindu Rashtra'. He said conversions took place because 'Hindus are too good and broad-minded'.

Deoras said the term Hindu had a broad connotation and it did not refer to any particular form of worship. Whoever accepted that there was a national cultural heritage in existence in our country, was a Hindu.

India could not be considered on the same level as countries like Egypt, Italy and Greece. 'The ancient cultural richness of those nations was in evidence only in the ruins, whereas in India, the Vedas, the Upanishads and the Kavyas continue to be interpreted even today, though nobody could say when they came into existence.'[31]

This was by no means the first or the last time that an RSS chief contradicted himself in the same single pronouncement: all Indians are Hindus versus Hindus are the majority community with Muslims and Christians as 'the Other'. Spreading the scare about the Hindus being reduced to a minority – in a steep decline from 85 per cent of the population to, say, 45 – had a purpose. It was to justify the drive for *ghar wapsi*.

The Thoothukudi speech also contained remarks typical of the ones RSS chiefs have made since Golwalkar; for instance recalls of history which no educated

[31] *The Hindu*, 30 January 1984.

person could possibly accept. If these do not repel the 'elite' among its followers it is because they share the RSS's core beliefs while condoning its verbal and other excesses. In this category fall Prime Minister Modi's claims of 'scientific achievements' in the Vedic Ages.

The RSS projects and protects the BJP. But the 1976 and 1984 precedents suggest that it would have supported Indira Gandhi if its support was acceptable. In 1976 it offered to ditch Jayaprakash Narayan. In the 1984 elections it ditched the BJP. The umbilical cord with the progeny ensured that the BJP would not retaliate. The BJP had nowhere to go. Its cadre came from the RSS. On the eve of the BJP's National Convention in Ahmedabad on 31 March, the RSS's general secretary Rajendra Singh said, 'We have said we have supported the Government on national issues. Even now, when we feel that the nation's integrity, sovereignty and security are in danger, or if Mrs. Gandhi presents a programme of action for nation-building, we would support her. We have no particular interest in electoral politics.'[32]

Deoras's rhetoric became sharper by the day. Afghanistan, Pakistan and Bangladesh were created because the Hindus in these areas allowed themselves to be wiped out, resulting in the division of Hindustan, he said.

Decrying the 'minority complex' which he said seems to have gripped our politicians, he said that the Christian and Muslim minorities in this country are not foreign ethnic groups. They are people of this country. If they are always referred to as minorities, or treated as minorities, they will never be assimilated. They will remain separate groups.

He said the concept of secularism had become such a holy cow and communalism such a phobia that India is today the only country in the world where the minority groups enjoy privileges and rights that the majority community does not.

The only way to keep this country united and strong is to treat minority groups in the same manner as the majority community and not as separate groups.

Defending his use of the term 'Hindu', he said the RSS does not use it in its narrow religious sense. It has a wider social connotation. This country, elaborated Deoras, has been referred to as Hindustan and its people as Hindus since ancient times. And it is this meaning the RSS wants to convey when it refers to India as Hindustan and its citizens as Hindus.[33]

As the crisis in Punjab became acute, the RSS began to oppose the Akalis. So did the BJP. A strong Hindu nation was vital for the survival of democracy, secularism and socialism. India was the only country where the minorities enjoyed more rights than the majority.[34]

[32] *Hindustan Times*, 25 March 1984.

[33] *The Indian Express*, 19 October 1984.

[34] *The Indian Express*, 22 December 1984.

On 16 November *The Telegraph* published on a full page a note by Nana Deshmukh praising Indira Gandhi and urging all sections of the people to support her successor, Rajiv Gandhi. This brought a sharp retort, two days later, from Vajpayee, Vijaya Raje Scindia, Jagannath Rao and L.K. Advani. They described him as 'an erstwhile colleague of ours in the BJP'. They spoke for the party. 'The BJP would like to dissociate itself from this article and, more particularly, from its conclusion.' Unlike his mother, Rajiv Gandhi was 'a prisoner in the hands of a small caucus of businessmen who have roots neither in the people nor in their own party'.[35]

Deshmukh's rejoinder came after two months; on 27 January 1985. He was 'not bothered' about incurring any one's displeasure. He had always advocated that persons above 60 should resign. He had himself renounced politics in 1978 to head the Deendayal Upadhyaya State Institute of Rural Development.[36]

In an interview to *Organiser* (17 February 1985) he blamed 'Atalji and others' for providing the Congress with an advantage by publicising his statement. Significantly the BJP's National Executive which met on 17-18 March 1985 was devoted to the question of revival of the Jana Sangh. Vajpayee rejected the suggestion. That the suggestion was made at all, five years after the BJP's establishment on 5 April 1980, indicates that the new venture had not struck roots. Vajpayee also said 'that the BJP had no truck with the Vishwa Hindu Parishad'.[37] Evidently the pressure was for revival of the Jana Sangh by the RSS cadres. Vajpayee was obliged to set up a Working Group with a wide remit in March 1985. Speculation mounted on the speculation genesis of Deshmukh's article. Prem Bhasin, a former general secretary of the Praja Socialist Party, retired from politics to emerge as one of the country's most astute political commentators. His modest means did not permit him to subscribe to many newspapers. He would repair to a public library in Aligarh and did a column for the *Janata*. The one in its May Day 1985 issue was widely noticed. It was entitled 'Lizard-in-Snake's Mouth'. It was prompted by the *Organiser*'s admonition to the BJP in an editorial on 7 April. It was for 'restoration of the leadership's rapport with a sizeable section of its selfless cadres', i.e. the RSS cadre. It also urged restoration of 'ideological clarity which got [blurred] by the BJP's stance of Positive Secularism and Gandhian Socialism'. The lesson was obvious. 'Heed the RSS if the cadres have to be enthused to work for the party in the old way.' The BJP was instructed to heed the lesson of its debacle in the Lok Sabha elections. It had won a mere two seats.

It is unlikely that Nana Deshmukh had fired his salvo without consulting the RSS's leader. He was not a maverick but a devoted member of the RSS, senior to Vajpayee and Advani with whom he evidently fell out in 1978. Nor was he an idealist. He was a quintessential operator; a fund collector and fixer both. He did

35 *The Telegraph*, 19 November 1984.

36 *The Indian Express*, 28 January 1988.

37 *The Times of India*, 19 March 1988.

not hesitate to tell a palpable falsehood on oath before the Justice Chandrachud Commission on Upadhyaya's murder; nor hesitate to put forth a document which he knew or ought to have known was forged. The Commission censured him on both counts.

Deshmukh's book *RSS, Victim of Slander* (Vision Books, 1979) tells us less about it than about his tiffs in the Janata Party. 'He was associated with the RSS since his childhood', the blurb tells us. It was he who forged a pact with Charan Singh on a division of the spoils of the Assembly elections of 1977 – the Bharatiya Lok Dal was to form governments in Uttar Pradesh, Bihar, Odisha and Haryana, the Jana Sangh in Madhya Pradesh, Rajasthan, Himachal Pradesh and Delhi.[38]

A newspaper tycoon introduced him to his friend Jayaprakash Narayan, whom he hosted in Mumbai. A city industrialist swore by Nana. It was an ego clash with Vajpayee and Advani which forced him to quit politics; save that unlike Madhok he did not criticise the RSS. For its part the mentor realised that Nanaji's talents lay in fields other than political leadership of the Vajpayee-Advani kind. Nagpur keeps all of them in hand.

In an interview to Coomi Kapoor, Deshmukh revealed a facet of his skills.

> Q. You were known not just as the great organiser but also the fund collector. How did you become close to Bombay's leading business families like the Tatas and the Wadias?
>
> Ans. I was made in-charge of the 1967 elections by my party. There was no money. I went to K.M. Munshi with whom I had close relations and who had just joined the Swatantra Party. At first, he protested that he was in a different party but then he introduced me to Dharamsibhai Khatau. Through Munshi and Khatau I came in touch with industrialists like J.R.D. Tata. Normally it would not have been possible for a person like me to enter their homes, but over the years close relations developed.
>
> Q. What do you think about the nexus between politicians and businessmen today?
>
> Ans. In my days they never expected anything in return from me. They never thought I am going to come to power. Today, I think they are controlling politics much more than before.[39]

It is a matter of record that Big Business always had a soft corner for the RSS, the Mahasabha, and later, for the Jana Sangh and the BJP. In 1922 Motilal Nehru bitterly complained to his son Jawaharlal about Lala Lajpat Rai and the Birlas' use of money power in the elections. He contemplated quitting politics.[40]

[38] Nana Deshmukh, *RSS, Victim of Slander*, Vision Books, 1979, p. 53.

[39] *The Indian Express*, 19 December 1999.

[40] Jawaharlal Nehru, *A Bunch of Old Letters*, Bombay: Asia Publishing House, 1960, p. 52.

G.D. Birla's sympathies for the group were pronounced. His biographer writes,

> Birla's deep involvement since the 1920s with Hindu cultural nationalism and his close links with Malaviya could not easily be forgotten. As seen earlier, 'Birla money' had been blamed by Motilal Nehru in 1922 as being behind the attempt to capture the Congress at the time of the crushing defeat which the Swarajya Party had suffered at the hands of Malaviya's Independent Congress Party. To further complicate matters had been the Birlas' close proximity to Patel.[41]

All was never well within the BJP or its relations with the RSS. A Working Group had been set up in March 1985. Its report of 47 pages came on 20 July 1985 in time for the Executive's meeting in Bhopal. It upheld all the three decisions in the past; namely, to merge with the Janata Party, to leave it and to form the BJP. A survey of electoral performances concluded that

> if we are to secure power the Party should be in a position to secure at least 42% of total votes polled which Janata Party got in 1977, if not 49% by Cong (I) in 1984. Leaving aside a margin of 10% vote swing at the time of elections for various reasons, then we must have an additional 20% to 25% of votes polled. How to go about securing this 20% to 25% votes must be definitely borne in mind while deciding upon our ideological, organisational, electoral etc. approach for the coming 5 years.[42]

The BJP faced a problem.

> The statement that BJP is a party with a difference means that the Party, amongst other things, possesses an ideology which is not fully shared by others. In ultimate analysis the strength and spread of a political party will also depend upon its ideological appeal. A party must, therefore, keep on reviewing whether the basic premises of its ideology are capable of resolving the various conflicts which confront the society at that point of time and also whether they are properly understood by those for whom they are meant. With this end in view, the Working Group tried to assess that, (a) to what extent during the past five years the party workers were able to assimilate the Party ideology and how far could they carry it to the masses, and (b) what further steps should be undertaken, including the updating of basic policy documents, so that the Party ideology is more clearly understood by different sections of the society? . . .
>
> But by and large the adherents of the political movement which culminated

[41] Medha M. Kudaisya, *The Life and Times of G.D. Birla*, Oxford University Press, p. 296.

[42] Pages 13, 14, 15.

> into BJP have not been able to identify the BJP ideology as a derivative of the political philosophy which they so assiduously formulated. Persistence of this hiatus during the past five years is yet another shortcoming in the domain of ideological training. In the opinion of the Working Group, incorporation of Integral Humanism as an ingredient of the Party ideology would go a long way to fill this void.[43]

In short, a return to the Jana Sangh's credo and ethos. The BJP depended on the cadres assigned to it by the RSS. It had yet to become a mass party. 'There can be a happy marriage between these two.'[44]

The Report concluded:

> For a political party growth basically means increased acceptance by voters, as reflected in election results. The ability of any party to get votes, is primarily based on its support of people. As more people feel the party represents them and speaks for them, the party grows. Why BJP failed to grow as expected is at the core of the whole exercise of our Working Group.

There was nothing in its Report which a competent political analyst could not have written without the assistance of its 12 stodgy members. Finally, on 9 October 1985 the executive bowed to the inevitable. It discarded the opportunistic slogan of 'Gandhian socialism' and went back to the Jana Sangh idol D.D. Upadhyaya's Integral Humanism. One wonders how many understood its connotations. *The Times of India* reported:

> In major ideological shift, the Bhartiya Janata Party, today abandoned 'Gandhian Socialism' as one of its major objective and resolved to follow 'integral humanism', pronounced by Pandit Deendayal Upadhyaya as the basic philosophy of the party. . . . About the party's relations with the RSS, Mr. Advani said that there was no basic change in the party's policy. 'We have parted company with the Janata Party over dual membership issue and the BJP had come into existence because of the RSS,' he added. He said that he was proud of his links with the RSS.[45]

The party decided to set up training camps for its workers. On 11 October the National Council endorsed the Executive's decisions.

The BJP was groping in the dark for, both, an appealing ideology and a winning strategy. The Meenakshipuram incident fizzled out after the official report

[43] Pages 13-15.

[44] Page 25.

[45] *The Times of India*, 10 October 1985.

revealed the truth. Riots in north India helped little. Nor did the enactment of the Aligarh Muslim University (Amendment) Act, 1981 which acknowledged the University character as an educational institution established by a minority and entitled therefore to the fundamental right to its autonomous governance by the Muslims as a minority under Article 30(1) of the Constitution. Nor did the Muslim Women's Act, 1986 help much except as a laboured debating point.

The Babri Masjid question helped Advani resolve his dilemma. The BJP can win on an 'ideological' (i.e. communal hate) programme in the country. Ideology can get strong without diminishing the appeal – by playing the Hindu card as the RSS always insisted. This issue was explosive in the extreme. It damaged the party which created it (Congress) and assisted its adversary (the BJP) to become a mass party charged with communal hate. It damaged India's secular credo with consequences that are still upon us. It was Arun Nehru's decision to secure the opening of the locks on the gates of the Babri Masjid. They were duly ordered to be opened by the Faizabad District Judge on 1 February 1986. TV cameras were present as if they had been tipped off earlier. This act of criminal folly led inexorably to the demolition of the Masjid on 9 December 1992, to the rise of the RSS and to the riveting of its control over the BJP, to installing the BJP in power at the Centre. Above all, it diminished the BJP. Essentially the RSS in action, in politics it had some autonomy. Now that was gone. Eventually, a pracharak, Modi, became prime minister.

There was not a tittle of merit in the RSS's demand. (1) In the entire litigation in the 19th century the Mahant claimed the Ram Chabutra *outside* the Masjid as Ram's birthplace; never the Masjid. (2) The RSS and the BJP admit that it is not possible to identify the place where Ram was born. (3) The issue is not susceptible to judicial determination. (4) The Sangh Parivar will not accept a judicial verdict. (5) If it was a 'matter of national honour', it is inexplicable why none from the days of Tilak and Lajpat Rai to Gandhi and Malaviya ever demanded it. (6) The demand thus exacted its compliance, not through a legal process, but by use of brute force.

16. Power in the Name of Ram

On 29 August 1964, the RSS set up in Mumbai the Vishwa Hindu Parishad which, in turn, set up the Bajrang Dal in May-June 1989. As with the BJP, RSS men were put in charge of both; Ashok Singhal of the VHP and Vinay Katiyar, formerly of the ABVP, of the Bajrang Dal. Amidst much fanfare on Ram Navmi day (31 March 1984), the RSS-VHP leaders resolved to take up the issue of Babri Masjid and wrest control of the Babri mosque site for the construction of a Ram temple. The Dharma Sansad, in a meeting on 7 and 8 April 1984 at New Delhi, resolved to 'liberate' the mosque.[1]

It was an RSS-driven campaign throughout with a clear political objective – capture of power. The locks to the gates of the Masjid were opened in 1986. Advani's presidential address to the BJP's National Council on 2 January 1987 was not able for the complete absence of any reference to the Ram temple project. There was an extensive reference to Punjab, Mizoram, advocacy of a Presidential system, electoral reforms, etc. but none of the so-called issue of 'national honour'. Silence was also conspicuous in the Executive's resolutions in October 1987, October 1988, and September 1989. There was no mention of Ayodhya even in the eight 'main issues of the Campaign' drawn up by the BJP in October 1987.

The RSS's Akhil Bharatiya Pratinidhi Sabha first adopted a resolution on the issue in 1987. It said, 'The Sabha calls upon the entire Hindu Society in general and the Sangh Swayamsevaks in particular to whole-heartedly take part in the task of putting up an imposing shrine at the Rama Janmabhoomi thereby making Mother Bharati stand resplendent with glory and honour.'[2]

The BJP Executive's Palampur Resolution came on the eve of the Lok Sabha polls. It spoke at the outset of 'the sentiment of the overwhelming majority in the country – the Hindus'. The rest was in this vein. The Hindu sentiments must be enforced. The Courts cannot decide.

> The BJP holds that the nature of this controversy is such that it just cannot be sorted out by a court of law. A court of law can settle issues of title, trespass, possession etc. But it cannot adjudicate as to whether Babar did actually invade Ayodhya, destroyed a temple and built a mosque in its place. Even where a

1 Ashok Singhal, quoted in Manini Chatterjee, 'Saffron Scourge: The VHP's Communal Fascism', *Frontline*, 10 September 1993; and Katju, *Vishwa Hindu Parishad and Indian Politics*, p. 45.

2 *RSS Resolves: 1950-2007*, p. 154.

court does pronounce on such facts, it cannot suggest remedies to undo the vandalism of history. . . .

The sentiments of the people must be respected, and Rama Janmasthan handed over to the Hindus – if possible through a negotiated settlement, or else, by legislation. Litigation certainly is no answer.

The RSS's fortunes soared thereafter.

During the decade 1979-89, the number of *swayamsevaks* of the RSS had swelled from 10 lakh to 18 lakh. The number of *shakhas* increased to 25,000 spreading over 18,880 cities and villages. It had 38 front organisations and 50 lakh people were connected with their activities. The RSS showed spectacular growth in south India. 3,000 daily *shakhas* and 900 weekly gatherings were organised in 12 out of 14 districts in Kerala.

A meeting of the top leaders of the Sangh Parivar took place at Ahmedabad on 24 March 1989. Besides the chief M.D. Deoras, other important leaders of the Parivar who attended it were H.V. Seshadri, Rajendra Singh, Yadav Rao Joshi of the RSS, Ashok Singhal of VHP, L.K. Advani, A.B. Vajpayee and S.S. Bhandari of BJP, D.B. Thengadi of BMS and Madan Das Devi of ABVP. A close coordination among the leading members of the RSS family was obviously required before going for the offensive. . . .

The event that became the eye of the storm was *Ramshila Pujan*. The VHP launched a campaign to carry consecrated bricks, called *Ramshilas*, from every village with a population of 2,000 or above for the construction of the Ram temple. This programme was meticulously planned out. The bricks were taken to Ayodhya through *panchayat* centres, district headquarters and state capitals.[3]

Poison was injected into the atmosphere; a fact noticed by many.

The beatific smile of Ram in VHP posters had been replaced by a war-like image – Ram with his trident and bow at ready. This new imagery of Ram came from television epics – Ramanand Sagar's *Ramayana* and B.R. Chopra's *Mahabharata*. The latter especially glorified a militaristic and virile Hinduism. The telecasting of these epics on *Doordarshan* resulted from the decision of an insecure Congress party. Though Ram existed all along, popular perceptions were vague and varied. The telecasting of *Ramayana*, which was primarily based on the *Ramcharitmanas* of Tulsidas, ignored the traditions of 'many *Ramayanas*' projecting a uniform version. The serial certainly concretised

[3] Kanungo, *RSS's Tryst with Politics*, pp. 195 and 197.

> certain perceptions of Ram. For instance, when people were asked about Ayodhya before the telecast, though they identified Ayodhya as the birthplace of Ram, their idea about the place was still vague. After the telecast they defined it as a town in UP. The broadcasting of *Ramayana* and *Mahabharata* helped to create a national Hindu identity, a form of consciousness that had not hitherto existed.
>
> It became easy for the VHP to project a militant Ram, a symbol of strength and power. Passionate slogans rent the air. '*Saugandh Ram ki khate hain hum mandir vaheen banayege* (We swear by Ram we will build the temple at the same site)', '*Bachcha-bachcha Ram ka, Janmabhoomi ke kaam ka* (Every child belongs to Ram and for Ram Janmabhoomi)' and *Jis Hindu ka khoon na khaule, khoon nahin vo pani hai; Janmabhoomi ke kaam na aye, vo bekaar jawanee hai* (That Hindu whose blood does not boil has water in his veins, youth that does not serve *Ram Janmabhoomi* is youth lived in vain)'. Therefore, the Ramshila campaign was not only mobilisational, it was confrontational as well. It became aggressively anti-Muslim and provoked communal violence.[4]

Lloyd I. Rudolph wrote that the telecast of the Ramayana and the Mahabharata played 'a leading role in creating a national Hindu identity, a form of group consciousness that has not hitherto existed'.[5]

What followed was choreographed by the mentor, RSS.

> Advani's Rath Yatra was not the decision of the BJP. It was a carefully designed strategy of the RSS. The yatra was a concerted effort of all the leading members of the RSS family. Bhaorao Deoras, brother of (M.D.) Balasaheb and a master political strategist of the RSS, reportedly spent two weeks in Delhi coordinating Advani's *Rath Yatra plans*. The motive of this yatra was clearly political rather than religious. The Toyota rath, carrying the party symbol prominently, made their political intentions very clear.
>
> Advani was ideally suited to the purpose. He was the chosen hero. Despite his insistence that it was the VHP who was leading the movement, it was Advani, who became identified as the leader of the movement. He was presented a *dharmadhwaja* by the priest of Somnath temple before he started his *dharma yuddha* (holy war). . . .
>
> At every place the most common offering was traditional weaponry: arrows, dices, maces, swords, trishuls and kripan. At Jetpur in Gujarat 101

[4] Ibid., p. 197.

[5] L.J. Rudoph, 'The Media and Cultural Politics', in *Electoral Politics in India: A Changing Landscape*, ed. S.K. Mitra and J. Chiriyankandath, New Delhi: Segment Books, 1992, p. 92; vide also Robin Jeffrey, 'Media Revolution & "Hindu Politics" in North India, 1989-99', *Himal*, July 2001. *Himal* is a Kathmandu monthly.

> Kshatriya youths offered him a bowl containing their blood. The slogans raised were highly inflammatory: '*Jab jab Hindu jaga hai, Desh me mulla bhaga hai* (When the Hindus have arisen, the mullahs have fled the country)'; '*Mussalman ko dono sthan, Pakistan aur kabarstan* (Muslims have two places – Pakistan or the graveyard)'.[6]

Jaffrelot has described how 'the triple network of the RSS, the VHP and the BJP worked with ever-increasing vigour as the election approached'.[7] This is not a work on the Babri Masjid.[8] The issue is relevant here only on the course of the RSS's politics.

It injected life into the RSS and the BJP. Since 1980 the BJP watched in dismay as the BJP under Vajpayee went into an apparently irreversible decline which its pact with Charan Singh in 1983 to form a National Democratic Alliance could not arrest. Indira Gandhi deftly checked its growth. So did the popularity of her son, Rajiv, after her assassination. Adversity caused fissures. Hence Nana Deshmukh's dissent. But for the Babri Masjid issue, the RSS and the BJP might have gone into a tailspin. The RSS sensed an opportunity too good to be missed, not only to secure the votes but also secure greater control of the BJP and to ensure that the BJP listened to the VHP and the Bajrang Dal.

Its objective was entirely political. Its leaders resided in Nagpur; not in Delhi. Success was slow in coming but when it did, it was plentiful – a BJP-led government at the Centre (1998-2004) and an RSS pracharak Narendra Modi as prime minister in 2014, resolved to beat the earlier BJP regimes' record.

The RSS faced a political challenge from the Congress and regional parties in its contest for power. But the ideological challenge came from intellectuals, and the Left parties the Communist Party of India (Marxist) and the Communist Party of India, academics, scholars and writers. They debunked the myths not only on Ramjanmabhoomi but also delved into history, archaeology and religion to present incontrovertible evidence. It speaks for the strength of the secular core in India's ethos that the best contributions came from Hindu scholars, not Muslims. The Ramjanmabhoomi movement gave a sharp edge to the Hindutva movement. It could not have gone far if political compromises had not facilitated its progress.

As always, it is the RSS supremo who leads the campaign. Deoras tried to appeal to critics by making absurd claims. Once he said at Gwalior on 11 November 1986 that the ideals sought by political parties such as democracy, socialism and secularism can be achieved only 'if Hindus are united, strong and in a majority in the country'. If the Hindus are reduced to a minority then the Hindu nation

[6] Kanungo, *RSS's Tryst with Politics*, pp. 202-3.

[7] Jaffrelot, *The Hindu Nationalist Movement and Indian Politics*, p. 383.

[8] Vide A.G. Noorani, *The Babri Masjid Question*, 2 Volumes, New Delhi: Tulika Books.

would meet the fate of Bangladesh, Pakistan and the Arab countries. To make the appeal attractive he said that Hinduism did not mean a form of worship but a broad culture and way of life.[9]

At every juncture in its history the RSS, while nursing its progeny, sought to woo the Congress as well. Its general secretary Rajendra Singh offered support to Prime Minister Rajiv Gandhi 'for his programmes on nation-building, unity and integrity', an expansive phrase which implied total support. Rajiv Gandhi had adopted a policy of 'cooperative politics' instead of 'confrontational politics'.[10]

Deoras pushed the offer further but with calculated ambivalence. He said on 6 April 1987 that there was no alternative to the Congress at the moment although there was a need to replace it. He did not rule out the possibility of entering into an understanding with the Congress in the future. 'If the Congress (I) approaches us, we will also seriously consider the possibility. But the chances are remote with the Congress (I)'s stand on minorities.'[11] Having failed on Meenakshipuram, the RSS hoped for an understanding on Punjab.

The Indian Express published on 7 September 1977 an article by 'A Swayamsevak' entitled 'RSS: A Realistic Assessment'. Described as 'a senior member of the RSS', he pleaded for opening the RSS's doors to Muslims. The appeal was ignored; the writer's identity remained obscure. He wrote:

> The RSS position is that whoever regards India as his motherland and a holy land, is a Hindu. Can anybody claim that no Muslim fits this definition? Was not Dara Shikoh a greater Hindu than, say, Jai Singh or Jaswant Singh? Were Rahim and Kabir, Farid and Latif less 'Hindu' than Tulsi, Mira or Sur? Mecca is the religious centre of Muslims, and Jerusalem that of Christians; but India is as dear to Muslim Indians and Christian Indians as to Hindu Indians. . . .
>
> If Shivaji could trust Madari, a Muslim youth, as his assistant in his captivity in and escape from Agra, why can't we allow Muslim young men to attend the RSS shakha? Why should the RSS fear to open its doors to Muslims? Why this diffidence, this touch-me-not-ism?

The identity of the writer can only be guessed.

The RSS's claim to being a 'cultural' body is refuted by the entire record of its conduct. Deoras's traditional annual address to the faithful at the Vijaya Dashami was a purely political lecture. 'The RSS Chief sought to dispel the notion that the RSS is anti-Congress. Many times we are portrayed as if we are anti-Congress, but this is a wrong notion. . . . He said it was the minority appeasement policy of the

[9] *The Statesman*, 12 November 1986.

[10] *The Times of India*, 30 December 1986.

[11] *Hindustan Times*, 7 April 1987.

Congress which is being opposed by the RSS. Otherwise we want that a strong Centre should rule the State.'[12]

The speech created a stir in the ranks. Vajpayee declined comment. The BJP was engaged in forging a united front against the Congress. Deoras played on both sides. His BJP's eyes were set on sharing power at the Centre; the RSS's on controlling any coalition set up there. In an interview to Pradip Kumar Maitra, Deoras said 'we have no enmity with the Congress; but this does not mean that we are in favour of it either. . . . I don't see any prospect of the Opposition parties coming together in the foreseeable future to provide a viable alternative to the Congress (I). The Opposition is as much divided as the Congress itself. . . . We are not permanent enemies'. He would not comment on V.P. Singh's campaign against corruption.

The BJP was then in opposition to the Congress in a tacit understanding with V.P. Singh. Not only the BJP even the RSS's members were confused. Maitra reported:

> The local RSS cadre, however, maintain that Mr. Deoras's adopting a soft line towards the ruling Congress party at a time when the public image was at lowest ebb, has pained many in the RSS. Resentment among some of the RSS hardliners over Mr. Deoras's pro-Congress stand is quite widespread.
>
> The sources also said that quite a few RSS workers were not happy with the RSS chief's pro-Congress (I) policy but the military-like discipline of the organisation prevents them from voicing out against it openly. The pro-Congress (I) elements in the RSS, however, defend their outlook by saying that this was not for the first time that the organisation had supported the Congress.[13]

A secret conclave of the RSS and the BJP was held at Nagpur on 15 October. Vajpayee and Advani tried to persuade Deoras not to support the Congress (I) at a time when its credibility was at its lowest thanks to Bofors and other scandals. The BJP's national executive had decided at Jodhpur to mount an agitation for the ouster of Rajiv Gandhi.[14]

Little did the BJP leaders realise that they were in the last days of the party's 'functional autonomy' from the RSS. Deoras clarified that all he had done was to make three points: 'The Congress party is totally disintegrated' and the process was 'irreversible'. His comments were not made out of prejudice. Lastly, 'no Opposition party has as yet developed a country wide base to be able to fill the void'. Nana Deshmukh and K.R. Malkani of the Deendayal Research Institute, Ashok Singhal

[12] *Hitavada*, 4 October 1987.

[13] *The Indian Express*, 7 October 1987.

[14] *The Indian Express*, 16 October 1987.

of the VHP and Ashok Modak of the ABVP and Rajendra Singh of the RSS participated in the conclave.

The *Hindustan Times* reported that the BJP leaders returned to Delhi 'much like chastened schoolboys'. There was no link between Deoras's speech on 30 October and the conclave. While M.M. Joshi and J.P. Mathur returned with Vajpayee and Advani, Nana Deshmukh stayed put at Nagpur, happy at the humiliation of his rivals. 'Who can deny that there is no alternative to the Congress, that too in the presence of Balasaheb? What is wrong in that statement to create such a controversy? We are so accustomed to telling lies that we become uncomfortable the moment someone speaks the truth.'

He added: 'How many seats can the BJP contest? The question is not of winning them, only contesting. We cannot befool ourselves, it is a simple question. When you are put in water either you know swimming or you don't.'

The former master strategist said the issues facing the country were discussed threadbare at the meeting. 'People call us fascist, but this was the most democratic discussion in which more than 200 persons participated and expressed their views frankly.'

Deshmukh said the reality was that the Congress was dead. It could not be revived, but the other reality was also true: that no alternative was forthcoming: 'That is why the situation is so precarious, and Balasaheb has simply stated this fact. We came together to discuss this situation and find out ways and means to face it. We have decided that all of us have to work together to solve the problems that are facing the nation.'

Later in the evening, RSS office secretary M.K. Chouthaiwale issued a statement on the meeting. The statement pointed out that for five days the Rashtriya Swayamsevak Sangh, the Bharatiya Mazdoor Sangh, the Akhil Bharatiya Vidyarthi Parishad, the Bharatiya Janata Party, the Vishwa Hindu Parishad and other like-minded organisations decided to jointly fight the danger posed to the nation by the anti-national and divisive forces. Expressing deep concern over the conspiracy hatched by these forces, the prominent office-bearers of these organisations decided to force their design through a joint effort.[15]

Organiser reported on the five-day conclave very briefly, listing eight items on its agenda; of them two were 'political situations' and 'Ramjanmabhoomi Mukti'.[16] *The Statesman* reported on 22 October 1987 the text of Deoras's speech. Advani flatly denied that Deoras's speech was discussed. There was nothing unusual about the conclave. 'After all there is a linkage. All these organisations consist of people belonging to the RSS. The BJP was founded on that issue – we refused to sever our own links with the RSS.'[17] Most comment was critical of the BJP.

15 *Hindustan Times*, 19 October 1987.

16 *Organiser*, 1 November 1987.

17 *Hindustan Times*, 22 October 1987.

Yubaraj Ghimire reported: 'You are a "swayamsevak" before anything else' was the theme of the five-day conclave which concluded on Monday at Nagpur. Top RSS activists, including the BJP president, L.K. Advani and Atal Bihari Vajpayee attended it.

This was probably an indication that the RSS would have an overriding authority over the BJP in case political turns compelled the party to take a new line. Prior to the conclave, a note had been circulated among top RSS activists seeking their opinion on whether the BJP should be reverted back to the old 'Jana Sangh pattern' or dissolved and merged for a broader opposition unity in case the 'Janata phenomenon' was repeated at the next general elections.

'The conclave did not take a decision on the issue. But RSS sources believe that the BJP would be asked to pass the resolution supporting the majority and the "accepted view". It was with this motive that the conclave sought "reaffirmation of the first loyalty" towards the Sangh from the activists dominating the BJP.'[18]

This was only one of the occasions on which RSS expressed its disquiet at the BJP's politics. Deoras went one step further on 16 November at Jaipur. The RSS had not taken a vow that it would not enter politics. That possibility cannot be ruled out.[19] Deoras attacked the minorities. 'Christians, Muslims, Parsis and members of other minority communities had been acting against the interests of the Hindu Rashtra which India is in reality.'[20]

At Pune on 26 December, Deoras clarified, 'A majority of Hindus felt that their interests were being harmed in the present circumstances and the RSS, therefore, would not even mind openly supporting deserving candidates in future elections.'

Commenting on the recent Assembly by-election at Vile Parle in Mumbai which was won by the Shiv Sena, the RSS chief said it was possible that members of his organisation had canvassed for the Shiv Sena, as the Sena had fought the election on a Hindu plank. But, added, 'We have no illusions about the Shiv Sena. We know that it was incepted to safeguard interests of Maharashtra and we also know that it is now trying to cash in on the awakening among Hindus brought about by us all over the country in the wake of the Meenakshipuram conversions.'

Deoras expressed happiness that the efforts to bring all eminent religious leaders together had succeeded and that they had now started travelling widely to propound the religious cause. He, however, did not expect them to assume leadership of society as a whole in the near future. They should, instead, strive for social reforms as it would have long-lasting positive effects.[21]

In retrospect the Nagpur conclave diminished the BJP's leaders. They could not have been happy at Deoras's running commentary on Indian politics far exceeding

[18] *The Telegraph*, 24 October 1987.

[19] *Hindustan Times*, 17 November 1987.

[20] *New Age*, 22 November 1987.

[21] *The Indian Express*, 27 December 1987.

in frequency and length as compared to that of predecessors or successors. The RSS was as unhappy with the BJP leaders as they were at his conflicting speeches. Anil Sharma reported:

> There is an increasing realisation in the Rashtriya Swayamsevak Sangh that the Bharatiya Janata Party (BJP) does not serve its objective of furthering the Hindu interest.
>
> The RSS leaders are not given to speaking in equivocal terms. Their statements lend themselves to several interpretations. The recent remark by the RSS Sarsanghchalak, Balasaheb Deoras, that the 'Congress culture' was spreading to other cadre-based political parties, observers felt was an indictment of the BJP.

Deoras's observations at the concluding session of the Akhil Bharatiya Pratinidhi Sabha are usually not disclosed to the press. This time, however, the secretary-general H.V. Seshadri, made a special mention of these remarks while briefing newsmen. 'When people come to us and tell us about these things, we feel sorry,' he said when asked whether the RSS leadership had received any specific complaints about the BJP functionaries.

> Insiders in the RSS camp point out that this disenchantment is much deeper and stems from the bitter realisation that the BJP has practically failed to deliver the goods as compared to other front organisations of the RSS like the Vishwa Hindu Parishad. 'The other frontal organisations have not only gathered strength on their own, but also contributed to the growth of the RSS, whereas the BJP is a sort of drag on the RSS itself,' remarked one observer.
>
> Organisations like the Vishwa Hindu Parishad have been able to attract much wider support from the people and have contributed much more towards the attainment of the 'Hindu awareness'. The BJP has not been able to play its role in the consolidation of the political forces in a manner that suits the RSS objectives.
>
> Constant attacks on the communists are part of the 'isolation drive' by the RSS aimed at ensuring that the leftists do not become partners in any power-sharing arrangement at the Centre. In another sense, the process that was first discussed at the October conclave soon after the controversial statement from Deoras that there was 'no alternative to the Congress' is expected to continue.

The BJP men were subjected to thorough grilling at that time and were foxed by some of the questions put to them by the RSS leadership. One of these being – how many Lok Sabha seats can you contest, leave alone win, if the elections are held?

> The RSS strategists want to play a major role in political developments. But after their experiences in 1967 and 1977, they were playing it on [their] terms and would not like to play second fiddle to anyone.[22] . . .

Advani's morale was boosted after the BJP's fourth plenary session at Agra on 8 April 1988. It marked a watershed between its declining fortunes since 1980 and its rise after the 11 June 1989 resolution on Ayodhya. Advani spoke of Hindutva in terms he had never used before; thus securing the RSS's confidence, its cadres' support and signalling a change. He demanded abolition of the Minorities Commission. 'For many politicians, secularism is only a euphemism for minority appeasement.' At the Janata Party Executive on 4 April 1980 he had pledged himself 'unconditionally' to 'preserving the composite culture of India'. Now in Agra, he said that the 'emphasis on the composite character of Indian culture is generally an attempt to disown its essentially Hindu spirit and content'.

This was a deliberate and deceptive misquotation as will be clear from a reference to Prof. Smith's work.

> One view simply equates Indian culture with Hinduism and Hindu culture; all non-Hindu aspects which have been assimilated are regarded as contaminating influences. The Hindu communal political parties are the most vocal exponents of this view.
>
> In an interesting speech a Hindu Mahasabha leader attempted to list the cultural changes which Indian Muslims would have to undergo in order to become acceptable nationals of the Indian (Hindu) state of the future. First, they would have to accept the *Ramayana* and *Mahabharata* as their epics and reject the Arabic and Persian classics. They would have to regard Ramachandra, Shivaji, and the classics and the Hindu gods Rama and Krishna as their heroes, and condemn various Muslim historical figures as foreign invaders or traitors. The Muslims would also need to discard their Arabic names (Abdulla, Mohammed, Ibrahim) in favour of Hindu names such as Ram, Krishna, Hari, etc. If the Muslims of India would accept the Hindu manner of dress, personal laws, and customs from birth to death, they could then retain their own religion! 'We would not much mind their following any path for their personal salvation.' The conception is clear; the extent to which cultural manifestations diverge from the Hindu norm is the measure of their un-Indian nature. Indian culture is identical with Hindu culture. . . .
>
> The Indian Muslim and Christian minorities have become increasingly sensitive to what they regard as the anti-national cultural exclusivism of some segments of the majority community. . . . A group of Protestant Christians expressed their concern over the widespread identification of Indian

[22] *The Times of India*, 17 March 1988.

culture with Hinduism. There has been a tendency to regard Indian culture as synonymous with the religious practices of the majority community. Consciously or unconsciously, those who wield authority seek to impose these outward forms of the religion of the majority on others. The statement urged the necessity of distinguishing between those aspects of Indian culture which are the possession of all and those aspects which are intimately associated with Hindu religion.

In an editorial entitled 'What Is Indian Culture?' the *Times of India* [13 August 1949] noted that the RSS (Rashtriya Swayamsevak Sangh) had declared that its aim was the revival of India's ancient culture. But the precise components of that culture which the RSS wanted to resurrect were not explained in any detail. 'So far as we can gather from its slogans and shibboleths its aim is the revival of militant Hinduism reaching not so much into an enlightened future but groping back to a past lost in the mist of mythology and time.' The writer saw the greatest danger lurking precisely in this extreme vagueness, for 'Indian culture then becomes a thing clothed in the airy fancies of its progenitors'. He deprecated the RSS's talk of Indian culture as if it were a 'special exalted cult'. . . .

Gandhi refused to narrow his cultural heritage as Indian. 'Indian culture,' he wrote, 'is neither Hindu, Islamic nor any other, wholly. It is a fusion of all.' Prime Minister Jawaharlal Nehru gave one of the clearest expositions of the composite nature of Indian culture in his book *The Discovery of India*. He wrote that it is entirely misleading to equate Indian culture with Hindu culture. An Indian Buddhist or Jain has roots only in the thought and culture of India, yet neither is a Hindu by faith. Nehru agreed that in ancient times, the Hindu religion, philosophy and way of life were largely synonymous with Indian culture; but later, cultural influences from outside the subcontinent became extremely important. During the Mughal period, Indian culture was profoundly influenced by Islam, yet remained distinctively Indian. Especially in northern India, music, painting, architecture, food, clothes, language and traditions were affected by the impact of Islam, and a composite culture emerged which was neither Hindu nor Muslim. Nehru wrote that 'some inner urge towards synthesis' has been the dominant impulse which has characterised India's long cultural development.

Our task is now to evaluate these two opposing views of Indian culture adhered to in present-day India. Hindu culture or composite culture – which view comes closer to the truth? If forced to choose between them, one would immediately select the latter. Indian culture is a complex pattern, a composite culture into which have gone many diverse elements, foreign as well as indigenous. To *equate* Indian culture with Hindu culture is factually wrong. However, a second statement must follow immediately, namely, that despite the composite nature of Indian culture, Hinduism remains by far the most

> powerful and pervasive element in that culture. Those who lay great stress on the composite nature of Indian culture frequently minimise this basic fact. Caught up in their enthusiasm for the idea of cultural synthesis, and with the best of motives (usually the desire to strengthen communal harmony and national unity), they seem to suggest that the cultural fusion is of a kind which might have resulted from blending together *equal quantities* of the principal ingredients. This, of course, is simply not the case.
>
> Hinduism has indeed provided the essential genius of Indian culture; this cannot be denied. Significant cultural synthesis has not taken place everywhere; with the exception of Christianity in the small state of Kerala, there is much less non-Hindu cultural influence in south India than in the north. Thus, while not denying the reality and importance of the composite culture, we must be prepared to deal with an Indian culture largely rooted in Hinduism. Those who equate Indian culture with Hindu culture can produce considerable evidence in support of their position, although that part of empirical Indian culture which they ignore or reject makes their equation factually wrong; *the use to which their argument is put is frequently disruptive and anti-national.*[23]

Advani unfailingly omits the paras which refute the thesis.

Vajpayee said that the BJP would take the RSS's help in the general elections as it did in 1977. He described the Shiv Sena as 'parochial' and anti-non-Maharashtrian, which was striving to become a pro-Hindu regional party.[24]

Amidst moves to unite the opposition parties, the CPI (M) sounded a timely warning. Its general secretary, E.M.S. Namboodiripad recalled the 1977 experience in a detailed article. It deserves quotation *in extenso*:

> The RSS-BJP concept of 'Hindutwa', 'Hindu Rashtra' and so on are irreconcilably opposed to the radical secular democracy for which the CPI (M) and other left parties stand. Furthermore the moral political values for which secular Opposition parties, like the components of the Janata Dal and the National Front, stand are opposed to the values for which the BJP-RSS outfit stands.
>
> We Communists, therefore, consider it our duty to caution our friends belonging to the secular Opposition parties against the evil consequences of any alliance, understanding or adjustments with communal and divisive forces, including the RSS and the BJP, and the three major issues raised by the BJP and the RSS [Article 370 on Kashmir, Babri Masjid and Uniform Civil Code], and [to show] the total incompatibility of these forces with the secular democratic forces.

23 Smith, *India as a Secular State*, pp. 374-9.

24 *The Indian Express*, 5 March 1989.

> Take the specific example of Ram Janambhoomi. There has for a long time been a dispute on whether it is the birth place of Lord Ram or a mosque built by Babar. Feelings have been running high on both sides. Should the dispute be allowed to break out in a conflagration or settled? We Communists stand for an amicable settlement which can be brought either through: (1) The transformation of the whole place as national monument, there being no temple or mosque there or (2) construction side by side of a temple and a mosque, so that followers of the two religions can offer prayers according to their light, or (3) leave the whole dispute to the judicial process of a court verdict.
>
> It is well known that, while the friends of the Babri Masjid committee are prepared for either of these three solutions, the Ram Janambhoomi people are not. We Communists are of the view that the stand of the latter, which Mr. Malkani and his friends also unfortunately advocate, is unreasonable. . . .
>
> This is connected with the general propaganda persistently carried on by the RSS and the BJP on their concept of Hindutwa or Hindu Rashtra. This land of 800 million inhabitants, they claim, is the land of Hindus; all those non-Hindus who are living in this country should either Hinduise themselves or go out of the country. This is the ideology preached from day to day at the various RSS shakhas which are used for the training of young boys and girls in the martial arts. . . . The RSS-BJP is at odds with the left and secular Opposition parties. Am I making a mountain out of it when I caution my friends of the Janata Dal and the National Front that, by having any alliance or adjustments with this Hindu chauvinist outfit, they will be committing themselves to positions which are contrary to the cause of national unity?[25]

EMS followed his article by a keynote paper for the National Conference on Minorities and Secularism in Thiruvananthapuram. Hindu revivalism represented fundamentalism of the majority and its major vehicle, the RSS, was a 'semi-fascist' organisation. 'The RSS can actively intervene and transform any tension into communal riots.' He perceptively warned that allowing the BJP to become a ruling party either singly or as a powerful force in a coalition would be the 'beginning' of national disintegration. United Fronts in the States (SVD) in 1967 and at the Centre in 1977 had made the BJP respectable. Along with the secular parties like the Janata Dal, the Telugu Desam Party, the DMK and others the Congress could be defeated in the next Lok Sabha elections.[26]

The RSS's 'principal intellectual' (boudhik pramukh) K.S. Sudarshan, who was to become chief shortly, confirmed in an interview to Pankaj Pachauri that while

[25] *The Statesman*, 24 March 1989.

[26] *The Times of India*, 24 April 1989.

the erstwhile members of the Janata Party plumped for 'Gandhian socialism' to acquire a bigger base, 'Our swayamsevaks felt differently. After the last elections' negative results they abandoned socialism.'

As the interview proceeded candour overcame discretion.

Q. Do you think the BJP can emerge as an alternative?

A. That will take some time. When we talk about an alternative, we talk about a new system. The present encourages casteism and separatism.

Q. But you talk about the control of the 'Hindu mat'. Don't you encourage separatism from the 17 per cent minorities?

A. These 17 per cent are not the nation. They are not connected with the culture of the country. Why don't they sing Vande Mataram?

Q. But we are a secular country.

A. It should have been made clear at the start that they were free only to worship differently, but they have to kowtow on other issues. If they want to stay citizens of this country, the minorities must give up all their special privileges.

Q. Then why have you taken up the Ram Janmabhoomi issue?

A. Beliefs never have rationale or logics. The Ram Janmabhoomi in Ayodhya is a symbol. If the Government can take a decision to renovate the Somnath Temple, why can't they do the same here?

Q. But this has led to bloodshed.

A. This is nothing. There will be more. We are not scared.

Q. What about your samrasata (peaceful co-existence) theory?

A. We do not want samrasata by appeasement. Babur broke the temple to build a mosque. If they want to live in peace they should give up the mosques in Ayodhya, Mathura and Varanasi. Peaceful co-existence has to be desired by both sides.

Q. But the Muslims have agreed to refer the matter to the court. After all it is a disputed property.

A. What will the court decide? Will it decide that Ram was born there? Beliefs and traditions cannot be logical. The dispute has been created. We will worry no more about any disorder.

Q. What about the Government?

A. The Government has to bow before the Hindus. It has done so before the Muslims in the Shah Bano case.

Q. Will you take militant action?

A. Everything has been decided by our leaders. On 30 September each village will start sending a brick and on 9 November the temple's construction will begin. We need no court orders.[27]

[27] *India Today*, 30 June 1989.

Not many supported EMS's critique. Chandra Shekhar was among them. He told Bhola Chatterjee,

> The tendency in this country seems to be that if any member of the minority community pleads for his own religion he is taken for a communalist but if that is done by any person belonging to the majority community, it is assumed to be the thing to do.
>
> I hold quite the opposite view. Minorities all over the world, whether religious, linguistic or ethnic, use more aggressive language and they assert themselves in a more intemperate manner. If one goes by the dictionary meaning of what they say, one would invariably reach the wrong conclusion. We should try to understand the emotions behind it, the sentiments which motivate them to speak that language and try to assuage their feelings.
>
> Q. Do you agree that in recent years there has been an alarming growth of Hindu-Muslim ill-feeling and both the ruling Congress and Opposition parties seem to have resigned themselves to it? How do you think the potentially explosive issue of Ramjanmabhoomi-Babri Masjid could be resolved?
>
> A. Not only Hindus and Muslims, but it is the tragic situation in this country that all the religious groups are feeling estranged from each other. The Sikhs are in no better position. Nobody seemed to have been concerned when the Sikhs were getting alienated from the national mainstream. At that time I made a statement but I did not see even one journalist who could appreciate the gravity of the situation.
>
> About Ramjanmabhoomi, just three days after the locks were opened I said that a grave mistake was being committed. One Amritsar (that is Operation Bluestar) was enough and there should be no repetition of that in regard to the Ramjanmabhoomi-Babri Masjid question. . . . You know that there has been a mosque at that place for five hundred years. Are you going to revise history? . . .
>
> I have not seen very many people in this country who are courageous enough to say that we should put a stop to amending history in this manner.[28]

It was an RSS show in play now. On 23 August 1989 Deoras declared at Mumbai that the VHP would play a major role in reviving the self-respect of Hindutva in the country as well as in the world. The VHP's chief organiser Moropant Pingle announced that the next international convention of Hindus would be held in London a week later.[29] The RSS and its affiliate have acquired impressive support

[28] *The Telegraph*, 24 March 1989.

[29] *The Indian Express*, 24 August 1989.

abroad, especially in the United States. An aspect which deserves more notice than it has received is its aspiration to make India, and at one remove itself, a Jagadguru – a guide to the whole world.

The campaign for a Ram temple was a cover under which the RSS went about its main campaign. Soon Vajpayee fell in line. 'National interests and Hindu interests cannot be separated,' he said on 24 September 1989 as the BJP draft manifesto was being finalised.[30]

Around this time a new and revealing slogan was coined which the RSS as well as Bal Thackeray relished, '*Garv se kaho, hum Hindu hain. Har Bharatvasi Hindu hai. Hindu jage desh jage* (Declare with pride "I am a Hindu". Everyone in India is a Hindu. If Hindus wake up so will India).' This line struck a response among some. Girilal Jain, former editor of *The Times of India* cited as 'a fundamental issue whether or not the vague, undefined and, for me, undefinable Hindu search for self respect is to develop along anti-Muslim lines'.[31]

The campaign resulted in riots. In a long editorial entitled 'Stop the carnage' *The Times of India* noted the revival of the Jana Sangh in the RSS's campaign. 'Mr. Advani while holding forth on "Bharat Mata" now goes on so far as to deny that Mahatma Gandhi was the Father of the Nation.'[32]

The political character of the 'cultural' RSS surfaces unfailingly at crucial moments. At his annual address in Nagpur Deoras called upon the people to vote in the general elections for those who would protect Hindu interests.[33] The election reaped a promising harvest for the BJP. The annual one-month camp of swayamsevaks held at Nagpur was addressed by Vajpayee. The cadres were elated, 'perceiving that there is an aggressive pride in being a Hindu: "We have to encash on this, or else we will never succeed," the leaders seem to feel.'

Encashed it was – by demolishing the Babri Masjid on 6 December 1992. 'The position of the RSS among the intellectuals' had also changed.[34] The BJP's leaders rode high on the wave. Its 'modern' face Jaswant Singh alleged in Mumbai at a meeting of the Indian Merchants Chamber 'the temple of Santosh Mehta is far more important than the temple of Nehru. We have to be idol breakers.' Nehru's policies whether in economics or foreign affairs must be rejected. He stopped short of mentioning secularism in this context but implied as much, as *The Times of India*'s report reveals.

> While claiming that the legacy of Nehru was essentially westernised, Mr. Singh regretted that never in the history of this country was everything so western

30 *The Telegraph*, 25 September 1989.

31 *Sunday Mail*, 19 November 1989.

32 *The Times of India*, 17 October 1989.

33 *The Indian Express*, 11 October 1989.

34 *The Times of India*, 13 June 1990; Anil Sharma's report from Nagpur.

> accepted. 'Somewhere the essence of India got eroded in the last 43 years. "Gai (cow), Ganga and Geeta" have now become communal symbols,' he lamented.
>
> Earlier, he said, political stability had no nexus with development and consequently had no bearing on economic growth. The accent on development hitherto had been on science and technology which was largely based on western systems.[35]

He was wooing Big Business; but more so the RSS by his diatribe against Nehru.

Advani told the BBC that it would not be wrong to call the BJP a 'Hindu Party'. To a question he replied it could be called a 'Hindu Nationalist Party'.[36]

The BJP won 85 seats in the Lok Sabha in 1989 as against the 4 it had won in 1984. Advani's letter to V.P. Singh and N.T. Rama Rao, as convenor of the National Front, dated 29 November 1989, contained this stipulation:

> If it is acknowledged by the Janata Dal that though the JD and BJP differ on issues like Article 370, Uniform Civil Code, Human Rights Commission, Rama Janmabhoomi, etc., the JD does not regard the BJP as communal, that would go a long way in removing misgivings in our rank and file. I hope the NF will take note of these reservations and exert to remove them. . . . Even while expressing these reservations, we have not made our support to you conditional to your agreeing to remove them. In response to your letter, the BJP wishes to convey to you its readiness to give general but critical support to the NF Government.[37]

Advani went back on this only a few months later when he launched the rath yatra which could not have failed to bring down the National Front government. The reference to the Human Rights Commission was a veiled demand for the abolition of the Minorities Commission. The BJP leaders were privy to the Janata Party government's decision to set up the Commission in 1979. The RSS demanded its abolition and replacement by an HRC. The BJP fell in line.

On 27 February 1990, elections were held to Assemblies of eight states. The BJP won the largest number; 498 seats, against the Dal's 458 and the Congress (I)'s 444. It formed governments in Madhya Pradesh, Rajasthan and Himachal Pradesh. On 7 August 1990 Prime Minister V.P. Singh announced his government's decision to implement the Mandal Report which had recommended that 27 per cent of government jobs be reserved for backward castes. Advani's riposte was sharp and calculated. He declared, on 12 September, that he would go on a *rath yatra* from

[35] *The Times of India*, 11 August 1990.

[36] *Organiser*, 5 August 1990.

[37] *The Hindu*, 30 November 1989.

Somnath to Ayodhya from 25 September to 30 October. The challenge to the National Front government could not have been more explicit.

Following Advani's arrest in Bihar by Laloo Prasad Yadav's government, the BJP withdrew its support from V.P. Singh's government on 23 October. It was voted out of office on a non-confidence motion on 7 November by 356 votes against 151 with 6 abstentions. Both the BJP and the Congress (I) voted for the motion. Chandra Shekhar split the Janata Dal on 5 November and formed a government with Congress (I) support. It was, predictably, withdrawn in March 1991. The Lok Sabha was dissolved. On Rajiv Gandhi's tragic assassination in May, P.V. Narasimha Rao became leader of the Congress (I) parliamentary party and was sworn in as prime minister on 21 June 1991.

On 29 December 1997 Singhal said, 'It is time to catch Muslims by their necks and tell them where their place lies.' He added: 'Kashi and Mathura are ours. If the Muslims want to avoid *further humiliation*, they should hand over those shrines quietly.'

Vajpayee did not denounce these remarks. Formal dissociation became necessary only because of the barbaric nature of the remarks. On the day on which Singhal was fulminating in Lucknow, Advani spoke at the temple town Tirupati. *The Hindu* reported:

> He took the occasion to affirm 'categorically and unequivocally' that Kashi and Mathura were not on the agenda of the BJP. He, however, said that Kashi and Mathura formed part of the BJP manifesto, while the dominant issue in the elections would be stability and good governance. He hastened to add that it did not mean that the two temple issues were put on the back burner but said that just as each election had its own 'key issues', it was 'stability' this time.

Advani himself had earlier, on 16 March the same year, explained what this meant: '[Kashi and Mathura] are not on the agenda. Ayodhya, to begin with, was also not on the agenda.' Predictably, on 1 January 1998, Singhal poured scorn on Vajpayee's denial. He 'knew very well the meaning of such statements . . . the decision of the Sangh parivar was final and binding'. A day earlier he had said in Ayodhya: 'There is no difference between the BJP and the VHP on the temple issue. Their language might be different, but ideologically we are one.' On 9 January, he pledged that 'there won't be any conflict between the two arms of the Sangh Parivar in this regard'.

RSS supremo Rajendra Singh's speech on 10 January made the situation crystal clear. He justified the BJP's ostensible shift in emphasis from Ayodhya, Article 370, and other contentious issues. 'If you are ill, you don't take a bath. But that does not mean that this will be the arrangement forever, in all circumstances.'

The other two mosques at Mathura and Varanasi still remain under threat.

Advani's speech in London on 29 July 1990 gave short shrift to secularism. 'Secular principles did not allow non-Hindus to undermine Hindu rights and traditions.'

The RSS set Advani on a collision course. A three-day study camp of BJP legislators was held in Bhopal which he inaugurated on 14 September 1990 with an attack on the National Front government. Qurban Ali, a seasoned correspondent, asked whether there were pressures to withdraw support from the V.P. Singh government. Advani saw the point and denied that the RSS had put any pressure on that point adding revealingly, 'We certainly do press them for their workers.'[38]

Advani set off on a *dharm yudh yatra* (religious war march) from Somnath on 25 September 1990. Richard H. Davis, in his incisive essay on the iconography of Rama's chariot notes how the VHP played a very important role in Advani's rath yatra in 1990:

> The procession was planned jointly, with the VHP leadership setting the stage and offering strategic advice behind the scenes. The hard-core imagery, for which the VHP and related groups were primarily responsible, was religious, allusive, militant, masculine, and anti-Muslim. Making much use of Rama as paradigm, it played out themes inherent in the primary terms of the mobilisation. The BJP and Advani placed themselves often in the position of trying to reframe this imagery or put a softer spin on it. . . . This message-doubling held advantages for both parties. For the VHP and kindred groups [such as the Bajrang Dal], the participation of the BJP insured coverage of the procession by major media, enabling them to project their message to a much larger audience than had been previously possible. The BJP, on the other hand, was able to disavow the more militant imagery as originating from the VHP and so attempt to maintain its electoral respectability, while at the same time profiting from the undoubted power and commitment that militant imagery evoked for some. . . .
>
> The Sangh campaign [was] an enormously successful mobilisation in which an aggressive, risky and adept manipulation of cultural symbols through a variety of mass media provoked wide-spread popular response, transformed the marginal VHP into a major religious-cultural organisation, and generated considerable electoral gains for the BJP.[39]

Peter van der Veer holds that

> the political success of the BJP depends squarely on its alliance with two Hindu nationalist movements, the Vishwa Hindu Parishad (VHP), an organisation

[38] *Sunday Observer*, 23 September 1930.

[39] Richard H. Davis, 'The Iconography of Rama's Chariot', in *Making India Hindu*, ed. David Ludden, Delhi: Oxford University Press, 1996, pp. 42 and 31.

> of religious leaders, and the Rashtriya Swayamsevak Sangh (RSS). . . . This alliance allows it to use religious discourse and mass-scale ritual action in the political arena.
>
> In 1989, the BJP made Ayodhya an 'absolutely central' issue.
>
> At least from this point onward – and probably already in 1986 – the political agenda of the BJP cannot be separated from that of the VHP. There is a direct coordination of rituals, agitation and political manoeuvring by the high command of the BJP, the RSS, and the VHP who in fact overlap to a significant degree. Vijaya Raje Scindia is a Vice-President of the BJP and a leader of the VHP; Lal Krishan Advani and Atal Behari Vajpayee are leaders of the BJP, but have a background in the RSS; an important leader of the RSS, Manohar Pingle, has the VHP in his portfolio. Significantly, the VHP leadership also draws extensively on the experience of the Indian bureaucracy, such as former directors-general of police, former Chief judges, and former ministers; it is not simply an 'extremist' organisation, far removed from the mainstream of Indian society. Obviously, the support of persons with strong links to the bureaucracy is critical in the planning and execution of mass-scale demonstrations.[40]

All these are scholars of impeccable credentials. Their research, and the reality as people in India know it, suffice to expose the deception which the BJP is practising so brazenly and sedulously about its separateness from the RSS and the VHP.

The Bajrang Dal turned 15 in 1999, to the delight of its grandparent, the RSS. An able work which sheds much light on the growth of the Bajrang Dal is *Creating Nationality* by Ashis Nandy, Shikha Trivedy, Shail Mayaram and Achyut Yagnik. They write:

> The Bajrang Dal first came into the limelight in December 1985, when it called for a general strike in U.P. to demand the removal of the lock on one of the gates of the Babri Masjid. In the following year it was in the forefront when the VHP organised a number of programmes in connection with the Ramjanmabhoomi Mukti Andolan. In October 1988, the Dal forcibly closed down for a day all educational institutions in U.P. to protest against the Ayodhya march organised by the Babri Masjid Action Committee and the latter's plan to read namaz at the mosque.
>
> The countdown to the events to 1990 began for the Bajrang Dal in July

40 Peter van der Veer, *Religious Nationalism: Hindus and Muslims in India*, Delhi: Oxford University Press, 1996, pp. 1-4.

> 1989. This was when the Dal held a Bajrang Bhakti Diksha Samaroh (a training programme given the form of an initiation ceremony) at Ayodhya 'To strengthen them [the boys] for the fight that lay ahead'. More than 6,000 volunteers, it is claimed, went through the initiation rites.

Vinay Katiyar claimed for the Bajrang Dal a membership of 100,000 in UP alone. All could not have been new adherents. Very many were seconded to it by the RSS. In 1988 the Bajrang Dal's men, armed with tridents, bows and arrows, stopped the Muslims' march towards the mosque at Ayodhya.

Besides the VHP, the Bajrang Dal had a central role in Advani's rath yatra from Somnath in Gujarat to Ayodhya in September-October 1990. The Bajrang Dal's volunteers offered him a cup of their blood as proof of their commitment and kept him company throughout. The riots that followed were their handiwork. At Ujjain they presented him with weapons, and as the scholar, Prof. Richard H. Davis of Yale, recorded, 'often welcomed him by applying a ritual mark (tilak) of blood on his forehead'. He tried to humour them at times: 'What are these weapons [bows and arrows] in the days of the AK-47?' The Dal, however, showed that it had the weapons which mattered when it came to the crunch. On the eve of the demolition of the Babri Masjid, on 30 November 1992, Katiyar said: 'If there is any sangharsh, we are ready for it. . . . *Kuch bigadane par hi kuch banta hai* (Only when something is destroyed, is something born).' These were not empty threats: the organisation was in the forefront of the attack on the Babri Masjid on 30 October 1990 and its demolition on 6 December 1992. As, indeed, were the leaders of the VHP and the BJP.

On 11 July 1993, the VHP put the Bajrang Dal within the confines of a written constitution, prescribed a uniform – blue shorts, white shirt and saffron scarf – and a handbook for the trainees.

The Bajrang Dal has deservedly acquired a formidable reputation. Paul R. Brass characterises it is as 'a fighting protection squad for the other organisations, a somewhat pathetic, but nevertheless dangerous version of the Nazi S.A.' Yogendra K. Malik and V.B. Singh make a similar assessment of this 'paramilitary wing' of the VHP:

> Bajrang Dal, the VHP's youth wing, is its fighting arm. Consisting of lumpen elements in reflects the contemporary political culture of India. . . . The steady rise in the number of unemployed educated youth in the urban areas has added to the degenerate segment of society. The Bajrang Dal, more than any other group in India, is able to mobilise all these elements in the cause promoted by the VHP.

There is an important aspect of this seemingly 'uncontrollable' body. The fact that the Bajrang Dal is known to recruit untrained, volatile, semi-lumpen elements in contrast to the handpicked and thoroughly-coached RSS cadres absolves the larger front and core organisations from direct responsibility for reckless acts of indiscipline or violence. Scholars of note have recorded the Bajrang Dal's role in the riots in 1990 and 1992. Yet, Justice P.K. Bahri of the Delhi High Court struck down on 4 June 1993, the government's notifications of 10 December 1992 banning the RSS and the Bajrang Dal, but upheld the one on the VHP. The bans were imposed after the demolition of the Babri mosque on 6 December 1992 by activists of these three bodies. A month after Justice Bahri gave a clean chit to two of the three organisations, the absurdity of his ruling was exposed by the evidence given by witness after witness before the Citizens' Tribunal on Ayodhya.

Advani knew he was playing with fire. The RSS knew also the Bajrang Dal was a tool in their hands. It was set up by the VHP in 1984, the year the VHP decided on its march to Ayodhya. Violence was freely threatened. Often, the threat was made good. The VHP's general secretary Ashok Singhal warned, 'If the Hindu sentiments sweep the whole country, the Muslims would realise that neither the police nor the government nor political parties would be able to save them from the wrath.'[41] But what *had* the Muslims said or done to incur the wrath? One fine day in 1964 the RSS sets up the VHP to make a demand and refuse to submit it to adjudication. It was preceded in December 1983 by the Hindu Ekatmata Yojna.

These political games exacted a toll which rose till 1993. On 8 January 1991 the Minister of State for Home Affairs, Subodh Kant Sahay, told parliament that 693 people were killed and 2,773 injured in communal riots 1990. They occurred in parts of Andhra Pradesh, Assam, Bihar, Delhi, Gujarat, Karnataka, Tamil Nadu, Rajasthan, Uttar Pradesh and Maharashtra.[42]

Poisonous rhetoric kept pace with the flow of blood. The BJP president, Murli Manohar Joshi, who replaced Advani on 1 February 1991, said,

> Hindu rashtra need not be a formal structure. It is the basic culture of this country. I say that all Indian Muslims are Mohammadiya Hindus; all Indian Christians are Christi Hindus. They are Hindus who have adopted Christianity and Islam as their religion. So long as we call this country India, so long as the majority believe they are Hindus, India will never go theocratic. It is my guarantee that India would remain secular as long as it remains a Hindu majority country.[43]

L.K. Advani referred to the 'so-called minorities'. He said, 'I object to the talk of

41 *The Times of India*, 15 November 1990.
42 *The Indian Express*, 9 January 1991.
43 *Sunday Observer*, 13 January 1991.

Hindu interest. It is not Hindu interest we should talk about but national interest. But no national interest can be different from Hindu interest.'[44]

The 'moderate' Vajpayee was as addicted to double-talk:

> The BJP has not endorsed the concept of Hindu rashtra, but we don't denounce this extreme demand made by some, including admittedly sections of our own party. We have called for a Bharatiya rashtra, the name Hindu rashtra is given by those who feel that all Indians, including Muslims, are culturally speaking Hindus. Let them remain Muslims as far as their religion is concerned but otherwise *let them not abdicate their identity as Hindus*. The name Hindustan was given by others to India and it symbolises the cultural heritage of the country. If somebody calls for a Hindu rashtra we don't quarrel with it.

His complaint was very extensive. 'Even Hindu girls and boys go to convents and get westernised.'[45]

This is the heart of the matter. The RSS does not mind Muslims praying five times a day provided that they pray for Ram as well in negation of their faith. This fundamental is spread over the pages of the writings of Savarkar, Golwalkar, D.D. Upadhyaya and his successors to this day.

One must face the question boldly. Such mumbo jumbo cannot possibly appeal to educated Hindus. Why then do they vote for the BJP and laud the RSS? The reasons are many. The RSS first instils an inferiority complex and, next exploits it to prod Hindus to become dominant. Political instability drives some to follow 'strong' leaders. Lastly, the RSS offers the vision of a Great India, economic revival, and military might. Demolition of the Babri mosque was to be a symbol of Hindu might; a revenge against 'the wrongs of history'.

Money was never a problem with the RSS and its fronts. Advani was presented with a purse of more than Rs. 1 crore in Jaipur in February 1991.[46] The RSS reduced the debate to an intra-Hindu debate in which the minorities had no place, as noted sociologist Dr. Victor D'Souza perceptively noted.[47] The minorities were kept out.

On 9 March 1991, after the Chandra Shekhar government fell, once Rajiv Gandhi withdrew his support, the BJP leaders rushed to the RSS's headquarters at Nagpur on 9 March. On the table was strategy for the snap polls and pleas to enlist the RSS's support.[48] The poll was to be dominated by Hindutva.

The trip was successful. *The Times of India* reported that the RSS 'will throw its full weight behind the BJP in the forthcoming Lok Sabha elections'. But the RSS

[44] *Hindustan Times*, 16 January 1991.

[45] *Illustrated Weekly of India*, 26 January 1991.

[46] *The Times of India*, 5 February 1991.

[47] *The Times of India*, 6 February 1991.

[48] Rita Manchanda, *Sunday Observer*, 10 March 1991.

imposed one condition. 'It will not publicly share its platform with the BJP leaders.' This was to maintain the facade of its being a 'cultural' body (12 March 1991). The Hindutva card was played openly. 'We always play the patriotic card and in India nationalism and patriotism divested of its Hindu element does not have any meaning.'[49]

The general elections yielded 120 seats in the Lok Sabha to the BJP. P.V. Narasimha Rao became prime minister and BJP's Kalyan Singh chief minister of Uttar Pradesh. The RSS was up to its old trick: open a line to the Congress. The RSS chief M.D. Deoras's younger brother Bhaurao told Prasun Sonwalkar a lot. He supported the idea of the BJP entering into a coalition at the Centre with the Congress leader P.V. Narasimha Rao's government to provide stability. Rao was a 'sober' person. He had met the Prime Minister. Once the Ram temple is built there would be a major change in the attitude of the Muslims.[50] M.M. Joshi pursued the Hindutva line vigorously. 'Muslims are Hindu because they live in Hindustan.'[51]

Meanwhile the Janata Dal split when 24 of its M.P.s led by Dr. Subramanian Swamy quit the party. *The Telegraph* of 23 December 1991 reported:

> It was ironical that the BJP was claiming to be a nationalist party and had embarked on a yatra to hoist the national flag in Srinagar, Dr. Swamy stated. He challenged the BJP to hoist the national flag in Karimnagar district of Andhra Pradesh, Batala district of Punjab and in some parts of Assam, where the PWG, the Khalistanis and the ULFA have respectively announced that the national flag would not be permitted to be hoisted on 26 January. The BJP was interested only in Srinagar because 'their intent is only anti-Muslim', he said.
>
> Dr. Swamy also pointed out that the RSS, the backbone of the BJP, had banned the national anthem at its shakhas and nor was the national flag allowed to be hoisted at the shakhas. He also charged that BJP, as a political party, had never hoisted the flag even once during Independence Day or Republic Day. Regarding Mr. Bhaurao Deoras's call for co-operation between the RSS-BJP and the Congress, Dr. Swamy said it was a ploy by the enemies of the Prime Minister Narasimha Rao, inside and outside the Congress.
>
> He also wanted to know why the BJP at its meeting with the Chinese Premier, Mr. Li Peng, had raised only the Ayodhya issue and not Kailas Mansarovar in Tibet – 'Only because there are no Muslims living in Mansarovar,' Dr. Swamy said.

The BJP president M.M. Joshi received a pat on the back from his patron, the RSS's chief M.D. Deoras. 'A Hindu Nation exists here from time immemorial. . . .

[49] *The Hindu*, 20 April 1991.

[50] *The Times of India*, 28 November 1991.

[51] *Hindustan Times*, 8 December 1991.

So this Ekta Yatra of yours will also spread Hindutva which is the national spirit of our country.'[52]

Two points deserve emphasis. First, there has been no dilution in any of the formulations since Savarkar's *Hindutva* in 1925. In the overall framework, which Deoras outlined in his letter, fall the other items – there are no minorities, Hindu culture is India's culture, the minorities can pray as they like provided they regard themselves as Hindus, adopt Hindu religion ('culture') and Hindu names, as M.M. Joshi insisted. Since the minorities do not entertain these demands, *ghar wapsi*, conversion miscalled 'reconversion', is the only way out. Finally, State power will be used gradually in aid of the programme. Its programme leaves the RSS no room for compromise or retreat. On the contrary its ambitions have grown. Deoras said at Kalyani on 25 January 1992 that the day was not far off when Hinduism would spread to other parts of the world. All over the world people would be content if they accepted Hindu philosophy and the Hindu way of life.[53]

These themes were voiced since 1925 and continue to be voiced even now in 2019. At the same camp Deoras insisted that Hinduism is the only viable alternative in the wake of phenomenal changes all over the world. The VHP chief Ashok Singhal was present. Earlier Deoras unfurled the saffron flag. The general secretary H.V. Seshadri had filled the details on 'Hindu resurgence' for the Bengali audience. Hinduism is not a particular religion or mode of worship. 'Instead, it is whole gamut of eternal human values and the concept of Hindu rashtra is entirely cultural and it comprises all those who adore their country as their motherland.'[54]

Hitler and Mussolini did not cover fascism under a 'spiritual' or 'cultural' garb. The RSS and the BJP had hit a rock by 1985-86. The slogan of 'Gandhian socialism' had to be dropped. The cadres yearned for the Jana Sangh. Capture and demolition of the Babri Masjid infused life. The RSS's spear arm, the VHP, was founded in 1964. It was set to work in the mid-eighties. That was to be symbolic of Hindu dominance.

The roots lay in the 19th century. The Congress disrupted the trend and gave the nation the ideal of a modern secular democracy. The RSS took its revenge. It has not fared too badly; but is none too successful. The secular ideal still holds sway in the country. The battle is still being fought. Cries never uttered before were heard. Rajendra Singh, the RSS general secretary said, with remarkable precision, that 98 per cent of Muslims were originally Hindus. 'They should not object if they were termed as Hindus as "Hindu" is not a religious but a cultural term.'[55]

In P.V. Narasimha Rao, India had its von Hindenburg who facilitated Hitler's assumption of power. The media helped the BJP. 'The gravitating towards it (the

[52] *Organiser*, 29 December 1991.

[53] *The Statesman*, 26 January 1992.

[54] *The Statesman*, 24 January 1992.

[55] *Organiser*, 16 February 1992.

BJP) of upper and middle classes and the rich and literate ruralites [sic] was basically due to the media hype.'[56]

Truth to tell, the RSS faced hardly any challenge. The Prime Minister was quiescent, if not complicit. Muslim leaders, such as they were, were inept. The issue demanded a secular approach. It concerned a national movement. They set up multiple Muslim 'Action' Committees at war with one another. Large sections of the media and some leading journalists supported the RSS. Even the Chief Justice of India, M.N. Venkatachaliah, was complicit. The RSS proceeded with its drive to demolish the Masjid unchecked. The parleys and the shilanyas and kar sevaks are outside the scope of this book. (They are set out in this writer's three-volume compilation *The Babri Masjid Question*, Tulika Books.) We are concerned here with the RSS's ideology and its politics. During this phase sadhus and sants were enrolled. An enormous Hindu vote bank was built. Muslims were not only marginalised but were derided and denounced as heirs of Babar and Muslim 'invaders'. The movement spread to rural areas where the RSS had little or no presence. In less than a decade since 1985, its year of frustration, the RSS had brought the BJP centre stage. The VHP prospered; so did the Bajrang Dal.

Predictably, industrialists, businessmen, the upper and middle classes supported the Ram temple movement. The underprivileged were not unmoved. Jaffrelot has described the impact on former members of the armed forces.

> A substantial number of retired military officers joined the BJP in 1991. Up till then, Jaswant Singh, a retired major from an aristocrat background in Rajasthan who was a member of the Rajya Sabha between 1980 and 1989 and the Lok Sabha from 1989 onwards, had been almost their only representative. Suddenly, former members of the armed services, most of whom had been high-ranking officers, began to enter the party; among those who joined in 1991 were 2 Air Marshals, 6 Lieutenant-Generals, 4 Major-Generals, 4 Brigadiers, 1 Air Commodore, 4 Colonels, 1 Lieutenant-Colonel, 2 Wing Commanders, 21 Majors, 3 Captains, 1 Squadron Leader and Flying Officer. Along with these servicemen, at least one retired Inspector-General of police and 2 retired Director-Generals of police joined the ranks of the party. The latter had already forged close links with the RSS: B.P. Singhal was the brother of Ashok Singhal and Shrish Chandra Dixit had joined the VHP after retiring in 1984. In fact, a number of servicemen who had gone over to the BJP since the late 1980s had been involved with the RSS combine for some time. Capt. Jagat Vir Singh Drona, who had unsuccessfully contested the Kanpur seat in 1989 on a BJP ticket, had been a member of the RSS since he was 12 and became a *sanghchalak* on leaving the Army.[57]

[56] Prabhu Chawla, then editor of *The Indian Express*, 9 May 1992.

[57] Jaffrelot, *The Hindu Nationalist Movement and Indian Politics*, pp. 433-4.

The Civil Services were no better. The question is inescapable. If Judges of the Supreme Court, men of the armed forces, civil service and the police join the BJP or the RSS after retirement what could one have expected of them when they were in service?

BJP leaders supported the demolition. The Babri Masjid 'was a symbol of shame and has been erased', Vajpayee said in December 1992.[58] None of the Muslims in the Narasimha Rao Cabinet – Salman Khurshid, Ghulam Nabi Azad and Jaffer Sharif – resigned. It is only fair to mention that large sections of Hindus disapproved of and even denounced the crime. The best research on history and archaeology was done by Hindu scholars and a Parsi archaeologist.

However, the BJP, no doubt at the behest of the RSS, gave party tickets to an array of sants.

> In early 1993 Swami Chinmayanand, the BJP member for the Uttar Pradesh seat of Budaun in the Lok Sabha and one of the leaders of the VHP, delivered a speech in Parliament in which he emphasised the role *sadhus* had played in the Ramjanmabhoomi movement from 1984 onwards and their participation in the demolition of the mosque . . .
>
> This expression of pride in the demolition provides a further indication of the way in which certain *sadhus* were claiming for themselves their own sphere of political action, a trend that was apparent even before 6 December 1992. First, more and more sadhus contested elections. In 1991, the BJP had 6 saffron-clad MPs: Swami Chinmayanand (Budaun), Mahant Avaidyanath (Gorakhpur), Uma Bharti (Khajurao), Swami Sureshanand (Jalesar), Swami Sakshiji Maharaj (Mathura) and Yoganand Saraswati (Bhind). Second, *sadhus* tried increasingly to influence purely political matters.[59]

The RSS always injected religion into politics in a big way; consistently.

The demolition was intended to mark a watershed in Indian politics. Girilal Jain, former editor of *The Times of India*, lauded it and warned that Muslims must learn a 'lesson' from it and remember that there would be no going back on the pre-6 December situation. Hindus had now mobilised as never before.[60] The message was clear. Muslims will not be heard to voice their grievances; they must accept what Hindus offer them. Ramkrishna Bajaj, a Mumbai industrialist, and former Congressman and admirer of Jayaprakash Narayan, sent a circular letter to many, this writer included, to assert that the Muslims should learn a 'lesson'.

Overwhelming evidence establishes prior concert. The demolition was pre-planned and finalised at a meeting held on 5 December 1992 and attended by H.V.

[58] Ibid., p. 475.

[59] Ibid., p. 479.

[60] *The Times of India*, 14 December 1992.

Seshadri, K.S. Sudarshan, L.K. Advani, M.M. Joshi, Vijaya Raje Scindia, Ashok Singhal, Vinay Katiyar, Uma Bharti, Sadhvi Rithambara, Acharya Dharmendra, Pramod Mahajan, B.L. Sharma, and Champat Roy, apart from Moreshwar Save of the Shiv Sena.[61]

The CBI filed a charge sheet in October 1993 against L.K. Advani, M.M. Joshi, V.H. Dalmia, Ashok Singhal, Vinay Katiyar, Uma Bharti and others. On 27 August 1994 Special Judicial Magistrate found that a prima facie case did exist and committed the case to the Sessions Court for full trial. On 9 September 1997, Additional Sessions Judge, Jagdish Prasad Srivastava framed charges against the accused after finding that a prima facie case existed, a finding also made by the Magistrate; two judicial findings on the existence of a prima facie case.[62]

The RSS, VHP and the Bajrang Dal were banned by the Central government; but as a matter of form. Such was the material produced before the tribunals under the Unlawful Activities Act, 1967 that all the bans were set aside. The Judges' reasoning was, to say the least, preposterous.

The BJP-ruled governments in Rajasthan, Madhya Pradesh and Himachal Pradesh were sacked and direct Central rule, called President's rule, imposed. Its validity was upheld by the Supreme Court.[63] Uttar Pradesh came under President's Rule shortly after the demolition.

In the 1996 general election the BJP won 161 seats in the Lok Sabha. Its government lasted for a mere 13 days from 16 to 28 May 1996. This did not deter it from signing a counter guarantee for Enron. The United Front governments headed by H.D. Deve Gowda and later I.K. Gujral lasted three years. The 1998 elections voted a BJP government to power as did the 1999 elections. The BJP boldly nailed its colours to the mast in its election manifestoes. It sought votes on the plank of Hindutva, i.e. 'cultural nationalism'. The 1996 manifesto said:

> The BJP is committed to the concept of one nation, one people, one culture – our nationalist vision is not merely bound by the geographical or political identity of India, but defined by our ancient cultural heritage. From this belief flows our faith in '*Cultural Nationalism*' which is the core of *Hindutva*. That, we believe, is the identity of our ancient nation – *Bharatvarsha*.
>
> *Hindutva* is a unifying principle which alone can preserve the unity and integrity of our Nation. It is a collective endeavour to protect and re-energise the soul of India, to take us into the next millennium as a strong and prosperous nation, *Hindutva* is also the antidote to the shameful efforts of any section to benefit at the expense of others. . . .
>
> On coming to power, the BJP Government will facilitate the construction

[61] Kanungo, *RSS's Tryst with Politics*, p. 208.

[62] Noorani, *The Babri Masjid Question*, vol. 2, pp. 102-23.

[63] *S.R. Bommai vs. Union of India*, (1994) 3 SCC 1.

of a magnificent Shri Ram Mandir at Janmasthan in Ayodhya which will be a tribute to *Bharat Mata*. This dream moves millions of people in our land; the concept of Ram lies at the core of their consciousness.

The 1998 manifesto elaborated on it.

The BJP is committed to the concept of 'One Nation, One People and One Culture'. The unique cultural and social diversity in India is woven into a larger civilisational fabric by thousands of years of common living and common and shared values, beliefs, customs, struggles, joy and sorrow, as well as symbols of high degree of unity without uniformity. Our nationalist vision is not merely bound by the geographical or political identity of Bharat but it is referred by our timeless cultural heritage. This cultural heritage which is central to all regions, religions and languages, is a civilisational identity and constitutes the cultural nationalism of India which is the core of Hindutva. This we believe is the identity of our ancient nation 'Bharatvarsha'.

The BJP is convinced that Hindutva has immense potentiality to re-energise this nation and strengthen and discipline it to undertake the arduous task of nation-building. This can and does trigger a higher level of patriotism that can transform the country to greater levels. It is with such integrative ideas in mind, the BJP joined the Ram Janmabhoomi movement for the construction of Shri Ram Mandir at Ayodhya. . . . The BJP is committed to facilitate the construction of a magnificent Shri Ram Mandir at Ram Janmasthan in Ayodhya where a makeshift temple already exists. Shri Ram lies at the core of Indian consciousness.

The 2004 manifesto said:

The BJP draws its inspiration from the history and civilisation of India. We believe that Indian nationhood stems from a deep cultural bonding of the people that overrides differences of caste, region, religion and language. We believe that Cultural Nationalism – for which Indianness, Bharatiyata and Hindutva are synonyms – is the basis of our national identity. . . .

The BJP reaffirms its commitment to the construction of a Ram temple in Ayodhya. As Maryada Purshottam, Ram is an inspiring cultural symbol of India. His birthplace in Ayodhya is also associated with the religious sentiments of crores of Hindus. The BJP remains committed to its stand that the judiciary's verdict in this matter should be accepted by all.

A remarkably consistent refrain from 1996 to 2004. The 1989 and 1991 manifestoes were cited in the Supreme Court's judgment on the dismissal of the BJP governments.

In 1998 the BJP won 180 seats in the 12th Lok Sabha and secured 250 with its regional allies' support. Vajpayee was sworn in as prime minister on 19 March 1998. Rajendra Singh, who had taken over from Deoras as RSS chief on 11 March 1994, openly claimed credit for the victory. 'A clear cut ideology, leaders of proven merit and a large number of devoted and committed workers are the main reason for the growth of the BJP.'[64] Hindutva and RSS cadres had won power for the BJP leaders.

The RSS lost no time in telling Prime Minister Vajpayee who was the boss. General Secretary K.S. Sudarshan 'reportedly stormed into Vajpayee's residence late at night at the time of ministry making in March 1998 to prevent Jaswant Singh from being inducted into the Union Cabinet as the Finance Minister'.[65] The episode was widely reported in the press.

Pralay Kanungo records:

> After the initial euphoria, the RSS did not feel satisfied by the way the BJP government was being run. It acted tough; even hardcore RSS men like L.K. Advani were not spared. After the killing of 26 Hindus at Doda in Jammu & Kashmir, Acharya Giriraj Kishore of the VHP said, if the government had the will the situation in the state could be brought under control in a month's time, but he would give six months more to Advani as the problem was complex. He did not accept Advani as the 'hero' of the Ayodhya agitation and said: 'It was not Advani who built the movement . . . naturally when politicians choose to jump in at the last minute they get the credit.' It was the VHP and not Advani, who did the hard work, but Advani ran away with the credit, grumbled Kishore. He also rejected Advani's comparison as the second Sardar Patel, saying that he had to demonstrate through action. *Panchajanya*, the RSS mouthpiece, pulled up Vajpayee for forgetting to include Janmashtami (birthday of lord Krishna) greetings in his Independence Day speech and for overlooking Deendayal Upadhyaya's name in the list of past national leaders.
>
> The RSS also tried to have its control in the states where the BJP was in power, either on its own or in coalition. In Uttar Pradesh, it ran a virtual 'super-cabinet' to oversee the performance of the ministers, including Kalyan Singh. Rajendra Singh, the *sarsanghchalak*, addressed over 60 top IAS and IPS officers, including the Chief Secretary and the Director-General of Police, on the state's declining law-and-order situation. In Delhi, the RSS was able to appoint its favourite as the Lieutenant-Governor. In Rajasthan, the RSS pressurised Bhairon Singh Shekhawat, a non-conformist saffronite, for induction of more RSS members into the cabinet and other important positions. In Madhya Pradesh, where the party was out of power, the Sangh

[64] *Organiser*, 22 February 1998.

[65] Kanungo, *RSS's Tryst with Politics*, p. 258.

strategy operated through the Governor Bhai Mahavir, a trusted RSS worker. In Bihar, Sunder Singh Bhandari, a RSS *pracharak* and seasoned politician was appointed to mastermind the saffron strategy to counter Laloo Yadav.

In December 1998

the RSS held a *chintan baithak* (brain-storming session), a rare introspective session held in the past only at extraordinary times like the aftermath of Gandhi's assassination and the Emergency and following the BJP's 1984-5 electoral rout. The four-day meeting was attended by leaders of important affiliates: BJP's President Kushabhau Thakre, General Secretaries Venkiah Naidu and Govindacharya, VHP's Giriraj Kishore, Bajrang Dal Chief Jiban Singh Powayya and SJM's S. Gurumurthy. Sudarshan said the RSS would not like to be treated as an 'appendage' of the BJP. The BJP's recalcitrant behaviour was discussed threadbare. Some of the saffron affiliates allegedly charged the RSS leadership for being lenient towards the BJP, and asked for a clarification – who was the master – the BJP or the RSS? Angry delegates even talked of teaching the BJP leaders a lesson for straying from the path. They asked the RSS not allow the BJP to dilute its Hindutva ideology.

At the *chintan baithak*, the RSS decided on asserting itself and strengthening its control over the BJP. Their affiliates wanted the BJP to stop playing to what they call the 'pseudo-secular gallery'. They charged that the government first compromised on core *Hindutva issues* – Article 370, Ram temple and the Uniform Civil Code – because of the compulsions of coalition politics, as well as dumping the swadeshi agenda. Dalmia warned that the government's repeated condemnation of the VHP might prove costly. There was also a demand that the RSS should replace the discredited BJP. Some hardcore workers threatened that the RSS could 'finish off' the BJP in the next election and reminded it of the 1984 electoral debacle.

'National interest is supreme' declared *Panchajanya* (27 December 1998) on its cover. 'Should the government act against the national interest, we will be compelled to speak out,' announced K.S. Sudarshan, and warned the Vajpayee government for going back 'on its own declared policies'.

In 1999 the BJP and its allies won 296 seats and formed the government.

Kuppalli Sitaramayya Sudarshan, the sah-sarkaryavah (joint general secretary) took over as sarkaryavah, the chief, from Rajendra Singh on 10 March 2000 on his resignation on grounds of ill health, H.V. Seshadri, the sarkaryavah, general secretary, having declined the post on the same ground. He was perhaps the most outspoken of all the bosses the RSS has had. Soon after he took over the rein Sudarshan 'warned of another "epic war" between Hindus and "anti-Hindus" after which every opposition to *Hindutva* will change'. Asserting that 'even otherwise confused people have now come to believe in Hindutva', he observed: 'But it is going to change. This is yet another epic war between Hindus and anti-Hindus, a veritable Mahabharat in which sometime Abhimanyu will fall, sometime Ghatotkacha or it may be Jayadratha's turn yet another day.' Sudarshan advocated the need to scrap the Constitution, which was a 'remake of the British model of 1935' and suggested its replacement with one based on the 'aspirations of the people'.[66]

The RSS's unhappiness with the Constitution of India and India's national flag is a suppressed aspiration which is certain to rise in a more congenial atmosphere. At the turn of the century India faced an increasingly assertive RSS, a submissive BJP, rising tensions and bitter political confrontations. Demolition of the Babri Masjid on 6 December 1992 did not assuage the RSS's animosities; only intensified them. The nearly two decades that have elapsed since leave the country divided with little hope of reconciliation as the RSS's fortunes rise menacingly. All for the RSS's grab at total power through the BJP as the BJP.

The temple movement was 'purely political in nature and had nothing to do with religion', Sushma Swaraj publicly admitted at Bhopal on 14 April 2000. Indeed, the whole thing has been about polls to secure power and dominance. Immediately on the passing of the Palampur resolution on Ayodhya on 11 June 1989, Advani said, 'I am sure it will translate into votes.' On 3 December 1989, after the general elections, he expressed satisfaction that the issue had contributed to the BJP's success. On 24 February 1991, as India teetered towards another election, he was confident that the issue would 'influence the electoral verdict in favour of the BJP'. On 18 June 1991, he made this pathetic confession: 'Had I not played the Ram factor effectively, I would have definitely lost from the New Delhi constituency.' Shortly after the demolition of the Babri mosque on 6 December 1992 and another wave of carnage that came in its train, Advani wrote that if the Muslims were to identify themselves with the concept of Hindutva there would not be any reason for riots to take place.[67] In July 1992, he argued in the Lok Sabha Speaker's chamber: 'You must recognise the fact that from two seats in parliament in 1985 we have come to 117 seats in 1991. This has happened primarily because we took up this issue [Ayodhya].' Behind the BJP's religio-cultural rhetoric, however, there has always been cold political calculation.

Suresh Nambath's report in *The Hindu* of 26 March 2011 is an eye-opener.

> Is Hindu nationalism the *raison d'être* of the Bharatiya Janata Party (BJP), or just another vote-catching device? In a private conversation with American diplomats in May 2005, senior BJP leader Arun Jaitley articulated the view that Hindu nationalism was an opportunistic issue for the party.

[66] *Hindustan Times*, 13 March 2000; Kanungo, *RSS's Tryst with Politics*, p. 268.

[67] *The Times of India*, 30 January 1993.

> Mr. Jaitley, who is now the Leader of the Opposition in the Rajya Sabha, met Robert Blake, the *Chargé* at the US Embassy, on 6 May 2005, and provided him and the Political Counsellor an insightful exposition on the politics of Hindutva. Pressed on the question of Hindutva, Jaitley argued that Hindu nationalism 'will always be a talking point' for the BJP. However, he characterised this as 'an opportunistic issue', the Chargé wrote in a cable dated 10 May 2005. . . .
>
> When Mr. Blake explained the 'rationale and legal basis' for the US decision (on a visa for Modi) 'Jaitley agreed with the Chargé's point that Modi was a polarising personality, but argued that it would have been better for the US to let the Chief Minister visit the US, where he would have attracted a few demonstrators and then nothing more would be said'.
>
> The Modi issue aside, the BJP leader was upbeat on US-India relations, 'emphasising that ties with the US were no longer a point of controversy in Indian politics'. Citing his own situation as typical, 'Jaitley noted that he has several nieces and sisters living in the US, and "five homes to visit between DC and New York".' . . .
>
> In response to the Chargé's pitch for opening of the Indian services sector, Mr. Jaitley, a Senior Advocate, agreed that legal services should be opened to foreign competition, 'noting that the performance of the Indian bar has begun to improve, even though the quality of judges suffers from a "Gandhian" mindset that leads to unreasonably low salaries'. On the retail sector, Mr. Jaitley 'argued that foreign competition should not seriously hurt the mom and pop stores that form a BJP constituency'.
>
> In a concluding comment, the Chargé wrote: 'Although visibly pained by the Modi visa revocation, Jaitley was gracious and open throughout. He clearly values his personal and commercial connections to the US (several US corporates are legal clients). As the competition for BJP leadership heats up, Jaitley will enjoy the advantages of a telegenic personality and strong ties to the New Delhi establishment.'

These politicians did not realise that their success itself will spell their doom. The RSS will swallow them and rule directly through its chosen functionaries. Advani's dismissal is warning enough. So is the RSS's statement on its role in politics.

This phase saw the RSS merrily cracking the whip on the BJP, whenever a crisis erupted. In October 1995, it was over the revolt in Gujarat. *The Times of India*'s chief correspondent, Mumbai, S. Balakrishnan went to Nagpur to report that the RSS had now 'decided to play a greater role in the affairs of the BJP'. A 'Bombay-based business house was behind the revolt'. As a consequence 'the RSS will have a major role in the distribution of tickets' for the 1996 elections to the

Lok Sabha. The RSS chief Rajendra Singh attacked Enron for padding the cost of its Dabhol projects by as much as Rs. 2,000 crores. 'Where has the colossal sum gone?' he asked. In its brief 13 days in office in May 1996 Vajpayee's government signed unconstitutionally the famous Enron Counter Guarantee without winning a vote of confidence. He also made Pramod Mahajan defence minister.[68]

The VHP continued with its Ekatmata campaign in which Vajpayee joined. Hindutva was synonymous with Hinduism and nationalism.[69] Odd slogans were heard from odd platforms. Ram Jethmalani, vice-president of the BJP, resigned and floated his own party, Pavitra Hindustan Kazhagam. Inaugurating this 'outfit' on 19 November 1995, he declared 'those Muslims who still see a difference between Ram and Rahim cannot stay in this country'.[70] Six months later he was minister in the Vajpayee government. It was typical of the RSS acolytes like him to assume a right to banish people from the country.

On the eve of the elections Rajnath Singh met the top leaders of the BJP in New Delhi in March 1996 to discuss strategy. Hindutva was to be the main guiding principle of the BJP and L.K. Advani was to continue as the leader. All the RSS organisations were to work wholeheartedly for electoral victory of the BJP through which alone the BJP hoped to establish a Hindu Rashtra with 'Hindutva' as its guiding ideology.[71] This is the real game. The RSS does not owe the BJP a living. It had always kept its channels with the Congress open. It seeks to rule the country; revise its Constitution, discard the tricolour as the national flag and instal a Hindu Rashtra. Advani was the RSS's preference. He had reluctantly, but sensibly yielded the crown to Vajpayee much earlier at Mumbai on 13 December 1995. Doubts about him persisted in the RSS though. 'There were many senior leaders within the party who were not quite convinced about Mr. Advani's innocence. It had been repeatedly stressed that not a paisa of the alleged Rs. 60 lakhs pay off to Mr. Advani had come to the party funds.'[72]

At the RSS end enthusiasm ran high.

> The RSS is of the view that time is ripe for it to take a plunge into the election arena, with all its manpower, to mobilise voters in the forthcoming Lok Sabha elections, in favour of the Hindutva forces.
>
> The General Secretary of the RSS H.V. Sheshadari, while presenting the annual report on the first day of their All India Pratinidhi Sabha meeting here on Friday called upon the 'awakened sections of Hindus and in particular to the Hindutva workers, to mobilise support for such parties and persons

[68] *The Times of India*, 4 October 1995.

[69] *The Asian Age*, 10 November 1995.

[70] *The Asian Age*, 20 November 1995.

[71] *The Hindu*, 7 March 1996.

[72] Ibid.

who were of sterling character and could be depended upon for successfully tackling the grave problems and threats confronting the nation'.

The report denounces the Christians' demand for extension of the Dalit reservation to the Christian converts as a ploy to open the flood-gates of Dalit Hindus to Christianity.[73]

The RSS had decided to take the 'plunge into the election arena' with all the massive manpower at its command.

In its annual report presented today at the All-India Pratinidhi Sabha here, the RSS, however, does not name any political party (more so the BJP) while calling upon all the 'awakened sections of the Hindus to mobilise voters in the coming Lok Sabha elections to elect only such parties and persons who are of character and who could tackle successfully the threats and problems confronting the nation'. . . .

The three-day conclave has all the top brass of the Sangh Parivar attending the deliberations including the RSS chief, Rajendra Singh alias Rajju Bhaiya, H.V. Sheshadri, Ashok Singhal representing the Vishwa Hindu Parishad, Sundar Singh Bhandari, Keshu Bhau Thakre and K.N. Govindacharya – all representing the BJP, besides the representatives of the Hind Mazdoor Sangh and the Akhil Bharatiya Vidyarthi Parishad, the Sangh Parivar's trade union and student wings.

The RSS has again tried to emphasise the interests of the nation being synonymous to that of the Hindus, when it expresses concern over 'the descending curve of the Hindu population is in contrast to the rising graph of the Muslim population'.[74]

After the exposure of the Jain diary on Advani, Rajendra Singh said, 'If we remove Mr. Advani it will send wrong signals, even if it is clean moral stand.'[75] At the conclusion of the meeting of the RSS's Pratinidhi Sabha on 9 March, it announced that 'the RSS would actively back the BJP in the election arena through its organisational strength and manpower'.[76]

Double talk persisted. On 12 March General Secretary H.V. Seshadri repeated 'the time is ripe to plunge into the electoral arena with all its might'. On the same day M.G. Vaidya said, 'The RSS is purely an educational social and apolitical organisation.'[77] It is impossible to take the RSS and the BJP or their leaders at their word.

[73] *Hindustan Times*, 9 March 1986.

[74] *The Statesman*, 9 March 1996.

[75] *The Telegraph*, 9 March 1991.

[76] *The Telegraph*, 10 March 1996.

[77] *The Telegraph*, 13 March 1996.

The *Organiser* of 7 April 1996 published the full text of an appeal.

> All of you also know that the country's worrisome condition is the result of *India's politics being divorced from the pure indigenous Hindu nation*. For 2,500 years the word Hindu has been used to describe this people's nationality. Every person who regards this land as his mother, its heroes as his ancestors and this culture based on unity in diversity as his own is a Hindu, a national of this land irrespective of his land, irrespective of his mode of worship. Recently the Supreme Court has once again accepted Hindutva as a liberal, all-assimilative way of life. But the nationalist people of this land have been a victim of dissension on account of caste, sect, language, etc. only because they lacked a sense of nationhood. For the same reason they failed to be fully conscious of their right to vote in a democracy. As a result they had to bear the cross of an anti-Hindutva political leadership. This same leadership has perpetuated in all spheres of national life the western philosophy and lifestyle which is fast decaying in the land of its origin. . . .
>
> The coming election is going to be a test of to what extent our countrymen have grown vigilant and enlightened with the right appreciation of Hindutva. We therefore appeal to you with great feeling that you too should contribute your time and mite to the fullest in this popular awakening which actually is God's work, so that our politics eclipsed by anti-Hindutva thinking can come out and shine forth.

This was more than a plea for a 'Hindu votebank'. It was a cry for the exclusion of non-Hindus from national life.

After his resignation as prime minister, Vajpayee made a revealing remark on 3 June. 'We are willing to love the Muslims but the Muslims too should learn to love us' – with Hindutva and the rest.[78] The threat was palpable. The RSS spokesman M.G. Vaidya warned that the mosques at Mathura and Varanasi were 'symbols of national shame' and should be removed.[79] Rajendra Singh repeated this but said 'Ayodhya was our *first* battle'.[80] The crime of 9 December 1992 had not affected the vile ardour.

Sudarshan threw a challenge at the BJP leaders as the 1997 elections drew close. The senior leaders must step down in favour of a 'new generation'.[81]

They would, of course, be more responsible to the RSS's wishes. Kushabhau Thakre took over as BJP president from Advani on 2 May 1998. The RSS threw its full force in the election campaign. Its chief Rajendra Singh hoped that the BJP government

[78] *The Times of India*, 4 June 1976.

[79] *The Telegraph*, 7 July 1996.

[80] *The Telegraph*, 9 July 1996.

[81] *The Asian Age*, 13 December 1996.

would change the face of the country. Though the country had completed 50 years of Independence, the mental slavery was continuing. The country has not yet thrown out the colonial system of education and English continues to dominate the national languages. There was no change either in the police or in judiciary. The only change is that the whole machinery has slowed down. The Sarsanghchalak called upon Muslims to change their mindset and to learn to live with Hindus.[82]

At this juncture, Subramanian Swamy fiercely attacked Vajpayee.

If the PM praises the RSS, then others in the Front have the right to criticise it for its negative role in the 1942 Quit India Movement, in the Mahatma Gandhi assassination, in the subversion of the anti-Emergency struggle, and of course in the national shame of the Babri Masjid demolition.

Besides, said Dr. Swamy, in a recent interview of the RSS general secretary H.V. Seshadri to a private TV channel, he had openly admitted that the Union ministers with roots in the RSS continued to take guidance from the organisation in their ministerial work as well. This only proves that the RSS will do backseat driving and seek to remote control the government. RSS cannot run a parallel government, this is not acceptable.[83]

To be sure Swamy knew what had been happening. As Yubaraj Ghimire reported, the RSS 'admitted that it had been consulted in the process of the formulation of the Vajpayee ministry'. Rajendra Singh's message to the RSS's Akhil Bharatiya Pratinidhi Sabha (General Council) was 'Sangh volunteers are expected to exploit such a pro-Hindutva atmosphere towards a durable and permanent growth'.[84] Make the gains permanent.

Between the general elections of 1996 and 1998 the BJP amended its constitution in June 1997. The effect was summed up in the *Hindustan Times* headline 'BJP gives RSS key role in organisation' (29 June 1997). 'The General Secretary would be a full time member who would be debarred from contesting any election.' A full-time worker is a euphemism for an RSS pracharak. The BJP's general secretary Kushabhau Thakre was a former pracharak. The RSS's man thus controls the BJP. After all Stalin was a mere general secretary of the CPSU. In time the RSS's general secretary becomes its supremo – to wield greater clout over the BJP. Madhok's complaint of the powers of the Jana Sangh's organising secretary was justified.

Sudarshan's election as RSS supremo fell in this scheme. Even before his election

[82] *Organiser*, 12 April 1998.

[83] R. Bhagwan Singh, *The Asian Age*, 6 April 1998.

[84] *The Indian Express*, 27 March 1998.

to the post on 28 March 2000, he delivered a fusillade of attacks on Muslims and Christians while courting the Sikhs. To get a flavour of his enterprise, it is best to read his remarks *in seriatim*.

15 October 1999:

> The Muslims had the 'blood of Rama and Krishna in their veins'. He told them, 'Why you are linking yourselves with the invader Babur whose mausoleum stands neglected even in Islamic Afghanistan? The ancestors of Muslims did not come from abroad except a handful. Their roots are Indian. Like the Iranian Muslims, who evolved Sufism, why don't they give a new form to Islam which can take everyone along?'[85]

His ignorance of the roots of Sufism apart, it is his aversion to his countrymen which stands out.

20 February 2000:

> The present Constitution is but an extension of the Government of India Act, 1935, enacted by the British to serve their imperialistic objectives. Some chapters, drawing from other Constitutions, have been added, making it the biggest written Constitution. But it has still needed nearly 80 amendments in 50 years. . . . The review commission will examine how far the Westminster type of parliamentary democracy has been beneficial to us, and whether it needs changes.[86]

11 March 2000: The RSS wanted a totally new Constitution.[87]

12 March 2000: 'These non-Hindus are not foreigners but ex-Hindus. They are Indians but their faiths will have to be Indianism.'[88]

12 March 2000: The constitution should be 'scrapped'.[89]

16 March 2000: 'Intellectual is that class of bastards which tries to implant an alien culture in their land.'[90]

15 March 2000:

> 'This is yet another epic war – between Hindus and anti-Hindus, a veritable Mahabharat in which sometime *Abhimanyu* will fall, sometime *Ghatotkacha* or it may be *Jayadratha's* turn yet another day. As prophesied by Vivekananda

[85] *The Indian Express*, 16 October 1999.

[86] *Hindustan Times*, 20 February 2000.

[87] *The Asian Age*, 12 March 2000.

[88] *The Hindu*, 13 March 2000.

[89] *The Statesman*, 13 March 2000.

[90] Quoting from RSS organ *Panchajanya*; *The Asian Age*, 17 March 2000.

and Mahatma Gandhi, this country's honour is surely going to shine forth one day,' he said.

He favoured a new code of conduct (dharma) based on the Hindu philosophy and a 'Hindu way of development' in India, which is passing through a 'transitional' period. Sudarshan also said India is a Hindu rashtra, which is based on dharma. 'Its identity lies in one motherland, one sanskriti (culture), common ancestry and heritage, and unity in diversity. It is these three that constitute the national culture. The mode of worship can differ from person to person.'

Holding that not only India but the whole world was undergoing a radical change, Sudarshan said India is passing through a transitional period. 'The Sangh grew on the basis of Hindu philosophy (chintan). It is now necessary to frame a new code of conduct again based on the same philosophy.'[91]

23 March 2000: 'Muslims in India should Indianise.'[92]

25 March 2000: 'We believe that without shasti (arms) shastra (ideology) has no meaning.'[93]

10 April 2000: The RSS 'agenda' of propagating the ideals of Guru Gobind Singh through their shakhas in the Punjab countryside is being viewed with suspicion by Sikh religious bodies and scholars.

'It is an attempt to subvert Sikh culture and identity. The RSS has reactivated institutions like mutts and ashrams which had become defunct. The sadhus and sants of these institutions have been mobilised and sent to rural areas by the RSS to impose its hegemonistic agenda on the Sikh community. Since April 1999, the RSS has been actively engaged in the Khalsa tercentenary celebrations to propagate the mission of Guru Gobind Singh as per its interpretation,' said Gurdarshan Singh Dhillon, President of the Institute of Sikh Studies.

Baba Hari Singh of Dera Baba Harnam Singh in Sira, Ferozepur, has warned the RSS not to distort Guru Gobind Singh's verses to suit their interests in shakhas and to lure Sikh youth into their fold.[94]

29 April 2000: To mix metaphors consciously, the Swadeshi Don Quixote of Nagpur met his Waterloo in Chandigarh. These reports tell the whole story.

Sikh women and men belonging to some 20 different religious, social and political organisations, brandished kirpans (swords) and chanted angry 'ban

[91] Interview to *Organiser* quoted in *The Times of India*, 16 March 2000.

[92] *The Asian Age*, 24 March 2000.

[93] To Harish Gupta, *The Indian Express*, 26 March 2000.

[94] *The Asian Age*, 11 April 2000.

RSS' slogans outside the Chandigarh venue where Rashtriya Swayamsewak Sangh chief K.S. Sudarshan arrived to address a conclave of the RSS sister organisations, Rashtriya Sikh Sangat, on Saturday.

Referring to the Rashtriya Sikh Sangat as 'a bastard child of the RSS', Kanwarpal Singh of the Dal Khalsa and Jagmohan Singh of the Shiromani Akali Dal (Amritsar) said that 'for the past one year RSS activists have embarked upon a dangerous design to subsume Sikh religion into Hinduism. Towards this objective, they have been publishing and distributing highly communal propaganda material of the kind that the Nirankaris did during the late 1970s. The setting up of the Rashtriya Sikh Sangat and by organising conclaves, they are now attempting to infiltrate into Sikh religion.'

Insisting that 'Sikhs are a separate nation, and any attempt to change this status in word or in deed will be contested and resisted', the leaders of the protesting Sikhs warned that 'though Sikhs are a peace-loving and god-fearing people, when all peaceful methods fail, then, as ordained by Guru Gobind Singh, it is righteous to take to the sword'. They said that 'if the RSS is permitted to continue with its nefarious activities in Punjab, this will inevitably sooner or later lead to violent communal clashes in the state'. The protesters sought 'a complete and immediate ban on the RSS in Punjab'.[95]

Over a dozen Sikh organisations held a protest march against Rashtriya Swayamsewak Sangh and its chief K.S. Sudarshan during his visit here today. Raising slogans against alleged RSS agenda of assimilation of Sikhs into Hinduism and demanding a ban on RSS, five leaders of these bodies also courted arrest.

Wearing badges proclaiming 'Hum Hindu Nahin (we are not Hindus)', the protestors raised slogans like 'KS Sudarshan Vapis Jao, RSS Hosh Mein Aao (K.S. Sudarshan go back, RSS wake up)'.

Protesters including representatives of radical Sikh organisations like Simranjit Singh Mann of Shiromani Akali Dal (Amritsar), Dal Khalsa, Human Rights and Democracy Forum, Sikh Missionary College, management committees of various gurudwaras of Chandigarh and Mohali marched about 7 km from the local Gurudwara in Sector 34 to venue site.

Prof. Jagmohan Singh of Mr. Mann's party stated that this was a tussle between a centric monolithic society propagated by RSS and plural multi-cultural society traceable to the revolt against the hegemonistic policies of the then Brahmanical order by Guru Nanak.

'The Sikh Nation will follow in their footsteps as it has not forgotten the role of RSS in early '80s and training given to lumpen elements who burnt Sikhs on the streets of Delhi in 1984.'[96]

[95] *The Asian Age*, 30 April 2000.

[96] *The Statesman*, 30 April 2000.

> 'At the appropriate time, we will form akhand (composite) Bharat. We have to regain the area which we lost in 1947. We have to regain Lahore – the capital of Maharaja Ranjit Singh's Khalsa Raj. We have to reclaim Nankana Sahib and several other religious places, as also Sindhu (Indus) and Kasoor. The feeling for "Akhand Bharat" has to survive because it is akin to the feeling that led to the unification of Germany, Vietnam and Poland. Partition of India was wrong.'[97]

> 7 October 2000:

> 'What the Indian Christians must do is set up a swadeshi Church, on the lines of the Orthodox Syrian Church and the Marthoma Church of Kerala. Wasn't a move started in 1962 towards that by Rev Fathers William, Rodrigues and Das?' Sudershan, speaking at a Vijaya Dashmi gathering here, also called for complete 'Indianisation of Islam' in the country, and urged Muslims to join the cultural mainstream.[98]

15 October 2000: 'Muslims had the blood of Rama and Krishna in their veins' and 'Indian Muslims should realise that their ancestors did not come from a foreign land. So, why don't they work for the Indianisation of Islam and give a new shape to their religion?'[99]

30 October 2000: Sudarshan asked the Central government to throw out all foreign Christian missionaries from India. He said the government should establish an indigenous church on the lines of the church in China.

> According to a senior RSS leader who was present at the occasion, the RSS chief said, 'It is advisable to have a totally Indian church like the one in China and all foreign churches and missionaries should be asked by the government to pack up and go.' . . .
>
> The RSS wants India to emulate the post-revolution Chinese government which, according to RSS leaders, threw out all foreign missionaries and established its own version of a Christian church.
>
> The idea of a 'government-sponsored church' that is being floated by the RSS implies that Indian churches will have to cut off their links with foreign churches and missionaries. For instance, if the plan is implemented, the Catholics will have to sever links with the Vatican.[100]

The list is long. To jump ahead, this bit on 12 February 2006 takes the cake:

[97] *The Statesman*, 30 April 2000.

[98] *The Statesman*, 8 October 2000.

[99] *The Telegraph*, 16 October 2000.

[100] *The Times of India*, 3 November 2000.

'Because we cannot throw out Muslims and Christians into the sea, we have to Indianise them.' The Jana Sangh's plank of Indianisation in 1969 remained relevant 37 years later in 2006; it was a euphemism for Hindutva.

Sudarshan faithfully adhered to the party line. The most faithful of the faithful in the BJP was Advani. His remarks on the Muslims reeked of communal poison. On the 50th anniversary of the country's independence he contributed a long article to the party organ *BJP Today* not on India but on his pet obsession, the Muslims of India.

It was left to Kalyan Singh, former chief minister of Uttar Pradesh to rip apart the RSS's pretexts after he was expelled from the BJP. On 8 February 2000, the PTI reported, he

> accused Prime Minister Atal Behari Vajpayee of trying to mislead the nation by saying RSS was not a political organisation and expressed surprise over BJP's secular allies maintaining a silence over 'contentions' issues.
>
> 'I have spent a greater part of my life in this organisation (RSS) and I can say that right from the distribution of election tickets, in the BJP, to selecting Cabinet Ministers, it is only the RSS which calls the shot. What else is political activity?'[101]

The former editor Bharat Bhushan deserves high praise for his meticulous tabulation of the members of the RSS's family, the Sangh Parivar.

> The only organisation which has consistently geared itself to micro-level politics, getting into almost every sphere of activity which influences social and political life is the RSS. In the field of education Vidya Bharati today is the largest educational organisation in the non-governmental sector with 13,000 educational institutes including Saraswati Vidya Mandirs, 75,000 teachers and over 17 lakh students. It has organisations, headed by RSS volunteers, addressing tribals (Vanvasi Kalyan Ashram), literature (Akhil Bharatiya Sahitya Parishad), intellectuals (Pragya Bharati, Deendayal Research Institute), historians (Bharatiya Itihas Sankalan Yojana), teachers (Bharatiya Shikshan Mandal and Akhil Bharatiya Rashtriya Shaikshik Mahasangh), language (Sanskrit Bharati), culture (Sanskar Bharati), slum-dwellers (Seva Bharati, Hindu Seva Pratishthan, Swami Vivekanand Medical Mission, National Medicos Organisation), leprosy patients (Bharatiya Kushta Nivarak Sangh), consumers (Akhil Bharatiya Grahak Panchayat), publication of newspapers and other propaganda material (Bharat Prakashan, Suruchi Prakashan, Lokhit Prakashan, Gyanganga Prakashan, Archana Prakashan, Bharatiya Vichar Sadhana, Madhav Prakashan, Rashtrotthan Sahitya, Sadhana

[101] *The Asian Age*, 9 February 2000.

> Pustak Prakashan and Akashvani Prakashan), scientists (Vigyan Bharati), caste integration (Samajik Samrasta Manch), religion and proselytisation (Vivekananda Kendra, Vishwa Hindu Parishad, Hindu Jagaran Manch, Bajrang Dal), industrialists (Bharat Vikas Parishad), lawyers (Akhil Bharatiya Adhivakta Parishad), Sikhs (Rashtriya Sikh Sangat), ex-servicemen (Poorva-Sainik Seva Parishad), small scale industrialists (Laghu Udyog Bharati), NRIs (Bharatiya Swayamsevak Sangh, Hindu Swayamsevak Sangh, Hindu Seva Sangh, Sanatana Dharma Swayamsevak Sangh, Friends of India Society International) – the list is virtually endless.
>
> These organisations are in addition to its political front (BJP), trade union wing (Bharatiya Majdoor Sangh), women's wing (Rashtriya Sevika Samiti), students wing (Akhil Bharatiya Vidyarthi Parishad), and its economic wing (Swadeshi Jagaran Manch). For the RSS, politics is not only about who can come into power and the quantum of patronage disbursed. That is why it does not see the battle for the hearts and minds of the people being fought only at the hustings but in almost all spheres of social activity.
>
> The Congress and Left parties do not have the vast variety of front organisations that the RSS has. At the same time, because of their centralised structures, they lack the ability to work with those organisations which occupy the new sites of politics in society – the autonomous NGOs (non-governmental organisations).
>
> However, if these parties are to survive and fight the retrograde and communal worldview of the Hindutva forces, then they have no alternative but to take up the challenge at all the social spaces which these forces are trying to occupy.[102]

Around the time he wrote of the situation, the RSS was occupied with an internal shake up. On 12 March Mohan Bhagwat was made the Rashtriya Swayamsevak Sangh general secretary in place of H.V. Seshadri. The new committee was to function for the next three years.

The other executive committee members of the organisation were as follows: Ranga Hari (chief of intellectual training cell), Dr. Sripati Shastri (joint-chief of intellectual training cell), Sakhal Chand (chief of physical training cell), Ramchandra Sahasrabhojne (joint-chief of physical training cell), Suresh Joshi (Seva Pramukh), Surendra Singh Chouhan (Sah-Seva Pramukh), Suresh Ketkar (Pracharak Pramukh), Jagmohan Garg (contact chief), Srikant Joshi (publicity chief), Suresh Soni (deputy chief of publicity cell), Kalidas Basu and Raghavendra Vir (members).

The Akhil Bharatiya Pratinidhi Sabha nominated outgoing RSS chief Rajendra Singh, Moropant Pingle, Suryanarayan Rao, Baburao Vaidya and Vishwanath as

[102] *Hindustan Times*, 3 March 2000.

special invitees. Mohan Bhagwat said the RSS would open its doors to people of all religions. 'RSS will bring together people from different faiths under the umbrella of Hindutva to sow the seeds of nationalism and patriotism.' Even Muslims and Christians were originally Hindus, he claimed. The RSS would first mobilise Hindus to come together for projecting the real image of the community which had 'eclipsed' due to unforeseen circumstances, Mr. Bhagwat said.

The next step, he said, would be to rope in people from other religions as well. In a resolution, the RSS condemned cinema and satellite TV channels for 'striking at the roots of Indian culture' and assailed forces which, it alleged, portrayed Indian goddesses in 'bad light in the name of freedom of speech and expression'.[103] It was a step towards Bhagwat's elevation as the chief. A man with a will to power and a hardliner with an outlook which Golwalkar would have endorsed, he aspires to make the RSS 'modern' without embracing modernity.

Soon after his election he gave an interview to *Organiser* of 19 March. Venkatesh Kesari of *The Asian Age* carefully reported his remarks.

> Although the RSS projects itself as a cultural organisation dedicated to the cause of nation building, its strategists differentiate the Sangh from Arya Samaj, Brahmo Samaj and other such organisations saying that the RSS's role is like that of Lord Krishna in Mahabharata who did not fight the epic war but played an important role and stood for dharma (justice).
>
> 'RSS considers politics as one of the aspects of life. Sangh is not concerned with day-to-day politics or what is generally known as election-oriented politics. But one thing is certain; the RSS cannot remain unconcerned about something that affects the nation or society even if it relates to politics. The Sangh engages itself in *rashtraniti* and not *rajniti*,' he said, adding he is concerned over growing politicisation of society and the increase in consumerism. Bhagwat's views on the role of the RSS in the changing situation have been published by *Organiser*, in its 19 March issue.
>
> The RSS network is expanding across the country with the number of its shakhas nearing 45,000 while the strength of full-timers has gone up to 5,000.[104]

A later interview to *Organiser* (22 October 2000) suggests that he chafes at the restraints on the RSS's political activity:

> When the late Mauli Chandra Sharma left Jana Sangh alleging that the RSS has started dominating the party, former chief minister of Madhya Pradesh Ravi Shankar Shukla asked Shri Guruji (Golwalkar) about it. Guruji said,

103 *Hindustan Times*, 13 March 2000.

104 *The Asian Age*, 18 March 2000.

Why only Jana Sangh, we would like to prevail over every political party. The whole society is ours. If you want to unite the whole society you should not let the ideological gap widen to the extent that it becomes difficult to bridge. We have to go to all people of all ideologies to develop a national perspective.

Q. It is alleged that the RSS is meddling in politics too much?

A. Politics has never been considered untouchable by the Sangh swayamsevaks. Our swayamsevaks have faith in the Sangh *adhikaris*. Earlier, the number of Sangh swayamsevaks in politics was very less so their presence was not felt. But, today several Sangh swayamsevaks have made their mark in the political sphere. Since swayamsevaks work in various fields, they normally come to the Sangh *adhikaris* to discuss their problems. Similarly, swayamsevaks who are in politics also come to the *adhikaris* to discuss their problems.

The BJP government in Gujarat tested the waters by amending the Civil Services Conduct Rules to remove the ban on its officials participating in the activities of the RSS with full support from Union Home Minister L.K. Advani.[105] Vajpayee supported the move on 5 February. However, President K.R. Narayanan strongly objected. On 8 March the government of Gujarat lifted the ban.

[105] *The Hindu*, 5 January 2000.

17. How Modi Profited by a Pogrom

Anyone who thought that the Chief Minister of Gujarat, Narendra Modi, on whose watch a pogrom of grave magnitude was staged in Gujarat would suffer in prestige did not understand the RSS's psyche and that of its faithful in the BJP. His culpable conduct received the Supreme Court's censure in the Best Bakery Case.

> Those who are responsible for protecting life and properties and ensuring that investigation is fair and proper seem to have shown no real anxiety. Large number of people had lost their lives. Whether the accused persons were really assailants or not could have been established by a fair and impartial investigation. The *modern-day 'Neros'* were looking elsewhere when Best Bakery and innocent children and helpless women were burning, and were probably deliberating how the perpetrators of the crime can be saved or protected. Law and justice become flies in the hands of these 'wanton boys'. When fences start to swallow the crops, no scope will be left for survival of law and order or truth and justice.[1]

Far from repenting, the RSS and its front the VHP became aggressive in Modi's defence. There were at least formal regrets after the demolition of the Babri Masjid in 1992. The pogrom of 2002, a decade later encouraged the Nero to shower insults at Muslims, L.K. Advani to defend him ardently, Vajpayee to denounce Muslims, and the RSS and the VHP to hurl warnings at Muslims.

Far from suffering politically, Modi emerged as a potential candidate for the prime minister's office sidelining Advani. To his consternation Modi repaid his help in the hour of need by putting him on the shelf with due ceremonies.

The questions which all Indians who believe in the secular values of the freedom movement must ask are whether such conduct represents truly the national mood; whether the ethos of old can be revived; and, if so, how. In a real sense the moral and political crises of 2002 are still upon us.

Nothing was left unsaid or undone. It was a repeat of the carnage and dance of hate half a century earlier during the Partition. We thought they would not occur again. They did.

The VHP's vice-president Giriraj Kishore called the carnage an 'awakening of Hindu Society'.[2] Its working president Ashok Singhal warned in New Delhi on

[1] *Zahira Habibullah H. Sheikh vs. State of Gujarat & Ors.*, (2004) 4 SCC 158.

[2] *The Asian Age*, 14 May 2002.

11 October 2002 that 'what happened in Gujarat will happen in the whole of the country. Hindus were not born to be cut like carrots and radishes ("*gajar mooli ki tarah katne ke liye nahin paida huye hain Hindu*")', and that 'the Hindukaran of the people of Gujarat was the direct result of the "jehadi" mentality of Muslims'. Neena Vyas noted, 'This is the second time that he has talked of the Gujarat massacres being replicated. Earlier, he had said that the "Gujarat experiment" would be repeated elsewhere.'[3]

The VHP's parent the RSS had delivered a similar warning on 17 March in a resolution on Gujarat adopted by its Akhil Bharatiya Pratinidhi Sabha. 'Let the Muslims understand that their real safety lies in the goodwill of the majority. . . . Winning goodwill means respecting, tolerating and cooperation with the majority community.'[4] The RSS was set on making political capital out of the bloodshed.

Modi had every reason to feel encouraged. As prime minister, Vajpayee went to Gujarat only as late as on 4 April, with a trip to Godhra first, calling the killings at the train 'a pre-planned conspiracy'. His famous and cryptic words to Modi were '*Rajdharma ka palan karein*' ('uphold the dignity of high office'). Modi's retort was curt, 'I am doing that.'[5]

In Goa, on 12 April, the BJP National Executive overruled Vajpayee by rejecting Modi's offer to resign. As ever Vajpayee attacked Muslims whenever he felt cornered by the RSS. Speaking at a huge public rally at Campal Maidan, organised as an election campaign kick-off by the Goa unit, Vajpayee said that wherever there are Muslims in the world, there is strife. 'Once Islam meant toleration, truth and compassion – from what I see now, it has come to mean forcing their opinion through terror and fear. Islam is run on jehad.'

Then to loud applause, he said, 'No one should challenge us about India's secularism and no one should teach us about tolerance. . . . We were secular even in the early days when Muslims and Christians were not here. We have *allowed* [sic] them to do their prayers and follow their religion. No one should teach us about secularism.'[6] This at a time when the world censured Modi and the Muslims of Gujarat had suffered grievously. Vajpayee did not suffer in popularity.

Two of the country's top police officials testified to the gravity of the carnage after visits to the sites, belying the apologias by the BJP. Julio Ribeiro wrote:

> I was in Ahmedabad earlier this month. I visited the Shah Alam camp where nearly 10,000 Muslims had been accommodated after their homes were burnt and looted and their relatives raped and killed. I had expected histrionics and wailing but I was astounded at the matter of fact manner in which young boys

[3] Neena Vyas, *The Hindu*, 12 October 2002.

[4] *The Indian Express*, 18 March 2002.

[5] *The Statesman*, 28 March 2002.

[6] Smruti Koppikar, who was present there, *Hindustan Times*, 13 April 2002.

and girls recounted the sordid details of what they had seen and experienced. It gave me an uneasy feeling that these young people were not going to forget the injustices heaped on them. . . .

The first thing that I noticed while talking to the inmates of Shah Alam was that the victims had lost all hope of justice. In most riots, justice is routinely denied by crafty politicians and self-serving officers but hope still lingers. If hope is lost nothing more remains, only a resort to criminality or, worse still, terrorism. The victims of Ahmedabad did not know to whom they could complain as no empowered authority was willing to listen to them.

In Gujarat, the VHP has been systematically advocating the removal of Muslims from private employment. They have ensured that Muslim businesses, factories and other means of livelihood are destroyed. This is going to alienate the Muslim community from the mainstream of Indian society. The results are going to be exactly the opposite of what the Hindu zealots had intended. The Muslims are not going to run away because they have nowhere to go.

The second thing that struck me after my interaction with various people and groups of people in Ahmedabad was that the state had not merely sat back and allowed the massacre to happen as in Delhi in 1984, but had actively encouraged and participated in the mayhem. On the night of the barbaric killing of 59 kar sevaks in Godhra, instead of going after the culprits and taking precautions to prevent revenge killings of innocent Muslims, the government joined the call for the bandh. *The Chief Minister, I learnt, called a meeting of officials that night and told them that they need not be too enthusiastic about preventive measures* because he said that the bandh would pass off peacefully. Then, one of his ministers sat in the city police commissioner's control room and another minister in the DGP's state control room, each with a band of supporters, to put subtle pressure on the police. . . . My inquiries showed that the BJP government of Narendra Modi, with a VHP activist named Govardhanbhai Zadapiya as minister of state for home, had systematically emasculated the leadership by placing pliable officers and men of its choice in every possible position at the cutting edge.

Gujarat is easily the worst (or best) case study of a police force becoming politicised by the misuse of the power of appointments and transfers. The phenomenon has been commonly noticed in every state since the eighties. Unless corrective measures are quickly taken, people are going to experience a worse breakdown of the law and order machinery leading to a threat to the security of life and property.

An immediate solution is available. The National Police Commission had recommended the setting up of state security commissions which would be vested with powers of appointments of officers at the senior levels and then giving them fixed tenures so that they would not have to look over their shoulders for approval from their political masters whenever they acted according to the law.

Last, my most important finding. There was a widely prevalent perception in the minds of the Hindu upper and middle classes that the revenge that was taken in Ahmedabad was for the good of the city, the state and the country as it would serve as a good lesson to recalcitrant Muslims. They harboured deep misgivings about the Muslim minority, its ethos, its absolutist religious dogma, its perceived penchant for violence and its belief in a brotherhood that extended beyond the borders of the country and [which] was possibly loyal more to this brotherhood than to the land of their birth. They had succumbed to the propaganda that Muslims were a pampered lot, that it was the Congress which had pampered them because of vote bank politics. . . . What I worry about most is that the communal poison has spread so deep in the hearts and minds of the Hindu middle class that it will have to be extracted by super-human efforts before we can hope to re-establish any semblance of communal unity.[7]

Hate speech leads to hate violence.

K.P.S. Gill told the press at Gandhinagar on 15 July 2002, as he packed his bags to return to Delhi, that 'it is the political leadership that needs to be re-educated'. There was no doubt as to who he had in mind as he ended his term as Modi's security adviser with a brief to modernise the state police force.[8]

Amidst all this the RSS family was plunged in fire fighting. Differences had cropped up within the BJP, especially with Vajpayee and between the BJP and the VHP, which took orders only from the RSS. The RSS's top brass met Vajpayee and other leaders for two days on 26-27 April. The BJP president K. Jana Krishnamurthi reshuffled the party to induct more RSS men. The BJP was split into five zones, each under an RSS pracharak.[9]

Vajpayee and Advani promised to 'try and formulate policy according to what the Sangh suggests'. Advani who was made deputy prime minister on 5 February went to the RSS HQs in Jhandewalan on 3 July to meet the RSS leaders including Sudarshan who were pleased at his elevation.

Backed by the RSS, Modi began wooing his constituency with rabidly communal propaganda and appeal to Gujarat's pride. He went on a 'Gaurav Yatra' on 8 September while attacking the Congress President in racist and religious idiom. He said on 8 September: 'Mahatma Gandhi, the most famous son of Gujarat, had fought against the domination of white-skinned people in our country. The Congress's ploy to bring Sonia Gandhi . . . a daughter of Italy . . . is an insult to the

[7] *The Times of India*, 24 April 2002.

[8] *The Times of India*, 16 July 2002.

[9] *The Asian Age*, 2 May 2002.

Mahatma.' Modi said Sonia Gandhi was abusing the Mahatma when she went to his birthplace at Porbandar and made references to Godse.

Defending the use of the word 'Gaurav' for his yatra, Modi played his pet political card – invoking the *asmita* (pride) of five crore Gujaratis, whose self respect, he claimed, has been insulted by the Congress. 'The history of the Congress began at Godhra.'

Dismissing Sonia Gandhi's political victory in getting the gaurav yatra deferred from July to September by writing to Prime Minister A.B. Vajpayee, Modi said: 'The Pope in Rome must have advised her to get our Gaurav Yatra postponed. But the delay turned out to be a boon for us since it rained in Gujarat thereafter, due to which the drought – which could have hampered the success of the Gaurav rath – was over.'[10]

Muslims were told: 'You have missed the bus again and again to improve your relations with Hindus and establish your secular credentials.' He added: 'Good and brotherly relations cannot be a one-sided affair, you cannot expect one side to always condone *your crimes* and still maintain good relations between the two communities . . . it must be a two-way traffic and one community alone cannot ensure peace and communal harmony.'

Claiming that the perpetrators of the train carnage were once felicitated by the Congress for upsetting the BJP control on the Godhra municipality, he said the Congress was still making efforts to get all the criminals arrested in connection with the train carnage released. 'Why is the Congress sending the criminals tiffins in jails?' he asked amid thunderous cheers from the crowd.

The Congress was playing 'negative politics', and it could not 'buy' the self-respect of the five crore people of Gujarat with 'US dollars' which its state leaders had gone to collect during their recent visit to the United States.

He alleged that the organisers of the Congress leaders' meetings in the US were the same people who had been felicitating the Pakistan President, Pervez Musharraf, during his trip to the US. 'The people of Gujarat must be careful during the December 12 elections, something sinister seems to be cooking between the Congress and Pakistan.'[11]

There were no depths to which the man would not stoop in his mudslingings, laced with malice and brazen lies. McCarthy would have been put to shame by Modi.

It was at Becharaji on 9 September that he delivered this tirade: '[S]hould we run relief camps? Open child producing centres?'[12] Correspondents nailed Modi's falsehoods to the counter. To quote a particularly detailed and contemporary one by Sujan Dutta:

[10] *The Statesman*, 9 September 2002.

[11] *The Hindu*, 12 November 2002.

[12] *The Indian Express*, 19 September 2002.

> The riots in Gujarat in the wake of the Godhra train carnage on 27 February were not only tacitly backed by the state administration, but chief minister Narendra Modi's government also gave the VHP/Bajrang Dal storm-troopers 24 hours to do the job.
>
> While it cannot be reported that the government set a deadline, investigations by *The Telegraph* over the past week reveal that the top men in the government moved in a fashion that made it clear to the VHP/Bajrang Dal that 'turant jawabi karvai' (quick punitive action in the words of the Bajrang Dal) must be taken by the evening of 28 February.
>
> In the event, much of the vengeance – if that is what the systematic pillage, looting and killing can be called – spent itself out within that time, but the violence spilled over to the districts, villages and smaller towns. It continues in small pockets more than a week after the Godhra burnings.
>
> That the VHP and the Bajrang Dal have organic linkages with the current rulers of Gujarat is public knowledge. Even so, the point man between the administration and the VHP leadership was the person entrusted with the peaceful running of the state: state home minister Govardhanbhai Zhadapia, himself a secretary of the VHP for six years before moving on to electoral politics and the BJP.
>
> The Modi government's decision to support the '*jawabi karvai*' was conveyed to the VHP/Bajrang Dal on the evening of 27 February in Godhra itself. That day, chief minister Modi, home minister Zhadapia, health minister Ashok Bhatt, VHP state joint general secretary Jaidipbhai Patel and VHP state organising secretary Arvindbhai Patel were in the town.
>
> They met and talked several times: in Signal Falia where the S-6 coach of the Sabarmati Express was torched, in the collectorate, in the hospital, in the run of things. It was not a formal, structured meeting in which the decision was made clear to the VHP. It was conveyed to them on-the-fly, as it were, but with the warning that a spiralling of violence could mean deployment of the army by midnight Thursday-Friday (28 February-1 March).
>
> Till late in the evening of 27 February, the VHP leadership was anxious to get support from the BJP for the state-wide bandh on 28 February, the day following the Godhra killings. The decision to call for a bandh was taken by the afternoon of 27 February, and across Gujarat, the VHP/Bajrang Dal cadre interpreted it as a call to action.[13]

On this, more later.

The aftermath distinguishes it from the pogrom in Delhi in 1984. In Gujarat the entire administration came under the grip of the RSS and the VHP.

[13] *The Telegraph*, 12 March 2002.

> The Public Prosecutor appointed to try the Sardarpura case in Mehsana district where about 33 persons were burnt alive, and the Dipda Darwaja case in Visnagar in the same district, where 11 persons were killed, was the VHP State general secretary, Dillip Trivedi. For the controversial Naroda-Patiya and Gulmarg Society cases in Ahmedabad, where over 140 persons were burnt alive, the Public Prosecutor appointed was Chetan Shah, who was in the VHP advocates' panel for over two decades. The Public Prosecutor for trying the 121 riot cases in the Panchamahals district was Piyush Gandhi, president of the district VHP. For the riot cases in Anand and Kaira districts, the Public Prosecutor was a known RSS and VHP sympathiser, P.S. Dhora. And the Public Prosecutor for the Best Bakery case was a close relative of the Vadodara city VHP president, Ajay Joshi.
>
> In almost all the riot-affected districts, the Public Prosecutors trying the cases in which VHP and other Sangh Parivar activists were the main accused happened to be VHP or Sangh Parivar supporters.[14]

While the VHP was busy making preparations for a Ram temple at Ayodhya, the RSS worked hard to bring the BJP to heel. Its strongest censures were made through the VHP. The RSS's organ *Panchajanya* declared war on the Vajpayee government on 8 October 2002, for its 'failure on all fronts'; adding, a 'government intolerant of criticism deserves a place in the dustbin of history' and sneered 'all our faults are heaped on Pakistan'. It reminded the leaders that the BJP came to power 'riding on the shoulders of the Parivar outfits'.

RSS-BJP meetings were held to 'remove misunderstandings'. The first in the series was on 15 October between Advani and the RSS's point man for talks with the BJP, Madan Das Devi. One of the issues was trifurcation of the state of Jammu & Kashmir, into the Valley, Jammu, and Ladakh, which the RSS-backed Jammu State Morcha demanded and the RSS itself did earlier.

The talks continued in the luxurious Centaur Hotel in Mumbai on 20 October. The RSS demanded that it and its outfits be 'taken into confidence'. The government agreed to consult the organisation on policy formation. The BJP leaders complained of the *Panchajanya* editorial and the VHP's attacks.[15] The government could no longer ignore the VHP, the Swadeshi Jagran Manch and the Bharatiya Mazdoor Sangh.

It was an uneasy time. Only a few days later Smita Gupta reported,

> The ongoing war of nerves between Prime Minister A.B. Vajpayee and the Sangh parivar is far from over. Speaking to this newspaper, a senior minister

[14] Manas Dasgupta, *The Hindu*, 21 September 2002.

[15] *The Asian Age*, *The Telegraph* and *The Hindu*, 25 October 2002.

> with strong RSS links said, 'I am ideologically close to the RSS. But it is becoming impossible to function at the governmental level and it's not just the ideological gaps with the NDA agenda. For instance, Sangh functionaries, from the lowest to the highest, are interfering in things as basic as postings and transfers of officials. You can't take a step without them.' The minister added that the electoral debacle in Jammu recently, where the BJP and a RSS-sponsored front effectively neutralised each other, summed up the state of the party and its sangh affiliates in the country. . . . What is clear is the RSS will no longer take the responsibility of restraining the VHP and the Swadeshi Jagran Manch hotheads. Mr. Advani and BJP president Venkaiah Naidu will have to do the job.[16]

2003 saw no improvement. The RSS was determined to keep Vajpayee and Advani unsettled. It began to see in Modi a possible replacement for both. On his part, Modi began quietly to endear himself to the RSS by advocating Hindutva more ardently than they.

Following an understanding between the BJP's president Venkaiah Naidu and Sanjay Joshi, the RSS general secretary, the terms needless to say, favoured the RSS.

> The BJP will soon start bringing in RSS cadres into its organisation. The inductions will be the first in about a decade. The RSS will reciprocate by dealing directly with the VHP to make it tone down its strident stand on the Ayodhya issue. . . .
>
> Under the new deal, the government and the BJP will have to stop distancing themselves from the VHP to appear modern or liberal. Neither side will publicly express divergent views on crucial issues. The RSS also got an assurance that the BJP will focus on the 'core issues' for which the sangh created the BJP. RSS pracharaks will move into BJP units in the districts after the two sides identify organisational gaps.
>
> The RSS wants the induction of its workers at the grass roots. They can then move up in the party organisation over a period of time. Senior RSS leaders rarely join the BJP. The RSS has had a long-standing grouse that its dedicated cadres have been ignored by the BJP, except for electoral mobilisation.
>
> Bhagwat, a hardliner, and Naidu did some plain speaking, sources said. Bhagwat said the RSS's commitment to a Ram temple in Ayodhya was no less than the VHP's and pointed out that the BJP had done nothing to help the parishad move forward on building it.[17]

[16] *The Times of India*, 29 October 2002.

[17] *Hindustan Times*, 14 February 2003.

The RSS's strategy had succeeded. It skilfully used the VHP to bark at the BJP which went running to their common master for relief. That was granted provided the BJP made peace with the VHP; but the rift remained for the RSS to squeeze the BJP whenever it so desired. At the 1,100-strong Pratinidhi Sabha, the supreme policy-making body, the RSS general secretary Mohan Bhagwat said 'normally the Ayodhya movement is spearheaded by the VHP and the RSS takes part in it whenever the need arises'. But 'the RSS is of the view that time has come for the swayamsevaks to join the movement once again', he said. Replying to a question about the performance of the BJP-led NDA government at the Centre, Bhagwat said 'the RSS is not willing to give full marks to it'. It is a '*kahin khushi kahin gam situation*', he said. 'The RSS view of the NDA government's performance does not vary much from popular opinion.'[18]

It is impossible to reason with people who prefer assertion to argument. The RSS denies the very existence of minorities in India and has its own concept of the term at sharp variance from the term which has been internationally recognised since the Polish Treaty after the First World War. But according to RSS General Secretary Mohan Bhagwat, Muslims and Christians cannot be termed minorities as they had not come from outside India but were Hindus before changing their religion.

Inaugurating a three-day national general council meeting in which over 1,200 delegates from all over India were participating, Bhagwat said by merely changing their way of worship, the Christians and Muslims could not acquire the tag of minorities. '99.9 per cent of Muslims and Christians were Hindus.'[19] Sudarshan repeated this on 16 March 2004.[20] Such a view admits of no compromise. It asks these minorities to shed their faiths and become Hindus. The coordination meet, or the Chintan Baithak, between the BJP and Sangh outfits received a minor jolt on the second day, with the VHP targeting Deputy Prime Minister L.K. Advani on the issue of 'trishul diksha'. The VHP at its media centre made it categorically clear that it would continue with trishul diksha, irrespective of likes and dislikes of the home ministry. The BJP explained to the VHP that legislation on the Ram Mandir issue was 'not possible without a majority in Parliament'.

However, when pointed out that the Deputy Prime Minister was not 'happy' with the VHP's trident distribution in various states, Surendra Jain a senior VHP leader, lashed out: 'We are not here to make anyone happy.' He added: 'Trishul diksha is not being carried out to please Advaniji or anybody else. We are not here to see whether the Centre is happy or unhappy. Society is happy, that is what matters. Trishul is gaining popularity.'

[18] *Asian Age*, 10 March 2003.

[19] *The Statesman*, 12 March 2003.

[20] *The Hindu*, 17 March 2004.

Jain quickly added that the outfit has taken permission from concerned authorities for 'trishul diksha' in Delhi, slated for 4 May. He refused to give details of the 'authorities concerned' from whom permission for the programme was taken by the outfit. For Jain, the trishul, which 'is less than six inches, does not come under purview of any Arms Act, is a symbol of Hindutva and is Lord Shiva's ornament'.[21] Quite a rise from the lathi to the trishul.

Vajpayee sought peace at the conclave by speaking from both sides of his mouth; a sport in which he excelled. He had not accepted Pakistan's offer of talks. The denial explains why he rejected the agreed Agra Declaration in July 2001. Ram Madhav claimed legislation on a Ram temple was promised, though it was a constitutional impossibility.[22] The RSS firmly snubbed Venkaiah Naidu when he pitted Vajpayee, as Vikaspurush, against Advani, the Lohpurush. Sudarshan phoned Naidu to advise him to focus more on 'ideology' and 'principles' and less on 'individuals'. Any kind of 'personality cult' should be avoided.[23]

Desperate, Advani brought Hindutva and the communal card in the election campaign. 'The BJP alone can find a solution to our problems with Pakistan because Hindus will never think that whatever we have done can be a sell-out. The Congress can never do this because Hindus will not trust it.'[24]

Modi injected his characteristically coarse language.

> The Chief Minister took his campaign to a new low on Wednesday, even as he shared the dais with DPM L.K. Advani who steered clear of any attacks on Congress leaders.
>
> 'The Congress symbol used to be gai and vaccharado (cow and calf) and people used to say gai (Indira Gandhi) and vacchharado (Sanjay Gandhi) are contesting. *Have to kheduto mane kahe chhe saheb have to jarsi vacchharado chuntani ladhva aavyo chhe* (Now farmers tell me a hybrid calf has come to contest the elections),' Modi told the gathering.

He said: 'A survey in Nadiad recently showed that none of the 20 shopkeepers replied in affirmative to a question whether they were ready to employ Sonia Gandhi as a clerk. They were also not ready to employ her son as a driver, and she wants him to become the Prime Minister.' The 'Congress in its 125-year history fought against the white-skinned people asking them to leave the country but now the party is out to welcome them'. The tirade continued as Advani looked on. As the yatra passed through Surendranagar and Patan, which elected Congress M.P.s

[21] *The Asian Age*, 3 May 2003.

[22] *The Hindu*, 4 July 2003.

[23] Harish Khare, *The Hindu*, 8 June 2003.

[24] *The Indian Express*, 14 March 2004.

in 1999, Modi asked the people to throw them away for 'they called us murderers, rapists and arsonists in Parliament. You settled scores in Assembly polls; an encore is needed in LS'.[25] The RSS shifted its point man Madan Das Devi from New Delhi to Mumbai. Joint General Secretary Suresh Soni was asked to liaise between the RSS and the BJP.

Sudarshan went public with the thought he had long nursed quietly. On 11 April 2004 he asked both Advani and Vajpayee to quit their posts. Shekhar Gupta, editor of *The Indian Express*, was told, 'Both of them should step aside. And after stepping aside, they should watch the new generation leadership come up. They should keep an eye on them and see if the new leadership is coming up properly.' Sudarshan renewed his attacks against the Prime Minister's confidante and principal secretary, Brajesh Mishra and his son-in-law Ranjan Bhattacharya. He had criticised them in March 2001 after the *Tehelka* exposés.[26] Hurt, Vajpayee ad Advani went into a huddle with colleagues on how to repair the damage of their prestige and that of the BJP. They did not dare publicly to criticise Sudarshan.

Advani did his bit to please the RSS by going to Ayodhya where he said: 'To Hindus, Lord Rama is more than an epic hero and a God. He epitomises the ideals of a perfect ruler. . . . I have often used *Ramarajya* to describe our goal of making India a developed economy and a world power by 2020.'[27] That he expected non-Hindus to accept Ram as 'a God' lies at the core of the RSS-BJP's policy on Ayodhya; a policy which no Hindu leader expressed before 1986. Ram Madhav evidently spoke for the RSS as its spokesman when, on 13 April, he officially endorsed Sudarshan's view of 'generational change in the BJP'.

Defeat at the elections to the Lok Sabha in 2004 shocked the BJP; particularly Advani who had long aspired to become prime minister. He invited little sympathy. In an editorial entitled 'Dirty Politics' the *Hindustan Times* noted on 27 July 2004, that 'the leader of the opposition in the Lok Sabha, L.K. Advani, reiterated his party's position that "religion is ingrained in politics as it is in Indian culture"'. If politics and religion 'are indeed so intertwined, is it too much for Advani and his colleagues to accept that the law too is – or should be – ingrained in our polity?'

Organisationally, the expected happened. The RSS used the BJP's electoral debacle further to tighten its own control. On 6 August the BJP

> announced the appointment of six kshetriya sanghatan mantris (zonal organising secretaries) belonging to the RSS. The RSS men will be the live link between the parent organisation and its political wing. They include Venugopal Reddy, V. Satish, Mukundan, Ram Pyare Pandey, Sudan Singh and

[25] *The Indian Express*, 2 April 2004.

[26] *The Indian Express*, 12 April 2004.

[27] *Organiser*, 12 April 2004.

> Prasanna Mishra. More appointments in the category are likely since all the zones were not covered today.[28]

The BJP President appointed full-time Rashtriya Swayamsevak Sangh 'pracharaks' as regional organisation secretaries, with each 'pracharak' to head a cluster of states to take care of all organisational issues in that region. Some of these 'pracharaks' have only recently been given to the party by the RSS, a senior party leader said. One of them was till recently more active in the Vishwa Hindu Parishad, the RSS spokesperson, Ram Madhav said.

'It seems that the decision to place the "pracharaks" in these newly-created "regional" positions is a signal of the new synergy between the RSS, the larger Sangh Parivar and the BJP.'[29]

In October 2004, Advani became BJP president and began touting the Hindutva line. 'I joined the RSS at the age of 14.' He went to its HQs in Nagpur on Vijaya Dashami Day. The VHP was not impressed by this 'change of label'. Advani and Vajpayee made the ritual journey to the RSS HQs at Jhandewalan in Delhi on 1 November; the second since the defeat in the election.

But, contrary to common impression, the RSS is not a monorail either. The challenge came from the VHP. Its leaders Ashok Singhal and Praveen Togadia boycotted the RSS National Executive at Haridwar on 5 November. The RSS claimed that the BJP gave it a solemn 'assurance that they will return to Hindutva. Let us see how they fulfil it'.[30] Months later this assurance spelt Advani's doom.

To Advani, the BJP was 'the chosen instrument of the Divine to take our country out of its present problems and to lofty heights of all-round achievements'. He pushed the Hindutva plank at the beginning of the party's national executive and tried to snatch away the Shankaracharya issue from VHP. He also raised the VHP demand of shifting all the cases on the Kanchi Shankaracharya from Tamil Nadu.[31]

By April 2005, it seemed that there was a grand reconciliation. 'The smiles are back', a correspondent noted. Vajpayee, Advani and Sudarshan were locked in mutual affection.[32] Apparently the RSS asked the VHP 'not to join issue with the BJP'. *The Indian Express* reported, on 15 April 2005,

> It's learnt that the Sangh has asked all its affiliates, VHP included, to remain silent and not to join issue with the BJP. VHP general secretary Pravin Togadia

[28] Manini Chatterjee, *The Indian Express*, 7 August 2004.

[29] Neena Vyas, *The Hindu*, 7 August 2004.

[30] *The Hindu*, 7 November 2004.

[31] *The Asian Age*, 27 November 2004.

[32] *The Asian Age*, 21 April 2005.

called up Sudarshan for 'instructions' immediately after the telecast of excerpts from his interview to Gupta.

But the RSS chief, sources said, advised him to maintain *maun* (silence). This was the reason why VHP working president Ashok Singhal and Togadia – they have been vocal in their criticism of the BJP – did not utter even a word when Sudarshan kicked up a controversy by saying both Vajpayee and Advani should step aside to let a younger leadership take charge of the BJP.

The RSS was not appeased. Sudarshan alleged, on 20 April 2005, that 'the attack on Hindutva forces has increased today'.[33] S. Gurumurthy alleged that the 'Hindus can never get justice in secular India'. He told a BJP think tank on 30 January that 'the secularists and English educated people have caused a great damage to the country. In fact, it is the English educated India that has become a problem for India itself'.[34]

Earlier, on 17 July, the RSS chief Sudarshan had said: 'The English culture connects our children to lesbianism and free sex which is not objectionable in West.' The RSS chief wants the medium of instruction in schools to be 'regional languages' and feels that people should 'demand that teaching of all subjects up to the research level should be only in Indian languages'. He wants English to be treated as a 'foreign language' in schools. Sudarshan's address in Delhi Prant Shiksha Varg has been published in the RSS mouthpiece *Organiser*.

The RSS chief also felt that by teaching children words like 'mummy and daddy', parents in the country are depriving them from learning about 'Indian bhavjagat' (forms of expression in Indian languages). Sudarshan pointed out the limitation of English language. 'There is no word for bua, nani, mami, kaki and tai in English. They have nothing beyond the words like father, mother, son, daughter, brother, sister, husband, wife, uncle, aunt, nephew and niece.'

The RSS chief wondered,

Will an Englishman understand the lotus-like hands, lotus-like face, lotus-like eyes, and lotus-like feet? We can understand the meaning of Giridhar Gopal in all Indian languages. But if you describe it in words of like mountain-bearer cow halter [sic] to an Englishman, what will he understand?[35]

This explains Modi's claim on plastic surgery in Vedic times. *Organiser* of 13 February 2005 had a whole page on how 'Ancient Hindus could navigate the

[33] *Organiser*, 1 May 2005.

[34] *Organiser*, 13 February 2005.

[35] *The Asian Age*, 18 July 2004.

air'. Revivalism is not confined to rewriting history to marginalise Muslims and Christians. It covers the entire span of modern thought.

Interestingly, attacks on Western educated persons did not include a distinguished and proud alumnus of St. Patricks at Karachi – Lal Krishna Advani. We need to face the question squarely – how do highly educated Hindus support an RSS or BJP which is led by such people? What is it that drives them to drown doubt and embrace such rubbish?

18. The Advani Episode

Woh baat saare fasane men jis ka zikr na thaa
woh baat unko bohat nagwar guzri hai

(The topic which never figured in the entire discourse
Was the one which offended her the most)
– Faiz

This immortal couplet by the legendary poet Faiz Ahmad Faiz, sums up the RSS's style of discourse with its political progeny, the BJP. It conveys hints; sends messages through liaison men, but speaks only when it wishes to do so. When all this fails, the RSS strikes hard and ruthlessly.

L.K. Advani was dear to the RSS because he was closer to it ideologically and otherwise. Atal Bihari Vajpayee was an asset. Advani was house trained. The greater the disappointment when he went about feathering his nest ignoring the RSS's quiet murmurings of disquiet in the last 25 years since the BJP was set up in 1980.

To begin with, as the cadre indicated, the RSS sought a clean, honest revival of the Jana Sangh. It thought poorly of clever ploys like acquiring bits from here and there. The name Bharatiya Janata Party was purloined from the Janata Party; Gandhian socialism, particularly. The RSS had no respect for Gandhi and no love for socialism. Its leaders did not understand what it meant anyway. Minor skirmishes took their toll on everyone's nerves. In power the BJP did not endear itself to the RSS.

Against this background, Advani took a fateful and risky course. The reason he gave was enough to annoy the RSS: it was to build up his own image. No leader can have a sharper or more appealing profile than the RSS. Narendra Modi has got away with his bid for self-promotion because he delivers; ideologically, administratively and, most of all, electorally. If he stumbles the RSS's surgery will be thorough.

Now, for the unspoken reason, the unmentioned lapse – his repeated, if insincere, expressions of regret at the demolition of the Babri Masjid. The RSS had rejoiced over it. More than anything else, this rankled in the minds of the RSS's boss and his senior colleagues.

To Advani, however, these expressions of regret were central to his new strategy to build himself up as a worthy successor to Vajpayee; a moderate, who appeals to all. The trip began on 30 May 2005 and ended on 6 June 2005. Explanations for the trip differed. It covered Islamabad, Lahore and Karachi, contemporaneous from the belated ones in his memoirs, *My Country, My Life* (2008).[1] *The Telegraph*'s

[1] *My Country, My Life*, p. 790.

correspondent Radhika Ramaseshan, who accompanied him, reported his remarks at a press conference in Islamabad.

> As he began his six-day tour of Pakistan, the former deputy Prime Minister was at pains to paint himself as a politician more sinned against than sinning.
>
> 'Every person who is in public life and politics has an image. I have been one of those whose image and real persona are not very identical.'

Three years later he asked in his memoir a revealing question. 'Had I done it for opportunistic reasons? Had I done it for reasons of an image makeover?'[2] No wonder he was disbelieved.

About the demolition of the Masjid, he said, 'It was the saddest day of my life.'[3] Advani had long been oppressed by his negative image which contrasted poorly to that of Vajpayee. What he left unsaid was that the image promotion was not targeted at Pakistanis. They did not vote for him. It was aimed at Indians. He overlooked the impact on Nagpur. It was, besides, a palpable lie. Correspondence of dailies of repute has seen and heard him directing the mob to seal the roads to prevent Central forces from arriving to prevent the demolition of the mosque.[4] Charge sheets in criminal cases he has yet to face. They record Advani's presence at conspirational meetings the day before the demolition.[5] On 27 August 1994 the Special Judicial Magistrate found that a prima facie case existed and committed the accused to trial in the Sessions Court. On 9 September 1997 the Sessions Court framed the charges.[6] Thus two courts have held that a prima facie case did exist. The trial never proceeded to conclusion.

Advani arrived in Karachi on 4 June. His first engagement was a visit to the monument in memory of the founder of Pakistan, Mohammed Ali Jinnah. He inscribed these words in the Visitors' Book:

> There are many people who leave an inerasable stamp on history. But there are very few who actually create history. Quaid-e-Azam Mohammed Ali Jinnah was one such rare individual. In his early years, Sarojini Naidu, a leading luminary of India's freedom struggle, described Jinnah as an 'Ambassador of Hindu-Muslim unity'. His address to the Constituent Assembly of Pakistan on 11 August 1947 is a classic, a forceful espousal of a secular state in which every citizen would be free to practise his own religion but the State shall make no distinction between one citizen and another on the grounds of faith. My respectful homage to this great man.[7]

[2] Ibid., p. 813.

[3] *The Telegraph*, 1 June 2005. Vide PTI report in *The Hindu*, 1 June.

[4] Vide Noorani, *The Babri Masjid Question*, vol. 2, pp. 5 and 7 for the reports by eye witnesses.

[5] Ibid., p. 99.

[6] Ibid., pp. 102 and 122.

[7] Advani, *My Country, My Life*, p. 813.

This was obviously written out earlier, after many drafts, calculatedly. It was slick as was the visit and its motive.

All hell broke loose as Indian TV channels telecast the event in 'Breaking News'. He denied it was for an 'image makeover'; contrary to his own admission at Islamabad on 31 May. Advani repeated the praise later in the day at a function organised by the Karachi Council on Foreign Relations, Economic Affairs and Law. He spoke in favour of a voice for civil society on foreign affairs, the composite dialogue between India and Pakistan, and for opening links between the two countries.[8]

By any test it was a highly successful visit. In India the reaction was mixed; utterly negative in the Sangh Parivar's circles. None defended him for his measured, calculated words. *The Times of India*'s instant report summed up the priorities in their ranks.

> Senior leaders of the Sangh Parivar have told the BJP that it will have to choose between Hindutva and Advani, who has been described by them as a 'grave liability who will have to be discarded soon'.
>
> The parivar is deeply upset with Advani's statement that the Babri masjid demolition was the 'saddest day' in his life. It's also sore with him for paying tribute to Mohammad Ali Jinnah at the latter's mausoleum in Karachi on Saturday. . . .
>
> The functionary said one of the items to be discussed at the camp would be Advani's visit to Pakistan and his various statements 'which have destroyed the Hindutva agenda'. A top RSS activist said on Saturday that *the VHP had been directed to lead the attack against Advani* for the various statements the BJP president has made in Pakistan. He said, 'The RSS never reacts to political developments directly. In this instance, the responsibility to mount the attack has been entrusted to the VHP.'
>
> The activist, a powerful leader who is regarded as a link between the BJP and the parivar, pointed out that VHP president Ashok Singhal was the first to target Advani. This was done on the direction of the RSS.[9]

As the English saying goes, why bark when you keep a dog. Not for nothing did the RSS set up VHP. On 5 June the VHP's president Ashok Singhal said: 'The era of Atal and Advani is over and the Sangh Parivar will now surely decide the new direction for the BJP. The question is about who will form national politics. Surely, it cannot be just Atal (Atal Bihari Vajpayee) and Advani.' He added that Advani, by making the remarks about Jinnah, was 'throwing dust in the eyes of the people of the country and distorting history. . . . If he (Advani) feels free to make such

[8] For the full text vide *The Indian Express*, 8 June 2005.

[9] *The Times of India*, 5 June 2005.

statements, that he is the lord of all I survey, then his survival in politics could also prove to be difficult'.

On Advani's statement that the demolition of Babri Masjid was the saddest day of his life: 'To make statements like these on Pakistani soil is a matter of concern for our nation, especially for Hindus. Such a statement is an insult to Hindus. Why did he take out the *rath yatra* if he now feels this way?' Singhal asked.[10] That was the more hurtful bit. The VHP leader spoke at the RSS's behest.

Advani resigned as BJP president on 7 June but retained the post of leader of the opposition. Narendra Modi's silence was deafening. Pankaj Vohra, an exceptionally well-informed reporter on the Sangh, explained Advani's calculations.

> Advani – who is trying for an image makeover to cast himself as a political clone of A.B. Vajpayee in order to succeed him as the NDA boss – has unfolded his Plan B, which is to appoint one of his acolytes as his successor so that he himself can continue to guide the party by remote control.
>
> The other ingredient of his Plan B is to make requests for the withdrawal of his resignation from his coterie appear as an expression of the support he was getting from the party even for his remarks on Jinnah – so that a perception is created that while the BJP was solidly behind him, it was only the RSS which was playing the villain. Advani's stand on his resignation – that it was irreversible – was taken after RSS chief K.S. Sudershan asked Sanjay Joshi, general secretary of the BJP who coordinates with the Sangh, to accept the resignation.[11]

Advani returned to New Delhi in the morning of 6 June. On 10 June the BJP's parliamentary board issued a statement which lauded Advani's efforts to improve relations with Pakistan. It praised him for his criticism of cross-border terrorism and the like. The last paragraph recorded its different views on Jinnah but without a word of criticism of Advani.[12]

Advani withdrew his resignation on 19 June realising that if he refused it was a matter of time before he lost the office of Leader of the Opposition. The RSS itself called it quits but its VHP continued to shout at Advani; to keep him in check. Sudarshan himself took a hand at it. In doing so he defined the RSS's role in India's public life. When he said that it keeps away from politics, he meant electoral politics since it was always neck-deep in politics through its front, the BJP. 'At its best, political power can protect the country from external and internal aggression. There was a need to mobilise and organise *society*, as distinct from the State. That alone, the State will comply with society organised by the RSS; especially if its men

[10] *The Asian Age*, 6 June 2005.

[11] *Hindustan Times*, 8 June 2005.

[12] For the text vide *Hindustan Times*, 11 June 2005.

were voted to power. The tasks of mobilisation and organisation would be done by the RSS and two front organisations whom he named specifically – the Vanvasi Kalyan Parishad and the Vishwa Hindu Parishad.' The BJP was not named.

It was a pursuit in piety. 'Our saints carried the message of Hindu culture to distant lands such as Mexico.' The RSS wanted 'saffronisation' of India. 'Saffron is a good colour. The country men should not have this feeling that we are a defeated race.'[13]

Sudarshan gave full vent to his suppressed feelings. 'We have kept ourselves away from politics as salvation cannot be attained through it. Politics keeps changing every minute. Like a prostitute who keeps changing her form, politics also keeps changing its appearance. There is no permanent element in politics,' he told RSS workers.

The RSS slammed Advani saying secular Jinnah was like saying Ravana was the symbol of goodness. In a lead article in the latest issue of *Organiser*, its editor said: 'It also shows how far the BJP has travelled, away from its moorings.'[14] The offending words added to the distrust which the entire 'opportunistic' venture had generated.

That the RSS was in a state of wrath became clear when, a day after Sudarshan's speech, its former spokesman M.G. Vaidya attacked Advani for *withdrawing* his resignation and his colleagues for rejecting his resignation. Ram Madhav was censured for his 'habit of speaking to the media daily'.[15] A habit, in which he still persists.

As if on cue, the VHP's Kendriya Margdarshak Mandal, the top decision-making body met at Haridwar on 13 June to demand that Advani 'take total sanyas from politics' and 'apologise' for his 'betrayal'.[16]

The Sangh Parivar was on the boil. The resignation drama had made the situation worse. Finally, on 15 July some BJP leaders – Sushma Swaraj, Jaswant Singh, and Pramod Mahajan – met the top RSS brass in New Delhi to plead for 'another opportunity' for Advani till the elections to the Bihar Assembly. They also assured the RSS leaders that the forthcoming meeting of the BJP's National Executive in Chennai would be a 'turning point' for the party. They were unnerved by the RSS leader Indresh Kumar's remark at a condolence meeting for Sundar Singh Bhandari, '*Sacrifice karoge to hero banoge* (If you sacrifice, you will become a hero).'[17]

Advani was not cut out for either; be it heroism or sacrifice. He thought he would ride out the storm. The grimness of a situation in which top leaders of a political party kowtowed before a bunch of arrogant, ignorant men who wielded

[13] *The Hindu*, 12 June 2005.

[14] *Hindustan Times*, 12 June 2018.

[15] *The Asian Age*, 13 June 2005.

[16] *The Hindu*, 15 June.

[17] *The Asian Age*, 16 July 2005.

authority like priests in medieval times was accurately described by Neena Vyas.

> The BJP has made it only too clear that it is accountable not to the people, not to Parliament, but to a bunch of people who set themselves up as super patriots, the super nationalists, who know what is best for the country. *Don't forget, that the RSS has never accepted the Indian Constitution.* If the BJP were to ever come to power on its own strength, it would mean rule by an unelected body, the RSS. Democratic India as we know it today may become a thing of the past.[18]

The RSS is a menace to India.

Advani persistently refused to read the writing on the wall which the RSS had engraved for him to read in bold letters. In the evening of 6 June, when Advani returned from Pakistan, Mohan Bhagwat made it plain to the BJP leaders who met him that Advani had to go. He responded on 7 June with his letter of resignation which he handed over significantly to an RSS man, Sanjay Joshi. On 8 June the BJP's parliamentary board's mealy-mouthed resolution paved the way for Advani to withdraw his resignation. But this was staged to help him save face. There was an 'unwritten understanding that Advani would soon quit as party chief'.[19]

Advani's supporters jumped into the fray to stave off the inevitable. The BJP's general secretary Pramod Mahajan criticised the RSS's interventions, asserted that 'in organisational matters we are sovereign', and pressed for the RSS's de-politicisation.

He went farther than anyone in the JS or BJP had gone ever before. 'I know I am not an RSS favourite; they will never allow me to become party president.' That did not deter him from outlining what he expected and what he did not from the Sangh headquarters in Nagpur.

> Mahajan maintained that in the last 10 to 12 years, interventions from the Sangh, 'at least at the level of the *sarsanghchalak*', have grown. He recalled that when M.S. Golwalkar was '*sarsanghchalak*', he would often give a 'direction in the national interest'. But today, the Sangh even dictates appointments to the state and district units of the BJP and lays down who should get tickets in an election.
>
> Mahajan recalled that about a decade ago, when asked if the BJP was dictated to by the Sangh, Advani, who was party president, replied that the Sangh went by the BJP's 'political judgment'.
>
> 'The Sangh is our mother but even the umbilical cord gets severed because nature ordains that a child must move and walk on his own. So let the Sangh

[18] *The Hindu*, 15 June 2005.

[19] Neena Vyas, *The Hindu*, 16 June 2006.

allow its child to walk on its own. As the mother, the Sangh should not keep scolding its child publicly and passing comments every day.

'The Sangh should realise that a section within it wants to de-politicise it. The norm of not crossing the Lakshman *rekha* does not apply only to the BJP. If the RSS crosses this Lakshman rekha, it will become a political party and then the sarsanghchalak's comparison of politics with prostitution will apply also to it.

'The real strength of the RSS and the BJP was that everyone spoke in one voice. We have lost that sense of brotherhood. Saffron is not important but brotherhood is.' Mahajan said it was a 'myth' that the BJP was dependent on the Sangh in an election. 'The media has perpetuated the myth that the BJP is 100 per cent dependent on the RSS. This may be true in certain tribal areas. I have run the BJP in Maharashtra for the last 20 years and I maintain that it is the best-run unit. There is no RSS intervention.

'If I get nine crore votes, the Sangh's contribution will be 1 or 1.5 per cent.' At worst, Mahajan said, in a 'tough' election, the Sangh could get the BJP defeated.[20]

This was factually untrue. It is unlikely that even the estranged Advani approved of this direct and unprecedented challenge to the RSS.

The very next day at Lucknow the RSS chief Sudarshan warmly praised Indira Gandhi in terms which suggested that the RSS had never discarded its plank, if the situation permitted, to team up with the Congress. Both Golwalkar and Deoras used with this option to keep the JS and BJP leaders in check. 'Indira Gandhi was a lady of firm determination *unlike* today's central leadership which lacks the same.'[21]

Sudheendra Kulkarni's approach was fundamentally different. He presented a paper at a closed-door 'Thinkers Meet' under the aegis of the RSS in Bhopal on 23 and 24 March. He criticised the 'Hindu-only' approach lest the BJP became a slightly larger version of the Hindu Mahasabha.

According to Kota Neelima and Manini Chatterjee 'the bulk of the paper is a passionate argument in favour of secularism and for respect and goodwill towards all non-Hindu faiths, especially Islam'. Turning Advani's pet 1980s slogan on its head, Kulkarni asked, 'If we are sincere about "Justice for All but Appeasement of None", isn't there a crying need for a non-appeasement approach to the welfare and development of the poor among non-Hindus, especially Muslims?'

Underlining that a pro-Muslim approach also made eminent political sense, Kulkarni wrote:

20 Radhika Ramaseshan, *The Telegraph*, 19 June 2005.

21 *The Statesman*, 20 June 2005.

> By now every objective election analysis has established, without the thinnest shadow of doubt, that with zero or insignificant support of our Muslim brethren, no political party in India can aspire to have a majority of its own in Parliament. And should a party like the BJP ever come to power in alliance with other parties, we'd be living in a fool's paradise if we thought that we can retain power from one election to another, by ignoring Muslims altogether.

The choice, Kulkarni asserted, was clear – a secular approach which ensures that BJP remains an important pole in Indian politics or a narrow 'Hindu-only approach' that makes it 'a slightly larger version of the Hindu Mahasabha'.[22] A decade later, Narendra Modi demonstrated that the Muslim vote can be dispensable if the Hindu vote is mobilised on the cry of Hindutva; albeit at a cost. India will cease to be the India dreamt of by the founding fathers. That is, only if Modi succeeds in fulfilling his dreams.

Kulkarni had served as aide to Vajpayee and Advani. Both M.M. Joshi and Jaswant Singh rejected his line. 'The BJP has an umbilical cord attached to the RSS.' Umbilical cords are cut. In this case it survives to control the offspring. Advani kept silent.

BJP leaders met their RSS counterparts ahead of the RSS conclave on 2 July. So did George Fernandes. The RSS stepped up pressure on Advani to resign. Mohan Bhagwat, Madan Das Devi and Suresh met Vajpayee and Advani on 11 July.

Meanwhile, Sudheendra Kulkarni kept up his campaign for reform of the RSS and curbs on the VHP. It is important to study his views because they mirrored sincerely what a lot of people had been advocating; especially since Jayaprakash Narayan in 1977 and Vajpayee's famous article in *The Indian Express* on 2 August 1979 – the RSS must cease to be what it has been since 1925, and discard its core beliefs. But its mentors' writings are remarkably consistent in espousing the beliefs since 1925 which well-meaning critics wish it to discard. They want the BJP not only to discard its skin but also its very heart. It will cease to be the RSS. That it finds impossible.

In a letter to Advani, Kulkarni urged the BJP to 'distance itself completely from extremist elements in the VHP who have derailed the Hindu movement, brought a bad name to the BJP and weakened the larger national cause'. He added: 'The BJP-RSS relationship will have to be recast. The RSS should not micromanage the affairs of the party. It must not make any public comments on the top leaders of the party.' Then came the sting. 'The RSS must realise that people of India do not like to see their *leaders remote-controlled by an external entity*.' He ought to know.

Reiterating views expressed at the Sangh meet in Bhopal a few months back, the letter stated, 'The party must make principled attempts to reach out to Indian Muslims. The fear that this would displease our core voters is misplaced. In any

[22] *The Indian Express*, 21 June 2005.

case, isn't it our duty to change the mindset of our core voters?' 'The RSS should not micromanage the affairs of the party.'[23]

On the day the RSS's conclave met at Surat on 3 July, Kulkarni resigned as BJP secretary and as member of its National Executive. The RSS was not mollified. An RSS leader told PTI the same day:

> 'Advani or Kulkarni is not the issue. If the BJP wants our support, don't dilute the ideology and don't be disrespectful towards the Sangh leadership,' an RSS leader told PTI earlier in the day.
>
> Besides 'erosion in ideology' by the BJP, the Sangh brass is concerned about the growing tendency among party leaders to attack the RSS and display personal loyalties, sources said.
>
> 'It is not the issue of Advani's statement. It is the tendency towards *personality-based politics*, polarisation of individual loyalties and the attack on the RSS even by small-time leaders that is worrying,' the RSS leader said. 'We don't want lip service. We want a categorical commitment towards ideology from the BJP and this time round we are in no mood to compromise.'[24]

Sudarshan reportedly told the gathering that some of those from the RSS ranks who had gone to the BJP had 'brought degeneration' not only to themselves but also to the organisation. While holding responsible positions in the government and in the BJP, some of them had not only become corrupt, they had also turned their back on the RSS, he said.

These leaders did not take any interest in the RSS shakhas or try to attract new blood to the organisation. The RSS membership was dwindling and the younger generation was shunning it because of the poor image created by the RSS-turned-BJP leaders.

He said the 'compromising attitude' adopted by the BJP for political reasons was also sending 'wrong signals' to the people. He praised Gujarat Chief Minister Narendra Modi and said the BJP should project him as a 'role model'.[25] The die was cast in favour of Modi nine years before the general election of 2014 and he acted accordingly.

Advani tried to forge a truce with the VHP when he met its president Ashok Singhal at Lucknow's Amausi Airport on 8 July. Pankaj Vohra, with his excellent contacts in the RSS reported on 8 July that its Surat conclave had decided to ask Advani to step down as BJP president.

> The decision taken at the RSS conclave at Surat is being conveyed to the BJP.

23 *The Indian Express* and *The Asian Age*, 2 July 2005.

24 *Hindustan Times*, 4 July 2005.

25 *The Hindu*, 5 July 2005.

> The delay in announcing is being attributed to the terrorist attack in Ayodhya. The RSS feels the BJP has deviated from the Hindutva ideology and Advani's remarks during the Pakistan visit were against the Sangh philosophy's basic tenets.
>
> The unanimous view was that the BJP had to set its house in order and it needed to be re-structured in tune with other Sangh outfits. Each of the 20-odd speakers who participated in the discussion on the political situation in the country were unanimous in condemning Advani.[26]

The RSS began working on an exit-Advani plan. The BJP's silver jubilee celebrations were due in Mumbai in December 2005. Its National Executive was due to meet earlier in Chennai. Time was fast running out to devise the plan for Advani's 'honourable exit'. According to one correspondent, it had all begun with the BJP electing Advani as its president in October 2004 'without taking the RSS into confidence'. His comments on Jinnah deepened the distrust. The Surat conclave sealed his fate.[27] In a statement issued at Nagpur on 9 July the RSS revealed the results of the Surat conclave. The 'prant pracharaks' had expressed 'serious concern over the ideological erosion, behavioural misdemeanour and violation of organisational discipline by some functionaries of a couple of like-minded organisations'.

> The Sangh, it added, 'has taken serious note of this and our elders will soon talk to the concerned people and convey the Sangh's reservations'. . . . Advani has already 'back-tracked' from his attempts at an image makeover over the last few days – first, by accepting the resignation of his aide Sudheendra Kulkarni and then by visiting Ayodhya (albeit belatedly) and reiterating his commitment to the old 'mandir wahin banayenge' line.
>
> However, the fact that the Sangh was impelled to issue the statement after his Ayodhya visit and after the 'sacking' of Kulkarni, shows that it has not forgiven Advani for his 'lapses' and wants a more unambiguous commitment from him, sources said. . . .
>
> The RSS, sources said, has been unhappy with the BJP leadership for a long time now because of its 'ideological deviations' during its years in power. But power had its own uses even for the Sangh and, therefore, it kept largely silent in the six years of NDA rule.
>
> But now that the BJP is out of power, the RSS wants to re-establish itself as the 'stern patriarch' and bring all errant members to heel. Advani's Jinnah remarks provided a perfect pretext to force a 'course correction'.[28]

[26] *Hindustan Times*, 9 July 2005.

[27] Dipankar Chakraborty, *The Statesman*, 15 July 2005.

[28] Manini Chatterjee, *The Indian Express*, 10 July 2005.

In the eyes of the RSS the Jinnah inscription was no solitary lapse. It was the culmination of its grievances against the top leaders of the BJP, Advani and Vajpayee, since they formed the BJP twenty-five years ago. To ideological deviation was added the hitherto unstated ire at the duos' 'personality cult which enabled them to ignore the RSS' advice upto a point'. A senior party leader revealed that 'the RSS has been keen that the BJP move away from politics based on personality cults built around the two big leaders, Mr. Vajpayee and Mr. L.K. Advani. It has recommended supremacy of ideology, the party organisation and a disciplined cadre'. It is not difficult to identify the 'senior party leader' who confided thus to *The Hindu*'s special correspondent (23 June 2005). He was obviously one who felt himself sidelined by them. Suspicion centred understandably on Murli Manohar Joshi.

Advani's lapse provided the RSS with an opportunity it had been waiting for, for years. As always, it would sing the tune of the BJP's 'internal matter' even as it tweaked its ears to follow the RSS's orders. *The charade that was played out from 7 June when Advani returned to India, till 31 December 2005, when he stepped down, reveals glaringly the true state of the relationship between parent and progeny.* Hence the need for a close and detailed analysis. By 17 July Advani's fate was sealed. That was when he went to the RSS HQs in Jhandewalan in New Delhi, in soak cloth and ashes, to beg for a reprieve. He went to the wrong people. Legally and morally it was for the BJP to decide on his position as president and the RSS to rule on his status as a swayamsevak. Yet the RSS's authority over the BJP none questioned, significantly.

Advani faced open defiance within the party from former President Jana Krishnamurthy, former Vice-President Pyarelal Khandelwal, Parliamentary Secretary Ashwini Kumar and, most tellingly of all, the towering veteran of Delhi BJP, Madanlal Khurana. In a letter to Advani he wrote:

> It is public knowledge that the Sangh leadership has lost confidence in you and had expected that you, as a disciplined swayamsevak, would resign from the presidentship of the party. I do not know whether you respect the sentiments of the Sangh leadership, or whether you prefer to go by the advice of people like Mr. Sudheendra Kulkarni. But, under the present circumstances, I find it impossible to continue under your leadership.[29]

Advani's supporters were Venkaiah Naidu, Sushma Swaraj, Sanjay Joshi and Jaswant Singh, whom he was to ditch over *his* book on Jinnah. Vajpayee was one of them; but he calibrated his support. The quartet had several rounds of talks with the RSS leaders Mohan Bhagwat and Suresh as had Soni, Vajpayee. They accompanied Advani to Jhandewalan. The RSS's spokesman Ram Madhav spelt out the terms.

[29] *The Asian Age*, 17 July, 2005.

'Swayamsevaks working in organisations inspired by the Sangh ideology should maintain [the] utmost commitment to ideology and also behave in a manner befitting Sangh traditions.' This was widely perceived as a direct reference to Mr. Advani.

> Madhav said that he was speaking on behalf of Mr. Bhagwat and Mr. Soni and that 'serious efforts' must be made in the coming days to address the views of the Sangh on 'issues like ideology, conduct, organisation [and the] emergency of [a] new generation [leadership]'. He laid stress on maintaining 'organisational discipline' and the need to 'avoid negative publicity' by restricting all discussions to 'the four walls of the organisation'. . . .
>
> In an article in a Marathi magazine *Tarun Bharat*, RSS leader M.G. Vaidya recently wrote that at the RSS Surat conclave 'it was clearly decided to ask Advani to step down [as party president]' and 'this was conveyed to the senior BJP leaders'. He added that the Sangh was not pressuring the BJP, it had conveyed its views, and it was 'for the BJP to decide whether a tarnished leader was an asset or a liability for the party'.[30]

Around the same time on 19 July Khurana declared, 'I had the approval of all the Sangh outfits, including the RSS, for writing the letter to Mr. Advani.' He was expelled from the BJP for six years. Vajpayee objected to it. At long last Advani decided to quit; but not quite, as we shall see. He said, on 18 September 2005, at the concluding session of the BJP's National Executive meeting at Chennai,

> From time to time, and depending on the issue at hand, the BJP leadership has had no hesitation in consulting the RSS functionaries. After such consultations, the party takes its own independent decisions. Some of these decisions may differ – and have indeed differed – from the stated positions of the RSS and certain constituents of the 'Sangh Parivar'.
>
> But lately an impression has gained ground that no political or organisational decision can be taken without the consent of the RSS functionaries. This perception, we hold, will do no good either to the party or to the RSS. The RSS too must be concerned that such a perception will dwarf its greater mission of man-making and nation-building. Both the RSS and the BJP must consciously exert to dispel this impression.[31]

He announced that he would demit the office of the BJP's president at its National Council meeting in Mumbai. The BJP had not had an election for its presidency ever since it was formed. Vajpayee said meaningfully on 21 October,

[30] Neena Vyas, *The Hindu*, 18 July 2005.

[31] Vide *The Hindu*, 19 September 2005 for the text.

that old leaders must go and new ones should take charge. 'I have started feeling that I am ageing fast.'

From the sidelines Nana Deshmukh vents his spleen. He had not left politics to seek sanyas but to register his rejection of the two BJP leaders. He said on 22 October that

> he was pained to see the state of political parties, none of whom were functioning properly. He had suggested in the Rajya Sabha in the aftermath of the Godhra incident that the then Prime Minister Vajpayee and Leader of Opposition Sonia Gandhi should together visit the state with a message of peace.
>
> 'When Muslims were being butchered in Gujarat, I emphasised in the RSS that political parties must make a joint effort to restore communal harmony in the country. But neither Vajpayee nor Sonia Gandhi took the initiative to respond to my appeal.'[32]

When he functioned as leader, in the Jana Sangh and the BJP, Deshmukh was the most communal of all; an operator to his finger tips.

The RSS began slowly to assert its role as patron. Mohan Bhagwat said on 23 October, 'Our job is to ascertain whether they are on the right path or not.'[33] He stood by the RSS's five-point agenda which it had suggested after its Haridwar session in November 2004 – the primacy to Hindutva, strengthening the organisation, training of cadres, ethical conduct and a consultation mechanism in the party.[34]

In a cryptic one-liner, Vajpayee distanced himself from Advani. 'The Sangh does not interfere.'[35] Advani stepped down as president on 31 December 2005. Rajnath Singh was formally declared his successor. But Advani was not taking sanyas. He would not only continue as leader of the opposition in the Lok Sabha (prime minister in waiting) but he would also be the party's 'face' in the general elections due in 2009.[36] Ambition made him deaf to the loud attacks on his leadership. The RSS burrowed deep into the ranks of the BJP on the eve of its Chennai meeting to garner support against him. M.G. Vaidya explained the RSS's grievances. Advani had, like Vajpayee before him in 1999, assured Pakistan that India respects its independence and, worse, that he felt sorry when the Babri Masjid was demolished.

In an interview to the noted scholar Jyotirmaya Sharma, Vaidya said:

32 Hemendra Singh Bartwal from Chitrakoot, MP, *Hindustan Times*, 23 October 2005.

33 *The Indian Express*, 24 October 2005.

34 *Hindustan Times*, 24 October 2005.

35 Manini Chatterjee, *The Indian Express*, 15 October 2005.

36 Manini Chatterjee, *The Indian Express*, 1 January 2006.

> We also believe that this partition of India is not final. If Germany can be unified, if Vietnam can be united, if the two Koreas can try unifying, why not India? We also believe that though we had no plan to demolish the Babri structure, we did not feel sorry when it was demolished. If someone says that the demolition was the saddest day in his life, then we do not share his perception. This is what the Surat meeting said and this is what was conveyed to Advani. . . .
>
> We have conveyed our concern and our perception that what he said in Pakistan is not shared by us. Now, whether he continues and for how long is for the BJP and Advani to decide. . . . The link between the RSS and the BJP is through the swayamsevaks who work in the BJP. *Our relationship with the BJP is a constitutional one*. Our swayamsevaks work there. We have sent some and some others have gone on their own. They are our medium of communicating with the BJP and putting forth our views. . . .
>
> I have written newspaper articles arguing that once Advani resigned in Pakistan, he ought not to have withdrawn his resignation. I wonder why he resigned in Pakistan. Why not after returning from there? He could have resigned after coming back and consulting his associates. This puzzles me. I believe that once he tendered his resignation, he should not have withdrawn it. . . . The BJP is not the life-breath of the Sangh. Our life does not depend on the BJP.[37]

Sudarshan became more candid. Vajpayee and Advani were no longer acceptable as they had 'become too big' for the Sangh Parivar. The RSS preferred 'a collective leadership' in their place; which the RSS could manipulate. 'They became individually too big and sidelined the concept of collective leadership by which the RSS swears.' He also demanded the '*Indianisation of the Constitution* and religion practised in country'.[38] The RSS is waiting for an opportune moment to make this a major plank in its campaigns – discard the Constitution of India and write a new one; in Nagpur, of course.

But if the RSS was so keen on showing a veteran the door, it could not have ignored the possibilities of his replacement. All the evidence suggests that *Narendra Modi had endeared himself to the RSS precisely because of the Gujarat pogrom of Muslims in 2002.*

When, at last, Advani resigned as president of the BJP at Mumbai on 31 December 2005, he declared Rajnath Singh as his successor and declared that he would continue as leader of the opposition in the Lok Sabha. The National Executive recorded its deep appreciation of his 'extraordinary contribution' to the party.

[37] *The Hindu*, 1 August 2005.

[38] *The Times of India*, 6 November 2005.

The RSS faced another problem meanwhile. Sanjay Joshi, its general secretary (organisation), resigned after the BJP's leader received a VCD that allegedly featured him in a sex scandal. The RSS stripped him of his post as *pracharak*. He had been seconded to the BJP in 2001. It was to him that Advani had submitted his resignation. Now, it was his turn to submit his resignation to Advani, on 27 December.

Vajpayee emerged from the drama with enhanced stature. Initially, Advani received his sympathy. Vajpayee did not want the RSS to become too powerful. He also wanted to distance himself somewhat from Advani lest he grew too big for his boots. Their relationship although friendly, was never close. It was marked by a certain reserve on both sides. As Vajpayee's successor to the office of BJP's presidentship, Advani carved out his own niche. He overruled Vajpayee to take up the Babri Masjid issue in 1989; all for votes as he said on 11 June 1989 after the Palanpur resolution. 'I am sure it will translate into votes.' He repeated this several times. He aspired to be prime minister. Advani yielded the palm to Vajpayee belatedly only in 1995 at Mumbai. He knew he did not command the following which Vajpayee did.

Vajpayee was too astute not to have noticed Advani's game. As de La Rochefoucauld said in one of his piercing Maxims, 'In the adversity even of our best friends, we always find something not wholly displeasing.'

No tears need be shed for Advani's multiple humiliations at the hands of the RSS and later by Modi. This is the one man who shamelessly exploited the Ayodhya issue to secure power, injected communal hate in our body politic, and rode in a rath yatra over a trail of human blood. All, to become prime minister. He still persists in this ambition in the hope that Modi will trip and he will be recalled. This is why despite the humiliation of being put on the rickety shelf of a Margdarshak Mandal he continues to present himself at all occasions, cutting a pitiable figure throughout. There is little to choose between them. Advani saved Modi from ouster for the pogrom of 2002. Advani it was who had said, at Ayodhya on 19 November 1990, in his brief moment of ecstasy, 'Henceforth only those who fight for Hindu interests would rule India'; complaining bitterly on 2 October 1990 that secular policy is putting unreasonable restrictions on Hindu aspirations.

None has shed any tears at his steep and deserved fall. Not a few recalled Ghalib's immortal couplet: *Nikalna khuld se Adam ka suntey aye they lekin/ Bohot beabroo ho kar terey kooche se hum nikle* (We had heard a lot of Adam's expulsion from paradise/ It was in utter disgrace that we were turned out of your quarters).

A detailed study of the Advani episode exposes the lies which the RSS the Jana Sangh and the BJP, Advani particularly, have retailed throughout the existence of these bodies; namely that the RSS is a 'cultural body', it does not interfere in the internal affairs of the BJP and both work democratically and according to their respective constitutions.

But over a period of months the RSS secured the ouster of the BJP's president just as it had, with ease, secured the expulsion of two presidents of the Jana Sangh, Mauli Chandra Sharma and Balraj Madhok; in the latter's case, ironically, by using Advani. The RSS's spokesman Ram Madhav, who later glided with ease to the BJP as its spokesman, falsely claimed on 7 June 2005: 'We have nothing to do with today's development (Advani's resignation). It is an internal matter of the Party.'[39]

Constitutionally, it was open to the RSS to expel Advani as its *swayamsevak*, leaving the BJP free to do what it pleased to do with its battered President. The official statements of both tell a different story. This record is of abiding relevance. On 9 July 2005 the RSS said in a statement:

> Several imaginary stories have appeared in the media about the proceedings at Surat. The Prant Pracharaks who have assembled at Surat expressed serious concerns over the ideological erosion, behavioural misdemeanour and violation of organisational discipline with impunity by some functionaries of a couple of like-minded organisations. The Sangh has taken serious note of this and our elders will soon talk to concerned people and convey Sangh's reservations.

A detailed fatwa by the RSS was issued on 17 July. The text reads:

> There have been discussions in our circles for some time now that the Swayamsevaks working in the organisations inspired by the Sangh ideology should maintain utmost commitment to ideology and also behave in a manner befitting the Sangh traditions. The very same things have been discussed at length at the recently concluded Surat meet also. After that meet, as per the instructions of the Sarsanghachalak, me [sic] and two of my colleagues had come to Delhi and met the functionaries of a couple of like-minded organisations. We communicated our sentiments and concerns to them.
>
> We expressed our desire that serious efforts be made in the coming days to address the sentiments expressed by us on issues like ideology, conduct, organisation, emergence of new generation, etc. We also expect that while doing all this our Swayamsevaks will be cautious in maintaining organisational discipline and do the needful in avoiding negative publicity by restricting all their discussions on these matters to the four walls of the organisation only.
>
> In the last few weeks there were several references to the Sangh in the media on this issue. I would like to make it clear that our objective was to convey above mentioned matters to concerned functionaries of the organisations and it is the responsibility of those organisations to bring in necessary reforms. The Sangh shall not interfere in that process.

[39] *The Asian Age*, 8 June 2005.

It was signed by Mohan Bhagwat; itself a rarity.

However, the BJP *exonerated* Advani completely. A resolution passed by a central office-bearers and parliamentary board meeting on 8 July 2005 said,

> The Parliamentary Board, Central Office Bearers and Chief Ministers of the BJP ruled States met today to discuss the resignation submitted by Shri L.K. Advaniji. Shri M. Venkaiah Naidu presided over the meeting. Shri Atal Bihari Vajpayee was present in the meeting.
>
> The meeting unequivocally rejected the resignation of Shri L.K. Advaniji, he has so ably led in the past. Shri Advani represents the best values in public life. He has scholarly [sic] articulated the debate on nationalism in the past few decades with rationality, logic and with powerful idioms. His contribution to our ideology is unparalleled. The party has benefited enormously from his leadership and needs his leadership in the future also.
>
> The party strongly condemns the use of highly objectionable language by some leaders of the VHP about Shri Advani. These statements have lowered the level of public discourse. Such outbursts, indecent protests and abusive language adversely affects the strength of the nationalist movement in the country. These statements also go against the very ethos of Hinduism.

A statement issued on 10 June 2005, after the meeting of the BJP parliamentary board, central office-bearers, and chief ministers of BJP ruled states said:

> The Bharatiya Janata Party lauds the path-breaking visit to Pakistan by its president, Shri L.K. Advani. The week-long tour has brought the people of India and Pakistan closer, helped remove a mountain of misunderstandings between them and taken the momentum of better relations to a new level, in continuation of the policy of friendship initiated by successive governments led by Shri Atal Bihari Vajpayee. The warm and enthusiastic response Shri Advani's visit elicited from both the officials and ordinary people of Pakistan proves the correctness of the NDA's policy of pursuing good neighbourly ties between the two countries.
>
> The party is happy to note that Shri Advani raised the issue of cross-border terrorism with the President of Pakistan and impressed upon him the need to immediately dismantle the infrastructure of terrorism and bring cross-border terrorism to an end. Shri Advani emphasised that lasting peace in South Asia would be possible only when such issues were satisfactorily resolved between India and Pakistan.
>
> The BJP appreciates the Pakistan Government's invitation to Shri Advani to inaugurate a project for the restoration of Katasraj Temples, revered by all Hindus of the Indian sub-continent as a resting place of the Pandavas. The

> overwhelming response to his Katasraj visit could well go down as a turning point in removing long-held misgivings between the people of the two countries. The BJP hopes that Pakistan will progress further along this path and ensure that the rights of Hindus and other religious minorities are fully protected and that official initiatives to restore and develop other mandirs and gurudwaras continue in the future.
>
> Shri Advani welcomed the event in Katasraj as a good beginning and in that context, without describing Mr. Jinnah as secular, reminded the people of Pakistan of its founder's address to the country's Constituent Assembly in which he had urged full freedom of faith for all its citizens on grounds of religion.
>
> The BJP reiterates that whatever may have been Jinnah's vision of Pakistan, the state he founded is theocratic and nonsecular, the very idea of Hindus and Muslims being two separate nations is repugnant to it. The BJP has always condemned the division of India on communal lines and continues to steadfastly reject the two-nation theory championed by Jinnah and endorsed by British colonialists. There can be no revisiting the reality that Jinnah led a communal agitation to achieve his goal of Pakistan, which devoured thousands of innocent people in its wake and dispossessed millions of their homes and livelihoods.

The sin was condemned. The sinner was exonerated. If the sinner was, nonetheless, thrown out unceremoniously as the party's president, on 18 September 2005, kicking and screaming at the RSS's interference, it was because of the RSS's pressures, as the record shows. The BJP bowed to its wishes on a major issue like this and revealed itself in its true colours. It was not an autonomous political party. It was the political department of the RSS. Can the BJP ever order the removal of the RSS chief?

19. The RSS in Triumph

With both the BJP stalwarts put in place, the RSS felt itself free to run the show without any compromises. Leaders in the BJP's second rank do as they were told without the occasional pleas which Vajpayee and Advani would offer.

In an editorial entitled 'The BJP Silver Jubilee', the RSS's mouthpiece *Organiser* sharply reminded the party's leaders that

> the real growth of the party as a pan-Indian force was the result of the Ramjanmabhoomi movement, which spurred an ideological debate in the country and attracted people from all strata of society cutting across caste, region, urban, rural divide. The agitation brought large goodwill, resources and youth involvement. The Janmabhoomi campaign was both innovative and creative. It was the time when women and tribals swelled its ranks. In power the BJP attracted more intellectuals and fence-sitters, setting the stage for a credible alternative to socialist secular sloganism that so far dominated the political space. . . .
>
> A sharp warning followed:
>
> A party like the BJP cannot exist only for power. When pursuit of power becomes the only goal, clash of personalities ensues. The recent sparrings in the BJP in state after state have nothing to do with ideology. Ideological commitment of the leadership is what inspired the cadre to serve, sacrifice and combat. Effective leadership has to balance between its core constituency and the other constituency. It is suicidal to believe that the committed constituency is a captive one and go about wooing the other.[1]

Rajnath Singh made haste to assure his RSS chiefs that he would not be found wanting, as the BJP's president, in his commitment to ideology.

> The foremost task before us is to widen our base. Cultural nationalism and integral humanism are the basis of the BJP. India's unity is not only based on politics, but also on the cultural aspects. Hindutva and cultural nationalism have a common basis. Hindutva never creates confrontation among human beings.[2]

[1] 1 January 2016.

[2] *Hindustan Times*, 2 January 2006.

To remove all doubt he said, 'We are all workers of the Sangh.'[3]

The RSS chief, never too restrained, held forth with abandon. Addressing the fourth Vishwa Sangh Shivir at Ahmedabad, in the presence of Modi, on 26 December 2005, *Organiser* reported that he

> extended shivirarthis to feel proud of their Indian origin. He said it was the Indian culture that had the power to raise a human being to the status of narayana (divine). Elucidating the nara rakshas (demon), nara (human), narottam (human of highest quality) and narayana, Sudarshan said Indian culture was capable of raising a human being from the existing status of narottam to the status of narayana. He raised a pointed question to the shivirarthis, 'Why do you call yourself Hindu? Is it only because you were born in a Hindu family or because your forefathers belonged to India?' He said every individual was born as Hindu and it was the religious rituals of various religions like sunnat or baptism that made one Muslim or Christian. Describing the Vedas as an ever-lasting source of knowledge, Shri Sudarshan pointed out that 22 of the total 40 points, on which the scholars at the World Environment Summit were unanimous, were already mentioned in the Bhoomisukt of Atharvaveda.
>
> Vishwa Sangh Shivir (VSS) is a gathering of Hindu Swayamsevak Sangh (HSS) activists once in every five years. The prime objective of the Shivir is to discuss the present state of HSS shakhas and their presence in these camps were 200 in Bangalore, 378 in Vadodara and 568 in Mumbai.
>
> There are about 120 countries in the world where seven crore Hindus live. Included in these 120 countries are England, America, Holland, Kenya, Germany, Middle East, West Indies, South Africa, Hong Kong, Singapore, Australia, New Zealand, Fiji, Nepal, Sri Lanka, Bangladesh, Pakistan, Myanmar and Surinam. These overseas Hindus have proved their existence in their respective countries through their excellence in world politics, spirituality and unique values of joint family system seen only in India.
>
> In most of these 120 countries, Hindus are understandably in minority. Parents are fighting hard for imparting education based on Hindu values and culture to their children. Already Western culture has virtually led the society to worst degradation, which has created biggest danger to young Hindu generation. Obviously, their parents are deeply worried as to how to inculcate good samskars in their growing youngsters. Under such perversity, Hindu Swayamsevak Sangh is busy in organising a series of camps for promoting yoga, Vedic mathematics and education based on Hindu values. Efforts are also being made to popularise Hindu festivals. These efforts have yielded the desired results.
>
> The first shakha of HSS was held on the deck of a ship sailing from

[3] *The Asian Age*, 2 January 2006.

> Mumbai to Kenya in 1947. Kenya took the lead in spreading shakhas of HSS to Tanzania, Uganda and elsewhere. Currently, the HSS work has spread to 32 countries and has 720 shakhas, of which 620 shakhas are weekly and 130 shakhas are daily.[4]

Rajnath Singh dutifully testified. 'RSS never interferes in the BJP's internal matters. Since I come from that family, I will seek its directions. For that, I do not feel any hesitation or shame,' he said in an interview to Aaj Tak TV news channel.

Not just that, in his interaction with reporters he also indicated the possibility of more full-time RSS pracharaks being inducted into the party's central team of office-bearers to oversee its organisational activities. 'Clearly, the RSS' Chitrakoot plan to tighten the grip on the BJP and "purge" it of its ills is on in a big way,' the *Hindustan Times* correspondent Hemendra Singh Bartwal remarked (7 January 2006). He said also, 'We should be more resolved in our ideological commitment.'[5]

Organiser exposed the 'Devils among us' in an editorial under that title (8 January 2006). It said:

> Much harm has been inflicted by individuals from within. The war on Hindutva has taken many forms. More saddening is that some of us are not seeing the woods for the trees.
>
> First it was the attempt to deny the BJP its legitimate role in the polity. As long as the BJP remained a peripheral entity everybody ignored it. When it gained some popularity the attempt was to ostracise and isolate it. When the party grew up to wield power, there was a sinister design to work to dilute its ideological and organisational commitment. In this they received solicitous encouragement from some in-house experts.
>
> Who are the people behind it? Is it part of a Congress strategy to enlarge its base? Or is it a gang up against Hindutva ideology to weaken the forces of nationalism? It started as a blame game, then the hardliners versus the moderates, the pro-RSS segment versus the no-RSS segment, the Gen-old versus Gen-next. And we have pundits prescribing the BJP to become a right wing tool for power, discarding all ideological baggages. . . .

This was aimed at well wishers who urged it to become a secular conservative party.

> In 80 years of its existence, the Rashtriya Swayamsevak Sangh has earned reputation for character building, austerity, discipline, patriotism and service. Even its worst critics have not disputed these qualities of the organisation.

4 *Organiser*, 2 January 2006.

5 *Organiser*, 8 January 2006.

And its affiliates including the BJP have proved how different they are in comparison to other organisations in upholding values and probity in public domain. Now a well-greased, highly-sophisticated campaign is on to tarnish this image. (In tackling these challenges, we need to be fully conscious of the mindset of the mafia. It is interesting to have a look at the science of their shenanigans as described in books like *Advise and Consent series, The Da Vinci Code, Mitrokhin Archives, In God's Name, Bias and Arrogance*, etc.)

Now, take the case of the former BJP General Secretary (Organisation) Sanjay Joshi. We have no doubt that he is a victim of an inhuman ploy. He is innocent. The CD, the audio-cassette and letters, all anonymous, were fake. But some people were at it systematically. A canard was spread tenaciously. We should not grant voyeurism the dignity of an expose. For anyone to sneak into somebody's alleged bedroom and record so-called intimate moments are criminal. And those responsible should be exposed and punished. Character assassination is a time-tested method in political arm-twisting. The targeted sting operations are meant to break the backbone of political opposition. Any leadership confronting such situations needs a very humane, generous and long-term perspective of the issue in hand. For, hypocrisy is the reigning ideology in politics.

Look at the glaring violation of an individual's right to privacy in the sting operations. *Old notions of morality are not tenable in the modern society where market forces* have invaded our private lives and attitudes. Is there a contradiction between very natural human instincts and the larger social mission of an individual? Should our perception of individuals undergo a U-turn after every sting operation? Correctives need to be enforced.

It was amusing to find the RSS organ inveighing against 'Old notions of morality'.

The RSS was going 'modern'. Its top leaders met at a five-star resort on the outskirts of Jaipur on 24 January 2006 for a brainstorming session on ideology and strategy. Vajpayee and Advani were absent; Murli Manohar Joshi, Sushma Swaraj, Venkaiah Naidu, Pramod Mahajan and Arun Jaitley participated. RSS sources told *The Indian Express*, 'The Sangh seems to have won the first battle for the control over the BJP after Advani's exit. It would now seek to strengthen it.'

Sudarshan

announced a strategy to ensure that India dominated the world by Year 2011: *Bharatiyakaran*. Indianisation of the 17 crore Muslims and 3 crore Christians residing here is the only way out, he said on day two of the Shabari Kumbh here.

'2011 will mark the end of sankraman kal for Bharat. We have to prepare ourselves for leadership. And because we can't throw our Muslims and Christians into the sea, we have to Indianise them. And for this, we have to communicate with them the importance of this objective. For *vanvasis*, we have to tell them that they are part of the extended Hindu family.' He was addressing an audience of sadhus at Shabari Kumbh site (Dangs) on 12 February. Pravin Togadia proposed to a gathering of tribals 'a grand Christian-Hindu alliance' against Muslims.[6]

In the BJP its new President put the RSS's stamp on his core team. It marked Narendra Modi's elevation to central bodies, a mere eight years ahead of his final triumph in 2014 as prime minister. Shekhar Iyer of *Hindustan Times* noted:

> Hardline Hindutva leaders like Gujarat CM Narendra Modi and former Bajrang Dal chief Vinay Katiyar got key slots on Wednesday as the new party chief Rajnath Singh's core team announced here bore the imprint of the RSS loud and clear.
>
> Modi was brought to the BJP's central Parliamentary board, the apex decision-making body, Katiyar, who played a prominent role in the Ram temple movement, was made the general secretary. Both Modi and Katiyar belong to the OBC. Their inclusion is also seen as a strategic move to contain the damage caused by the expulsion of Uma Bharati, who is also an OBC.
>
> Though Modi has no intention of leaving Gujarat, his inclusion is seen as an acknowledgement of his growing appeal within the Sangh Parivar. He is considered to be the next undisputed Hindutva face of the BJP after the decline of L.K. Advani, whose influence was on the wane ever since he tried to adopt a moderate image during his visit to Pakistan. . . . Madan Lal Khurana, who crossed swords with Advani last year, is back in the BJP's national executive.[7]

But if Christian Democrats and Social Democrats could form a 'grand coalition' in Germany, why cannot the Congress and the BJP 'think on similar lines. Coalition does not mean abandoning one's own principles', M.G. Vaidya, a senior RSS ideologue said.[8]

A Congress-BJP (read: RSS) alliance has always been a recurring theme in the RSS's pronouncements. It was no compliment to the Congress. *Organiser* proposed an alliance with the Samajwadi Party in Uttar Pradesh (8 February 2006).

One is at a loss to understand how the RSS was able to garner support from some well-educated persons despite its strange views which are contrary to modern thought and knowledge on history, the present world order, on population control

[6] *The Indian Express*, 12 February 2006.

[7] 26 January 2006.

[8] *The Times of India*, 31 January 2006.

and on much else besides. As general secretary, Mohan Bhagwat, the RSS boss now, held that

> It is because of the rapid decline in Hindu population that the whole world is today in the grip of terrorism. The reason of growing terrorism in Afghanistan, Pakistan, Bangladesh, Myanmar and Tibet is their separation from India. . . . He said there are all-round onslaughts on Hindus. After the Kanchi Shankaracharya, Swami Ramdev has been targeted. Describing the Sangh work as God's work, he said after 80 years the Sangh has become a formidable force, which is very difficult for anyone to ignore. He said the country would be strong and developed with the unity of Hindu society. 'The solution to all problems lies with India and the key to development of India is the Sangh.'[9]

Sudarshan predicted on 10 July 2006

> a nuclear war of supremacy between the West and backers of jihadi Islam. He also picked a bone with the Supreme Court's view that mixed marriages were the most effective way to blot out the inequalities engendered by caste divisions, and went on to resolutely defend the Hindu caste system. Speaking on the occasion of the birth centenary celebrations of the Sangh's second sarsanghchalak, M.S. Golwalkar (better known as Guruji), Sudarshan said a nuclear holocaust in four-five years was imminent largely because tension between the West and the backers of jihadi Islam had reached a decisive stage. After which India, home to 73 different Muslim groupings, would emerge an island of peace, and a world power. In essence, the rivalry was quite pointless since both the Bible and the Quran stood for the same values. . . . His open defence of the caste system took many by surprise. Historically, he said, the caste system had been the most effective guarantor of jobs. There was no friction because everybody knew his/her place in society.
>
> 'Everybody had a role. The staying power of the system alone enabled it to withstand the forays made by 700 years of Muslim and English rule. Ironically, it was only after Independence that organised efforts to break the caste edifice began?'[10]

The Sangh Parivar is deeply committed to the caste system. Its eulogies to Dr. B.R. Ambedkar are as false as they are belated. It is against family planning because of its communal phobia. Sudarshan wanted mothers who could produce 10 children. He said at New Delhi on 27 November 2006, 'Forget the two-child norm. Produce three at the very last, more than that are more than welcome.' The

[9] *Organiser*, 6 February 2006.

[10] *The Asian Age*, 11 July 2006.

punchline came a while later. 'We have, in fact, instituted awards for our mothers who produce 10 children.'[11]

Sanjay Basak's report was of the same tenor.

> '*Teen se kam nahin, aap jitna zyada kar sakte utna achcha* (Not less than three. The more you produce the better).' He called upon Hindus not to 'get trapped' into the slogan of '*hum do, hamare do*' and '*hum do, hamare ek*'. He warned that going by the way the population of the minority communities was growing, Hindus would soon become a minority in India, and hence they should start breeding to retain their majority status.
>
> He tried to drive home his point by coming up with some saffron brand of mathematics. The Sudarshan theory suggested: 'A couple with 12 sons were likely to be survived by a 1,200-strong progeny after 1,200 years. The one with 11 sons would have 1,100 successors. Those with three would have 38 descendants, while couples with two sons would show a zero increase.' A BJP leader quipped: 'There is going to be a leadership change in the BJP. Lalu Yadav, with 11 children, fits the bill!'[12]

Some BJP leaders disagreed. But none of the top leaders dared to go on record. At Guwahati, on 10 December 2006, Sudarshan asked Hindus to do away with family planning.[13]

It is an organisation whose leaders spoke thus which

> tightened its grip on every level of decision making in the BJP with a series of crucial appointments in the party. Of the 35 new office-bearers, the appointments of as many as 11 are seen as directly guided by the Sangh. Frustrated senior leaders, who do not wish to be quoted, are now questioning BJP president Rajnath Singh's ability to resist Sangh pressure. . . .
>
> The various social bodies and cells, too, now have a disproportionate presence of Sangh favourites, mainly from Maharashtra. They include Devdas Apte, president of the Scheduled Tribe Front, Gajendra Chauhan (cultural cell), Kirit Somaya (investors cell), Anand Pandit (commerce cell) and Poornima Advani (NGOs cell).
>
> 'What can we possibly do? The president doesn't have the stature or inclination to deny anything that the Sangh wants done. Beyond a point, it's difficult to resist,' he said.[14]

[11] Poornima Joshi, *The Telegraph*, 18 November 2006.

[12] *The Asian Age*, 19 November 2006.

[13] *The Indian Express*, 11 December 2006.

[14] Poornima Tripathi, *The Asian Age*, 24 February 2006.

The RSS's ideological trimming took a strange turn. It disowned one of its three guide books, *We or Our Nationhood Defined* by Golwalkar, but not officially. A booklet, 'Shri Guruji and Indian Muslims', authored by a Delhi University lecturer Rakesh Sinha and published by RSS's Suruchi Prakashan and formally released by the Sangh in Nagpur on 24 February, argues that in his lifetime Golwalkar had 'revealed that the book carried not his own views but was an abridged version of G.D. Savarkar's Rashtra Mimansa'.

Former RSS spokesperson M.G. Vaidya, while approving the removal of *We or Our Nationhood Defined* from the Sangh's pantheon of texts, says the book that is central to 'us is Golwalkar's "Bunch of Thoughts" since it consists of his views after he became sarsanghchalak on 21 June 1940'. . . .

> According to Vaidya, *We or Our Nationhood Defined* is a collection of Golwalkar's experiences with religion and spiritualism from the time he was a biology lecturer in BHU to his meeting the first sarsanghchalak K.B. Hedgewar in Benaras in 1931, his joining the RSS, taking over of the Sangh's Officers' Training Camp in Nagpur, subsequently abandoning Sangh to join Swami Akhandananda and finally returning to RSS in 1937 after Akhandananda's death.[15]

Passage of time induced in Advani's mind thoughts of return to favour. He returned to his favourite tactic, the Yatra, in March 2006. He went to Nagpur to solicit support from Sudarshan and Bhagwat. VHP leaders opposed it.[16] Sudarshan snubbed him. Rajendra Singh was also on a yatra of his own. Sanjay Basak reported that Sudarshan gave Advani a thorough dressing down.

> As the meeting went on, Sudarshan attacked Advani for other things. He said Advani deliberately delayed his resignation as BJP chief by nine months so that Sangh would get only a year and three months at the helm till March 2007. He also accused Advani of interfering in the BJP's list of nominations for the Rajya Sabha.
>
> The sarcastic Sudarshan said the yatras appeared to be a political gimmick with no obvious end. 'Whose ekta are you trying to achieve?' he asked Advani. 'Hindu-Muslim? India-Pakistan? Or the unity of parties you are talking to in order to become PM?'
>
> He reminded Advani of the breakfast meeting they had on 6 March at Jhandewalan, New Delhi, where no plan for attacking 'Muslim appeasement' was discussed. Advani had only apprised Sudarshan of the party's position on Iran and other peripheral issues.

15 Akshay Mukul, *The Times of India*, 8 March 2006.

16 *The Statesman*, 14 March 2006.

> He accused Advani of deliberately keeping the RSS in the dark about his intentions. A stung Advani was told finally: 'You have no credibility. You're not to take the Sangh agenda forward. Rajnath is.'[17]

The BJP had launched seven yatras in the past 16 years.

The BJP reinstated Sanjay Joshi as general secretary (organisation) within 24 hours of the RSS bringing him back as pracharak. Modi forced both to reverse their decision.

The RSS's Akhil Bharatiya Pratinidhi Sabha (All India General Council) met at Nagpur from 24 to 26 February and reviewed the progress in the implementation of directives its Akhil Bharatiya Karyakari Mandal (National Executive) had issued when it met at Chitrakoot in October 2005. The BJP had come in for a drubbing then. The RSS now made a clever move 'to boost the importance of other organisations in its fold such as the VHP, the Bharatiya Mazdoor Sangh (BMS) and the Swadeshi Jagran Manch (SJM)'.[18] The VHP's vote bank need not be the same as the vote bank of the BJP. It now ceased to be *primus inter pares*, the first among equals. If Advani thought that he could revive the personality cult that he had promoted around his name, he was swiftly disillusioned.

In these internal wranglings Muslims were not neglected. Sudarshan asked them to regard Krishna as one of their gods, a demand none outside the RSS had ever made before.[19] The BJP began to rewrite its own history as well, as Sanjay Basak reported in detail.

> The 'Party Document' detailing the birth of the Bharatiya Jan Sangh between 1952 and 1980 claims that 'atrocities' committed by Muslims against Hindus were responsible for the rise of the RSS.
>
> The sixth volume of the document, authored by saffron historian Makhan Lal and senior BJP leader J.P. Mathur, quoted ideologue Deen Dayal Upadhyaya describing the Muslims as 'goondas, ruffians, thugs and hoodlums'. It also spoke of the 'advent of Gandhi and Muslim appeasement'. With the RSS now embarrassed by its 'negative documentation', the BJP has withdrawn copies of the volume from all its book stores and will re-launch it after 'necessary corrections'.
>
> Copies of the controversial chapter being sent for 'necessary correction' are in the possession of this newspaper. The foreword, written by the then BJP chief, L.K. Advani, states, 'As a major political party, the BJP is accountable to the people, to students and scholars, and to history for providing an official account of the evolution of the party. The footprints of the evolution of the party may be seen in these documents.' . . .

[17] *The Asian Age*, 11 March 2006.

[18] Venkitesh Ramakrishnan, *The Hindu*, 4 April 2006.

[19] *The Asian Age*, 12 April 2006.

The controversial volume begins with an attack on the 'elite and educated class of Muslims', who, according to the authors, 'do not think that they have anything to do with the Vedas, the Upanishads, the Ramayana, the Mahabharata, Kalidasa, Panini and so on'. . . .

Then follows Deen Dayal Upadhyaya's statement:

'Muslim goondas (ruffians, thugs, hoodlums) may at a single stroke besmirch the honour and the reputation of the highest citizens. This is so because even though they stand high, the samaj to which they happen to belong is weak and degenerate, devoid of power and steeped in selfishness. . . . Do you believe samaj will stand by you in case of an emergency? No, it will not, and for the simple reason that it is disorganised. . . . Our sisters and daughters are carried away by Muslims, they are victims of assault by British soldiers in broad daylight, and we, who are never tired of boasting of our honour and our exalted position in society, are obliged to look on in utter helplessness.' The chapter adds that the 'same was the reason for such leaders as Rajendra Singh, alias Rajju Bhaiya, A.B. Vajpayee, L.K. Advani, J.P. Mathur and scores of others joining the RSS'. It then claims that it was due to the communal riots, particularly the 1923 Nagpur riots, that Dr. K. Baliram Hedgewar founded the Rashtriya Swayamsevak Sangh on the 'day of Dashara, which signifies the victory of righteousness over evil, i.e. the victory of Rama over Ravana.'[20] . . .

Rajnath Singh was re-elected president of the BJP for three years on 26 November 2006. There were few rounds of applause during his inaugural address to the party's National Council on 23 December 2006; though not for want of demagogy on his part. 'Give us a clear majority and 10 years' time – five years will not do – and I promise that the BJP will put an end to the politics of Muslim appeasement that is ruining the nation.'[21]

In 1997 the BJP had obligingly amended its constitution to call for the appointment of only a 'full-time worker' as a general secretary in charge of the organisation. In the RSS-BJP terminology a 'full-time worker' or a 'whole-timer' is a 'pracharak' of the Sangh who is delegated to the BJP or another such organisation and devotes himself totally to the propagation and spread of the Sangh ideology and organisation.

The amendment significantly maintains that the appointment of a full-time general secretary (organisation) be made in the party organisation starting from the district to the state and the national levels. It paved the way for the revival of the post of the organising secretary at the national level which was there in the Jana Sangh, an earlier avatar of the BJP. Only a full-time worker will be appointed

[20] *The Asian Age*, 16 May 2006.

[21] *The Asian Age*, 24 December 2006.

as general secretary (organisation) at the national, state and district level.

Neena Vyas reported:

> The BJP national council amended the party constitution to give more powers to the president and clear the way for the induction of Rashtriya Swayamsevak Sangh 'pracharaks' (propagandists) in positions that would give them control of the party machine. The key positions of secretaries at the national, State and district levels would be given only to whole-time party workers (euphemism for RSS 'pracharaks') who would not contest any elective post or have any political ambition.
>
> One of their functions would be to ensure 'harmony' and 'cooperation' with the various frontal organisations of the RSS such as the Vishwa Hindu Parishad and the Bajrang Dal.[22]

The Vajpayee-Advani era which began with the expulsion of their rival, Balraj Madhok, and Nana Deshmukh's political sanyas around 1980, was now over. In 2014 emerged another figure, Narendra Modi, who promoted *his* personality cult. His impact on the RSS machine deserves careful study.

[22] *The Hindu*, 23 December 2006.

20. RSS Selects India's Prime Minister

On 20 October 2013, *The Indian Express* carried this interesting report from Mumbai:

> RSS Chief Mohan Bhagwat has said: the Sangh Parivar has not yet decided on a PM candidate. Bhagwat was in Mumbai to attend a Conclave on nation building through social sectors. Last week, BJP national president L.K. Advani had met Bhagwat in Nagpur. Advani said he was holding discussions with the top RSS leadership on his proposed rath yatra against corruption.

Neither was being truthful. Bhagwat and the RSS had already selected Modi for the job. Advani was not seeking Nagpur's approval for his favourite ploy, the yatra; but to canvas support for his candidature to the office of prime minister. What escaped notice was the RSS's arrogation publicly of a right to select India's future prime minister from one of its own fold.

He would be one who had taken this oath on admission to the RSS:

> Before the All-Powerful God and my ancestors, I most solemnly take the oath, that I have become a member of the Rashtriya Swayamsevak Sangh in order to achieve all-round greatness of Bharatvarsh by *fostering the growth of my sacred Hindu religion*, Hindu society and Hindu culture. I shall work for the Sangh honestly, disinterestedly, with my heart and soul, and I shall adhere to this oath all my life.

This is in total contradiction to the oath he would take as prime minister of India. It would bind him to regard all equally – 'I will do right to all manner of people in accordance with the Constitution and the law without fear or favour, affection or ill-will'. The provisions of the Constitution will not permit him to foster the growth of Hindu religion as prime minister or for that matter as a minister.

There is a wider aspect. The Constitution of India establishes a secular and democratic polity. Fundamentally, as the RSS chief Sudarshan repeatedly said, the RSS is for scrapping this Constitution which it says is imbued with Western values. Not only these two oaths but the entire Constitution and the values it represents clash with the RSS's ideology and the values it fosters. Yet it is this fascist body which functions in secret and on the leader principle which will select a person who will preside over India's democratic and secular polity.

Tightening its control over the BJP was not such a difficult problem for the

RSS. Its assets were many. With Vajpayee and Advani out, there was none to seek accommodation for his 'political judgment'; i.e. tactical compulsions. The path was not a smooth one, though. The RSS had not reckoned with the ferocity of Advani's ambition, his talent for intrigue and his capacity to struggle doggedly, shamelessly to return to his former pre-eminence. He fought hard from 2006 till 2014 when Narendra Modi was confirmed in the post of prime minister. As Adlai Stevenson said of Estes Kefauver, 'There is such a thing as wanting to be President of the United States too badly.'

Nor did Modi have an easy ride. Rajnath Singh, who had taken over from Advani, was formally elected for a full three-year term as BJP president, with Vajpayee's support, on 26 November 2006.

Two months later, he dropped Modi from the parliamentary board on 29 January 2007. Sanjay Joshi was replaced by an RSS pracharak Ram Lal. He had been inducted into the BJP in October 2006. This was perceived as a blow to his supporter Advani.

Nearer the Lok Sabha elections 'a senior Sangh Parivar leader' said, 'Our aim is to develop a Hindu vote bank by the 2019 Lok Sabha elections. No political party will be able to ignore the Hindus' concerns if it wants to do well in the elections.'[1] It was Golwalkar's year-long birth centenary celebrations. Invites were sent to all the parties for a massive show of saffron strength. None outside the Parivar came.

Political equations change with the change of fortunes at the polls. The RSS came under strong criticism after the BJP's debacle in the Uttar Pradesh elections. A senior leader squarely blamed the RSS: 'You can say that the Sangh was in charge of everything from election management to media affairs. They have to share some responsibility.' The Sangh interfered in distribution of BJP's tickets as well. 'The BJP suffered in a number of constituencies . . . because the RSS insisted on their favourites being fielded, the sources said.'[2] The 'cultural body' is not invincible despite its long-held position as a monitor of the Hindutva class. M.M. Joshi, for example, rushed to Nagpur to explain 'differences' among the BJP leaders; none of whom, apparently, thought much of him. Rajnath Singh was then in New Delhi for talks between the RSS and the BJP's 'organisational leaders'. Joshi bitterly complained, 'The party has turned into a divided house, which is getting divided everyday.'[3] A 'cultural' body is uniquely qualified to inject culture in a political party.

It was a messy situation to which Rajnath Singh made his own contribution. He said that 'the Sangh was influencing crucial appointments in the party'. RSS had played a role in the ouster of Gujarat Chief Minister Narendra Modi from the central parliamentary board as well as the removal of Arun Jaitley as chief spokesperson as part of the reshuffle he effected earlier that year.

[1] *The Hindu*, 19 February 2007.

[2] Poornima Joshi, *The Hindu*, 19 May 2007.

[3] *The Statesman*, 30 June 2007.

Responding to a question about his controversial move against Modi and Jaitley, the BJP chief made light of the issue and said that he had taken the concurrence of the Sangh leadership. 'The media made too much of it. These were routine changes. Okay, the RSS was consulted. In Modi's case, it was 70% RSS and 30% my decision. In Jaitley's case, the responsibility was 50:50.'

The Sangh leadership was not amused by the statement which could be a weapon in its critics' hands. Approached by *The Times of India*, an RSS leader Ram Madhav said, 'He has to clarify what he means by 70% and 30%. Decisions are taken by the party. You can consult anyone including the RSS, that's a normal practice, but on what basis do you say that the decisions were taken by the Sangh . . . of course there is a possibility that he (Singh) may have been misquoted'[4] – the last refuge of a politician.

Gujarat was also set for elections. Modi's battle cry was that it was the 'number one State in Asia'. Vidya Subramaniam, who interviewed him, reported:

> Yet the Chief Minister was to turn hostile on the question of Muslims. Asked where Muslims figured in his vision of Gujarat, he flared up. 'I don't like this thinking. I work for five-and-a-half crore Gujaratis. For me, anyone who lives here is a Gujarati, and I will not allow politics to come into this.'
>
> If only this were true.
>
> In Vadodara, Professor Ganesh Devi, a literary critic, activist and director of the Tribal Academy at Tejgadh, took me on a tour of Tandalja and Vasna Road, two parallel streets only six metres apart. The first was a mostly Muslim area, the second housed Hindus. The contrast wrenched the heart. Mounds of rotting garbage, dark, damp, crowded homes, and desolate young men standing in groups made the Muslim part instantly recognisable. The brightness of Vasna Road equally identified it as a Hindu area. The divide is as much physical as mental – and as much in Vadodara as in other Gujarat cities. It is a symbol of complete, absolute Muslim isolation in a State that Mr. Modi claims is 'number one in Asia'.
>
> It is perhaps a consolation that unhygienic and wretched as their living conditions are, those Muslims at least live in their own homes. There are many who don't. In October 2006, the National Commission for Minorities reported that over 5,000 displaced Muslim families live in 'sub-human conditions' in 46 makeshift colonies spread across the riot-affected districts of Gujarat. The NCM team, which visited 17 camps, accused the Gujarat Government of refusing to fulfil 'its constitutional responsibility'.[5]

[4] *The Times of India*, 31 July 2007.

[5] *The Hindu*, 9 October 2007.

Modi asked minority leaders of the BJP not to take part in campaigning in the state, which the party has described as a 'Hindutva laboratory'.

A senior minority leader of the party said,

> 'We have been barred from entering Gujarat till the polls,' recalling how minority leaders were kept aside in the Uttar Pradesh Assembly elections a few months ago. If BJP insiders are to be believed the fight is not against the Congress. It is 'BJP versus BJP. Modi is an asset as well as a liability'.[6]

But Modi had an impact at the national level in the BJP. Rajnath Singh could declare, as he did on 27 January 2008, that Vajpayee had passed on the baton to Advani. But Vajpayee was absent from the conclave of the top BJP leaders and did not send a message either. Modi 'was the star attraction winning accolades on his victory in the recent Assembly elections'.[7] Not one to miss an opportunity for self-projection, Advani presented himself as the natural choice for prime minister while describing Modi as a 'truly secular leader'. The theme of the conclave was 'Good Governance, Development'. But as Varghese K. George noted it 'had substantial component of conventional Hindutva repackaged in contemporary idioms'.[8]

Shortly thereafter Advani anointed Modi as his likely successor in the BJP. He had proved his mettle much better than his peers. A correspondent Hemendra Singh Bartwal, perceptively noted:

> There is already a sense of unease in a section of the party's central leadership over Modi's enhanced stature and his soaring popularity with the party cadres after the BJP's resounding victory in the Gujarat assembly elections under his charge. The victory had sparked speculation that he may even pose a threat to Advani's claim as the NDA's prime ministerial candidate. This was, however, quickly quashed with the official announcement shortly thereafter that Advani would lead the alliance in the next parliamentary election as its prime ministerial candidate.
>
> That Modi had been accepted in the party as an important leader whose stature and clout extended much beyond Gujarat became evident when he was invited to participate in a meeting of the BJP's core strategy group at Advani's residence soon after the party victories in Gujarat and Himachal Pradesh. He was the only BJP chief minister asked to the distinguished gathering of top party leaders headed by Advani and Rajnath Singh.
>
> Subsequently, at the BJP national executive meet in Delhi lavish praise was showered on Modi by Advani and other senior leaders for the developmental

6 *The Asian Age*, 1 December 2007.

7 *Hindustan Times*, 28 January 2008.

8 *The Indian Express*, 30 January 2008.

> achievements and administrative acumen. This ruffled the feathers of other chief ministers like Rajasthan's Vasundhara Raje, Shivraj Singh Chouhan of MP and Raman Singh of Chhattisgarh.[9]

This was six years before Modi pipped Advani to the post.

Advani kept hammering at his pet theme oblivious of the fact that the ground was slipping away beneath his feet. In an interview to N. Ram, editor of *The Hindu*, he said:

> In independent India, we want India to be a secular country in which all citizens are equal. Hindutva should be equated to Bharatiyata. Bharatiya is a Hindu. Indianness and Hindutva are synonymous. Don't make a distinction between the two. It should mean nationalism essentially. Therefore it is that I grew up with cultural nationalism.[10]

Votes melt hearts. Advani went back on his earlier assertion on primacy of Hindu interests when he wooed a gathering of Muslim women in New Delhi on 13 July 2008. He said he always disapproved of the slogan raised by his partymen during his famous 'Rath Yatra', when they used to say, '"*Wahi desh par raj karega, jo Hindu heet ki baat karega* (Only those who talk in favour of Hindus will rule the country)." I always suggested that they say, "*Wahi desh par raj karega, jo rashtra heet ki baat karega* (Only those who talk of national interest will rule the country)", and I feel this holds true even today,' he added.

Asserting that neither he nor his party have anything against the minority of the country, Advani said, 'Irrespective of what percentage of Muslims vote for the BJP and NDA, our government, if voted into office by the people of India, will work for the welfare, development and security of Muslims.'[11] The RSS quietly returned to Sudarshan's demand for an age barrier to high posts – 54 to 60 years and no more.

But Advani's overtures to Muslims annoyed the hardliners especially Indresh Kumar, an Akhil Bharatiya Prachar Pramukh of the RSS who manages also the Muslim Rashtriya Manch, an RSS outfit. This is not unusual. On 4 October 1998, Prime Minister Vajpayee addressed a convention of Muslim women and assured them that the BJP sought friendship with Pakistan.[12]

There was also a calculated effort at acquiring respectability as a party with a modern outlook. Security experts were enlisted at a brainstorming session on 24 January 2009 to 'formulate the policy of a future BJP-led Government'. The

9 *Hindustan Times*, 21 March 2008.

10 *The Hindu*, 12 July 2008.

11 *The Asian Age*, 14 July 2008.

12 *The Statesman*, 5 October 1998. Vide also Noorani, *The Muslims of India*, p. 279.

one that came to power in 2014 under Narendra Modi had little use for any but the ones recommended by Ajit Doval, his National Security Adviser. In 2009 the ensemble was impressive. The party president Rajnath Singh, General Secretary Arun Jaitley and the former union minister, Arun Shourie, were present. Among the experts were retired armed services officers including Air Chief Marshal A.Y. Tipnis, Admiral Arun Prakash and Lt. Generals R.K. Sawhney and N.S. Malik. The former Intelligence Bureau directors, Ajit Doval and K.P. Singh; the former defence secretary, Yogendra Narain; the former home secretary, Anil Baijal; and the former Director-General of Police, Punjab, K.P.S. Gill, were part of the team. A few journalists were also present. . . .

Arun Jaitley said 'some' of the retired officers and bureaucrats might well join the BJP before the Lok Sabha election and some might even contest. However, not all of them were supportive of the BJP, nor all corporate heads who had interacted with Advani earlier were BJP admirers or supporters. It was, nonetheless, an impressive show.[13]

This modernism went hand in hand with revivalism which masqueraded as part of a global movement. That the RSS aspires to make India, under its teaching, of course, as a *jagadguru* or *vishwaguru* (mentor of the world) is an aspect neglected by students of the RSS. Towards the end of 2008 Mohan Bhagwat declared:

> We are creating a world order in such a way that all nations can benefit from it and every nation becomes fit to contribute for good of the humanity. This view itself is our national view and that is why though we profess to organise Hindus we have termed our organisation Rashtriya Swayamsevak Sangh because it is our nationality. The term Hindu does not apply to any religion or particular people living in particular land. The term applies to this ancient glorious tradition, to this world-view. This will become a panacea for the whole world in modern times.[14]

He knew he was close to the top post in the RSS.

Advani's venture to re-brand himself as a moderate obsessed him. At the concluding session of the BJP conclave on 29 January 2009, he 'acknowledged that the BJP needed to work hard to re-brand as it is not like the rest of parties' – an image it acquired in office between 1998 and 2004.

'The best way of creating a nation-wide urge for a BJP-led NDA government is to effectively tell the people how we are going to be different from the Congress and the UPA,' Advani said. He wanted the BJP to send out a strong message that the days of weak leadership are over. Advani concluded: 'Can the NDA win a clear majority?

[13] *The Hindu*, 25 January 2009.

[14] *Organiser*, 11 January 2009.

My answer is yes. We can.'[15] The voter disagreed, destroying his ambitions.

Shifting gears was not easy for him for two reasons; his own outlook and the RSS's 'umbilical cord'. A week later he was compelled to assure a meeting at Nagpur, 'We never left Ram.' His quaint notions of secularism are understandable. He said that

> it was during the partition that he had asked the then RSS chief, M.S. Golwalkar, what secularism meant. 'It was from Guruji [Golwalkar] that I learnt about secularism when I talked to him soon after the assassination of Mahatma Gandhi,' Advani admitted. He added that he had told him India was a Hindu majority state, therefore, a Hindu state.

Modi followed him with a speech full of vitriol.[16]

The RSS's revivalism is not aimed at Muslims and Christians alone. It rejects modernism and modern thought as well as Sudarshan made clear in a speech in Pune on 15 February 2009. He advocated

> an educational system which is free from the English and makes the generation proud of its heritage. Bharat was a rich and prosperous country. Britishers brought Macaulay's educational system, as a well-planned strategy to rule India. Even after 60 years of Independence, parents still force their children to study in 'convent' schools. But children lose their much valuable time to understand the language, as English is very difficult and sometimes confusing in terms of grammar, pronunciation and spelling. Developed countries like China, Japan, France and Russia never used English as development tool! But Government Officers in our country fear of getting distracted if English is removed from the system.[17]

The election campaign had begun. The BJP launched its campaign from Gorakhpur in Uttar Pradesh on 15 February 2009 fielding Advani who promised, once again, to build a Ram temple at Ayodhya. 'It was the mandir issue that finally took the BJP to power at the Centre and in several States, and changed the course of Indian politics'[18] – and poisoned the atmosphere in the country, he might have added.

At the RSS's All India Pratinidhi Sabha it was announced that Mohan Bhagwat (59) would succeed Sudarshan (78) as the RSS's sarsanghchalak on 21 March 2009. He is a veterinary doctor by education. His father was a pracharak. Immediately

15 *Hindustan Times*, 30 January 2009.

16 *The Hindu*, 9 February 2009.

17 *Organiser*, 1 March 2009.

18 Ibid.

after his anointment he announced 'India as a Hindu Rashtra and all people living here are Hindu'.[19]

He spoke less than Sudarshan but proved to be far more authoritarian. Advani had trained in the RSS under his father Madhukar Rao Bhagwat. He had, like Advani, nursed a desire to change the image while leaving the core intact. Suresh Joshi, not Suresh Soni, succeeded him as sarkaryavah. General Secretary Bhagwat sent a message to cadres – '100 per cent voting in the interest of Hindus' – the RSS's 'vote bank'.

Advani rushed to Nagpur by a chartered plane the very next day, on 22 March. After discussion with Bhagwat he addressed the Pratinidhi Sabha and urged members to work actively for the BJP in the Lok Sabha elections. He had begun life as a swayamsevak and without their support it would be difficult for him to become prime minister of India. The BJP president Rajnath Singh had preceded him in the journey to Nagpur.

The BJP's defeat in the 2009 election to the Lok Sabha strengthened the RSS's hands. It had deferred to Vajpayee and Advani because they had a mass following. On 1 June Advani went to the RSS's Delhi headquarters at Keshav Kunj to meet Bhagwat.

For once, disagreements with the RSS proved easier to resolve than the dissidence within the party. Arun Jaitley was made leader of the opposition in the Rajya Sabha and Sushma Swaraj, Advani's deputy in the Lok Sabha. Jaswant Singh sought a debate once he failed to secure any post. There must be 'some correlation between *inam* (reward) and *parinam* (result)'. Two successive defeats, in 2004 and 2009, and no accountability for them? he asked. Advani was in the dock now; so was Arun Jaitley. The RSS watched with amusement. M.G. Vaidya had his own line to pursue. He blamed Advani for not enthusing the Hindus.[20] The RSS has no use for moderation, even one in Advani's style. Finally, Bhagwat publicly cracked the whip in a press conference and asked the BJP leaders to stop the infighting.[21]

Not one to accept defeat, Advani tried to turn the tables on his critics by claiming that Bhagwat had asked him to oversee the transition process to the younger generation. He declined to comment on his own plan.[22]

Bhagwat gave an interesting interview to *The Times of India* and the TV channel Times Now. The RSS had reached out to over 25,000 out of the 60,000 revenue circles. The rest would be covered in 'the next four to five years'. He added: 'We have been saying to Advaniji since 2003 that you have sufficient young workers, bring them slowly forward.' Transition is at all levels. There is an average age group at every level and that average age group must be maintained.

[19] *The Asian Age*, 22 March 2009.

[20] *The Indian Express*, 11 June 2009.

[21] *The Times of India*, 28 August 2009, and *The Telegraph*, 28 August 2009.

[22] *The Indian Express*, 3 September 2009.

I am not in politics. But, I would say that at my level we say 55-60 not more should be the average age group. I believe that BJP has received a nasty jolt in the elections and so it was a bit destabilised. So, they lost their balance. They have to regain that. Whatever has happened was not very good not only I am saying it. All the leaders in BJP feel bad about it and they have to gain back their balance quickly and they have to think about it and make amends about it. How did it happen? What was the mistake? They should give thought to this in their 'Chintan Baithak'. . . .

We have been asking our swayamsevaks in the BJP for five things. You should be reasonably sound and articulate about the ideology; you should have a collective work pattern, team work; you should have dialogue with all well-wishers and many swayamsevaks who are with the BJP and are working for them; fourth, they should be a party with difference; and fifth, they should bring in the young generation.[23]

Jaswant Singh paid for his labours. The Chintan Baithak at Shimla was confused about the existence of a report entitled 'Analysis of Election Results' by a three-member committee headed by Bal Apte. On 19 August the parliamentary board decided to expel Jaswant Singh for his book on Jinnah – *Jinnah: India, Partition, Independence*. It was in fact a shoddy work, a vicious attack on Nehru, rather than one in praise of Jinnah; replete, like his earlier book, with grave factual errors and shameless plagiarising. Prof. C.M. Naim of Chicago University exposed both mercilessly. It was a lapse, not an offence which warranted expulsion from the party. In 2005 he had defended Advani for his praise of Jinnah. Advani was privy to his expulsion, revealing the flawed character of a weak but ambitious man. Modi was also for the expulsion.

As always the BJP's leaders make a beeline for the RSS's headquarters; Nagpur, for a grave crisis, to Jhandewalan in New Delhi for lesser ones. Arun Jaitley, Sushma Swaraj, Venkaiah Naidu and Ananth Kumar rushed to meet Bhagwat in New Delhi on 27 August and to Advani's residence thereafter. 'Party leaders here are of the view that the resignation of Advani as leader of the opposition cannot be postponed for too long.' He had dishonestly shifted the blame for the Kandahar episode.[24]

The RSS itself was growing apace, however, as Radhika Ramaseshan reported:

As BJP leaders vie with each other for a shrinking political space, the Bharatiya Mazdoor Sangh (BMS), the Akhil Bharatiya Vidyarthi Parishad (ABVP), the Bharatiya Kisan Sangh (BKS) and the Vanavasi Kalyan Ashram are bursting with good health. They have some way to go yet before they can match the

[23] *The Times of India*, 19 August 2009.

[24] Neena Vyas, *The Hindu*, 28 August 2009.

BJP's numbers, but the day that happens, the BJP would lose its rank in the parivar, a Sangh source warned.

The BMS, India's largest trade union, has over one crore members – about half the BJP's 2.14 crore. According to the last official count by the labour ministry in 2002, the BMS had 62.2 lakh members while the Congress affiliated Indian National Trade Union Congress (INTUC) had 38 lakh and the CPI's AITUC, 33 lakh.

Both the BMS and INTUC now claim they have a crore each. But when quizzed hard on what accounted for the leap, INTUC president and Rajya Sabha member G. Sanjeeva Reddy became cautious and said: 'A Congress government at the Centre has certainly helped us make us inroads into the organised and unorganised sectors.'[25]

How Sangh outfits' memberships are rising

Organisation	*Year*	*Membership*
Bharatiya Mazdoor Sangh	1989	31.1 lakh
	2002	62.2 lakh
	2009	1 crore
Bharatiya Kisan Sangh	2008	8 lakh
	2009	9 lakh
Rashtriya Seva Bharati	1997	16,063
	2004	43,386
	(till 31 March) 2009	157,776
Akhil Bharatiya Vidyarthi Parishad	2008	15.8 lakh
	2009	19 lakh
Vanavasi Kalyan Ashram (seva projects)	2007-08	13,065
	2008-09	14,441

Note: Earlier BMS figures from labour ministry, latest from BMS. Rest from RSS annual report.

By now Bhagwat had had enough of Advani. He said on 14 November, 'A divided house cannot function properly . . . I have suggested to the party leadership to look for a young candidate who can restore its organisational set-up.'[26]

The entire Sangh Parivar was nettled by the exposure of what came to be called 'Hindu Terrorism'. Sadhvi Pragya's arrests, the Malegaon blasts and the like deserve a book by itself. The crimes did not cease as Gauri Lankesh's murder on 5 September 2017 revealed. The Supreme Court has suggested that a single agency, the CBI,

[25] *The Telegraph*, 19 October 2009.

[26] *The Indian Express*, 2 November 2009.

should probe all the murders, namely Narendra Dabholkar's on 20 August 2013, Govind Pansare's on 16 February 2015, M.M. Kalburgi's on 30 August 2015 and Gauri Lankesh's on 5 September 2017, respectively at Pune, Kolhapur, Dharwad and Bengaluru.[27] This is significant.

Rajnath Singh's three-year term as BJP president ended in October 2009. Nitin Gadkari replaced him on 19 November, a day after Advani stepped down as leader of the opposition in the Lok Sabha in favour of Sushma Swaraj. A special post of Chairman of the BJP Parliamentary Party was created for him by amending the constitution. At 52, Gadkari fulfilled Bhagwat's stipulated dates – between 55 and 65 years. Advani made it plain that he was not about to retire. He would continue to do a political 'rath yatra' till the end of his life.[28] Memories of the heady days of 1990 never ceased to possess him.

He was grooming Narendra Modi as his successor. Asked: 'Didn't the RSS force you to accept Nitin Gadkari as party chief?' He replied: 'That is not so. When we discussed the issue, I told the Sangh that Modi (Gujarat Chief Minister) is the best choice since he can revitalise the morale of the party, which was down after the elections. The Sangh agreed with me and I talked to him. But he was not inclined to leave the state and come here now. Then, we decided that Nitin is the best choice.'[29] Gadkari was a stop gap. But Modi was expected to *succeed* Advani; not *oust* him, as he did in 2013 to Advani's dismay.

How far could the BJP distance itself from the RSS's worldview? On Pakistan, for instance? Speaking on India's partition on 15 December Bhagwat unfolded his views with chilling clarity. He traced the partition to India's break with Hindutva (Hindu-ness), the 'central link' that made India indivisible. He added that Partition was transitory and India would re-unite to become Akhand Bharat (undivided India).

The RSS's conception of Akhand Bharat includes Afghanistan, Pakistan, Tibet, Bhutan, Nepal, Bangladesh, Myanmar and Sri Lanka. 'Partition is not a settled fact. We will cancel it, as this will be in everyone's interest, including Pakistan's,' he said. 'Rivers of blood have flown in Afghanistan, once Gandhara. Look at the state of Pakistan, Bangladesh, Tibet, Myanmar and Sri Lanka. What happiness have they experienced after separation from Akhand Bharat?'

Bhagwat's reason for the 'separation': a break with Hindutva. '*Hindu bhaav ko jab jab bhoole, aayee vipada mahaan* (great calamity has struck whenever the Hindu sentiment has been forgotten),' he said. 'We have never lost. Even invasion that began from Arabia and went up to Spain, expelling Parsis from Iran, could not destroy our nationalism, Hindutva,' he said, in an oblique reference to 'Islamic' invasions, a central theme in the RSS's idea of history.

[27] *The Hindu*, 27 December 2017.

[28] *The Hindu*, 18 December 2009.

[29] Shekhar Iyer, *Hindustan Times*, 20 October 2009.

Bhagwat added that Partition took place because India forgot its soul, Hindutva. 'The more important question is what was responsible for Partition, rather than the much-discussed "who",' he said.

He said Hindutva was the link that united India despite Panthic (religious community) differences: 'There are no minorities in India, all are Bharat Mata's sons, as they come from Hindu ancestors. Hindutva teaches that all can live together. Politicians are dividing the country on the minority card for political purposes.'[30]

The trend was visible to all. The RSS was on the rise and so was Modi; though not altogether with its backing. Each tried gimmicks of its own. In April 2011 Bhagwat and 'Bhaiyya' Joshi the joint general secretary firmed up the basis of support for 'Baba' Ramdev's Bhrashtachar Mitao (Remove Corruption) Satyagraha. 'RSS sources said their support for Ramdev carried an unstated understanding. It was agreed that Ramdev would support BJP candidates in the northern states and have an understanding in case he floated his own party.'[31]

There is no evidence of any understanding as such with Anna Hazare. However, on 6 October 2011, Mohan Bhagwat, the RSS chief 'revealed that RSS actively participated in the Anna Hazare-led anti-corruption movement', reported Pradip Kumar Maitra from Nagpur.[32]

Gadkari was elected BJP president in 2010. The RSS sought a second term for him. But the top leaders of the BJP, opposed to Gadkari, relented on the ouster of Sanjay Joshi from the National Executive to secure Modi's support. Joshi had to quit as general secretary in 2005 after some CDs, allegedly portraying him in an 'embarrassing situation', surfaced at the Mumbai session. So powerful was Modi's clout that he went off to Udaipur rather than attend the meeting of the National Executive in Mumbai. He had skipped its meeting in September after Joshi's return to the party.

Thus already by May 2012 Modi had acquired a powerful standing within the BJP and, to some extent, vis-à-vis the RSS. The feat was accomplished gradually as this chronology demonstrates:

In March 2002, the then prime minister Atal Bihari Vajpayee stated that Gujarat Chief Minister Narendra Modi had not followed 'Rajdharma'. Instances of Modi's 'Rajhatta' (royal obstinacy) are, however, plenty since then.

November 2002: Modi gets Keshubhai Patel evicted from the election committee. Gets himself admitted to a hospital complaining of chest pain to ward off pressure to give Haren Pandya a ticket to contest the Assembly polls.

June 2003: When the RSS-affiliated Bharatiya Kisan Sangh took to the streets over the farmers' issues, he got BKS office operating from a government bungalow vacated and threw their belongings out on the street.

[30] Vikas Pathak, *Hindustan Times*, 12 December 2009.

[31] Radhika Ramaseshan, *The Telegraph*, 3 June 2011.

[32] *Hindustan Times*, 7 October 2011.

June 2005: When the VHP protested, Modi got the police to raid VHP offices and arrested leaders and workers.

December 2007: Modi tells central leaders to stay away from Gujarat Assembly poll campaign. Selects all the candidates himself, instead of allowing the BJP parliamentary committee to have the last say.

August 2011: Fights with Gadkari over the appointment of Sanjay Joshi as BJP's UP election in-charge. Refuses to allow L.K. Advani to take out a rath yatra in Gujarat against corruption and black money.

September 2011: Boycotts BJP National Executive meeting over Joshi.

January-February 2012: Refuses to campaign for BJP in the Assembly elections in UP, Punjab, Uttarakhand and Goa.[33] In June 2012 Sanjay Joshi resigned from the BJP.[34]

Modi had exacted his revenge. When he was banished from Gujarat by then chief minister Keshubhai Patel in 1998, it was Sanjay Joshi who succeeded him as the BJP's organisation secretary in Gujarat. Joshi took a firm grip on the party and kept Modi loyalists at bay. He opposed Modi's elevation as chief minister in October 2001 and became a rallying point for anti-Modi activities, especially after the 2002 Gujarat riots. Joshi's closest aide and ex-minister Haren Pandya was gunned down in March 2003. The sleaze CD of 2005 that saw Joshi resigning from the party was later found to be manipulated. It had originated from Gujarat and was distributed by the state's crime branch officials in Mumbai.[35]

Advani, no less vengeful than Modi, attacked Gadkari in the National Executive. The RSS's organ *Kamal Sandesh* attacked Modi, very perceptively, for being a 'man in a hurry' reminding him that the 'party does not function on the basis of any individual's contribution alone'. Its editor, Prabhat Jha, a Rajya Sabha M.P., was close to the RSS. It was reported to be unhappy with Modi's 'individualistic' attitude.

The editorial also reminded the party leaders that they should not forget that the organisation has put them in the top position. It stated that some leaders of the party appeared to be in a hurry to occupy high posts and in the process even harming the party.

'Sometimes in crowded situation even traveller having urgency is compelled to stay back. He has to wait for another train. In his rush, he never pulls out any other traveller, nor he wrecks the track or stones the train.'[36]

Panchajanya was more direct. It mentioned Modi by name and his 'style of functioning'. Questioning Modi's prime ministerial ambition, the article stated that the party has 'several chief ministers and central leaders, who could be the PM candidate'.

[33] *The Times of India*, 24 May 2012.

[34] *The Indian Express*, 9 June 2012.

[35] *The Times of India*, 25 May 2012.

[36] *The Asian Age*, 2 June 2012.

'It is not unnatural for several workers of the BJP to have confidence and ambitions in their mind for the Prime Minister's post,' the article said. It, however, went on to state that since BJP's organisational structure is democratic, the present constitutional formation demands that after the election results are declared the parliamentary party of the victorious group chose its leader.[37]

This was obvious to journalists; strange that it escaped Advani's notice. He not only failed to stop Modi's rise but at crucial moments boosted him up. Advani did not acquire a supporter but a successful rival who had acquired an enviable mass base. He wooed Muslims to seek 'Sadbhavana Effect'. In the 2012 Assembly elections communal polarisation was complete. Muslims were marginalised. Even the Congress could not seek their support for fear of losing the majority vote.[38]

Nitish Kumar, head of Janata Dal (United), was opposed to Modi. But after the victory in 2015, in concert with Laloo Prasad Yadav's Rashtriya Janata Dal, he broke the coalition and preferred the BJP as partner.

At long last on 13 September 2013 the parliamentary board of a divided BJP named Gujarat's chief minister Narendra Modi as prime ministerial candidate for the alliance (the National Democratic Alliance [NDA]) for the general elections to the Lok Sabha in 2014. *The Indian Express* published a detailed report on 22 September 2013 on how the decision was arrived at.

> Sources, however, said that in meetings at the Royal Tiger Resort at the Tadoba-Andhari Tiger Reserve, five top leaders of the RSS had decided to support Narendra Modi as the BJP's prime ministerial candidate, and to ask Advani to play mentor.
>
> The five leaders – Bhagwat, Dattatraya Hosabale, Suresh Soni, Madan Das Devi and Bhaiyyaji Joshi – had gone on a visit around TATR on the morning of 16 September before continuing discussions in the afternoon, the sources said.
>
> It was only after this meeting that Soni was sent to meet the fasting Narendra Modi and extend the support of the Sangh for his Sadbhavana mission, . . .
>
> The RSS, the sources said, had all but made up its mind to throw its weight behind Modi as PM candidate. 'It is only logical that the Sangh, which had earlier taken the stand that top BJP leaders like Advani and Vajpayee should pave the way for younger leaders, and also led by example by appointing Mohan Bhagwat in place of the ageing K. Sudarshan, should ask Advani to play mentor,' said a source.
>
> The sources, however, underscored that while lending its support to

[37] *The Asian Age*, 3 June 2012.

[38] Vide Mohammed Wajihuddin's perceptive analysis in *The Times of India*, 21 December 2012.

> Modi, the Sangh would not like leaders like Gadkari, Sushma Swaraj or Arun Jaitley to play the 'second fiddle' to him. 'In fact, the RSS wants the party to be multipolar, or at least bipolar,' they said.
>
> According to these sources, Gadkari himself could be a potential PM candidate after entering the poll fray in 2014 from Nagpur with RSS backing. 'He has been preparing himself, and has visited some foreign countries to familiarise himself with international relations,' they said.
>
> Some in the RSS, however, support the one-man-one-post principle, and would prefer that Gadkari stays out of the race as long as he is party president. Sangh parivar sources in Delhi said the RSS brass was unhappy over the unnecessary debate over leadership that Advani's yatra announcement had triggered at a time when the BJP should be focused on cornering the UPA.
>
> At a meeting with Advani last week, Bhaiyyaji Joshi had conveyed to him the RSS position that he must 'de-link' his yatra from the leadership issue, these sources said. The RSS would support the yatra as a political campaign against corruption, but wanted no focus on the leadership question now.
>
> The decision had been reached earlier. The Parliamentary Board adopted it on 13 September. The RSS finally endorsed it two days later.

Advani voiced his 'dissent' and skipped the meeting. His protégé Sushma Swaraj was visibly upset. Jaitley, once an Advani favourite, now jumped on the Modi bandwagon. Rajnath Singh, who had taken over as BJP president from Gadkari, supported Modi. Advani withheld his precious 'consent' despite the pleadings of colleagues. He had burnt his bridges with the RSS. They had long ceased to be in good repair. It was not the BJP but the RSS which appointed the BJP's president as the well informed Sanjay Basak and Yojna Gusai reported:

> It was the RSS which had made it clear to BJP chief Rajnath Singh that Modi be anointed at the earliest.
>
> Despite hectic parleys, cajoling, persuasion by top leaders for the last few days, Advani refused to relent. In his letter to the BJP chief, Advani made it clear that he was 'unhappy' with the decision. 'This afternoon, when you had come to my residence to inform me about the parliamentary board meeting, I had said something about my anguish as also my disappointment over your style of functioning,' Advani did not even spare the BJP chief who, apparently under RSS pressure, decided to go ahead with the parliamentary board meeting. Modi, who flew down from Gujarat, entered the meeting, which started at 5.30 pm, slightly late. Singh moved the proposal naming Modi as the PM candidate and it was endorsed by all. The meeting was a mere formality.[39]

[39] *The Asian Age*, 14 September 2013.

It is to this state that the RSS ('cultural body') effectively reduced the BJP – its Political Department.

Advani's tantrums were as undignified as they were belated. He had built up Modi. He saw Modi's rise till he ceased to be a protégé. Only six months earlier Modi became an accepted figure at the BJP's headquarters in New Delhi where only a few years earlier he held a humble post.

> [On 31 March] BJP president Rajnath Singh . . . inducted Narendra Modi into the party's apex decision-making bodies, parliamentary board and central election committee, marking the gradual ascent of the Gujarat Chief Minister in the BJP.
>
> Singh also inducted Modi's key political confidant Amit Shah as well as Rajiv Pratap Rudy, Varun Gandhi and Muralidhar Rao as general secretaries, to handle organisational affairs, along with six old faces. While Gujarat leader Shah is facing charges of criminal conspiracy in the Sohrabuddin encounter case, Varun was only cleared recently in hate speech cases filed against him in 2009 (another case, of violence outside a district jail, is pending).
>
> Modi will now share stage at the centre with 11 previous members – Rajnath Singh, Atal Bihari Vajpayee, L.K. Advani, Murli Manohar Joshi, Venkaiah Naidu, Nitin Gadkari, Sushma Swaraj, Arun Jaitley, Ananth Kumar, Thawar Chand Gehlot and Ramlal – in steering the BJP's national affairs, including the choice of its prime ministerial candidate for the next elections.
>
> Indicating that the BJP is keeping options open on future role for Modi, a senior party office-bearer said: 'Things happen gradually.'[40]

So they did, in September. Three other Modi allies were inducted, namely Smriti Irani, Balbir Punj and C.P. Thakur.

What Advani failed to notice was that he had long ceased to be an RSS favourite. It kept silent as the Vajpayee-Advani duo played their own games since 1980.

The RSS was worried. It had decisively rejected Advani. But would Modi repeat in the country what he had performed in Gujarat? Taking no chances it began to consider placing around 2,000 of its hardcore cadres in the BJP at the various levels in the next turn – three years to mould the BJP in the desired image. 'A very senior leader' told Shyamlal Yadav of *The Indian Express*,

> 'Once our ideologically committed workers join the BJP, some of them will gradually reach the top levels in the next few years,' . . . adding that these cadres would behave 'differently'. The time frame the RSS is looking at is five-six years. . . .
>
> The RSS has also appointed coordinators in all 3,108 Assembly

[40] Ravish Tiwari, *The Indian Express*, 1 April 2013.

segments and 543 Lok Sabha segments in the country. On February 16, RSS sahsarkaryawah (co-general secretary) Suresh Soni held a nearly two-hour online conference from Delhi with all the state pracharaks.[41]

The RSS's Annual Report presented to the General Body by Bhaiyyaji Joshi, said 'The nation expects a change'. The Report did not name Modi. But Joshi said, 'Modi is a strong leader. He is a swayamsevak himself and we are proud of it.'[42] Leaders of the students' wing, the Akhil Bharatiya Vidyarthi Parishad, were involved in the election campaign. Their cadres reached out to people in every booth. The leaders were attached to the candidates. The VHP was tasked with mobilising sadhus as well.

By the middle of May 2014 it seemed that the BJP was all set to win the elections. The results declared on 16 May 2014 catapulted Modi to the highest executive position in India's government.

41 *The Indian Express*, 24 February 2014.

42 *Hindustan Times*, 18 March 2014.

21. RSS Raj Under Modi

Narendra Modi made it all too clear to friends and foes alike that he would be his own man. The RSS was equally clear, soon after the Lok Sabha polls, that it would not play second fiddle to him. On 17 July 2014, it made clear to the BJP leadership that it should not expect its help in the forthcoming Assembly elections in some states, including Maharashtra. The RSS stand was conveyed to Amit Shah, whom Modi got appointed as BJP's president a few days back. Shah was on his maiden visit to Nagpur after becoming party president to seek blessings from the RSS chief Mohan Bhagwat.

During his one-to-one meeting with Shah, the RSS chief explained to him that during Lok Sabha polls, where the party had recorded a landslide win, the situation was altogether different as the country was passing through a difficult phase and needed a stable government with a strong leadership. He advised Shah to strengthen the party and prepare its workers for the polls, instead of depending on the Sangh's help.[1] It wanted to keep the government and the BJP in check.

On 9 October, the BJP's National Council endorsed Shah's appointment as BJP president. He set the tone of his performance by declaring, 'Now the time has come to spread our ideology and to leave an imprint on the nation's politics.' When Modi declared that the aim was a 'Congress Mukt' India, an India freed of Congress, he had in mind the total erasure of Jawaharlal Nehru's legacy and a totalitarian rule without any opposition.

There soon began a systematic assault on the walls which protected the institutions' autonomy, separated the State from the government of the day, and the government from its party.

Bharat Bhushan, who had given a detailed account of the RSS's off-springs, reported:

> The Dharam Jagran Samiti, an RSS body, is seeking donations for conversions – Rs. 5 lakh to convert a Muslim and Rs. 1 lakh to convert a Christian – to Hinduism. Its letter soliciting cash contributions claims that Christians and Muslims have become a 'problem' for the country and says, 'Bandhuwar (Friends) lots of money will be required in the "ghar wapsi" because the work of conversion is increasing – more workers and more people need to be covered.' . . .
>
> Moreover, foreign funds for conversion are used just as Christian missionaries are said to do. The activities of the RSS in tribal areas have been

[1] *The Times of India*, 18 July 2014.

> funded by a US-based body, International Development Relief Fund (IDRF). According to the Campaign to Stop Funding Hate, also based in the US, 82 per cent of all IDRF funding goes to the RSS in India and 70 per cent of the monies are used for 'Hinduisation/tribal/education' work, aimed at spreading Hindutva ideology among tribals.
>
> The main focus of the RSS had been the reconversion of Christians. Its prominent organisations which work among the tribals are: Vanvasi Kalyan Ashram, Ekal Vidyalaya, Sewa Bharati, Vivekananda Kendra, Bharat Kalyan Parishad and Friends of Tribal Society. Vanvasi Kalyan Ashram, Ekal Vidyalaya and Sewa Bharati have been implicated in the past in anti-Christian violence in Madhya Pradesh. . . .
>
> It is part of the ideological expansion of Hindutva politics that we are witnessing in the banning of German from school curricula and making Sanskrit compulsory in some states and schools, providing a historical 'date' for the Mahabharat war and demanding that the Bhagavad Gita be declared a national scripture.
>
> The response to the RSS expansion has been tremendous, with everybody and his uncle trying to project some real or imaginary family connection to the RSS. Spearheading this expansion of Hindutva ideology are men who wear non-Vedic khaki short-pants, borrowing their militaristic ideology from the Brown Shirts [sic] of Mussolini, clearly a product of Kalyug.[2]

'Our time has come,' an RSS pracharak declaimed.[3] In Mumbai, on 14 December 2014, the Virat Hindu Sammelan heard some of the most vicious slogans in speeches brimming with hate.

> Stressing India's identity as a Hindu rashtra, calling for a law against conversions, construction of the Ram Temple at Ayodhya, culling 'gaddars' (traitors), scoffing at Mahatma Gandhi's leadership of the freedom movement, fears of Hindus being under threat, preventing cow slaughter and ensuring that the entire world was converted to Hinduism – these were some themes that found prominence in the Vishwa Hindu Parishad's (VHP) 'Virat Hindu' sammelan in Mumbai as Hindutva demagogues and religious leaders addressed the faithful.
>
> RSS sah-sarkaryavah (joint general secretary) Dattatreya Hosabale, VHP international working president Pravin Togadia and senior leader Ashok Singhal, Kanchi mutt pontiff Jayendra Saraswathi, Narendra Maharaj of Nanji and Buddhist and Jain religious leaders we present.[4]

[2] *The Asian Age*, 13 December 2014.

[3] *The Indian Express*, 15 December 2014.

[4] *Daily News and Analysis*, 15 December 2014.

Togadia's imagination took unprecedented flights. 'At a point of time, the entire world was Hindu. There were 700 crore Hindus, and now there are just 100 crore. Currently, there are 82 per cent Hindus in this country. If we don't create awareness and take steps now, in a few decades this number will drop to 46 per cent.'[5] Soon love jihad made its way to a charge sheet with familiar charges – cow slaughter, ghar wapsi (conversions to Hinduism), etc.

Strange voices were heard M.G. Vaidya, the RSS's ideologue, asked on 21 December 2014, 'Who were the Muslims in India? 99 per cent of them were Hindus. How they were converted history knows. We are only doing their "ghar wapsi".' He defended mass conversions of Muslims in Agra that had kicked up a hornet's nest across the country.[6]

As during the Vajpayee regime, history was singled out for attack. In March 2015 the Indian Council of Historical Research became the first of the learned institutions to be 'reconstituted' to suit the tastes of the saffron rulers.

The RSS believed that its hour had arrived. Mohan Bhagwat said on 9 February 2015 that this was a 'favourable time'. He asserted that 'the idea of Hinduism is the only idea in the world which brings all together. . . . Hindustan is a Hindu rashtra, which is a fact. We are going ahead with this (idea). All Hindus have to be organised to make this nation great. When our country will become great that will benefit the entire world'.[7] He was being modest; for the usual refrain was that a 'Hindu India' would be a Vishwaguru or a Jagadguru (world teacher). The world expected the RSS to lead. 'The job of the organisation is to unite Hindus and this cannot be done through speeches alone. The time has come when the whole society wants the RSS, and has expectations from us. The organisation must grow in order to fulfil these expectations. We have to unite Hindu society, make it fearless, self-reliant and selfless.'

Talking about its shakhas, the RSS chief asked: 'What is the meaning of the RSS shakha? We come together and forget everything else. It is only the "bhagwa" (saffron) flag that remains in focus and becomes a symbol of pride.'[8]

The RSS was not too happy with Modi's behaviour and said as much to the BJP president Amit Shah when he met Bhagwat in Nagpur on 6 March on the eve of the Akhil Bharatiya Pratinidhi Sabha's meeting on 13 March. The RSS's main grouse was the 'autocratic' style of functioning of Prime Minister Narendra Modi.[9]

It was a tense equation. The RSS was never happy with a BJP man who projected the image of a 'strong leader'. Its distaste for the personality cult, practised outside

[5] *The Indian Express*, 15 December 2014.

[6] *The Asian Age*, 22 October 2014.

[7] *The Asian Age*, 10 February 2015.

[8] *The Asian Age*, 16 February 2015.

[9] Pradip Kumar Maitra, *Hindustan Times*, 7 March 2015.

the RSS, is well known. Modi knew that he owed his job to the RSS. He shared not only its ideology but also its worldview. Neither can do without the other.

The Akhil Bharatiya Pratinidhi Sabha (ABPS) retained Bhaiyyaji Joshi. Contrary to speculation, Dattatreya Hosabale, perceived to be close to Modi, did not replace him even though he dispelled any doubt on that point. 'Asked if the Prime Minister's strong personality and image had contributed to the growth of the RSS in recent years, Hosabale said, "The increasing spread of the RSS in the past few years is not because of any individual. It is the hard work of our workers and emphasis on increasing contacts which has taken us closer to the people."' The message was clear.

If some RSS sources are to be believed, Hosabale's 'perceived' closeness to Mr. Modi and his health condition were the main obstacles to his elevation as the executive head of the organisation.

'Bhaiyyaji's re-election is signal that the RSS top brass does not want any individual [PM] to dominate the entire Parivar. When a son tries to assert himself, the father has to come forward and tell the family that he is in command,' an RSS office-bearer told *The Hindu* when asked to analyse Bhaiyyaji's re-election.

> The larger Sangh Parivar, despite the convincing victory of the BJP last year, has been facing many internal conflicts over the decisions of the Modi government, be it on the Land Acquisition Bill or the 'uneasy alliance' in Jammu and Kashmir (with the PDP).
>
> The Bharatiya Mazdoor Sangh, the Bharatiya Kisan Manch and the Swadeshi Jagran Manch, all RSS organisations, have openly criticised the Modi government over one issue or another – a clear signal that all is not well in the Parivar.[10]

Bhaiyyaji Joshi retained Dattatreya Hosabale, Suresh Soni and Krishna Gopal as the sah-sarkaryavah (joint general secretary). Bhagaiah was appointed as the fourth joint general secretary of the RSS, a post which fell vacant the previous year when K.C. Kannan was sacked – for getting married.

He was the RSS's boudhik pramukh (in charge of intellectual training) in the previous RSS team, a post which went to Swata Ranjan in the new team. The RSS leader Mukunda was appointed as the deputy to Ranjan and Sunil Kulkarni was given the post of Akhil Bharatiya Sharirik Pramukh (in charge of physical training).

Jagdish Prasad retained his post as the sah-sharirik pramukh of the organisation. Manmohan Vaidya, the son of the most senior RSS ideologue M.G. Vaidya, was retained as the chief spokesperson of the organisation and J. Nandkumar continued to be his deputy.

[10] Pavan Dahat, *The Hindu*, 15 March 2015.

Joshi's new team also included Aniruddha Deshpande as the Akhil Bharatiya Sampark Pramukh (in-charge of communication) and Mangesh Bhende as the Akhil Bharatiya Vyavastha Pramukh (management in charge).

Indresh Kumar, Madhubhai Kulkarni, Shankar Lal, Dinesh, Mukunda Rao Panashikar, Sankal Chandra Bagrecha, Hastimal, Sunilpad Goswamy, Mahavir, Ashok Bheri, R. Vanarajan, Srikrishna Maheshwari, Purushottham Paranjape, Bajarangalal Gupta, Darshan Lal Aroda, Ishwar Chandra Gupta, Siddhanath Simha, Ranendralal Banerjee and Aseema Kumar Goswamy were elected members of the Central Executive Council of the RSS. Balkrishna Tripathi, Sethu Madhavan and Madan Das Devi were appointed invited members of the Central Executive Council.[11]

The RSS had every reason to be pleased with Modi's ventures which were based on three fundamentals. First, wipe out the secular national consensus evolved since the 19th century by the leaders of the freedom movement such as Dadabhai Naoroji, Badruddin Tyabji and Surendranath Banerjea. It was also enunciated by Vallabhbhai Patel in his presidential address to the Congress in 1931 and by Maulana Azad in his presidential address in 1940 as a retort to the Muslim League's clamour for the partition of India. Nehru faced the reaction thereafter. The tragic situation brought out the best in him and he emerged as the most articulate exponent of and the icon of the secular State.

Secondly, next only to Ashoka and Akbar, Nehru became a great builder of the Indian State. He won the nation's love and confidence and the world's admiration. But his concept of that State was that of a secular, democratic State based on a tolerant, pluralist society. This was in direct contradiction to the ideology of the RSS and its political progeny. He fought them tooth and nail. He is the one Congressman the RSS has always hated the most. On the partition of India it wanted to establish a Hindu State. Gandhi, Nehru and Patel opposed it. It fell to Nehru to expound the ideal by word and deed. He did so by a relentless campaign of educating the people and by building institutions cast in the secular mode. He espoused the concept of a composite culture of India. The former Jana Sangh leaders accepted this very concept in 1979; only to resile from it a few years later.

The RSS and its creature the BJP want to wipe out and demolish the secular State and erect a Hindutva State based on the fascist 'Leader' principle. It would be sustained by a society from which religions tolerance is banished as was done, one hopes momentarily, in Gujarat before and after the 2002 pogrom. This is 'The Gujarat Model' which the RSS and its pracharak Modi seek to replicate at the Centre. Not only will India's democracy and secularism suffer, the India which the nation loves and the world admires will perish. The RSS is a menace to India; and not only to its minorities.

The RSS has set before itself this, the second, task – the destruction of the

[11] *The Hindu*, 15 March 2015.

Gandhi-Nehru State after brainwashing the nation into acceptance of Hindutva. Soon after the 1989 elections, Jaswant Singh went about campaigning for an ideological 'idol-breaking'. Modi is at work on this ignoble venture.

Lastly, the RSS wants to eliminate the minorities, chiefly Muslims and Christians as minorities, and reduce them politically to being nonentities. Mobilise 'the Hindu vote bank', denounce the 'appeasement' of a 'Muslim vote bank' and either eliminate all opposition parties ('Congress Mukt', Modi's ideal) or absorb them; the willing ones are too small and too contemptible to mention. The Sikhs are not overlooked. Sudarshan's characteristically Quixotic venture to Punjab earned him a loathing.

Sudarshan became RSS chief on 10 March 2000. He advised, 'The Prime Minister should bring in economic advisers who believe in the swadeshi concept.' He also demanded that the Constitution of India be scrapped. 'This "remake" of the British model in [sic] in 1935' should be replaced with one based on the 'aspirations of the people'. In drafting the present Constitution 'Indian ethos and aspirations were not taken into account'. He added that 'the RSS did not expect the Review Committee appointed by the Government to do this [take a fresh look] as it has been asked not to alter the basic structure of the Constitution'.

On the same day, in his first address to RSS activists in Nagpur, Sudarshan said: 'These non-Hindus are not foreigners but ex-Hindus; they are Indians but their faiths will have to be Indianised.' He repeated this admonition in New Delhi on 23 March:

> This is yet another epic war – between Hindus and anti-Hindus, a veritable Mahabharat in which sometime Abhimanyu will fall, sometime Ghatotkacha or it may be Jayadratha's turn yet another day. . . . This is Hindu Rashtra. It is based on dharma. Its identity lies in one Motherland, one sanskriti, common ancestry and heritage and the unity in diversity. It is these three that constitute the national culture. The mode of worship can differ from person to person.[12]

He attacked Gandhi as well as Nehru. 'Even Gandhi blamed the Hindu community for creating an environment congenial to communal conflicts.' He asserted that the 'third phase in RSS history was marked by Jawaharlal Nehru's efforts to curb the organisation'.[13] The demolition of the Babri Masjid, he claimed on 19 March, 'has made Hindus all over the world proud'. For a man who extols the use of violence, his language is befittingly coarse and vulgar. 'Intellectual is that class of bastards, which tries to implant an alien culture in their land,' he said on 17 March.

Sudarshan was a man on the move. Sanjay Basak's report of 17 March said:

[12] *Organiser*, 19 March 2000.

[13] *Organiser*, 19 March.

'With a friendly government at the Centre, the RSS intends to step up its activities for the "creation of a Hindu rashtra".'

'Operation Khalsa' was revived once Modi became prime minister, targeting Dalit Sikhs.[14]

State help gave a fillip to the RSS's activities. The number of shakhas rose by 2,000 per year from 2012 to 2014.[15] By 2015, 51,335 shakhas held daily sessions across India. Mumbai saw a 34 per cent increase in daily shakhas and 70 per cent in weekly shakhas. 'The largest increase in shakhas across India over the last five years took place between 2013-2014 and 2014-2015,' *The Times of India* reported (16 August 2015).

There were, to be sure, those who joined the shakhas in the ordinary course but the appeal of power cannot be denied as the graphic which the newspaper published shows. It successfully used social media, with over 15 lakh 'Likes' on its Facebook page and 1.5 lakh followers on Twitter. 'The spread of RSS is being experienced not only in cities but in almost every tehsil and over 55,000 villages of our Bharat,' an RSS source told Anahita Mukherji.[16]

Shubhangi Khapre's report was detailed.

> The RSS membership is growing at 10,000 to 15,000 recruits every month and says it has reached every district except parts of Kashmir and Assam.
>
> 'With the change in the political atmosphere, many people or organisations who earlier supported us but hesitated to join us are now openly working with us. This is a big change,' RSS sahasarkaryavah V. Bhagaiah said in an interview to RSS organ *Organiser*. 'About two years ago, just 8,000 to 10,000 people would join the RSS (every month) but now it is 10,000 to 15,000 joining us every month.'
>
> RSS members attributed the growth to their 'join RSS' initiative. In interview, Bhagaiah said the response from college students and IT professionals had been huge. An office-bearer said, 'The RSS has expanded its base to all districts of the country except 14 districts of Kashmir and some remote areas in Assam. Of 55,000 mandals in the country, we are active in 25,000.'
>
> The RSS hopes to reach every mandal this year. According to plans charted out at the RSS meeting in Nainital from 22 to 24 July, prants and kshetra-level karyakartas and adhikaris will tour every khand, previously called talukas or blocks. At every village, they will try and engage farmers and labourers in organisational work.[17]

14 Chander Suta Dogra, *The Indian Express*, 22 December 2014.

15 *The Times of India*, 3 November 2014.

16 *The Times of India*, 16 August 2015. Vide the graphic which illustrate her able report.

17 *The Indian Express*, 17 August 2015.

The RSS's aspiration to become the world's teacher (Jagadguru) drove it to open branches abroad creating splits in the Indian diasporas there; especially in the United States. What results its mission to impart instruction in 'Vedic science' accomplished is not known.

The *Hindustan Times* reported:

> Maharishi Bharadwaj's Vaimanika Shastra prescribes a chemical formula that can make a flying plane invisible; the 100 Kaurava brothers were the first evidence of human cloning; cow urine can cure cancer. . . .
>
> Set up in 1991, Sangh-affiliated science organisation Vijnana Bharati, says it plans to expand in the Muslim-dominated Gulf countries to acquaint children of Indian families there with the country's rich scientific and cultural heritage.
>
> With eminent scientists G. Madhavan Nair and Anil Kakodkar as patrons, the organisation is headed by Vijay P. Bhatkar who developed India's first supercomputer.
>
> Vijnana Bharati identifies promotion of 'swadeshi science', intertwining traditional and modern sciences, as well as natural and spiritual sciences, as its founding principle.
>
> 'What is available in the Vedas and Upanishads can give India a big leap. The Government should promote research based on them,' [Dr. Somdev] Bhardwaj [of Vijnana Bharati] said.
>
> While Vijnana Bharati wants to expand to the Gulf, the Vishwa Hindu Parishad (VHP) is pushing the government for steps to protect and develop indigenous cows.
>
> The [agriculture] ministry is already in overdrive. It has allocated Rs. 500 crore to protect and promote desi cows. Projects worth Rs. 378 crore have been sanctioned and Rs. 123 crore released in this financial year. Two breeding centres in Mathura and south India have also been proposed [by the end of 2014].[18]

The RSS had spread its wings in 39 nations.

Overseas, the RSS becomes the Hindu Swayamsevak Sangh, Ramesh Subramaniam, Mumbai coordinator of the Jagadguru's work abroad told Anahita Mukherji. Its overseas wing was bigger than that of its affiliate the Vishwa Hindu Parishad. Since outdoor shakhas are forbidden in the Gulf countries, meetings are held in people's homes. Finland has one e-shakha for people from over 20 countries living in countries where HSS units are absent.

'While Nepal has the largest number of shakhas outside India, US comes

[18] *Hindustan Times*, 5 January 2015.

> second with 146. We are present in every state of the US. We have shakhas in cities like New York, Washington D.C., Seattle and Miami,' said Satish Modh, who was associated with RSS work abroad for over 25 years. While shakhas in India take place in open maidans, in the US, most shakhas are held in university campuses or hired parking lots, says Modh.
>
> Most overseas shakhas are held once a week. In London, they are held twice a week. The UK has 84 shakhas. 'The Sangh parivar got a boost in the UK under Blairite "multiculturalism" in which culture was identified with religion and religion with its most hardcore version,' says [Subir] Sinha [of SOAS].[19]

Growth boosted confidence; electoral debacles shatter them. Elections in Bihar in 2015 did just that. They shook faith in Modi. Speaking to *The Indian Express*, a senior BJP functionary said, 'The Parliamentary Board of the party and other experts will come out with a comprehensive report on what went wrong in *caste* permutations and combinations, and whether there was any shortcoming in Prime Minister Narendra Modi's campaigns.' Caste appeals were approved to form caste 'vote banks'.

> 'In any cadre-based party, when individuals grow larger than life and undermine the collective role of die-hard karyakartas, one cannot expect positive outcomes,' said the leader who has always played the role of coordination between his party and the RSS.
>
> Though the BJP had emerged the largest political party in India, having registered more than 10 crore members across the country including 1 crore in Maharashtra, there cannot be an alternative to the secret and silent role of RSS workers during elections. Any attempt to undermine or engage in conflict with the RSS would never work to BJP's advantage, feel senior functionaries. Acknowledging that RSS chief Mohan Bhagwat's statement on reviewing reservations will be debated threadbare, a BJP leader pointed out, 'There is no practice in the organisation to seek any explanation from the RSS. Whether it was design or coincidence will be left for endless debate.' . . .
>
> A senior BJP Minister said, 'The Bihar elections would work as a wake-up call for all of us. To begin with, we will have to learn once again to speak and work unitedly as a team. No matter how great your past achievements are, individuals cannot pull a victory.'[20]

What effect the BJP's defeats in November 2018 in Rajasthan, Madhya Pradesh and Chhattisgarh had on its morale and Modi's image is not clear. Certainly Modi's aura of invincibility is gone.

[19] Anahita Mukherji, *The Times of India*, 21 December 2015.

[20] *The Indian Express*, 9 November 2015.

By the end of 2018, the Modi government had worked hard to turn institutions upside down, planting favourites from the RSS wherever possible especially in ones which would shape public opinion. The Jawaharlal Nehru University (JNU) was an obvious target; it bore Nehru's name, and cherished his ideals and his record.

Three institutions spread the official doctrine. First, the Deendayal Research Institute set up by Nana Deshmukh. It has languished somewhat lately. Two other became prominent since 2014. The Vivekananda International Foundation has already lent heavyweights to government, including National Security Adviser Doval, Principal Secretary Nripendra Misra, and A. Surya Prakash. Bibek Debroy, was appointed as a full-time member of the NITI Aayog on Monday.

The VIF is run under the aegis of the Vivekananda Kendra, which was set up by the RSS leader Eknath Ranade. The other is the India Foundation. Its director, Shaurya Doval, is son of Ajit Doval. It is one of the most active 'think tanks' in New Delhi. Railways Minister Suresh Prabhu; BJP's general secretary and former RSS spokesperson Ram Madhav; Minister of State for Finance Jayant Sinha; Minister for Commerce (independent charge) Nirmala Sitharaman; Rajya Sabha M.P. Chandan Mitra; Chairman of Prasar Bharati A. Surya Prakash are on the board.

> In December [2015], the IF organised an India Ideas Conclave in Goa where almost the entire intellectual elite of India's right was present. The idea, as participant after participant stated, was to create a 'centre-right ecosystem', which would question the established 'left-liberal' consensus on economy, culture and religion and polity. The event ran into trouble when one foreign scholar castigated Islam, prompting key Muslim delegates to walk out.[21]

This was an impressive record in seven months. Important changes followed. On 2 March 2015 Baldev Bhai Sharma, former editor of the RSS's organ *Panchajanya*, was appointed chairman of the National Book Trust, ousting its incumbent in the post whose term had yet to end. Five days later the Indian Council of Historical Research (ICHR) was reconstituted. Vikas Pathak explained the reasons for the changes.

> The discourse on medieval India is witnessing a heated debate as the composite culture theory that highlights Hindu-Muslim syncretism is being challenged by an assertion that Hindus were persecuted during the period.
>
> Saradindu Mukherjee, a member of the new panel, embodies the shift. 'Hindus suffered at the hands of their Islamic conquerors. Look at the records and not the propagandist books and you find destruction of temples, discrimination, forced conversions either smothered or rationalised, if not justified,' he says.

[21] *Hindustan Times*, 6 January 2015.

In recent months, statements by some in the government about ancient Indian knowledge of planes, advanced mathematics and medical sciences invited controversy and were disputed by well-known academics.

[Irfan Habib] alleged that some new members were known for their RSS leanings. One had been a BJP candidate, some weren't qualified enough to make it to university departments, and some were not even historians by training. The historian, however, said veteran Cambridge archaeologist Dilip Chakrabarti was an exception.

Veteran historian K.N. Panikkar also told *Hindustan Times* the panel seemed to lack diversity and RSS leanings were perhaps considered crucial.

Habib said there was little representation of medieval India on the panel, adding that a new member Meenakshi Jain had written an NCERT textbook 'full of errors' during the Vajpayee government.

Jain, however, questioned Habib's claim, saying only half the tale was being told.[22]

Strange people surfaced in the changed clime.

RSS ideologue and Haryana's school and higher education consultant Dina Nath Batra said he wanted to 'saffronise' education across the country.

'I am working for saffronisation of education in the whole country and I want to complete it at the earliest,' said Batra [who had forced pulping of a distinguished American scholar Wendy Doniger's book on the Hindus]. 'Let us teach the world about the contribution of our experts and expertise towards global growth.' Batra dismissed the allegation that his strategy was part of a larger agenda of the Sangh. . . .

[He insisted] that his definition of saffronisation was not related to any community or religion, [and added it was] a set of ideas which gives an independent identity to a person. . . .

He clarified that the existing school teachers will teach the Hindu scripture. 'The students will be taught a compilation of two shlokas from every chapter of the Bhagwat Gita,' he said.

The state government had announced plans to introduce the Gita in schools in December 2014.[23]

An ex-official of the Archaeological Survey of India who led the digging in Ayodhya was appointed director-general of the National Museum on 25 July 2016. He was Buddha Rashmi Mani. The 'Jobs for the Boys' policy was extended to land

22 *Hindustan Times*, 8 March 2015.

23 *The Times of India*, 7 November 2015.

allotment as well. Allotment of prime plots in the capital to 26 bodies was cancelled by the UPA government. They got them back in 2016.[24]

The new Indian Council of Historical Research proved helpful in defending Modi's absurdities on history. *The Telegraph* reported:

> Historians were divided today on Prime Minister Narendra Modi's statement that Hindu kings used to lose battles because Muslim rulers 'cunningly placed cows at the head of their troops'.
>
> An eminent historian described Modi's claim as a 'falsehood' and another said it was an uncorroborated claim spread by the Rashtriya Swayamsevak Sangh.
>
> 'If we go back to history, whenever the rajas fought the badshahs, the badshahs cunningly placed cows at the head of their troops,' Modi [had said on 6 August]. 'That put the rajas in a quandary because there was no way they would kill the cows. That's how they lost the battles.'
>
> Irfan Habib, Professor Emeritus at Aligarh Muslim University and a specialist on ancient and medieval India, dubbed Modi's statement a 'falsehood'.
>
> 'It's a falsehood; (it's) nonsense. Neither in ancient India nor in medieval India is there any evidence of cows being placed as a first line of defence by any army,' Habib said.
>
> Historian Arjun Dev said: 'This is the kind of history that is taught in the shakha (Sangh camp) schools.' He added: 'I have never come across any historical material that corroborates what the Prime Minister said but I have a recollection of hearing something like this at a shakha school in my early childhood.' . . .
>
> Vishwa Mohan Jha, who teaches history at a Delhi University college, said that historical references to certain rulers being anti-cow or anti-Brahmin were 'figurative'.[25]

The minister for human resources and development, Prakash Javadekar held a last closed door consultation with senior functionaries of the RSS on 27 July 2016. Sources said that Javadekar interacted with members of Vidya Bharati, Akhil Bharatiya Vidyarthi Parishad, Rashtriya Shaikshik Mahasangh, Bharatiya Shikshan Mandal, Sanskrit Bharati, Shiksha Bachao Andolan, Vijnana Bharati and Itihas Sankalan Yojana for close to six hours at Gujarat Bhawan. RSS Joint General Secretary Krishna Gopal, BJP President Amit Shah and Aniruddha Deshpande, the RSS Akhil Bharatiya Sampark Pramukh, were also present at the meeting.

'Sources told *The Indian Express* that the meeting was held to share the Sangh's

[24] *Hindustan Times*, 1 August 2016.

[25] *The Telegraph*, 8 August 2016.

inputs on the new education policy and to plan measures to "instil nationalism, pride and ancient Indian values in modern education".'[26]

Shakti Sinha who had served in Atal Bihari Vajpayee's PMO, was said to be the RSS's choice. He was a director in the RSS-aligned think tank India Foundation. Sangh leaders such as Ram Madhav are learnt to have pushed his candidature in the world famous Nehru Memorial Museum & Library in New Delhi.

Madhav is on the board of directors of India Foundation. Two members, including the chairperson of the search-and-selection committee for NMML director, are also on the same board.

'The search committee, headed by vice-chairperson and BJP M.P. M.J. Akbar, had Mehta, Prasar Bharti CEO A. Surya Prakash, Kumar Sanjay Krishna and Makhan Lal as members. Akbar and Prakash sat on the board of an institution with Sinha as director. Sinha left India Foundation a few days ago.'[27]

> In one stroke the Modi government reconstituted the board of trustees of Indira Gandhi National Centre for the Arts (IGNCA) and replaced the members with its own favourites.
>
> The incoming members are known for their proximity to BJP. They included Odissi dancer Sonal Mansingh, film director Chandraprakash Dwivedi, also a member of the Censor Board, lyricist and adman Prasoon Joshi, former chairperson of Khadi and Village Industries Corporation Mahesh Sharma, former Andhra Pradesh DGPK Aravinda Rao, also author of 'How to Tell Hinduism To Your Child', portrait artist Vasudeo Kamath, author of 'Thulasidasarum Thulasiramayanamum' M. Seshan, and industrialist and art aficionado Harsh Neotia. . . .
>
> Two relatively unknown names are Bharat Gupta and Viraj Yagnik. The previous trust was headed by the former diplomat Chinmaya R. Gharekhan and consisted of art scholar Kapila Vatsyayan, a former foreign secretary Salman Haidar, artist A. Ramachandran, writer Namita Gokhale, retired bureaucrat Subas Pani, former home secretary, G.K. Pillai, educationist Sukanya Bharatram, danseuse Shovana Narayan and former model and businesswoman Feroze Gujral [among others].[28]

Academics of impeccable credentials were singled out for hostile treatment – Jean Drèze and Amartya Sen. Jean Drèze was dropped from a high level conference, the Delhi Economic Conclave, organised by the Finance Ministry while he was on the train to Delhi. Amartya Sen, a Nobel Laureate, was ousted

[26] *The Indian Express*, 28 July 2016.

[27] *The Indian Express*, 14 August 2016.

[28] *The Times of India*, 15 April 2016.

from the chancellorship of the Nalanda University. In a scathing well-documented statement he said: 'Nothing on this scale of interference has happened before. Every institution where the government has a formal role is being converted into one where the government has a substantive role.' Sen pointed out that at the Tata Institute of Fundamental Research the government refused to ratify the appointment of director Dr. Sandip Trivedi. 'This has never happened under any previous PM,' he said, adding that it's not just the HRD ministry but the entire Modi government which is to blame, as Nalanda comes under the MEA.

He pointed out that at the National Book Trust, its head A. Sethumadhavan was asked to step down and an RSS ideologue appointed instead. He also said that at the ICCR, Dr. Lokesh Chandra, who has been appointed, believes Modi is a greater personality than Mahatma Gandhi. At the ICHR, he said, the head, Yellapragada Sudarshan Rao, has not done any historical research, but has written an article saying the caste system was wrongly blamed for being exploitative when it did a lot of good for India.

> Delhi IIT Director Raghunath Shevgaonkar resigned, the IIT Bombay Board Chairman, Anil Kakodkar, expressed that he could not help the government in anything in the future, for the IIMs they have introduced a Bill where instead of having indirect power of withholding the signature – which they did in my case or in Trivedi's case – they can now directly appoint the director. That's the new bill. Instead of having effective power, it becomes direct control.[29]

All this fell into a planned pattern. It bore Modi's imprint.

There was trouble within the Sangh. In May 2015 Hosabale, the RSS's joint general secretary appealed to its affiliates not to attack the Modi government publicly.[30] A list of 72 economic issues had been handed over by the RSS to the concerned ministries.

A statement issued by L.K. Advani, Yashwant Sinha, Murli Manohar Joshi and Shanta Kumar was issued on 10 November 2015 over Sinha's signature. It said:

> The principal reason for the latest defeat (in Bihar) is the way the party has been emasculated in the last year. A thorough review must be done of the reasons for the defeat as well as of the way the party is being forced to kow-tow to a handful, and how its consensual character has been destroyed. This review must not be done by the very persons who have managed and who have been responsible for the campaign in Bihar.[31]

[29] Sagarika Ghose, *The Times of India*, 7 July 2015.

[30] *The Telegraph*, 18 May 2015; vide also *Hindustan Times*, 19 May 2015.

[31] *The Asian Age*, 11 November 2015.

The quartet relapsed into silence bar a rare squeak. Yashwant Sinha kept up his dissent, though.

Mohan Bhagwat promoted his ghar wapsi programme. He said at Kolkata on 20 December, 'We are not involved in conversion but ghar wapsi.'[32] The RSS had plans for the BJP as N.J. Nair reported:

> The Rashtriya Swayamsevak Sangh (RSS) is set to further deepen its influence over the BJP's organisational structure by delegating more powers to its nominees assigned to play a pivotal role in the party. Party sources told *The Hindu* here that as in the case of the Jan Sangh, organising secretaries, mostly deputed by the RSS, would eventually micro (manage) activities.[33]

Modi actively pursued his well tried Gujarat strategy – isolate Muslims, by denouncing them, and mobilise Hindus. At the conclusion of the BJP's National Council at Kozhikode on 25 September 2016, he placed Deen Dayal Upadhyaya on the same pedestal as Gandhi and Nehru. 'Fifty years ago, Pandit Upadhyaya said "do not reward/appease (puraskrit) Muslims, do not shun (tiraskrit) them but purify (parishkar) them". Do not treat Muslims like *vote ki mandi ka maal* (vote banks) or *ghrina ki vastu* (object of hatred). *Unhe apna samjho* (regard them as your own).'

Upadhyaya's views on Muslims were anchored in the Sangh's classical perspective on minorities. 'Purification' was premised on the Sangh theory that Indian Muslims had not come from a foreign land but were Hindus who had been coerced into conversion to Islam.

Upadhyaya had said: 'The Muslims are the flesh of our flesh and blood of our blood.' K.S. Sudarshan, a former RSS sarsanghchalak, had once said that Muslims had the 'blood of Rama and Krishna coursing through their veins'.

According to the RSS, 'purification' involves a process called 'shuddhikaran' that calls on Muslims to 'reclaim' their 'Hindu origin' – by forsaking Islam and embracing Hinduism.

Modi's Upadhyaya citation was not confined to Muslims. He recalled the ideologue to take the BJP back to its roots. In 1967, Upadhyaya was anointed as the Jana Sangh president at Kozhikode, then called Calicut.

> 'Our yatra (journey) has been from the Bharatiya Jana Sangh to the BJP, from Calicut to Kozhikode. Calicut's name was changed because it was important to connect the place to its roots. Somehow Calicut did not have a sense of being rooted. Similarly we may have journeyed from the Jana Sangh to the BJP

[32] *The Asian Age*, 21 December 2015.

[33] *The Hindu*, 24 September 2016.

> but it is important to rediscover our roots, to rekindle the mantra that Pandit Upadhyaya gave us to fire our hope and enthusiasm.'[34]

This is the man whom the RSS considers an intellectual and a peer of Nehru.

Bhagwat wanted just such a leader. He enjoined the RSS to work for the BJP in the Assembly elections in Uttar Pradesh and Uttarakhand. 'We have faith in swayamsevaks in government.'[35] The relationship was not free of tension, though.

It was too late in the day to correct Modi, however. His silence on the cow lynchings and on ghar wapsi and his rhetoric especially during the elections in Bihar and Uttar Pradesh had spawned a climate which gave a licence to hate speeches and hate crimes, unheard of before. In very many ways Modi blazed a new and fiery trail. The women's branch of the RSS, Rashtriya Sevika Samiti, said on 6 July 2016, 'Islam is not a religion. It is a political aggression.'[36] Mohan Bhagwat was no better: 'We have to take advantage of this favourable situation in India' – an RSS man as prime minister. India had led the world in the past as a 'world leader' and there was peace during the period.[37] To which period was he referring when Pax Indica preserved the world's peace as its Jagadguru? This was not a solitary remark. Both Modi and Bhagwat – indeed, all the RSS chiefs since 1925 – indulged in such historical absurdities. If educated persons followed them it was not because of their erudition but their appeal to national pride. The RSS injects an inferiority complex in the minds by playing on historical falsehoods and then pleads for restoration of 'national pride' by suppressing Muslims and Christians.

Playing on this theme, Amit Shah said on 5 March 2016, 'If we have to elevate Bharat Mata to the status of Vishwa Guru (the world's teacher) . . . it is important that the country has a BJP Government for 25 years.'[38] It is a painfully recorded theme.

> Suruchi Prakashan, a publishing house run by the RSS, has brought out a map called '*Punyabhoomi Bharat*' in which Afghanistan is called 'Upganathan', Kabul 'Kubha Nagar', Peshawar 'Purushpur', Multan 'Moolsthan', Tibet 'Trivishtap', Sri Lanka 'Singhaldweep' and Myanmar 'Brahmadesh', among others.
>
> Outside the RSS's headquarters in Keshav Kunj in Jhandewalan, west Delhi, a book titled *Pratyek Rashtrabhakta Ka Sapna: Akhand Bharat* (Dream of every patriot: Akhand Bharat), written by one Dr. Sadanand Damodar Sapre, is on sale. The book says: 'We can put the map of Akhand Bharat in our home so that it is always before our eyes. If the map of Akhand Bharat is in

[34] Radhika Ramaseshan, *The Telegraph*, 26 September 2016.

[35] *The Times of India*, 25 July 2016.

[36] *The Asian Age*, 7 July 2016.

[37] *The Indian Express*, 5 January 2016.

[38] *The Indian Express*, 6 March 2016.

> our hearts, we will be offended every time we see the map of divided India on Doordarshan, newspapers and magazines, and remind us of the resolution of Akhand Bharat.'[39]

How do people who spew hate at Muslims within and outside India, hope to accomplish a reunion of South Asia? Modi never ceased electioneering and did so in the very coarse idiom that he had used in the election campaigns for the Gujarat Assembly. The language he used in the Bihar, Uttar Pradesh, Rajasthan, Madhya Pradesh and Chhattisgarh elections was never used by any prime minister in the seven decades of our independence. He was shamelessly communal. On 2 November 2015 Modi said at Forbesganj that Nitish Kumar and Laloo Prasad Yadav wanted to take away reservations from Dalits and Adivasis and give them to 'those people' ('*unko*'), i.e. Muslims. Earlier, on 26 October, he was explicit: 'give it to members of other religion'. Repetition of this theme reflected his mindset. Muslims were always the 'Other' to him.

In February 2015 a communist leader Govind Pansare was killed. In August 2015 a 77-year-old scholar, M.M. Kalburgi, an outspoken critic of idol worship, was murdered. Sonia Faleiro, co-founder of the writers' cooperative Deca wrote a detailed analysis entitled 'India's Assault on Free Speech' in an international daily *The International New York Times* on 30 October 2015. It bears quotation *in extenso* especially because she touched on an important point – Modi's calculated silence. She wrote:

> The harassment is front-page news, but the government refuses to acknowledge it. Indeed, Prime Minister Narendra Modi's silence is being interpreted by many people as tacit approval, given that the attacks have gained momentum since he took office in 2014 and are linked to Hindutva groups whose far-right ideology he shares.
>
> Earlier this month, a leader of the Sri Ram Sene, a Hindu extremist group with a history of violence including raiding pubs and beating women they find inside, ratcheted up the tensions. He warned that writers who insulted Hindu gods were in danger of having their tongues sliced off. For those who don't support the ultimate goal of these extremists – a Hindu nation – Mr. Modi's silence is ominous.
>
> This is a turning point for India, a country that has taken pride in being a liberal democracy and that often adopts a high-minded tone when neighbours fall short of the same standards. . . .
>
> Some of the killers are still on the loose, and while in one hand they wield a gun, in the other they wave a list. On 20 September, Mr. [Nikhil] Wagle, the journalist, learned from a source that intercepted phone calls had revealed

[39] *The Indian Express*, 4 January 2016.

that members of yet another right-wing Hindu group, Sanatan Sanstha, had marked him as their next victim. The extremists who celebrated the murder of Mr. Kalburgi were more direct: They used Twitter to warn K.S. Bhagwan, a retired university professor who is critical of the Hindu caste system, that he would be next.

The goal of transforming India from a secular state to a Hindu nation, which seems to be behind the murders, is abetted not just by the silence of politicians, but also by the Hindu nationalist policies of the ruling BJP.

Over the past few months, the government has purged secular voices from high-profile institutions including the National Book Trust and the independent board of Nalanda University. The government is not replacing mediocre individuals: The chancellor of Nalanda was the Nobel laureate Amartya Sen. It is replacing luminaries with people whose greatest qualification is faith in Hindutva ideology. The new appointees are rejecting scientific thought in favour of religious ideas that have no place in secular institutions.

One of the government's chief targets is the legacy of India's first prime minister, Jawaharlal Nehru, who laid the foundation for a secular nation. Last month, having nudged out the director of the Nehru Museum and Library in New Delhi, the government announced plans to rename the museum and change its focus to highlight the achievements of Mr. Modi. This is akin to repurposing the Washington Monument as an Obama museum.

In addition to erasing the contributions of long-dead liberals, BJP leaders are busy promoting violent Hindu nationalists. Sakshi Maharaj, a BJP member of Parliament, described Nathuram Godse, the man who assassinated Mahatma Gandhi, as a 'patriot'. Although Mr. Maharaj later retracted his statement, his opinion is shared by many of his party colleagues. Gandhi's assassin was a former member of the Rashtriya Swayamsevak Sangh, an armed Hindu group, with which Mr. Modi has been associated since he was 8 years old.

The BJP's efforts to reshape institutions that embody secular values – values they dismiss as 'Western' – was certainly anticipated. It came as no surprise when the culture and tourism minister, Mahesh Sharma, recently promised to 'cleanse every area of public discourse that had been Westernised'. Mr. Sharma is well aware of the connotations of the word he used.

It's also not surprising that Hindu fundamentalists would feel empowered in the shadow of a Hindu nationalist government. . . . But the country is undergoing a tectonic shift that will have long-term repercussions.

The attacks in India should not be seen as a problem limited to secular writers or liberal thinkers. They should be recognised as an attack on the heart of what constitutes a democracy – and that concerns everyone who values the idea of India as it was conceived and as it is beloved, rather than an India imagined through the eyes of religious zealots. Indians must protest these

> attacks and demand accountability from people in power. We must call for all voices to be protected, before we lose our own.

Over the months this newspaper, widely read the world over criticised Modi's record on free speech. Beginning with an editorial entitled 'Modi's Dangerous Silence' published on 6 March 2015. Since it is a journal which was not unsympathetic to Modi, its editorial is quoted in full for its citation in the record in grim detail.

> What will it take for Prime Minister Narendra Modi to speak out about the mounting violence against India's religious minorities? Attacks at Christian places of worship have prompted no response from the man elected to represent and to protect all of India's citizens. Nor has he addressed the mass conversion to Hinduism of Christians and Muslims who have been coerced or promised money. Mr. Modi's continued silence before such troubling intolerance increasingly gives the impression that he either cannot or does not wish to control the fringe elements of the Hindu nationalist right.
>
> Recently, a number of Christian churches in India have been burned and ransacked. Last December, St. Sebastian's Church in East Delhi was engulfed in fire. Its pastor reported a strong smell of kerosene after the blaze was put out. On Monday, St. Alphonsa's Church in New Delhi was vandalised. Ceremonial vessels were taken, yet collection boxes full of cash were untouched. Alarmed by the attacks, the Catholic Bishops' Conference of India has urged the government to uphold the secular nature of India and to assure its Christians they are 'protected and secure' in their own country.
>
> There is also concern about the mass conversions. Last December, about 200 Muslims were converted to Hinduism in Agra. In January, up to 100 Christians in West Bengal 'reconverted' to Hinduism. Hard-line Hindu nationalist groups, like the Vishwa Hindu Parishad (V.H.P.) and the Rashtriya Swayamsevak Sangh (R.S.S.), make no secret of their support for a 'homecoming' campaign designed to 'return' non-Hindus to the fold. More than 80 per cent of Indians are Hindu, but Pravin Togadia of the V.H.P. says his organisation's goal is a country that is 100 percent Hindu. The only way to achieve that is to deny religious minorities their faith.
>
> The V.H.P. is reportedly planning a mass conversion of 3,000 Muslims in Ayodhya this month. The destruction of the Babri Mosque there in 1992 by Hindu militants touched off riots between Hindus and Muslims across India that left more than 2,000 people dead.
>
> Mr. Modi has promised an ambitious agenda for India's development. But, as President Obama observed in a speech in New Delhi last month: 'India will succeed so long as it is not splintered along the lines of religious faith.' Mr.

Modi needs to break his deafening silence on religious intolerance.

It noted the toll which the 'cow protection' propaganda exacted in an editorial of 15 October 2015 entitled 'The Hindu Hardliners'. It censured the killing of Mohammed Akhlaq and the implication of severe injuries on his son at Dadri in Uttar Pradesh. Another son, Sartaj, who belonged to the Indian Air Force, sensibly appealed for calm.

> By mid-October, 35 Indian authors and poets had returned their awards to India's National Academy of letters. Since then, Indian sociologists, scientists, filmmakers and more than 300 Indian artists have published public statements of concern and outrage. On the occasion of his 50th birthday on Monday, the film superstar Shah Rukh Khan spoke out against intolerance and warned, 'We will never be a superpower if we are not going to believe that all religions are equal.'
>
> The plain truth is that India is being riven by hatred and held hostage to the intolerant demands of some Hindu hard-liners. This is not the India a vast majority of Indian citizens want and it is not an India that will attract the foreign investment Mr. Modi has worked hard to drum up on his many trips abroad.[40]

The distinguished actors Aamir Khan and later, in December 2018, Naseeruddin Shah expressed their anxieties for the future of their children. They were subjected to vile attacks. In speaking as they did they simply followed the tradition of actors in the West speaking up on issues of national concern especially during crises like the Vietnam War.

Critics were not wrong. Haryana's chief minister and Modi's close friend Manohar Lal Khattar said, on 15 October 2015, 'Muslims can continue to live in this country, but they will have to give up eating beef,' because the cow is an article of faith here.[41]

Whether it is eating beef or a temple at Ayodhya the tacit assumption underlying them is the same – the land belongs to the Hindu. Muslims and Christians live here on sufferance ('allowed' is the word commonly used). They must submit to the diktat of the Hindus; regardless of the country's laws and the Constitution. Conversions of Muslims and Christians to Hinduism is 'ghar wapsi' (return to home); conversion from Hinduism is a heinous crime.

There was a surge in the occurrence of communal riots for which the RSS has a formidable record. A report by a correspondent of *The Asian Age* (3 August 2015) was disturbing; but not surprising.

40 *The International New York Times*, 4 November 2015.

41 *The Indian Express*, 16 October 2015.

The Modi government has witnessed a rise in incidents of communal violence in the country since it came to power with official figures revealing that such incidents have gone up in the first six months of 2015 compared to the corresponding period last year.

Figures with the Union home ministry show that while 330 riots were reported till June this year in which 51 people lost their lives, there were only 252 such incidents in the first six months of 2014. A total of 51 people lost their lives and 1,092 others were injured in communal violence so far this year.

Last year, as many as 33 people had lost their lives in the first six months. There were a total of 644 riots in the entire 2014 in which 95 people were killed and 1,921 injured, according to the figures collated by MHA (Ministry of Home Affairs).

The last word on this hate campaign belongs to Julio Ribeiro:

Today, in my 86th year, I feel threatened, not wanted, reduced to a stranger in my own country. The same category of citizens who had put their trust in me to rescue them from a force they could not comprehend have now come out of the woodwork to condemn me for practising a religion that is different from theirs. I am not an Indian anymore, at least in the eyes of the proponents of the Hindu Rashtra.

Is it coincidence or a well-thought-out plan that the systematic targeting of a small and peaceful community should begin only after the BJP government of Narendra Modi came to power last May? '*Ghar wapsi*', the declaration of Christmas as 'Good Governance Day', the attack on Christian churches and schools in Delhi all added to a sense of siege that now afflicts these peaceful people.

It is tragic that these extremists have been emboldened beyond permissible limits by an atmosphere of hate and distrust. The Christian population, a mere 2 per cent of the total populace, has been subjected to a series of well-directed body blows. If these extremists later turn their attention to Muslims, which seems to be their goal, they will invite consequences that this writer dreads to imagine.

He rightly pinned his hopes on the millions of Hindus who do not share the hate.[42] Fortunately, none denounced him as a communalist.

Academia reacted early furiously to the State's assaults on its freedom. On 29 October 2015 a group of 53 historians, under the banner of Sahmat, a brave organisation which has been fighting for the secular ideal, came out in protest.

The historians' protest came on the day when scientists P.N. Bhargava, Ashoke

[42] *The Indian Express*, 16 March 2015.

Sen and P. Balaram announced their decision to return their Padma Bhushans with Bhargava alleging RSS interference in key appointments. Among the historians who signed the statement were scholars of international repute like Romila Thapar and Irfan Habib. They said:

> These days, differences of opinion are being sought to be settled by using physical violence. Arguments are met not with counter arguments but with bullets. . . . When writer after writer is returning their award of recognition in protest, no comment is made about the conditions that caused the protest; instead the ministers call it a paper revolution and advise writers to stop writing. This is as good as saying that intellectuals will be silenced, if they protest.[43]

Their reference to 'physical violence' was perfectly justified. In Mumbai Sudheendra Kulkarni's face was blackened the day he was to preside over the launch of the former foreign minister of Pakistan Khurshid Mahmud Kasuri's book *Neither a Hawk nor a Dove*, a powerful plea for conciliation between India and Pakistan. In Kashmir the fearlessly independent M.L.A., Engineer Rashid, was assaulted by BJP M.L.A.s in the Assembly.

The U.S. has produced outstanding intellectuals. But, as Richard Hofstadter points out, an anti-intellectual tradition has also flourished in its political life. His books *Anti-intellectualism in American Life* (1963) and *The Paranoid Style in American Politics and Other Essays* (1965) remind one of the pronounced anti-intellectual elements in the Sangh Parivar's (the RSS family's) discourse. The assertions are sweeping and palpably untrue. The language is coarse. The accusations are demonstrably false. Narendra Modi revels in all three.

Since Nehru was an intellectual of strong secular commitment he bears the main thrust of the attacks. The RSS's organ *Panchajanya*'s attack on him on 13 October 2015 strikingly reflects this outlook. 'Some pen artists afflicted with the disease of secularism have returned their medals to protest attempts at distorting Hindu religion and destroying India. No matter which government the country wants, nothing but the Nehruvian model is acceptable to them.'[44]

Read that with this informed national analysis of India's population problem.

> The growing population is responsible for the benefits of development not reaching the poor. In 1947, the country's population was 30 crores, after 1947 we gave up Hindutva and the population burgeoned to 100 crores. In those days, there were no other means of entertainment other than (procreation) yet Hindutva taught restraint and the population was under control. Today India

[43] *The Hindu*, 29 October 2015.

[44] *The Asian Age*, 14 October 2015.

has the highest number of AIDS patients in the world. If people had followed the footsteps of Lord Ram we would not have had AIDS at all. Abandoning Hindutva has resulted in the breakdown of families.

The speaker was Narendra Modi.[45] The man is not only uneducated but uneducable. He had exposed himself fully over a decade before he became prime minister. In Mumbai, shortly after he assumed office, he spoke at a hospital of the use of plastic surgery in India in ancient times.

Once he reached the high office flattery flowed aplenty in our accordance with our rich tradition since feudal times. To his urban development minister Venkaiah Naidu, Modi was 'God's gift to India'.

He ably listed Modi's accomplishments in two decades of power. 'PM Modi made it to *Time* Magazine's list of 100 most influential people in 2015 and now, this year, to the top 30. The Prime Minister is seen as the leader of the largest democracy, with over 18 million Twitter followers and 32 million Facebook likes.'[46] In turn, Modi recognised his abilities and made him vice-president. Amit Shah's praise had a clear target. 'Modi has been working to protect the true traditions and culture of this country and this is a proud moment for Hinduism (sanatan dharma).' Shah, who visited the famous Banke Bihari Mandir to seek blessings and later inaugurated the Priyakantju Temple, said by performing arti at Kashi, Modi had ignited hope in the hearts of millions of people that he would protect 'our' culture.[47]

Flattery and partisanship governed Modi's decisions. The board of trustees for the Indira Gandhi National Centre for the Arts was reconstituted. A respected and veteran diplomat Chinmaya Gharekhan was dropped as chairman and a Hindu journalist Ram Bahadur Rai was appointed in his place. At least four of the new appointees had supported his government during the 'awards wapsi' movement. Rai, a long RSS associate, was a Padma Shri awardee in the first round of honours and was reputed to be close to the RSS's general secretary Krishna Gopal 'who has a big say in the functioning of cultural institutions'.[48]

The trend depressed people who followed it in India and abroad. Every other day news of actions motivated by 'cultural nationalism' came in. A note by National Council for Promotion of Urdu Language (NCPUL) handed out to the writers read: 'I (name of author) confirm that my book/magazine (name of publication) does not contain anything against the policies of the government of India or the interest of the nation.'

Criticising the HRD ministry's proposal, Congress leader Digvijaya Singh said,

45 *The Telegraph*, 13 January 2003.
46 *The Times of India*, 26 March 2016.
47 *The Times of India*, 8 February 2016.
48 *The Telegraph*, 15 April 2016.

'If they have introduced such a clause, it should be for writers of all languages. Why are they only targeting Urdu writers? It is being done because their only agenda is to divide the country on communal lines and rule.'[49]

> In its annual report, the Congress-mandated US Commission for International Religious Freedom (USCIRF) asked the Indian government to publicly rebuke officials and religious leaders that make derogatory statements about religious communities.
>
> 'In 2015, religious tolerance deteriorated and religious freedom violations increased in India,' the report said.
>
> 'Minority communities, especially Christians, Muslims, and Sikhs, experienced numerous incidents of intimidation, harassment, and violence, largely at the hands of Hindu nationalist groups,' the report alleged.
>
> USCIRF alleged that members of the ruling BJP tacitly supported these groups and used religiously-divisive language to further inflame tensions.
>
> 'These issues, combined with longstanding problems of police bias and judicial inadequacies, have created a pervasive climate of impunity, where religious minority communities feel increasingly insecure, with no recourse when religiously-motivated crimes occur.'[50]

In Delhi, as in Mumbai, Muslims were denied accommodation, an offence under American as well as British laws.

> From Bollywood actors not finding apartments in Mumbai over the years to the latest IAS entrant, who took on a Hindu surname to find accommodation in Pune, there have been a number of stories about Muslims finding it difficult to rent houses.
>
> Now, a full-fledged study stands testimony to this discrimination – in the national capital.
>
> Released last week by the Helsinki-based United Nations University World Institute for Development Economics Research (UNU-WIDER), the study confirms that Muslim applicants find it more difficult than their counterparts to rent a house in Delhi, Gurgaon and Noida.[51]

With such a performance neither the RSS nor Modi had any difficulty in getting along. Pradip Kumar Maitra made a fair assessment of their equation.

> Bhagwat and Modi go back a long way. Both were born in September 1950

[49] *Hindustan Times*, 20 March 2016.

[50] *The Indian Express*, 3 May 2016.

[51] *The Indian Express*, 18 May 2016.

and Modi was groomed in the Sangh by Bhagwat's father – Madhukar – who was the prant pracharak of Gujarat. Bhagwat is known to have pushed Modi's candidature as the BJP's candidate for Prime Minister over L.K. Advani. His reasoning was that the old order had to change. His preference for younger leaders was clear when he ensured that Nitin Gadkari became the BJP President in December 2009. At 52, he was the youngest ever party chief.

Even as RSS number two, Bhagwat had felt it would be difficult to deal with senior functionaries. At an RSS meeting at Kolkata in 2004, he had suggested that Vajpayee, Advani and other senior leaders step aside and let the younger leadership take charge of the BJP. Ten years later, this plan had been accomplished.

Bhagwat publicly mentioned his doubts on the policy of reservations.

His success in effectively mobilising the RSS ahead of the 2014 elections added to his stature. The RSS believed the BJP could win 272 Lok Sabha seats on its own and form a government. Led by Bhagwat, RSS strategists and key BJP leaders sifted through data and noticed that the BJP had won at least once from 278 seats across the country. There were 70-75 where the party was a close second. RSS chalked out a strategy to focus on these 350-odd seats. The results were unprecedented. . . .

The formation of the Modi cabinet and its expansion in November 2014 also had a visible RSS imprint with over a dozen ministers associated with the Sangh Parivar being inducted. Among them, Hansraj Ahir, a four-time MP from Chandrapur – Bhagwat's native place – found a place in Modi's team. Ahir, known for exposing the coal block allocation scam, is considered to be very close to Bhagwat. The inclusion of Manohar Parrikar in the Union cabinet and the promotion of Prakash Javadekar to the HRD ministry recently also show the rising clout of the RSS within the government. By elevating Javadekar as HRD minister, a close associate, he wanted to push the RSS agenda in the education system. . . .

There are bound to be differences between the Sangh and the way Modi's government functions. But both seem to be accommodative. While the government allowed the Sangh's views in education, culture and to a certain extent dealing with troubled neighbours, the Sangh on its part has been supportive of the government's economic policies that it may not subscribe to in entirety. Having a familiar government in Delhi was a necessity felt by the Sangh after the poor show in assembly polls and now, there seems to be a clear understanding between the two – to let Modi govern the country and Sangh pursue the Hindutva agenda. . . .

A veterinary doctor, Bhagwat left a post-graduation course in veterinary

> medicine from Akola half way and became a full-time pracharak in 1975. His family has been associated with the RSS for three generations. A senior RSS swayamsevak close to Bhagwat said that both Modi and Bhagwat would turn 75 when the saffron organisation celebrates its centenary in 2025 and could step down to set an example regarding their policy of a retirement age for Sangh Parivar leaders. Bhagwat is known to be ruthless in pursuing the Sangh's goals. . . .
>
> A voracious reader of detective books in his student days, Bhagwat, a Maharashtrian Brahmin, was a non-vegetarian till his elevation to the post of sarkaryavah in 2000. A good singer, he rarely misses his yoga and routine exercise, whether he is in Nagpur or elsewhere.
>
> However, a section of RSS activists here also feel how a leader of Bhagwat's stature failed to keep the flock together in the RSS Goa unit and failed to rein in Subhash Velingkar who decided to float a political party against the BJP.[52]

Modi deployed Amit Shah to iron out the differences.

Time did not mellow the RSS or Modi; nor, following their example, their followers. One sample will suffice to illustrate the trend. Hari Om Pandey, a BJP M.P. from Uttar Pradesh said on 27 July 2016:

> Terrorism, murders and rapes are prevailing because of the rising Muslim population. There has been a rapid increase in Muslim population since Independence. Muslims marry 3-4 times and have 9-10 kids, they don't get any education and end up unemployed. It will obviously lead to anarchy. Their population is increasing rapidly, they are demanding Sharia now, later they will demand new Pakistan.

Pandey, a father of four, is a first time M.P. A BJP M.L.A., Surendra Singh had appealed to Hindus to 'have at least five children and make the country strong'.[53]

Such people took their cue from those in command who constantly harped on their pet themes. Bhagwat propounded this definition of the Hindu. 'Everyone who respects Bharat Mata is a Hindu. Despite following different faiths and modes of worship, we are all one,' he told a 'Hindu Sammelan' in Madhya Pradesh's Betul. 'If India were to become world leader (vishwa guru), Hindus will have to take responsibility. If something goes wrong questions will be asked *only of Hindus*. India is the only country for Hindus.'[54]

As in Bihar, Modi waged communal propaganda during his election campaign in Uttar Pradesh. He said on 19 February 2017 that

[52] *Hindustan Times*, 31 October 2016.

[53] *The Times of India*, 28 July 2016.

[54] *The Indian Express*, 9 February 2017.

Gaon mein agar kabristaan banta hai, to gaon mein shamshaan bhi banana chahiye. Agar Ramzan mein bijli milti hai, to Diwali mein bhi milni chahiye. Agar Holi mein bijli milti hai, to Eid par bhi bijli milni chahiye. Bhedbhav nahin hona chahiye (If a village gets a graveyard, it should get a cremation ground too. If there is electricity during Ramzan, there should be electricity during Diwali too. If there is electricity during Holi, there should be electricity during Eid too. There should not be any discrimination).[55]

Small wonder that Modi picked Yogi Adityanath to be the chief minister of Uttar Pradesh. It was interpreted as 'the strongest signal in the run up to the 2019 elections'. Amit Shah spoke of the BJP's 'willingness to go for Hindu consolidation'.

The Telegraph published a selection of his *bon mots*:

Has it happened anywhere in the world that Gauri and Ganesh are placed inside a mosque? Every time a Hindu visits the Vishwanath temple, the Gyanvapi mosque taunts us. If given a chance, we will instal statues of Goddess Gauri, Ganesh and Nandi in all mosques of the country. (February 2015.)

Demolition of the Babri Masjid was only the first step.

Muslims who want to become Hindus will be purified and we will form an entire new caste for them. . . . If they take one Hindu girl, we will take 100 Muslim girls. (Undated video that surfaced in 2014.)

Those who don't want to do yoga can leave India. People opposed to surya namaskar should drown themselves in the sea. (June 2015.)

Shah Rukh Khan should remember that if a huge mass of people in the country boycott his films then he would also have to wander on the streets like a normal Muslim . . . I think there is no difference between the language of Shah Rukh Khan and Hafiz Saeed. (November 2015.)

There have been 450 riot cases in western Uttar Pradesh in two-and-a-half years of Samajwadi Party rule because the population of a particular community is rising manifold. Why are there no riots in eastern Uttar Pradesh? You can easily understand. In places where there is 10-20 per cent minority population, stray communal incidents take place. Where there are 20-35 per cent of them, serious communal riots take place and where they are more than 35 per cent, there is no place for non-Muslims. (August 2014.)[56]

It is a clear signal that the RSS and Modi will fight the 2019 elections viciously with sheer communal propaganda. At the concluding session of the RSS's Pratinidhi

55 *The Indian Express*, 20 February 2017.

56 Compiled by *The Telegraph*, 18 September 2017.

Sabha at Coimbatore on 21 March 2017, Mohan Bhagwat asked swayamsevaks to be ready to perform their tasks.

The general secretary (organisation) Ram Lal said that the party needs to work much harder in 2019 Lok Sabha polls since it faces a possible scenario in which all opponents will join hands to fight it. He pointed out that the BJP-led NDA may have secured more than 42 per cent votes in the Uttar Pradesh Assembly election but the opposing parties polled a combined 55 per cent or so votes.[57] An RSS 'leader' made an ominous comment. 'The RSS has better influence in urban areas and places with Muslim-Hindu conflicts.'[58] Riots help the RSS. It was born out of one in Nagpur in 1925.

A survey of BJP-ruled states revealed the items on their agenda – text book changes; surya namaskar; cow vigilantism; lifting bans on State employees participating in RSS shakhas; changing names of cities; curriculum drive; and renaming institutions.[59] How any of these can improve the lot of the people is never explained.

Their leaders had set their sights on a different goal – making India a super power and thus reclaim its glory as a Hindu Rashtra. Bhagwat repeatedly advocated this line drawing attention to India's ability to provide a cure to the world's ills. 'The world today is plagued by various problems due to loss of dharma. The spread of radicalism shows that the world is losing the principle of good for all. Against this backdrop the rise of Bharat assumes significance as dharma is its core (prana). A strong and prosperous Bharat can lead the world to Vishwa Dharma,' he said on 5 August 2017.[60] The RSS's doctrines are meant for the whole world.

In his view, 'Hinduism was the only true religion in the world and other religions were just sects which emerged from Hinduism.' Also, 'People hailing from other sects were originally Hindus who had drifted to these sects over the course of time. RSS does not support conversion, but our doors are open for those who want to come back to Hinduism from other sects.' Bhagwat added that 'the ancestors of all those who are living in the country today were also Hindus'. So much for his claims to tolerance. He also pitched for changes in the Constitution and jurisprudence in line with the value systems of the country, a stance which is sure to invite brickbats from the opposition, which has often expressed fears about the current dispensation's implicit agenda.

> 'Our Constitution was written based on the understanding of the "Bharatiya" ethos of our founding fathers, but many of the laws that we are still using are

[57] *The Indian Express*, 22 March 2017.

[58] Ibid.

[59] *Hindustan Times*'s survey of Rajasthan, Haryana, Madhya Pradesh, Gujarat and Jharkhand, 26 March 2017.

[60] *Organiser*, 20 August 2017.

> based on foreign sources and were made as per their thinking. Seven decades have passed since our independence . . . this is something we must address.'
>
> The RSS chief suggested that the country's legal system should be based on such an ethos. 'A discussion and debate should be held on this. After a comprehensive national debate, we will have to arrive at a consensus and such system should be made available to people. It should be such that it not only benefits our country, but also sets an example for other countries.' . . .
>
> He said the country's justice system was under the ambit of the legal framework, but what was legal may not be morally right. Laying emphasis on the importance of law and legislation in running society, Bhagwat said a society should be built where its morality was at a level where society in general and the law were not at loggerheads.[61]

The RSS never accepted India's Constitution. Bhagwat was simply following the line laid down by Golwalkar and Sudarshan.

The murder of Gauri Lankesh in September 2017 shook India. She was a fearless critic of Hindu nationalist militancy. Investigations revealed that the crime was part of a conspiracy which took the life of Kalburgi. *The International New York Times* squarely put the blame on Modi in an editorial of 8 September 2017. It said,

> Prime Minister Narendra Modi has let a climate of mob rule flourish in India, with his right-wing Hindu supporters vilifying 'secularists'. The venom that reactionary social media trolls direct at journalists, or 'presstitutes' as they call them, is especially vicious, but not entirely new. At least 27 Indian journalists have been killed since 1992 'in direct retaliation for their work', according to the Committee to Protect Journalists. Only one of the killers has been convicted. . . .
>
> This has not happened so far in the murders of other outspoken critics of right-wing Hindu nationalists. Narendra Dabholkar, whose campaigns against superstitious practices angered many Hindu religious activists, was shot to death near his home in Pune in 2013. Two years ago, Malleshappa Madivalappa Kalburgi, a former vice-chancellor of Kannada University who spent decades debunking peddlers of superstition, was fatally shot in his home in Dharwad.
>
> Ms. Lankesh had voiced concern about the climate of menace against journalists who didn't toe the Hindu-nationalist line. If Mr. Modi doesn't condemn her murder forcefully and denounce the harassment and threats that critics of Hindu militancy face daily, more critics will live in fear of deadly reprisal and Indian democracy will see dark days.

[61] *The Times of India*, 12 September 2017.

Modi kept his grief strictly to himself.

Writers who do not toe the Hindutva line suffer; so does India's reputation. There are few in the world who can match the erudition and scholarship of Wendy Doniger as a Sanskritist and Indologist. She is the Mircea Eliade Distinguished Service Professor of History of Religions at the University of Chicago, and has taught there since 1978. Her major works include *Asceticism and Eroticism in the Mythology of Siva*, *Hindu Myths: A Sourcebook*, *The Origins of Evil in Hindu Mythology*, *Women, Androgynes, and Other Mythical Beasts*, and *The Rig Veda: An Anthology, 108 Hymns Translated from the Sanskrit*.

Her 2009 book, *The Hindus: An Alternative History*, flung her into the spotlight when right-wing Hindu groups filed a lawsuit under India's colonial-era anti-blasphemy law, Section 295A of the Indian Penal Code, which forbids 'deliberate and malicious acts intended to outrage the feelings of any religious community'. India had previously banned James Laine's book on Shivaji, Joseph Lelyveld's book on Gandhi and Salman Rushdie's *Satanic Verses*, among many others.[62]

A *Times of India* survey by Subodh Varma published on 30 June 2017 said:

> A review of media reports shows 32 cases of attacks by mobs or vigilante groups on Muslims since May 2014. In these attacks, 23 people were killed, including women and children. This is a conservative estimate because many attacks may not have been covered in national media. In most cases, the issue of cows has been the proximate cause – allegations of cow slaughter, smuggling, eating or even possessing beef.
>
> Between June 2014 and December 2015, 11 such attacks took place, but after that, the pace has increased with 2016 recording 12 cases and 2017, 9 cases in six months. Most such attacks have occurred in north India.
>
> Clearly, the spurt has taken place after the NDA government took over. This may be because of the advocacy of cow protection by the BJP and its associated organisations, changes in laws related to cow slaughter in several states ruled by the BJP and a sense of impunity felt by cow vigilantes. In many cases that caused extensive protests, like the lynching of Akhlaq in Dadri in 2015 or the stripping and beating of Dalit youths in Una, in 2016, the Centre and state's response was perceived to be delayed and tepid.
>
> According to home ministry reports, there have been 1,454 communal incidents over 2015 and 2016, in which 183 people have been killed and 4,585 injured. The categorisation of a case as 'communal' or not is largely up to local police and often incidents like lynching or similar attacks motivated by communal poison may not be recorded as a 'communal' incident.
>
> In some cases, mob frenzy was characterised by unprecedented barbarism. In March 2016, Inayatullah Khan, 12, was hanged along with Mohd. Majloom

[62] Vikram Zutshi, *The Hindu*, 17 December 2017.

by a mob, for suspected cattle trading. In the Mewat rape, a 14-year-old girl and her 20-year-old cousin was raped by four men. One of the survivors told the media later that the rapists told her they were going to punish her for eating beef. In most cases, victims have denied allegations of cow slaughter or beef eating, but in vain.

The BJP and the RSS intellectuals are no more enlightened than its leaders. One Dr. Jay Dubashi's lament in *Organiser* (28 August 2011) explains the psyche of the family – its quarrel with history or rather with the past it imagines. He recalled how Hindus suffered for a thousand years.

> Now the Hindus are going out and running other people's estates – the so-called multinationals. Personally, I don't think much of this. Why should Indians put themselves on the back on running other people's companies – banks, hotels, software and investment banks? This is what we did for the Moghuls and, later, for the East India Co. and its successor, the British crown. And what did we get out of it? Nothing. It is ridiculous that people as talented as Hindus – or Indians, if you like it that way – should be content behaving like Munshis, which is what they have become. . . . We have to shed our inferiority complex – the complex all slaves suffer from. But we are not a subjugated race now, and we should take our destiny in our own hands and aim for the moon. This is what Shivaji did. And it is time we repaid our debt to our ancestors.

Inject an inferiority complex based on a false historical narrative and then cry that the injected complex must be 'shed'.

But what is the state of their historical 'tormentors', the Muslims in India today, against whom the RSS and Modi have launched a campaign?

> The Muslim community is being targeted and vilified in the backdrop of the bomb blasts across the country, Union Agriculture Minister Sharad Pawar said, speaking on Day 2 of the Nationalist Congress Party (NCP) conclave in Alibag. The party chief said this trend of targeting one community would lead to its isolation and was dangerous for the country.
>
> 'I didn't see Hindu extremists being masked and paraded by the police after the blasts in Thane and Panvel by some members of the Sanathan Sanstha. I have read their literature and it is vile,' he said. 'Hindus don't have to prove their secular credentials, despite the activities of, say, the Sanathan Sanstha. But the same is not the case with Muslims.'[63]

[63] *The Times of India*, 6 October 2017.

An authoritative report is quoted *in extenso*:

> Gujarat accounts for over a third of the total Muslim detainees in the country, Union home ministry figures show. Of the country's 658 Muslim detainees, 240 are in PM Narendra Modi's home state. Tamil Nadu is a close second with 220. India has 82,190 Muslims in its jails and police custody. These include 21,550 convicts, 59,550 undertrials in prisons and 658 in lock-ups.
>
> The state has 58.61 lakh Muslims who account for 9.7% of 6 crore Gujaratis. The number of Muslim detainees is disproportionate to the state's share in India's Muslim population. Gujarat is home to 3.4% of 17.2 core Muslims in India. Yet it accounts for 36.5% of Muslims detainees. The number of Muslim detainees in TN is also disproportionate to its share in India's Muslim population, which stands at just 2.5%.
>
> Gujarat has 846 convicts – 3.9% of Muslims convicted. For undertrials, this figure stands at 1,724 or 2.9% of Muslim undertrials.
>
> Uttar Pradesh, which has the highest number of Muslims behind bars – including 5,040 convicts and 17,858 undertrials – has just 45 detainees. The state accounts for 22.4% of India's Muslim population.[64]

Let alone the Sachar Report, impeccably researched studies by internationally respected scholars reveal a most distressing state of affairs. What Christophe Jaffrelot and Kalaiyarasan A. wrote in *The Indian Express* on 20 April 2018 is shocking.

> In a report it released last month on the 'aspiration districts', the Niti Aayog showed that 11 of the 20 most backward districts were Muslim-dominated. Yet this body continues to focus on districts when the relevant units of analysis are communities, as shown by another commission appointed under Manmohan Singh, the National Commission for Religious and Linguistic Minorities, known as the Ranganath Misra Commission, which had recommended positive discrimination policies for the minorities which were losing ground. But its report was not even tabled in Parliament. Any move in favour of minorities looks illegitimate in the era of majoritarianism.[65]

Jaffrelot and Shweta Bhutada documented the under-representation of Muslims in police and the army as the late Omar Khalidi of the MIT had done.[66] Himanshi Dhawan has described the fear and sense of alienation that has gripped

[64] Ashish Chandan, *The Times of India*, 4 May 2016.

[65] *The Indian Express*, 20 April 2018.

[66] *The Indian Express*, 12 July 2018.

Muslims since Modi became prime minister. It covers the contents of the lunch box: Does it include beef? After the Supreme Court's judgment on the right to privacy no government has a right to ban consumption of beef.

Marginalisation is reflected in the steep drop in Muslim representation in parliament and the state Assemblies. Jaffrelot and Gilles Verniers analyse this calculated elimination.

> The BJP's decision not to field any Muslim candidates aims to liberate the party entirely from the 'Muslim vote' that it accuses other parties of wooing for electoral gain at the expense of the Hindu majority. The low representation of Muslims also stems from other parties, who are reluctant to field Muslim candidates in constituencies other than those with a high concentration of Muslim voters. This tactic was especially clear in the Congress' case, which the BJP accused of cultivating a Muslim vote bank by showing concern for their social and economic condition – a false concern if one goes by the impoverishment of Muslims in the UPA regime.
>
> The BJP's accusation of minority favouritism falls flat when one considers that the Congress hasn't fielded more than 7 per cent Muslim candidates since the early 1990s, when its decline accelerated. In 2009, the Congress, unwilling to embrace its traditional secularism, only endorsed 29 Muslim candidates (or 7 per cent of the total), of whom only 10 won seats. In 2014, only 7 of the 31 Congress Muslim candidates won. The Congress is hardly a 'Muslim party' if one goes by factual evidence. . . .
>
> Each time the BJP conquers a new state, the number of Muslim MLAs drops. The most spectacular example is found in UP where, in 2017, their proportion went from 17 to 6 per cent. While the figure of 17 per cent, achieved in 2012 mainly thanks to the success of the SP, had brought the share of Muslim MLAs closer to their share of the population in UP, the figure of 6 per cent, associated with the BJP's landslide victory, reflects an under representation comparable to that of 1991, when the party had already taken control of the state.
>
> The drop in Muslim representation is less stark in bipolar states where the BJP and Congress are opposed to each other, particularly in northern and western India, where the Hindu nationalists traditionally have the greatest influence. In those states, the attempt to form a Hindu vote bank by the BJP has prompted the Congress (and other parties) to nominate few Muslim candidates, for fear of a Hindu backlash. . . .
>
> The dwindling representation of India's largest minority in elected assemblies matters because in India, substantive representation (of the interests of a group) is linked to descriptive representation (their numerical presence

> in elected assemblies). An analysis of Lok Sabha parliamentary questions conducted by Saloni Bhogale reveals that the number of questions concerning minorities is linked to their presence in Parliament. In other words, institutions care about minorities as long as their members are represented in them.[67]

Irfan Ahmad Sofi and Santosh Mehrotra establish that there is no respite from poverty for Muslims. The educational attainment of Muslims is the least among the major religious communities surveyed by the National Survey Office.[68] Any action by the State to provide redress is branded 'appeasement of a vote bank'. The only vote bank that can function is that run by Hindutva. The other parties dread this charge – and do nothing.

Students imbibe RSS-brand instruction. Sonia Sarkar's exposé should alert all.

> Mythology is in, history is out. Announcing a new trend in varsities across the country. It's 'Rashtravaad' (nationalism), Hindutva, Golwalkar, Savarkar, Modi and Indian mythology that have caught the imagination of research scholars post-2014. Looks like Prime Minister Narendra Modi's 'Make in India' cry carries a deep Indic ring in academic circles.
>
> 'This is the time for Indian researchers to move beyond (German revolutionary) Karl Marx and (Russian communist) Vladimir Lenin and research Indian personalities and Indian polity, Indian culture and consciousness,' asserts Kaushal Kishore Mishra, professor of Political Science at the Banaras Hindu University (BHU). Mishra's students are writing papers on 'Cultural nationalism of (RSS icon) M.S. Golwalkar', and 'Relevance of Hindu Mahasabha leader Vinayak Damodar Savarkar in Political Science'.
>
> More and more MPhil and PhD students are being encouraged by faculty in various universities to explore Hindutva-related subjects. . . . Eulogising Modi in research papers is a growing trend too. Scholars in BHU are writing papers on the 'Role of Modi in the empowerment of Muslim women', and 'Modi and (US President) Trump – a case study of the two personalities vis-a-vis their elections'. In Gujarat University, researchers are working on papers such as 'Improvement in India-US relations, post Modi', and 'Emergence of the Bharatiya Janata Party (BJP) in national politics, post Modi'.
>
> Other state-run higher education institutions such as the Ram Manohar Lohia Avadh University in Uttar Pradesh's Faizabad and Maharaja Ganga Singh University in Rajasthan's Bikaner are championing the 'Hindu' cause in a big way too. A scholar in the Bikaner university is writing a paper on 'Sarsanghchalaks of the RSS (Heads of the RSS)'; another is working on 'The

[67] *The Indian Express*, 30 July 2018.

[68] *The Hindu*, 6 November 2018.

Cultural Outlook of the RSS'. At the Faizabad University, grants have been sanctioned to a PhD student to write a paper on 'Deendayal Upadhyaya and his Hindutva ideology'.

This is not to suggest that all research work in the social sciences in every university revolves around the Hindutva ideology these days. But surely, there is a pattern – young researchers are being nudged towards themes and personalities attached to the notion, and politics, of Hindu nationalism, whose unabashed mascot Prime Minister Modi is.

There is good reason for this to have become a trend. Many academics believe smart researchers are trying to cash in on the Hindutva vogue to secure easy grants. 'Research grant funds allotted to universities are poor. Given the current political scenario, receiving grants, either from universities or from the central funding institutions, for Hindutva-related topics would be easier,' argues Vijay Kumar Rai, head of the Department of Political Science at Allahabad University. . . . 'A young scholar would shape the academic terrain of the country in the coming years. Projects with preconceived conclusions should not be entertained by universities,' Rai stresses. . . .

With Modi in power, the likes of Golwalkar are replacing Nehru in research bibliographies. Hindutva-related ideologues tried to craft their narrative in educational institutions once before – during the Ram Janmabhoomi movement in the early 1990s. That's happening in a big way now. 'Modi's radical approach is reassuring for the right-wing academia; we feel encouraged,' says Manoj Dikshit, professor of Public Administration at Lucknow University. It is no coincidence that academics with Sangh affiliations are being handpicked to head major institutions – Y. Sudarshan Rao (ICHR), Girish Chandra Tripathi (BHU), Chandrakala Padia (Indian Institute of Advanced Studies), Vijay Bhatkar (Nalanda University).

Rai, however, warns universities that they should not compromise standards by welcoming run-of-the-mill work merely to appease the government. 'Churning out research papers like factories could affect the credibility of the universities. . . . Academics, with any leaning, shouldn't try to prove their loyalty towards the government through their work,' he adds.

But few on the Right are interested in listening, it would appear. They are marching on, regardless, taking cue from a dispensation that is positively urging them on. The presence of RSS members in university seminars and workshops is becoming a norm. For instance, many of them attended the Indian Political Science Association's annual conference at BHU in 2015, where research papers on subjects such as the theory of Ram Rajya and the relevance of Manuvaad in the current political scenario were released. Last year, Hindu spiritual guru Shankaracharya Swami Nischalananda Saraswati

> addressed students of Lucknow University where he claimed that the computer has its origins in the Vedas.
>
> RSS leaders were invited at the DU convocation in November last year. Many witnessed the varsity vice-chancellor, Yogesh Tyagi, touching RSS joint general secretary Krishna Gopal's feet before moving to the dais.
>
> RSS leader Indresh Kumar and a few others have been regularly invited to speak at orientation courses in DU. In all these sessions, RSS leaders tried to indoctrinate teachers by giving lectures on their idea of nationalism. A teacher who attended one says, 'One speaker likened atomic particles – electrons, protons and neutrons to Hindu gods – Brahma, Vishnu and Maheshwar.' IIT Delhi has received close to three dozen research proposals on the potential of panchgavya, a concoction of cow dung, urine, milk, ghee and curd.

She cites case after case in her excellent exposé.[69]

Modi's cult figure is Deen Dayal Upadhyaya. In September 2016 he said in tribute, 'Fifty years ago, Pandit Upadhyaya said, "Do not reward/appease (puraskrit) Muslims, do not shun (tiraskrit) them, but purify (parishkar) them."'

BJP-ruled states poured lakhs to propagate Upadhyaya's views. The Haryana government bought 5,000 sets of his collected works for Rs. 2 crores. Chhattisgarh bought 900 copies; Madhya Pradesh, nearly 500. Amit Shah asked all BJP-ruled state governments to ensure that their public schools and colleges bought the books. Amazing that the writ of the head of a political party extended to the government run by that party.

The Ministry of External Affairs did not lag behind. Sachin Parashar reported:

> Many Indian missions across the world – from London to Moscow to Port of Spain – held events late last month to mark the 100th birth anniversary of Upadhyaya, who was an important leader of the Bharatiya Jana Sangh.
>
> While the missions celebrated his birthday with gusto, MEA even launched an e-book on Upadhyaya calling it Integral Humanism. According to the official BJP website, Integral Humanism, a doctrine developed by Upadhyaya, is among the guiding precepts of the ruling party and was first presented by Upadhyaya in the form of four lectures delivered in Bombay on 22-25 April 1965. In a foreword to the readers, foreign minister Sushma Swaraj compliments MEA officials for their efforts in ferreting out some 'pearls' from the thoughts of Upadhyaya to publish the e-book. She further says that the e-book will prove to be useful for both national and international leaders. . . .
>
> The e-book published by MEA's External Publicity Division is now facing

[69] *The Telegraph*, 19 February 2017.

> criticism from several former foreign secretaries for what has been described by some as MEA's unacceptable venture into domestic politics.[70]

Sushma Swaraj spoke, as she always does, with all the zeal of a convert. She was a socialist once. A booklet on Upadhyaya was also published by the MEA's External Publicity Division.[71]

What, indeed, did this convenient cult figure propagate? He was set up, incredibly as a rival to Nehru. He was the general secretary of the Jana Sangh, UP branch in 1951; became the BJP's president in 1967 and died in 1968. Upadhyaya sought, indeed, to 'purify' Muslims by getting them to shed their faith and identity; very much as Modi and Bhagwat hope to accomplish. Upadhyaya asserted:

> Undivided Bharat is not a Utopian idea, but a carefully thought-out ideal. Some people consider the Partition of India a settled fact. . . . These people have forgotten history and have never properly understood its implications. The country was divided into many parts during Muslim domination but our Hindu leaders never accepted that as a settled fact and continued to fight against it . . . there is only one nation in this country. There is no minority in this nation . . .

He further stated:

> . . . there exists only one culture here. There are no separate cultures here for Muslims and Christians. Culture is not related to mode of worship or sect; it is related to the country. Kabir, Jayasi and Rasakhan should serve as models for Muslims. Today their centre of loyalty is outside Bharat. The Muslims must completely change their sentiment and view.

During the 1965 war he advocated a Muslim-free corridor along the India-Pakistan boundary.

In no way was this politician different from others in the Jana Sangh. But a cult figure was needed. Advani & Company plumped for him. None outside the Sangh parivar misses him. He propagated hate. By the end of 2017 Modi had made impressive strides in this direction.

In less than five years since he became prime minister, he had undermined and subveiled institutions, refused to make himself accountable to parliament or the press, promoted Hindutva with State power and created a divisive atmosphere of suspicion and hate. Gujarat was steadily being replicated.

[70] *The Times of India*, 6 October 2017.

[71] *The Hindu*, 6 October 2018.

22. Endgame in 2018

Neither Narendra Modi nor the RSS ever stopped electioneering. A massive victory in the 2014 elections did not mellow either of them. Modi began to put the RSS's imprint on public institutions, vilify the opposition parties, denigrate Nehru and suborn the constitutional and administration systems. Cabinet ministers were by-passed as the Prime Minister reached out directly to civil servants; both were reduced to being servitors. His eyes were fixed on imposing the gains of 2014 in 2019, set up a one-party State, *Congress-mukt Bharat* (Congress-free India) which means just that; well in time for the RSS's 100th anniversary in 2025.

Conduct of foreign policy became a highly personalised affair to earn domestic support. Large sections of the media cooperated.

The RSS could now operate under more favourable conditions. No RSS chief went about projecting its views more systematically and virulently than did Mohan Bhagwat. Smaller ones followed his example. Never in all the years of independence has the country heard such calumnies on Muslims and Christians triggering off violent attacks on them.

This utterance by an M.L.A. from Bairia in Uttar Pradesh, Surendra Singh was typical. He said at Balliah on 14 January 2018: 'There are a very few Muslims who are patriotic. Once India becomes a Hindu rashtra (Hindu nation), Muslims who assimilate into our culture will stay in India. Those who will not are free to take asylum in any other country,' Surendra Singh told reporters. Describing Prime Minister Narendra Modi as an 'avatar purush' (reincarnation of a deity), Singh said, 'By the grace of god, India is going to be a global superpower thanks to the leadership of Modi and Uttar Pradesh Chief Minister Yogi Adityanath. Not only will India become a "vishwa guru", it will also become a Hindu rashtra by 2024.'[1]

The RSS-BJP establishment maintains a group of persons who were expected to spread communal hate while praising Modi; Sakshi Maharaj being foremost among them.

The theme of *Vishwaguru*, hitherto neglected by scholars, increasingly acquired prominence. Bhagwat said at Guwahati on 21 January that the RSS's aim was to bring about social transformation to make India 'vishwa guru'.[2] The RSS, he said at Patna on 11 February, can raise a force in three days as compared to the Army which needs 'six to seven months'. Since the usual denial followed, as is the norm with the RSS's more hare-brained utterances, it is best to set out the exact words.

[1] *The Asian Age*, 15 January 2018.

[2] *The Asian Age*, 22 January 2018.

> *Hamara military sanghatan nahin hai, military jaisi discipline hamari hai. Aur agar desh ko zaroorat padey, aur desh ka samveedhan . . . toh sena tayyar karne ko chhe saat mahine lag jayenge, Sanghke swayamsevakon ko leke teen din me tayyar honge, yeh hamaari kshamata hai.* (Ours is not a military organisation, but we have military discipline. And if the country requires it and the Constitution . . . then the Army would take six to seven months to get ready, our volunteers will take three days. This is our capability.)[3]

He is so ignorant as not to know that the lathi or trishul training, suited to street fighting in riots, may not quite suffice in modern warfare. State officials were inducted into RSS and BJP events. Derek O'Brien, an articulate Trinamool Congress M.P. voiced strong objections at one such event. 'What is the serving BSF DG, K.K. Sharma, doing in uniform at the "RSS-backed" NGO's function in Kolkata? Will take the issue to the Home Minister.'[4]

Modi intensified his rhetoric in a speech at Gonda on 24 February 2018. Earlier, on 21 November 2017, there was a train derailment in Kanpur, killing 150. It took India's Prime Minister two months to allege that it was not an accident but a conspiracy. He said:

> 'Kanpur rail accident in which hundreds were killed was a conspiracy and conspirators carried it out sitting across the border . . . Gonda is adjoining Nepal . . . if the cross-border foes want to carry out their work, is it not necessary that more vigil is maintained in Gonda?'
>
> The change in tone marks a tactical escalation in Modi's speeches, which has gone from being focused on development to being more shrill and communal, from his *kabristaan* and *Ramzan vs. Diwali* comments to Friday's Pakistan targeting. . . .
>
> Eleven districts, including Gonda, that account for 52 seats were to go to the polls on 27 February in Phase 5 of the Uttar Pradesh Assembly elections.
>
> The PM also took a broadside against the UP administration, saying: 'If such people, who will help them (conspirators) get elected from here, will Gonda be safe then, will the nation be safe then?'
>
> Continuing in the same vein, Modi asked people to vote only for 'patriotic' candidates.
>
> 'Gonda needs to elect only those who are full of patriotism, only then we can do anything good for Gonda. There should not be any mistake in this election . . . be it the SP or the BSP, not a single seat should go to them. . . . 100 per cent seats should be won by the BJP,' pressed full confidence about the party's victory.[5]

[3] *The Indian Express*, 11 February 2018.

[4] *The Telegraph*, 12 February 2018.

[5] *DNA*, 24 February 2017.

He said, 'BJP will celebrate kesariya Holi in [UP].'[6] The Uttar Pradesh police maintained there was no sabotage. No craters or explosives were found on the track. Playing with national security for votes is typical of Modi's electioneering in Joseph McCarthy's style. If the integrity and patriotism of the opposition are challenged the very basis of parliamentary democracy is destroyed. Why would the opposition co-operate with the government?

The RSS held the three-yearly meeting of its Akhil Bharatiya Pratinidhi Sabha at Nagpur from 9 to 11 March 2018, comprising 1,300 members. An 'RSS functionary' said:

> The RSS will engage its affiliated organisations at the three-yearly Akhil Bharatiya Pratinidhi Sabha (APBS) meeting, scheduled from 9 to 11 March, to ensure unity in the Sangh Parivar ahead of the 2019 general elections.
>
> Over 1,500 delegates from various organisations under the Sangh parivar will also take a call on their next team of office-bearers for the next three years.
>
> Sources in RSS said that no major changes were expected in the organisation. Speculation was rife that Sahsarkaryawah Dattatreya Hosabale would replace incumbent Sarkaryawah Suresh alias Bhaiyyaji Joshi. At least two middle-level RSS functionaries told *The Indian Express* that no such move seems to be afoot. 'Bhaiyyaji hasn't given any indication that he wants to step down. So, it is unlikely that he will be replaced,' said one.
>
> Hosabale's name had been making the rounds since the last ABPS at Nagpur. He was said to be a favourite of the BJP, too, and was preferred by Narendra Modi and Amit Shah. 'That itself may be a deterrent for the RSS, which won't like to give primacy to the choice of the BJP ahead of the 2019 elections. If BJP returns to power under the Modi-Shah duo next year, the RSS would prefer to have its own chosen team at the helm. Joshi may make way for his successor in the middle of his next term,' said a source.
>
> The RSS's stature as the BJP's patriarch has grown by leaps and bounds due to its prime role in ensuring the party's victory in the north-east. 'This will certainly keep the RSS a notch above the individual charisma of Narendra Modi, something that can never be compromised within the organisation,' the source added. Amit Shah's visit to the RSS headquarters immediately after the BJP's north-east victory, is also significant from this point of view.
>
> Apart from having its chosen Sarkaryawah, the RSS will also try to engage its sparring constituents like the Bharatiya Majdoor Sangh (BMS) and Vishwa Hindu Parishad (VHP) to ensure complete unity ahead of the 2019 the general election. 'The RSS would like to ensure that the BJP wins the election. It is extremely crucial for it in the wake of its 100th anniversary celebrations in 2025.'[7]

[6] *The Indian Express*, 24 February 2017.

[7] Vivek Deshpande, *The Indian Express*, 5 March 2018.

Modi blew the trumpet ahead of the event. So did Bhagwat.

'Say with pride that you are a Hindu. As Hindu, we have to unite because the responsibility of this country is upon us. From ancient time it is our home. We have nowhere else to go in this world. If anything wrong happens with this country, we will be responsible,' Bhagwat told a gathering of RSS workers in Meerut.

He was speaking on the occasion of 25th Swayamsevak samagam, called Rashtryoday. The assembly was touted as the biggest gathering of RSS workers in recent years with close to three lakh registrations.

He said hardline Hindutva stands for commitment to truth and commitment to Ahimsa. 'When we become hardliners we will celebrate diversity more,' he said, before adding a note of caution: 'But the world has a rule that it listens to good things only when there is a power standing behind them.'

Emphasising that it was important to be strong, but that the gathering was not a show of strength, Bhagwat said, 'Even gods take sacrifice of lambs because it is powerless. Even, gods do not respect those without strength. You don't need to show strength, it is visible when it is there.'[8]

Representatives of 60,000 shakhas met to elect the new sarkaryavah (general secretary). Shyamlal Yadav lucidly explained the working of the mammoth RSS machine.

Apart from the Akhil Bharatiya Pratinidhis, the ABPS has delegates nominated by front organisations of the Sangh, the largest of which is the Vishwa Hindu Parishad (VHP), which has around 40 delegates, the most among the front organisations. All former Prant Pracharaks (state leaders) of the RSS are invited to the ABPS. The BJP is normally represented at the meeting by its national president and general secretary (organisation).

According to the annual report presented by Sarkaryawah Suresh Bhaiyyaji Joshi at last year's ABPS meeting in Coimbatore, the RSS's work has now reached 59,136 places in India, where it is holding either a daily shakha, or a weekly Milan, or a sangh mandli.

While the annual meetings of the ABPS are held in cities across the country; every fourth meeting of the ABPS must necessarily be held in Nagpur, the headquarters and birthplace of the Sangh. It is at the meetings in Nagpur that the Sarkaryawah is elected.

The normal practice is for the new Sarkaryawah to be chosen from

[8] *The Indian Express*, 26 February 2018.

among the three Sah-Sarkaryawahs who are deputies to the general secretary. Bhaiyyaji Joshi's Sah-Sarkaryawahs are Suresh Soni, Dr. Krishna Gopal and Dattatreya Hosabale.

Soni, who is from Madhya Pradesh, was on leave last year due to bad health, but has now recovered. He looks after RSS organisations involved in education. Krishna Gopal, from Uttar Pradesh, is in charge of the BJP, and is closely involved in the day-to-day coordination with the party. Hosabale, from Karnataka, is relatively young, and earlier worked in the Akhil Bharatiya Vidyarthi Parishad (ABVP), the BJP's student wing.

However, those who understand the Sangh say it is also possible that someone else altogether may be chosen. In theory, it is possible for Joshi to get another term; however, given that he is already 70 and has been Sarkaryawah thrice already, this seems unlikely. There is no election for the post of Sarsanghchalak. The chief of the RSS appoints his successor, who holds the position for life.

The executive head of the RSS has full control over the organisation's every activity. This weekend's meeting is extra important because of the remarkable growth and spread of the BJP, which now rules 22 states either on its own or as part of an alliance, apart from being in power at the Centre. Close coordination between the party and its ideological parent is crucial, given that Lok Sabha elections are due next year. While the RSS insists that it is not a political organisation, the fact is that swayamsevaks play a very important role in the BJP's election campaign. The RSS also seeks to play big brother to the BJP, with pracharaks attempting to influence policies and appointments made by BJP governments at the Centre and the states. A heavyweight Sarkaryawah at this stage is essential for the RSS to maintain the line between its cadres and the policies of the BJP.

The election officer explains the election process, after which a senior functionary proposes a name for the new Sarkaryawah. This name is generally accepted, and the Sarkaryawah is declared elected unopposed. The formal process of the election notwithstanding, the decision on the new Sarkaryawah is taken by consensus among the top leaders of the RSS. After he is elected, the new Sarkaryawah announces his team.

The present system of holding the Sarkaryawah election was adopted in the early fifties. Three Sarsanghchalaks, Balasaheb Deoras, Prof. Rajendra Singh alias Rajju Bhaiya, and the current chief, Mohan Bhagwat, served multiple terms as Sarkaryawah (Deoras, 1965-73; Rajju Bhaiyya, 1978-87; Bhagwat 2000-09). Between Rajju Bhaiya and Bhagwat, H.V. Sheshadri was Sarkaryawah from 1987 to 2000, the longest tenure on the post.

Deoras became Sarkaryawah after Madhavrao Mule passed away in office.

Rajju Bhaiya quit in 1987 due to ill-health, and became Sah-sarkaryawah under Sheshadri.[9]

Suresh aka Bhaiyyaji Joshi was 're-elected' general secretary for the fourth term, the permissible maximum. He was first elected in 2008, succeeding Bhagwat. At 70 he is five years short of the maximum age limit 75 which Modi deftly imposed on the BJP to keep Advani and M.M. Joshi out; no doubt with RSS support. An RSS 'insider' explained:

> The RSS is planning centenary celebrations in 2025. It is all for the BJP returning to power in 2019 to facilitate a smooth passage to 2025. It's true that some Sangh outfits like Bharatiya Mazdoor Sangh, Vishwa Hindu Parishad, Bharatiya Kisan Sangh and Swadeshi Jagran Manch have crossed swords with the Narendra Modi government on some issues. But the attempt in the ABPS is to bring about a peace among all at least till 2019. Joshi served the job better than anyone else.[10]

The RSS's membership had peaked; though report of its actual strength varied. J.P. Yadav's report reveals a lot.

> The Rashtriya Swayamsevak Sangh's presence has grown by more than 30 per cent since Narendra Modi became Prime Minister, successive annual reports of the organisation show.
>
> The Sangh's 'activities are now being held in 96 per cent of the geographical mass of India', the organisation's joint general secretary, Krishna Gopal, told reporters at the Akhil Bharatiya Pratinidhi Sabha meeting.
>
> 'We have a presence across the country, except for a few pockets in Nagaland, Mizoram and the Kashmir valley.' According to the Sangh's latest annual report, it now holds a record 58,976 shakhas or daily gatherings at neighbourhood parks in 37,190 locations in the country. In March 2014, two months before the Modi government came to power, it had 44,982 at 29,624 locations. By March 2015, the figure had leapt to 51,332 shakhas at 33,223 locations. In March 2016, it was 56,859 at 36,867 locations and last March, 57,165 at 36,729 locations.
>
> It is widely believed that the BJP's electoral entry into areas where it previously had little presence is preceded by silent spadework by the Sangh in these places. . . . It adds that a record 1.25 lakh urban Indians, including professionals in India and abroad, had expressed an interest in joining the

[9] *The Indian Express*, 8 March 2018.

[10] *The Indian Express*, 11 March 2018.

Sangh in the current financial year. 'We had never before seen such interest in the Sangh (from the urban idle class),' an official said.[11]

According to another account:

> The RSS is the world's largest non-governmental association, it claims. Close to 1.5-2 million take part in 57,000 daily shakhas, 14,000 weekly shakhas, and 7,000 monthly shakhas in 36,293 different locations, according to a report in 2016. On top of that, the RSS has six million alumni and affiliate volunteers. Without doubt, this is a formidable organisation, but its rise has been dramatic in recent years.[12]

The *Hindustan Times* reported on 3 July 2018 that 'the Sangh registered its highest growth rate between March 2015 and 2016. 10,143 Shakhas were introduced at 5,161 new places in the country between 2012 and 2015, and the number rose to 57,233 in April 2017'. The RSS's current strength is 5 million. Its target 'is 10 million by 2025'.

Vikas Pathak's report said:

> The RSS seems to have expanded its sphere of influence in 2018, with the number of shakhas (branches) – daily gatherings in neighbourhood parks – increasing by about 1,800 this year.
>
> A report presented by RSS general secretary Suresh (Bhaiyyaji) Joshi at the ongoing Akhil Bharatiya Pratinidhi Sabha here said 58,967 shakhas were functional at 37,190 places across the country. The number in 2017 stood at 57,165, functional at 36,729 locations. . . .
>
> The rising shakha numbers is a reversal of the trend in the first decade of the millennium. The Sangh's annual report in 2010 had admitted a decline of 4,000 shakhas from the 2009 figure of 43,905 shakhas. The 2009 figure, too, was much lower than the figure of 51,000 in 2005-06. There was, however, a slight increase in the numbers in 2011.[13]

The only resolution which the Sabha, the general body, passed expressed its concern at the vanishing dialects and the need to preserve Indian languages.

> To ensure that RSS is not seen as ceding ground, a subtle message was delivered that the outfits will continue to press for their demands. Joshi said the government may have concerns about implementing certain measures,

[11] *The Telegraph*, 11 March 2018.

[12] Andersen and Damle, *The RSS: A View to the Inside*, Penguin Viking, 2018.

[13] *The Hindu*, 10 March 2018.

> but that the RSS expects ideology to drive organisations to pursue their cause without any compromise.
>
> A senior RSS functionary said that the government had largely accommodated the organisation's demands; the BJP's response to the call for the construction of a Ram Temple at the disputed site at Ayodhya was also favourable, this person added on condition of anonymity.
>
> By allowing the government greater flexibility in policy making, the Sangh has opted for a mentor's role, but will continue to monitor as well.[14]

All the reports agree on one point; namely that the RSS flourished *after* the Modi government came to power in May 2014.

It is this formidable force which its chief claims to be able to launch into the field of action in a mere three days. Meanwhile, this rabidly communal, secret, militant and fascist body sets out the BJP's agenda. Without its help the BJP cannot win elections. Bhagwat's confidence grew with the RSS's strength.

> Criticising those from other religions who he alleged try conversion of Hindus, Bhagwat said, 'When you are saying that all religions have a common teaching, then why ask people to change their religion? I would tell Hindus to be prepared for a confrontation when it comes to religion. Hindus need to remain alert when people start a sweet talk. I would appeal Hindus to spend one third of their time for the country.'[15]

Grew also a sense of insecurity among the minorities.

> Cardinal Oswald Gracias, President of the Catholic Bishops' Conference of India, [the Indian Catholic Church's apex decision-making body,] said that there is 'growing anxiety' among minority communities 'because the government is not acting enough' to protect them . . . there have been 'more attempts' to polarise society in the last four years. . . .
>
> 'Fear would be an exaggerated word. I would say there is anxiety, a growing anxiety among the minorities that things would get worse. It will be exaggerated to say the Church is being attacked everywhere in the country. It is not. But there is an anxiety because the government is not acting enough (in protecting minorities) and not conveying the right message. My complaint with the government is that they are not giving the message that it (attacks on minorities) is not acceptable.'[16]

[14] *Hindustan Times*, 13 March 2018.

[15] *DNA*, 15 April 2018.

[16] *The Indian Express*, 7 June 2018.

Goa's Archbishop Filipe Neri Ferrao advised Catholics to play an 'active role' in politics while warning that 'the Indian Constitution is in danger' and that 'a kind of monoculturalism' has gripped the country.

In his annual pastoral letter for 2018-19, which was released Sunday, Ferrao wrote:

> It is advisable that the lay faithful play an active role in the political field; they should, however, follow the dictates of their conscience while doing so and shun 'sycophantic' politics. They should thus strengthen democracy and, on the other hand, help to improve the functioning of the state administration. The ideals of social justice and the fight against corruption are of utmost importance.

Stating that people across the country are being 'uprooted from their land and homes in the name of development', the Archbishop warned that human rights are being trampled as 'in recent times we see a new trend emerging in our country which demands uniformity in what and how we eat, dress, live and even worship: a kind of monoculturalism'.

> Ferrao's letter [came] weeks after Delhi's Archbishop Anil Couto wrote in a letter that India is 'witnessing a turbulent political atmosphere' and the community should begin a 'prayer campaign' ahead of the elections. Couto's remarks faced criticism, including from Home Minister Rajnath Singh, following which he clarified that they were not directed at the BJP-RSS. . . .
>
> In the letter, Ferrao wrote that the Catholic Bishops' Conference of India had declared in its plenary assembly that the Church should 'diligently promote and stand by values like secularism, freedom of speech and freedom to practise one's religion enshrined in the Indian Constitution'.
>
> While focusing on poverty, Ferrao wrote that the need to 'work hard to protect the Constitution' is more urgent now.[17]

Archbishop Ferrao exercised his rights as an Indian citizen. A similar plea by a Muslim cleric would have been denounced.

Relations between the RSS and the BJP grew closer in the pre-election year. Smriti Kak Ramachandran explained the mechanics of growing collaboration.

> [Rashtriya Swayamsevak Sangh's] sangathan mantris (organisational general secretaries) . . . will have a role in all election-related decision making ahead of the 2019 general elections and the assembly polls in four states this year, people familiar with the developments said.

[17] *The Indian Express*, 5 June 2018.

RSS functionaries said the organisational general secretaries are involved in decision making, but now a 'concerted move' has been made to ensure their participation in every aspect of electoral preparations.

[The Bharatiya Janata Party's ideological parent, the RSS, deputes] organisational general secretaries to the party to oversee coordination. They are the central link between the RSS and the BJP.

'To strengthen coordination between the Sangh and the party, the role of sangathan mantris will be reinforced and this decision has been taken after a series of meetings between the RSS brass and BJP president Amit Shah,' a Sangh functionary said, who did not want to be identified.

The process of involving sangathan mantris in candidate selection, zeroing in on key poll planks and the precise details of campaigning was first tried out during the 2017 Uttar Pradesh (UP) assembly elections and in the Karnataka elections in May.

'In both the states, the experiment was a success. BJP won with an unprecedented mandate in UP, where it bagged 312 of the 403 seats and in coastal Karnataka and Malnad regions, it won 28 out of 33 seats in the assembly elections. It has now been decided to allow sangathan mantris to have a greater say in decision making,' the functionary said. . . .

RSS functionaries, who provide feedback to the BJP about the mood of the electorate, have also relayed concerns of their volunteers and those of the BJP workers . . . 'When tickets were given to those who came from other parties, it led to resentment within the cadre. So to avoid recurrence of such disagreements, there will be coordinated decision making,' the functionary said.

The second functionary said new sangathan mantris would be appointed in states, where the BJP units are 'considered weak' and that those who have 'grown too close to the party' would be replaced.[18]

The RSS expects its men to keep a distance from and within the BJP and not 'get mixed up'. It is equally clear that the RSS has no love for the BJP's allies. If circumstances permit the RSS will secure the demise of the NDA; although the NDA has only a shadowy existence.

The BJP has freely sought the RSS's support for the polls. Amit Shah

sought the active support and coordination of the RSS to win the upcoming elections in four states, Rajasthan, Madhya Pradesh, Chhattisgarh and Mizoram, besides a possible early election in Telangana. Shah also wanted the Sangh's feedback and inputs on expanding the party's footprint in Andhra which may go to polls in April/May 2019.

[18] *Hindustan Times*, 9 July 2018.

> Shah was addressing a three day BJP-RSS 'chintan baithak'; a coordination meeting at a famous pilgrim centre Mantralayam on the banks of Thungabhadra river in Kurnool district of Andhra Pradesh . . . BJP senior functionary Kapileswaraiah [said] over the phone that this was a routine annual meeting between the BJP and RSS functionaries. Representatives from close to 55 outfits including Viswa Hindu Parishad would be joining the discussions and review their activities in social, political and educational fields.
>
> Shah is understood to have sought the cooperation of the RSS and its front outfits in testing the public pulse and explaining to them the good work done by the Narendra Modi led BJP government in the last four years.[19]

A determined attempt was made by the RSS at its highest lead to win respectability, not among the minorities, but among Hindus and foreigners who doubted its credentials. It invited diplomats of 60 countries, bar Pakistan, to a lecture series. Invited also were representatives of national and regional political parties, of the media, industry and other sectors.[20] The RSS was coming out of the purdah to work harder for its goal of 'vishwa guru' on which Bhagwat had expatiated on 9 August. In this it received same help from ex-President Pranab Mukherjee's visit to the RSS HQs on 7 June 2018.

There followed Bhagwat's much hyped oration; significantly at the Vigyan Bhawan in New Delhi on 17 September 2018. It was part of a three day series called 'Bharat of Future: An RSS Perspective'. He was at pains to deny that the RSS wielded a remote control on the Modi government. The statement which aroused keenest interest was that there can be no Hindu Rashtra without Muslims.

> 'A Hindu Rashtra (nation) does not envision the exclusion of Muslims and the Rashtriya Swayamsevak Sangh (RSS) has not gone against the Constitution and the law of the land.' . . .
>
> On the second day of his lecture series, an outreach exercise aimed at those who were not familiar with the Sangh, Bhagwat sought to clarify that the RSS is not anti-minorities and doesn't propose to change the framework of the Constitution, as is often alleged by the Opposition.
>
> 'We think everyone must abide by the Constitution. . . . The RSS has never gone against the Constitution. [Sure,] the words secular and socialist were added later, but now they are there,' he said. The RSS is the ideological parent of the Bharatiya Janata Party (BJP).
>
> In 2017, Bhagwat's statement that the Constitution was based on an understanding of the 'Bharatiya' (Indian) ethos, but that there are several laws in use based on foreign sources that need a rethink, was perceived by the

[19] S. Rama Krishna, *Sunday Guardian*, 1 September 2018.

[20] *The Indian Express*, 12 September 2018.

Opposition as an indicator of the Sangh's intent to change the Constitution.

Speaking at length on the issue of Hindutva, as defined by the Sangh, Bhagwat said the concept of a Hindu Rashtra, or Hindu nation, does not rest on segregation or rejection of any community or faith. 'Hindu Rashtra doesn't mean there's no place for Muslims. The day it becomes so, it won't be Hindutva. Hindutva talks about one world family.' . . .

Jawaharlal Nehru University professor Badri Narayan said Bhagwat's statement that a Hindu Rashtra cannot be without Muslims was part of a 'discursive strategy to appropriate, absorb and include all sections and fragments that were considered opposed to their ideology'.[21]

To quote the speech in the original Hindi:

'*Hum kehte hain ki hamara Hindu Rashtra hai. Hindu Rashtra hai iska matlab isme Musalman nahin chahiye aisa bilkul nahin hai . . . jis din yeh kaha jayega ki yahan Musalman nahin chahiye . . . uss din woh Hindutva nahi rahega. Woh toh vishwa-kutumb ki baat karta hai* (We say ours is a Hindu Rashtra. Hindu Rashtra does not mean it has no place for Muslims. The day it is said that Muslims are unwanted here, the concept of Hindutva will cease to exist. Hindutva believes that the world is a family). . . .

'The image of Bharat is that we accept and welcome diversity . . . global dharma was nurtured here. Bharat is the trustee of all this knowledge, and has given it to the world from time to time,' he said.

He did, however, equate organising the society with organising Hindus. 'Like an examination in which we solve the easy questions first and then pick the hard ones later . . . we will organise those first who admit they are Hindus . . . There might be people who consider us enemy . . . our objective is not to finish them but to take them along . . . that is Hindutva in the real sense,' he said.[22]

He had once earlier remarked, addressing a gathering in Jammu:

'Our country is Hindu Rashtra and our ancestors are Hindus. This is what the world knows and identifies us with. Ours is a Hindu Rashtra and our ancestors are Hindus,' adding, 'We are all sons of Bharat Mata.'

'Our country is Hindu Rashtra not because one practices a particular religion or not. It is Hindu Rashtra because it accepts all practices and this is what the world has known us since thousands of years and identifies us with.'[23]

21 *Hindustan Times*, 18 September 2018.

22 *The Indian Express*, 18 September 2018.

23 *Greater Kashmir*, 13 November 2016.

Two days later the mask dropped. Bhagwat said on 19 September that the RSS had reservations on the word 'minority' which is used in Articles 29 and 30 of the Constitution. He proceeded to demand construction of the Ram temple at Ayodhya.

> 'Lord Ram is not only a god for the majority of this country but is also the protector of this country's traditions and its dignity and is also an Imam-e-Hind for many . . . all sections of Indian society have faith in him . . . We are not talking about any Ram mandir as many such mandirs were demolished . . . we are talking about the birthplace of lord Ram and only a mandir should come up there,' asserted Mr. Bhagwat, as he said if the temple was built, it would resolve contentious issues between Hindus and Muslims.[24]

On the last day, confronted with Golwalkar's *Bunch of Thoughts*, he said:

> *Rahi baat* 'Bunch of Thoughts' *ki, batein jo boli jaati hain woh paristhiti vishesh, prasang vishesh ke sandarbh mein boli jaati hain. Woh shashwat nahin rehti hain. Ek baat toh yeh hai ki, Guruji ke jo shashwat vichar hain unka ek sankalan prasiddh hua hai* 'Sri Guruji: Vision and Mission' *usme tatkalik sandarbh se aane waali saari batein humne hatakar usme jo sada kaal ke liye upyukt vichar hain woh rakhe hain. Usko aap padhiye. Usme aapko aisi baatein nahin milengi.*
>
> (As far as *Bunch of Thoughts* goes, every statement carries a context of time and circumstance . . . his enduring thoughts are in a popular edition in which we have removed all remarks that have a temporary context and retained those that will endure for ages. You won't find the (Muslim-is-an-enemy) remark there.)

The correspondent Ravish Tiwari noted that 'though the omission of Golwalkar from the RSS chief's address is not exactly the "repudiation" that Ramamurti sought in 1982, Bhagwat's prescription of an edited version of Golwalkar's thoughts is possibly the first public signal of an RSS rethink on some of its contentious issues'.[25] It is odd that the RSS waited till this extravaganza to distance itself from Golwalkar. In a sworn affidavit, it swore by this very *Bunch of Thoughts*.

Meanwhile, the RSS and the VHP stepped up their campaign for a temple at Ayodhya as the election drew closer. It was also at work on elimination of Article 370 of the Constitution on J&K's autonomy, and on a uniform civil code.

Bhagwat also expressed his fears about State power.

> 'State has power, nobody can deny that. It is needed. But because the state

[24] *The Asian Age*, 20 September 2018.

[25] *The Indian Express*, 20 September 2018.

> has the power you need to have control over it. The state's power is controlled by the Constitution but there is no guarantee that the state will abide by the Constitution. For that, you need an aware public opinion and public organisations who represent that public opinion.
>
> 'That is why public organisations should never be subservient [to] state power. They should keep away from the politics of state power. They cannot be the organisations of political parties,' said Bhagwat at a function organised to mark the 99th birth anniversary of RSS ideologue and founder of Swadeshi Jagran Manch, Dattopant Thengadi. . . .
>
> 'There are people within the government who want this change. But such is the arrangement of state power that it does not allow them much room,' said Bhagwat asserting change would occur only if public outfits keep on track in the long haul.[26]

The RSS will help the BJP government; but it will never relinquish its role as its guru.

[26] *DNA*, 11 November 2018.

23. RSS & Violence

The RSS was conceived in sin; the sin of criminal violence. Its 'historians' never fail to emphasise that its founder Hedgewar was prompted by the riots in Nagpur. The Hindu Mahasabha was there to project the Hindu viewpoint, led as it was by men like Lala Lajpat Rai and Madan Mohan Malaviya. It was Mahasabhaites who helped to found it. The difference lay not in ideology. Both submitted to Hindutva. The difference laid in the RSS's commitment to recourse to violence whenever it thought it necessary to do so. Its rejection of non-violence was announced from house tops. It was set up not only to conduct an ideological campaign but much more besides. Disdain for Gandhi was no secret. 'Here we had leaders who were, as if, pledged to sap all manliness from their own people.'[1] Golwalkar refers to 'the docile Hindu'[2] and castigated those who 'committed the most heinous sin of killing the life-spirit of a great and ancient people. To preach impotency [sic] to a society which gave rise to a Shivaji . . . and to break the self-confident and proud spirit of such a great and virile society has no parallel in the history of the world for the sheer magnitude of its betrayal.'[3]

If the secular Hindu was a traitor, the Muslim was an alien foe with whom no reconciliation or peace was possible.

> Then came the question of Muslims. They had come here as invaders. They were conceiving themselves as conquerors and rulers here for the last twelve hundred years. That complex was still in their mind. History has recorded that their antagonism was not merely political. Had it been so, they could have been won over in a very short time. But it was so deep-rooted that whatever we believed in, the Muslim was wholly hostile to it. If we worship in the temple, he would desecrate it. If we carry on bhajans and car [sic] festivals, that would irritate him. If we worship cow, he would like to eat it. If we glorify woman as a symbol of sacred motherhood, he would like to molest her. He was tooth and nail opposed to our way of life in all aspects – religious, cultural, social etc. He had imbibed that hostility to the very core.[4]

The lathi was an integral part of the volunteers' training kit. He has since

1 Golwalkar, *Bunch of Thoughts*, p. 153.

2 Ibid., p. 150.

3 Ibid., p. 152.

4 Ibid., pp. 147-8.

acquired the trishul. 'In Punjab sharpened trishuls have become standard wear for Hindu youths.'[5]

On 11 June 1970, Golwalkar waxed eloquent before a group of journalists. The communal atmosphere was tense in the wake of the Ahmedabad and Bhiwandi riots. *Organiser* reported this exchange:

> Q. Who will teach Muslims to identify themselves completely with the country and its culture?
> A. You and me, all of us.
> Q. Can you teach by beating?
> A. Beating is of two kinds: mother beating her child and an enemy sticking a man. We have not done any beating. But if, as and when we do teach by beating, it will be like the mother's beating of her child – out of love and solicitude for the child's welfare.

Yet he complained, 'misunderstandings are sought to be created about the training in the use of *danda* (lathi), *yogchap* (lezim), *khadga* (sword), *vetracharma* (canefight) etc. that is imparted in the RSS branches'. 'What has our good behaviour towards Muslim faith and the Muslim people brought us?' Golwalkar asked. The alternative is propounded openly. Is there any place for violence in the life of a society?

> Yes, but it should be used as a surgeon's knife . . . to cure society of any malady that needs such a surgical intervention. . . . In this task of self-protection we might have to destroy evil persons. . . . If these Asur [evil forces] are to be defeated through the use of force, force should be used. . . . Generally speaking, it is a matter of common experience that evil forces do not understand the language of logic and sweet nature. They can be controlled by force.[6]

According to K.R. Malkani, member of the RSS and BJP, Golwalkar invested violence with religious sanction. He thought it was ridiculous to describe India as a land of *ahimsa*. 'Obviously we did not expand into Central Asia and South-East Asia by sermons alone. It is significant that every Hindu god is armed.' He ridiculed the suggestion that Alexander had defeated king Puru (Porus of Greek historians) of India. Fact of the matter, he said, was that Puru had more territory at the end of that war than before – and Alexander was forced to beat a hasty retreat.

He thought that a proper history of India had not yet been written. 'It is

[5] Inderjit Badhwar, Prabhu Chawla and Farzand Ahmed, 'Militant Revivalism', *India Today*, 31 May 1986, p. 76.

[6] *Spotlights*, pp. 44, 45, 110, 188.

> ridiculous to divide our national history into Hindu period, Muslim period and British period. History can't be named after rulers; a proper history has to be a history of the people. And so our entire history is Hindu history.'[7]

In December 1948, the British High Commissioner in New Delhi, Sir Archibald Nye, characterised the RSS in a report to London as 'a Hindu right wing semi-military party'.[8]

The chief secretary to the government of Uttar Pradesh, Rajeshwar Dayal recorded in his memoirs how Golwalkar was detected with a 'smoking gun' but was allowed to go scot-free by the chief minister Govind Ballabh Pant.

> When communal tension was still at fever-pitch, the Deputy Inspector-General of Police of the western Range, a very seasoned and capable officer, B.B.L. Jaitley, arrived at my house in great secrecy. He was accompanied by two of his officers who brought with them two large steel trunks securely locked. When the trunks were opened, they revealed incontrovertible evidence of a dastardly conspiracy to create a communal holocaust throughout the western districts of the province. The trunks were crammed with blueprints of great accuracy and professionalism of every town and village in that vast area, prominently marking out the Muslim localities and habitations. There were also detailed instructions regarding access to the various locations, and other matters which amply revealed their sinister purport.
>
> Greatly alarmed by those revelations, I immediately took the police party to Premier's house. There, in a closed room, Jaitley gave a full report of his discovery, backed by all the evidence contained in the steel trunks. Timely raids conducted on the premises of the RSS had brought the massive conspiracy to light. The whole plot had been concerted under the direction and supervision of the Supremo of the organisation himself. Both Jaitley and I pressed for the immediate arrest of the prime accused, Shri Golwalkar, who was still in the area.
>
> Pantji could not but accept the evidence of his eyes and ears and expressed deep concern. But instead of agreeing to the immediate arrest of the ring leader as we had hoped, and as Kidwai would have done, he asked for the matter to be placed for consideration by the Cabinet at its next meeting. It was no doubt a matter of political delicacy as the roots of the RSS had gone deep into the body politic. There were also other political compulsions as RSS sympathisers, both covert and overt, were to be found in the Congress party itself and even in the Cabinet. It was no secret that the presiding officer of the Upper House, Atma Govind Kher, was himself an adherent and his sons were openly members of the RSS.

[7] K.R. Malkani, *The RSS Story*, New Delhi: Impex India, 1980, p. 42.

[8] Lionel Carter (ed.), *Towards a Ceasefire in Kashmir*, Manohar, 2018, p. 680.

> At the Cabinet meeting there was the usual procrastination and much irrelevant talk. The fact that the police had unearthed a conspiracy which would have set the whole province in flames and that the officers concerned deserved warm commendation hardly seemed to figure in the discussion. What ultimately emerged was that a letter should be issued to Shri Golwalkar pointing out the contents and nature of the evidence which had been gathered and demanding an explanation thereof. At my insistence, such a letter if it were to be sent, should be issued by the Premier himself to carry greater weight. Pantji asked me to prepare a draft, which I did in imitation of his own characteristic style. The letter was to be delivered forthwith and two police officers were assigned for the purpose.
>
> Golwalkar, however, had been tipped off and he was nowhere to be found in the area. He was tracked down southwards but he managed to elude the couriers in pursuit. This infructuous chase continued from place to place and weeks passed.
>
> Came 30 January 1948 when the Mahatma, that supreme apostle of peace, fell to a bullet fired by an RSS fanatic. The whole tragic episode left me sick at heart.

Timely action by Pant would have saved Gandhi's life.[9]

Painstaking researches by the Italian scholar Marzia Casolari have revealed that fairly early in its life the RSS took a fancy to Mussolini's Fascism. B.S. Moonje was president of the Hindu Mahasabha in 1927 and was close to the RSS as well. He travelled to Italy in 1931, six years after the RSS was set up, and was dazzled by what he saw. He met Mussolini (Mahasabha's Savarkar preferred Hitler's Germany). Moonje founded the Bhonsala Military School in 1934 and began to work on the foundation of the Central Hindu Military Education Society, whose aim was 'to bring about military regeneration of the Hindus and to fit Hindu youths for undertaking the entire responsibility for the defence of their motherland'.[10]

Casolari writes:

> The links between the RSS, the Hindu Mahasabha and the military institutions connected with Moonje were fairly close. Hedgewar was a member of the board of governors of the aforementioned Central Hindu Military Education Society, together with Jayakar, Kelkar, Aney and Khaparde (all leading members of the Hindu Mahasabha) and, of course, Moonje. The chairman was Shreeman Motilal Manakchand, also known as Pratap Seth, and the vice-chairman was Khaparde. The rules of this new society included a provision whereby if it were to be disbanded, all real estate and other properties including liquid assets and

9 Rajeshwar Dayal, *A Life of Our Times*, pp. 93-4.

10 Marzia Casolari, *In the Shade of the Swastika*, p. 79.

donated goods were to be devolved to the Rashtriya Swayamsewak Sangh.

British sources confirm the existence of close links between Moonje and the RSS, as well as the fascist character of the latter. According to an Intelligence report of 1933, 'Note on the Rashtriya Swayam Sewak Sangh', Moonje had re-organised the Sangh in the Marathi speaking districts and in the Central Provinces in 1927. The report, describing the activity and the character of the RSS, warned that 'It is perhaps no exaggeration to assert that the Sangh hopes to be in future India what the "Fascist" are to Italy and the "Nazi" to Germany'. Moonje advocated a policy of 'Strike First'. As early as 1935 the Government of India's Home Department perceptively noted: 'It is, however, capable of being used for any purpose the organisers decide on, and is a potential danger. The Sangh is essentially an anti-Muslim organisation aiming at exclusively Hindu supremacy in the country.'[11]

By any test Golwalkar's coarse denunciation falls within the ambit of what has come to be known as 'hate speech' or, 'group libel'. The RSS has spread hate speech for nearly a century from 1925 to 2018. It plans to 'celebrate' the 100th anniversary of its birth in 2025; hopefully with a Modi regime in power.

A classic work on hate speech establishes beyond doubt that speech has consequences.[12] Jeremy Waldron is University Professor, New York University School of Law and Chichele Professor of Social and Political Theory, All Souls College, University of Oxford. He quotes from the posters put up in some cities in the United States. One of them is relevant to the situation in India.

> Don't be fooled into thinking you are welcome here. The society around you may seem hospitable and non-discriminatory, but the truth is that you are not wanted, and you and your families will be shunned, excluded, beaten, and driven out, whenever we can get away with it. We may have to keep a low profile right now. But don't get too comfortable. Remember what has happened to you and your kind in the past. Be afraid.[13]

Waldron writes:

> The harm that expressions of racial hatred do is harm in the first instance to the groups who are denounced or bestialised in the racist pamphlets and billboards. It is not harm – if I can put it bluntly – to the white liberals who find the racist invective distasteful. Maybe we should admire some lawyer who says he hates what the racist says but defends to the death his right to say it, yet this

[11] Ibid., p. 89.

[12] Jeremy Waldron, *The Harm in Hate Speech*, Harvard University Press, 2012.

[13] Ibid., p. 2.

> sort of intellectual resilience is not what's at issue. The question is about the direct targets of the abuse. Can their lives be led, can their children be brought up, can their hopes be maintained and their worst fears dispelled, in a social environment polluted by these materials?[14]

Speech has consequences, especially if hate speech has been spoken in an orchestrated manner for decades. As Catharine A. MacKinnon remarks in her book *Only Words.*[15]

Waldron puts it neatly: 'The issue is publication and the harm done to individuals and groups through the disfiguring of our social environment by visible, public, and semi-permanent announcements to the effect that in the opinion of one group in the community perhaps the majority members of another group are not worthy of equal citizenship.'[16]

Political scientists have studied the anatomy of riots. One of them is Professor Paul R. Brass at the University of Washington. He has tirelessly done extensive field work in Uttar Pradesh. His work *Theft of an Idol* is of seminal importance (Princeton University Press, 1997). He holds:

> The riotous events I have here documented were not primarily 'spontaneous' occurrences or chance happenings and that there were identifiable culprits who had conspired to produce or who had committed acts either designed to produce or whose effects were to produce riotous and murderous results. . . .
>
> Although most people everywhere are capable of committing acts of violence under a variety of circumstances, the kinds of violence that are committed in 'communal riots' are, I believe, undertaken mostly by 'specialists', who are ready to be called out on such occasions, who profit from it, and whose activities profit others who may or may not be actually paying for the violence carried out. Such regions have developed what I call 'institutionalised riot systems', in which known actors specialise in the conversion of incidents between members of different communities into 'communal riots'. Even here, however, not every such incident is allowed to develop into a 'riot'. When full-fledged riots develop, the local politicians and authorities are often either incompetent or they themselves desire the riots to take place, and are willing to place a communal interpretation on the precipitating incidents.[17]

Brass amplifies:

14 Ibid., p. 33.

15 Catharine MacKinnon, *Only Words*, Harvard University Press, 1993, p. 30.

16 Waldron, *The Harm in Hate Speech*, p. 39.

17 Paul R. Brass, *Theft of an Idol: Text and Context in the Representation of Collective Violence*, pp. 8-9.

I believe that all riot-prone cities and towns do have to a greater or lesser degree such informal organisational networks. They also have something else, which is central to the notion of institutionalised riot systems, namely, a network of persons who maintain communal, racial, and other ethnic relations in a state of tension, of readiness for riots. Here I part company definitively with the 'sequence' theorists of collective action, who imagine a state of tension arising out of grievances, frustrations, and discriminations in the relations between two communities, which requires only the proverbial spark to ignite it. On the contrary, there are regular fire-tenders who maintain the fuel at a combustible level, sometimes stoking it, sometimes letting it smoulder. They are the conversion specialists, who know how to convert a moment of tension into a grander, riotous event.

These fire-tenders occupy formal and informal roles in existing organisations and outside them. In the most riot-prone cities, one is certain to find community organisations, cultural organisations, and/or political parties devoted to the advancement of their community, who also depict members of another, designated community as either an enemy, an oppressor, or a threat to their own community. Such organisations in India include especially the RSS and the BJP, the former a Hindu cultural organisation and the latter a party of militant Hindu nationalism, whose leading positions are occupied by RSS-persons. Other organisations in the RSS 'family' include the Vishwa Hindu Parishad (VHP) and the Bajrang Dal. The former organisation is devoted to mobilising the Hindu community in India to 'rectify' alleged past wrongs committed against Hindus by Muslims, notably the construction of mosques upon temples allegedly destroyed for the purpose. The Bajrang Dal is a fighting 'protection' squad for the other organisations, a somewhat pathetic, but nevertheless dangerous, version of the Nazi SA.

In other towns in some parts of India there are Muslim organisations of this type, but they are far less widespread and less well organised, disciplined, and directed. There are other organisations as well, most of whose members are honestly devoted primarily to cultural activities and/or religious reform within their communities, whose members also may nevertheless play roles, deliberate or inadvertent, in riot systems. Such organisations include the Arya Samaj among Hindus in north India. Some towns known to be riot-prone do not necessarily have a full panoply of organised groups or the groups may be in an early stage of organisation. But they all have individuals, formally affiliated or informally associated with such organisations or the ideas for which they stand, who play the roles of fire-tenders.[18]

A new situation was created, Brass points out:

[18] Ibid., pp. 16-7.

> What is new, though there are precedents for it in previous days of Hindu-Muslim conflict, is the deliberate inculcation among the RSS cadres who provide the shock troops for the entire 'family' of its organisations, including the BJP, the VHP, the Bajrang Dal, and others of a cult of violence aimed at the intimidation of Muslims, their selective killing, and the destruction of their properties during riots. In this cult of violence, the Muslims are portrayed as the aggressors, the Hindus as defenders, the Muslims as experts in the wielding of knives and in the art of killing, the Hindus as novices who must learn the art of their enemies. Those well-skilled in the practices of violence, prepared to use them against Muslims, are portrayed as heroes. (. . . a strong state must have a single, unified nation, they insist, and the Muslims are an obstacle to that goal until they become political Hindus.)[19]

This is only partly true. Like Savarkar, the RSS and the BJP propagate 'cultural nationalism'. It requires Muslims and Christians to adopt the Hindu religion in the name of 'Hindu culture' and Hindu values.

This explains why communal riots erupt over insignificant incidents. They were discussed at the National Integration Council when it met in Srinagar in June 1968. Y.B. Chavan, union home minister, reposed to this phenomenon. 'Coming to the causes of communal riots, we know they always start from some insignificant incident, but suddenly they spread to the whole community. Therefore, we have come to the conclusion that this cannot be explained by these small insignificant incidents, but there are some dangerous spots in the minds of men like distrust which ultimately erupt into communal riots.' He put it neatly: 'It is not merely what starts the riots that should be considered but what is *behind* the riots.'

It is not possible for any government to anticipate the immediate cause of the eruption of violence but it should be possible for a reasonably vigilant government to be aware of a situation conducive to such an outbreak. As the Jaganmohan Reddy Commission on the Ahmedabad disturbances of 1969 put it (para 6.59, page 67 of the Report):

> Whilst this is so, whether from such a communal atmosphere to expect that the Government should anticipate with any precision that communal riots will erupt, and, if so, when, would be to attribute to its agencies a sixth sense, a sense of anticipation well-nigh difficult to postulate, inasmuch as communal riots erupt on such insignificant and minor incidents which in themselves are difficult to predict. What could be expected from law-enforcing and Governmental agencies is a proper appreciation of the communal atmosphere prevailing in a State, in a Town or in any particular place or locality, to anticipate trouble and to take steps to nip it in the bud or to deal with it firmly when such

[19] Ibid, pp. 282-3.

> a situation does arise. In our view, on the facts disclosed by the Governmental and other records already referred to, the law-enforcing agencies could not but have known that the communal atmosphere in Ahmedabad had become tense.

Culpability then rests, therefore, on those who create communal tension. The Home Ministry presented to the Council a comprehensive review of the riots. It put paid to the view that the riots were but a continuation of those that engulfed the entire north in 1947 during the Partition. It said, instead, that

> From 1954 to 1960 there was a clear and consistent downward trend, 1960 being a remarkably good year with only 26 communal incidents in the whole country. *This trend was sharply reversed in 1961.* The increase was, however, largely in Bihar, Madhya Pradesh, Uttar Pradesh and West Bengal. There was a substantial fall during the next two years indicating stabilisation of the situation. 1964 was an abnormal year when largely as a repercussion of serious communal riots in East Pakistan there was large scale communal violence in West Bengal, Bihar and Orissa. There was no marked rise in communal incidents in other parts of the country.

Reversal of the trend in 1961 was due to the riots in Jabalpur which Brass calls 'the turning point' in the rise of communal violence.[20]

In February 1961, Usha Bhargava, a student at a local college in Jabalpur was raped by two Muslim youths. Overcome with shame she soaked herself in kerosene oil and set her clothes to fire and died. The next day there was a 'hartal' by shopkeepers and angry students demanding action against the culprits. Disturbances followed the demonstrations – shops were looted, buildings set on fire. The Jabalpur riots had begun. They soon spread to some other towns of Madhya Pradesh.

The Congress parliamentary party sent a four-man committee to investigate into the riots. Its members were Giani Gurmukh Singh Musafir, Ansar Harvani, Sushila Nayar and Surendra Mohan Ghosh. *The Times of India* reported (23 March 1961) that 'allegations that the recent riots in Jabalpur were organised and not sporadic are understood to have been generally upheld' by the Committee.

Prof. Mahesh Dutt Misra of Jabalpur ascribed the violence to the local press which had poisoned the minds of the people. The riots spread to UP, whose home minister, Charan Singh, bluntly accused the Jana Sangh of inciting communal violence in his speech in the Vidhan Sabha on 6 April 1961. He also drew attention to the fact that elections were not far away. Jabalpur shook India.

Donald E. Smith mentions it in his work *India as a Secular State*:

[20] Ibid., p. 39.

> One of the most distressing aspects of the situation is the continued eruption of large-scale Hindu-Muslim violence from time to time. Regardless of which side starts the riot (this is often impossible to determine objectively), the Muslims are generally the relative losers in terms of lives lost and property destroyed. The serious communal riots in Jabalpur and other cities and towns of Madhya Pradesh in February 1961 resulted in the loss of fifty-five lives, mostly Muslims. Muslim leaders charge that police and administrators, frequently under the influence of communally-minded politicians, allow the disturbances to go unchecked for some time, since the minority group will in most cases bear the brunt of the violence. In a number of such disturbances, local Hindu communalist newspapers have played a major role in fanning the flames of anti-Muslim sentiment.[21]

The RSS might be proud of the fact that it has won international notice. Apart from Paul R. Brass other distinguished scholars have censured it strongly. Professor Donald L. Horowitz of Duke University and author of scholarly works writes:

> The program of the RSS has been decidedly anti-Muslim, and the RSS has been involved in an enormous range of riots, alone, in combination with Jan Sanghis or BJP members, or in a broad coalition of extremist groups. The Meerut riot of 1968 was inspired by a combination of the Jan Sangh, the RSS, and the Hindu Mahasabha.
>
> The Gujarat riots of 1969, in which more than 1,000 people were killed, were preceded by the formation of a 'Committee to Defend the Hindu Religion'. Organisers were Jan Sanghis and Hindu religious leaders. RSS people distributed inflammatory handbills. A similar common front, the Rashtriya Ustav Mandal (RUM), was founded by the RSS, the Jan Sangh, and the Shiv Sena (a Maharashtrian paramilitary-cum-political party) before the riots in Kausa and Bhiwandi, in Maharashtra (1970). The RUM managed to have a Hindu procession pass in front of a mosque – a time-tested provocative tactic that also produced violence in Jamshedpur (1979).
>
> From its inception, the RSS had a narrowly Brahmin orientation, but it has since widened its reach considerably. Riot coalitions, such as one with the Shiv Sena, have been a means of broadening support for the RSS and for its affiliated party, currently the BJP. In Meerut (1982), the RSS apparently recruited ex-untouchables (in this case, Bhangis or sweepers) for anti-Muslim violence.[22]

[21] Smith, *India as a Secular State*, p. 414.

[22] Donald L. Horowitz, *The Deadly Ethnic Riot*, Oxford University Press, 2002, pp. 244-5. Vide also Ashutosh Varshney's able work *Ethnic Conflict and Civil Life: Hindus and Muslims in India*, Oxford University Press, 2002; Iqbal A. Ansari (ed.), *Communal Riots: The State and*

Ward Berenschot of the Royal Netherlands Institute for Southeast Asian and Caribbean Studies in London has written an extremely able study entitled *Riot Politics: Hindu-Muslim Violence and the Indian State* (London: Hurst & Company, 2011). He conducted extensive interviews in Mumbai in 2001 and in Ahmedabad (2005-6) besides careful research. In his view,

> A fairly closely-knit network of VHP and RSS activists, municipal councillors, MLAs, the police, party workers and local social workers facilitated the organisation and perpetration of the violence. The MLA Shailesh Macwana was a central figure in this network, as he coordinated and communicated with a range of different contributors to the riots.
>
> Such descriptions suggest the existence of what Brass (1997, 1998, 2003, 2004) called an 'institutionalised riot system'. The descriptions above corroborate Brass' observations about specialisation within such networks: among the different actors who contributed to the rioting in Isanpur, one can identify certain 'fire tenders' who spread rumours and maintained a certain level of communal tension in the area, while neighbourhood leaders functioned as 'conversion specialists' who, by using their authority to provide interpretations of preceding triggers of unrest and of the rioting itself, helped to legitimise the violence. Similarly, the *goondas* whom politicians recruited for the violence could be labelled 'riot specialists' or 'riot captains' whose specialised role lay in providing mobs into committing acts of violence. Above I also tried to emphasise, like Brass, the established communication links that facilitated the operation of this 'riot system'.[23]

He explains:

> An important element in the lead-up to rioting is the dissemination of prejudices and grievances against the target population. During meetings, discussions, rituals, training etc. the perception of a 'threatening' other is slowly built up by a constant stream of accusations and rumours. Such meetings contribute to what Tilly (2003) called 'boundary activation': a repeated emphasis on differences between religious communities serves to bring one aspect of one's identity to the fore, at the expense of other identity dimensions, thereby heightening awareness of tensions between an 'us' and a 'them'.
>
> Such speeches are relatively rare compared to the regular activities that organisations like the VHP and RSS organise. The RSS organises shakhas ('branches') throughout Gujarat in which participants get not only a workout but also a daily dose of Hindu-nationalist ideas. The VHP and its youth wing,

Law of India, New Delhi: Institute of Objective Studies, 1997.

23 Ward Berenschot, *Riot Politics*, pp. 166-7.

> Bajrang Dal, organise weekly training and meetings for local youths, where, in addition to religious texts, the threats posed by Muslims are a recurring topic of discussion. Such discussions are often accompanied by a more military type of training in which youths are instructed on how to fight. These organisations have been very effective in spreading Hindu-nationalist ideology; the organisations now command an unsurpassed grassroots network of thousands of local activists.
>
> Hindu-nationalist organisations stepped up their activities in the months preceding riots. According to several informants the VHP and the RSS started organising new weekly meetings inside the chowks in Isanpur in the months before the riots, which were then discontinued after the riots. This increased activity of VHP, RSS and Bajrang Dal units was also noted in other parts of Gujarat, which suggests that the preparation for the violence had been under way before the burning of the train coach in Godhra.[24] . . .
>
> The grassroots-level activity of organisations like the VHP and RSS and the Bajrang Dal is impressive: there are people throughout Ahmedabad, whose activities infuse a daily dose of Hindu-nationalist ideology into the hearts and minds of the city's inhabitants. There are good arguments for attributing the popularity of these organisations – and their command over a large number of local activists – to the attractiveness of their ideas: the ideas discussed at the RSS' shakhas, or during the VHP discussion and the Bajrang Dal training-camps can generate an attractive sense of self-esteem, of pride, in a threatening changing world. . . . The links between Hindu-nationalist organisations and government institutions are not only visible at the top; at that level one can point to the infiltration of the RSS and the VHP into government bureaucracies and the judiciary, as well as universities, or to the many state-level politicians like Chief Minister Narendra Modi.[25]

At the shakhas, *boudhiks* (intellectuals) indoctrinate the faithful. The most notorious among them was one Nathuram Vinayak Godse, who assassinated Gandhi. The Sangh Parivar has always been uneasy about Gandhi. It could neither accept him nor reject him publicly. It took the plunge in 1997 and began a campaign for 'adopting' Gandhi.

Sushma Swaraj, the BJP's general secretary, said on 17 October 1997, 'Mahatma Gandhi is not the monopoly of the Congress party.' Two decades after the assassination, the RSS mouthpiece (*Organiser*), then edited by K.R. Malkani, could remember Gandhi, on 11 January 1970, only in these terms in its editorial: 'It was in support of Nehru's pro-Pakistan stand that Gandhiji went on fast and, in the process, turned the people's wrath on himself.' So, Nathuram Godse represented

[24] Ibid.

[25] Ibid., p. 178.

'the people', and the murder he perpetrated was an expression of 'the people's wrath'. In 1961 Deen Dayal Upadhyaya said: 'With all respect for Gandhiji, let us cease to call him "Father of the Nation". If we understand the old basis of nationalism, then it will be clear that it is nothing but Hinduism.'

The Times of India editorially noted on 17 October 1989: 'Mr. Advani, while holding forth on "Bharat Mata", now goes so far as to deny that Mahatma Gandhi was the Father of the Nation.' The RSS chief Rajendra Singh said, 'Godse was motivated by the philosophy of Akhand Bharat. His intention was good but he used wrong methods.'[26] Voice of India, publishers in New Delhi, turn out the Sangh Parivar's propaganda material. It published in 2001 and 2012 a book *Gandhi and Godse* by one Koenraad Elst, a Belgian favourite of the Sangh Parivar. At page 175 he wrote: 'Numerous contemporaneous and later observers shared Nathuram Godse's criticism of Gandhiji's character and politics to a large extent.' He listed seven of them. Godse's murder cannot be defended. His defenders diminish his crime by lauding his political views which they share, to diminish, if not erase, the gravity of Godse's crime.

There is another and largely neglected aspect. The shakha has been much discussed; not so the *akhara* (gymnasium) in which physical prowess is tested. John Zavos of the University of Manchester draws attention to it.

> The *akhara* is most commonly associated with physical fitness gymnasiums and the art of wrestling but also with forms of cultural performance (theatre, music, poetry), medicine, and even 'the organisational structure used by mendicants'. . . .
>
> Certainly the way in which the RSS emerged confirms the connection between *akharas* and the shakha unit. Before the daily shakha was introduced in May 1926, Hedgewar encouraged his volunteers to attend an akhara. Early swayamsevaks interviewed in relation to this project all stated either that they had joined the RSS via an akhara, or that they had been attracted by the 'physical tricks' of shakha activity and viewed it as 'a new kind of akhara'. This reflects very much the increased prominence of akharas as a feature of politics in the mid-1920s. Anderson and Damle note a leap in the number of akharas in Nagpur district over this period from 230 to 570. It is also evident that the sangathan movement had to some extent encouraged the idea of akhara attendance as a feature of the revitalisation of Hindu society. . . . With its implication of physical, or even quasi-military, preparation (the Kanpur akharas had been started 'to teach the art of warfare') . . . the adaptation of the akhara model in the RSS has a clear implication: it was an appropriate form for an organisation which resisted the trajectory of Gandhian ahimsa.[27]

[26] *Outlook*, 19 January 1998.

[27] John Zavos, *The Emergence of Hindu Nationalism in India*, Delhi: Oxford University Press,

This completes the riot system which Paul Brass described so well. The boudhik at the shakhas injects poison in the minds of the young recruit. The akhara trains him to act on what he was taught. The RSS chief Deoras wrote to Prime Minister Indira Gandhi from his prison cell on 22 August 1975: 'In none of the court judgments or in the Report of any Commission of Inquiry has it been said that the volunteers of the Sangh were involved.' This was false to his own knowledge. There were reports aplenty censuring the RSS when he wrote. In 1979 he was censured personally. Here is the record:

1. Jabalpur, 1961: *Report of the Disturbance which took place at Jabalpur, Sagar, Damoh and Narsimhapur in February 1961*, by Justice Shiv Dayal Srivastava (Bhopal: Government Central Press, 1962). In this case, it was not the RSS but the RSS influenced press which inflamed the public. In the afternoon of 3 February 1961, a Hindu girl was allegedly ravished by two Muslim young men when she happened to be all alone in her father's house at Jabalpur. Between the 4th and the 15th of February widespread disturbances (Hindu-Muslim) occurred not only in the town of Jabalpur and certain rural areas of that district but also in the three neighbouring districts, Sagar, Damoh and Narsimhapur. A Commission of Inquiry comprising Justice Shiv Dayal Srivastava was set up on 6 March. He submitted his Report on 26 February 1962.

Usha Bhargava poured kerosene oil on her body and set herself on fire. When enveloped in flames she cried. The shrieks brought neighbours to her rescue and removed her to a hospital where she died. Among those present at the hospital was a correspondent of a local Hindu daily *Yug Dharma*, a revealing title. It published the news of the rape incident with banner headlines: 'MUSALMAN GOONDE DWARA CHHURI DIKHA KAR HINDU LADKI SE BALATKAR. ASAHAI CHHATRA MITTI KA TEL DAAL KAR JAL MARI. ABHIYUKTA UDYOGPATI KA BETA. SARE NAGAR MEN SANSANI VA TANAVPOORNA VATAVARAN' (Hindu Girl Raped by Muslim Scoundrel at the Point of Dagger. Helpless Student Poured Kerosene Oil and Burnt Herself. Accused is Son of Industrialist. Sensation and Tense Atmosphere in the Whole City).

It was reported in the news item that Usha Bhargava, a first year student of the Hitkarini College, was raped at about 14.30 hours in her house. When she returned to her relation, Chhote Lal Bhargava, the accused entered her house and a rape was committed on her at the point of a dagger. Thereafter, she burnt herself because of dishonour and helplessness. People removed her to the hospital where she eventually died. This newspaper was distributed in the town in the early hours of the 4 February. Other local dailies, '*Nai Dunia*' and '*Nav Bharat*', also published the news but, relatively, not in that sensational strain. They scrupulously avoided to indicate that the girl was a Hindu while the alleged offenders were Muslims. . . . On the morning of the 4th, local students decided to take out a procession to condemn the rape episode and to voice their demand for severe legal action against the

2000, pp. 188-9.

offenders. They reached the Anjuman-e-Islamia School and demanded its closure. The inmates there replied with pelting of stones. Communalising the heinous crime was coupled with communalising of the protest and response. The Judge's description of the course of the riots is as fair as his analysis of the causes. He never censures but errs on the side of restraint. Even the *Yug Dharma* is spared deserved censure. All that the Judge would say is that its reportage 'must have contributed'.

A heartening feature of the inquiry is the absence of any communal divide in the representations. The Town Congress Committee appeared through its lawyer. Nehru was outraged by the riots. Hindu Sahayata Samiti appeared. The most encouraging feature was the appearance of nine advocates for the Secularist Committee, three of whom were Muslims, including Nuruddin Ahmed of the Supreme Court Bar who became mayor of Delhi. Two other members of that Bar also appeared, M.K. Ramamurthi and A.S.R. Chari, a brilliant and forceful advocate who participated actively. Chari was formerly a member of the Communist Party of India.

2. Ahmedabad Riots, 1969: *Report of the Inquiry into the Communal Disturbances at Ahmedabad and other places in Gujarat on and after 18 September 1969*. It was appointed by the Government of India and comprised three sitting Judges; namely, Justice P. Jaganmohan Reddy of the Supreme Court, one of the finest who served that Court, and Justices, Nusserwanji K. Vakil and Akhar S. Sarela of the Gujarat High Court.

Next to Jabalpur, the Ahmedabad riots created a lot of disquiet in the country. Jayaprakash Narayan aimed his gun at Muslims. H.M. Patel, I.C.S. told this writer that Muslims must now decide whether they wished to live at peace in India.

The Report, a masterpiece, demolished all such notions. By now the Jana Sangh had become powerful. Its technique of forming united fronts was exposed. The Commission was set up on 13 October 1969. Its massive report was submitted on 21 October 1970. Among the political parties the Congress, Jana Sangh, Hindu Dharma Raksha Samiti (Committee to protect the Hindu religion), Hullad Pidit Sahayata Samiti (Committee to assist riot victims), Hindu Mahasabha, the CPI, the CPI (M) and the SSP and the Jamiat Ulema-e-Hind appeared. Balraj Madhok, M.P., former president of Jana Sangh, was summoned as the Commission's witness.

The charge against Muslims which went viral was that they had attacked the Jagannath temple. It created a lot of bad blood. The Commission found it to be false.

> The evidence, in our view, does not disclose that the incident at the Jagannath temple can be said to be an attack on the temple as such. If that was so, there was nothing to stop serious damage being done to the temple, both outside and inside. On the other hand, the damage to it was negligible. The persons who are involved were merely concerned with the 'Sadhus' in respect of the

> incident caused by the shying of the cows. The incident initially arose because of this circumstance, namely of the shying of the cows and not because the people in the crowd wanted to attack the 'Sadhus' or Hindus as such. But, as the Commissioner of Police said, the Jagannath temple got involved in this incident because the 'Sadhus' with whom the fight took place belonged to the temple, the altercation took place near the temple, and the stone-throwing was near the temple. The shouting by the crowd, the chasing of the 'Sadhus' into the temple, and the breaking of the glass facade in front of the main gate with photo figures of Shri Narsinhdasji and SHREE KRISHNA with a cow and of SHREE KRISHNA in the side facade – all this was construed as an attack on the temple.

Even Muslim leaders at the time and in the atmosphere then existing believed it to be so, because, in the apology given by them, as admitted by Peerzada, which he said had been made voluntarily, though he took the stand that it was not established that the Muslims had done it, they had stated that there was an 'assault on the temple' by certain anti-social elements, while the joint appeal of Hindus and Muslims stated that there was an 'attack on the Jagannath temple and its Sadhus'. Though according to Peerzada, it is not correct to say that some section of the Muslims did not like the expression of sorrow, there are some who say that when he expressed the sorrow he had given the impression that the Muslims had attacked the temple.

There was no doubt that the 'Sadhus' and the Mahant of the temple were all agitated about it and the Muslim leaders including Peerzada realised the serious mischievous potentialities arising out of the situation. Peerzada in his evidence had stated that when he went there after the incident, there was no 'Mela', the road was empty, the 'Medni' procession was on its way at Jamalpur chakla consisting of about 150 to 200 persons, the road was clear and he felt that something untoward had happened because usually, during the Urs, thousands gather but this time there was no one. There was tension near the temple. He also thought that the whole incident might flare up into a communal clash. That the situation was considered to be serious is evident from the fact that the Hindu leaders started arriving and going into the temple.

The Commission added:

> While this was the stand taken by the police initially, we find that in the evidence, the Commissioner sought to deny that the Hindu Dharma Raksha Samiti was formed with the participation of Jan Sangh, but instead asserted as pointed out by us in paragraph 6.57 that it was formed as an independent organisation. It is apparent that the police were attempting to resile from the stand taken by them in their reports that Jan Sangh, Hindu Mahasabha

> and other communal minded Hindus were involved in the agitation and had contributed to communal tensions just before the Jagannath temple incident. We have earlier pointed out that one of the Jan Sangh workers was said to be participating in the riots. . . . This evidence as a whole indicates that the police had reason to believe that some local Jan Sangh leaders and workers were actively participating in the riots though these officers, in their affidavits, had not given any such indication and even in cross-examination attempts were made to prevaricate and plead ignorance of such participation.[28]

3. Bhiwandi Riots, 1970: *Report of the Commission of Inquiry into the Communal Disturbance at Bhiwandi, Jalgaon and Mahad in May 1970*, by Justice D.P. Madon of the Bombay High Court runs into seven volumes. He rose to be a Judge of the Supreme Court.

Here again two standard features were repeated; a provocative procession through Muslim areas hurling abuses and the Jana Sangh's united front tactics. Trouble arose over a Shiv Jayanti procession on 1 May 1970. The Jana Sangh had forged as in Ahmedabad a united front under another name, the Rashtriya Utsav Mandal (National Festival Group). The Judge found:

> (1) The shouting of provocative, abusive and obscene anti-Muslim slogans was the most intense in the Bhusar Mohalla-Old Thana Road locality, and so was the brandishing of fists and the making of indecent gestures at the Muslims. (2) There was excessive throwing of 'gulal' by the processionists not only on one another, but in the air, and on the bystanders who were all Muslims. (3) The police officers and policemen on duty with the procession or posted on picket duty at various points in and around Bhusar Mohalla and Old Thana Road made no attempt to check the misbehaviour of the processionists.
>
> (4) The disturbances commenced in Bhusar Mohalla near the Old Fish Market. As a result of the provocation given by the offensive behaviour of the processionists and the provocative and abusive anti-Muslim slogans shouted by them, an altercation took place near the Old Fish Market between some processionists and some Muslim bystanders. In the course of this exchange of words, some of the Muslim bystanders started throwing stones on the processionists. The processionists immediately started pelting stones at the Muslims and their houses, shops and factories, and attacked the Muslims on the road with the lathis which they had brought with them with Bhagwa flags tied to them, and a free fight took place between the processionists and the Muslims. Other Muslims who had come to watch the procession, and who were in the lanes and by-lanes, or had collected there on learning what was

[28] *Report of the Inquiry into the Communal Disturbances at Ahmedabad and other places in Gujarat on and after 18 September 1969*, p. 218.

> happening during the progress of the procession, as also some of the residents of the locality came out and joined in the fight. (5) Within a short time the disturbances spread to the rest of Bhusar Mohalla and to Old Thana Road. (6) The processionists attacked Muslim properties and broke into and looted and set fire to several of them. (7) The weapons and missiles used by the Muslims were stones, brick-bats, soda-water bottles, lathis and some acid-bulbs. A few Muslims were carrying spears and at least one Muslim rioter had a sword. Stones, brick-bats and some acid-bulbs were also thrown on the processionists from some houses on Old Thana Road.[29] . . .
>
> The organisations operating in Bhiwandi which have fomented communal tension in the said places are: (1) the Bhiwandi Branch of the All-India Majlis Tameer-e-Millat, (2) the Bhiwandi Branch of the Shiv Sena, (3) the Bhiwandi Branch of the Bharatiya Jan Sangh, (4) the Bhiwandi Seva Samiti, (5) the Rashtriya Utsav Mandal.
>
> The organisation responsible for bringing the communal tension in the said places to a pitch is the Rashtriya Utsav Mandal. The majority of the leaders and workers of the Rashtriya Utsav Mandal belonged to the Jan Sangh or were pro-Jan Sangh and the rest, apart from a few exceptions, belonged to the Shiv Sena.[30]

In Jalgaon the Jana Sangh formed a Shree Ram Tarun Mandal. 'The RTM was merely an organisation of the Jalgaon City Jan Sangh.'[31]

The Commission found: 'The organisations which have fomented communal tensions in Jalgaon are: (1) the Jalgaon City Branch of the Jan Sangh, and (2) Shree Ram Tarun Mandal which was completely controlled and managed by the Jalgaon City Branch of the Jan Sangh and the Jalgaon District Branch of the Jan Sangh.'[32] The Mahad riots were fomented by Bal Thackeray, the Shiv Sena leader.[33]

4. Thalassery, 1971: *Report of the Commission of Inquiry on the Tellicherry Disturbances on 28 December 1971*, by Justice (Retd.) Joseph Vithayathil of the Travancore-Cochin High Court.

> Although the Jan Sangh and RSS are not numerically strong in the places where the occurrences took place, it is in evidence, that they have taken part in comparatively large numbers in the third phase of the disturbances. Many witnesses speak to that. P1W1 Sri Ramdas who is a leading member of the

[29] *Report of the Commission of Inquiry into the Communal Disturbance at Bhiwandi, Jalgaon and Mahad in May 1970*, Vol. II, Part II, p. 270.

[30] Ibid., Vol. III, Part III, p. 308.

[31] Ibid., Vol. IV, Part IV, p. 24.

[32] Ibid., Vol. IV, Part IV, p. 380.

[33] Ibid., Vol. V, Part V.

Tellicherry Bar and who resides in Thiruvangad swears that he saw RSS workers known to him taking part in the attack of Muslim houses in Thiruvangad. At the same time there have been instances of members of the Jan Sangh Party also giving succour to their Muslim neighbours when their houses were attacked by rioters. P3W3 Ramesh was one who gave such succour. There is no evidence to show that any recognised leader of that party took part in the disturbances.

Members of the Ruling Congress and CPI and also of the organisation Congress have taken part in the incidents that took place during this phase of the disturbances, as sworn to by some witnesses. P6W1 the President of Tellicherry Block Congress Committee (O) admits that members of his party have taken part in the disturbances.[34] . . . But none of the leaders of those parties has taken part in the disturbances. The fact is that Hindus belonging to all political parties have taken part in the disturbances.

(At pages 86 and 88 the Judge discussed the RSS and Jana Sangh's propaganda and Golwalkar's *Bunch of Thoughts.*)

5. Jamshedpur, 1979: *Report of the Three-Member Commission of Inquiry* headed by Justice (Retd.) Jitendra Narain of the Patna High Court, P.P. Agarwal, I.C.S. (Retd.) and S.Q. Rizvi, I.P.S. (Retd.). The Commission was set up on 15 May 1979 to inquire into the disturbances in and around Jamshedpur since 11 April 1979.

It is stated in para 4 of the written statement dated 22nd September 1979 filed on behalf of the RSS that 'nowhere in India, by any Judicial Commission, the RSS has been found guilty or responsible for the outbreak of any communal riot'. This is, however, not correct. There is a definite finding in the report of the Commission of Inquiry on Tellicherry Disturbances of 1971 that 'the RSS had taken an active part in raising anti-Muslim feeling amongst the Hindus of Tellicherry and in preparing the background for the disturbances'.[35]

The facts deserve to be quoted *in extenso*.

The pattern of administration of oath and the manner of enlistment etc. and other materials on the record indicate the militant character of the RSS. Designedly an attempt was made to conceal the existence of the Register of members of the RSS. The purpose was to withhold a document which would

[34] *Report of the Commission of Inquiry on the Tellicherry Disturbances on 28 December 1971*, p. 27.

[35] *Report of the Three-Member Commission of Inquiry headed by Justice (Retd.) Jitendra Narain of the Patna High Court*, p. 29.

establish connection of certain persons with this communal organisation. In this connection, the evidence of the Secretary of the district Branch of RSS, who alone has been examined as a witness on behalf of the RSS, makes an interesting reading. He has admitted that at Jamshedpur the Sangh has 400 to 500 members. The witness is categorical that no register is maintained of members and claims to recall the names of all these persons – a remarkable feat of memory indeed. He has also admitted that there is no ban on maintaining a Register but assigns no reason why such a register is not maintained at Jamshedpur. . . .

It is important to observe that the Divisional Conference of the RSS was held in Jamshedpur in the campus of the Co-operative College on the 31st March and the 1st of April, 1979 i.e. only 5 days before the Ram Navami festival. Permission to hold the camp there was accorded by the Vice Chancellor of the Ranchi University despite strong objection on the part of the students and staff of the College. So vehement was the opposition of the student community to the holding of the conference in the College campus that special precaution had to be taken in the public meeting addressed by Shri Deoras. The Report of the Intelligence Branch (Ext. RSS/12) mentions that there was apprehension that the student community would voice such a protest in the public meeting. In fact, leaflets etc. were distributed but no untoward incident, however, occurred on this account. The Commission feels that permission to hold the conference in the campus of an educational institution should never have been accorded. Shakhas, which also means drills conducted by the RSS were held on 31st of March and 1st of April. Shri Balasaheb Deoras, the Sar Sangh Chalak, attended the function and addressed a huge public meeting in Regal Maidan at 4.30 p.m. on the 1st of April, 1979. Before the meeting started, 1,000 Swayamsewaks stood in formation, several rows deep, and gave a display of lathi exercises and drill accompanied by music.

According to the S.P. Shri Deoras spoke in the meeting that it was said that Hindus in their own country are not allowed to take out religious processions freely and that the number of mosques are increasing day by day and in the Arabian countries Hindus are not allowed to construct temples. Shri Deoras also referred to the controversy regarding Road No. 14. . . .

The point for consideration is the kind of effect the above speech produced on the large gathering that had collected to hear Shri Balasaheb Deoras. It may be recalled that the communal atmosphere of Jamshedpur was already disturbed on the day Shri Balasaheb made the above speech. The communal issue centred round the controversy regarding Road No. 14 which passed through a Muslim residential area and a mosque, known as the Jhonpra Masjid. The speech, in the opinion of the Commission, must have made the stand of the extremists amongst the Hindus all the more rigid in respect of their previous stand regarding Road No. 14 and the Commission has found that the proximate cause of the disturbances was the controversy regarding Road No. 14.

Communal propaganda is a powerful weapon in the armoury of the communalists. Mr. Justice D.P. Madon, in his Report on Communal disturbances at Bhiwandi, Jalgaon and Mahad has listed 27 items as important items of communal propaganda. One of them is 'The decrying of the religious customs and traditions of the other community'. This is exactly what was done in the public address of Shri Balasaheb five days before the day on which the Ram Navami procession was to be taken out. Extolling tolerance amongst the Hindus and highlighting the absence of it amongst the Muslims, manifestly amounts to communal propaganda. . . .

This is the kind of situation that the administration had to reckon with at the time the communal tension prevails in a locality. In the first instance, the speech of Shri Balasaheb tended to encourage the Hindu extremists to be unyielding in their demands regarding Road No. 14. Secondly, his speech amounted to communal propaganda. Thirdly, the Shakhas and the camps that were held during the Divisional Conference presented a militant atmosphere to the Hindu public. In the circumstances, the Commission cannot but hold the RSS responsible for creating a climate for the disturbances that took place on the 11th of April, 1979 and thereafter.

After giving careful and serious consideration to all the materials that are on record, the Commission is of the view that the RSS, with its extensive organisation in Jamshedpur and which had close links with the Jan Sangh and the Bharatiya Majdoor Sangh, had a positive hand in creating a climate which was most propitious for the outbreak of the communal disturbances.

That contributed to the disturbances at the Ram Navmi festival on 11 April 1979 after speeches by the RSS chief Deoras only five days before the festival. It was the same old story of a provocative procession.

The Commission, therefore, concludes with the observation that the communal passion aroused amongst the Hindus by the intractable and domineering attitude of the Hindu communalists over the question of the route for the Dimna Basti Akhara procession which expressed itself in various overt acts, was the proximate cause of the riot that broke out in Jamshedpur during the Ram Navami Festival of 1979. And, the RSS played their role in this matter, motivated by the long-term political objective of gaining strength for their political wing, simultaneously with propagating their doctrine, by arousing the communal sentiments of the large majority [of] Hindus.[36]

[36] Ibid., p. 104.

6. Kanyakumari, 1982: *Report of the Commission of Inquiry into the Firing Incidents on the Clashes between Christians and Hindus at Mandaikadu in Kanniyakumari District on 1 March 1982 and 15 March 1982*, by Justice (Retd.) P. Venugopal (Tamil Nadu Legislature, 1986). Kanyakumari is the land tip of India at the confluence of three seas, Bay of Bengal, Arabian Sea and the Indian Ocean. From this tip, to the North Pole, the entire area is covered by land and the entire area from this tip to the South Pole is covered by sea. From this southernmost tip of India, one can witness both sun-rise and sun-set. Kanyakumari district has a plethora of temples and churches of various denominations.

In 1963, a memorial was planned to be erected for Swami Vivekananda on the rock embedded in the sea, near Kanyakumari. The Christians put up a Cross on the rock and began to claim it as St. Xavier's Road. Then the Kanyakumari Devaswom approached the Government of Tamil Nadu for permission to erect a memorial on the rock for Swami Vivekananda. The permission was granted. A memorial tablet was put on the rock on 7 January 1963. It was damaged by the Christians and a wooden Cross was installed in its place. Ultimately, the Hindus succeeded in erecting the Rock Memorial for Swami Vivekananda and the foundation was laid on 6 November. This was one of the earliest starting point of friction between Hindus and Christians.

> The RSS route-march, proposed to be conducted from Manglam to Kulasekaram on 30th August 1981, though banned, was later permitted to be taken on 11 October 1981. On the evening of 21 December 1981, the Christians of Madathattuvilai, took out a procession of the sacred Image of St. Sebastian in a decorated 'sapparam' which was put in a jeep illuminated with electric lights. The procession was disturbed by the Hindus near Pettukulam.
>
> On 15 March 1982 the police opened fire killing two persons.
>
> The Commission in the earlier part of this Chapter has observed that any amount of constitutional safeguards, or conferring legal rights or creating new police stations and vesting them with more powers, will not help the safety or promote the prosperity of the minority community if they lose the goodwill and sympathy of the majority community. *The RSS propaganda and methodology aim exactly in striking and destroying the goodwill, sympathy and understanding, which the majority community has for the minority community.* The Indian concept is Composite Nationalism, which recognises that all religious communities have contributed for the development and growth of this country. This concept is enshrined in the Constitution by granting equal rights to all, irrespective of their religious creed and it provides protection to minority cultures and languages. The RSS concept of Nationalism is that

all Christians are aliens as they have changed their religion. The concept of Nationalism by RSS excludes all non-Hindus. . . .

The RSS adopts a militant and aggressive attitude and sets itself as the Champion of what it considers to be the rights of Hindus against minorities. It has taken upon itself the task to teach the minority their place and if they are not willing to learn their place, teach them a lesson. The RSS has given respectability to communalism and communal riots and demoralised the administration. The RSS methodology for provoking communal violence is: (a) rousing communal feelings in the majority community by the propaganda that Christians are not loyal citizens of this country; (b) deepening the fear in the majority community by a clever propaganda that the population of the minorities is increasing and that of Hindus decreasing; (c) infiltrating into administration and inducing the members of the civil and police services [into] adopting and developing communal attitude; (d) training young people of the majority community in the use of weapons like dagger, sword and spar; (e) spreading rumours to widen the communal cleavage and deepen communal feelings by giving a communal colour to any trivial incident.

A review of the clashes and riots that have occurred in Kanniyakumari District would show that the same techniques have been followed. The RSS is a paramilitary organisation believing in centralised direction, regimentation of thought, uniformity of dress and some sort of regular drill and parade and a separate flag. As a result of these pernicious communal propaganda indulged by the RSS in Kanniyakumari District, suspicion arose between the two major communities, Hindus, and Christians. . . .

The RSS concept of renaissance and resurgence of Hinduism will take the country backwards towards the cowdung age. The Twenty Points programme formulated by its ally the Hindu United Front shows that it wants to retain the caste system. . . .

The RSS Shakhas include in their programmes training in lathis, swords, javelin throw. Drills, exercises, parades and other activities are organised, in playgrounds and other public places. All these activities are organised in the name of physical training. The aim behind these activities appears to inculcate an attitude of militancy and training for any kind of civil strike. They often cause apprehension, fear and a sense of insecurity among the minorities. It prejudicially affects maintenance of public tranquillity. The Commission is of the view that such activities like drills, exercises, parades, etc., enumerated above in public places by the RSS and its other allied organisations should be prohibited.

7. Bhagalpur Riots, 1989: Not till 1995 was the *Report of the Bhagalpur Riot Inquiry Commission* produced. It comprised Justice Ram Nandan Prasad

as chairman and Justices Ram Chandra Prasad Sinha and S. Shamsul Hasan, as members. Communal riots began in the riot torn city on 24 October 1989 as a Ramshila procession wended its way through Bhagalpur and continued intermittently till March 1990. Nearly a thousand persons were killed.

The Commission split unprecedentedly. The Chairman's remarks on the BJP's innocence and its non-linkage with the VHP reveal his bias. In all decency he ought to have recused himself. His daughter, Reeta Verma, was a BJP M.P.

His colleagues' Report censured the police officials, the magistrate and the judiciary. The procession was an offshoot of the Ayodhya movement. The atmosphere had been fouled for days.

> In regard to pre-riot period, no steps whatsoever were taken to prevent building up of anti-Muslim psyche in the villagers by BJP workers. Evidence in regard to this has already been set out. No effort was made whatsoever by the district authority to prevent the activities of the criminal elements in the town of Bhagalpur whether they were Hindus or Muslims or fanatics like Sallan and Ansari or Mahadeo and Kameshwar Yadav and Bajoria. Most of them are accused in criminal cases which were filed for the numerous criminal incidents that related to the massacre of Muslims that took place.[37]

> At page 15 of the Report occurs this damning nugget.

> The matter really reached a peak when Mr. Advani really spilled the beans and revealed the real intention of the BJP. In his statements reported in the *Panchjaniya* and copied by the *Times of India*, dated 30th January 1993, he states as follows:
>
> 'RIOTS WILL STOP IF MUSLIM . . . IDENTIFY WITH HINDUTVA': ADVANI
>
> If the Muslims in the country identify themselves with the concept of 'Hindutva', there would not be any reason for riots to take place, the Senior BJP leader L.K. Advani, has said. In a write-up appearing in the forthcoming special issue of *Panchjaniya*, considered a pro-RSS publication, he said acceptance of the 'Hindutva' concept by the Muslims would have an impact on the psychology that leads to riots, and disturbances would not take place on the slightest pretext, he added. Claiming that India is a Hindu Rashtra (Nation) Advani wrote that those residing in the country are Hindus even if many of them believed in different religions. He extended this contention to state that those following Islam were Mohammadi Hindus. Likewise, in his perception, Christians living in the country were Christian Hindus while Sikhs

[37] *Report of the Bhagalpur Riot Inquiry Commission*, p. 111.

were termed Sikh Hindus. The respective identities were not undermined by such a formulation, he wrote.

'Similarly someone is Sanatani Hindu while the other is an Arya Samaji Hindu. It would be better if such a formulation comes to be accepted. As part of the same concept, I consider this country to be a Hindu Rashtra. There is no need to convert it into a Hindu Rashtra. This needs to be understood. But certainly do not believe in forcing people to believe in this,' Advani wrote. The term Hindu Rashtra, he said, was never used during the Jan Sangh days, neither has it ever been mentioned in any manifestoes of the BJP. *But the term has gained currency in the wake of the Ayodhya movement, he wrote.* It is due to this that he wanted to make it clear that he had no hesitation whatsoever in using the term. If the ordinary Muslims do not accept the concept of Hindu Rashtra, he would like to tell the community that there was no difference in the three terms: Hindu Rashtra, Bharatiya Rashtra and Indian nation. If the attempt is to undermine the basic Hindu nature of the country by using the term Indian nation, Advani said such an attempt was wrong. The basic ethos of the country can only be described by the word Hindu, he claimed.

Coming from a person of Advani's stature to say the least the statements were distressing. We do hope that Advani did not really mean what he had said. Speaking for ourselves were distressed to read that statement not out of fear because our life and our religion are both safe in this country but because an eminent national leader should resort to threat of rioting, unless the norms set by him are followed.[38]

The Report says, 'The Muslim fanaticism also did not lag behind.'[39]

Incensed, Advani and leaders of the Bihar BJP moved the Patna High Court to quash the Report and restrain the Government of Bihar from taking any action on the basis of its censures. The Report simply quoted his remarks in his RSS organ *Panchajanya*. Advani's poisoned mind on Muslims was revealed in his own essay, 'A Four-point Appeal to Muslims of India'.[40] On the fiftieth anniversary of the country's independence, he had nothing else to write about but on his bête noire, the Muslims.[41]

A more insightful study is provided in *Splintered Justice: Living the Horror of Mass Communal Violence in Bhagalpur and Gujarat* (Three Essays Collective, 2016). Its authors are Warisha Farasat, a noted lawyer in Delhi, and Prita Jha, a legal activist and researcher based in Ahmedabad.

Reports by Judges, reportage by correspondents, lawyers and scholars touch,

38 Ibid., pp. 15-6.

39 Ibid., p. 16.

40 *BJP Today*, 1997.

41 Vide Appendix 13 for the text of his article.

at best, the obvious tip of the iceberg. For nearly a century the RSS has conducted a sustained propaganda in its shakhas, its journals, and public statements against Muslims and Christians. Prof. Sara Lipton of the State University of New York asked in an article entitled 'Brutal Speech, Violent Acts':

> Do harsh words lead to violent acts? At a moment when hate speech seems to be proliferating, it's a question worth asking. Attorney General Loretta E. Lynch recently expressed worry that heated anti-Muslim political rhetoric would spark an increase in attacks against Muslims. . . . When a group is labelled hostile and brutal, its members are more likely to be treated with hostility and brutality.[42]

Since 2014 India has had none other than its prime minister Narendra Modi leading the hate mongers. I have advisedly refrained from citing in detail reports and documents on his culpability in the Gujarat pogrom. The material is voluminous. Two, however deserve mention. The Chief Justice of India Justice V.N. Khare's remarks on the 'Nero' of Gujarat in the Best Bakery Case stirred the country. He wrote after his resignation, a brief article which is reproduced.[43] The fearless and honest Rana Ayyub's devastating exposures in her sting operation is a classic of its kind; utterly indispensable.[44] Also deserving of mention are the memoirs of R.B. Sreekumar, *Gujarat: Behind the Curtain* (Manas Publications, 2016). He was Additional D.G.P. (Intelligence) of Gujarat from April to September 2002; was penalised yet rose to be Director General of Police. It was most unfortunate that the Supreme Court appointed none other than R.K. Raghavan, former chief of CBI to head the Special Investigation Team. The amicus curiae Raju Ramachandran's report is able and thorough as one would expect of an upright lawyer.

Indians who cherish the values that have informed our public life for nearly two centuries should ponder on why and how a man with his record became prime minister of India. Communal appeal is only a part of the answer. The root goes deeper in our body politic.

In a famous incident in Britain's House of Commons, Prime Minister Harold Wilson referred to an M.P. who had just got elected by spreading racist hate. Wilson called him 'a moral leper'. One refrains from using words which can aptly describe persons who, for years around, spread communal poison against their fellow citizens; their fellow humans.

[42] *The International New York Times*, 12 December 2015.

[43] Vide Appendix 14.

[44] *Gujarat Files: Anatomy of a Cover Up*; published by herself in 2016.

24. RSS's Progeny: ABVP, VHP & Bajrang Dal

No management consultant could have done a better job than the RSS did in arranging its expanding activities. The ban in 1948 taught it the necessity of a parliamentary wing distinct from it but under its control. Thus was born the Jana Sangh, ancestor to the BJP. But the ban, which came as a shock, also drove it to have an alternative at work immediately again, distinct but under firm control. It was the Akhil Bharatiya Vidyarthi Parishad (ABVP). The brainchild of Balraj Madhok, founded on 9 July 1949. It was a students' body but quite unlike any students' organisation just as the BJP is unlike any other political party. The RSS appoints its president and runs it through its officials whom it seconds. The ABVP sought to counter the All India Students' Federation, a left body.

It must not be overlooked that the shakha system is a big help. It is informal and can meet during a ban by oral directives and messages. Each of the trio – the ABVP, VHP and the Bajrang Dal functions like Hitler's Storm Troopers, ready to use violence at any time.

ABVP

Narendra Modi, Arun Jaitley, K.N. Govindacharya and Sushil Kumar Modi were all members of the ABVP. The ABVP led Jayaprakash Narayan's Nav Nirman Samiti in Gujarat. In Bihar it joined the Chhatra Sangharsh Samiti during the JP Movement.

In 1995, the ABVP had working units in 415 out of a total of 483 districts of the country. Of India's 167 universities, 121 had branches of the ABVP.[1]

The Caravan is an Indian monthly which has won international notice for its fearlessness, integrity and thoroughness. Its issue of October 2017 carried a detailed exposé on 'The Age of ABVP' by Priyanka Dubey.[2]

In 2017, the ABVP had a young 49-year-old Sunil Ambekar as its head; formally he was national organising secretary appointed by the RSS. The ABVP, the VHP and the Bajrang Dal are all independent of the BJP. To bridle the BJP, the VHP hurls abuses at it, driving the BJP to seek Nagpur's protection. That is granted and the BJP begins to adhere to the RSS's line.

Rajkumar Bhatia, who had served the ABVP for four decades and was once its national president, told Priyanka Dubey:

[1] Yogendra P. Malik and V.B. Singh, *Hindu Nationalists in India: The Rise of the Bharatiya Janata Party*, New Delhi: Vistaar Publications, 1994, p. 156.

[2] *The Caravan*, October 2017, pp. 37-55.

The ABVP constitution, he said, written in 1949 by the RSS ideologue Eknath Ranade, states 'that this is an organisation for the glory of the country'. Once, he said, the country – 'Bharat' – was a '*vishwa guru*', a teacher for the world. It used to be said, he continued, that the country was very rich, that rivers of milk flowed through it – '*yahan doodh ki nadiyan beheti thi*' – and that it was a golden bird – '*Bharat ek sone ki chidiya thi*'. He insisted that 'these were not mere metaphors', but literally true. The ABVP, Bhatia said, wants to bring back those '*ache din*', those good days.

K.N. Govindacharya, not noted for modesty, claimed that he and Ram Bahadur Rai, ABVP leader in Patna, 'had been instrumental in Narayan's rise to the leadership of the resistance' to Indira Gandhi.

The controversies in Hyderabad and Delhi drew greater scrutiny to the ABVP's activities elsewhere. In the preceding year alone, ABVP activists had, among other things, vandalised a statue of the Catholic priest and educator Don Bosco in Guwahati, assaulted a leader of a rival student organisation in the town of Sikar, Rajasthan, been accused of assaulting the principal of a government college in Shimla, and been suspected of spurring the administration of the Indian Institute of Technology in Chennai to 'derecognise' a group called the Ambedkar-Periyar Study Circle. Shortly before Vemula's suicide, a lecturer at Banaras Hindu University was dismissed after being accused of 'anti-national' activity. He later wrote that the University's decision was 'based on rumours floated and sustained by the Sangh Parivar', and described 'irregularities going on in the BHU (Banaras Hindu University)' in terms of regular appointments of unqualified people associated with the Rashtriya Swayamsewak Sangh (RSS) as faculty members and admission of undeserving students associated with the Akhil Bharatiya Vidyarthi Parishad (ABVP).

During the controversy over Vemula's death (in 2011), the ABVP forced the cancellation of a seminar on 'democracy, media and freedom of expression' organised by the student union at Allahabad University. . . . ABVP members stormed the History Department at Delhi University while campaigning to have the essay 'Three Hundred Ramayanas', on the many existing versions of the epic, dropped from the curriculum. After further ABVP protests, in 2011 the university administration acceded. . . .

A literary society at Ramjas College, which forms part of the university, invited two students closely involved in the 2016 controversy at JNU – including Umar Khalid, one of the three students arrested – to speak at a seminar on the 'culture protests'. The university's student union, then dominated by the ABVP, objected, and the university administration cancelled the invitations.

The ABVP's map modestly includes Pakistan, parts of Tibet and Bangladesh within India. The RSS goes far beyond that. It includes Afghanistan and South-east Asia as well.

VHP

We have a full account of the Vishwa Hindu Parishad in two books by Manjari Katju of the University of Hyderabad; namely *Vishwa Hindu Parishad and Indian Politics* (Orient Longman, 2003) and *Hinduising Democracy* (New Delhi: New Text Publications Pvt. Ltd., 2017). There is also a meticulously documented article by Vandita Mishra of *The Indian Express* on 24 February 2002.

The VHP was founded at Mumbai on 29-30 August 1964 by RSS leaders M.S. Golwalkar and S.S. Apte as well as K.M. Munshi. 150 were invited. 60 came to the inaugural conference which was held at the Sandipani Sadhanalaya (Ashram) of Swami Chinmayananda. Vandita Mishra wrote:

> The declared object of Christianity is to turn the whole world into Christendom – as that of Islam is to make it 'Pak', warned Shiv Shankar Apte, who had joined the RSS in 1939 and who became the first man to head the VHP in 1964. 'Besides . . . there has arisen a third religion, communism . . . and all these three consider the Hindu society a very fine rich food on which to feast and fatten themselves. It is therefore necessary in this age of competition and conflict to think of, and organise, the Hindu world, to save itself from the evil eyes of all three.'

These are the very three threats to internal security on which Golwalkar expended his wrath in his *Bunch of Thoughts*. It was a pseudo-religious body with clear political aims. It brought in sadhus into politics.

Chetan Bhatt records:

> It was decided at the inaugural VHP meeting to organise a world Hindu *sammelan* during the Kumbh Mela on 22-24 January 1966 in Allahabad. This event was attended by a claimed 25,000 delegates, of which some 250 were from abroad. By this stage, the VHP had secured the attendance of two *shankaracharyas*, from Sharda peet in Dwarka and Govardhan peet in Puri, as well as the ex-*shankaracharya*, 'Mahamandaleshwar' Satyamitranand Giri. Satyamitranand was of considerable significance both in furthering the aims of the VHP, especially outside India, and in developing an early and distinctly territorial form of devotionalism – a 'geopiety' that sacralised symbolic devotion to the land, and was the precursor to the VHP's 'semiological' political strategy from 1979. At the sammelan, he called on Hindu society to kindle brahmatej

> and kshatriyatej. The resolutions passed at the sammelan included: making Sanskrit teaching compulsory in secondary education; banning cow slaughter; reconversion of those who had left Hinduism through 'violence, coercion and temptations exerted on them by people of other faiths', particular attention being focused on 'the sinister activities of Christian missionaries amongst the Tribals'; and strengthening ties and promoting dharma among Hindus in India and abroad.
>
> The sammelan resolved to appoint a Vidvat Parishad ('Council of the Learned') 'to compile a minimum code of conduct and cultural guide' for Hindus to strengthen Hindu samskars in society. This was framed as the preparation of a charter of 'Hindutva', to prescribe a common code of 'Laukika' [mundane or ordinary] and 'Daivika' [extra-mundane or religious] conduct in conformity with our ancient heritage and in consonance with the needs of the modern world.[3]

The VHP cut its teeth on the anti-cow slaughter movement in New Delhi in 1966 on the eve of the 1967 general election. In April 1984 it declared for the first time its resolve to 'liberate' the birth place of Ram at Ayodhya.

> A meeting of the top leaders of the Sangh Parivar took place at Ahmedabad on 24 March 1989. Besides Deoras, other important leaders of the Parivar who attended it were H.V. Seshadri, Rajendra Singh, Yadav Rao Joshi of the RSS, Ashok Singhal of VHP, L.K. Advani, A.B. Vajpayee and S.S. Bhandari of BJP, D.B. Thengadi of BMS and Madan Das Devi of ABVP. A close coordination among the leading members of the RSS family was obviously required before going for the offensive. Soon after the VHP's decision to construct a temple in Ayodhya, the ABKM of the RSS appealed to all Hindus to extend their generous help for the purpose.[4]

Presence of the top brass of the BJP indicates resolve.

In 1982, it formed a Central Margdarshak Mandal whose members would 'direct and guide the religious ceremonies, morals and ethics of Hindu society'. Its 39 members represented different sects of Hinduism. Alongside, almost like an executive committee, a Sadhu Sansad came up, whose 17 sadhus would enable the 'shakti of the sadhus to play an enlarged role in the activities of nation-building'.[5]

By the '90s, the Central Margdarshak Mandal had grown into a permanent institution, a twice a year gathering of around 200 members. The Sadhu Sansad

[3] Bhatt, *Hindu Nationalism*, pp. 181-2.

[4] Kanungo, *RSS's Tryst with Politics*, p. 196.

[5] Vandita Mishra, 'VHP in brief: The Sangh's right fist', *The Indian Express*, 24 February 2002.

became a Dharma Sansad in 1964, with hundreds, thousands, of participants who meet at irregular intervals to deliberate on 'vital problems'.

> Cleverly playing upon the two symbols of Ganga and Bharat Mata, the Ekatmata Yatra in 1983 was the first campaign of the resurgent VHP. Three processions – from Kathmandu in Nepal to Rameshwaram in Tamil Nadu, from Gangasagar in Bengal to Somnath in Gujarat and from Hardwar in Uttar Pradesh to Kanyakumari in Tamil Nadu – distributed water from the Ganga (50 centilitres for Rs. 10). Jaffrelot points out that the yatra represented a tactical innovation; till then, the only symbol that had been manipulated for political purposes was the cow.
>
> Then, the first Dharma Sansad unanimously adopted the resolution demanding the 'liberation' of the Ramjanmabhoomi at Ayodhya in 1984 and there was no looking back for the VHP, and the BJP. The Bajrang Dal was formed under the leadership of Vinay Katiyar, organisational secretary of ABVP in 1970-74, an RSS pracharak since 1980. Ram Janaki Raths toured Uttar Pradesh and Bihar in November-December 1985. The gates to the Babri Masjid were thrown open in February 1986 to facilitate 'puja' and 'darshan' in the presence of a crowd of VHP supporters and a DD crew. The VHP organised Ram Shila Pujans in 1986. The Congress government permitted it to conduct the shilanyas in 1989. BJP leader L.K. Advani led the Rath Yatra.[6]

The VHP drew up an 18-point code of conduct: 'Achar Samhita for Individuals, Families and Political leaders'. It read:

> Object No. 1: To prescribe the order of Dharma relevant to the modern age for developing the unity of Hindu Society. Object No. 2: To re-affirm deep faith in our Dharma, culture, language and glorious traditions established by our great men, removing misunderstanding about them . . . Object No. 4: To get Dharma Shiksha (the education of Dharma) introduced as a compulsory part of education in schools and to arrange publication of suitable literature thereof and also to promote Sanskrit as the language of daily usage and to have it enthroned as our national language. . . .
>
> Object No. 7: To develop Maths, Mandirs and other places of worship of different religious sects as powerful Sanskar Kendras, as symbols of Hindus and to renovate ancient Kendras. Object No. 8: To prescribe the order of Dharma to preserve the cultural heritage behind every Hindu festival. Object No. 9: To strengthen the faith in Hindu life values, of Hindus living abroad, which is faltering in the absence of living contact with the Hindu values of

[6] Ibid.

> life. . . . Object No. 10: To prescribe the order of Dharma for the acceptance in Hindu Society of those brothers who had for some reasons got converted to foreign faiths and now wish to come back to their ancestral fold. . . . Object No. 12: To compel the State to safeguard Hindu interests and to take effective steps to defeat by all possible means the conspiracy of foreign religionists to diminish Hindu population.
>
> Achar Samhita for Political Leaders: 1. Dharma shiksha should be made compulsory. 2. Teaching of Sanskrit should be made compulsory throughout the country. 3. All Hindu social and charitable organisations should be exempted from Income-tax. 4. Government interference in the management of Maths and Mandirs must be ended. 5. Legal ban should be imposed on conversion of Hindu to foreign religions. . . .
>
> 11. Shri Rama and Sri Krishna Janmasthans, Kashi Vishwanath Mandir and all other historic temples should be restored to Hindus. . . . 13. Human Rights Commission should be constituted in place of a mere Minority Commission. . . . 16. Total ban should be imposed on such activities of minorities which are aimed at disrupting national unity. . . . 18. Cinema-films should not be allowed to ridicule Hindu Dharma, Hindu culture, Hindu gods and goddesses and Hindu life-values.[7]

Yubaraj Ghimire reported on 'The rise of the Sadhus' in the wake of the BJP's Ram Mandir movement. The sadhus were, in fact, propelled to the forefront by the BJP through a resolution in its National Executive meeting in June 1989. Subsequently, the BJP accepted the sadhus' supremacy, agreeing to the resolutions adopted at the Dharma Sansad and Margdarshak Mandal, and to the decision of holding kar seva on December 6. The dominance of the sadhus has perhaps taken even the BJP leadership by surprise. At the *shilanyas* in Ayodhya on 9 November 1989, the sadhus were confined to religious rituals. But by 1999, the tally of saffron-clad BJP M.P.s went up to 22. Emboldened by their political acceptability within the BJP, the sadhus promulgated the suggestion for rewriting the Constitution. Swami Niranjan Teerth even advocated constitutional sanctity to the caste hierarchy, with unquestioned supremacy to the Brahmins.

> The growing participation of sadhus in the decision-making process while electorally beneficial was proving a heavy cross for the BJP to bear, especially among its lower caste and minority members. An emergency meeting of the national executive of the BJP's Scheduled Caste Morchas dissociated itself from the move to go back to the varna system. The sadhus reacted announcing the construction of a Valmiki temple near the disputed site. This would stop the alienation of Harijans who trace their lineage to Valmiki and would counter

[7] VHP publication: *Dimension of Thought*, Part - I, 1985.

Laloo Prasad Yadav's decision to appoint Harijans as priests in Bihar.

The servility of the BJP became apparent when Acharya Vamdeo demanded that Delhi's Jama Masjid be put on the list of mosques to be demolished. Party Vice-President S.S. Bhandari lacked the courage to decry the demand. 'It's not on our agenda *at present*. But I cannot rule out the possibility in the future,' was his weak-kneed response.

Yubaraj Ghimire listed the heroes of the hour. 'A Who's Who of the powerful sadhus dictating the BJP's agenda'; Ramchandra Paramhans: chairman of the Ram Janmabhoomi Trust; Mahant Nritya Gopal Das: militant sadhu of Ayodhya chhawni; Acharya Vamdeo: chairman of the Ram Janmabhoomi Renovation Trust; Vishwesha Teerth: Pejawara (Udupi)-based swami with unparalleled influence over the Ayodhya movement; Acharya Dharmendra: pro-demolition and VHP loyalist, prominent member of the Dharma Sansad; Swami Muktanand: BJP-VHP's new-found Ambedkar, prominent member of the All-India Sant Samiti; Mahant Avaidyanath: BJP M.P. and chairman of the Ram Janmabhoomi Mukti Samiti; Swami Chinmayananda: BJP M.P. who influenced the BJP into agreeing to give an affidavit limiting kar seva to bhajans and kirtan on December 6; Swami Yoganand: BJP M.P. and member of the Dharma Sansad.[8] Since 1991 sadhus entered parliament in large numbers.

Being a *world* organisation, 'Vishwa Hindu Parishad' staked a claim to a 'General' consultative status to the United Nations' Economic and Social Council. South Asia Human Rights Documentation Centre of New Delhi, which enjoys that status, filed a devastating 'Briefing Note' refuting the VHP's claim. Its meticulous documentation bore the imprint of its director Ravi Nair whose research is world-class. This document of 33 pages deserves widely to be read.

Bajrang Dal

The RSS is not father to the Bajrang Dal but its grand-father. It was set up by the VHP, at the RSS's instance to be sure, in May and June 1984 under the leadership of Vinay Katiyar. He was organising secretary of the ABVP (1970-74) and an RSS pracharak since 1980. The move was linked to the Ram Mandir movement. The Bajrang Dal was to serve as the spear arm. Jaffrelot records:

> On 11 July 1993, the Bajrang Dal became an all-India body with a more rigid organisational structure that resembled that of the RSS in several respects. Uniforms were introduced (blue shorts, white shirt and saffron scarf) and in 1993 some 350 training camps were held. A handbook was published discussing the ways in which 'the trainers should give mental and physical training to the

[8] *India Today*, 31 January 1993.

trainees', . . . more and more sadhus contested elections. In 1991, the BJP had 6 saffron-clad MPs: Swami Chinmayananda (Budaun), Mahant Avaidyanath (Gorakhpur), Uma Bharti (Khajurao), Swami Sureshanand (Jalesar), Swami Sakshiji Maharaj (Mathura) and Yoganand Saraswati (Bhind). Second, sadhus tried increasingly to influence purely political matters.[9]

Prof. Yogendra Malik and V.B. Singh describe the Bajrang Dal in these terms:

> Bajrang Dal, the VHP's youth wing, is its fighting arm. Consisting of lumpen elements, it reflects the contemporary political parties and politicians in India have become dependent upon muscle power. Gangsters, criminals, and hired hands are used frequently to achieve political goals. Vandalism displayed by the Ram Bhakts (devotees of Ram) and karsevaks (volunteers) in recent years are the BJP, RSS, and VHP versions of the vulgarisation of Indian politics. The steady rise in the number of unemployed educated youth in the urban areas has added to the degenerate segment of society. The Bajrang Dal, more than any other group in India, is able to mobilise all these elements in the cause promoted by the VHP.
>
> The Bajrang Dal has been successful in raising large amounts of money in the name of Ramjanambhoomi not only from the traders and small-scale manufacturers but also from the countryside, primarily of north India but also from south and east India.[10]

It is easy to involve religious heads in political mobilisation. Once they arrive and acquire a taste for politics, they will not quit. Witness their roles in Pakistan, Sri Lanka and Myanmar. The blame lies squarely on L.K. Advani's shoulders.

Professor Richard H. Davis of Yale University described Bajrang Dal's street power:

> Conspicuous in all coverage of the Rath Yatra were young men holding primitive weapons like bows and tridents. Here it was the young militants of the youth wing of the VHP, the Bajrang Dal, who challenged the BJP elders. Employing a Shaiva ritual vocabulary, Bajrang Dal activists were given an initiation prior to participating in the procession, during which they received a trident and took a vow 'to protect women, temples, and religion from "the irreligious"'. As Neeladri Bhattacharya (1991, p. 129) notes, the god Shiva here more suitably expresses 'the new militant, aggressive spirit of Hindutva', willing to destroy in service of a subsequent recreation, where Rama is seen as too constrained by his duty as a ruler to maintain the existing order of things. Yet the Bajrang

[9] Jaffrelot, *The Hindu Nationalist Movement and Indian Politics*, pp. 478-9.

[10] Malik and Singh, *Hindu Nationalists in India*, p. 169.

> Dal militants who located themselves within the guiding narrative of the Ramayana by naming themselves 'Hanuman's Troops', Rama's monkey army. To enforce the analogy, Hanuman himself – or one of the activists dressed up as the great monkey warrior – frequently accompanied the procession.
>
> The young activists tried to incorporate Advani into their iconography of violence. At Ujjain, they presented him with weapons, and they often welcomed him by applying a ritual mark (tilak) of blood on his forehead. Sometimes Advani went along with the atmosphere of youthful enthusiasm and pageantry. Unlike the Bajrang Dal youth, however, Advani was aware of a large audience he hoped to reach with a more moderate political message. Early on in the procession, the *Times of India* chastised him in an editorial for wielding a replica of Vishnu's irresistible discuss weapon (*sudarshana chakra*), and so, most commonly, Advani maintained the posture of a respectable upper-class urban Hindu, in starched white traditional garb (kurta and dhoti), seeming to disdain the more fervid displays surrounding him. When a ritual potful of blood was presented to him, Advani asked his party functionaries to send out word that such offerings were not acceptable. In Delhi, he publicly scolded the Bajrang Dal for overzealousness and urged them to put away their weapons.
>
> Of course, the ambiguity of these symbolic armaments posed an interpretive as well as practical challenge for the civil authorities, since tridents could indeed serve as rather effective implements in the street battles that often surrounded the procession. When does an icon become a weapon? . . .
>
> The iconography of ancient warfare and Advani's soft-peddling of it corresponded to two different ways of situating the Rath Yatra and the Ayodhya campaign into overarching structures of historical meaning. These two narratives in turn identified two different enemies. The mythical war against demonised Muslims that the Bajrang Dal and the VHP were fighting was not quite the same as the political struggle that Advani and the BJP were waging against the Indian government. Yet in the end they were two parts of a single agenda.[11]

It 'belonged to the world's inventory of black deeds'. President K.R. Narayanan's remark, on 24 January 1999, is indelibly imprinted on the minds of the people because it captured in one unforgettable phrase the deep revulsion which the nation felt at the burning alive of the Australian missionary, Graham Stewart Staines, and his two sons, Philip and Timothy, aged 9 and 6, respectively. The crime, perpetrated on the night of 22-23 January 1999 in a remote village, Manoharpur, in Keonjhar district in Odisha, aroused international concern. Staines had devoted his life to the succour of leprosy patients.

[11] Davis, 'The Iconography of Rama's Chariot', pp. 47-8.

On 29 January, the Government of India appointed Justice D.P. Wadhwa of the Supreme Court as Commission of Inquiry to inquire into the crime. Doubt on the wisdom of this exercise was expressed by many at the very outset. For, there was not the slightest doubt in any quarter on the identity of the prime culprit, Dara Singh alias Rabindra Pal Singh, on his criminal antecedents and his rabid communal outlook. He fled after the crime. However, he did appear on a private TV channel, on 29 March, to assert, 'I do not have any connection with any organisation.'

This was in reply to a specific question: 'Now, as is presently appearing in papers, what is your connection with BJP, RSS and Bajrang Dal?' On 25 January, five days before the Commission was appointed, the home minister L.K. Advani gave a clean chit to the Bajrang Dal and blamed the press for the outrage. 'I have known these organisations for a long time and they do not have criminal elements.' In the Lok Sabha, on 23 February he rejected pleas for widening the terms of reference to cover all incidents of attacks on Christians.

His debt to the Bajrang Dal for its role during his yatra does not excuse Advani's certificate of good conduct ahead of the inquiry. As it happened, Justice D.P. Wadhwa lived up to Advani's expectations. His Report was a white-wash. Exertions of the counsel for the Commission, Gopal Subramaniam of the Supreme Court Bar, a counsel of integrity, proved in vain. Dara Singh's loyalties and affiliations were known. *The Statesman* reported on 28 May what the CBI thought of their links. Dara Singh 'had campaigned extensively for the Bharatiya Janata Party in the 1998 general elections'. He was a fugitive from the law, then. 'The CBI, which is inquiring into the case, says that though Dara Singh was not a primary member of the BJP, RSS or the Bajrang Dal, he had a long, active association with the BJP and was deeply involved in many of its projects.'

Vikas Pathak of *The Hindu* described the Bajrang Dal's network on 12 December 2015.

> At the central level, the Dal has activists below the age of 45, while at the State level, the cut-off age is 40. A similar arrangement exists for the women's forums – those below 35 are part of Durga Vahini, the VHP's young women's wing, while those above 35 are part of Matru Shakti (mother power), clearly aligning to the idea of women's primary role being necessarily of a 'mother' beyond a cut-off-age.
>
> The Sangh's allied organisations are functionally autonomous but the link with the RSS never snaps. The Akhil Bharatiya Vidyarthi Parishad (ABVP) works on campuses, the Bharatiya Mazdoor Sangh (BMS) among workers, the BJP in the electoral arena, the Vanvasi Kalyan Ashram among tribals, and so on. Representatives of the entire ideological family (Vichar Parivar) meet routinely and exchange notes on their activities.
>
> People also move from one organisation to another. While a chunk of

BJP leaders come from the ABVP, leaders such as Katiyar have come from the Bajrang Dal. Sharma, the Dal's convener from 2002 to 2009, is now vice-president of the BJP's Uttar Pradesh unit. The organisational structure of the Bajrang Dal has several tiers – the national, zonal, State, zilla and prakhand (up to one lakh population) levels; each has conveners and co-conveners.

There are some key activities that bind its cadre. Once a week, there is a Hanuman Chalisa recital, generally in temples. This apart, a Dal worker is expected to be part of a local Balopasana (worship of physical strength) Kendra, which is generally a wrestling akhada, or gymnasium.

The Dal also has a vidyarthi pramukh, an activist who is expected to spread its influence among students. But this work is strictly non-political, as the ABVP is active in the sphere of student politics – of course, the reach of the Dal is not a patch on that of the ABVP. While these activities are seen by the Dal as organisational work, it also sees work involving agitation as crucial to its scheme of things, its involvement in the Ram temple campaign is one such example. Another is cow protection, which has been in the news through the year. The Dal mobilises opinion against cow slaughter and even captures vehicles apparently transporting cows for slaughter. They file police complaints but are open to courting confrontation when required, said a Dal functionary. The Bajrang Dal also counts helping organise an Amarnath Yatra in 1996 as a major milestone in its activity involving agitation, Mr. Sharma said.

The organisation claims a 'softer side' that it seeks to showcase, though few take this seriously. 'We do constructive social work too, like organising blood donation camps and offering service in hospitals,' he added.

The Bajrang Dal observes Hanuman Jayanti as Balopasana Diwas. Dal insiders say that the ideal activist should be in the image of Hanuman, strong in body and character, and ready to punish evildoers. Of course, it is a confrontational Hindutva line that informs its definition of character, leading to the viewing of potential stand-offs over cow protection or a Ram temple as central to its vision.[12]

Like its parent, the VHP, the Dal is also independent of the BJP, while all three function according to the RSS's dictates. As the BJP gets weaker organisationally, thanks to Modi's personality cult, these two bodies become more powerful. The RSS has gained by letting loose these creations; but they have carved out a life of their own meanwhile. It is not a comforting prospect. With limbs like these, the RSS has no rival.

[12] *The Hindu*, 12 December 2015.

25. RSS's Self-Revelation to Tax and Charity Authorities

In 2019, it is not necessary to trace the course of the protracted litigations which the RSS faced, in the late seventies, before the income-tax authorities and the Charity Commissioner. It is, however, of the utmost importance to note the admissions it then made, its contradictory stands before the two fora, and its proud acknowledgement of its Bibles, Golwalkar's *We or Our Nationhood Defined* and *Bunch of Thoughts*. What is more, this avowedly cultural body warned explicitly that its commitment to 'culture' was a matter of 'policy' and it might, should it so choose, descend into the political arena as a political party.

The proceedings were initiated by Dr. Manoharkant Dayalji Kamdar of Nagpur who belonged to the RSS since 1942, was a devotee of its founder Hedgewar but rejected the leadership of Deoras and his colleagues. He freely provided the documents among which the most revealing is a 15-page application (Application No. 17 of 1978 dated 1 February 1982) by Rajendra Singh as sarkaryavah of the RSS (Applicant No. 1) and Bhaurao Deoras as its sah-sarkaryavah (Applicant No. 2). It contains damning admissions and self-revelatory statements.

Dr. Kamdar alleged that the RSS's statement in the preamble to the constitution it presented to Home Minister Vallabhbhai Patel, that 'the Sangh had till now no written constitution', was false. There did exist a constitution of 1933. The 1949 constitution, he alleged, was, in turn, amended in 1972 'to give a legal status to the Guru Dakshina' among other changes. The constitution of 1949 was amended in 1972 to give a legal status to the term 'Guru Dakshina' and its division into individual shakhas or branch funds. Article 5 said, 'While recognising the duty of every citizen to be loyal to and to respect the State flag, the Sangh has its Flag, the "Bhagwa Dhwaj" the age old symbol of Hindu Culture.' The Amendment of 1972 read: 'While recognising the duty of every citizen to be loyal to and to respect the state Flag, the Sangh has as its Flag the "Bhagwa-Dhwaj" the age-old symbol of Hindu culture, *which the Sangh regards as its Guru*.'

The constitution of 1949 said in Article 22: 'All offerings, gifts, donations, etc. received for Sangh purposes by the branches, shall constitute the *Sangh Funds*.' The 1949 Amendment said 'The Guru Dakshina' received for Sangh purposes by a Sangh shakha, shall 'constitute the *funds of that Shakha*'. Tax liability was passed on to each shakha.

These amendments were made on legal advice and during the litigation. What emerged in the long-drawn litigation was the RSS's proneness to lie and to deceive. It claimed before the Bombay High Court that it was 'a charitable institution under Section 10(22) of the Income-Tax Act, 1961' and before the Charity Commissioner that the 'RSS is not a charitable trust but a political institution under Section 12(13) of the Bombay Public Trusts Act, 1950'. To the public at large it pretended to be a 'cultural' body. While the tax proceedings were on, it amended its constitution in order to avoid tax liability. But it suppressed the fact from the Charity Commissioner and was less than candid to the tax authorities.

We owe a lot to Dr. M.D. Kamdar of Nagpur, for exposing the RSS's mendacity. It all began on 11 December 1970, when a notice under Section 139(2) was issued to the RSS. It was challenged by its sarkaryavah, M.D. (Balasaheb) Deoras – who became supremo in 1973 on the death of M.S. Golwalkar (sarsanghchalak) – in a Special Civil Application (No. 525 of 1971) filed on 22 April 1971. He recalled earlier proceedings in 1965 in which, apparently, nothing happened. Deoras claimed to be an 'agriculturist'. So did co-petitioner Pandurang B. Kshirsagar. Two tax returns were filed under protest. They claimed that the work of the RSS 'was *solely* educational work and it was not taxable as an association of persons or body of individuals' who had come together to earn income. Its prime source of income, according to the statement of receipts and expenditure sent with the balance-sheet, was *gurudakshina* – donations to the guru – collected by different shakhas (branches).

On the same day, 22 April 1971, Deoras replied to the Income-Tax Officer (ITO) who had sent another notice dated 27 January 1971. He claimed:

> The Sangh is devoted to *purely cultural* work and its faith being in the orderly evolution of the society, the nature of RSS work is *solely educative*. The programme of training and educating Hindu youths in the cultural heritage of the Hindu Samaj and the propagation of national self-discipline through the process of drilling, organising physical activities and arranging for lectures of learned men on subjects touching the above aspects, is a purely educative process. The RSS is therefore an institution covered by Section 10(22) of the Indian Income-Tax Act, 1961.

The gurudakshina collected by the shakhas came to Rs. 2,68,370; proceeds from the sale of old newspapers, Rs. 527; and 'surplus receipts on sale of old scooter', Rs. 1,851. For the activities of the Kendra Karyalaya, the central unit, there was the Hedgewar Bhawan in Nagpur. 'This property is held by the Institution [sic] for its charitable activities.'

The RSS was impaled on the horns of a dilemma of its own creation. As a 'cultural' body, it was liable to pay tax and be registered as a public charitable trust under the Bombay Public Trusts Act, 1950. To avoid tax it pleaded that its object were educational which brought it within the ambit of a charitable trust. But it resisted registration pleading that its work was 'akin to political purposes'.

On 25 April 1972 a sworn affidavit was filed on behalf of the RSS by its Akhil Bharatiya Nidhi Pramukh, Pandurang Baliram Kshirsagar before that ITO. He said that the RSS 'is devoted *purely* to cultural work'; in the context it clearly meant 'exclusively'. The next sentence fortifies. The RSS is carrying on purely educational and cultural activities as stated above.'

He estimated 'the number of shakhas at about 20,000 or more'. The attempt was to show that it was the shakhas that collected the money but for their own use – so, do not tax Nagpur.

The RSS 'is devoted purely to cultural work' and

> each Shakha maintains its own separate register of its members called Swayamsevaks. Each Shakha maintains its own separate account of receipts and expenditure. All these units manage and utilise their own funds for the objects of the Sangh. The only source of receipt of money by every Shakha is out of voluntary offering styled as Guru Dakshina. Only a few units of big cities who have some surplus out of Guru Dakshina have short term fixed deposits and on which some interest is earned. All these moneys are inclusive of interest it earned spent away in the same year for the object of the Sangh. Each unit of a city or town maintains account of its receipt and expenditure. Each unit is free to utilise the money for the object of the Sangh as they like. If they have surplus they send a portion of Guru Dakshina to the Provincial units or to the Kendra (the centre at Nagpur). In turn the Kendra may send the portion of Guru Dakshina received by them to other units which may require money for carrying out the objects of the Sangh. The so-called Nagpur Head Office has no financial control over the Shakha of different provinces. The Nagpur Office cannot compel any Shakha or Prantiya Office to send to them any portion of Guru Dakshina received by them. Shakhas do not send their accounts to the Nagpur Office. Nor are the reports of Shakha's accounts incorporated in the Nagpur Office. Nor has the Nagpur Office got to do anything with the accounts maintained by the Shakhas. The function of the Kendriya Mandal, is merely advisory. It has no control over the finances of Shakhas or Prant. In fact the Nagpur Office does not know about the financial affairs of Shakhas. Only one thing is certain that all units of town or city do maintain their accounts and that the funds received by way of Guru Dakshina etc., are utilised by them for the object of the Sangh, which are purely educational and cultural. The details of receipt and expenditure statements of every unit of city or province can be obtained from respective units.

On 30 March 1974, the ITO, Central Circle III, Nagpur made an Assessment Order for 1971-72 against the assessee, the RSS. He observed in para 5:

> At the hearing on 15.10.73, when asked from those present how the RSS organisation throughout the country was controlled and managed from the

Kendriya Artha Vibhag, it was explained that there were 18 prant offices. Under the prant offices were the zilla offices and under each zilla office were shakhas. It was stated that the Kendriya Artha Vibhag has the lists of only the prant offices. All policy decisions were communicated to these prant offices, which in turn informed the zilla offices under them. Each zilla office then communicated the same to the shakhas. At my request a list of prant offices and the persons in charge of them was filed. A letter dated 16.10.73, was then issued to the assessee to confirm what was explained at the hearing. *In their letter dt. 31.10.73, the assessee, however, resiled from this position* and once again took the same stand which was taken in the earlier year, that the Kendriya Artha Vibhag of RSS had no control over the finances of the branches and all branches were independent units and ultimately it is shakhas who decide their course of action keeping in view the objects of the Sangh. It was also stated that there is hierarchy of offices or control of one over the other.

On 31.10.73, an amended constitution of the Rashtriya Swayamsevak Sangh was also filed before me. It was stated that the constitution of RSS was amended on 1.7.72 and the proposals for amendment come from the Karnataka Prantiya Karyakari Mandal. On 21.11.72 the assessee filed a note reiterating that: 'All the shakhas are independent units by themselves. They have their own executive bodies, they receive Guru Dakshina from Swayamsevaks and they are free to utilise the same in the manner they like keeping in view the ideals of the sangh. There is nothing like head office nor there is anything like branches.'

The RSS had tied itself into knots.

It is admitted that the Central office can call for funds from the Branches. Thus to this extent the head office does not have the control over the finances of the branches. Besides the major policies are laid down by the Central Working Committee and the Central Office which have to be pursued by the shakhas. The centre also organises training camps for officers who work for the branches. Thus it is clearly established that the Central Office has control over each and every shakha. This finds further support from the fact that in the year under consideration the head office received a sum of Rs. 70,800/- from some prant offices. It also paid Rs. 38,000/- to 2 other prant offices which were in deficit. I have had occasion to examine the books of accounts of the Nagpur prant office of the RSS. It is seen from these books that the Nagpur prant office received the collections made by various shakhas under it, by way of Gurudakshina and passed it on to this prant office. This demolishes the assessee's case that the shakhas keep the amounts collected by them to themselves and spend it as and when they like. The books of the Nagpur prant office clearly indicate

> that the Gurudakshina collected by various small shakhas was in the year under consideration, passed on to the prant office. Although in the year under consideration, the Nagpur prant office has not contributed any amount to the centre, but the other prant offices have. All this leads me to the irresistible conclusion that the organisation is one as a whole and therefore, I hold that the incomes earned by the shakhas, the Zilla office, and the prant offices would definitely be taxable in the hands of the organisation which I am assessing through its Central office.

He estimated receipts from gurudakshina at Rs. 20 lakhs. That was in 1974; nearly half a century ago. How much 'gurudakshina' does it receive now?

To turn from the tax authorities to those under the Bombay Public Trusts Act, 1950, on 11 January 1978, M.S. Vaidya, the Joint Charity Commissioner, Maharashtra, at Mumbai held that the 'RSS is proved to be a public religious and charitable trust. It is registered as such'.

He thus reversed the finding and order of V.P. Behere, the Deputy Charity Commissioner, Nagpur Region at Nagpur that the RSS was not liable to be so registered because it had 'a patriotic purpose which is neither religious nor charitable. The objects of the organisation of the RSS are *akin to political* objecs [sic], as distinct from religious or charitable objects'. It taught 'Nationalism'. Dr. Kamdar alleged that Behere was related to Deoras. Certainly his judgment reads like a defence statement of the RSS.

If the RSS played games before K.H. Chaimani, the ITO, it did not spare Vaidya, either. He censured it; albeit in moderate terms. He referred to the correspondence between the Home Minister Vallabhbhai Patel and the RSS supremo Golwalkar published in the RSS's publication *Justice on Trial* and said:

> The subsequent correspondence included in the said book itself indicates that what was submitted to the Minister was only a draft which was discussed at length in the correspondence. It was specifically referred to as such in letter dt. 3.5.49 sent by Shri H.V.R. Iyengar, the then Secretary to Government of India, Ministry of Home Affairs and letter dated 10.7.1949 issued by Respondent No. 9 to Moulichandra Sharma (pp. 56 to 61 of the book). The final form of the constitution appears at Exhs. 23 (typed) & 47 (printed) in the record of the proceeding before the Deputy Charity Commissioner, Nagpur. The appellant admitted in his cross examination (page 6 at Exh. 64) that ex. 47 is the final form of the constitution. It appears that some amendments were affected since the finalisation of the constitution in 1949, but, I was told that they did not pertain to objects, preamble etc. but they were meant to effect some organisational changes. It is indeed, not known why the Respondent

> (RSS leader) failed to bring on record a copy of the constitution containing up to date amendments. The allegation of the applicant appellant that the respondents want to be secretive in the matter of certain particulars about the constitution gains ground due to this omission and also the production of documents, Exhs. 23 and 47 which bear no date or final adoption of the constitution, not even the date of typing or printing and publishing. Whatever that be, for the purposes of this case, the decision is to proceed principally on the basis of the constitution as it appears at Exhs. 23 and 47 in the proceeding . . . before the Deputy Charity Commissioner, Nagpur Region, Nagpur.

These proceedings are not merely of historical relevance. They bear on the politics of today; for, they reveal the RSS's techniques, its contradictory claims, and/or its proneness to prevaricate. The limit was reached in Miscellaneous Application No. 17 of 1978 made by Rajendra Singh, sarkaryavah of RSS jointly with Bhaurao Deoras, its sah-sarkaryavah and younger brother of the chief M.D. Deoras (vide Appendix 8 for the full text).

It was filed in the court of the District Judge, Nagpur in an appeal against M.S. Vaidya, the Joint Charity Commissioner's decision. It attacked Gandhi without mentioning his name, affirmed the binding force of Golwalkar's books *We or Our Nationhood Defined* and *Bunch of Thoughts*; and said that 'it is possible for Sangh to change its policy and even participate in politics' (para 14). The RSS's objects are 'akin to political purposes'. Abstinence from formation of a political party was a matter of '*policy*' (para 17). It emphasised that 'tomorrow the policy could be changed and the RSS could participate in even day to day political activity as a political party because *policy* is not a permanent or irrevocable thing' (para 18). This document was filed on 6 March 1978. Singh and Deoras recalled (in para 8) that the RSS was founded on Dussehra Day 1925 by Dr. K.B. Hedgewar for a particular reason: 'The concept that [sic] nation with a glorious past which indeed, was a "Hindu Rashtra" was being wiped out from the people and its interest was being ignored by the then political leaders particularly after the eclipse of Lokmanya Tilak from the political horizon after his death in 1920.' The attack on Gandhi and the Congress was fairly clear.

The concept of 'Hindu nation' of the founder of RSS was on the basis of cultural unity of the entire people living in the Bharatvarsh. Lest any imagine that 'the entire people' were truly included, they emphasised that 'It is significant to note that the name was not chosen as "Hindu Swayamsevak Sangh" though the Sangh is open to Hindus only. This is because of the faith of the Sangh that in India "Rashtriya" (national) means "of Hindus" which are the mainstream of the Nation'. Another reason for the name was 'to reflect the political ideology of the organisation, though the Sangh as such never had politics of its own as of policy'.

Failure to appreciate this fundamental stand of the RSS lies at the root of the continued misunderstanding of the RSS by some to this day. The RSS itself has, however, never wavered in its stand.

The Application stated some important features of RSS ideology. Para 13 noted that

> The first feature is that the terms used have special significance and meaning as understood by the Organisation in view of its philosophy as distinct from the ordinary meaning. In brief . . . one has to look as to how [the said terms] are understood by the organisation and not how such terms are commonly used or interpreted by others. Such terms are Rashtriya, Dharma (religion), Sanskriti (cultural), Hindu Dharma, etc.

This enables the RSS to practise duplicity freely.

Secondly, the chief (sarsanghchalak) is 'the guide and philosopher', and his writings and speeches are important. The written constitution came into existence for the first time in June 1949. The third feature of the constitution is its flexibility. The fourth feature is that aims and objects are distinguished from *policy* since 'policy is not a permanent feature and changes or is changed from time to time'. The RSS does not participate in 'day to day politics though the Sangh has a political philosophy within its wide sweep of cultural work. It is possible for Sangh to change this policy and even participate in politics'.

There is the special importance of the flag, 'the "Bhagwa-Dhwaj", the age-old symbol of Hindu Culture'. Another feature is 'the limited democratic form and machinery' provided for carrying out the work of the Sangh. 'There is no election at all levels but selection and nomination except the posts Sakaryawaha (General Secretary) and Prant Sanghchalaks (State Chiefs)'.

The document concluded that the work of the RSS is neither religious nor charitable but its objects are cultural and patriotic as contra-distinguished from religious or charitable.

> It is akin to political purposes though RSS is not at present a political party inasmuch as the RSS Constitution quoted above bars active political participation by RSS, as such, as a policy. . . . Tomorrow the policy could be changed and RSS could participate in even day to day political activity as a political party because policy is not a permanent or irrevocable thing.[1]

Individual members were, however, free to join any political party (Article 4). The document boldly asserted that the RSS was free to proclaim itself a political party some day. This stand has never been altered. It has been reaffirmed repeatedly;

[1] Paras 18 and 19.

including by Deoras, the supremo, on 15 and 16 November 1987.

The character of this 'cultural body' was fully explained by the definition which the Sangh assigns to culture:

> [It] does not mean the popular or governmental limited meaning as pertaining to art, drama, music, dance, etc. The word 'Sanskritik' or cultural used in the Sangh work has a very wide sweep and has to be understood as expounded by the Guide and Philosopher of the RSS Shri Golwalkar in his speeches and writings. These include all aspects of society or nation; viz. political, social, economic, customary, morality, language, script and in general the Hindu way of life, inclusive of faiths of various groups in distinct tenets, practices, etc.

Contrast this assertion in para 26 of the document with that in Article 4(b) of the constitution – 'the Sangh as such, has no politics and is devoted purely to cultural work'. But, if 'cultural' means what the RSS's Application solemnly said it does, is not Article 4(b) of its constitution calculated to deceive?

In an appeal filed before the Appellate Assistant Commissioner of Income Tax, Nagpur (29 May 1972), Deoras solemnly stated the direct opposite; namely, that it held the funds on trust for charitable purposes (Grounds 35, 36 and 37):

> The learned ITO erred in holding that the objects of the Sangh are not charitable . . . erred in holding that the funds were not proved to have been utilised for 'charitable purpose' . . . has not properly appreciated the connotation of the words 'Trust' and any other 'legal obligation' . . . failed to see that the assessee was under a *legal obligation* to spend the money for the objects specified in the Constitution.

On 16 September 1979 UNI reported that Deoras said that his organisation would in ten years gain the popularity needed to form a government at the Centre. 'Nobody can grudge such an eventuality in a democratic set up, he told a closed-door meeting attended by nearly 100 people [in Bhopal].' Three days later, Deoras rushed back to Bhopal to contradict the reports. The RSS's mouthpiece *Organiser* angrily denied the report and quoted Deoras as saying that it was not a closed-door meeting at all and the entire proceedings had been taped and played back 'a few days back to local correspondents and they were all satisfied . . .' The UNI, however, carried another story on 20 September which said that Deoras 'refused to oblige newsmen who insisted on listening to the taped version' despite the RSS local unit's promise to play the tapes at his press conference.

That the RSS won its appeal in the Court of S.M. Mandika, 'Extra Assistant Judge, Nagpur', on 1 February 1987 is less relevant than its conflicting claims and dubious tactics. The Charity Commissioner at Mumbai appealed to the High Court

(First Appeal No. 697 of 1991). Kamdar did not know its result. Apparently it was pending in 1999.

These traits still persist. Confession of political ambition is of abiding relevance. Why should it dirty its hands if it can act through its creature, the BJP? It will continue to test the political climate. The day it changes its 'policy' and decides to step into the political arena, its cadres in the BJP will quit it to join the RSS's new political venture; the BJP's leaders will retire to their abodes, abandoned and humiliated; and the ABVP, VHP and Bajrang Dal will serve the new party set up by the RSS. It is most unlikely that the politicians who run the BJP will give a grave provocation to their masters at Nagpur.

Hedgewar's ingenuity seems to have won the day. The RSS is flush with money as the *Organiser* of 11 December 2016 reported.

> Dr. Hedgewar evolved another innovative method that is 'Guru-Dakshina'. Sangh decided that it will not ask donation from anybody. Nor here is any membership fee. Each Swayamsevak once in a year would pay back to the Guru (preceptor) with the sense of gratitude. The Guru is also not any individual but the symbol of purity, sacrifice and valour, *Bhagwa Dhwaj* (*Saffron Flag*). No individual is considered as Guru nor is there any sloganeering in anyone's name. Sangh decided to say 'Bharat Mata Ki Jai' (Let there be Glory of mother Bharat) after the daily prayer in Shakha. This is the only slogan that is chanted in RSS Shakhas for the last 91 years. Money contributed with a sense of gratitude was really beneficial for Sangh functioning as RSS remained self-reliant and autonomous. Today there are many Swayamsevaks who can contribute Lacs of rupees, no one except Shakha level office bearer comes to know about these amounts.

The RSS is the richest organisation in the country. Its Political Department is the richest in the field.

Bibliography

Books

Abdullah, Sheikh. *The Blazing Chinar*. Srinagar: Gulshan Books, 1995.

Advani, L.K. *My Country, My Life*. New Delhi: Rupa.

Ahmad, Waheed (ed.). *The Nation's Voice: Speeches and Statements*. Karachi: Quaid-i-Azam Academy, 1992.

Ambedkar, B.R. *Pakistan or the Partition of India*. Bombay: Thacker and Co., 1946.

———. *What Congress and Gandhi Have Done to the Untouchables*. Bombay: Thacker & Co., 1946.

Andersen, Walter K., and Shridhar D. Damle. *The Brotherhood in Saffron: The Rashtriya Swayamsevak Sangh and Hindu Revivalism*. New Delhi: Vistaar Publications, 1987.

———. *The RSS: A View to the Inside*. Penguin Viking, 2018.

Ansari, Iqbal A. (ed.). *Communal Riots: The State and Law of India*. New Delhi: Institute of Objective Studies, 1997.

———. *Readings on Minorities: Perspectives and Documents*, 2 volumes. New Delhi: Institute of Objective Studies, 1996.

Baxter, Craig. *The Jana Sangh: A Biography of an Indian Political Party*. London: Oxford University Press, 1969.

Berenschot, Ward. *Riot Politics: Hindu-Muslim Violence and the Indian State*. London: Hurst & Company, 2011.

Bhagwat, Mohan. *The Hindu Renaissance*. Translated by S.D. Mohan. New Delhi: Suruchi Prakashan, 2008.

Bharatiya Jana Sangh: Principles and Policy. Delhi: Bharatiya Jana Sangh, Arjun Press, 1965.

Bhatt, Chetan. *Hindu Nationalism: Origins, Ideologies and Modern Myths*. Oxford, New York: Berg Publishers, 2001.

Brass, Paul R. *Theft of an Idol: Text and Context in the Representation of Collective Violence*. Princeton: Princeton University Press, 1997.

Cardozo, Benjamin N. *The Nature of the Judicial Process*. New Haven: Yale University Press, 1921.

Carter, Lionel (ed.). *Towards a Ceasefire in Kashmir*. Manohar Publishers, 2018.

Casolari, Marzia. *In the Shade of the Swastika: The Ambiguous Relationship Between Indian Nationalism and Nazi-Fascism*. Bologna: I Libri di Emil, 2011.

Chand, Feroz. *Lajpat Rai: Life and Work*. New Delhi: Publications Division, Ministry of Information and Broadcasting, 1978.

Chandra, Bipan. *Communalism in Modern India*. Delhi: Vikas, 1987.

Chatterji, Joya. *Bengal Divided: Hindu Communalism and Partition, 1932-1947*. Cambridge: Cambridge University Press, 1994.

Chopra, P.N. (ed.). *Sardar Patel: Muslims and Refugees*. Konark Publishers, 2004.

Congress Presidential Addresses: Second Series, 1911-1934. Madras: G.A. Natesan & Co., 1934.

Constituent Assembly Debates, Volume 7.

Das, Durga (ed.). *Sardar Patel's Correspondence 1945-50*. Ahmedabad: Navajivan Publishing House.

Dayal, Rajeshwar. *A Life of Our Times*. Orient Longman, 1998.

BIBLIOGRAPHY

Deshmukh, Nana. *RSS, Victim of Slander*. Vision Books, 1979.

Dimension of Thought, Part - I. VHP publication, 1985.

Dutt, Brahm. *Five Headed Monster: A Factual Narrative of the Genesis of Janata Party*. New Delhi: Surge Publications, 1978.

Garrett, H.L.O. (ed.). *The Trial of Muhammad Bahadur Shah*. Lahore: Punjab Government Records Office Publication, 1933.

Golwalkar, M.S. *Bunch of Thoughts*. Bangalore: Sahitya Sindhu, 1968.

———. *Shri Guruji Samagr Darshan* [Collected works of Golwalkar in Hindi]. Nagpur: Bhartiya Vichar Sadhna.

———. *The Answer to All Questions*. New Delhi: Rashtriya Swayamsevak Sangh, 1968.

———. *We or Our Nationhood Defined*.

Gopal, S. (ed.). *Selected Works of Jawaharlal Nehru. Second Series*. Jawaharlal Nehru Memorial Fund.

Goyal, D.R. *Rashtriya Swayamsewak Sangh*. Radha Krishna Prakashan, 2000.

Graham, B.D. *Hindu Nationalism and Indian Politics: The Origin and Development of the Bharatiya Jana Sangh*. New York: Cambridge University Press, 1990.

Gundevia, Y.D. *Outside the Archives*. Sangam Books, 1984.

Gupta, Partha Sarathi (ed.). *Towards Freedom: Documents on the Movement for Independence in India 1943-1944*, Part III. Delhi: Oxford University Press, 1997.

Hay, Stephen (ed.). *Sources of Indian Tradition*, Volume 2. Columbia University Press, 1988.

Historic Statements by Veer Savarkar. Bombay, 1967.

Horowitz, Donald L. *The Deadly Ethnic Riot*. Oxford University Press, 2002.

Inamdar, P.L. *The Story of the Red Fort Trial, 1948-49*. Popular Prakashan, 1979.

Integrate Kashmir: Mukherjee, Nehru & Abdullah Correspondence. Delhi: Publicity Department, Bharatiya Jana Sangh.

Islam, Shamsul. *RSS Primer*. Pharos, 2014.

Jaffrelot, Christophe. *The Hindu Nationalist Movement and Indian Politics*. Viking, 1996.

Kanda, K.C. *Allama Iqbal: Selected Poetry*. New Delhi: New Dawn Press, 2006.

Kanungo, Pralay. *RSS's Tryst with Politics: From Hedgewar to Sudarshan*. Manohar Publishers, 2002.

Katju, Manjari. *Hinduising Democracy: The Vishwa Hindu Parishad in Contemporary India*. New Text, 2017.

———. *Vishwa Hindu Parishad and Indian Politics*. Orient Longman, 2003.

Keer, Dhananjay. *Veer Savarkar*. Popular Prakashan, 1966.

Kudaisya, Medha M. *The Life and Times of G.D. Birla*. Oxford University Press.

Limaye, Madhu. *Janata Party Experiment: An Insider's Account of Opposition Politics, 1975-1977*. Delhi: B.R. Publishing Corporation, 1994.

MacKinnon, Catharine. *Only Words*. Harvard University Press, 1993.

Madhok, Balraj. *Indian Nationalism*. Bharati Sahitya Sadan, 1969.

———. *Indianisation?: What, Why and How*. New Delhi: S. Chand & Co., 1970.

———. *Portrait of a Martyr: Biography of Dr. Shyama Prasad Mookerji*. Jaico Pub. House, 1969.

Malik, Yogendra P., and V.B. Singh. *Hindu Nationalists in India: The Rise of the Bharatiya Janata Party*. New Delhi: Vistaar Publications, 1994.

Malkani, K.R. *The RSS Story*. New Delhi: Impex India, 1980.

Malsiani, Arsh. *Abul Kalam Azad*. New Delhi: Publications Division, 1976.

Mehta, Asoka. *1857: The Great Rebellion*. Bombay: Hind Kitabs, 1946.

Mookerjee, S.P. *Awake Hindusthan*. Calcutta: Ramesh Chandra Banerjee, 1944.

———. *Leaves from a Diary*. Oxford University Press, 1993.

Naqvi, Saeed. *Reflections of an Indian Muslim*. New Delhi: Har-Anand, 1993.

Nehru, Jawaharlal. *A Bunch of Old Letters*. Bombay: Asia Publishing House, 1960.

Noorani, A.G. *Badruddin Tyabji*. New Delhi: Publications Division, Government of India, 1969.

———. *Savarkar and Hindutva*. New Delhi: LeftWord Books, 2002.

———. *The Babri Masjid Question*, 2 volumes. New Delhi: Tulika Books.

———. *The Muslims of India: A Documentary Record*. Oxford University Press, 2003.

Philips, C.H., with the cooperation of H.L. Singh and B.N. Pandey. *The Evolution of India and Pakistan, 1858 to 1947: Select Documents*. London: Oxford University Press, 1962.

Prabhu, R.K. (ed.). *An Anthology of Modern Indian Eloquence*. Bharatiya Vidya Bhavan, 1965.

Prasad, Bimal (ed.). *Jayaprakash Narayan: Selected Works*. New Delhi: Manohar.

Purohit, B.R. *Hindu Revivalism and Indian Nationalism*. Bhopal: Madhupriya, 1990.

Ralhan, O.P. (ed.). *Hindu Mahasabha*. Delhi: Anmol Publications, 1997.

Reorganisation of Jammu & Kashmir State: Problem and the Solution. Delhi: Indraprastha Vishwa Samvad Kendra.

RSS Resolves: 1950-2007: Resolutions passed by ABPS and ABKM of the RSS from 1950-2007. New Delhi: Suruchi Prakashan.

Savarkar, V.D. *Hindutva: Who is a Hindu?*. Mumbai: S.S. Savarkar, Veer Savarkar Prakashan, 1969.

———. *Hindu Rashtra Darshan: A Collection of his Presidential Speeches*. Bombay, 1949.

———. *The Indian War of Independence of 1857*. London, 1909.

Scarfe, Allan, and Wendy Scarfe. *J.P.: His Biography*. New Delhi: Orient Longman, 1997.

Seervai, H.M. *Constitutional Law of India*, Volume 1. Bombay: N.M. Tripathi Pvt. Ltd., 1975.

Shauq, Sumat Prakash. *Thus Spoke Firaq*. New Delhi: Allied Publishers, 1992.

Singh, Amarinder. *The Last Sunset: The Rise and Fall of the Lahore Durbar*. Roli Books, 2009.

Singh, Neerja (ed.). *Nehru-Patel: Agreement within Differences (Select Documents and Correspondences 1933-1950)*. National Book Trust, 2010.

Sitaramayya, Pattabhi. *The History of the Indian National Congress*, Volume 1 (1885-1935). Bombay: Padma Publications, 1946.

Smith, Donald Eugene. *India as a Secular State*. Princeton University Press, 1963.

Smith, Wilfred Cantwell. *Modernisation of a Traditional Society*. New Delhi: Asia Publishing House, 1965.

Spotlights: Guruji Answers. Bangalore: Sahitya Sindhu, 1974.

Sunderlal, Pandit. *The Gita and the Quran*. Hyderabad: Institute of Indo-Middle East Cultural Studies, 1957.

Swarup, Ram. *Hindu-Sikh Relationship*. New Delhi: Voice of India, 1985.

Thapar, Romila. *Communalism and the Writing of Indian History*. Delhi: People's Publishing House, 1969.

———. *Historical Interpretations and the Secularising of Indian Society*. Bangalore: Visthar, 1999.

van der Veer, Peter. *Religious Nationalism: Hindus and Muslims in India*. Delhi: Oxford University Press, 1996.

Varshney, Ashutosh. *Ethnic Conflict and Civil Life: Hindus and Muslims in India*. Oxford University Press, 2002.

Waldron, Jeremy. *The Harm in Hate Speech*. Harvard University Press, 2012.

Weiner, Myron. *Party Politics in India*. Princeton University Press, 1957.

Why Bharatiya Jana Sangh. Daryaganj, Delhi: Bharat Mudranalaya.

Zavos, John. *The Emergence of Hindu Nationalism in India*. Delhi: Oxford University Press, 2000.

Select articles and book chapters

Badhwar, Inderjit, Prabhu Chawla and Farzand Ahmed, 'Militant Revivalism'. *India Today*, 31 May 1986.

Casolari, Marzia. 'Hindutva's Foreign Tie-up in the 1930s'. *Economic & Political Weekly*, vol. 35, no. 4, 22-28 January 2000.

———. 'Role of Benares in Constructing Political Hindu Identity'. *Economic & Political Weekly*, vol. 37, no. 15, 13 April 2002.

Chatterjee, Manini. 'Saffron Scourge: The VHP's Communal Fascism'. *Frontline*, 10 September 1993.

Davis, Richard H. 'The Iconography of Rama's Chariot'. In *Making India Hindu: Religion, Community, and the Politics of Democracy in India*, edited by David E. Ludden. Delhi: Oxford University Press, 1996.

Dillard, James E. 'The Fortune of Nehru's Mass Contacts Campaign and the Rise of Muslim Separatism'. *Journal of South Asian and Middle Eastern Studies*, vol. XXXI, no. 2, Winter 2008.

Dubey, Priyanka. 'The Age of ABVP'. *The Caravan*, October 2017.

Graham, B.D. 'Syama Prasad Mookerjee and the Communalist Alternative'. In *Soundings in Modern South Asian History*, edited by D.A Low. Berkeley: University of California Press, 1968.

Jeffrey, Robin. 'Media Revolution & "Hindu Politics" in North India, 1989-99'. *Himal*, July 2001.

Mohan, Lalit. 'RSS' invisible machinery wooing HP voters'. *The Tribune*, 6 November 2017.

Naim, C.M. 'The Maulana Who Loved Krishna'. *Economic & Political Weekly*, vol. 48, no. 17, 27 April 2013.

Noorani, A.G. 'Muslims & Police'. *Frontline*, 12 and 26 December 2014.

Rai, Lala Lajpat. 'The Hindu-Muslim Problem'. Chapter in *Writings and Speeches*, Volume 2, comprising articles he wrote for *The Tribune* and other newspapers, edited by Vijaya Chandra Joshi. Jullundur: University Publishers, 1966.

Rajagopal, Arvind. '"He did not leave the RSS": Interview with Gopal Godse'. *Frontline*, 28 January 1994.

Rudoph, L.J. 'The Media and Cultural Politics'. In *Electoral Politics in India: A Changing Landscape*, edited by S.K. Mitra and J. Chiriyankandath. New Delhi: Segment Books, 1992.

Sarkar, Tanika. 'Imagining Hindu Rashtra'. In *Making India Hindu: Religion, Community, and the Politics of Democracy in India*, edited by David E. Ludden. New Delhi: Oxford University Press, 1996.

Reports and Supreme Court Cases

Union Home Ministry review prepared for the National Integration Council, June 1968.

Mitra, N.N. (ed.). *The Indian Annual Register*, 1941, Volume 1. Calcutta: Annual Register Office.

Report and Proceedings of the Second Indian National Congress.

Report of the Disturbance which took place at Jabalpur, Sagar, Damoh and Narsimhapur in February 1961.

Report of the Inquiry into the Communal Disturbances at Ahmedabad and other places in Gujarat on and after 18 September 1969.

Report of the Commission of Inquiry into the Communal Disturbance at Bhiwandi, Jalgaon and Mahad in May 1970.

Report of the Commission of Inquiry on the Tellicherry Disturbances on 28 December 1971.

Report of the Three-Member Commission of Inquiry headed by Justice (Retd.) Jitendra Narain of the Patna High Court.
Report of the Commission of Inquiry into the Firing Incidents on the Clashes between Christians and Hindus at Mandaikadu in Kanniyakumari District on 1 March 1982 and 15 March 1982.
Report of the Bhagalpur Riot Inquiry Commission.
Abhiram Singh vs. C.D. Commachen & Ors., (1996) 3 SCC 665.
Abhiram Singh vs. C.D. Commachen, (2017) 2 SCC 692.
Dr. Ramesh Prabhoo vs. Prabhakar K. Kunte, (1996) 1 SCC 130.
Manohar Joshi vs Nitin Bhaurao Patil, (1996) 1 SCC 169.
Mohammad Aslam vs. Union of India & Ors., (1996) 2 SCC 749.
Mohammed Ahmed Khan vs. Shah Bano Begum, (1985) 2 SCC 556.
Narayan Singh vs. Sunderlal Patwa, (2003) 9 SCC 300.
S. Aziz Basha vs. Union of India, AIR 1968 S.C. 662.
S.R. Bommai vs. Union of India, (1994) 3 SCC 1.
Zahira Habibullah H. Sheikh vs. State of Gujarat & Ors., (2004) 4 SCC 158.
Fullilove vs. Klutznick, 448 U.S. 448 (1980).

Newspapers and Journals referred to

Daily News and Analysis
Economic & Political Weekly
Free Press Journal
Frontline
Greater Kashmir
Hindustan Times
Hitavada
Illustrated Weekly of India
India Today
Janata
Journal of South Asian and Middle Eastern Studies
Mahratta
New Age
Organiser
Outlook
Panchajanya
Secular Democracy
Sunday
Sunday Guardian
Sunday Mail
Sunday Observer
Tehelka
The Asian Age
The Hindu
The Indian Express
The International New York Times
The Times of India
The Tribune

Appendices

Appendix 1

RSS Prayer and Oath

(D.R. Goyal, *Rashtriya Swayamsewak Sangh*, pp. 246-9.)

The Hindi-Marathi Prayer which was sung in the RSS shakhas till 1939 when the present Sanskrit prayer was introduced. In English it would read:

Salutations to you, O Motherland where I am born;
Salutations to you, O the Land of Aryas where I have grown;
Salutations to you, O Sacred Land where I have worked;
My body will ever and again bow to you in salutation.
O Guru, the messenger of Rama, grant us good character;

Give us soon all the virtues to become full Hindus;
Induct us to your grace and make us followers of Rama:
May we become celibate, defenders of faith and men of brave determination.
Victory to Samarth Shri Ramdas, the Guru of the Nation
Victory to Mother India

The English version of the above Sanskrit prayer which is sung in the RSS shakhas these days is given below:

O Affectionate Motherland, I eternally bow to you.
O Land of Hindus, you have reared me in comfort.
O Sacred Land, the Great Creator of Good, may this body of mine be dedicated to you
I again and again bow before you.

O God Almighty, we the integral parts of Hindu Rashtra salute you in reverence;
For your cause have we girded up our loins,
Give us your blessings for its accomplishment;
Give us also the invincible power, the purity of character which may win the respect of entire world and the wisdom which may facilitate the thorny path that we have consciously adopted.
Let our hearts be inspired by the bold determination to achieve salvation along with prosperity which alone is the outstanding means;
Let undying and intense devotion to the goal be ever alive in our minds;
With your blessings let our all-conquering organised force meet with eminent success in taking this Nation of ours to the highest pinnacle of glory while defending our dharma.
Victory to Mother India!

The English version of the oath which every candidate is made to take for admission in the Sangh.

Before the All-Powerful God and my ancestors, I most solemnly take this oath, that I have become a member of the Rashtriya Swayamsewak Sangh in order to achieve all-round greatness of Bharatvarsh by fostering the growth of my sacred Hindu religion, Hindu society and Hindu culture. I shall perform the work of the Sangh honestly, disinterestedly, with my heart and soul, and I shall adhere to this oath all my life.
Bharat Mata ki Jai.

(Before 1939 the slogan in the oath was 'Jai Bajrang-Bali Balbhim-ki-Jai'.)

Appendix 2

Constitution of the RSS

Translated from original in Hindi
(As given in D.R. Goyal, *Rashtriya Swayamsewak Sangh*, pp. 256-68.)

Preamble

WHEREAS in the disintegrated conditions of the country it was considered necessary to have an Organisation

(a) to eradicate the fissiparous tendencies arising from diversities of sect, faith, caste and creed and from political, economic, linguistic and provincial differences among Hindus;

(b) to make them realise the greatness of their past;

(c) to inculcate in them a spirit of service sacrifice and selfless devotion to the Hindu Samaj, as a whole;

(d) to build up an organised and well-disciplined corporate life; and

(e) to bring about an all-round regeneration of the Hindu Samaj;

AND WHEREAS the Organisation known as 'THE RASHTRIYA SWAYAMSEWAK SANGH' was started on the Vijaya Dashmi day in the year 1982 Vikram Samvat (1925 A.D.) by the late Dr. Keshav Baliram Hedgewar;

AND WHEREAS Shri Madhav Sadashiv Golwalkar was nominated by the said Dr. Hedgewar to succeed him in the year 1997 Vikram Samvat (1940 A.D.);

AND WHEREAS the Sangh had till now no written constitution;

AND WHEREAS in the present changed conditions, it is deemed expedient to reduce to writing the constitution as also the Aims and Objects of the Sangh and its Method of work;

THE RASHTRIYA SWAYAMSEWAK SANGH hereby adopts, the following constitution:

The Rules and Regulations

Name
Article I
The name of the Organisation is 'THE RASHTRIYA SWAYAMSEWAK SANGH'.

Head Office

Article 2

The Head Office of the Sangh is at NAGPUR.

Aims & Objects

Article 3

The Aims and Objects of the Sangh are to weld together the diverse groups within the Hindu Samaj and to revitalise and rejuvenate the same on the basis of its Dharma and Sanskriti, that it may achieve an all-sided development of the Bharatvarsha.

Policy

Article 4

(a) The Sangh believes in orderly evolution of the Society and adheres to peaceful and legitimate means for the realisation of its ideals.

(b) In consonance with the cultural heritage of the Hindu Samaj, the Sangh has abiding faith in the fundamental principle of tolerance towards all faiths.

The Sangh, as such, has no politics and is devoted purely to cultural work. The individual swayamsewaks, however, may join any political party, except such parties as believe in or resort to violent and secret methods to achieve their ends; persons owing allegiance to such parties or believing in such methods shall have no place in the Sangh.

Flag

Article 5

While recognising the duty of every citizen to be loyal to and to respect the State Flag, the Sangh has as its flag, the 'Bhagwa-Dhwaj' – the age-old symbol of Hindu Culture.

Swayamsewaks

Article 6

1. (a) Any male Hindu of 18 years or more, who subscribes to the Rules and Regulations of the Sangh and takes its pledge, set out in Appendix (a), be registered as a swayamsewak.

(b) A swayamsewak shall be deemed to be an active swayamsewak, if he attends a Sangh shakha regularly or performs specific work duly assigned to him.

(c) A swayamsevak shall cease to be swayamsewak, if he resigns his membership or is expelled for misconduct or indiscipline or any act prejudicial to the interests of the Sangh.

2. *Bal swayamsewak*: Any male Hindu below the age of 18 may be admitted and allowed to participate in the Sangh programmes. They will be classified according to their ages and given suitable training in accordance with the Rules framed for the purpose.

A list of the bal swayamsewaks will be maintained in the units to which they are admitted.

APPENDICES

Register of Swayamsewaks

Article 7

(a) Each village, town, city and the provincial centre having a shakha, shall constitute a primary unit of the Sangh.

(b) Every shakha shall maintain a register of all its swayamsewaks – active or otherwise.

Constituent Units

Article 8

(a) For organisational purposes, the country, shall be divided into provinces.

(b) Every province may be further subdivided according to their order of subordination as indicated below:

Province (Prant)

Division (Vibhag) | Provincial Centre (Prantiya Kendra)

Dist. (Zila) | City (Nagar) (Place with a population of 1,00,000 and ovcr)

Town (Shahar) (Place having a population of 5,000 and over) | Mandal (Group of villages (Gram (Village))) (Place below 5,000 population)

Elections

Article 9

(a) Elections shall be held after every three years. (b) The date, method and venue of elections shall be determined by the Kendriya Karyakari Mandal.

Qualification for Voters and Candidates for Elections and Appointments

Article 10

(A) Voters:

Every active swayamsewak of at least one year's standing immediately prior to the date of preparation of electoral lists for the elections, shall be entitled to vote in the elections.

(B) Candidates:

(1) He (i.e., a swayamsewak), who is an officer-bearer of a political party, shall not be eligible as a candidate for election or as an appointee to any post so long as he is such an office-bearer.

(2) A candidate for election, for an appointee to any Akhil Bharatiya post, shall be:

(a) An active swayamsewak of at least six years' continuous standing; and

(b) Shall work full time without any remuneration.

(3) An appointee to a provincial post shall be an active swayamsewak of at least three years' continuous standing.

(4) A candidate or appointee for Sangha chalakship shall be an active swayamsewak of at least one year's standing.

Order of Authorities and Bodies

Article 11

There shall be the following authorities and bodies constituted as provided in the Articles shown against their names:

1.	Sar Sangha chalak	: Art. 12
2.	Sar Karyavaha	: Art. 13
3.	Kendriya Karyakari Mandal	: Art. 14
4.	Akhil Bharatiya Pratinidhi Sabha	: Art. 15
5.	Prant, Vibhag, Zila etc. Sangh chalaks	: Art. 16
6.	Pracharaks	: Art. 17
7.	Prantiya, Vibhag, Zila, etc. Karyakari Mandals	: Art. 19
8.	Prantiya Pratinidhi Sabha	: Art. 19

Sar Sangh Chalak

Article 12

Late Dr. Keshav Baliram Hedgewar, the Founder of the Sangh, was the Adya (First) Sar Sangh chalak. Shri Madhav Sadashiv Golwalkar was nominated Sar Sangh chalak by him in consultation with the then Kendriya Karyakari Mandal. He is the Sar Sangh chalak since then. The Sar Sangh chalak will nominate his successor, as and when the necessity arises, with the consent of the then Kendriya Karyakari Mandal.

The Sar Sangh chalak is the guide and philosopher of the Rashtriya Swayamsewak Sangh. He may attend, summon or address any assembly of the swayamsewaks, prantinidhi sabhas, and karyakari mandals, severally or jointly.

Sar Karyavaha

Article 13

(a) The elected members of the Akhil Bharatiya Pratinidhi Sabha (vide Art. 15) shall elect the Sar Karyavaha.

(b) The Sar Karyavaha shall act in consultation with the Sar Sangh chalak.

Kendriya Karyakari Mandal

Article 14

(a) The Sar Karyavaha shall form the Kendriya Karyakari Mandal. The Mandal shall consist of the following office bearers:

(i) Sar Karyavaha (he will preside)

(ii) One or more Sah-Sar Karyavahas.

(iii) Akhil Bharatiya Sharirik Shikshan Pramukh

(iv) Akhil Bharatiya Bauddhik Shikshan Pramukh

(v) Akhil Bharatiya Prachar Pramukh

(vi) Akhil Bharatiya Nidhi Pramukh

(b) The Kendriya Karyakari Mandal shall have in addition not less than five members who shall be chosen from among the Karyakari Mandal of the provinces.

(c) *Functions*

The following will be the functions of the Kendriya Karyakari Mandal:

(i) The KKM is the highest executive authority of the Sangh and as such, will carry into effect the policy and programme laid down by the ABP Sabha. The KKM shall supervise the working of the units.

(ii) The KKM shall control the finance of the Sangh. It may take from the several provincial units such amounts of money, as may from time to time be required for the general advancement of the Sangh work. The KKM may finance such of the units as have insufficient funds of their own.

(iii) The KKM shall appoint one or more auditors to audit the accounts of the Sangh annually.

(iv) The Kendriya Karyakari Mandal may shift the Head Office to or establish one or more sub-head office at places wherever it may deem proper.

(v) The KKM in consultation with the Prantiya Karyakari Mandals concerned, may redistribute the provinces.

(vi) The KKM shall be the highest authority for taking such disciplinary action against any swayamsevak as may be necessary.

(vii) The KKM will frame rules and bye-laws, in consonance with the Constitution, for the purpose of uniformity in rules and procedure and for the proper functioning of the Sangh.

Akhil Bharatiya Pratinidhi Sabha

Article 15

(a) The elected members of a Prantiya Pratinidhi Sabha shall elect from amongst themselves one-eighth of their number as representatives of the province on the Akhil Bharatiya Pratinidhi Sabha.

(b) Akhil Bharatiya Pratinidhi Sabha shall consist of:

(i) Representatives of the delegates.

(ii) Sangh chalaks and pracharaks of divisions and provinces and provincial centres.

(iii) Members of the Kendriya Karyakari Mandal.

(c) The Sar Karyavaha shall preside over the ABPS.

(d) The Akhil Bharatiya Pratinidhi Sabha shall meet at least once a year.

(e) The Akhil Bharatiya Pratinidhi Sabha shall review the work and lay down the policy and programme of the Sangh.

Sangh Chalaks

Article 16

(a) Every province, provincial centre, division, district, tehsil, city and town may have a Sangh chalak.

(b) The Prant Sangh chalak shall be elected by delegates elected as per Article 19(a).

(c) The Sangh chalaks for the constituent units in the provinces shall be annually appointed by the Prant Sangh chalak in consultation with the prant-pracharak.

(d) In case a suitable person is not available for the office of Sangh chalak, the prant Sangh chalak may appoint a karyavaha. The karyavaha, so appointed, shall perform the duties of a Sangh chalak.

(e) In case of death, departure, prolonged illness or resignation of the prant Sangh chalak the Kendriya Karyakari mandal shall appoint a person to discharge the duties of the prant Sangh chalak.

Pracharaks

Article 17

(a) (i) Pracharaks shall be full-time workers selected from amongst those devoted workers of high integrity whose mission is to serve the society through the Sangh and who of their own free will, dedicate themselves to the Cause.

(ii) They will receive no remuneration.

(b) Appointment of pracharaks:

(i) The Akhil Bharatiya Prachar Pramukh will appoint prant pracharaks with the consent of the Sar Karyavaha and in consultation with the Sangh chalaks concerned.

(ii) The prant pracharak will appoint pracharaks for different units in the province in consultation with the prant Sangh chalak.

(c) The ultimate authority for the appointment, transfer or discontinuance of the service of the pracharaks shall vest in the Sar Karyavaha.

Prantiya Subordinate Karyakari Mandals

Article 18

(a) Sangh chalak of a province, provincial centre, division, district, tehsil, city or town will form a karyakari mandal consisting of the following office-bearers:

(i) The Sangh chalak (he will preside).

(ii) Pracharak [appointed under Article 17(b)].

(iii) Karyavaha.

(iv) Bauddhik Shikshan Pramukh.

(v) Sharirik Shikshan Pramukh.

(vi) Nidhi Pramukh.

(b) Each karyakari mandal shall also have in addition not less than three members chosen from amongst the karyakari mandals of the subordinate units, if any.

(c) Karyakari mandals will be the highest executive authorities in their respective units, responsible to the immediately superior karyakari mandal for implementing the policy and carrying out the programme laid down by the ABP Sabha. They shall supervise the Sangh work in their respective units and control the finances.

(d) Karyakari mandals will have the power to take disciplinary action against any individual swayamsevak for breach of discipline or behaviour prejudicial to the interests and honour of the Sangh. Such an action is subject to confirmation by the Karyakari Mandal of the superior unit.

(e) The PKM with sanction of the KKM may change the provincial centre.

(f) The Prantiya Karyakari Mandal may, if necessary reconstitute the various units in the province.

(g) The Prantiya Karyakari Mandal may frame rules in consonance with the Constitution and the rules framed by the Kendriya Karyakari Mandal for the proper functioning of the Sangh in the province.

(h) For mandals and places with a population of less than 5,000 a karyavaha will be appointed by the Sangh chalak of the superior unit. He will be responsible for the Sangh work in his unit.

Prantiya Pratinidhi Sabha

Article 19

(a) Districts, cities and the provincial centre will send for every fifty swayamsewaks entitled to vote, one such swayamsewak as delegate to the Prantiya Pratinidhi Sabha.

(b) The Prantiya Pratinidhi Sabha shall consist of:

(i) The elected delegates.

(ii) Sangh Chalaks and pracharaks of divisions, districts, cities and of the provincial centre.

(iii) Members of the Prantiya Karyakari Mandal.

(c) The Prant Sangh Chalak will preside over the Prantiya Pratinidhi Sabha.

(d) The Prantiya Pratinidhi Sabha shall meet at least once a year.

(e) The Prantiya Pratinidhi Sabha shall review the work in the province and make such recommendations to the PKM as it may deem fit.

Programmes

Article 20

The existing branches of the Sangh will continue subject to the provisions of the Constitution.

New branches may be opened.

Physical training will be given by means of exercises and games organised at a convenient hour every day.

Occasional talks and lectures will be arranged for imparting intellectual training and inculcating love for ideals of Hindu dharma and culture.

Periodical classes for swayamsewaks to be trained as instructors and workers will be arranged.

Festivals of cultural importance will be celebrated and members of the public may be invited on such occasions.

Agencies and institutions may be established to disseminate knowledge of the ideals and activities of the Sangh and to educate the people generally.

In general, the Sangh may do all such things and carry on any other work capable of being undertaken in connection with and calculated, directly or indirectly, to promote and achieve any of the objects mentioned in Art. 3.

Meetings, Conferences, Rallies and Training Classes

Article 21

(a) All karyakari mandals will meet as often as necessary but at least once in the period shown below against each:

KKM	-	Four months.
PKM	-	Four months.
VKM	-	Three months.
ZKM	-	Three months.
Teh. KM	-	Two months.
Other KMs	-	One month.

(b) The workers or swayamsewaks of any unit or of two or more co-ordinate units may have combined programmes and meet together in conferences, rallies or training classes, with the previous permission of the proper authorities of the superior unit.

(c) The KKM may arrange Akhil Bharatiya Conference and rallies of workers and swayamsewaks.

(d) The KKM shall organise training classes called Adhikari Shikshan Varga at different places in the country to impart training in the Sangh work. Swayamsewaks thus trained in the prescribed three years course will be qualified instructors.

Funds

Article 22

(a) All offerings, gifts, donations, etc., received for Sangh purposes by the branches shall constitute the Sangh Funds.

(b) On the 'Vyas Poornima' function of every year or any other sacred day fixed for the purpose, every branch will celebrate the 'Dakshina Day' and will receive voluntary offerings.

(c) The funds received by the branch will be entrusted by the Sangh chalak to the nidhi pramukh of the branch concerned, who will be responsible for maintaining proper accounts, which shall be annually audited.

(d) The funds received by a village branch will remain with the karyavaha of that branch. The Tehsil Nidhi Pramukh will supervise the management of funds of all such branches within the tehsil.

(e) The KKM and PKM shall issue such directions for the disbursement of the funds collected by its subordinate units as it may from time to time think necessary for the general advancement of the Sangh work.

Quorum

Article 23

One half of the total strength shall form the quorum for the meetings of the various karyakari mandals, and one-fifth for the Prantiya and Akhil Bharatiya Pratinidhi Sabhas.

Undeveloped Units

Article 24

(a) In case of provinces in which the work has not yet developed to an appreciable level, elections shall not be held, and the Prant Pracharak appointed shall be in sole charge of the work.

(b) The province shall be deemed to be developed when:

The number of active swayamsewaks reaches one thousand in that province.

Provided the KKM is satisfied with the general progress of the work in that province.

The KKM, however, may provide to such provinces due representation on the Akhil Bharatiya Sabha in a manner it deems fit.

Interpretation and Amendment of the Constitution

Article 25

(a) The interpretation of the Constitution and its clauses by the Kendriya Karyakari Mandal shall be final.

(b) An Amendment to the Constitution can be proposed to the KKM by any PKM or by any other karyakari mandal with the recommendation of the respective PKM of any twenty-five members of the Akhil Bharatiya Pratinidhi Sabha. The KKM will put the proposal of an amendment before the PKMs, and the amendment will be deemed carried if two-thirds of the provinces agree by a simple majority.

(c) The decisions of the PKMs over such amendments may be brought for reconsideration before the ABP Sabha on a requisition by any twenty-five members of that Sabha. The decision of the ABP Sabha in this behalf, taken by two-thirds majority shall be final.

Appendix B

Abbreviations

Sangh	:	Rashtriya Swayamsewak Sangh.
ABPS	:	Akhil Bharatiya Pratinidhi Sabha.
KKM	:	Kendriya Karyakari Mandal.
PKM	:	Prantiya Karyakari Mandal.
VKM	:	Vibhag Karyakari Mandal.
ZKM	:	Zila Karyakari Mandal.
TKM	:	Tehsil Karyakari Mandal.
KM	:	Karyakari Mandal.

Appendix 3

RSS Declared Unlawful

Text of Government communiqué dated February 4, 1948
(D.R. Goyal, *Rashtriya Swayamsewak Sangh*, pp. 250-2.)

In their resolution of February 2, 1948, the Government of India declared their determination to root out the forces of hate and violence that are at work in our country and imperil the freedom of the Nation and darken her fair name. In pursuance of this policy the Government of India have decided to declare unlawful the Rashtriya Swayamsevak Sangh in the Chief Commissioner's Provinces. Similar action is also being taken in the Governor's Provinces.

As democratic governments, the Government of India and the provincial governments have always been anxious to allow reasonable scope for genuine political, social and economic activities to all parties and organisations including those whose policies and purposes differ from, or even run counter to their own, subject to the consideration that such activities should not transgress certain commonly recognised limits of propriety or law. The professed aims and objects of the Rashtriya Swayamsevak Sangh are to promote the physical, intellectual and moral well-being of the Hindus and also to foster feelings of brotherhood, love and service amongst them. Government themselves are most anxious to improve the general material and intellectual well-being of all sections of the people and have got schemes on hand which are designed to carry out these objects, particularly the provision of physical training and education in military matters to the youth of the country. Government have, however, noticed with regret that in practice members of the Rashtriya Swayamsevak Sangh have not adhered to their professed ideals.

Undesirable and even dangerous activities have been carried on by members of the Sangh. It has been found that in several parts of the country individual members of Rashtriya Swayamsevak Sangh have indulged in acts of violence involving arson, robbery, decoity [sic], and murder and have collected illicit arms and ammunition. They have been found circulating leaflets exhorting people to resort to terrorist methods, to collect fire arms, to create disaffection against the government and suborn the police and the military. These activities have been carried on under a cloak of secrecy, and the government have considered from time to time how far these activities rendered it incumbent on them to deal with the Sangh in its corporate capacity. The last occasion when the government defined this attitude was when the Premiers and the Home Ministers of provinces met in Delhi in conference towards the end of November.

It was then unanimously agreed that the stage when the Sangh should be dealt with as an association had not yet arrived and that individuals should continue to be dealt with sternly as hitherto. The objectionable and harmful activities of the Sangh have, however, continued unabated and the cult of violence sponsored and inspired by the activities of the Sangh has claimed many victims. The latest and the most precious to fall was Gandhiji himself.

In these circumstances it is the bounden duty of the government to take effective measures to curb this reappearance of violence in a virulent form and as a first step to this end, they have decided to declare the Sangh as an unlawful association. Government have no doubt that in taking this measure they have the support of all law-abiding citizens, of all those who have the welfare of the country at heart.

Appendix 4

Golwalkar's Interaction With Home Minister Sardar Patel

Press Note dated November 14, 1948, issued by the Home Ministry of the Government of India (D.R. Goyal, *Rashtriya Swayamsewak Sangh*, pp. 252-3.)

Soon after his release from prison in Nagpur after the statutory period of six months, Mr. Golwalkar, head of the RSS organisation, made approaches to the government which indicated a possibility that the activities of that organisation might be diverted and confined to channels which would have no harmful effect on the communal situation in the country. He also expressed a desire to interview the Home Minister. In order to enable him to do so, the Government of India requested the CP government to cancel an order issued by them under which Mr. Golwalkar's movements had been restricted to the city of Nagpur and to facilitate his departure for Delhi for the specific purpose of seeing the Home Minister.

Mr. Golwalkar accordingly came to Delhi and had his first interview with the Home Minister soon after his arrival. There was an exchange of views and Mr. Golwalkar wanted some time to consult his followers in an attempt to influence them on the right lines. Some days later he had his second interview during which he expressed his inability to bind himself to any change until the ban was lifted. He felt that the lifting of the ban would strengthen his hands in dealing with his followers. Simultaneously, however, the Government of India had got in touch with provincial governments to acquaint themselves with their views and the latest information about the activities of the RSS. The information received by the Government of India shows that the activities carried on in various forms and ways by the people associated with the RSS tend to be anti-national and often subversive and violent and that persistent attempts are being made by the RSS to revive an atmosphere in the country which was productive of such disastrous consequences in the past. For these reasons, the provincial governments have declared themselves opposed to the withdrawal of the ban and the Government of India have concurred with the view of the provincial governments.

This position was conveyed to Mr. Golwalkar towards the end of the last month and he was told that since the purpose for which he had been allowed to come to Delhi had been served, he should now return to Nagpur. Mr. Golwalkar was not prepared to accept this position and expressed a desire to see the Home Minister and the Prime Minister on their return to Delhi. The Home Minister declined to grant a further interview, but in order to give him a chance to interview the Prime Minister on his return, if the latter so desired, he was allowed to remain in Delhi under certain restrictive orders issued by the District Magistrate of Delhi. Mr. Golwalkar declined to accept the orders of restrictions, but has made no attempts to contravene the restrictions imposed on him. He has written letters both to the Prime Minister and Home Minister explaining inter alia that the RSS agrees entirely in the conception of a secular state for India and that it accepts the National Flag of the country and requesting that the ban imposed on the organisation in February should now be lifted. These professions of the RSS leader are, however, quite inconsistent with the practice of his followers and for the reasons already explained above, the Government of India find themselves unable to advise provincial governments to lift the ban. The Prime Minister has, therefore, declined the interview which Mr. Golwalkar had sought.

Mr. Golwalkar is accordingly being informed that he should make immediate arrangements to return to Nagpur. The Government of India are also taking appropriate steps to ensure that Mr. Golwalkar complies with these instructions.

Appendix 5

Justice On Trial

A collection of the Historic Letters between Sri Guruji and the Government (1948-49)
(Prakashan Vibhag, RSS, Karnatak, 1969)

A WORD PLEASE

All is well that ends well. Even memories of the most terrible and fatal accidents, when overcome, become a sweet and precious treasure of joy and happiness. Is it not an universal experience shared by all?

The imposition of ban on the R.S.S. immediately after the assassination of Gandhiji resulting in the arrest and detention of thousands of its workers along with their leader Sri Guruji under suspicion; clearance of the mist of murder followed by the release of all the workers; release of Sri Guruji after imprisonment for six months; the failure of his all-out efforts because of the obstinate attitude of the Government to persuade them through personal interviews and correspondence either to lift the ban on the R.S.S. or to institute an impartial public inquiry; his subsequent detention under the notorious Bengal Regulation Act of 1818 at Delhi; the courting of arrests and facing of all trials and tribulations by thousands of Swayamsevaks from Himalayas to Kanyakumari to establish the Truth and Justice of their Cause; the failure of the mediation of third party leaders like the venerable Sri T.R.V. Sastry and others due to the highly unjust and obdurate attitude adopted by the Government even after the submission of the draft Constitution of the R.S.S. by Sri Guruji; the unequivocal declaration by the Government on 9th July 1949 that the ban on R.S.S. could not be withdrawn because of the fundamental differences between the R.S.S. and the Government; and the taking of the people by surprise by lifting the ban unconditionally only after three days i.e., on 12th July '49 and all such happenings, have now become sweet memories of the past, though at the time of their occurrence every moment seemed to be most disquieting, extremely perilous and highly explosive. After all, it is history now.

The grave charges levelled by the Government at the time of the imposition of ban on the R.S.S., such as robbery, dacoity, loot, murder, arson etc., all evaporated and the mere presentation of the Constitution already in vogue (though in unwritten form) was sufficient for the Government to withdraw the ban subsequently. Let it be noted that there was no mention of this point in the communique issued by the Government when it banned the R.S.S.

But the most surprising part of the whole affair was the unhappy wording of the Government communique when it removed the ban, insidiously implying humiliating commitments by Sri Guruji on behalf of the R.S.S.

Justice therefore demands that all facts be placed before the discerning public for their impartial scrutiny. It is to meet that demand that the historic correspondence between Sri Guruji and the Government during those crucial times is compiled here, with some of the letters in Hindi original rendered into English. Certain connected material is also furnished as Appendix. These will, we are sure, lay bare the true picture of the story.

Facts speak for themselves. Let the people judge.

– PUBLISHERS

PREFACE TO THE THIRD EDITION

One more relevant addition has been made to the already published material in the 2nd revised edition – which itself had included a few new additions to the 1st edition.

The Present Addition is an extract from the statement of Bharat Ratna Dr. Bhagawan Das, who was a renowned thinker and philosopher and the revered father of Sri Sri Prakasha, our Ex-High Commissioner for Pakistan.

We are confident that the present edition, with its fuller contents, will evoke an even wider response from all over the country than the first two editions – the rapid selling out of which has only proved the alert and appreciative eye of our people for Truth and Justice.

APPENDICES

THE TEXT OF THE CORRESPONDENCE

Nagpur,
31st January, 1948

My dear Hon'ble Pandit Jawaharlal Nehru,

Pranams.

Yesterday at Madras I heard the shocking news that some thoughtless perverted soul has committed the heinous act of putting a sudden and ghastly end to the life of Poojya Mahatmaji by the bullet. This vile act is a blot on our Society in the eyes of the world. Even if it had been at the hands of one from an enemy country, this act would have been unpardonable, for the life of Mahatmaji was dedicated to the good of the entire humanity crossing the borders of particular groups of people. No wonder that every one of our countrymen will be filled with unbearable agony to see that one of our own countrymen has perpetrated this most inconceivable, abominable act. Since the moment I heard the news a void has pervaded my heart. My heart is laden with anxiety at the terrible prospects of the near future due to the absence of that great unifier. The attack on such a deft helmsman who held so many diverse natures in a single string bringing them to the right path, is indeed an act treacherous not merely to an individual but to the whole country. No doubt you, that is the Government authorities of the day, will deal suitably with that traitorous individual. However severe that dealing be, it is bound to be too mild when compared to the loss sustained. About that, it is not for me to say anything. But now is the testing time for all of us. The responsibility of safely steering the ship of our Nation ahead in the present troubled times with an unruffled sense of judgement, sweetness of speech and single-minded devotion to the Nation's interest is upon all of us. On behalf of the Organisation which has been moulded on these very lines, and intensely sharing the bereavement of the Nation at this crucial hour and invoking the sacred memories of that departed soul, I pray at the Feet of the All-Merciful Almighty that He bless us with the necessary inspiration and wisdom to establish a real everlasting oneness of our people.

Yours in the Service of the Mother,
(*Sd.*) M.S. GOLWALKAR
(*Rendered from the original in Hindi*)

Nagpur,
31st January, 1948

Hon'ble Sardar Patel,

Pranams.

Yesterday at Madras I heard the news of the ghastly incident which has shaken all humanity. Such a heinous and abominable incident has probably never been witnessed before. My heart is wrung with extreme agony. It is difficult to find words to condemn the person who has committed this crime. Even the idea of such an unprovoked wickedness passes comprehension. What can be said about the man who has thus plunged the whole world into indescribable grief? But let us shoulder the responsibility that has fallen upon us by the untimely passing away of that great unifier, keeping alive the sacred memories of that soul who had tied diverse natures in a single bond and was leading them all on a single path. And let us with the right feelings, restrained tone and fraternal love conserve our strength and cement the national life with everlasting oneness.

On behalf of the Organisation which is built on this faith and on this basis of oneness I pray at the Feet of the All-Merciful Lord to guide all the children of this Nation on the right path and inspire them for the building up of a pure and powerful national life.

Yours in the Service of the Mother,
(*Sd.*) M.S. GOLWALKAR
(*Rendered from the original in Hindi*)

Camp: Nagpur,
11th Aug. 1948.

My dear Hon'ble Pt. Nehru,

Prior to my arrest on 1-2-1948 and in the extraordinary atmosphere created by the assassination of Pujya Mahatmaji I had written a letter to you. After my release from prison on 6th August 1948, I am again writing to you with the same love, respect and spirit of honourable co-operation.

It is a fact that I could not then understand why a very large number of my friends and I were arrested and detained and the subsequent steps taken in respect of the work I was representing. I have tried to convince myself by the oft repeated argument that the times were extraordinary and hasty and unbalanced action was its result. I do not wish to believe that persons occupying the places of highest importance can or should be susceptible to impatience, hastiness or loss of mental balance. But that is the only conclusion forced upon me when after six month's detention, when sufficient evidence has come to light and I and my work have been absolved from all the astounding allegations laid at our door, I have been served with an order interning me in Nagpur and restricting my activities in such a manner that my release has become only a fresh imprisonment in a more extensive jail.

But whatever the mental condition of the authorities in general and yourself in particular may have then been and may now be, I am grateful to the Almighty that he has not let my mind turn sour and that I maintain my spirit of love and friendship and oneness. I hope and expect all my co-workers share my sentiments. I would have spread this message of love to all, preaching to all not to let feelings of hurt or rancour poison their hearts, but the restrictions laid upon me prevent me from doing this necessary duty. I would also have appreciated if instead of being placed under such unwarranted restrictions, I would have been given a chance to clear my position and to convince you of my feelings and readiness to cooperate with the Government in these crucial times. Even now I hope our rapproachment [sic] is not afar.

But times do change, everything regains its balance and I have no doubt the Great God who has been our support all down these centuries will give us the necessary strength, courage and large-heartedness to march on to greatness, each along his path but all united in common reverence to the Motherland.

Meanwhile, let us cherish now and forever cordial friendly relations, not allowing the ghastly dream of the last few months to embitter our mutual love.

With regards
Yours in the Love of the Mother,
(*Sd.*) M.S. GOLWALKAR

Nagpur,
11th Aug. '48

Nagpur,
11th Aug. 1948

Hon'ble Sardar Patel,

I was released from jail on the 6th of August 1948. Immediately thereafter, certain restrictions were imposed upon me, because of which I am remaining at Nagpur alone. I have tried to convince myself that it was because of the disturbed mental condition of the authorities (in the circumstances at the time when I was put behind bars) that such an unexpected step was taken. Of course it was extremely difficult for me, and so is it even now, to believe that persons occupying places of the highest importance can be susceptible to loss of mental balance and thus act improperly. And now after the lapse of sufficient time and especially after sufficient evidence to clear up the whole atmosphere has come to light, it is almost impossible for me to think that their mental condition can remain the same. But the fact of the needless restrictions now imposed upon me, betraying the same lack of mental equilibrium, has shown the impossible to be possible.

All the same, the cherished sentiments of love and friendship to you all which I have ingrained in my very nature have not suffered in the least. The feelings of mutual love and co-operation that I had expressed in my letter which I wrote to you on 1st February 1948 before entering the jail, have been the constant texture of my mind. It is also with the same spirit of goodwill that I am writing this letter.

After having thought from all angles, I feel it would be proper that the friendship and identity that has grown between us both, in person and in our attitude, should be made firm for all time. For my part, I believe that all of my friends of the now disbanded work, also look to you with the same feelings. I am only sorry that because of restrictions I have been denied the chance to do my duty of disseminating in all others those sentiments of friendship. Also, I am intensely pained that because of restrictions, I am unable to meet you in person and give a clear idea of our work so as to wash off the misconceptions in your mind. For the same reason I am also unhappy, that in these difficult times of our Nation I am denied the opportunity of discharging my duty of co-operating with the Government. I hope that the day is not far off when we will be able to come together and foster a healthy atmosphere of co-operation.

This is all for the present. I close this letter with prayers to the Presiding Deity of Bharat that our mutual affection be always on the increase and by the co-operative efforts of all, the future be one of all round joy and glory.

More in person when the occasion arises.

Yours with best wishes,
(*Sd.*) M.S. GOLWALKAR
(*Rendered from the original in Hindi*)

Camp: Nagpur,
Date: 24th Sept. 1948

My dear Hon'ble Pandit Jawaharlalji Nehru,

It is over a month-and-a-half since I wrote to you my last letter. I have not had the happiness of receiving any reply yet. I have been putting off writing again since the Hyderabad question had come to head and action seemed imminent. Now, however, the most important part of the question has been successfully solved and I feel it time to write to you.

In the clear atmosphere created by the success in the Hyderabad question, I request you kindly to reconsider the question of the ban imposed on the R.S.S. It is now almost eight months and nothing can remain to be investigated into. I am sure you are convinced that the allegations against the R.S.S. have been found to be without foundation in facts. It is, therefore, a case for simple justice, which we have a right to expect from a Government which we have always considered our own.

During this period, the R.S.S. having been disbanded, the intelligent youth are rapidly falling into the snares of Communism. With the alarming happenings in Burma, Indo-China, Java and other neighbouring States, we can envisage the nature of the menace. The one effective check of the R.S.S. no longer exists. The Communists had always considered the R.S.S. as their main obstacle and had tried to denounce and vilify it. In Mahatmaji's assassination and the ban on the R.S.S. they got their life's opportunity which they exploited to denounce the R.S.S. and push forward their work. News of their progress is alarming. I hope you will consider this problem coolly and help create an atmosphere in which the R.S.S. will be able to work honourably and help the Government fight the menace – on its own cultural lines. A candid withdrawal of the charges levelled against the R.S.S. and generous lifting of the ban imposed upon it will go a long way in bringing about the desired atmosphere.

For myself, I cannot persuade myself to sit still and helplessly watch the growing danger when I feel confident of triumphing over it with my cultural organisational work – freed from the unwarranted stigma of the charges levelled against it and from the legal disability to carry on its work. It is therefore that I am writing this to you, requesting you to consider the situation and lift the ban on the R.S.S.

Waiting for favour of an early reply,

I am,
Yours in the Love for the Mother
(*Sd.*) M.S. GOLWALKAR

No. 10(12)–47/P.M.

Prime Minister's Secretariat,
New Delhi,
27th September, 1948.

Dear Shri Golwalkar,

The Prime Minister has received your letter of the 24th September. He desires me to inform you that the question of continuing or not continuing the ban on the R.S.S. is a matter for the Home Ministry to deal with. Your letter is, therefore, being forwarded to them.

But he wants me to inform you also that he is not prepared to accept your statement that the R.S.S. are free from blame or that the charges against them are without foundation. Government have a great deal of evidence in their possession to show that the R.S.S. were engaged in activities which were anti-national and prejudicial from the point of view of public good. Just before the banning of the R.S.S. he is informed that the U.P. Government sent you a note on some of the evidence they have collected about such activities of the R.S.S. in U.P. Other provinces have also such evidence in their possession. Even after the ban we have received information about the undesirable activities of old members of the R.S.S. This information continues to come to us even now. You will appreciate that in view of this, the Government cannot consider the R.S.S. as a harmless organisation from the public point of view. It is the Government's policy to root out communalism from this country and, therefore, not to encourage any movement which aims at the encouragement of the communal outlook. The approach of the R.S.S. as well as their activities have been definitely communal. What sometimes their leaders say is not borne out by what is done and there is a great disparity between outward precept and real practice.

Yours sincerely,
(*Sd.*) A.V. PAI.

Shri M.S. Golwalkar,
Hedgewar Bhavan,
Nagpur, C.P.

20, Barakhamba Road,
New Delhi, 3rd November, 1948.

To
The Hon. Pandit Jawaharlal Nehru,
Prime Minister of India.
Sir,

I am in due receipt of your favour dated the 27th September 1948, and signed on your behalf by Shri A.V. Pai. I received the letter – a reply to my letter to you of the 24th September 1948, on the 4th October 1948, when it was too late for me to reply to you before you left for England. I am, therefore, sending this now, when you are due to be back in Delhi, in the hope that you will pay kind and considered attention to it.

2. Let me first point out that the Central Government is not fully informed by the Provincial Government of the U.P. in the matter of the note alleged to have been sent to me. Neither myself nor any of my former co-workers in the U.P. ever received any such note. What must have happened to it, if at all it was despatched, is a mystery to me! Long before the R.S.S. was banned, I too had heard much about a 'charge sheet' the U.P. Government was preparing against us. But months rolled by and it was not forthcoming. May I infer that much of the so-called evidence in the possession of the Governments of the U.P. and other provinces is as authentic as this mysterious 'note'?

3. In connection with this 'evidence', allow me further to point out that Shri Govind Sahay, Parliamentary Secretary to the Premier of the U.P., has written a pamphlet entitled 'Nazi Technique and the R.S.S.' (in Hindi) and he is widely circulating it in his position of a ranking Government official. Even a cursory glance at it is enough to show that from cover to cover it is pure fabrication and libel. Such is the nature of the 'evidence' in possession of the U.P. Government.

4. Again if really the Central and Provincial Government are in possession of incriminating evidence against the R.S.S. or certain of its members, is it not right to expect at least a few successful prosecutions against the alleged wrong-doers? So far as I know all down these many months the various Governments have taken recourse to the extraordinary special legislations

and not proceeded against any person or group of persons under the substantive penal law. The one case in District Muzaffarnagar – upon which the whole super-structure of the so called 'charge sheet' of the U.P. Government seems to have rested has been decided only in the last week. A look at the learned and well-balanced judgement is sufficient to prove the falsity of the 'great deal of evidence' against 'certain members of the R.S.S.'.

5. Also in a Government by law in a free State, which propounds and maintains the fundamental rights of citizens and their right to associate and peacefully propagate their views, we claim it as a right to be placed in possession of the 'evidence', so that we may meet the charges. It is unfair for a civilised Government that ours is, to charge any person or body of persons with crimes of a serious character, without laying sufficient weighty evidence on the table and giving the accused a chance to vindicate his innocence. In the case of the R.S.S. I am constrained to state that it is most unfair to level charges against us, allow private individuals and parties to carry on a campaign of vilification against us under cover of the Government ban and at the same time gag us by use of Emergency Legislations like the Public Safety Acts. I fail to see how this course is calculated to do credit to the Government which we want to love and hold in esteem.

6. In the short space of this letter, I have only tried to indicate that the 'evidence' on the face of it is unreliable. It deserves to be sifted and assessed for what it is worth. May I appeal to you, our Prime Minister and First Gentleman of the State, to apply an impartial, judicious and objective mind to this question and allow me and my friends the chance to disprove the allegations and vindicate our innocence? May I appeal further that, in view of the untenability of the charges, the ban on the R.S.S. be lifted? May I also appeal that no new matters be now introduced as it will be a deviation from the established canons of law and justice?

7. I shall be grateful if I am given an early chance to meet you in person and personally explain my position to you. The date and time when I may be able to have an interview may kindly be communicated to me.

Hoping for favour of an early reply,

I remain,
Yours in the Service of the Mother,
(*Sd.*) M.S. GOLWALKAR

20, Barakhamba Road,
New Delhi, 8th November, 1948.

Hon. Pandit Jawaharlalji Nehru,

Pranams.

Immediately after the removal of the restrictions laid upon me by the C.P. Government, I came here to Delhi to meet necessary persons. All these days I have been waiting for your return from abroad so that I may have the honour of a personal interview with you. Whatever may be the result of the interview, I feel it necessary to try to clear away the many misunderstandings about me and the work I stood for.

When in October 1947, I had the happiness of meeting you, I had said I would come again. But my ceaseless wanderings made it impossible. Now I hope the chance has been offered to me and I shall be very grateful if you will kindly communicate to me the date and time when I may have the interview and be given the chance of reiterating my assurance of last October 1947 of unstinting support to the Government in these delicate times.

Expecting early reply,

I am,
Yours in the Love for the Mother,
(*Sd.*) M.S. GOLWALKAR

No. 1396–P.M.

New Delhi,
10th November, 1948.

Dear Shri Golwalkar,

I am in receipt of your letters of the 3rd and 8th Nov.

The Home Ministry of the Government of India are concerned with internal matters and thus have to deal with the problem of the R.S.S. I understand that they have given a great deal of attention to it and have consulted Provincial Governments also. I suggest that you should deal with that Ministry and I am forwarding the papers you sent me to them.

In the course of the last year both the Central Government and the Provincial Governments have received a mass of information in regard to the objectives and activities of the R.S.S. This information does not fit in with what has been stated by you in this behalf. Indeed it would appear that the declared objectives have little to do with the real ones and with the activities carried on in various forms and ways by people associated with the R.S.S. These real objectives appear to be completely opposed to the decisions of the Indian Parliament and the provisions of the proposed Constitution of India. The activities, according to our information, are anti-national and often subversive and violent. You would appreciate, therefore, that mere assertions to the contrary do not help very much.

I would gladly see you but, apart from my being very fully occupied since my return from Europe, I do not think such an interview will serve any useful purpose. As the matter is in the hands of the Home Ministry, it is desirable that you should deal with them directly.

Yours sincerely,
(*Sd.*) JAWAHARLAL NEHRU

Shri M.S. Golwalkar,
20, Barakhamba Road,
New Delhi.

20, Barakhamba Road,
New Delhi,
12th Nov. 1948.

Hon. Pandit Jawaharlalji Nehru,

Pranams.

I am grateful for the kind and prompt reply sent to me on the 10th instant. I hope it was after full consideration that it was written. After its reaching me I need not have carried on this correspondence since it depicts that your mind is practically closed on the question.

But I must point out a few things arising out of your favour of the 10th instant. It appears to me that the Government are making an extravagant claim in stating that they have more knowledge of the R.S.S. than all of us – its members – put together, and have a mass of information come to them in the course of the last year. Out of this period, for the last nine months and more, the R.S.S. is not functioning at all and as for the individual members, all the prominent ones were in jail for most of this period and not in a position to do any activity about which adverse information, as suggested, could be given with any trace of truth in it. I hope you will note this palpable discrepancy in your letter.

Next: The information seems to show that these activities have been 'anti-national'. This is a grave charge and does not deserve to be made lightly. It calls for proof weighty and substantial. Mere feelings and opinions have no value in this behalf. Reiterating that the Government have information in their possession without allowing those against whom the charges are made to test it, to subject it to searching scrutiny, means nothing. Let it be appreciated by both of us that 'mere assertions do not help much'. So long as the Government continue to make assertions and allegations without discharging their onus of supporting the same with unrebuttable evidence, we can only continue to assert and with justification that the charges are untrue and that injustice is being perpetrated against us.

If a magistrate convicts a person for an offence, however small, without disclosing to him any evidence, merely stating that there is a 'lot of information' against him, the magistrate's conduct stands self-condemned. And when such grave charges are made without bringing forward one iota of proof, what shall we say? Have we retrogressed into the dark ages, when the feelings, opinions and will of some one individual or group were alone just and rational and any person or group of persons could be awarded even capital punishment just for the fun of it? Is not this arbitrary course much more in opposition to the decisions of the Indian Parliament than any act which we could ever imagine?

So far as my knowledge goes, there is nothing in the objectives of the R.S.S. to which the Indian Parliament can take exception, nothing which is contrary to the decisions of the Parliament so far published. As for being 'opposed to the provisions of the proposed Constitution', it would have been better if this had not been written by you – our Prime Minister. It is queer as to punish a man for attempted murder of an individual due to be born in a year or so.

One more point: We are all ignorant of what you have been pleased to call 'real objectives and activities, as distinguished from the professed ones'. To us our professed objectives are real and our real objectives have always been openly given expression to. To wear a mask hiding the reality within, to express what is not meant and mean what is never expressed, to maintain and cherish complete discord between thought, word and deed are facets in the art of dissimulation – the quality of the wily diplomat and politician – maybe a necessary quality. By the grace of God, we are humble servants of our people in the cultural field, aloof from politics, building character, building unity. There is no room in our work for the art which maintains discrepancies between the 'professed' and the 'real'.

Excuse me for having been a little frank. But the continued injustice, the constant harping upon 'the mass of information' which dare not face the sun of scrutiny and the fact that each of your letters has some original and previously unthought of allegations have made me express a fraction of my feelings at the gross injustice done to my work and at the Government's peculiar attitude which, in the long run, is bound to set such bad precedents that, I am afraid, this unfortunate country will be involved in interminable party feuds and mutual distrust. The history of the last thousand years is full of these feuds and their resultant defeat and degeneration. Now when for the first time the country is emerging from the heap of ruins of the past ten centuries, I hope we rise wiser and saner and not allow that unfortunate portion of our history to repeat itself under different denominations.

That is all. I would have felt very happy and grateful to have been given the chance of an interview with you. But it seems you would rather not have it. Be it so. We appear to be at the parting of ways. The Mother can be worshipped in various ways, all sooner or later converging, meeting at Her Sacred Feet. I had hoped and tried that our ways converge and meet sooner but that does not seem to be Her Will. I obey Her Command and with all love and respect for you, prepare to step upon the course which the Great Mother may indicate.

A considered reply will be a great favour.

I am,
Yours in the Service of the Mother,
(*Sd.*) M.S. GOLWALKAR

20, Barakhamba Road,
New Delhi,
13th Nov. 1948.

Hon. Pandit Jawaharlalji Nehru,
Pranams.

The accompanying letter was almost ready yesterday, when in the evening I received a letter from the Home Ministry communicating to me that the ban would not be lifted in pursuance of your letter to me of the 10th instant. It is surprising to note that you say that the Home Ministry is solely responsible for deciding this question whereas the Home Ministry came to a decision not independently but on the strength of your letter.

Let me also point out that the Home Ministry wishes unjustly to compel me to leave Delhi and go to Nagpur. You know I have come here to demand justice from the Central Government, as I have a right to. Arbitrary decisions can have no value. Let all charges be proved conclusively or withdrawn unconditionally and the ban be lifted forthwith.

We profess to be a civilised State. Such arbitrary acts may fit in with the autocratic rule of barbaric ages or to a certain extent to a foreign bureaucratic domination. But it does not, in my opinion, become a modern civilised democratic Government which professes to uphold and maintain the rights of the people with impartiality and justice.

I have, therefore, decided to stay over in the Capital till the wrong done to us is redressed.

With regards,

I am,
Yours in the Service of the Mother,
(*Sd.*) M.S. GOLWALKAR

Nagpur,
Date: 24th Sept. 1948.

Hon'ble Sardar Vallabh Bhai Patel,

Sadar Pranams.

It is over a month and a half since I wrote my last letter to you. I have not had the pleasure of receiving any reply from you as yet. For some time past I had been thinking of writing to you again. In the meanwhile, however, the Hyderabad problem was becoming graver everyday and the situation too so developed that intervention by the Government had become inevitable. That step was also taken. Fortunately the most important part of the question has been solved successfully in a very short time. In spite of the fact that various groups and parties were trying to act in their own ways with regard to the Hyderabad problem, I and my co-workers had always maintained that the Government alone should tackle the issue and set it right; and that the people would whole-heartedly support such a move. My cherished desire has been fulfilled, although in the present disbanded condition of our work I was unable to offer any help. All the same, my heart longed to see the success of our Government's action. Happily, victory has ensued and I wired to your good self and to the Prime Minister my heartfelt congratulations. I had put off writing this second letter to you till now, only because I thought that you would be engrossed in the Hyderabad problem. As that question is now solved for the most part, I am penning this letter.

It is now almost eight months that Rashtriya Swayamsevak Sangh has been banned. Doubtless, you are fully aware as to how far there is truth in the allegations made against the Sangh. I am quite certain that you have not the least doubt regarding the innocence of Sangh. There have been country-wide searches and investigations. Now, no more proof is needed to show that all the charges levelled against the Sangh were baseless even though the Government at that time might have thought otherwise. It now behoves [sic] the Government to withdraw all these charges and thus express their love of justice.

This, however, is only from the point of view of justice. From the point of the nation's situation I request you to consider it from two angles. The Hyderabad problem, because of which there was apprehension on the part of some that communalism would grow, is being successfully solved. Our Government's hand has proved strong enough and all of us are happy and free from anxiety as such a bold policy on the part of the Government will effectively checkmate the evil of communalism. The present success has wrought a change in the atmosphere and there can be no objection now to declare the charges against the Sangh to be baseless and allow it to function as before.

The other way of looking at the situation is this. Reports received from the South and the United Provinces reveal that the youths, especially the student section has, since the banning of Sangh, begun to lean more and more towards communism. Their propaganda is on the increase. It is not as if I have to give this indication of peril to you. But you will appreciate how much I have to control myself to sit idle and be a mere helpless spectator of the growth of foreign 'isms' when I feel confident that if Sangh is allowed to come out without the least stigma and function normally, the youth can be saved to a very large extent. I for one feel that if you with Government power and we with organised cultural force combine, we can soon eliminate this menace. I am intensely worried at the waves of victory of that foreign 'ism' which are sweeping over our neighbouring countries. It is that anxiety that makes me appeal to you with earnest urgency to create the necessary atmosphere for the functioning of the Rashtriya Swayamsevak Sangh as before.

Indeed you bestow deep thought on each and every question of importance. This too is one such, fit for your generous and comprehensive power of vision.

One more request to you. I am under restrictions! It is not impossible that it may be due to Central Government directives. But I feel it my duty to tour the whole of Bharatavarsha in order to protect our nation, our national life and our Government and save our young men from becoming extra-territorial in their loyalty. On that account even if I have to suffer, I have got to go out touring in a short time.

Kindly consider all these things. This is not the time to keep on discussing about the justice or injustice of the Government's actions against the Sangh. Nor do I possess so much of intellectual leisure. As such, removing all these things from before the eyes and in answer to the call of the times alone, please take a decision. I and all my co-workers have been striving from the very start to co-operate with you to bring the situation under control and make our Motherland invincible.

Expecting your reply at the earliest,

With best wishes,
Yours
(*Sd.*) M.S. GOLWALKAR
(*Rendered from the original in Hindi*)

Aurangzeb Road,
New Delhi,
Date: 11th Sept. 1948.

Brother Sri Golwalkar,

Received your letter dated 11th August. Jawaharalal [sic] has also sent me your letter of the same date.

You are very well aware of my views about the R.S.S. I have expressed those thoughts at Jaipur in December last and at Lucknow in January. The people had welcomed those views. I had hoped that your people also would accept them. But they appear to have had no effect on R.S.S. persons, nor was there any change in their programmes. There can be no doubt that the R.S.S. did service to the Hindu Society. In the areas where there was the need for help and organisation, the young men of the R.S.S. protected women and children and strove much for their sake. No person of understanding could have a word of objection regarding that. But the objectionable part arose when they, burning with revenge, began attacking Mussalmans. Organising the Hindus and helping them is one thing but going in for revenge for its sufferings on innocent and helpless men, women and children is quite another thing.

Apart from this, their opposition to the Congress, that too of such virulence, disregarding all considerations of personality, decency or decorum, created a kind of unrest among the people. All their speeches were full of communal poison. It was not necessary to spread poison in order to enthuse the Hindus and organise for their protection. As a final result of the poison, the country had to suffer the sacrifice of the invaluable life of Gandhiji. Even an iota of the sympathy of the Government or of the people no more remained for the R.S.S. In fact opposition grew. Opposition turned more severe, when the R.S.S. men expressed joy and distributed sweets after Gandhiji's death. Under these conditions it became [inevitable] for the Government to take action against the R.S.S.

Since then, over six months have elapsed. We had hoped that after this lapse of time, with full and proper consideration the R.S.S. persons would come to the right path. But from the reports that come to me, it is evident that attempts to put fresh life into their same old activities are afoot. I once again ask you to give your thought to my Jaipur and Lucknow speeches and accept the path I had indicated for the R.S.S. I am quite certain that therein lies the good of the R.S.S. and of the country and moving on that path we can join hands in achieving the welfare of our country. Of course, you are aware that we are passing through delicate times. It is the duty of every one from the highest to the lowliest in the country to contribute his mite, in whatever way possible, to the service of the country. In this delicate hour there is no place for party conflicts and old quarrels. I am thoroughly convinced that the R.S.S. men can carry on their patriotic endeavour only by joining the Congress and not by keeping separate or by opposing. I am glad that you have been released. I hope that you will arrive at proper decision after due consideration of what I have said above. With regard to the restrictions imposed upon you I am in correspondence with the C.P. Government. I shall let you know after receiving their reply.

Yours,
(*Sd.*) VALLABH BHAI PATEL
Offers Vandemataram
(*Rendered from the original in Hindi*)

Aurangzeb Road,
New Delhi,
26th September, 1948.

Brother Sri Golwalkar,

Received your letter of the 24th. I had sent a reply to your first letter on 11th September. I do not know why it did not reach you. I am sending a copy of the same. As the first letter did not reach you, I have thought it advisable to send this letter to you through Shuklaji.

2. From the reply which I had given to your letter, you will appreciate the whole situation. It is in consultation with all the Provinces that action has been taken against the Sangh. Only recently, the suggestions of the Provinces were again taken. But their opinion is still the same, that the notification imposing ban on the Sangh cannot be withdrawn. You are aware that our own men are there in all the Provincial Ministries. When it is the unanimous opinion of all of them that the notification be kept in force, then there must be some defect in the organisation itself. No one has any animosity against the organisation. If even then their opinion is like this, there must surely be some real basis for it.

3. After viewing all the things my only suggestion to you is that the Sangh should be brought to adopt fresh lines of technique and policy. That new technique and new policy can be only according to the rules of the Congress. If there is enthusiasm among the youth or the students it cannot be that it should be expressed in aggression and violence. There are other beneficial paths on which youth and students can be taken, to which I personally and the Government will offer heartiest sympathies.

4. With regard to your coming here, I have written to Shuklaji. After receiving his reply, I shall write to you again.

Yours,
(*Sd.*) VALLABH BHAI PATEL
(*Rendered from the original in Hindi*)

20, Barakhamba Road,
New Delhi,
5th November, 1948.

Hon'ble Sardarji,

Sadar Pranam.

After your departure to Bombay from here, I have received some instructions sent at your own instance. Their substance is as follows. The purpose of my coming to Delhi is over. The opinion of the Provinces was called for and they have sent their opinion against the removal of the ban. Now I need not remain here but should return to Nagpur, because the restrictions imposed upon me were removed only to enable me to proceed to Delhi to meet and request you in person to lift the ban. Now that work is over. Since the opinion of all the Provinces is unfavourable, there is now no need for further talks. As such, you are not even going to meet me now. It is with the knowledge that you have decided not to meet me again that I am forwarding this small letter for your kind perusal.

At the very outset, I wish to make one point very clear. I am not aware that the restrictions upon me were removed only for any limited purpose. As early as in August alone I had made it quite clear to the Hon'ble Pandit Dwaraka Prasadji Misra that I did not want the restrictions to be removed only for the limited purpose or on the condition of going to Delhi. After considering the pros and cons, if the Government removes the restrictions unconditionally, well and good. Of course, I had said that in my efforts to see that the Sangh was legalised I would first go to Delhi. But I was not prepared to accept any removal of restrictions on that condition. Therefore, it was only after reading the intimation of unconditional removal of restrictions that I started for this place.

Secondly, so many persons have been asking many a time so many types of questions. I have tried to give a consolidated answer to them all in the two statements published on 2-11-48. I have herewith enclosed copies of both statements. My request is that you go through them carefully.

Thirdly, you had asked for opinions from the various Provinces regarding the removal of ban on the Sangh and you had also told me of it. Then alone, I had pointed out that this is the concern of the Central Government especially of yourself alone. So far as all of us are aware, when the ban was imposed it was the Central Government which took initiative in promulgating the order. On the next day the other Provinces, and a few days later the States, only enforced that order. To my co-workers who had approached the ministers of various Provinces, the ministers declared that they were not concerned. Of course, some Provinces did express their opposition. But all finally said that it was a central question and they would act according to the Central Government's directions. I had also said the same thing, that in fact this question comes under the jurisdiction of the Central Government alone and that the other Provinces will only follow the Central Government's directions.

And now for the Provincial Governments to point their finger to the Central Government and the Central Government in their turn to point to the Provincial Governments, is something which will only result in evading the issue and can never lead to any satisfactory solution. How far is such a state of affairs desirable, is for you to consider.

The innocence, usefulness and the urgent need of the Sangh is bound to be, as is already being done, proved. Malpropaganda cannot suppress the truth for long.

Once again, I want to submit that the charges levelled against the Sangh are, one and all, baseless, fictitious and false. It appears that due to the virulence of their propaganda, even the mind of such a balanced person as yourself has been disturbed. I know the nature of our work.

It has been a matter of daily experience to me how individuals, especially youths, inspired with the noblest of sentiments, cultural integrity, spirit of selfless sacrifice and service to the people are moulded here and how the purest of love and sublime character blossom forth in them. That mean allegations should be laid at the door of this sacred organisation has caused me intense pain and surprise. After so much of wild propaganda against them and even after suffering dastardly attacks from so many thoughtless people, the exemplary restraint that the Sangh swayamsevaks have displayed even up to this day and have, by their wise and dignified conduct, avoided internecine quarrel and ill-will – even this single instance should suffice to prove the pure intentions of the Sangh.

Keeping in mind the delicate situation in the country and with a view to remove dissensions for the sake of a glorious future, I had instructed all my swayamsevak brothers to be peaceful and I strove for a peaceful settlement. I tried my utmost to see that between the Congress, which is capable of delivering goods in the political field and is at present the ruling party, and the Rashtriya Swayamsevak Sangh in the cultural field, which has achieved success in creating a matchless spirit of patriotism, brotherhood and selflessness among the people, there be no bad blood, there be only everlasting mutual love, one supplementing and complementing the other, both meeting in a sacred confluence. I extended my hand of co-operation. With utmost regrets I have to say that you have chosen to ignore my best intentions. My heart's desire to see the converging of both the streams has remained unfulfilled. Maybe that the All Merciful Lord is indicating to me a different path and maybe the seed of future glory of this divine Bharatavarsha is imbedded therein.

At this juncture, when our ways are parting, I have a longing to have your darshan once. Although you have thought of not seeing me, I pray that you give me an opportunity so that I can take leave of you according to our traditional custom. Even though there has arisen some difference of opinion regarding the issue of legalising the Sangh, I have personally the highest esteem for you. It is because of it that at this point of taking, however unwillingly, a separate course, I am desirous of meeting you.

One small thing. On the evening of 2-11-48, the Delhi District Magistrate had sent me an order of restriction. From what is written in the first paragraph, I surmise that it was done with your consultation and as per your instructions alone. I had not expected such a treatment. I had to reject that order with a feeling of utmost regret, as I thought it to be unprovoked and unjust.

That is all. May the Lord who is the Bestower of the power of discrimination, shower good on all. Expecting the favour of an early reply.

With best wishes,
Yours,
(*Sd.*) M.S. GOLWALKAR
(*Rendered from the original in Hindi*)

New Delhi,
12th November, 1948.

Dear Mr. Golwalkar,

Sardar Patel has asked me to acknowledge the receipt of your letter dated the 5th November, 1948 and the enclosures thereto and to say that he is very sorry that due to his preoccupations he is unable to reply to you himself.

2. You have doubtless received the Prime Minister's letter dated the 10th November, 1948, which deals fully with the main points which you have made in your letter to Sardar Patel. Sardar Patel regrets he is unable to depart from the position which he took in his last interview with you and the verbal communication which was made to you through Mr. Bedekar of the Home Ministry. The Provincial Governments have expressed themselves unable to lift the ban imposed on your organisation, and for the reasons communicated to you in the Prime Minister's letter of the 10th November, the Government of India are unable to advise the Provincial Governments to adopt a contrary course. Since the purpose for which the restrictions imposed on you by the Central Provinces Government were removed has been served, it is no longer necessary for you to stay in Delhi.

3. I am, therefore, to request you to make immediate arrangements to return to Nagpur. I should like to know, as soon as possible, but not later than tomorrow evening, what arrangements you are making in this behalf, so that we may inform the C.P. Government accordingly.

Yours sincerely,
(*Sd.*) H.V.R. IYENGAR
Secretary,
Ministry of Home Affairs.

20, Barakhamba Road,
New Delhi.
13th November, 1948.

Hon. Sardarji,

Pranams.

Received with thanks a letter signed by Shri Iyengar on your behalf yesterday evening. I have noted your decision not to lift the ban on the R.S.S. relying on the letter sent to me by the Hon. Prime Minister on the 10th November. I was surprised to find that whereas in his letter the Hon. Prime Minister has informed me that it is the Home Ministry alone which has to decide, you have taken your stand on the Hon. Prime Minister's letter to me.

Allow me to point out that I came to Delhi to get justice done to my work. In its place I have an arbitrary decision unbecoming of a civilised Government which professes to uphold the fundamental rights of the people. Since the case has been entrusted solely to the Home Ministry there are only two courses left open to them.

1. To limit their attention to the charges mentioned in the communique of the Government of India dated the 4th February, 1948, declaring the R.S.S. an illegal body and prove those charges by incontrovertible evidence, allowing us the right to subject the evidence adduced through scrutiny. Mere assertions of information which is not so proved and arbitrary decisions based upon such information which is kept a jealously guarded secret will not help in this matter; or
2. to withdraw unconditionally all the charges as being baseless and lift the ban. I intend staying on in the Capital till either of these two courses is taken and justice done to my cause.

As for my leaving Delhi and going to Nagpur, I had explained in my letter of the 5th November that it was only after an unconditional withdrawal of all restrictions on my movements and activities by the C.P. Government that I decided to come to Delhi. I was never prepared for a temporary relaxation of the restrictions for the limited purpose of coming here to see you. The suggestion that it was a temporary relaxation contained in your yesterday's letter is totally wrong. Under these circumstances it is improper to try to compel me to leave Delhi and go only to Nagpur. As I have said I wait for justice being done to me and stay on in Delhi till, as a civilised State, the Government fulfils the demands of justice.

I hope you will give considered attention to what is written above and do what is just and proper and not what is autocratic and arbitrary.

With regards,

I remain,
Yours in the Service of the Mother
(*Sd.*) M.S. GOLWALKAR

The following is the letter written by Shri Guruji while presenting the Draft Constitution of the R.S.S. to the Govt. of India:

Sub-Jail, Seoni,
11th April, 1949.

To
The Hon'ble Home Member,
to the Govt. of India,
New Delhi.

Through:
The Hon'ble Minister for Home Affairs,
Govt. of C.P. and Berar,
Nagpur.

Sir,

Enclosed is the written Constitution of the R.S.S. The body will hereafter function in accordance with its terms. They were substantially the terms on which the Sangh work was carried on in the previous years.

I hope the Constitution as now framed will be found unobjectionable and will satisfy a much felt want. With the hope that the Government of India will find it so, I expect that the Government of India will be good enough to pass early orders lifting the ban on Sangh and enabling it to function as before, subject to the Constitution now framed and submitted and to be duly published as soon as I am enabled to do so. All consequential orders may also be passed to facilitate the work of the Sangh.

I am painfully aware that the Government of India have viewed my words and attitude in general with suspicion; but time will show that my work of welding together in cultural bonds our loosely knit and largely divided population, by associating them in common pursuits and common discipline, will benefit the country as a whole and that my attitude is one of co-operation and goodwill to all and not one of conflict with any group.

Expecting an early and favourable response,

I remain,
Yours sincerely,
(*Sd.*) M.S. GOLWALKAR

Seoni Sub-Jail,
11-4-1949.

GOVERNMENT OF INDIA

(Ministry of Home Affairs)

No. 28/23/48 POL.
New Delhi,
May, 3, 1949.

From
H.V.R. IYENGAR, I.C.S.,
Secretary to the Government of India.

To
SRI M.S. GOLWALKAR,
C/o The Chief Secretary
to the Govt. of C.P. and Berar,
Nagpur.

Sir,

I am directed to refer to your letter dated the 11th April enclosing copies of the draft Constitution of the R.S.S. and requesting that the ban on the organisation be lifted.

2. The Government of India are in consultation with the Provincial Governments on the draft submitted by you and the request you have made and it will be some time before their replies are received and considered. In the meanwhile, they are disposed to think that it may be of advantage if they communicated to you at this stage the views they have themselves formed. In presenting these views, they have kept in mind the consideration which Sardar Patel mentioned to you in the course of interviews with him last October. You will recall his telling you that the gravamen of the charges against the R.S.S. was that it functioned in secrecy, that whatever the professions of its organisers might have been, it derived its main inspiration in the minds of the people from the doctrine of communal hatred, that it exalted a communal party above State and that in practice its followers indulged systematically in violence. The Government of India feel that the Constitution as drafted does not fully safeguard the organisation against these defects. In particular they have noticed the points mentioned in the following paragraphs.

3. You have stated in your letter that the R.S.S. has in the past adhered to the principles laid down in the draft Constitution. One of these is that the Sangh adheres to 'peaceful and legitimate means' for the realisation of its ideals. Unfortunately the history of R.S.S. activities in recent times shows that this profession has in practice been systematically violated by your followers.

Incidents have occurred in all Provinces and many States where the methods adopted by the Sangh were anything but peaceful and legitimate, and where the advancement of the interest of Hindu religion and culture took the form of violence against those who happen to profess some faith other than Hinduism. The Government feel therefore that positive and explicit declaration in the Constitution for the abjuration of violence would be necessary.

4. A specific declaration, under Article 4, of allegiance to the Constitution of India as established by law and an explicit acceptance in Article 5 of the National Flag (with the Bhagva Dhwaja as organisational flag of the Sangh) would be necessary for satisfying the country that there are no reservations in regard to allegiance to the State.

5. The charge of surreptitious functioning of the organisation cannot, in the Government's view, be adequately met without a provision in the Constitution of the Sangh stating that all rules and instructions shall be written and published and all its activities shall be open. A specific provision regarding the publication of annual audited accounts would also be desirable.

6. On the organisational side, the various committees of the R.S.S. at all levels seem to contain a substantial element of persons who are virtually nominated from above. This is a principle of organisation which is fraught with great danger and the Government of India consider that the democratic elective principle should be unequivocally recognised and acted upon. In particular, the functions of Sarasanghachalak have not been defined with any degree of precision. In the interest of democratic working, these functions should be specifically listed, and all vestiges of a dictatorial character should be removed. You are doubtless aware of the general criticism that in positions of importance the R.S.S. has persons belonging to a particular community from a certain area. You will have to ensure that this preponderance is removed and that there is generally local autonomy in regard to office-bearers etc.

7. In regard to the pledge, the acceptance of a life obligation in connection with membership of an association is more common with secret societies than with democratic groups functioning in full public view. To this extent, therefore, the pledge incorporated in the draft Constitution is retrograde.

8. The Constitution should contain a provision to the effect that minors can be enrolled as members, only with written consent of their parents or guardians and their membership should be terminated if at any time such parents and guardians desire it. The minors should not be required to take any oath or pledge.

9. These criticisms have been communicated to you at this stage because the Government want you to appreciate that their approach to this, as indeed to other political problems, is constructive and helpful rather than merely destructive and hostile. But it rests entirely with you to decide what action should be taken on this letter. Government will consider the matter further after receiving your further reply.

Yours faithfully,
(*Sd.*) H.V.R. IYENGAR.
Secretary to the Government of India.

Seoni Jail,
17th May, 1949.

To
The Hon'ble Home Member,
Government of India,
NEW DELHI.

Sir,

Received with thanks the letter No. 28/23/48 of 3-5-49 over the signature of Shri H.V.R. Iyengar, I.C.S., Secretary to the Government of India.

I feel it would have been advisable for the Government not to have referred to the so-called charges against the R.S.S. In this, this letter takes us back to the February '48 days, an unhappy retrogression. All the same everything that need be said in answer to the 'charges' has been said in detail in the memorandum submitted to the Government by some of my co-workers where it has been shown that there is no basis for the allegations. If the Government believed that the information on which they had based these charges was reliable, they should have in response to my request in my letters to the Hon'ble Prime Minister (written during Aug., Sep., Oct., 1948) and yourself, come forward to prove them before any impartial tribunal. This would have given us a chance to know what stuff the information was made of. But the Government have chosen to keep all this 'information' a jealously guarded secret and have not risked an open scrutiny of the same. It is over 16 months that the charges were levelled and over 6 months I asked for proof. But no such proof has been forthcoming and now it is too late. The one legitimate inference is, therefore, that the so-called 'information' is incapable of being proved and as such deserves to be rejected. Under the circumstances it is unbecoming of a Government claiming to be civilised, to continue to reiterate the so-called charges even at this late stage and does not derive any respect for the Truth, Justice or due process of law on the part of the Government. This is an uncomfortable deduction and it is to avoid this embarrassment to the Government, that I had in my last letter of 11-4-49 scrupulously avoided any reference to these 'charges' etc., and had not even requested the Government to make a statement withdrawing the 'charges', though I believe such a declaration will greatly enhance the prestige of the Government. This with reference to the paragraphs 2 and 3 of your kind letter.

Regarding para 6 of the letter, I am not aware of any general criticism that the R.S.S. has 'in all positions of importance persons belonging to a particular community from a particular area'. On the contrary I know that communal, sub-communal or provincial considerations do not vitiate the work of the R.S.S. or play any part in any person occupying any position of importance. To-day the Government have before them a substantial portion of members of the R.S.S. whom they have been pleased to put in jails. Even a cursory glance will suffice to show that this remark has been made without due consideration. There being, therefore, no preponderance of any particular class of people and local workers having always enjoyed full freedom in conducting the work of the R.S.S., I do not see that any specific provision in this connection is called for.

As regards 'appointments from above', let me with all humility, point out that this does not indicate any want of 'democratic element', since in all provinces and the centre, the bodies laying down the policy guiding and controlling the work are composed of elected members. Only the day to day routine is in charge of persons 'appointed from above'. This ought to satisfy the Government's solicitude for the democratic elective principle, seeing that the Government themselves are composed of a small elected body, the Assembly, whereas the great bulk are all 'appointed from above' – right from H.E. the Governor General to the last peon. And yet no one can say the Government of India is undemocratic.

About the functions of the Sarasanghachalak I have not been able to see what 'vestiges of dictatorship' there are in the draft Constitution. The central elected body is the sole authority and has alone the responsibility of discharging all necessary functions regarding the work. There seem to be only two rights which the Sarasanghachalak possesses: (1) of nominating his successor and (2) of calling and addressing meetings of members in any locality etc. For the rest he is a general guide. But it rests solely with the Central Body to decide how far, if at all, to follow that guidance. These are the only functions of the Sarasanghachalak and these have been stated quite clearly in the draft Constitution.

Regarding the minors mentioned in paragraph 8 of the letter, I am sorry to note that Government have not carefully considered what is stated about the minors in the draft. The minors are not members, hence the question of Pratigna (not oath) does not arise. They are encouraged to take part in out-door activities of the R.S.S. and imbibe abiding qualities of sound character. That is all. Regarding the necessity of the written permission of their parents these are minor details which can be worked out later.

Regarding paragraph 5, let me first state that the R.S.S. has always functioned in the open. The charge of 'surreptitious functioning' is untrue and born out of misunderstandings. At the same time I have said in my letter of 11-4-49 that the Constitution shall be duly published. When it comes to that stage, I shall ask my co-workers to consider the advisability of incorporating such provision in the Constitution.

The contents of para 4 of the letter are wholly out of place in the matter under consideration. I request the Government to recognise the difference between a Constitution and an oath of allegiance. If this difference is appreciated the suggestion contained in the paragraph becomes uncalled for. Even so Art. 4 and 5 of the Constitution are sufficiently unambiguous. In this connection let me draw the attention of the Government to my statements of 2nd Nov. '48 where these points have been unequivocally answered. I think that should suffice.

One more point remains, regarding the Pledge (Para 7 of the letter). The R.S.S. bases its work upon Hindu Culture. In Hindu Culture a Pledge is always a life obligation and not a temporary contract. If the life-pledge is the quality of secret societies only and retrograde, then in the opinion of Government the whole Hindu Society must be akin to a secret society and the Hindu Culture, retrograde in its nature. Do the Government think it will be right or creditable to accept this conclusion seeing that you the Hon. Home Member (and through you the Government) have declared in one of your recent speeches that you knew and respected Hindu Culture?

I have tried to explain the criticisms. Indeed a full answer is not possible without consulting my co-workers for after all they have as much voice in the matter as I have. I pray the Government to consider my answers calmly and without prejudice. I feel it serves no useful purpose to take recourse to dilatory methods. All the same the Government may take their own time.

I have always believed and with all the emphasis at my command maintain that these 'charges' are wholly untrue and that violence, secrecy, communal hatred etc., had never any place in the R.S.S. in the past and can have no place in its work in the future. As for the somewhat new and original charge of 'exalting a communal party over State', I can only say that the expression is meaningless and in the present set-up such a condition can never arise, whatever party be in question.

As I close this letter, let me point out that there is no Constitution which cannot be found fault with in one respect or the other. All Constitutions are capable of improvement in course of time. I think, therefore, that it is not proper to criticise a Constitution immediately it is framed and expect it to be perfect like the word of God. The Government, I was told, wanted that the Constitution of R.S.S. be reduced to writing and that has been done. If we expect it to be perfect before allowing it to be worked and go on suggesting improvements and alterations, I think it is likely to remain unfinished and unworked till the end of time. The only proper course to my mind is to allow it to work, and as circumstances demand, to alter and improve. This could be an approach really constructive and helpful.

Yours faithfully,
(*Sd.*) M.S. GOLWALKAR.

GOVERNMENT OF INDIA

(Ministry of Home Affairs)

NEW DELHI,
24th May, 1949.

From
H.V.R. Iyengar, I.C.S.,
Secretary to the Government of India.

To
Shri M.S. Golwalkar,
C/o The Govt. of C.P. & Berar.

Sir,

Please refer to your letter dated the 17th May addressed to Sardar Patel.

The Government of India regret that you should have used in your reply phrases like 'meaningless expression' and charged the Government with indulging in 'unbecoming behaviour and lack of respect for truth, justice or due process of law'. Such language constitutes a complete disregard of the ordinary rules of courtesy and propriety, more particularly in reply to the Government where letters are written, as my previous letters were written, with a full sense of responsibility that attaches to Government communications.

2. Coming to the substance of your reply, the Government of India regret to note that your attitude in regard to the activities of organisation of the R.S.S. seems to have undergone no change. Not only do you see nothing wrong in the ideologies and the activities of the R.S.S. in the past but you suggest that the organisation would be guided by the same ideology and pursue the same methods in future. In regard to your argument that an impartial tribunal should judge the charges made against the R.S.S., the Government of India would like you to understand that they are and must be the final judge of whether the activities of an organisation or an individual are prejudicial to or subversive of the State and they cannot share that judgement with any tribunal. Indeed any suggestion that a matter like this be referred to an impartial tribunal can only come from an unrealistic appreciation of the very elements of Public Administration. I am to repeat that the Government of India have ample evidence in their possession implicating both the

R.S.S. and its individual members in systematic acts of violence. They held their hand for a long time hoping that the organisation would mend its ways and they took action only when their patience was exhausted.

3. The Government had hoped that after some calm thinking you would appreciate the correctness and soundness of the attitude taken by them but they regret to notice that you continue to show an obstinate attachment to those very defects in the organisation and functioning of the R.S.S. which have proved so harmful to the interests of the country. You have carried this attachment to such an extent that you ignore even the patent fact that in key positions in your organisation in every province, you have persons belonging to a particular community from a particular area. The Government of India had expected that you would appreciate the constructive approach which they made to the draft Constitution of the R.S.S. but find that you have either misunderstood that approach or are deliberately adhering to the objectionable features of your Constitution in the hope that they will enable you to carry on the activities of the R.S.S. on the same undesirable lines as in the past.

4. The policy of the Government in regard to the R.S.S. is quite clear and unequivocal. They are and must be the custodian of public interests and it is their duty to safeguard those interests against the unhealthy and undesirable encroachments. Unless and until they are satisfied that the R.S.S. will not be in a position to repeat the happenings and disastrous consequences which flowed from their activities in the past, they cannot relax their present attitude towards the organisation.

Yours faithfully,
(*Sd.*) H.V.R. IYENGAR,
Secretary to the Government of India.

SEONI JAIL,
1-6-1949.

To
The Hon'ble Home Member,
Government of India,
NEW DELHI.

Sir,

1. I am very grateful for the letter dated 24th May, 1949, over the signature of Shri H.V.R. Iyengar, I.C.S., Secretary to Government of India.

2. I am thankful for being told that 'any suggestion that a matter like this be referred to impartial tribunal can only come from an unrealistic appreciation of the very elements of Public Administration'. I admit my ignorance in this behalf which I have the honour of sharing with no less a personality than Mahatma Gandhi. If this is meant to be an abiding principle of administration – well, it is dangerous.

3. I have tried to understand the spirit of the letter, as evidenced by the last paragraph. This letter as well as the last one of 3rd May, 1949, gives me great satisfaction in that they prove that my reading of the mind of the personalities vested with the power of the Government has not been incorrect.

4. Regarding the first paragraph of the present letter I am sorry that my language has offended

the Government. I am a plain man brought up in an organisation wherein the sense of high or low does not predominate and wherein, therefore, there is no occasion to study and use a style of language suitable for addressing rulers and masters. Hence I could use only plain and straightforward expressions for expressing what I believed to be right and true. All the same I beg to be excused for having unwillingly offended the Government by a direct expression of the truth.

5. I also beg to be excused for not being able to persuade myself to confess to charges which I know to be untrue, even to humour the Government, in spite of my regard for the persons now in charge of the Government.

6. Since my direct and truthful words seem to be unpalatable to the Government, I think it best to desist from writing any further for the present.

7. And yet I request the Government to reconsider the matter in the light of the last paragraph of my last letter of 17th May, 1949.

8. For the rest, I am happy as I am.

Thanking you again for the prompt reply,

Yours faithfully,
(*Sd.*) M.S. GOLWALKAR.

GOVERNMENT OF INDIA
(Ministry of Home Affairs)

No. 335/49/Ps.

Camp: SIMLA,
11th June, 1949.

From
H.V.R. IYENGAR, I.C.S.,
Secretary to the Government of India.

To
SRI M.S. GOLWALKAR,
C/o Government of C.P. & Berar.

Sir,

I am writing with reference to the correspondence resting with your letter of the 1st June, 1949, addressed to the Honourable Home Member. Your letter indicates that you are so much imbued with your own idea of truth and justice and the righteousness of your conduct that you are not in a position to receive with good grace any unpleasant truths or to appreciate any helpful and reasonable approach to the difficulties created by yourself. In these circumstances the Government do not consider that any useful purpose would be served by continuing the correspondence. So far as the Government are concerned, the position remains as stated in my two previous letters.

Yours faithfully,
(*Sd.*) H.V.R. IYENGAR,
Secretary to the Government of India.

APPENDICES

Hereunder, we produce the letter addressed by Sri Guruji to the person of Pandit Moulichandra Sharma once again restating in unequivocal terms the stand of the R.S.S. On the strength of this letter, it is said, the ban was withdrawn. Let it not be forgotten that Sri Guruji had stopped all correspondence with the Government.

10th July, 1949.

My Dear Pandit Moulichandraji,

I am thankful to you for having come to see me and put me in possession of the trends of thought current about the R.S.S. in certain sections of society in the country. I am surprised to learn that in spite of my public statements made before my arrest and the correspondence through friends who have met me in jail and direct with the Home Ministry, there are still doubts about the position I take on the points that have been raised concerning the R.S.S. at various times by the spokesmen of the Government. You think that in view of the critical times through which the country is passing, it is necessary that all those who wish for a strong, well knit and stable society in this country should sink their differences and close their ranks, and therefore you have taken the trouble of coming to see me to get from me a clear statement, of the ideological, constitutional and practical stand of the Sangh, so that doubts that still persist may be removed and conditions favourable for the consolidation of the forces of stability be created. I deeply appreciate your goodwill and the spirit behind your move and I have not the slightest hitch in restating the position of the R.S.S. on the points that you have raised.

1. Loyalty to the Constitution of India and the State Flag:-

This question should not arise in an independent country. Every national of India claims loyalty to his country and that is his proud birth-right. Every member of the Sangh pledges to dedicate his all to the service of the motherland. Like every other citizen of India every Swayamsevak of the Sangh is loyal to the country, its Constitution and all the emblems of India's national independence and glory. The Flag is such an emblem and it is, as has been stated before, the proud duty of every swayamsevak as of every national of India to stand by this flag and keep up its honour. As you know, this has already been stated in the draft Constitution in Article 5. Although it was not necessary to do so, it was advisably mentioned to emphasise the importance that the Sangh attaches to this point. I am sure nobody will mix up the question of our institutional flag, the Bhagava Dhwaja, with the question of the State Flag, adopted by the Constituent Assembly. As you know, even the Congress has its own flag separate from the State Flag. In fact according to law, no party, institution or individual can use this State Flag except under rules laid down by the Government. This being the spirit, I can have no objection to this point made more explicit in the Constitution itself.

2. Policy of Violence and Secrecy:-

Such policy has been alleged by the critics of Sangh. But neither violence nor secrecy has been proved. The Sangh has not believed in violence except in National War, when every loyal citizen must fight the enemies of the country under the command of its Government. Except for that, violence has no place in an orderly democratic society and in the ideology or the working of the Sangh. This is clear from Article 4.

As for secrecy, the draft Constitution of the Sangh is a positive proof that there is nothing secret in the working of the policy of the Sangh. It is a public body working in the open. In view of the emergence of certain political parties believing in and resorting to violence and secret methods, I would like that at the end of Article 4, it is made clear that persons believing in or resorting to violent and secret methods have no place in the Sangh.

3. Election to Sangh Bodies:-

As you would see from the draft Constitution of the Sangh, it follows broadly the Constitution of Indian National Congress. The A.B.P.S. is a purely elected body comparable to the A.I.C.C. The Pranteeya [sic] Pratinidhi Sabhas are similarly modelled on the Provincial Congress Committees. The Sarkaryavaha is like the Congress President, elected by the All India Elected Body viz., the Akhila Bharitiya [sic] Pratinidhi Sabha. Again like the Congress President, he appoints his whole executive which is called the K.K.M. This is comparable to the All India Congress Working Committee. Similarly P.K.M. is on par with Provincial Congress Executive. The A.B.P.S. lays down the policy and programme of the Sangh and the Karyakari Mandals are merely to carry out that policy. Thus you will appreciate that the Constitution is completely based on the elective principle. Whole-time workers meant to do technical training and such other specialised work are bound to be appointed for their knowledge and skill in that job, but their existence does not affect the predominance and controlling of the elected bodies.

4. The Life-long Pledge:-

The misunderstanding about the Sangh Pledge is probably due to the fact that it is in Hindi and few people have cared to look into it thoroughly. The Pledge is for loyalty to 'Bharata Varsha', our motherland and for dedication to her service, not loyalty to the Sangh or any institution or person. Accordingly a swayamsevak can leave the Sangh without breaking the pledge, if he feels that he can serve the country by doing so. Article No. 6 (i) d of the Constitution provides for it.

5. Admission of Minors to the Sangh:-

The Sangh is, by its Constitution, restricted to working in the cultural field and has nothing to do with politics. It aims mainly at the formation of national character, healthy bodies and healthy minds. The most formative period is between 14 and 20 years of age. All cultural organisations dealing with the youths try to mould them at that age. So long as there is no law to regulate such activities of cultural organisations, there can be no reason for asking the Sangh not to instruct minors under the age of 18. Let me make it clear that the Sangh has always worked among minors strictly in accordance with law. If a guardian writes to request the Sangh authorities that he does not want his ward to be given instructions, his name is struck off the rolls.

6. Sarasanghachalak nominates his successor:-

If you read the wording of relevant article, you will see it clearly stated that the present Sarasanghachalak i.e., myself was nominated by my predecessor, Dr. Hedgewar, 'in consultation with the then K.K.M.' In future, the Sarasanghachalak will nominate his successor 'with the consent of the then K.K.M.' You will see that the word 'consent' has replaced 'consultation' in future. So this nomination is a formal declaration of the person elected by the K.K.M., which is the Executive working under the control of the Central elected body viz., A.B.P.S. You will also see that the constitutional head of the Sangh is the Sarkaryavaha, who is elected by the elected A.B.P.S. The Sarasanghachalak is only a 'Philosopher and Guide' as Article 12 declares.

7. That Sangh is dominated by persons belonging to a particular community from a particular area:-

The Sangh originated in Nagpur and its first workers were trained here. They spread over different provinces and organised shakhas there. As such, for historical reasons, such workers were mostly Maharashtrians from Nagpur. But as the work spread, a large number of workers from other provinces have come up and some of them have been in the top ranks of the Sangh. More will come up and with the draft Constitution with its elected bodies coming into operation, this tendency will find full expression as a majority of the Swayamsevaks are non-Maharashtrians. Like every other public body, people most popular with the rank and file in their own provinces will be elected to the Prantiya Pratinidhi Sabhas and then to A.B.P.S. Such criticism is not correct even at present, but to future conditions it will have no application at all.

8. Auditing of Accounts:-

If you see Article 14 Clause C (iii) you will find that an annual audit of accounts has been provided for as a compulsory measure in the draft Constitution. On this point the Sangh is really very strict that not a penny of public funds remains unaccounted for.

I trust, this clarification will set at rest the doubts that may be entertained by certain people and will bring about a true understanding of the real position of the Sangh.

With best wishes and thanks for the trouble that you have taken.

I remain,
Yours sincerely,
(*Sd.*) M.S. GOLWALKAR.

APPENDICES[1]

APPENDIX I

Wire sent by Sri M.S. Golwalkar, to Pandit Jawaharlal Nehru, Sardar Vallabhbhai Patel and Sri Devdas Gandhi after the assassination of Mahatma Gandhi.

30th January, 1948.

Shocked at the news of cruel fatal attack and tragic loss of greatest personality. Country's loss unbounded in these critical times. God help shoulder responsibilities grown heavier and fulfil the void caused by the loss of incomparable unifier.

M.S. GOLWALKAR.

[1] This series of Appendices, from I to XX, are from *Justice on Trial.*

APPENDICES

APPENDIX II

Instructions sent to different branches of the R.S.S. by telegram:

Nagpur,
30th January, 1948.

Out of respect and sense of sorrow at the tragic demise of Mahatmaji observe mourning till the thirteenth day by suspending normal routine.

M.S. GOLWALKAR.

APPENDIX III

Statement of Sri M.S. Golwalkar, Sarsanghachalak of the R.S.S. issued to the press before his arrest.

Nagpur City,
1st February, 1948.

A deed of exceptional brutality having been perpetrated resulting in the death of the most revered and beloved personality of the times, I feel it my duty to depart from our usual abstinence from making public statements and give vent to the feelings of horror and grief which the news has awakened in my mind. It is a tragedy of unparalleled magnitude, the more so because the evil genius is his countryman and a Hindu. Every rightminded countryman will feel, on top of inexpressible grief at this bereavement, a sense of shame in that this preverted [sic] being happens to be his countryman.

Living in these critical times, the country needed a great unifier and pacifier that the great soul was, and encompassing his death is a deed of unpardonable national disservice. With outraged feelings, we mourn the loss and look to the future.

In the presence of this appalling tragedy I hope people will learn the lesson and practice [sic] the doctrine of love and service. Believing in this doctrine, I direct all my brother Swayamsevaks to maintain a loving attitude towards all, even if there be any sort of provocation born out of misunderstanding and to remember that even this misplaced frenzy is an expression of unbounded love and reverence in which the whole country held the great Mahatma, the man who made our motherland great in the world. Our salutations to the revered departed one.

APPENDIX IV

Instructions sent to different branches of the R.S.S. by telegram, dated 3rd Feb. 1948, from Nagpur.

Guruji interned; Be calm at all costs.

M.N. KALE.

APPENDIX V

Text of Government communique dated 4th February 1948, declaring the R.S.S. unlawful.

In their resolution of February 2, 1948, the Government of India declared their determination to root out the forces of hate and violence that are at work in our country and imperil the freedom of the Nation and darken her fair name. In pursuance of this policy the Government of India have decided to declare unlawful the Rashtriya Swayamsevak Sangh in the Chief Commissioner's provinces. Similar action is also being taken in the Governor's Provinces.

As democratic Governments, the Government of India and the Provincial Governments have always been anxious to allow reasonable scope for genuine political, social and economic activities to all parties and organisations including those whose policies and purposes differ from, or even run counter to their own, subject to the consideration that such activities should not transgress certain commonly recognised limits of propriety of law. The professed aims and objects of the Rashtriya Swayamsevak Sangh are to promote the physical, intellectual and moral well-being of the Hindus and also to foster feelings of brotherhood, love and service amongst them. Government themselves are most anxious to improve the general material and intellectual well-being of all sections of the people and have got schemes on hand which are designed to carry out these objects, particularly the provision of physical training and education in military matters to the youth of the country. Government have, however, noticed with regret that in practice members of the Rashtriya Swayamsevak Sangh have not adhered to their professed ideals.

Undesirable and even dangerous activities have been carried on by members of the Sangh. It has been found that in several parts of the country individual members of Rashtriya Swayamsevak Sangh have indulged in acts of violence involving arson, robbery, dacoity, and murder and have collected illicit arms and ammunitions. They have been found circulating leaflets exhorting people to resort to terrorist methods, to collect fire arms, to create disaffection against the Government and suborn the Police and the Military. These activities have been carried on under a cloak of secrecy, and the Government have considered from time to time how far these activities rendered it incumbent on them to deal with the Sangh in its corporate capacity. The last occasion when the Government defined this attitude was when the Premiers and the Home Ministers of Provinces met in Delhi in conference towards the end of November.

It was then unanimously agreed that the stage when the Sangh should be dealt with as an association had not yet arrived and that individuals should continue to be dealt with sternly as hitherto. The objectionable and harmful activities of the Sangh have, however, continued unabated and the cult of violence sponsored and inspired by the activities of the Sangh has claimed many victims. The latest and the most precious to fall was Gandhiji himself.

In these circumstances it is the bounden duty of the Government to take effective measures to curb this re-appearance of violence in a virulent form and as a first step to this end, they have decided to declare the Sangh as an unlawful association. Government have no doubt that in taking this measure they have the support of all law-abiding citizens, of all those who have the welfare of the country at heart.

APPENDIX VI

The following is the text of the Statement issued by Sri Guruji disbanding the Organisation, as reported in 'Bharat Jyoti' – Bombay, Sunday 8th Feb. 1948.

Mr. M.S. Golwalkar (Guruji) Sarasanghchalak of the R.S.S., has issued a statement saying 'It has always been the policy of the R.S.S. to be law-abiding and carry on its activities within the bounds of law. Therefore since the Government has declared the R.S.S. an unlawful body it is thought advisable to disband the R.S.S., till the ban is there, at the same time denying all the charges levelled against the organisation.' Mr. Golwalkar is in custody and the statement was issued through his counsel Mr. D.G. Deshapande and was addressed to Pt. Ravi Shankar Shukla, Premier of C.P. and Berar.

APPENDIX VII

The report, as appearing in 'Organiser' Aug. 12, 1948, of the restrictions imposed upon Sri Guruji, immediately after release from Nagpur Central Jail on 6th August 1948.

Restrictions:

1. To live within the Municipal limits of Nagpur, not to leave the same without the previous consent of the District Magistrate of the place in writing.
2. Not to address any public meeting.
3. Not to publish directly or indirectly any matter in any newspaper, journal or magazine without the previous approval of the District Magistrate.
4. Not to engage himself or associate with any person engaged in any activity tending directly or indirectly to excite disaffection against or to embarrass the Provincial or Central Government or to promote a feeling of hatred or enmity between different classes and subjects of the Indian Dominion or to disturb public peace.

APPENDIX VIII

After the breakdown of his talks with the Central Government, Sri Guruji issued the following two statements to the Press, on 2nd Nov., 1948.

STATEMENT I

I and my co-workers of the Rashtriya Swayamsevak Sangh, now under ban and disbanded, have been doing our bit to serve the Hindu people for the last 22 years since the Vijayadashami of 1925. The aims and objects of the Sangh have been pure and holy. I restate them in brief.

1. This land of Bharatvarsh is our holy land, our Motherland and the one object of our adoration and loyalty.

2. In this holy land we the Hindu People have been living for countless centuries for which reason it is also known as Hindusthan.

3. Living in this holy land we built a great Dharma (which word has no counterpart in the English language) combining highest material prosperity with purest spiritual beatitude. In this confluence we tried to build great empires, consolidating the people into a well ordered Society, striving to make every individual happy and free from want and to offer him opportunities to achieve the highest flights of philosophy and spiritual peace – each according to his own genius, inclination and persuasion and in this endeavour we set up lofty ideals of individual purity and holiness, of love and service, of sacrifice and selflessness, of devotion and dedication. A whole race of great personalities embodying these ideals have been gracing our people.

Purity of Character

4. Our material life with its manifold experiences, our spiritual outlook, our philosophical attitude, our insistence on purity of character and the stamp left on us by our great personages developed our great culture and welded us into a nation.

5. Unfortunately the great latitude allowed to all individuals and groups resulted in the creation of many faiths and sects. The vastness of our Motherland fostered many dialects which in time became so many sister languages. And gradually the grand unity in all the diversities of life began to crumble away.

6. Invaders a thousand years ago found us thus a disrupted people, easy to conquer and to rule over. A thousand years' subjugation hastened the disintegrating process to such a degree that we seemed to have lost memory of having been one people, with one culture, and one Motherland – one Nation.

7. Our ideals were lost. Foreign ideals, foreign ways of life, foreign types of social, economic, and political ideals took their place. It began to look as if the Hindu people, the cultural leader of the world, was about to exchange its place of honour for the abject condition of servile imitator of foreigners who have not even yet passed the stage of experimentation of trial and error, whose philosophy of life has not yet led them to break the shackles of the dross worship of Mammon.

Decision to Mend Matters

8. Believing that a people which thus does violence to its own past can have but a doubtful future, believing that a people divided against itself can achieve nothing, nor if anything happens to be achieved can it hold it for long, believing also that mere imitation is not progress we decided that matters needed to be mended.

9. We, therefore, started our work naming it the Rashtriya Swayamsevak Sangh to rouse a just appreciation of our past, to note its greatness for emulation and its evils for avoidance, to revive the memory of our being one people, with one holy Motherland, one heritage, one culture and therefore one Nation, to wipe off all fissiparous tendencies whether based on sects and faiths, caste and creed, or on political, economic or linguistic differences, to create absolute purity of character in all individuals, to inculcate in them the spirit of service, sacrifice and selfless dedication to the people, to teach that individual interests need to be subordinated to those of the people, as a whole, to build up an integrated, organised and disciplined corporate social life in place of the present disintegrated, disorganised, undisciplined life of individual self-seeking, to establish inviolable ties of abiding brotherhood in this great ancient Hindu People – thus to bring about an all-round regeneration of this greatest of all peoples and set it up once again on its high pedestal of the Cultural Guide of the World.

A Solid Brotherhood

Thus we worked for over 22 years. We have succeeded in rising above provincial, linguistic, sectarian and other differences and in building up a real solid brotherhood.

During this period, considering the holy nature of our work, we never expected anything would come in our way. Even under the very suspicious foreign Government we could carry on our work without hindrance.

Now after attainment of freedom, party power politics came to the forefront and we were also spotted out for being destroyed as a 'possible political rival'. But the holy nature of our work offered no chance. Then came the unfortunate assassination of Mahatma Gandhi and the party in power got the much-awaited chance. Small-minded leaders of various parties let hell loose against us and divided brother against brother, created bitter hatred in the minds of sections of our own brothers. I thank my Swayamsevak brothers for having maintained their balance and averted a fratricidal conflict.

R.S.S. Wrongly Charged

The R.S.S. was banned on February 4, 1948, by the Central Government and the Provincial Governments followed suit with a number of charges which are now too well-known to need repetition. We knew the charges were baseless. All the same, we disbanded the organisation for the time being, at the same time denying all the charges. Time has amply proved that the R.S.S. had been wrongly charged with all sorts of acts.

We believed that the ban was laid under stress of circumstances in haste and hope that in time the Government could retrace their steps. We have waited for over nine months and abided by the law, suffering imprisonment and restrictions on personal movements and activities. Our waiting was in vain.

I had hoped to place my case before the Central Government and ask them to redress the wrong. So when the restrictions laid upon me were lifted the first thing I did was to come to the capital and meet the Hon. Deputy Prime Minister, Sardar Patel. I met him twice and explained the whole position but I was told that opinions were invited from the Provinces about lifting the ban.

Centre's Responsibility

I cannot see why this course has been taken now when, while imposing the ban the Centre took the lead and the Provinces only followed suit. From the statements of various Chief Ministers and Home Ministers of different Provinces we understand that it is the look-out of the Central Government only, the Provinces may only follow up the directions.

It seems that since the charges for which the ban was laid are untenable this attitude is taken as a shield to perpetuate the wrong and unjust act.

Recently, new questions and so-called conditions are also mooted. In fact the Government ought to apply its mind only to the charges in the communique banning the R.S.S. and should not unnecessarily mix matters.

But this seems to be another ruse to mislead the people and make a show of justifying the continuance of the ban.

Unbearable Position

One more idea has been suggested that the R.S.S. convert itself into a political party – which will mean that besides political parties nothing else, not even pious cultural works have any right to exist. This position is unbearable and does no credit to those who may hold it.

I believe that cultural work should be entirely free from political scramble for power and should not be even tagged on to any political party. I, therefore, must say that their suggestion is not in the best interests of the people.

I, therefore, appeal to all my erstwhile brother Swayamsevaks to note that my attempts at bringing about an honourable settlement seem to have borne no fruit.

Two courses are open to them –

I. To vindicate their right to associate as R.S.S. by disregarding the ban and calling upon the Government to prove their charges. But it will mean creating unrest and disturbance which in the delicate conditions through which the country is passing, will be injudicious. I, therefore, advise them to desist from any such idea and give further evidence of their patriotic restraint and high culture, of which they have already given incontrovertible evidence in February last.

II. The next course for them is to find out lawful and peaceful avenues for utilising their strength, energy and selflessness in the service of the Hindu people. I suggest this latter course. As to the avenues of work they will be the best judges and best in a position to decide.

I appeal to my Hindu people not to be prey to misleading propaganda any more. We have already suffered much due to disintegration during the last thousand years. Now let us come together and build up a healthier, stronger and noble life of mututal love, trust and regard and make our ancient Hindu people happy and glorious in their home – their holy Motherland Bharatvarsh.

May the Almighty be our guide. Truth will triumph and our people under His guidance shall emerge from the present abject condition.

APPENDIX IX

STATEMENT 2

Certain of my interviews with pressmen having been reported in some papers, I feel it will be useful to state my views in a consolidated form before my brother countrymen, on some questions about which there seem to be many wrong notions and on which much stress has lately begun to be laid, and on the satisfactory explanation of which the question of the ban on the R.S.S. being lifted, it is suggested, mainly depends.

Imaginary Grounds

The impression I have gathered during my fortnight's stay in the Capital is that the question of the continuance or lifting of the ban on the R.S.S. does not seem to depend on the truth or untruth of the grounds mentioned in the communique of the Central Government on February 4, 1948, or on my explanation of the new questions, now appearing to be set up, being satisfactory or otherwise. From what I have been able to understand, other interests are at work and when it is clear to all people that the grounds in the communique of February 4 are wholly imaginary and untenable and cannot bear the light of impartial enquiry, these interests, finding the ground slipping from under their feet, have now begun inventing new and totally uncalled for grounds for continuing the ban on the R.S.S. and depriving the people of the urgently needed services of a trained band of selfless workers.

The least that can be said in this connection is that it is unfair now at this late stage to try to shift the ground and continue a wrong. All the same I place my views on the questions newly mooted, for the consideration of my countrymen.

APPENDICES

Not a Political Party

At the outset let me make it clear the R.S.S. is not a political party with any ambitions for political power in the country. All these years of its existence it has steered clear of politics with its party rivalry and scramble for power. Its doors are open to all Hindu brothers irrespective of their political persuasions. It leaves all its members free to choose and to subscribe to whatever political outlook they prefer and to join and work in the party of their choice. The one thing expected of all members is that they believe and work for the culture and unity of the Hindu people and strive to mould themselves to establish an abiding fraternity in the people on the solid basis of the one cultural heritage.

With this background let me explain our position regarding the questions surreptitiously raised in the way of our normal growth.

1. THE FLAG:– Much studied misunderstanding is spread about the R.S.S. in this connection. The State Flag has been decided upon by the Constituent Assembly and adopted by the State upon the attainment of Independence and as such has become the object of reverence to all citizens of the country and the R.S.S. is no exception to this.

The R.S.S. has its own flag distinctive of its aims and objects – creation of cultural unity of the Hindu People – and it is naturally the ancient ochre coloured emblem, depicting the Hindu culture of dedication and sacrifice. All private bodies have their own distinctive flags, even the Congress has one, which is different from the State Flag. Indeed this is as it should be. The State Flag should be used only for functions and occasions on State-buildings and by authorised State officials and not by any and every private person or body. As a matter of fact no private body or party, however big or popular, is to use the State Flag or anything so closely resembling it as to create reasonable misapprehension in the minds of the people, as its emblem. Thus with all its devotion to its particular emblem, as Part of the State, the R.S.S. holds the State Flag in all reverence and I can unhesitatingly state that every individual member of the R.S.S. shall willingly lay down his life to guard its honour from any aggressor.

2. BELIEF IN THE DEMOCRATIC FORM OF GOVERNMENT:– Time has proved that democracy is by far the best type of Government and more enduring than other methods. In politics and for political parties, therefore, the democratic way is beneficial and necessary. The R.S.S., however, being outside the political area and being a purely cultural organisation has built itself in a frame of an extensive family life. So far this system has worked to our complete satisfaction.

3. BELIEF IN THE SECULAR STATE:– We are a Hindu body. To a Hindu, the state is and has always been a secular fact. It was only a departure from the Hindu way of life that brought about, for the first time, a non-secular theocratic concept of State under Ashoka. Later on non-Hindu States of the various Mohammedan dynasties and the empire of the Mughals ran theocratic States. It must be noted that the Hindu power which rose under Shivaji against this foreign domination founded a secular State in conformity with Hindu heritage, where Hindu as well as Mohammedans could hold posts of high responsibility, the faith they professed being no bar to their civic life. Indeed emphasising the secular nature of the State by the adjective 'secular' is redundant in our country and exhibits a sad lack of understanding of the traditions and culture of this country, especially of the Hindu people.

4. HINDU RAJ:– The R.S.S. does not advocate a Hindu Raj to the exclusion of non-Hindu citizens of the country. We used to treat this idea as a phantasm created by over-strained nerves

and a too lively imagination, deserving only to be ignored as not worthy of consideration.

5. SECRECY:- No organisation worth the name can exist or grow to any extent for any appreciable length of time if it works in secret. That is our belief. The R.S.S., therefore, has conducted its work in the open, in the public eye. Also the R.S.S. being only a cultural work [sic] without any ambition for political power the question of working in secret simply does not arise.

6. PRIVATE ARMY:- Maintenance of the army is a function of the State, not of any private body. The R.S.S. did utilise stick-play and such other well-established Indian physical exercises and also simple drill, so long as the Law allowed it to all citizens, for inculcating a spirit of brotherhood and civic discipline. As such it is not proper to confuse orderly working of the R.S.S. with the Army and its structure.

7. AIMING AT OVERTHROW OF THE PRESENT GOVERNMENT AND CAPTURE OF POWER BY VIOLENCE:- This idea is pure fiction. Considering the cultural nature of the R.S.S. and its keeping itself free from political ambitions this question does not at all arise.

These have been the questions about which it was said by many responsible persons, misunderstandings needed to be cleared. I hope this will convince my brother countrymen that the R.S.S. has been unjustly charged and misrepresented, and induce them to appreciate my lawful endeavours to revive the organisation for their service.

APPENDIX X

Press Note dated 14th November, 1948 issued by the Home Ministry of the Government of India.

Soon after his release from prison in Nagpur after the statutory period of six months, Mr. Golwalkar, head of the R.S.S. organisation, made approaches to the Government which indicated a possibility that the activities of that organisation might be diverted and confined to channels which would have no harmful effect on the communal situation in the country. He also expressed a desire to interview the Home Minister. In order to enable him to do so, the Government of India requested the C.P. Government to cancel an order issued by them under which Mr. Golwalkar's movements had been restricted to the city of Nagpur and to facilitate his departure for Delhi for the specific purpose of seeing the Home Minister.

Mr. Golwalkar accordingly came to Delhi and had his first interview with the Home Minister soon after his arrival. There was an exchange of views and Mr. Golwalkar wanted some time to consult his followers in an attempt to influence them on the right lines. Some days later he had his second interview during which he expressed his inability to bind himself to any change until the ban was lifted. He felt that the lifting of the ban would strengthen his hands in dealing with his followers. Simultaneously, however, the Government of India had got in touch with Provincial Governments to acquaint themselves with their views and the latest information about the activities of the R.S.S. The information received by the Government of India shows that the activities carried on in various forms and ways by the people associated with the R.S.S. tend to be anti-national and often subversive and violent and that persistent attempts are being made by the R.S.S. to revive an atmosphere in the country which was productive of such disastrous consequences in the past. For these reasons, the Provincial Governments have declared themselves opposed to the withdrawal of the ban and the Government of India have concurred in view of the Provincial Governments.

This position was conveyed to Mr. Golwalkar towards the end of the last month and he was told that since the purpose for which he had been allowed to come to Delhi had been served, he should now return to Nagpur. Mr. Golwalkar was not prepared to accept this position and expressed a desire to see the Home Minister and the Prime Minister on their return to Delhi. The Home Minister declined to grant a further interview, but in order to give him a chance to interview the Prime Minister on his return, if the latter so desired, he was allowed to remain in Delhi under certain restrictive orders issued by the District Magistrate of Delhi. Mr. Golwalkar declined to accept the orders of restrictions, but has made no attempts to contravene the restrictions, imposed on him. He has written letters both to the Prime Minister and Home Minister explaining *inter alia* that the R.S.S. agrees entirely in the conception of a Secular State for India and that it accepts the National Flag of the country and requesting that the ban imposed on the organisation in February should now be lifted. These professions of the R.S.S. leader are, however, quite inconsistent with the practice of his followers and for the reasons already explained above, the Government of India find themselves unable to advise Provincial Governments to lift the ban. The Prime Minister has, therefore, declined the interview which Mr. Golwalkar had sought.

Mr. Golwalkar is accordingly being informed that he should make immediate arrangements to return to Nagpur. The Government of India are also taking appropriate steps to ensure that Mr. Golwalkar complies with these instructions.

APPENDIX XI

Statement issued to the press by the Delhi Provincial Organiser, R.S.S., dated 3rd December, 1948.

The Government of India issued a Press Note at about 1 A.M., on 14th November, 1948, detailing the reasons for their decision not to lift the ban on the R.S.S. About two hours later Sri Guruji was arrested. This made it impossible for him to answer the note. Since then many persons have approached me to ascertain the truth or otherwise of certain impressions the said Press-note has created in the public mind.

As I had the opportunity to be in Guruji's company during the short period of his stay in Delhi and as I had also the privilege to accompany him at the time of his talk with Sardar Patel, I can surely throw some light on some of the points mentioned vaguely and incorrectly in the Press-note.

It is not my purpose, of course, to meet old assertions in the Government note, because Shri Guruji himself has conclusively dealt with the same in his correspondence with the Government since published. I would like to invite the attention of the public to the first few sentences in the second paragraph of the note which run thus –

> There was an exchange of views and Mr. Golwalkar wanted some time to consult his followers in an attempt to influence them on right lines. Some days later he had his second interview during which he expressed his inability to bind himself to any change until the ban was lifted. He felt that the lifting of the ban would strengthen his hands in dealing with his followers.

The above is likely to create an impression that Sardar Patel had made some proposal for change and that Guruji's unwillingness to bring about any change before the ban was lifted was a reason for Government's decision not to lift the ban.

I would like to make it clear that Sardar Patel never made any such proposal and so the question of its acceptance or otherwise did not arise. The only desire Sardar Patel expressed or the advice he gave in one of his letters was that the R.S.S., a cultural organisation, should be merged in with the Congress, a political party. But then that advice was too queer and unreasonable to be termed a proposal for change.

There is another very incorrect and misleading expression in the same paragraph. In that connection it would be enough to say that Shri Guruji neither happened to receive any so called right lines from the Government nor did he, therefore, demand any time for consulting his followers. It was on the contrary the Home Department which wanted time to consult the Provincial Governments on whose favourable attitude alone, he was told, rested the probability of the ban being lifted.

One word more. It is true that Shri Guruji always consulted his co-workers or followers on all matters of policy. But to suggest, through the Press note, a sort of gulf or discord between himself and his followers by putting out an imaginary story that he wanted some time to consult his followers in an attempt to influence them on the right lines or that he wanted to strengthen his hands in dealing with his followers or by falsely asserting further that his professions were quite inconsistent with the practice of his followers, is, indeed, regrettable. The suggestion is no less mischievous than it is funny.

APPENDIX XII

Sri Guruji's clarion call to Swayamsevaks to restart the Organisation in spite of the ban.

Shree

20, Barakhamba Road,
New Delhi,
13th November, 1948.

To all my brother Swayamsevaks,

1. You are all aware of the conditions under which we disbanded our Organisation. I am happy to find that you have all strictly adhered to that decision all these days.

2. It was then hoped that the unwarranted ban upon our R.S.S. would be removed, the charges made against us being entirely baseless and imaginary would be withdrawn and we would be in a position to carry on our healthy cultural activity building up a pure Hindu brotherhood at an early date. It was hoped that the Government being manned by persons who are our very own, would not continue the wrong which they, in the heat of a particular moment, did to us, for time would sober them and induce them to do justice to us. It was also hoped that they being in such responsible positions would realise their mistake and be able to take a more far-sighted view; that they would exhibit a broad patriotism rising above party interests and be induced to right the wrong and pave the way for integrating all national interests. It was expected that at least the Government would follow the ways of a civilised State and come forward with their evidence against us, allow us to examine and disprove it, and, then come to a decision in accordance with established cannons of justice.

3. It is in this hope of justice being done to us ultimately that we quietly suffered imprisonments and personal restrictions. And when after the lapse of over eight months I was free to move out of Nagpur I came to the Capital to seek redress. All my efforts at an honourable

and just settlement have been in vain. Accordingly on the 2nd November, 1948, I issued two statements publicly answering all old and new allegations levelled against us, restating our aims and objects and expressing my reactions at the atmosphere prevailing in the central Govt. In the second statement I had pointed out two courses open to you all to follow and had distinctly discountenanced the course of disregarding the ban and continuing our work.

4. I would have been happy to stick to that decision but a little later, on the 2nd November itself in the evening I was presented with an order by the District Magistrate, Delhi, restricting my movements and activities. It was grave injustice and an unwarranted course on the part of the Govt. and now last evening (12th Nov.), I received a letter from the Home Ministry informing me of their arbitrary decision of not lifting the ban on our work. Added to this I have been told to return to Nagpur, and that the C.P. Govt. had, only conditional to my seeing Hon'ble Home Minister Sardar Patel, relaxed the restrictions imposed upon me. Now this suggestion is wholly untrue and the Govt. is trying to compel me unjustly to leave Delhi and proceed to a particular place, to infringe upon my fundamental right as a free citizen. Such unwarranted infringement of right has been the lot of a number of our workers also. The indication is clear; the Govt. appears to pursue a course of tyrannical suppression of which even old barbarian rulers would be ashamed, to deny us the natural rights of existence and mutual association, in a manner to deprive us of even elementary 'citizen' rights.

5. This state of affairs is humiliating. To continue to submit meekly to this atrocious tyranny is an insult to the honour of the citizens of free India and a blow to the prestige of our civilised free State. As patriotic citizens it is our sacred duty to refuse to submit to arbitrary tyranny. We have, therefore, to discharge our duty, to stand up and vindicate the honour and rights of the State and the citizens.

6. We appreciate that we are passing through delicate times. Our patriotic instincts have made us suffer meekly many wrongs in order that internal disintegration of the people be avoided. But the responsibility of appreciating the gravity of the times is equally, if not more, on the Government too. We have tried every effort to reach peacefully a just settlement. The Government on the other hand have been more and more unjust and autocratic. They appear to have been trying to exploit our patriotic sentiments to strengthen the position of their party. They take our restraint, actually born out of a grave concern for our country, as a sign of our weakness and plan to wipe us, in our individual as well as corporate capacity, out of existence. We can no longer allow these evil sentiments to work, for that will ultimately mean complete ruin of our country. To avert that grave catastrophe, it is an absolute necessity that today we stand up and risk a little upheaval so that greater calamities ahead may not overtake our State.

7. I, therefore, request you to stand up for our great Cause. Truth and Justice are with us. And where Truth exists the Almighty showers His Blessings. With absolute faith in Him and unswerving devotion to our holy Motherland let us start on our peaceful campaign of vindicating justice of our Cause. However unwilling, we have been forced into this only course by the narrow-mindedness of the Government, their greed for perpetuation of party domination and their intolerance of the existence of every other form of thought and action. The responsibility of creating the unfortunate situation rests solely on the Government, and on the Government alone.

8. Hence after full consideration I hereby withdraw my directive of disbandment of the R.S.S. dated the 6th February, 1948 and request you to resume our work in the normal manner. Utmost efforts should, at the same time, be made to maintain peace and prevent discord.

9. I have directed our General Secretary Sri Bhayyaji Dani to communicate this decision

to you and indicate to you the day and the date on which to resume our work.

10. We stand for Truth. We stand for justice. We stand for our National Rights. With implicit faith in the Just God of Truth let us march on and stop not till the goal is reached.

Glory to God. Glory to the holy Motherland.

Your brother,
In the Service of the Motherland,
(*Sd.*) M.S. GOLWALKAR.

APPENDIX XIII

The following is the statement of Sri T.R.V. Shastry [sic] of Madras issued before receipt of the news of the lifting of the ban published in 'The Hindu' dated 13th July, 1949, wherein he has traced in detail the history of all his attempts in negotiating between the R.S.S. and the Government.

Within the last two months I have received numerous letters, and am still receiving many more from all parts of India, calling upon me to say what had become of my efforts on behalf of the R.S.S. and at what stage the negotiations were. I did not respond to their call, lest an inopportune word hinder rather than help the cause they had at heart. Now I think the time has arrived for me to make a statement without impropriety.

My connection with the affair practically ended with the framing of the Constitution for the R.S.S. The draft was approved by Mr. M.S. Golwalkar on my second visit to Seoni Jail. It had to be fair-typed before it could be sent to the Government of India. So in order to save time, Mr. M.S. Golwalkar gave me a letter addressed to the Government of India that he had authorised me to send the Constitution to them. Accordingly I sent to the Government two copies of the Constitution, one in English and one in Hindi, and Mr. M.S. Golwalkar's letter, with a covering letter of my own. The procedure was disapproved by the Government as, in their opinion, it might seem to the public and to the R.S.S., that I was an intermediary between the Government and Mr. M.S. Golwalkar and such an impression would have undesirable consequences. They said that the move should come from Mr. M.S. Golwalkar himself and he should address the Government through the Government of C.P. and Berar. But this attitude of the Government of India had to be made known to Mr. M.S. Golwalkar, in order that he might take the correspondence with the Government into his own hands.

Being uncertain of a letter directly addressed to Mr. M.S. Golwalkar in gaol reaching his hands safely and in time, I addressed my communication to the Home Minister of the C.P. Government forwarding along with it two copies of the English and two copies of the Hindi Constitution and a letter addressed to Mr. M.S. Golwalkar, giving him full directions as to what he should say in his communications to the Governments, as I had formed the opinion that he requires guidance in such matters. I asked the Home Minister to read my letter to Mr. M.S. Golwalkar and then to take one of two courses as he thought proper, either send the communication to Mr. M.S. Golwalkar through the Government's own subordinates for action to be taken by him as advised in my letter to him or if that course was unsuitable, allow my messenger who carried the communication to deliver it at the gaol gate, obtain Mr. M.S. Golwalkar's communication and deliver it at the jail gate, leaving further action to the jail authorities. My communication was dated the 27th of March, and it was delivered at the gaol gate on the 30th March. That ended my connection in the matter.

I received a letter from Mr. M.S. Golwalkar, dated April 11, passed by the Censor and the Superintendent of the gaol on April 12th, despatched to me from Pachmarhi on May 3rd and received by me on May 5th. In that letter, he said that he had received my letter, dated March 27th only on the 9th April and that he had followed my directions. In the circumstances disclosed by the dates I became confirmed in my decision to keep aloof from the matter, taking no further part in it.

That is all I have to give by way of information to the public of my part in it.

On June 5th, there was an A.P.I. message reported in the pages of 'The Hindu', stating that the correspondence between the Government of India and Mr. M.S. Golwalkar had reached an impasse and that I was expected to go to Delhi to smoothen matters, not knowing that I had been warned off from further connection with the affair. It contained certain objections to the Constitution as raised by the Government and replied to by Mr. M.S. Golwalkar. In that matter an explanation is owing from me as the person who framed the Constitution and passed it on to the Government of India.

One important objection was stated to be that the Head of the Organisation, Sarsanghachalak, was to be chosen by his predecessor, a method which was said to be undemocratic and fascist in character. I think the nomination was to be in consultation with a council of members. I confess that the objection never occurred to me and it appears to me to mistake the nature of the organisation. A Government or a State can be characterised as fascist, but not a private association to which no one is compelled to belong. One may join it, or, refuse to join it, or, having joined it, may resign at will. To call it fascist is merely to express strong disapproval of it. There are many institutions in this country in which successors are nominated by the predecessors or in default of such nomination, selected by the close associates and disciples of the Head, not elected by all members of the institution. Democratic election is a device for dismissal, if need be, at the next election. In the realm of spirit, election by the population is not quite in place. If it is now a question of election, a competitor with the Head will only get an ignominous [sic] defeat. In any case, it is a question for the followers and not for an outsider to insist.

The other serious objection is to the admission of minors into the organisation. In the first place they are not admitted as members. They are only admitted to training and discipline preliminary to admission on attaining age should they then desire it. This was present to my mind and I insisted on a provision that if the parent or guardian objected, the boy should not be taken up for training in discipline. It was pointed out to me that it would be invidious to insist on an express provision in the case of R.S.S. while other organisations had no such provision. I then agreed to omit the provision and leave it to the law as in the other Constitutions they showed me. In the A.P.I. note it is said that Mr. M.S. Golwalkar pleaded that he should not be singled out and subjected to an express provision while others were exempted from it. I considered it a just plea then and I do so now. During all the years of their work, no complaint has been made that they have decoyed boys into their organisation against the parents' will.

The National Flag has been accepted in the Constitution and Mr. M.S. Golwalkar's acceptance is repeated by him according to A.P.I. Note. I do not think any serious objection remains under this head.

There is then the charge of communalism in spirit if not in letter. The organisation admits Hindus of all sorts and denominations. Boys of all communities meet in its many activities without discrimination. The objects and nature of this association do not admit of non-Hindus being members. The spirit of their work is bound to change in the changed conditions of the times under a self-governing India.

The tone of Mr. M.S. Golwalkar's reply is said to have been such as to give offence to the Government of India. I can well believe it. Mr. M.S. Golwalkar is a blunt man, innocent of the etiquette required in a correspondence with Government. The soft word that turneth away wrath is not among his gifts. In his letter to me he says that he followed my directions lest he commit any mistakes and adds, 'It is because of my ignorance of forms and formalities that I would have liked your coming in person . . . but I have given you too much trouble . . . I would, if I could, have been running to and fro from you. That would have been in the proper order.' That is why I gave him definite instructions as to what to write to the Government of India, which I guess the Government did not like.

If the Government had released all of them without even lifting the ban, Mr. M.S. Golwalkar would have had the opportunity to consult his followers and friends. Deprived of all movement he had and has no advice or guidance. The Government ought not to lay too much stress on the tone of his letter. The A.P.I. Note itself shows that in substance and in effect he assures the Government that he had always respected the National Flag, that he had not done anything in secret, that he had not harboured any ill-will towards anyone and that faith is in the Constitution he had submitted, and that he should not be treated with undue suspicion.

Living as I do in the midst of Communalism 'in excelsis' I cannot but feel that the R.S.S. was doing good work in trying to weld the much-divided Hindu community. It may also be helpful in counteracting other evils growing under our very eyes and requiring the attention of the Government.

If I proceed to say anything more, it is because I feel that there is a question of Civil Liberties involved in it.

In forming my judgement, I have taken into account the following facts – that they have worked for over twenty years under the predecessor Government openly and without any objection, that public men have associated themselves with their work and celebrations in more or less degree and openly, that even Government servants have taken part in their work without objection, that even our Government saw no reason for taking action till the assassination of Gandhiji, and the suspicion of their complicity in it and of their apprehended aim at other lives also. I take it that the suspicion has now been recognised to be without any real foundation. The arrest of Mr. M.S. Golwalkar under the odious Bengal Regulation was the result of the refusal of Mr. M.S. Golwalkar to leave Delhi and go to Nagpur, a regulation which I expect to come to an end on the passing of the Indian Constitution. Those who could apply for the Statutory Habeas Corpus have succeeded in invoking the aid of court; charges implicating the R.S.S., in some cases have been found un-sustainable. I do feel that, if the ban is lifted and the organisation is allowed to work as it did for over two decades before the recent troubles arose, there is no reason to apprehend danger to the State or to public security.

I have seen the comment in the press that the Constitution was right enough, but that the leaders of this organisation cannot be trusted to function within its scope. It would be hard on any organisation to say that, in anticipation of a not unlikely un-lawful action on the part of its members, it is not allowed to begin work. The power of a mighty Government is there to go into action when necessity arises.

I have seen another comment that though they profess to be a non-political body they may turn into one over-night. And so they may. If they did, it would be no crime. But I am sure that these people know better than to commit such a mistake. They know that this organisation would disrupt and break into fragments directly they attempt to convert it into a political organisation. That is the reason why they refuse to join any political group. At the last elections I am told that the vast mass of them voted Congress and the complaint of the Maha Sabha was that the weight of this organisation was not thrown on their side. What effect this action of the Government will have on the R.S.S. at the next election, I cannot say.

Now I must end with the expression of the hope that the Government will see their way to lift the ban and allow the R.S.S. to work as they used to do of old. The continuance of the ban and the detention of the chief men in jail is, in my opinion, neither just nor wise, nor expedient.

APPENDIX XIV

Government communique dated 11th July, 1949 announcing the lifting of ban.

In consultation with the Provincial Governments, the Central Government have had under consideration the question of removal of the ban on the R.S.S. The factors governing the problem clearly emerged during the discussion which the leader of the organisation had with Sardar Patel in October last year. In brief, they were that the R.S.S. should function under a written and published Constitution, restricting its activities to the cultural sphere, abjuring violence and secrecy, professing loyalty to the Constitution of India and the National Flag, and providing for a democratic organisation. The public is already familiar with the history of the break-down of these talks and the course which events took thereafter.

In spite of this, the Government's attitude to this organisation was never prompted by any spirit of vindictiveness and, when certain non-official gentlemen approached them with requests to interview the R.S.S. leader in jail, with a view to persuading him to fulfil the above mentioned conditions, the Government offered them facility to do so. In March this year, the R.S.S. leader wrote to the Government forwarding a draft Constitution, the terms of which were examined by Government in consultation with the Provinces. The Government of India conveyed to the R.S.S. leader their reactions on the draft and he has now generally accepted the suggestions made by the Government of India and the clarifications made by him indicate that the relevant provisions of the Constitution are intended to be worked in the spirit contemplated by the Government.

The R.S.S. leader has undertaken to make the loyalty to the Union Constitution and respect for the National Flag more explicit in the Constitution of the R.S.S. and to provide clearly that persons believing or resorting to violent and secret methods will have no place in the Sangh. The R.S.S. leader has also clarified that the Constitution will be worked on a democratic basis. In particular, the office of the Sarsanghachalak would in effect, be elective in that the successor would be nominated with the consent of the then Karyakari Mandal. It would be open to any member of the Sangh to leave it at any time without breaking the pledge and the admission of minors will be subject to the option of the guardian to withdraw his ward under a written request sent to the Sangh authorities.

In the light of the modifications made and clarifications given by the R.S.S. leader, the Government of India have come to the conclusion that the R.S.S. organisation should be given an opportunity to function as a democratic, cultural organisation owing loyalty to the Indian Constitution and recognising the National Flag eschewing secrecy and abjuring violence. Indeed the Government feel that, under a Constitution embodying these principles and worked in the right spirit, no reasonable objection can be taken to such functioning. They have accordingly decided to withdraw the ban on the organisation in the Centrally administered areas and to release as soon as possible, all R.S.S. men at present under detention or undergoing sentences of imprisonment in connection with the R.S.S. activities, and have requested the Provincial Governments to take similar action in their own areas.

APPENDICES

APPENDIX XV

The following is a pertinent extract of the report of the press conference addressed by Sri Guruji at Madras published in 'The Hindu' dated 22nd July, 1949.

'In what respects has the R.S.S. Sangh changed from what it was in the past?' asked a press reporter.

Mr. Golwalkar said that they had 'given up nothing' of their original principle and added, 'The Government of India wanted us to put down our Constitution in writing. We have done so. People might call it clarification if they chose.'

APPENDIX XVI

The following is an extract from the speech of Sri Guruji in a reception given in his honour at Nagpur by some of the dignitaries just after lifting of the ban on the R.S.S. when Sri A.D. Mani, Editor, 'Hitavada' English Weekly, while proposing the toast referred to the Government communique and asked if Sri Golwalkar had given any undertaking or assurances (Report published in 'Hitavada' dated 1st August, 1949).

Replying to the toast Sri Guruji said he had not intended to speak about the Government communique which the Government from their own point of view had considered proper, but since the question had been asked, he wanted to assure all concerned that in his negotiations he had not acted in his individual capacity. He would have preferred to lay down his life rather than do anything derogatory to the great organisation.

Mr. Golwalkar declared, 'There was no compromise. There was no undertaking of any kind given to the Government.'

He emphasised that nobody has a right to ask for the Constitution of any organisation. In his view it was transgressing the limits of administration. 'Mr. T.R.V. Shastry, who is just a year younger than my father, approached me and desired that I should give a written Constitution – just put down in writing what was so far unwritten. It was not that I was anxious, but I had to bow out of sheer respect to the wishes of one so much older in years.' He was unhappy, he said, when there was a deadlock. But later the doors opened by themselves without any gesture from the R.S.S. side and the ban was removed.

APPENDIX XVII

The following is an extract from the proceedings of the Bombay Legislative Assembly of 14th October 1949. Vide page No. 2126.

1503 (24-9-1949) Mr. Lallubhai Makanji Patel
(Surat District)

Will the Hon. Minister for Home and Revenue be pleased to state:–

(a) Whether it is a fact that the ban on R.S.S. has been lifted.
(b) If so what are the reasons for lifting the ban.

(c) **Whether the lifting of the ban is conditional or unconditional.**
(d) If conditional, what are the conditions?
(e) **Whether the leader of the R.S.S. has given any undertaking to the Government.**
(f) If so, what is the undertaking?

Mr. Dinkarrao N. Desai for Mr. Morarji R. Desai:

(a) **Yes.**
(b) The ban was lifted as it was no longer considered necessary to continue it.
(c) **It was unconditional.**
(d) Does not arise.
(e) **No.**
(f) Does not arise.

APPENDIX XVIII

The following is an extract of the report of the speech delivered by Gandhiji to the workers of the R.S.S. at the Bhangi Colony, Delhi, on the 16th Sept. 1947 ('The Hindu', Madras, dated 17th Sept. 1947.)

He had visited the R.S.S. Camp years ago, when the founder, Sri Hedgewar, was alive. He had been very well impressed by their discipline, the complete absence of untouchability and the rigorous simplicity. Since then the Sangh had grown. Mahatma Gandhi was convinced that any organisation which was inspired by the high ideal of service and self-sacrifice was bound to grow in strength.

APPENDIX XIX

The following is an extract of the report of the speech delivered by Sardar Patel at Lucknow prior to the assassination of Gandhiji ('The Hindu', Madras dated 7th Jan. 1948.)

Sardar Patel realised that they (R.S.S.) were not actuated by selfish motives. The situation demanded they should strengthen the hands of the government and assist in maintaining peace. He also had a word of warning 'to those who were in power in the Congress'. He said, 'In the Congress those who are in power feel that by virtue of their authority they will be able to crush the R.S.S. You cannot crush an organisation by using the "danda". The danda is meant for thieves and dacoits. After all the R.S.S. men are not thieves and dacoits. They are patriots who love their country.'

APPENDIX XX

The following is the extract of the statement of Bharat Ratna Dr. Bhagawan Das, a profound thinker and philosopher and the revered father of Sri Prakasha, Ex-High Commissioner for Pakistan.

('Organiser' dated October 16, 1948, Delhi)

'I have been reliably informed that a number of youths of the R.S.S. . . . were able to inform Sardar Patel and Nehruji in the very nick of time of the Leaguers' intended "coup" on September 10, 1947, whereby they had planned to assassinate all Members of Government and all Hindu Officials and thousands of Hindu Citizens on that day and plant the flag of "Pakistan" on the Red Fort and then seize all Hind.'

'. . . If these high-spirited and self-sacrificing boys had not given the very timely information to Nehruji and Patelji, there would have been no Government of India today, the whole country would have changed its name into Pakistan, tens of millions of Hindus would have been slaughtered and all the rest converted to Islam or reduced to stark slavery.

'. . . Well, what is the net result of all this long story? Simply this – that our Government should utilise, and not sterilise, the patriotic energies of the lakhs of R.S.S. youths.'

Appendix 6
'Guruji-Indiraji Correspondence'

(*Organiser*, 16 June 1973)

Rashtriya Swayamsevak Sangh, Kendra Nagpur
Tithi: Pousha Shukla 5,
Saka 1893,
Letter No. 232.
Dated 22.12.71

Prime Minister Smt. Indira Gandhi,

Respectful Namaskar.

The atrocities perpetrated on the innocent people of Bangla Desh were a blot on humanity. It was natural that they should infuriate every decent person and country. As succouring the distressed has been a traditional mission of Bharat, it was also expected that the people of Bharat should feel grief and anger. At the same time, the warlike rulers of Pakistan started to aggress on the sacred land of Bharat under the pretext that the loyalties of the people of Bangla Desh lie in Bharat. All the three wings of the armed forces of Bharat met this aggression with unanimity, skill in warfare and high bravery, defeating the enemy and liberating distressed Bangla Desh from the slavery of Pakistan. The biggest measure of credit for this achievement goes to you. At first you tried with restraint for an agreement and showed your peaceful intentions. But when war became unavoidable for the security of our country, you inspired the armed forces to meet the situation fearlessly and made a successful appeal to the people to strive for victory with all will. The opposition of so called friendly countries, the policy of pressurising through the stoppage of aid, the tendency to aggravate the situation by giving arms aid to Pakistan – ignoring all these you exhibited the determination to stand up to the situation with confidence in your own self and meet the calamity with courage. As this self-confidence has enhanced the prestige of Bharat the entire country is showing unprecedented enthusiasm in congratulating you.

The declaration of cease-fire on the achievement of the goal of the liberation of Bangla Desh would be considered a manifestation of the peaceful policy of Bharat. A cease-fire has come into being, but the danger is not yet over. Hence it is necessary for the country to be on the alert and ready to use its might. I think you are also quite aware of this. This might has to be kept ready in three ways . . . by means of a population strung together by the thread of national unity, economic prosperity and a capable armed force. It is also necessary to be very much on the guard against internal tendencies striking at the security and spirit of the nation.

Now that Bangla Desh is free it would be legitimate to make arrangements under which the refugees driven out from there during the last 24 years can return to their homes, get back the material possessions of which they had been robbed, and can dedicate themselves with enthusiasm to the development of their newly-freed country. May the assurances that you have given in this connection from time to time be fulfilled quickly, and may you have the good fortune of earning the gratitude of crores of distressed people.

May the unity of the country, a realistic assessment of the situation, and the determination to preserve the honour and prestige of the country continue like this. This is necessary not only in times of danger but for all time and for all activities of national renascence. In the creation of the strength of national unity infused with national pride, the Rashtriya Swayamsevak Sangh is and will always be with you. I have confidence that as the representative of the country you will take all these factors into consideration while determining our domestic and foreign policies. May the prestige of Bharat grow like this under your leadership.

On behalf of the Rashtriya Swayamsevak Sangh I heartly [sic] congratulate you and your minister colleagues on today's victory, which has enhanced the prestige of the nation, and salute our invincible armed forces.

Yours sincerely,
M.S. Golwalkar

No. 14 P.M. 0/72
New Delhi.
13 January, 1973.

Dear Shri Golwalkar,

Your letter of December 22 reached me through Shri Hansraj Gupta on January 6. I thank you for your good wishes.

Along with the daring and bravery of our armed forces the unity that the country has exhibited in this hour of trial also played an important role in the victory of our country. As the danger is not yet completely over, it is in the interest of the nation to preserve this unity.

The refugees who had come from Bangla Desh are going back to their country. The Government had given an assurance to the people that the refugees who had come over to escape the cruelty of the Pakistani forces in Bangla Desh would be sent back to their homes when the situation became normal. It is a matter of gratification that this task is being completed with the co-operation of the Government of Bangla Desh.

Yours sincerely,
Indira Gandhi

Rashtriya Swayamsevak Sangh
Uttar Pradesh
No. 363, 18.1.72

Received your letter of 13.1.72 today. Thank you so much.

It is true that feeling of unity should always be present in the nation. Everyone has to know his responsibility and endeavour to this end.

One has to realise the unity in diversity in the life-stream of Bharat and act accordingly. The beauty and vitality of diversity is not to be destroyed by putting everyone in the same mould. I wish that we would all keep this truth in mind. I pray to the Mother of the Universe that everyone should achieve the beneficial undertaking to work for this purpose.

Yours sincerely,
M.S. Golwalkar.

Appendix 7

Deoras's Correspondence during the Emergency with Indira Gandhi, S.B. Chavan and Vinoba Bhave

V.N. Bhide
Yeravada Central Jail
15-7-75

To
Hon'ble Shri Shankarrao Chavan,
Chief Minister,
Maharashtra,
Bombay.

I was the organiser of the RSS in Maharashtra (excluding Vidarbha) until the ban on it throughout the country by the Central Government on 4-7-75. Hence the work of the Sangh has come to a complete halt in Maharashtra and will remain suspended as long as the ban is in force. I understand that the central office-bearers of the Sangh in Delhi have also issued a circular stating that it will remain defunct for the duration of the ban.

I have been detained here as a security prisoner since 6-7-75. Like me, many other RSS workers in the state have been detained. Also, charges have been framed against some persons under the D.I.R. The cases will go on in the courts. The government will take prompt action against any one who carries on any work in contravention of the ban. We would like to urge that so long as the ban remains in force it is neither necessary nor desirable to keep any RSS worker in detention.

I think that you are fully aware of the nature and extent of the work of the RSS in Maharashtra. I had met you in Bombay after you became the Chief Minister. You had asked me to meet you during your subsequent visit to Pune. Accordingly, I tried to meet you when you first visited Pune but I was not given an opportunity because of your heavy schedule. However, if you think it necessary, I will come to meet you at any time. The Sangh has done nothing against the government or society even remotely. There is no place for such things in the Sangh's programme. The Sangh is engaged only in social and cultural activities. There have been some allegations against the Sangh. But these have been proved to be baseless. Since I trust, that you will take all this duly into consideration, I would request you to release the Sangh workers held in detention.

With regards,

(*Sd.*) [V.N. Bhide]

Yarvada Central Jail,
Pune-6.

Dated 22.8.1975
25.8.1975

Respected Mrs. Indira Gandhi,
Prime Minister, India, New Delhi.

I have heard the speech you delivered on August 15, 1975 from the Red Fort, Delhi on A.I.R. The speech was balanced and befitting to the occasion and has prompted me to write this letter to you.

I was arrested at Nagpur on 30-6-75 and was brought to Pune after some days and was put in this jail.

Thereafter, on 4-7-75, the Central Government banned the R.S.S. by issuing a special order. The reports published in newspaper regarding this ban show that the activities of the Sangh, its Volunteers and responsible workers are a danger to the Internal Security of the country, public peace and law and order situation. Such are the reasons given for the ban on R.S.S. According to the press reports about 2300 workers and officials of the Sangh have been arrested at different places throughout the country.

I am writing this letter to you on the basis of whatever little I have gathered [from] the speeches made by you and other senior leaders and officials and some of the interviews published in the newspapers.

The orders do not give the definite reason for banning the Sangh. The Sangh has never indulged in any activity which could be dangerous for the internal security of the country or for the law and order situation. The aim of the R.S.S. is to unify and organise Hindu society. The Sangh has also been active in maintaining discipline in the society. This is what we preach and practice [sic] in the Sangh. Therefore, there is nothing in the Sangh which could be harmful for the law and order situation and internal security.

It is not possible to refute all the charges in this letter, yet it is necessary to make it clear that the Sangh has never involved itself in any violent action, nor has Sangh the incited anyone to indulge in violence. The Sangh does not believe in such things. Not a single instance of violence or destruction can be cited in which the volunteers of the Sangh were involved during the last fifty years. Many a time, violence has erupted in the country. But in none of the court judgments or in the report of any commission appointed by the Government, has it been said that the volunteers of the Sangh were involved. The reason is obvious – the Sangh has never preached or practised such things.

In spite of this some people make allegations against the Sangh because of their prejudices. For example, some people tried to involve the Sangh in the murder of late Lalitnarayan Mishra. But now the enquiry has proved that it was [an] utterly false allegation. Similarly, even today there are people who try to involve the Sangh in the murder of Mahatma Gandhi. It has been proved that the Sangh was in no way related to this incident. Therefore, I don't think there is any need to write more about this in this letter. All the office-bearers of the Sangh are respectable members of the society and are playing a leading role in the social, cultural and educational fields. I am sure that their police record will bear this out.

There are people who allege that R.S.S. is a communal organisation. This also is a baseless charge. Although at present the activities of the Sangh are confined to the Hindu society, the Sangh never preaches anything against any non-Hindu. It is absolutely wrong that the Sangh is anti-Muslim. We don't even use an improper word regarding Islam, Mohammad, Kuran, Christianity, Christ or the Bible. The Sangh believes in the theory of 'Sarva Dharm Sambhav' (all religion are equal) and 'Ekam Sat Vipra Bahudha Vadanti' (Almighty God is one but he has been described in many ways). The Sangh believes that everyone should have the freedom of worship in one's own way. Many of the volunteers of the Sangh have very intimate relations with Muslims, Christians, Parsis and followers of other religions.

The social problems of the Hindu society and non-Hindu society are different. That is why the Sangh has kept its activities limited to the Hindu society. The Sangh is endeavouring to unite the Hindu society by removing the feelings of low and high, mutual distrust and separatism which have erupt [sic] into Hindus because of the difference of castes, sect and language and other reasons. You too will appreciate the need of this task. This shows that the Sangh is neither communal nor is casteist.

The R.S.S. has been working in the direction of making every individual of Hindu society a good citizen, patriotic and virtuous. It is the irony of the fate that it has been banned by its own rules.

You have correctly pointed out in your speech of 15th August that 'the task of the upliftment of the society, which includes tribes, the down trodden and the poor, is not the one which can be accomplished immediately. This is a long, difficult path, which demands sacrifice. For this we need the co-operation of many. All the forces of the society should start working honestly in their respective fields'.

The activities of the R.S.S. are spread throughout the country. Its members are from all the strata of society. It has many selfless workers – in fact the whole work of the organisation is based on the feeling of selflessness. This power of the Sangh must be utilised in a planned way for the development of the nation.

I request you to please reconsider the case of the Sangh without any prejudice. In the light of the democratic right of freedom to organise, I beseech you to rescind the ban imposed upon the R.S.S.

I would be pleased to meet you if you so desire.

Yours,
Sd/- M.D. Devras
Sirsanghchalak, R.S.S.

Address:
M.D. Devras,
[MISA] prisoner No. 308,
Class I,
Andheri Yard,
Yarvada Central Jail,
Pune-6.

(Brahm Dutt, *Five Headed Monster*, pp. 141-4)

Respected Smt. Indira Gandhiji,
Prime Minister,
Government of India,
New Delhi.

Yarwada Central Jail
Pune-6.
Dated 10-11-1975.

Respectful Namaskar,

Let me congratulate you as five judges of the Supreme Court have declared the validity of your election.

I wrote a letter to you from Ekhra jail on 22-8-75. That letter ought to have reached you directly but contrary to that the letter went to the Maharashtra Government and from there it was despatched to you – I have been intimated so. You might have received the same. I am waiting for the reply from your end.

I am not going to repeat now in this letter of mine the contents of my letter, dated 22-8-75. But in the meantime I could go through the Maratha edition of two government publications in the form of booklets in which your speech delivered in the Parliament on 22nd July, 1975, and your narration of causes in support of the Emergency were published.

Many allegations have been introduced in your speech and in the booklets, basing the facts on the wrong interpretations. They are definitely incorrect.

Some sentences from the books of the late respected Golwalkarji's two books 'Our Nationhood Defined' and 'Bunch of Thoughts' have been quoted in the aforesaid booklets. Late Golwalkarji was a greater thinker like Mahatma Gandhi and Pt. Jawaharlal Nehru. It was also natural for him to speak and to write on various subjects other than the clear-cut policies of the Sangh. Those thoughts of his cannot be understood without any context. Mahatma Gandhi once said, 'A Muslim is a bully and a Hindu is a coward.' Pt. Nehru pleaded the cause of the Muslims only to avail the support of Muslim Brothern [sic]. To speak thus or to criticise thus tantamounts [sic]to the criticism in respect of a particular profession. Guruji never criticised either the Muslim religion or Mohammad, the Prophet, or the KURAN, either Christianity or Jesus Christ or the BIBLE.

You have mentioned in your speech about the reports of one or two Commissions. Attempt has been made to implicate the Sangh with disturbances, after taking one or two words from those reports. Several disturbances or riots have occurred till now. Commissions were appointed in connection with the same. But those Commissions declared that the Sangh had no hand in such riots. There is no such example wherein any worker or the official of the Sangh had been sentenced in any legal cases after the riots.

You have mentioned about a letter of Sardar Patel in connection with the murder of Mahatma Gandhi. Sri Patel was the Home Minister and it was natural for him to write such a letter in support of the government policy. But a published booklet containing his opinions includes also a letter written to the Prime Minister in which he has expressed his conviction about the Sangh having no connection in the least with the assassination of Mahatma Gandhi. You might have no knowledge about this letter.

You have called the Sangh 'a Fascist Organisation'. You have also said that the meaning of Fascism is 'Propaganda of Lies'. Whatever charges you have levelled against the Sangh for spreading rumour etc. they are all baseless. Examples abound all over the world regarding rumour-mongering which spread in the society even after the censorship is clamped over newspapers. Hence it is improper to allege against the Sangh for spreading rumours.

There is always a programme of action along with the thoughts on Fascism. From these two stand-points the Sangh bears no relationship with Fascism. The Fascists of Italy and the Nazis of Germany called themselves 'National Socialists'. The thinking process of the Sangh is mainly based on Hindu spiritualism. From the practical stand-point they are fascists who do not fall in line with those who disagree with them and are oppressive, those who question the power to rule and those who oppress the others after achieving power. Fundamentally the Sangh keeps itself aloof from the power politics. People are inspired by the aims and objects of the Sangh and they feel attracted to it voluntarily. Under this circumstance to term the Sangh as a fascist organisation is utterly improper.

The Sangh has been referred to in connection with the movement of Jayaprakash Narain [sic]. The name of the Sangh has been linked with the Bihar and the Gujarat movements again and again and without any cause. To speak about the same from my end had been in progress. In reference to the clarification of the fact that the Sangh has no connection with these movements I have mentioned mainly two points. The first, these movements took place as the result of growing dissatisfaction among the public in general. Hence you and we all are responsible for the same. Second, it is improper and discourteous to call Jayaprakash Narayan as a CIA agent, a party to capitalists or a traitor. He is also a patriot. Such ideas have often been expressed in many of your speeches.

Everytime in my lectures I have protested against the lawlessness in our country. The Sangh and the lawlessness are two contradictory words.

'Arajakeshu Rashtreshu Dharmo Na Vyavatishthate
Parasparam Cha Khadanti, Tasmat, Dhik Arajakam'

Quoting this from Mahabharata, I myself have opposed and forbidden such disloyalty.

This is not the place to reply to all the charges against the Sangh. It is not even possible through letters. It can possibly be clarified during our meetings. But still it should be made explicit that legislation or law made by you is far from the reality. It is just the same to beat the ground in pretence of a sanke [sic]. Your legislation is based on wrong conception. This has so happened as a result of your being conversant with wrong or imaginative information given to you by some persons interested in politics.

This is my belief that you might have been informed by your administrative machinery that the officials and the RSS volunteers are honourable citizens. They initiate at their own places in the fields of public work, of education, of culture, etc. The work of the Sangh has all along been spotless and innocent. Such informations [sic] too, you might have received.

Hence this is my request to you that you kindly assume the correct impression about the Sangh, after taking into consideration its correct position and after giving up your bias against it. Set free thousands of RSS workers and remove the restrictions on the Sangh. If done so, power of selfless work on the part of lacs of RSS volunteers will be utilised for the national upliftment (Government as well as non-Government) and as we all wish, our country will be prosperous.

Awaiting the reply of my letter,

Yours faithfully,
Sd/- (MADHUKAR DATTATREYA DEORAS)

Central Jail
Yeravada, Pune
24-11-1975

Hon'ble Shankarraoji Chavan

I had written a letter to the Prime Minister, Mrs. Indira Gandhi on 22-8-1975 from Yeravada jail. I now learn that the letter was forwarded to Delhi by your home department on 9-9-1975.

Since then, I have written another letter to Mrs. Indira Gandhi on 10-11-1975. On inquiring from the jail officials, I learn that my second letter has still not been sent on to the Prime Minister.

Really speaking, my letters from jail addressed to the Prime Minister should go directly to her. Any citizen should be free to write directly to the Prime Minister. Even if my letter has had to be sent to the state home department in accordance with its rules, it should be possible to have it forwarded to Delhi in not more than two, or three days, considering that it will take a day to reach Bombay from Pune.

May I request you to go into this question personally? I will be obliged if you let me know what action is being taken in this connection.

With best wishes and regards,

Yours
(Sd/-)
Chief Organiser,
Rashtriya Swayam Sevak Sangh

22-12-1975
Madhukar Dattatreya Deoras
Yeravada Central Jail,
Pune-6.

Hon'ble Shankarraoji Chavan,
Chief Minister, Maharashtra,
Bombay.

The activities of the R.S.S. have been brought to a halt throughout the country as a result of an order banning these. I have also been promptly detained.

Since the ban on the RSS concerns the whole country, I wrote two letters to the Prime Minister, Mrs. Indira Gandhi but routed these through you. I thank you for having forwarded the letters to Delhi. Many days have passed since the despatch of the letters but I have not received even an acknowledgement from the Prime Minister. This is both surprising and regrettable.

It was in Nagpur that the RSS was inaugurated and its central office is also situated there. The work of the organisation has been going on for many years. So you must be fully aware of this work. In spite of this, however, there is a misunderstanding in the mind of the Prime Minister about the RSS. It is necessary to remove it soon.

Since the ban on the RSS five or six months ago, thousands of RSS workers have been detained in various places. It is understood that in your state their number exceeds 1200.

Among these workers are persons from all walks of life. Many of them are in straitened circumstances. Some of them are very old and infirm. It will be wholly wrong to prolong their agony for an indefinite period. I would, therefore, request you to take the initiative and try to remove the Prime Minister's misconceptions about the RSS and thus facilitate the use of its strength for various constructive activities.

I think that it will be better if I could meet you in person and talk about this.

Yours
(Sd.) M.D. Deoras

V.N. Bhide
Advocate,
Detenu Class I
2181, Nasik Road Central Jail,
Nasik Road
24-1-76

Hon'ble Shri Shankarraoji Chavan,
Chief Minister, Maharashtra.

I have been detained since 6-7-75. First, I was kept in Yeravada Central Jail and since 19-1-76 I have been here in the Nasik Road Jail. Many other workers have also been similarly detained. I have already written to you stating that these detentions are wholly uncalled for. You may have given some thought to it.

These detenus include old and even sick persons. I learn that your attitude towards them is sympathetic. But before releasing them you seem to propose to ask them to give an undertaking . . . relating to politics and emergency. In my view, such an undertaking will be improper. No one will like to secure his release in this way. If anyone wants to give an undertaking out of a sense of despair, it is a different thing. It will not be graceful to ask anyone to give an undertaking if he is to be released on the compassionate ground that he is either old or sick. So, I request that the workers be released but the release should not be conditional on . . .

With regards,

Yours,
(Sd/-)

V.N. Bhide,
Advocate,
Detenu No. 2181,
Nasik Road Jail,
12-7-1976

To
Hon'ble Mr. Shankarrao Chavan,
Chief Minister, Maharashtra,
Bombay.

Sir,

I have been troubling you with letters from time to time. In my letter dated 16-6-76 I had asked for release on parole with a view to clarifying certain issues directly to you. But that letter has still remained unanswered.

I will now explain why I am writing this letter. It is now over a year since many people have been detained. No one thought that the detention will be so prolonged. Possibly you too feel that the detenus should now be released and it seems that you are trying to take action for this purpose very gradually.

About seven months ago you expressed the view that detenus over 60 years of age and those who are not in good health should be released. Accordingly a list of such detenus was prepared. Also, after making due enquiries they were made to give an undertaking that they would not do anything against the emergency. Of the 150 detenus of over 60 years of age, only 10 to 12 were released. On my suggestion a similar concession was made to some detenus under 60 years. As I said in my previous letter the fact that a beginning in releasing detenus on the basis of an undertaking has been made should satisfy both sides. As regards the working of the undertaking, it will not be proper to use the expression 'good behaviour'. I hope you will agree and delete this expression.

On July 6, 1975, Rule No. 33 under the Defence of India Act was applied to the R.S.S. Following this the office-bearers of the Sangh have notified suspension of all activities of the Sangh. Therefore there is no need to make non-participation in R.S.S. activities a condition for the release. This indeed is the purpose of this letter. I hope you will give due thought to this question.

Our stand should be clear from what I have written above. I have made this request without any ill-feeling against the government. The government should make the best use of the urge to work for the good of the society felt by many people. The country will benefit immensely from this.

It is clear from Mrs. Indira Gandhi's latest interview that the decision on the release of the detenus has been left entirely to the states.

I request that all detenus be released without delay. May I again request to give me an opportunity to talk over this question directly to you?

M.D. Devras,
Yarvada Central Jail,
Pune-6.

Dated 16-7-76.

Respected Mrs. Indira Gandhi,
Prime Minister, Govt. of India, New Delhi.

Sadar Namaskar. I have already written two letters to you, but I am sorry to say that neither have I received the acknowledgement nor any reply. In those letters I had given some explanations regarding the allegations made by you and some other senior leaders against the R.S.S. The nature of the allegations was the same and no proof was ever given to substantiate them.

After banning the Sangh, all its main offices were taken-over by the Govt. All the papers found must have been investigated. It was expected that on the basis of those papers, the Govt. would produce some solid proof against the R.S.S. In place of that the Govt. republished and distributed the books already published by M/s. D.R. Goyal & Subhadra Joshi years ago. The Govt. have not produced any fresh proof.

After the brutal murder of late Lalitnarayan Mishra and the incident of throwing a bomb on Justice Mr. Ajitnath Ray of the Supreme Court, you and some others, alleged in the speeches that the Sangh was connected with these violent incidents. Now the incidents have been investigated and the names of the culprits have been announced. Legal proceedings have already began against them. This proves that the allegation of violence against the Sangh was not true.

Only a few days ago you had been to Russia, East Germany and Afghanistan. In your lectures and statements there, you had given a call to all the nations of the world to remain united irrespective of the difference in their political thinking and social setup. Besides you had promised to work to ease the tense situation of the world. This call of yours was congruent to the Indian tradition, India's independent foreign policy and world peace. In this regard your effort to improve the relations with Pakistan and China are also praiseworthy.

While trying to reduce the tension between the nations, it is not possible that you are not thinking of reducing the tension prevailing in your own country. We are a democratic nation and you also believe that it should remain democratic. Therefore, you would agree that in spite of difference of opinion the tension between the different ideologies and various organisations upholding them should be reduced. Time and again you have said that the meaning of Democracy is not uniformity but unity of diversity.

Therefore, I request you to please rise above the misunderstandings prevailing regarding the Sangh, reconsider the matter and lift the ban imposed upon the Sangh. For the reduction of the tension prevailing in the world, it would be necessary that the tension in the country also reduces. This will enhance the prestige of your efforts and make them significant.

I shall be expecting a reply from you.

Yours,
Sd./ M.D. Devras.

(The following have been taken from Brahm Dutt, *Five Headed Monster*, pp. 144-8.)

[*Letter sent on 12 January 1976*]

At the feet of Respected Acharya Vinobaji,

A meeting of the Acharyas of our country under your guidance has been scheduled to be held on the 16th, 17th and 18th January and it has been informed that discussions regarding the deteriorated condition of country are going to be held. I am happy to learn this; I have started believing that, during these discussions, some ways are to be found out of the emergent situation. On this occasion, what smaller role is to be played by me is the content of this brief letter.

After the death of the most reverent Guruji, the responsibility of the Sangh's activities was shouldered on me. I had also come to Pavnar for your 'darshan'. You gave me your 'darshan' and blessed me. I remember this daily. I am trying my level best to discharge my responsibilities on the strength of your sacred blessings.

Both you and Guruji were well-acquainted. At times when both of you met, matters relating to the State, the time and the activities of the Sangh were discussed. When I came to meet you, such discussions were held. Not only this, you inspired and blessed me for the working of the Sangh by saying, 'please take me to be an uncivilised member of the Sangh'.

As before, an unforeseen restriction was clamped down on the Sangh on account of my association with the same and after being arrested, I was kept in the Ekhra jail. Thus all over the country at different places thousands of workers and officials were thrust into jail. The sequence of such arrests is still continuing.

From my point of view such ban on the Sangh and the arrests of so many volunteers is based on a wrong conception. Particularly it appears that many people around Smt. Indira Gandhi were made to harbour a wrong idea about the Sangh. No opportunity was availed regarding the removal of this wrong impression about the Sangh and the presentation of its real picture as a result of which this calamity befell on the workers of the organisation.

From this jail, I attempted twice to let Srimati Indira Gandhi know about what my role was but it did not appear if that had received her attention as yet. Not only this, I had not been even informed about the receipt of my letters.

Many charges are levelled against the Sangh and the Sangh is put to harsh and one-sided criticism. All these charges against the Sangh are false and baseless. The contents of this letter are not meant for the reply to those charges. You are well acquainted with the goal of the Sangh, its work and the process of the work.

This is true that the Sangh wants to organise the Hindu community but that does not make it communal or national. It is beyond one's understanding how the outlook of Hinduism can be narrow and communal. The matter would have been different if at the time of organising the Hindus we would have done anything wrong against the non-Hindus. Not a single word of aspertion [sic] is uttered against followers of other religions. Neither it is taught to hate others than those of Hindus. In as much as the [lectures] of Respected Guruji have referred respectfully to the KURAN, the Prophet Mohammad, the Islamic religion, to Jesus Christ, the BIBLE and the Christianity.

For these last 50 years, the work of the Sangh is being done openly on the open fields. During this period some riots broke out between the Hindus and the Muslims but even in such a fray the Sangh never took part. Commissions were appointed after such communal disturbances. Reports of the same had also been received. The Sangh never was found responsible and no one was ever sued at the Court.

Some persons think, without rhyme or reason, that the Sangh encourages violence. But this is a very wrong notion. The Sangh does not have faith in the least on the creed of violence. The Sangh has neither been violent nor encouraged acts of violence.

The main function of the Sangh is to rectify man. The RSS volunteers are asked to observe, control and discipline, hence it can have no place for violence. In the lectures of Respected Guruji and mine too disloyalty and violence have been criticised vehemently.

'*Arajakeshu Rashtreshu Dharmo Na Vyavatishthate*
Parasparam Che Khadanti, Tasmat, Dhik Arajakam'

Quoting the above as a proof, stress has been given on non-violence and peaceful transition.

The Sangh is alleged of becoming a fascist organisation. How can that organisation become a fascist one when it has all along been far from politics of grabbing power and where people being inspired by the ideal can come and do come, voluntarily?

Those who create awe amongst people after achieving power and status and utilising the same power oppress and repress others are called Fascists. The Sangh can never be termed so. The view of the Sangh is based on ethical principles and spiritual heredity. As it is, it is totally wrong, unjust and false to call the Sangh as a fascist organisation. This is our mode of thinking and our behaviour that the voluntary organisations should keep themselves aloof from the government and should try to change the society after rectifying the people. This is all known to you. Hence, now you and the educated people of our country are about to discuss the present critical and dangerous situation of our country. It is natural, discussions will now be going on regarding RSS. You are in the know of everything about the Sangh. So this is my prayer that you should come at the forefront and find out such worthy ways by following which the Sangh can work as before so that its power can be utilised in constructive work.

Praying for your blessings,

Yours faithfully,
Sd/- (MADHUKAR DATTATREYA DEORAS)

ACHARYA Vinoba Bhave,
Pavnar Ashram,
Wardha,
District Wardha.

[*Undated letter*]
MADHUKAR DATTATREYA DEORAS
St. George's Hospital
Prison Ward No. 14,
BOMBAY.

At the feet of Respected Acharya Vinobaji,

I wrote a letter to you from Ekhra Jail on 12-1-76. You might have received that at the time when the Conference of the Acharyas was going to begin. I hope so. I wrote in that letter what the Sangh had to say in reply to the recent charges levelled against it, and I prayed to you that you should help for the removal of the Ban on the Sangh.

All of our friends became hopeful about the future, bright prospect as a result of your guidance at the Conference of the Acharyas, of deliberations and of unanimous verdict which we could read in the newspapers.

As far as I remember I think you and Guruji met at Keljhar (Nagpur-Wardha Road). When you had asked Guruji whether his angle of vision in respect of other religions was that of tolerance, Guruji had told you that we were not only tolerant to other religions, more so, we respected even those religions.

When you have walked on feet for BHUDAN in U.P., Bihar and other states, the RSS volunteers met you every where and participated in every programme of yours. What type of behaviour and thoughts of the Swayam Sewakas of Sangh have, you are well acquainted with that.

It has been published in the newspapers that the Hon'ble Prime Minister is going to meet you at the Pavnar Ashram on the 24th. Discussion relating to the present-day situation of our country will be held. This is my prayer to you that you kindly try to remove the wrong notion of the Prime Minister about the Sangh, and as a result of which the RSS volunteers will be set free, the ban on the Sangh will be lifted and such a condition will prevail as to enable the volunteers of the Sangh to participate in the planned programme of action relating to country's progress and prosperity under the leadership of the Prime Minister.

Praying for your blessings,

Yours faithfully,

Sd/- (MADHUKAR DATTATREYA DEORAS)
Rashtriya Swayamsevak Sangh.

N.B.:

You might not have received my letter dated 12/1; hence I am sending you the copy of the same.

Sd/- (M.D. DEORAS)

Appendix 8

In the Court of the District Judge, Nagpur

Miscellaneous Application No. 17/1978.

(Emphasis in original; notes in margins included in square brackets.)

APPLICANTS:

1. Rajendrasinghji, aged about 53 years, Sar Karyawah, R.S.S., Dr. Hedgewar Bhavan, Mahal, Nagpur.
2. Bhaurao Deoras, aged about 55 years, Sah Sar Karyawah, R.S.S. Office, Zandewala, New Delhi.

VERSUS

NON-APPLICANTS:

1. Manharkant Dayalji Kamdar, r/o Sitabuldi, Nagpur.
2. The Charity Commissioner, Maharashtra State, Bombay.
3. Shri N.R. Kanhe, Secretary, Dr. Hedgewar Smarak Samiti, Nagpur, C. No. 7, Ruikar Road, Nagpur.
4. Shri Eknath Ranade, C/o Vivekanand Rock Memorial, Kanya Kumari (Tamil Nadu)
5. Shri Madhorao Mule, R.S.S. Office, Samskriti Mandir, Zandewala, New Delhi-55.
6. Shri Yadaorao Joshi, Keshav Kripa, Sheshadripuram, Bangalore-20.
7. Shri Dattopant Thengadi, M.P. South Avenue, New Delhi.
8. Shri Madhav Narayan Ghatate, C/o Hedgewar Bhavan, Mahal, Nagpur.
9. Shri Laxmanrao Inamdar, C/o Hedgewar Bhavan, Mahal, Nagpur, now at R.S.S. Office, Ahmedabad.
10. Shri P.D. Talatule, 50, Gokulpeth, Nagpur-1.

Application under Section 72 of the Bombay Public Trust Act, 1950, for setting aside the decision of the Joint Charity Commissioner, Shri M.S. Vaidya, Maharashtra State, Bombay, holding that the Rashtriya Swayamsevak Sangh is a Public Trust in Appeal No. 89/1974 against the order of the Assistant Charity Commissioner, Nagpur.

The applicants named above beg to state as under:–

1. The Non-Applicant No. 1 filed an application U/S 19 of the Bombay Public Trust Act, which was registered as Inquiry No. 45/1972 dated 7-2-1972 praying that the Rashtriya Swayamsevak Sangh, hereinafter referred to as the 'R.S.S.' or the 'Sangh' be declared as a 'Public Trust' within the meaning of Section 2(13) of the Bombay Public Trust Act, 1950, hereinafter referred to as the 'Bombay Trust Act'. Shri M.D. Deoras who was then General Secretary of the R.S.S. and others who were impleaded as non-applicants in the said case filed written statement

denying that the R.S.S. was a Trust and submitted that the R.S.S. was not a Public Trust and much less a religious or a Charitable Trust.

2. The Deputy Charity Commissioner at Nagpur recorded the oral evidence of the Non-Applicant No. 1 while the applicants filed several documents as per list which amongst others included the 'Biography of Dr. K.B. Hedgewar', the Founder of the R.S.S. 'Bunch of Thoughts' a collection of the speeches delivered from time to time by the then R.S.S. Chief Shri M.S. Golwalkar and a book entitled 'Justice on Trial' which is a correspondence between Pandit Jawaharlal Nehru, the then Prime Minister of India and the late Sardar Vallabhai [sic] Patel and the various Government authorities on the one hand and Shri M.S. Golwalkar, the then R.S.S. Chief on the other, during the period of the first ban on the R.S.S. in the month of February, 1948.

3. The learned Deputy Charity Commissioner, Nagpur after going through the oral and documentary evidence by his order dated 22-5-1974 rejected the application holding that the R.S.S. was not a Public Trust. The learned Deputy Charity Commissioner observed in his judgement as follows:-

> 'Documentary and oral evidence on record shows that the R.S.S. is having a patriotic purpose which is neither religious nor charitable. The objects of the Organisation of the R.S.S. are akin to the political objects as distinguished from religious or charitable objects. Teaching about nationalism as contemplated by the preamble and the aims and objects and the activities of the Organisation of the R.S.S. will not be a religious or charitable purpose. It is an object of patriotism. In this view of the matter, I hold that the R.S.S. is not a Public Trust within the meaning of Section 2(13) of the Act and does not require registration under the Bombay Public Trust Act, 1950'.

4. Against the said decision the Non-Applicant No. 1 preferred an appeal which was registered as the Appeal No. 89/1974 and ultimately disposed of by the Joint Charity Commissioner, Maharashtra State, Bombay on 11-1-1978. The learned Joint Charity Commissioner held that the R.S.S. was proved to be a Public Religious and Charitable Trust and that it should be registered as such. On this view of the matter, the case was remanded to the Deputy Charity Commissioner with a direction to conclude the inquiry under Section 19 of the Bombay Trust Act by recording findings on the remaining statutory issues.

5. The applicants submit that the decision of the Joint Charity Commissioner is contrary to law and is liable to be set aside. Hence this application under Section 72 of the Bombay Trust Act and the submissions of the applicants for setting aside the said decision are as follows:-

6. The two important submissions on behalf of the R.S.S. are that;

i) that the R.S.S. is not a Trust, and

ii) that the R.S.S. is neither a Charitable Trust, nor a Religious Trust, nor was it created by its founder Dr. K.B. Hedgewar as a Trust for any such purposes and consequently it does not fall within the ambit and scope of Section 2(13) of the Bombay Public Trust Act, 1950. It is, therefore, in any event not a charitable or religious Organisation.

7. The work of the R.S.S. is 'Cultural' and 'Patriotic' and its object is to create cultural unity of Hindu Samaj and inspire them with patriotism, so as to stand as a strong Hindu Rashtra for all sided development of Bharatwarsha [sic]. Reference is invited to Ex. 30 W.S. dated 26-10-72. In this context, it will be necessary to refer to a biography of Dr. K.B. Hedgewar, the Founder of the R.S.S. written by Shri. N.H. Palkar Exh. (68) and the one published by Kendra Karyalaya at Nagpur as also to the various marked quotations from the book 'Bunch of Thoughts' placed

on record to clarify and understand the true purpose, the exact nature, the ambit and scope of the R.S.S. work and to get the correct perspective of the background of the formation of the organisation and its activities.

8. The founder of the R.S.S. late Dr. K.B. Hedgewar was amongst those few revolutionaries who worked for the emancipation of India from the then British Rule. In his youth and as a student in Calcutta, he came in close contact with revolutionary movement and himself was actively associated with their activities. Thereafter, he was an active, constructive worker of the Indian National Congress. However, after actually remaining in contact with the revolutionaries as well as after having participated in the Congress movement in the year 1921, he came to the conclusion that in the disintegrated condition of the country, an organisation of the Hindus based on the feelings of brotherhood and oneness without any distinction as to sect, faith, caste, colour or creed imbibed with the patriotism with a realisation of the greatness of their past can alone win independence for the nation. In the twenties, the political situation was fast changing and there was confusion writ large on the political scene. The concept that nation with a glorious past which indeed was a 'Hindu Rashtra' was being wiped out from the people and its interest [sic] were being ignored by the then political leaders particularly after the eclipse of Lokmanya Tilak from the Political horizon after his death in 1920. The Founder of the R.S.S. Dr. Hedgewar then visualised the idea of founding the R.S.S. as a movement with a view to fearlessly propagate that India was a 'Hindu Rashtra' (Nation), as contra-distinguished from 'Hindu Raj'. The concept of 'Hindu Nation' of the founder of R.S.S. was on the basis of cultural unity of the entire people living in the Bharatvarsh. Thus was born the R.S.S. as a movement founded by late Dr. K.B. Hedgewar on the Vijaya Dashmi day in 1925. In this context it is significant to note that the name of the movement or organisation was also chosen with a particular vision so as to reflect the political ideology of the organisation though Sangh as such never had politics of its own as of policy. It is significant to note that the name was not chosen as '"Hindu" Swayam Sevak Sangh' though the Sangh is open to Hindus only. This is because of the faith of the Sangh that in India 'Rashtriya' means 'of Hindus', which are the main stream of the Nation.

9. On 26-1-1929, the Indian National Congress the then Premier Political Organisation of this country adopted a resolution at the Lahore Congress stating in unequivocal terms that complete independence was the ultimate aim of the National congress. The founder of the R.S.S. late Dr. Hedgewar was extremely happy and issued a circular letter to all the R.S.S. Branches welcoming this resolution and directing them to work with that end in view. The documents on record will clearly establish that the R.S.S. propagated a distinct political philosophy to the effect that India was and is a Hindu Rashtra.

10. With a view to give a scientific base to propagate the idea [of] India being historically from time immemorial a Hindu Nation, late Shri M.S. Golwalkar had written a book entitled 'We or our nationhood defined' which was published in 1933. The political parties in those times were not enthusiastic about this philosophy and in fact in those days there was even a controversy as to whether India was a Nation or merely a 'State'. It was in these circumstances that the R.S.S. was founded by the late Dr. Hedgewar in 1925. This political philosophy of India being a Hindu Rashtra had gained tremendous momentum. In the year of Indian independence (1947) i.e. within a short span of 22 years, the R.S.S. had become a strong positive force in the social and political life of the Nation which could not be ignored. Political parties who were opposed to the concept of Hindu Rashtra had therefore started to raise a hue and cry that the Sangh be banned.

11. Due to political tensions and social commotion then prevailing on the eve of Independence and the consequent partition of the motherland on 15th August, 1947 and the

misunderstanding about the real mission of the R.S.S. the Government of India by a communique dated 4-2-1948 declared the R.S.S. as an Unlawful Organisation. A historical correspondence between late Pandit Jawaharlal Nehru, the then Prime Minister of India and late Sardar Vallabhai Patel, the then Deputy Prime Minister and Home Minister and various other Government authorities on the one hand and the late Shri M.S. Golwalkar, the then R.S.S. Chief on the other, took place during the period of the first ban on R.S.S. The entire correspondence is published in a book 'Justice on Trial' which forms part of the record exhibited as Ex. 73. A reference to the entire correspondence which is full of false and motivated charges made by the Government and its clarification in a forthright manner made by the R.S.S. Chief and which ultimately resulted in an unconditional withdrawal of the ban by the Government's communique dated 11-7-1949, announcing the lifting of the ban, will throw a flood of light on the nature of the work and activities of the R.S.S. as understood by the Government, the R.S.S. leaders, and the General Public opinion as was then represented by Shri T.R.V. Shastry [sic]. The relevant portion of page 101 which is reproduced below will clarify the circumstances under which the activities of the R.S.S. were resumed after lifting of the ban:-

> 'In the light of the modification made and clarifications given by the R.S.S. Leader, the Government of India have come to the conclusion that the R.S.S. Organisation should be given an opportunity to function as a democratic, Cultural Organisation owing loyalty to the Indian Constitution and recognising the National Flag eschewing secrecy and abjuring violence. Indeed the Government feel that under a Constitution embodying these principles and worked in the right spirit, no reasonable objections can be taken to such functioning. [T]hey have accordingly decided to withdraw ban on the organisation in the centrally administered areas and to release as soon as possible, all R.S.S. men at present under detention or undergoing sentences of imprisonment in connection with the R.S.S. activities, and have requested the Provincial Governments to take similar action in their own areas'.

12. Thus it would be obvious that even the Central Government had no doubt that the R.S.S. was to exist and to be given an opportunity to function as a 'Democratic Cultural Organisation' which was its sole purpose. It may be pointed out here that although various false and motivated allegations such as the R.S.S. was communal and anti-Muslim organisation carrying on para-military and violent activities etc. were made, no reasonable or sensible person in or outside the Government took at any time the view that the R.S.S. was a religious or charitable organisation or a Trust for such purpose. Govt. all along was of the view that it is a political party which label the organisation denied as it as of policy had never participated in the day to day politics, elections and formation of Government etc. It is submitted that the view taken by the Joint Charity Commissioner is wholly perverse and liable to be set aside.

13. It is in aforesaid context of inhibitions on the mind of Government that the Written Constitution came into existence for the first time in June 1949. Some salient features of the said written constitution have to be borne in mind when one tries to understand by interpreting the Constitution as to why R.S.S. was started, what is the nature of Sangh work, what is the meaning of terms used in the Constitution by the Organisation. The first feature is that the terms used have special significance and meaning as understood by the ORGANISATION IN VIEW OF ITS PHILOSOPHY as distinct from the ordinary meaning. For instance there is no definition clause in the constitution as we normally find in any constitution and clause 25(a) makes it

clear that the interpretation of the constitution and its clauses by the K.K.M. shall be final. In brief for interpretation of the said terms one has to look as to how they are understood by the Organisation and not how such terms are commonly used or interpreted by others.

14. Such terms are Rashtriya, Dharma, Sanskriti, Hindu Dharma etc. The second feature is as it is impossible to put in a nut shell in a written constitution all the philosophy, aims, objects, programmes of the Sangh work, the constitution provides the office of the Sarsanghchalak who is the Guide and Philosopher of the R.S.S. (Art. 12). It is he who is to expound the Philosophy and vide [sic] sweep of the Sangh work. As such we have to take into consideration his utterances or thesis in this behalf from the lectures, writings of the R.S.S. Chief, while understanding the constitution till there is contrary decision of K.K.M. under article 25(a). That is why in these proceedings the R.S.S. relies on the various books and writings to follow what is Sangh work. The third important feature of the Constitution is its flexibility as provided in Art. 25(b) and (c) under which the R.S.S. can modify or amend the constitution by following the procedure provided. In this behalf it would be borne in mind that this right or power of amendment or modification specifically reserved by the R.S.S. Organisation is not restricted to a few clauses. As such the organisation can add to, amend, alter, abridge, delete any of the clauses. In fact this right has been exercised from time to time and extends to even changing aims and objects, policy. The Fourth feature is aims [and] objects are distinguished from policy by providing two independent clauses in the constitution. It is common knowledge that policy is not a permanent feature and changes or is changed from time to time. It is evident that this clause was included in the constitution so as to protect the organisation from the misconceived allegations and charges. That is why faith in evolution and peaceful and legitimate means is expressed. So also tolerance towards all [faiths]. So far as politics is concerned it is made clear that it does not indulge in politics i.e. day to day politics though Sangh has a political philosophy within its wide sweep of cultural work. It is possible for sangh to change this policy and even participate in politics.

15. The fifth feature is the Flag mentioned in Art. 5 [and] pledge in Art. 6a(a). The sixth important feature is the programmes as provided in Art. 20. A perusal of the said clause will make it clear that the sweep of Sangh work is very wide and it can do any thing which directly or indirectly promote the general objects mentioned in Art. 3. The seventh feature is utilisation of funds and it will be clear from Art. 22 is an enabling clause that the funds can be used for general advancement of Sangh work which has a very wide sweep and the clause as such does not create any obligation express or implied to utilise the funds as in the case of the Trust for religious or charitable purposes. The eighth feature is the limited democratic form and machinery provided for carrying out the work of the Sangh with K.K.M. and A.B.P.S. whereunder the A.B.P.S. elects the Sarkaryawaha who is bound to act in consultation with the guide and philosopher viz. Sar Sangh chalak as per Art. 13. The Sarkaryawaha forms K.K.M. as per Art. 14 and similar arrangement is provided at the provincial levels. It may be noted that there is no election at all [levels] but selection and nomination except [for] the posts [of] Sarkaryawaha and Prant Sanghchalaks. The ninth feature is the Pracharaks who are full time workers who have dedicated their lives for the service of the country and society through the Sangh and working without remuneration. The tenth feature is Swayamsevak as described in Art. 6. In the Organisation right from Sarsanghchalak to the lowest cadre everybody is a Swayamsevak i.e. one who has voluntarily offered himself in service of the society by accepting the rules, regulations and taking the pledge. Art. 6(c) provides for expulsion of any one whose acts are prejudicial. The right to expel any body makes it clear that there is no right of admission to everybody.

The last and eleventh feature is the insistence of daily shakha and coming together of the

Swayamsevaks of the shakha and recital of prayers as one of the programmes. The Prarthana (which is on record) and the songs that are recited also throw a light on the Sangh work.

It is in the light of all the aforesaid features that one has to understand why [sic] Sangh, what is Sangh, what is Sangh work and then examine whether R.S.S. is a trust in law and whether it is a public trust either [of] religious or charitable nature or of both. The learned Joint Charity Commissioner totally ignored the aforesaid features of the constitution and rules and has drawn erroneous conclusions which are not at all supported by the evidence on record.

16. An important fact brought to the notice of the courts below and which the applicants crave leave to reiterate here is that in the letter dated 11-9-1948 Sardar Patel had appealed to the R.S.S. leader that they should join the Congress Party to carry out their patriotic endeavour. To clarify the exact position of the R.S.S. vis-a-vis day-to-day politics of power, the following provision was made in Article 4(b) of the R.S.S. Constitution:–

> 'The Sangh as such has no politics and is devoted to purely cultural work. The individual swayamsevaks, however, may join any political party except such parties as believe in or resort to violence and secret methods to achieve their ends, persons owing allegiance to such parties or believing in such methods shall have no place in the Sangh'.

That it would be clear that the work of the R.S.S. is not political in the sense of taking active interest in the game of 'power politics' but is merely of the nature, cultural and patriotic renaissance, which even excludes political activity subject to the policy laid down.

17. Now the submission of the R.S.S. in the context of all the material placed on record viz. the various books such as 'The life of Dr. Hedgewar', 'The Bunch of Thoughts', 'We or our Nationhood defined', 'The Nation its malady and remedy' etc. it is clear that the work of the R.S.S. is neither religious nor charitable but its objects are cultural and patriotic as contra-distinguished from religious or charitable. It is akin to political purposes though R.S.S. is not at present a political party in as much as the R.S.S. Constitution quoted above bars active political participation by R.S.S. as such, as a policy.

18. The material on record and the admission of the Respondent and the various public speeches and expression of views expressed by the leaders of the R.S.S. will clearly show that the Sangh work and its activities which [have] not been defined, nor is it possible to give the exact connotation thereof, are social and secular and inclusive or akin to political, but in any event not religious or charitable. The R.S.S. does not come under the religious or charitable Trust in as much as the activities if properly examined on the material on record are purely secular as distinct from religious as there are no religious beliefs or tents [sic] that are propagated or rites performed or any religious deity worshipped or to which the Organisation is devoted or any religious practices are followed. The activities like coming together, playing together games, performing drill or giving lectures, singing songs of love towards nation and patriotism have nothing to do with the Hindu Religious activities and consequently they are purely secular. The learned Joint Charity Commissioner has, therefore, misdirected and misconstrued the scope and ambit of the R.S.S. activities and recorded a perverse finding.

19. For existence of a trust there must be property, confidence reposed by settler and accepted as such by trustees, an obligation attached to such property that the same or income thereof shall be used by the trustees for the benefit of the beneficiaries. In the case of religious or charitable trusts the obligation should be that the funds or income shall be used for charitable purposes. So far as the R.S.S. is concerned Dr. Hedgewar, the Founder, never created [a] trust by any express deed. He started a movement or organisation. Initially there was no deed or any

constitution. The constitution framed in 1948 or so was for the satisfaction of the Govt. as to remove the misunderstandings. It does not and cannot depict the whole concept of Sangh and its work which has a very wide sweep. It is not an instrument of trust as contemplated for a trust but some documents to show some of the rules, aims, objects and policy and working of the R.S.S. It is not, therefore, proper to look to it as instrument of trust to spell out the Trust. Apart from it this document is not an irrevocable document which is an essence of a public religious and/or charitable Trust. The constitution and rules are liable to be changed, modified, etc. including its aims, objects, policy and as such it is not of such a nature which alone could be looked into to determine the purposes of the activity. Tomorrow the policy could be changed and R.S.S. could participate in even day to day political activity as a political party because policy is not a permanent or irrevocable thing. The R.S.S. had to launch satyagraha movement twice for getting the ban on its activities removed viz. once in 1948 and secondly during the emergency in 1975, which was against emergency and restoration of democracy and incidently [sic] for lifting the ban. This was a purely political object and clearly illustrates that objects are not charitable or religious in the sense contemplated by the B.P.T. Act. The Court cannot, therefore, merely look to the constitution by ignoring all the aforesaid aspects or facts of constitution to draw a conclusion that the purposes are religious or charitable. Apart from this nobody gives offerings, gifts or donations by reposing any confidence that the same should be used for a particular religious or charitable purpose, nor the shakhas accept the same by accepting any such obligation. The clause in the constitution viz. Art. 22 about funds is only on enabling provision which enables the authorities to give directions as to for what purposes the funds can be spent. It is not at all an obligation attached to the funds that they shall be used for religious or charitable purposes or for Sangh work alone. In this behalf the case of Andhra Chamber of Commerce decided by Supreme Court can be seen. In that case there was a clear mandatory provision creating an obligation as to utilisation of funds. Apart [from that] that constitution was a rigid constitution under Indian Companies Act and could not be changed by overriding the provisions of the Companies Act. That is not the case in the constitution or Rules and Regulations of the R.S.S. Again if we see the article 20 of programmes it would be clear that as per Art. 22 the funds could be spent or utilised for any of the programmes mentioned therein which already cover a very wide field and are liable to be still widened by modification and amendments. For example the programmes include establishment of agencies or institutions and the funds can be diverted or used for any such establishment or agency distinct or different from actual R.S.S. work. Similarly Sangh can do (under the last sub-clause in Art. 20) anything or undertake any other work which is calculated directly or indirectly to promote the object mentioned in Art. 3. Under this activity the funds of the R.S.S. could be used or expended by the authorities even though the work or activity may not form a direct activity of R.S.S. It may donate, gift, grant any fund or amount to any institution or body of person or individual which even indirectly promotes the objectives of R.S.S.

In brief the clauses in the constitution do not spell out any obligation as regards funds which are essential before holding the R.S.S. as a trust. In this behalf the decision of the Bombay High Court in Gonshala case is relied [upon] by the applicants. In the light of submissions made above the findings of the learned Joint Charity Commissioner attempted to be spelled out from [the] constitution, that a trust exists is erroneous and cannot be supported at all. In fact the learned Joint Charity Commissioner has not recorded any finding as to what is Sangh work and has erroneously observed that there is no mention of programme any where in the constitution when in fact Art. 20 clearly describes the programme for the time being.

20. The learned Joint Charity Commissioner ought to have seen that the R.S.S. activities,

aims and objects, pledge of the R.S.S., the name of the R.S.S. and the prayers offered every day in every shakha would all go to show that it is working for advancing an opinion or political philosophy not for any charitable purpose or religious purpose which can legally fall within the category of 'advancement of any other object of public utility' within the meaning of the definition in sub-clause(4) of Section 9 of the Bombay Public Trust Act.

21. The learned Charity Commissioner has ignored that the activity or movement of the R.S.S. mentioned in the aims and objects are so wide that it will be impossible to administer it as a Public Trust as in the case of an institution in as much as the scope and activity of the organisation as rightly observed by the Joint Charity Commissioner are so vague and [cover] everything on the face of the earth and consequently such an organisation or movement even if held as a Trust will not be covered in the ambit and scope of the definition of either a Trust for the Religious purpose or the Charitable purpose.

22. Thus, the dominant purpose of the R.S.S. activity is propogation [sic] of a particular philosophy as was held by the Supreme Court in the marginally-noted decisions [AIR 1967; SC P. 1553; AIR 1965; SC P. 1281.], it is the dominant purpose which must be examined to find out whether the activities fall within the definition of Section 2(13) and although some incidental or ancillary object or activities undertaken are charitable the said organisation cannot be declared to be for a predominantly charitable object.

23. The Public Trust Act is framed on the lines of the English Law. English Law or British Courts are yet unable to precisely define what is a charity or a charitable purpose. The attempt if any is of an enumerative nature. So [is] the case under Indian law especially the Income-Tax Act and the Public Trusts Act. S. 2(15) of the Income-Tax Act and S. 9 of the Bombay Public Trusts Act 1950 are analogous except the addition of recreational charities and facilities in S. 9(1)(3A). As such the decisions under Income tax Act would be attracted [sic] to decide whether R.S.S. is charity or not. In this behalf it may be mentioned that recently the Income tax Commissioner has held in an appeal that R.S.S. activity is neither religious nor charitable. The applicants rely on the said decision to the extent of the reasoning given by the said authority. In view of the enumerative nature of the definitions prevailing both under English law and Indian law there is no fixed principle or ingradients [sic] laid down by any court as to what is charitable purpose. If we look at the English authorities it would by clear that the principle of ejusdem generis or analogous principle is used in deciding whether any activity or purpose is charitable or not. That is why political purpose, sports or activities which are not benefiting the public are held to be not charitable. There are rulings that every object of general public utility is not charitable. In brief even if any activity [is] of the nature of general public utility there must be something more in it in order that it may be stamped as charitable. That something though no where laid down must be analogous to the purposes mentioned in clauses 9(1)(2)(3) and (3A). In brief the rule of ejusdem generis shall have to be applied while interpreting clause 9(1)(4) of the Bombay Public Trusts Act. The learned Joint Charity Commissioner has observed in para 20 of his judgement that there are 5 categories of charitable purposes mentioned. It appears that the learned Joint Charity Commissioner could not fit in the R.S.S. activity in any of the said 5 categories and as such attempted to widen the scope of S. 9 so as to include R.S.S. activity in the said definition. The interpretation given by the learned Joint Charity Commissioner to S. 9 is wrong and erroneous. Similarly his finding that the activity falls within the scope of S. 9 is erroneous. In any event in order that the R.S.S. should be considered a public Religious Trust, it must be established that it is a trust for advancement of religion. It is now settled law that the society engaged in advancing an opinion is not charitable. In this context, the marginally noted cases [(1943) ch. 535; (1958) ch. 406; (1924) (45) PLR 344.] support the submissions of the R.S.S.

24. During the pendency of Appeal No. 89/1974, the R.S.S. was banned for the second time by the Central Government by communique dated 4-7-1975 on the self-same charges of indulging in alleged violent activities and actively participating in the movement launched by Shri Jayaprakash Narayan, which obviously was a political movement aiming at total Revolution for emancipation. The ban was withdrawn with the formation of Janata Government in the Centre and the R.S.S. resumed its activities as usual. Then followed a spurt of political activity by the Janata Party higher-ups for merger of R.S.S. with that party. The press statements issued by various political party leaders including the Prime Minister on one hand and the R.S.S. Chief and other prominent personalities on the other proves the hollowness of the finding given by the learned Joint Charity Commissioner, Bombay. These recent events were brought to the notice of the Joint Charity Commissioner during the course of hearing of the appeal. The Joint Charity Commissioner was in error in not taking judicial notice of these events and its decision has been vitiated and liable to be set aside. The applicant craves leave to produce the relevant material for perusal of this Court at the Time of hearing.

25. With a view to substantiate this contention, the R.S.S. points out and [relies] upon the principle laid down in the marginally noted leading case [AIR 1962 (S.C. 1589).] of the Supreme Court of India. In this case, the Supreme Court examined the political life work and political philosophy of Late Lokmanya Tilak and in the light of his life mission and carved out a new and distinguishable head of work viz. 'The political work' or 'Political purpose' and took the view that the Kesari-Maratha Trust was created by the late Lokmanya Tilak for achieving a Political purpose and as such, it fell outside the ambit of the Bombay Public Trust Act, 1950. In view of the Supreme Court decision a contention was raised that R.S.S. was founded neither for a charitable nor a religious purpose but for a wholly cultural and patriotic purpose which is neither charitable nor religious and [consequently] falling outside the ambit and scope of Section 2(13) of the Bombay Trust Act, 1950. In the Supreme Court case cited supra the emphasis was on the political philosophy and background of late Lokmanya Tilak and on the analogy of the said case, a reference on the basis of the biographies and other literature filed in this case was made to the revolutionary patriotic life and philosophy of Dr. Hedgewar and Shri M.S. Golwalkar and a contention to the effect that the R.S.S. does not fall within the ambit of the Bombay Public Trust Act, 1950 or any other similar statute enacted in different states in India, was raised before the Joint Charity Commissioner, Bombay who rejected the same on a totally unjustifiable ground. The decision is, therefore, liable to be set aside.

26. In view of the R.S.S. EMPHASIS on the cultural aspect of the Sangh, it would be pertinent to point out the connotation of the word 'culture'. The definition of 'Sanskriti' given by Dyankoshkar Dr. S.V. Katkar [sic] is as under:–

> 'ज्ञानि राष्ट्रादि संघांनां साफल्यं चरितस्य यत्
> व्यक्तं संस्कृति शद्बेन भाषा शस्त्रात्मकं मनु' (ज्ञानकोष)

It is difficult to define 'culture'. It is possible to give connotation of the word 'culture'. The word 'culture' denotes a trend of impression on the mind of the society which is peculiar to its own and which again is a cumulative effect on its passion, emotion, thought, speech and action throughout the ages. The term 'Sanskriti' includes the sum total of the characteristics of human [groups] such as communities, nations etc. It is pertinent to note that the word 'Sanskriti' used in the activity of the Sangh does not mean the popular [or] Governmental limited meaning as pertaining to act [sic], drama, music, dance etc. The word 'Sanskritik' or cultural used in the Sangh work has a very wide sweep and has to be understood as expounded by the Guide and Philosopher of the R.S.S. Shri Golwalkar in his speeches and writings. These include all aspects of society or nation viz. Political, social, economic, customary, morality, language, script and in general the Hindu way of life inclusive of faiths of various groups in distinct tenets, practices etc.

27. Now if this is the Sanskritic work which the R.S.S. founder postulated to carry out in the country through the medium of R.S.S. read with the 'Pratidyna' incorporated in the Constitution and the Prarthana daily recited, it must be held that the R.S.S. activity is akin to a work for a political purpose, though the R.S.S. as an Organisation eschews participation in active politics of power as of policy. Nevertheless its members may and do take part in politics subject to the present policy limitations of the Constitution. It is undisputed that several members of the R.S.S. are actively participating in political activity and many of them are even members of Parliament and several of them are in the Union and State Cabinets.

28. In view of this position in fact and in law it is submitted that by no stretch of imagination the cultural (Sanskritic) patriotic and the social work of R.S.S. can be dubbed either as charitable or religious so as to be regulated, supervised and restricted by an authority appointed to supervise the working of charities. In fact it is because of such subtle nature of such purpose that the Law Courts had decided that Trusts of political purposes cannot be enforced or supervised by Courts and as such they do not fall within the concept of charitable trusts or religious trusts.

29. The position in law, it is submitted, has been well settled by English as well as Indian decisions. Our Law is in a way based on English decision. The R.S.S. had cited all the following decisions and relied upon the principles of law, pronounced by the Courts, but the learned Joint Charity Commissioner completely overlooked them and even failed to refer to them in his judgement. The decision is, on this ground alone, liable to be set aside. The R.S.S., therefore, craves leave to reproduce some of them hereunder. In England cases did arise as to what were charitable purposes and which were non-charitable [purposes]. Education was taken to be charitable purpose, being covered by the words 'General Utility'. According to the Halsbury's Laws of English [sic] IIIrd Edition, Vol. IV the Statement of law in regard to Educational purpose vis-a-vis the political purpose is summarised in the following terms:–

> 'In England a Trust for educational purposes where they are subordinated to political purposes are regarded as non-charitable'.

There is another decision in Public Trustees vs. Dey 1957(I) All E.R. 705. reported in 1957(I) All E.R. 705 in regard to a Trust where moneys were required to be utilised for the purposes of a particular hobby of the creator of the Trust for a certain scientific research in the manner he desired, the Court observed:–

> '. . . Instant trust was only to conduct a research into an aspect which can be considered to be a task of General Utility, *but was akin to a Trust for political purposes.*'

30. In Bonar Law Memorial Trusts vs. Commr. of Inland Revenue (1933) Seventeen Tax Cases 508 [1933 17 T.C. 508.], it was observed as under:–

> 'The fact that education was entrusted to Conservative Party would not, I think, affect the validity of the trust, if in truth it was a trust for education, but on the other hand if the true view is that it was a trust for education, lectures and so forth were subsidiary

to that which was the main and dominating purpose, then the fact that lectures and so forth would be educative would not be sufficient to make the trust a trust for Charitable purposes only'.

31. In re. Hopkinson Lloyds Bank Limited vs. Baher reported in 1949(1) All E.R. 346 it was observed:–

'. . . an educational fund to be utilised at the absolute discretion of the trustees for the advancement of adult education with particular reference, *to the following purpose, that is to say, the education of men and women of all classes on the lines of the Labour party's memorandum headed "A note on Education in the Labour Party"*. It was held that the direction to the trustees to have particular reference to memorandum of the Labour Party dominated the whole Trust'.

32. The learned Judge pointed out that 'Political [propaganda] masquerading, using the [word] not in any sinister sense, as education is not charitable'.

33. In Halsbury's Laws of England, 4th Edn. Vol. V. para 558, the position is summarised thus:–

'558. Political purposes. A trust for the attainment of political objects is invalid, not because it is illegal (for everyone is at liberty to advocate or promote by any Lawful means a change in the Law), but because the Court has no means of judging whether a proposed change in the Law will or will not be for the public benefit and therefore, cannot say that a gift to secure the change is a charitable gift. Any purpose with the object of influencing the legislature is a political purpose; and a trust for furthering the views of a particular political party, whether under the guise of an educational centre or a fund for adult education on party lines, is not charitable; but a trust for a purpose which is charitable is not rendered non-charitable even if the trust instrument envisages the use of political means to achieve the charitable object'.

34. In Titley's case reported in (1923) 1 Ch. 258 House of Lord's decision by Lord Haldane pointed out that 'a distinction exists between a patriotic intention and charitable intention and this intention is not only in language but in substance'.

'In the case of gift for a charitable purpose, there is a desire to profit people who would not be profited without a gift that is the dominant motive. In the case of patriotism there is desire to fulfil one dominant purpose – that is to benefit the cause of the country to which you belong. These are two different heads of intentions, different perhaps not in such a way that they never overlap but in such a fashion as to distinguish the one from the other'.

35. The learned Joint Charity Commissioner has in clear terms accepted that the work of R.S.S. is for the uplift of people of Bharat Varsh, that is patriotic, and further that in their present day activity no religious ritual are observed. These findings it is submitted take away the jurisdiction of the Charity Commissioner, as these are different distinct heads of intention falling outside Sec. 2(13) of the Act. The view taken by its Joint Charity Commissioner is against the Law of the land, and the decision is liable to be set aside.

These prepositions have been accepted by the Indian High Court, as well as Supreme Court of India. See 1962 S.C. 1589 supra, and the marginally-noted cases.

36. The Joint Charity Commissioner has taken a totally erroneous view and misconceived the entire concept of 'Religion' and 'Religious purpose' and appears to have widened the scope with a view to bring in the R.S.S. within S. 2(13). This observation at the end of para 16 to the effect that 'the aims and objects of R.S.S. as stated above have so wide a connotation that they can be interpreted to cover ritualistic activities laid down by Hinduism as commonly understood. It is this capability which is decisive of religious nature of the trust', shows his wholly erroneous approach. The learned Joint Charity Commissioner did not follow that the word Hindu or Hindu Dharma as used in the activity, constitution and working of R.S.S. has not the slightest shade of any religious activity as understood under the B.P.T. Act, 1950 or Constitution of India and as decided by Courts of Law. The work, activity of R.S.S. is purely and predominantly secular in its nature. The learned Joint Charity Commissioner was wrong in interpreting the [word] 'Dharma' as religion. Dharma is a way of life which sustains the society. Similarly it appears that the learned Joint Charity Commissioner has bias and prejudice for the [word] Hindu that is why his conclusion of identifying the word as connoting and pertaining towards religion is totally erroneous.

37. The learned Joint Charity Commissioner has again confused Religion and Culture. The function held by R.S.S. on Guru Poornima or Sankranti are social and as such 'Cultural' and not 'Religious'. The non-applicant 1 has in his cross examination in para 19 admitted that 'in all functions of R.S.S. the ultimate idea is to tell swayamsevaks that nation is God and to perform a Puja of nation'. Hence merely holding the cultural functions with above objects the R.S.S. cannot be called a public trust for Religious or Charitable purpose. In respect of the festivals performed by the R.S.S. it may be noted that the festivals chosen are from the social content and not from religious content. The functions or festivals of 'Hindu Samrajya' in 'Mahotsava' 'Dashera or Vijaya Dashimi' and 'Padava or Varsha Pratipada' has a political and social connotation for inspiring in the Swayamsevaks the dream of Hindu Rashtra on the fact that in historical past such a dream was visualised and fulfilled and as such one could do so again by organising the Hindu society. The festivals of 'Raksha Bandhan' and 'Sankrant' are merely social functions to inculcate the feeling of brotherhood and unity in the society. The festival of 'Guru Poornima' is also a political function in the sense that the Flag as mentioned in the constitution is just before the society as symbol of R.S.S. and symbol of age-old culture and as such should be dear to the society as Fod [sic] and everybody should be prepared even to die for the respect and dignity of the said flag. The [word] puja in the said festival has no religious connotation whatsoever but a connotation that we should work for the flag, which stands as symbol of Hindu Rashtra and be ready to sacrifice not only body and mind but also financially. In brief the learned Joint Charity Commissioner totally failed to appreciate these connotations and as such has erred in recording the finding that the activity has religious purpose.

38. In the course of his judgement the learned Joint Charity Commissioner after referring to various passages from the Bunch of Thoughts took the view that the [objects] of R.S.S. are religious. But [from] a perusal of the various passages particularly entitled 'Our World Mission' if understood in proper perspective, and interpreted in its true concept, the R.S.S. cannot be held to be carrying the activity with a religious purpose. '. . . the mission of reorganising the Hindu people on the line of their unique national genius which the Sangh has taken up is not only a great process of true national regeneration of Bharat but also the inevitable precondition to realise the dream of world unity and human welfare'. This indicates that the R.S.S. desires

to dominate the world by cultural conquest by a great process of true national regeneration. The learned Joint Charity Commissioner has failed to properly appreciate and [understand] the sweep of R.S.S. work and activities and arrived at totally misconceived findings and misdirected himself in holding that the R.S.S. work is religious or charitable.

39. According to the definition given in Webster's Dictionary, 'Religion' is the outward act or form by which men indicate their recognition of the existence of a 'God' or 'Gods' having power over their destiny to whom obedience, service, and honour are due. 'Religion' in its accepted sense is a system of 'Divine Faith and Worship' (Refer even to para 7 of Shah's Bombay Public Trust Act, 1950, 3rd Edition, and page 66 para 18 – Religious and Charitable purposes).

40. In this context, it will be interesting to note what is the connotation of its word 'Religion'. 'Religion' in general may be said to have three aspects viz. 'Theology', 'Mysticism' and 'Rituals' [sic] on the other hand, deals with certain [acts] and processes in the physical plane which are regarded [as] establishing links between the visibles and the invisibles. In 'Mysticism' the yearning of the human soul to realise the 'supreme' to obtain union with absorption in 'Brahma' either by introspection or by unifying vision either by contemplation or self-surrender is contemplated. 'Religion' is a state of life bound by monastic vows or action or conduct indicating a belief in reverence for a desire to please a Divine Ruling power or the exercise of practice of rights or observation implying this. Religion would be also recognition on the part of man [of] some higher unseen power, as having control of his destiny and as being entitled to obedience, reverence and worship and the general, mental and moral attitude resulting from this belief, with reference to its effect upon the individual or the community.

41. It is none of the non-applicants averment that religion as expounded above or religious practices as contemplated above are the objects of R.S.S. practices and programmes. The objectives of R.S.S. are mentioned in the Constitution of the R.S.S. to which reference is already made. The learned Joint Charity Commissioner has expressly held that these rituals are not a part of R.S.S. programmes. Nonetheless by a queer process of reasoning and misconception of legal position he arrived at erroneous view of law, which is liable to be set aside. R.S.S. craves leave to refer to and rely upon the commentary of Kanga and Palkhiwala and Income Tax Act Vol. I page 283, at the time of hearing.

42. The learned Joint Charity Commissioner was in error of fact and law in holding that the R.S.S. was covered under Section 9 of the Bombay Public Trust Act, 1950 as its activities fall within the ambit of Section though he has recorded a finding that the activities are for the purpose of promoting patriotism, nationalism and other cultural activities. The entire reasoning and approach is erroneous and liable to be set aside.

43. As already submitted in earlier paragraphs, the concept of 'Dharma' is altogether different from 'Religion' and the use of the words 'Dharma' and 'Sanskriti' in the Constitution of the R.S.S. is to be understood in the sense it has been expounded in the 'Bunch of Thoughts', the life of Dr. Hedgewar and other documents on record for interpretation of these words vis-a-vis the R.S.S. Constitution.

44. The Joint Charity Commissioner is also in error of law and fact in assuming that the word 'Hindu' is synonymous with Hindu Religion. The true position is in the words of Dr. Radhakrishnan, the philosopher politician, 'The term Hindu had originally a territorial and not a credal significance'. The view generally accepted by scholars is that the word Hindu is derived from the River Sindhu, and the people on the Indian side of the Sindhu were called the Hindu by the Persian and later western invaders. Thus 'Hindu' word does not necessarily refer to bond of Religion as has [been] erroneously held by the Joint Charity Commissioner.

45. The decision of the learned Joint Charity Commissioner further suffers from his failure to consider all evidence on record, and [vitiates] its final order. The learned Joint Charity Commissioner is in error [in] not considering the effect of the several admissions made by the non-applicant no. 1, in his pleadings and deposition. He was bound to consider the legal effect of the admissions on record, particularly because that was the main evidence regarding the actual practice and programme of R.S.S. The findings are vitiated as they are mere conjunctures.

46. The reasoning of the learned Joint Charity Commissioner in paras 17, 18 and 20 of his judgement is based on misapprehension of law and facts. The view that holding of cultural mass programme of Samkrant, Dassera, Vyas Puja with patriotic aim is a religious activity, it is submitted [is] perverse. The observation that such functions amount to outward expression of acts of religious faith and belief is equally misleading.

47. The learned Joint Charity Commissioner failed to correctly appreciate the submissions made by the R.S.S. during the course of hearing, and his approach appears to be biased by his own personal views about the concept of the words 'Dharma', 'Sanskriti', 'Religion', Dhamma Shastra etc. Though he referred extensively to the passage from Bunch of Thoughts, he failed to grasp the correct meaning, the context and the concept given to it by the R.S.S.

48. The judgement/decision of the learned Joint Charity Commissioner from paragraphs No. 12 to 18 is wholly erroneous and it is apparent that the interpretation made by him of the Constitution of the R.S.S., 'Hindu', 'Religion', 'Dharma', 'Sanskriti' and such other words, and phrases, aims, objects and purpose and the ultimate finding that the R.S.S. is proved to be Public, Religious and Charitable Trust is liable to be set aside.

50 [sic]. In any event the order saddling costs of Rs. 200/- for no fault on the part of the applicant is a grave miscarriage of justice and erroneous exercise of jurisdiction, assuming any such power existed to award costs. The order is totally wrong as the appeal was heard on the day it was fixed for hearing. The Court has acted perversely in saddling costs on applicants for the acts [of] commission and omission, if any, of the respondents themselves.

PRAYER:–

It is prayed that:–

(1) The record of the Assistant Charity Commissioner and Joint Charity Commissioner be sent for and after perusal thereof.

(2) Decision of Joint Charity Commissioner, dated 11-1-78 be set aside and the order dated 22-5-74 passed by the Deputy Charity Commissioner, Nagpur be restored,

(3) Pending hearing of the matter, operation of the appellate order dated 11-1-78 be stayed by appropriate direction, and

(4) be pleased to grant such other relief as may be permissible including that of saddling heavy costs on the Respondents.

Nagpur,
Dt.

General Secretary,
R.S.S.
Advocate,
Counsel for R.S.S., Nagpur.

VERIFICATION

I, professor Rajendrasinghji, Sar Karyawah, R.S.S., Nagpur, do hereby verify that the contents of paras 1 to 50 are true to my knowledge derived partly from my knowledge and the record of the case, and the submissions of law made therein are true from information received from my Counsel and believed to be true by me. Verified and signed this 6th day of March, 1978 at Nagpur.

Applicant

Appendix 9

'Limaye for consensus on RSS, other affiliates'

(*The Times of India*, 21 August 1977)

New Delhi: Mr. Madhu Limaye, a Janata Party general secretary has said his party should consider all aspects of the integration of volunteer-cum-cultural organisations, consult Mr. Jayaprakash Narayan and achieve integrated thinking on the subject.

These views were expressed by him in a note circulated to the members of the party's working committee, which concluded its three-day meeting here yesterday.

The following is the full text of Mr. Limaye's note:

During the long stay of Mr. Jayaprakash Narayan in Bombay, I had an occasion to discuss with him the question of volunteer organisations and youth training programmes. He asked me whether I had any dialogue with the leaders of the RSS in this regard.

I told him of my discussions with Mr. B. Deoras in the early seventies. He asked me to take up the question of integration of volunteer organisations with the leaders of the RSS. I met Mr. Deoras and Mr. Madhavrao Mule in the month of May in Bombay, I placed before them the following points.

NO RELIGIOUS CURB

1. That the coming together of the large number of RSS workers and other supporters of the JP movement under the roof of Mrs. Indira Gandhi's jails had promoted better understanding among the RSS cadres and other people. We should take advantage of this and try to achieve the integration of all volunteer-cum-cultural organisations who were in agreement with the principles of the JP movement.

   By way of illustration, I mentioned bodies like the Rashtra Seva Dal, Tarun Shanti Sena, Chatra Sangharsha Wahini and the RSS. I said that the formation of an integrated volunteer organisation would immensely strengthen the cause of national reconstruction in India.
2. The integrated volunteer organisation, if and when set up, should be open to all citizens of India, irrespective of their faith and religion.
3. The volunteer organisation should not be subordinate to any political party. It should be a fully independent, autonomous voluntary-cum-cultural organisation.
4. There should be friendly relations between the Janata Party and this integrated volunteer organisation. There should not be any organisational tie between the two, but only ideological affinity and a community of ideals; and
5. The main task of this integrated organisation should be character building and training of dedicated workers for national service.

Mr. Deoras and Mr. Mule did not express any dissent from any of these propositions. They, however, felt that integration, would necessarily be a long process. In the meanwhile mutual understanding and co-operation should be promoted.

As to opening the doors to people professing different faiths, the RSS leaders said the RSS itself was having an internal discussion on this question. Mr. Deoras related to me his tour experiences and also told me about his future tour programmes. He said he would return to Nagpur during the monsoon and that we could have further discussions at Nagpur during the rainy season.

NO QUICK RESULTS

They had apprehensions about the volunteer organisation being treated as a subordinate agency of the Janata party. This would not be helpful, they held. I told them that I was quite clear in my mind about this and I did not think of this volunteer organisation as an agency of the party or its subsidiary.

I also said that I had no doubt that the process of integration would be a long one, and that it could not be achieved within the space of a few months.

I further suggested that an informal meeting of six or seven representatives with long experience of the working of volunteer organisations should be called to discuss the problem. Some leading Sarvodayis should also be associated with these efforts. I requested both of them to discuss the matter with Mr. Jayaprakash Narayan. They told me that they themselves wanted to meet JP and exchange ideas with him.

After these talks, there have been no further discussions with the RSS on this subject. I once mentioned the matter to the Prime Minister. He was in favour of the idea of integration of volunteer organisations and said that if the RSS leaders so desired, he would be glad to meet them.

He, however, made it clear that such discussions would be fruitful if the desire for a get-together was mutual.

The RSS is a very old organisation. It has been in existence now for more than 50 years. Its founder was a nationalist and took an active part in the freedom movement. It was only after differences arose over the communal award that the RSS people gradually drifted away from the mainstream of the Indian freedom movement.

In the last few years since persistent efforts were being made to bring the various opposition parties together, inevitably some understanding developed between the RSS people, with their close links with the Jana Sangh, and members of other political parties. We worked together in the JP movement.

Within a few days of the proclamation of the emergency, the RSS was banned and a large number of its leaders and workers was arrested. Because of the common sufferings undergone by the victims of the emergency, a basis exists for further understanding and integration.

In the course of its 50 years of existence, the RSS people have developed a number of family organisations, such as Vidyarthi Parishad, Rashtriya Sevika Samiti, Bharatiya Mazdoor Sangh, Vishwa Hindu Parishad and so on.

Integration of student and youth organisations, women's organisation and trade union federations and, finally, the integration of volunteer organisations, including the RSS, will greatly strengthen the process of integration within the Janata party.

If we begin to work together in all departments of national life, sources of discord will be eliminated. Otherwise, there will be a conflict of loyalties and tension will inevitably increase.

The Janata Party should consider all aspects of the problems, consult Mr. Jayaprakash Narayan and achieve integrated thinking on this subject.

Appendix 10

'All responsible for Janata crisis'

(By Atal Bihari Vajpayee, *The Indian Express*, 2 August 1979)

The revolution of March 1977 demonstrated the unshakable faith of our people in democracy. With the establishment of the first non-Congress Government at the Centre, hopes were aroused that a new chapter will unfold in our history. Within 27 months, however, those who had suffered during the Emergency in jail or outside and who had been voted to power at the crest of unbounded public enthusiasm, squandered this opportunity for petty, personal and factional reasons.

In retrospect, the responsibility to this state of affairs must be shared in differing degrees by all groups and their leaders in the Janata Party. Group loyalties and personal ambition marked the very first steps of the infant party.

It is no secret that when the PM was to be elected in March 1977, members of the erstwhile Jana Sangh and the Socialists were in favour of Mr. Jagjivan Ram. They felt that the elevation of a Harijan to the Prime Ministership of our country would have a positive impact and that his proven administrative acumen as well as his ability to get along with people of diverse backgrounds would be an asset to the new administration.

However, when this proposal was put before Chaudhry Charan Singh, he rejected it outright and indicated that he would support Mr. Morarji Desai who had suffered during the Emergency rather than accept a person who had moved the motion in Parliament for approval of the Emergency. Once two of the three senior leaders had come together, the claim of the third was not further pressed. This pattern was to be repeated more than once in the ensuing two years.

Chaudhry Saheb has [nurtured] since then a deep grievance against the erstwhile Jana Sangh. Perhaps he is unaware that even if he had commanded a numerical majority (which he clearly did not command), neither Mr. Morarji Desai, nor Mr. Jagjivan Ram would have joined the cabinet and the state of affairs reached today would have come to prevail from the very beginning.

In fact, even at that time Chaudhry Charan Singh's letter supporting Mr. Desai came as relief of a kind to many of us since we more confident of persuading Mr. Jagjivan Ram to work under Mr. Desai than of persuading Chaudhry Saheb or Mr. Desai to work under Mr. Jagjivan Ram.

No formal vote

The manner in which this crisis and was 'resolved' contained an important portent of how crises would be handled in the Janata Party in the coming years: the sad fact is that in this as in later crises, the Members of Parliament and the national executive of the party were not taken into confidence about the negotiations that were going on behind the scenes.

When the Janata MPs assembled in the Gandhi Peace Foundation Hall they were taken by surprise at the announcement that the leader of the Parliamentary Party would be chosen by consensus. Among those who were opposed to election was Mr. Raj Narain who even threatened to walk out of the party meeting. Initially it had been decided to leave the matter to Mr. Jayaprakash Narayan. But at the suggestion of Chaudhry Charan Singh, Acharya Kripalani was also included. The two were asked to ascertain the wishes of the members, avoiding the need for a formal vote.

I vividly recall the dilemma that confronted the Acharya and JP in deciding the crucial leadership issue. It was also suggested that the person chosen as leader should relinquish office after two or three years and the other person should become PM for the remainder of the term.

The wrangle was not confined to the Prime Ministership. Having conceded the Prime Ministership to Congress (O), the BLD group sought the party presidentship for themselves. However, the others could not be persuaded and with great reluctance, Chaudhry Charan Singh agreed to Mr. Chandra Shekhar's nomination.

The Janata Government was formed in a situation without precedent before the five constituents had merged into one party. Each constituent, with an eye on the next election, sought to capture the party apparatus and in this the Jana Sangh with its disciplined cadre and the BLD with its large caste base in some northern States were the main contenders. Controversies arose over enrolment forms and the party constitution controversies which the Executive took long to sort out. Meanwhile, mass enthusiasm for the party evaporated.

Infrastructure

Although the Janata Party had been formed by the merger of five parties, the Cabinet was constituted on the basis of quota for each, Congress (O) getting a disproportionate share. Group loyalties hardened further during the formation of the State Governments. The former BLD and Jana Sangh came to an understanding which excluded other constituents. By this time the power struggle within the Janata Party had taken deep roots. It acquired a new dimension with Chaudhry Charan Singh's inability to reconcile himself to being No. 2 in the Central Cabinet.

An active and imaginative leadership would have created an infrastructure for the party all over the country by convening State and district level conferences by holding workers' camps at divisional level, by drawing towards it a large number of intellectuals, trade union leaders, youth leaders and women's organisations who had worked for the restoration of democracy and the victory of the Janata Party.

But with the Party President immersed in the distribution of State Assembly tickets and, along with the general secretaries, engaged in handling innumerable internecine quarrels, all these steps so crucial to the consolidation of the party were altogether neglected.

The performance of the Janata Governments both at the Centre as well as in the States, was better than that of the earlier Congress regime. But it fell short of public expectations. Factional quarrels within the party and public airing of grievances, even by ministers, vitiated the atmosphere and sullied the image of the Janata Party and prevented proper projection of the achievements of the governments.

Chaudhry Charan Singh's statement describing his colleagues as 'a pack of impotent men', and his subsequent ouster from the Cabinet along with Mr. Raj Narain, are events which do not need recapitulation. Mr. Advani and I have been blamed by some for being instrumental in Chaudhry Charan Singh's return to the Cabinet. It is true that we were active on his behalf. We were motivated solely by the desire to maintain the unity of the party. Little did we realise that our good intentions would lead to such an unforeseen, unwelcome destination.

Much time was lost in the process and ultimately Mr. Raj Narain was not taken back –

an act that could hardly have increased his identification with the party, or his love for the Prime Minister. Meanwhile, the Kisan Sammelan was formed and very large sum of money was collected. The Sammelan quickly assumed the proportions of a rival party set-up.

On the very day of Chaudhry Saheb's return to the Cabinet, by a grievous coincidence, Mr. Ram Naresh Yadav dropped four Ministers in UP. These included two junior Ministers of the erstwhile Jana Sangh. The Jana Sangh group, in its turn, reacted out of all proportion to this slight.

Mr. Yadav had earlier on several occasions given evidence of his inability to lead efficiently such a large State as UP. This had been acknowledged by Chaudhry Charan Singh himself but he could not bring himself to agreeing to a change in the UP leadership. Yadav lost his Chief Ministership through a vote in the JLP and Mr. Banarasi Das, not from the BLD was proposed by Chaudhry Saheb.

Having succeeded in displacing Mr. Yadav, the dissidents should have co-operated with Mr. Banarasi Das. However, Mr. Das raised the question of dual membership and refused to include the Jana Sangh in his Cabinet till this matter was resolved.

In a chain reaction, the dissidents voted with the Opposition in the Legislature to try and bring him down – an act of gross indiscipline. Accordingly, the relaxation of tensions that had followed Chaudhry Charan Singh's reinduction died out swiftly, and gave way to intensified recriminations. Thereafter the RSS bogey was bandied about by Chaudhry Saheb's men systematically, persistently and abusively.

The UP crisis swiftly engulfed the neighbouring States, amidst allegations that the States were being destabilised from Delhi.

Indiscipline in the party was in fact pervasive. It was connived at by senior leaders, and such disapproval as was expressed from time to time was purely verbal and for the record.

The Big-4, particularly the PM, had it in their power to rise above the petty considerations of the factions, to enforce discipline in the party and to ensure stability in the States and an effective government at the Centre. Such direction, alas, was never forthcoming.

Rumour

Much has been said about the political role of the RSS and its alleged involvement in recent communal riots. In the communal riots at Sambhal, the majority community was the target. In Aligarh, riots erupted after a quarrel between two wrestlers of different communities – a situation that a district administration of minimum competence should have easily controlled. In Jamshedpur, it started with an attack on a Ram Naumi procession.

In Purnea, a Congress (I) notable sent men galloping on horse-back in the night to spread a rumour that three girls – a Harijan, an Adivasi and his own daughter – had been raped by Muslims and to obtain firm pledges of revenge. In Nadia, riots followed the depredations of dacoit gangs. Even if some individual RSS youth, as those belonging to other groups were subsequently involved can one on that account tar the whole organisation with the communal brush?

The truth is that communal riots have their origin in minor incidents. These are blown up by anti-social elements of both sides and petty politicians also play their part. Passions are aroused, and if the local administration is inept, partisan or demoralised, there is bloodshed, looting and arson. There remains, however, in India fundamental amity between all communities who have lived side by side over the centuries by and large in harmony and peace.

Apprehensions about the RSS aiming at capturing political power are without foundation.

Its very character, its composition, the social strata from which it draws its cadre, its day-to-day activities, are such that it cannot mobilise support from the masses of a country like India where there is so much diversity of religion, language, caste, etc., even though it has built up a country-wide organisation of patriotic disciplined youth which is the envy of many.

Recently the RSS bogey has been assiduously built up by some BLD leaders as retaliation for the refusal by the erstwhile Jana Sangh to destabilise the Centre. So far has their obsession for office carried them that those who were calling their colleagues 'impotent' for not acting against Mrs. Gandhi yesterday are today seeking and appreciating her support ostensibly to fight the danger of the RSS. Having said that I must also add that the RSS, claiming to be a social and cultural organisation, should have taken greater pains to demonstrate that they did not seek a political role. Patronising a press that take sides in the sordid politics of power, involvement in youth bodies that interact with political parties, participating in trade union rivalries such as the one which recently brought enormous misery to the people of Delhi by callously cutting off the water supply – these do not help an organisation to establish apolitical credentials.

Challenge

It is possible that some people genuinely feel apprehensive about the RSS. A certain onus accordingly devolved on the RSS, an onus that has not been discharged effectively by the RSS. Its repudiation of the theocratic form of the State was welcome, yet the question could legitimately be asked – why does it not open its doors to non-Hindus? Recent statements of the RSS Chief, Mr. Deoras, indicate that non-Hindus are being encouraged to join the organisation. A national corollary of this process would be clear enunciation by the RSS that by 'Hindu Rashtra', it means the Indian nation which includes non-Hindus as equal members.

The other course of action open to the RSS could be to function only as a Hindu religion-cum-social-cultural organisation wedded to the task of eradicating the evils prevailing in Hindu society and revitalising it to face the challenges of modern times. The kind of selfless service that the RSS has rendered in times of natural calamities has endeared it even to its critics and has established beyond doubt its capacity for constructive work for ameliorating the suffering of those who are in need of help. Such an organisation will draw support and sustenance from members of various political parties as has been the case with institutions like the Arya Samaj.

The Indian polity cannot survive unless it is rooted in certain ideals. Among these are commitment to democracy, secularism, the equal participation of all communities and religions in national life, the upliftment of Harijans, Adivasis and the millions of the desperately poor. The country must develop on modern, scientific lines, ensuring at the same time social and distributive justice.

Today we face a crisis of a magnitude which nations face only once in several centuries. The pursuit of personal ambition, factional interest and self-aggrandisement, so blatantly displayed by some politicians recently has not only made politicians as a class the object of ridicule but also undermined faith in our political system. Let all politicians search their souls, acknowledge their failings and mend their ways. What is now at stake is not the fortune of a handful of individuals or parties. At stake is the survival of our nation.

Appendix 11

'Modern Hate'

(By Susanne Hoeber Rudolph and Lloyd I. Rudolph, *The New Republic*, 22 March 1993)

On Inauguration Day, Bill Clinton told the country and the world a story about how 'a generation raised in the shadows of the cold war assumes new responsibilities in a world warmed by the sunshine of freedom but threatened still by ancient hatreds'. The new president seemed to have in mind such things as ethnic cleansing and religious fundamentalism, the first a deceptive metaphor invented by extreme nationalist Serbs, the second a ubiquitous term that relieves politicians, news anchors and policy intellectuals from thinking about the complexities of the 'other'.

One event that fed the country's growing preoccupation with ancient hatreds occurred last December, when 'Hindu fundamentalists' tore down a mosque built in the sixteenth century by the first Mughal emperor, Babur, in Ayodhya, a small town in eastern Uttar Pradesh, India's most populous state. Its destruction was the climax of three tumultuous years during which Hindu nationalist Bharatiya Janata Party piqued emotions over the mosque. It held that Babur had destroyed a temple on Lord Rama's birthsite in order to build what came to be known as the Babri Masjid (Babur's Mosque); thus, Hindus should reclaim their heritage by building a new temple to Lord Rama on the site of the mosque. More than 2,500 people were killed in the retaliatory violence that followed the destruction of the Babri Masjid. In January violence erupted again in Bombay, where the police openly abetted burning and vandalism. At the end of February, the BJP attempted to hold a mass rally in New Delhi to bring down the Congress party government.

But recent news accounts that depict the violence as an outgrowth of old animosities are misleading. Hindus and Muslims in India under the Mughal emperor Akbar, the nationalistic leadership of Mahatma Gandhi and the Congress governments of Jawaharlal Nehru have gotten along more often than they have gone for each other's throats. So did Serbs, Croats and Muslims under Tito in Yugoslavia. Clinton and others too easily invoke 'ancient hatreds' to explain what are really contemporary conflicts. The question, in other words, is not why old conflicts are flaring up anew, but rather why traditionally harmonious mosaics have been shattered.

Before Christmas, the Hanukkah card section of the University of Chicago bookstore featured a seasonal card depicting two Santas, one with a white beard, one with a brown one, the first carrying the regulation Santa bag, the second carrying a menorah. A scholar of India looks at that card and says, 'How Indian!' St. Nicholas integrated into a Jewish festival! Societies with a plurality of religions can and often do work out symbolic settlements. Until recently, the ability to reach such settlements was the dominant theme in Indian history and in its post-independence politics. Friendships are as 'ancient' as hatreds. The face we see depends on what human agents cause us to see.

Looking at that Hanukkah card, we were reminded of a friend of ours, an observant Muslim, one of the numerous South Asian diaspora in Chicago. As a child in India, she was once asked to participate in a small community drama about the life of Lord Krishna. Krishna is the blue 'Hindu' god adored by shepherdesses, who dance for his pleasure. They exemplify through their human passion the quest of the devout soul for the lord. Not exactly a Muslim monotheist's theme. She was invited to dance as a shepherdess with other schoolgirls. Her father forbade it: Muslims don't dance. In that case, said the drama's director, we will cast you as Krishna. All you have to do is stand there in the usual Krishna pose, a flute at your mouth. Her father consented. She played Krishna.

Line-crossing seemed as natural to that Krishna-playing child as it did to Mahatma Gandhi. In his autobiography, *The Story of My Experiments with Truth*, he recalls that his devout mother regularly visited the tomb of a Muslim *pir* and followed Jain ideas about self-suffering and non-violence. Her un-self-conscious ecumenism was common in Gandhi's birthplace, Kathiawad, a cosmopolitan entrepôt area bordering the Arabian sea. Gandhi began his historic career in South Africa, working for migrant Muslim businessmen from the same region.

With about 110 million Muslim citizens, India is the second-largest Muslim country in the world, after Indonesia. Islam takes many forms, from the most severe monotheism to a Sufi mysticism and devotion that features worship of saints and their relics – practices repugnant to a more austere orthodoxy. Sufi *pirs* and their magnificent tombs attract Hindu as well as Muslim pilgrims from all parts of the subcontinent. None is more renowned than the Dargah at Ajmer, the burial place of Kwaja Nuin-ud-din Chisti [sic], founder in the twelfth century of a family of saints and courtiers, a shrine second only to Mecca in the eyes of South Asian Muslims. Cultural practices mingle and mix. Hindu practices persist among converts to Islam – dietary laws are followed, marriage boundaries observed, festivals celebrated. Aristocratic north Indian culture, its language and manners, its music and cuisine, remained distinctively Persian at least until the time of Nehru, embodying the idioms of Mughal court culture. The region's leading performers of Hindu devotional music, the Dagar brothers, are Muslims. Village Muslims, like their urban brothers, share in local or neighbourhood Ramayana performances and watch as eagerly as the rest of the nation when Doordarshan, Indian state-run television, airs the eighteen-month-long megaseries on the ('Hindu') Ramayana and Mahabharata.

But not all practices promote a composite culture and unity in diversity. Hindu and Muslim religious sensibilities have vacillated between tendencies to naturalise and demonise differences. Political language in the nationalist era sometimes used religious symbols to make politics meaningful to common people for whom religion was a natural idiom. Religious language, however, is capable of many different forms of expression.

Some nationalists used Hindu religious symbolism that excluded Muslims. B.G. Tilak, India's most influential popular leader before Mahatma Gandhi, led the way in inventing 'communalism', the term Indians use for community exclusivism and chauvinism. In the 1890s, keen to build a mass following, he revived a Maharashtrian festival commemorating the birth of Shiva's elephant-headed son, Ganesh, Hinduism's most beloved deity. For ten days each year villagers poured into cities and towns to celebrate and hear recitations of Hindu epic poetry. Ganapati festivals became occasions for clashes with Muslims when paramilitary 'Ganesh guards' directed noisy parades past mosques at prayer time. Muslims began to retaliate by acts of profanation and desacralisation, 'killing cows' and cutting auspicious peepul trees. Bengali nationalists wrote plays and songs that alienated Muslims by using the theme of opposition to Muslim kings as a surrogate for opposition to British rule.

Secular nationalism took different forms: Nehru maintained that science should ask and answer all questions; Gandhi believed that spiritual truth could be found in all religions. At Gandhi's prayer meetings, the Gita, the Koran and the Bible were read. He favoured a national language – Hindustani – which could accommodate Urdu, the language of North Indian Muslims, and Hindi, the language of North Indian Hindus.

'Ancient hatreds' are thus made as much as they are inherited. To call them ancient is to pretend they are primordial forces, outside of history and human agency, when often they are merely synthetic antiques. Intellectuals, writers, artists and politicians 'make' hatreds. Films and videos, texts and textbooks, certify stories about the past, the collective memories that shape perceptions and attitudes.

Before democracy, modernisation and the nation-state, Hinduism was loose, open and diverse, a web of local and regional sectarian groupings defined by a sacred geography of places and events, deities and temples. The very term 'Hinduism' was an abstraction, a word used by outsiders to describe a place and a people, not an institutionalised religion. Travellers – Hsuan Tsang, the seventh-century Chinese Buddhist pilgrim, and Alberuni, the eleventh-century Arab savant accompanying Mahmud of Ghazni – designated trans-Indus peoples as Hindus.

Instead of Hindus, there were followers of saints (*sants*): Kabir followers and Dadu followers, Vaishnavites in Gujarat and Bengal, Lingayats in Karnataka and Shivites in Tamilnadu, pursuing distinctive doctrines and practices. It is a truism to say Hinduism had no church. There was no pope, no ecclesia, no bishops to enunciate what was orthodox and heterodox, much less heretical or blasphemous. Great debates at Banaras reverberated through the centuries. Great teachers such as Shankara in the eighth century and Ramanuja in the twelfth were revered. But there was no all-India, transhistorical authority. Even today a local religious teacher in Jaipur or Bangalore is likely to be the person of greatest authority for her followers; no one is in a position to discipline her or to question her doctrine or ritual practices.

If there was no standard version of Hinduism until yesterday, then when and how did the day before yesterday end? How did it happen that the Bharatiya Janata Party was able to hijack Hinduism, replacing its diversity, multivocality and generativity with a monotheistic Ram cult? An answer can be found in the history of storytelling. The ancient legend of Ram, the virtuous god-king, incarnation of Vishnu, who wandered in exile for twelve years with his wife Sita before vanquishing the Southern demon Ravana, can be found all over India. It is a moral tale, exemplifying what right conduct should be between a king and his subjects and among generations, genders and relatives. Ram was an intimate deity, his representations infinitely diverse by region and locale. He was the subject of thousands of *Ramayanas* in many languages, of village drama cycles, of stories told by grandmothers, and today of epic comic books.

In time, Ram stories became consolidated. In *The Life of a Text: Performing the Ramcharitmanas of Tulsidas*, Philip Lutgendorf writes that this sixteenth-century *Ramayana* was regarded 'not merely as the greatest modern Indian epic, but as something like a living sum of Indian culture'. Lutgendorf details how during the nineteenth century the recitations of the *Ramayana* became the vehicle for the 'rise of the eternal religion' and how, through the *manas*, Hindus became a 'people of the book'. In 1984 the vastly popular recitals of the text, boxed in a set of eight audio cassettes, was the 'hottest-selling recording in the thriving cassette stalls of Banaras', hotter even than the immensely popular cassettes of Hindi film music.

In January 1987 an eighteen-month-long serial of the *Ramayana* based on the *manas* began airing at 9:30 a.m., prime time, on state-run T.V. *Ramayana* episodes quickly became the most popular programme ever shown, attracting an estimated 100 million viewers, roughly the size of the audience for presidential debates in America. On Sundays streets were deserted throughout India. Everyone was watching, even knots of cycle rickshaw drivers crowded in front of T.V. store windows.

The *Ramayana* 'megaseries' took advantage of a new space for religious discourse in India, Pakistan, Iran, Oman and elsewhere, a public space outside the private arenas of family and village, temple and mosque. In this space a new public culture is being created and consumed. Distant persons, strangers, create representations of public culture for anonymous viewers. Values and symbols, meaning systems and metaphors, can be standardised for national consumption.

And what did the series do to grandmother's version of the Rama tale? Or to the village performance? In Gatiali, located in the state of Rajasthan, the local village production of *Ramayana* wasn't performed in 1989. Village leaders who watched the television version had been impressed. The local version seemed to them amateurish by comparison. Why take the trouble and expense to put on an unworthy, moth-eaten version? Other Hinduish megaseries followed – such as the great epic *Mahabharata*, *Chanakya*, a Hindu nationalist reinvention of the Mauryan empire's cunning prime minister. Together they helped stamp out diversity and localism, replacing them with a national, standardised version of Hinduism, what historian and social critic Romila Thapar has characterised as syndicated, semitised Hinduism, a Hinduism of one God, one book, one place, one people, a religion resembling exclusivist versions of Judaism, Christianity and Islam.

Ten months after the *Ramayana* megaseries, the Vishua [sic] Hindu Parishad (World Hindu Council) called on Hindus throughout India to make holy bricks, inscribed with Rama's name, for use at Ayodhya. There, at the site of Rama's birth, and on the place of the Babri Masjid, they would build a temple to Rama. Construction was deferred during the national elections of 1989. The Bharatiya Janata Party, which had captured only two seats with 8 percent of the vote in 1984, now garnered eighty-six seats with 11 percent. Its modest 3 percentage point increase in electoral votes suggests that the party gained eighty-four seats more by virtue of making electoral alliances than by an increase in popular support, but its electoral gains put religion in the political spotlight. After another two years the BJP emerged from the May-June 1991 election as India's second-largest party, its vote share bounding upward from 11 percent to 20 percent and its seats in Parliament increasing from eighty-six to 118. L.K. Advani told India's electorate that if the countries of Western Europe and the United States can call themselves Christian, India should be free to call itself Hindu.

One of the ways to think about the recent savaging of the Babri Masjid by young Hindu men is to see it as a renegotiation of political and economic power and status, or rather as a sign of the pathology of renegotiation. The youths we saw standing on the domes of the doomed mosque were wearing city clothes, shirts and trousers, not the *kurta* and *dhotis* of villagers or the urban poor. They looked like clerks, boys from urban lower-middle-class families. They are the educated unemployed, not the poor and illiterate. Frustrated by the lack of good jobs and opportunities, they are victims of modernisation, seeking to victimise others – like 'pampered' Muslims. In an India where, despite its problems, the number of persons under the poverty line has been declining and entrepreneurship expanding exponentially, their expectations have run well ahead of available opportunities.

Social mobility in India has become a widespread phenomenon. Liberalisation and economic growth have enormously expanded the opportunities for many Indians. The '80s witnessed the highest economic growth rates of the last five decades. Green revolutionaries have grown prosperous on high-yielding varieties of wheat; doctors and engineers educated at government expense find public sector jobs; craftspeople who have parleyed workshops into lucrative enterprises supply large manufacturers. Such mobility is unhinging a severely hierarchical society, creating social stress bred of envy and resentment. Old, established Hindu middle classes, mostly from the upper literate and landed castes, suddenly see a whole range of Johnny-come-latelies at their side who only yesterday were their inferiors in status and income, both low-caste folk and Muslims. The hatred that led Nathuram Godse to kill Mahatma Gandhi was bred in the resentment of upper castes on the way down. Gandhi had mobilised the periphery against the centre, the lower castes and village poor against Brahmanical orthodoxy. These are conflicts generated by individuals using the opportunities of recent history.

The short-lived Janata party government of 1990, under V.P. Singh, recognised the political implications of the emergence into politics and social power of these new forces, forging an alliance of the 'Backward Classes' (a *raj* euphemism for the disadvantaged lower groups) and Muslims. The Backward Classes, many of them are agricultural castes who have profited from the green revolution, have been demanding quotas in government jobs and education for decades. Their demands threaten the position of urban upper castes who respond to an appeal to Hindu identity, whose long traditions of literacy have given them the advantage in merit-based competitions, and who disproportionately control such jobs.

How is that relevant to the position of Muslims? They do not have such quotas, either in government jobs or in education. The main 'privilege' they have in independent India is immunity for their religiously based family law, which allows 'privileges' such as multiple marriages for men and easy divorce. Muslims also have had tacit guarantees, imperfectly enforced, from state and federal governments to be represented in Cabinet and party posts. These may not be substantial privileges, but to the upper castes in the midst of backlash against their slipping position, it is easier to resent minority 'privileges' for Muslims than for other minorities. At 11 percent, Muslims are a more vulnerable target than the proportionately more numerous and politically more powerful 'Backwards'.

North India's Muslim population was decapitated at independence in 1947, when Muslim landowners and educated professionals, many descendants of Mughal court families, went to Pakistan. They left behind silk weavers in Banaras, gem cutters in Jaipur, poor cultivators and unskilled labourers, hewers of wood and drawers of water. But in recent years Muslims have found new opportunities through migratory labour to the Middle East.

A major component of India's foreign exchange has come from remittances of guest workers in the Gulf, Iraq and other Middle East countries. When several hundred thousand fled the Gulf war in early 1991, the precipitous fall in remittances that followed triggered a foreign exchange crisis that drove India into the arms of the International Monetary Fund and the World Bank. A large proportion of India's guest workers were (and are again) Muslims. For years they sent their earnings home to poor relatives scattered all over India. Their relatives built fancy houses and mosques cheek by jowl with the ostentatious homes and temples of newly rich Hindu neighbours. As Muslim youths joined the sons of green revolution farmers in sporting jeans and sunglasses, as their parents joined Hindu traders in wearing terry-cotton bush suits and driving Rajiv Gandhi's car of choice, the 'Gypsy' off-road vehicle, newly rich Muslims elbowed their way ahead rather than lagging respectfully behind.

Prosperity has also bred resentment and anger among those in North India, Kerala and Bombay accustomed to Muslim invisibility and deference. Hindu professionals and businessmen expect Muslims to serve them as tailors and bakers. Industrial and office workers seeking jobs, better pay or promotions expect them to stick to their traditional occupations – weaving, gem cutting, brass tooling. Hindus often respond to Muslim mobility and wealth by challenging Nehru-style secularism that offers special protection to Islam and Muslims. They decry it as privileging Muslim communalism and stigmatising Hindu communalism. The Hindu backlash to minority protectionism asks, whose country is this anyway? In Bombay in early January, a month after the destruction of the Babri Masjid, the militantly Hindu, Muslim-hating Shiv Sena acted out the fiery images and language of its campaign videos by torching Muslim homes and shops. The Bombay elite's sense of being in charge and safe in India's most cosmopolitan city was shattered when roving bands searched for Muslim names in elegant apartments along hitherto sacrosanct Marine Drive, Club Road and Malabar Hill.

The prospect that the aspiring poor might receive yet another boost from government action helped precipitate the Ayodhya crisis. In August 1990 Prime Minister Singh's minority government implemented the Mandal Commission report. The report recommended 'reservations' – quotas – in federal government employment for Backward Classes. Singh, who had campaigned on the issue, announced that 27 percent of federal jobs were to be reserved for Backward Classes. Together with the current 15 percent for untouchables (those at the bottom of the caste system) and the 7 percent for tribals, roughly their proportions of the population, reservations now totalled 49 percent, a ceiling set by the Supreme Court to maintain the credibility of the equal opportunity clause of the constitution.

Singh's minority government had been held in place by support from a number of left and right parties, including the Hindu-oriented BJP. The BJP leaders, who had not been consulted on the implementation, thought that Singh was ditching their party's support with a view to holding a midterm election that would give him a clear majority. He would appeal to the 'minorities' – untouchables, lower castes, Muslims, tribals who together constituted some 60 percent of India's population. The BJP set out to trump Singh's social justice platform, which pitted the disadvantaged against the advantaged, with a Hindu communal unity appeal.

Indian politics began to polarise around *mandir* (temple) versus Mandal. Within a week, anti-Mandal, anti-reservation violence backed by the Congress Party and the BJP began in New Delhi and spread throughout northern India. Upper-caste students, fearful of lost job opportunities, protested the job reservations by blocking traffic, burning buses, forcing shopkeepers to close their businesses and staging immolation rituals that sometimes ended in tragedy. Building on the discontents, BJP president L.K. Advani set out on a 10,000-kilometre chariot pilgrimage to arrive at Ayodhya for the proposed construction of a Ram temple. The country was convulsed as pro- and anti-pilgrimage violence joined anti-reservation violence and refocused attention from Mandal to *mandir*. Advani was arrested on October 23, 1990, and the BJP formally withdrew its support of Singh's government, which fell on November 7. Advani had succeeded in polarising Indian politics on communal rather than caste-class lines.

The Babri Masjid destruction and the ensuing violence tells us something about the making of 'ancient' hatreds: that they are being made in Lebanon, Bosnia, the republics of the former Soviet Union, Iraq, Israel, South-Central Los Angeles and Crown Heights – all those places where neighbours and friends have turned into foreigners and enemies. The enlightenment's vision prophesied human progress, modernisation predicted affluence with equality and democracy promised fellow feeling and shared citizenship. Together they foretold a world in which Santa Claus would join the menorah in Hanukkah cards, WASPs eat pizza and Anglos tacos, Muslim performers sing Hindu devotional music and Colin Powell could be chairman of the Joint Chiefs of Staff.

Thinking people are less sanguine about rationality, modernisation and democracy reducing ethnic and religious solidarities to harmless dietary differences. Religion has not retreated with increasing media exposure and political participation. The reverse seems to be the case. Religion is on the rise everywhere, from the religious right in Colorado springs to Islamic fundamentalism in Tehran. It exhibits benign enthusiasm, spiritual exaltation and neo-communitarianism on the one hand, exclusionary and even deadly intolerance on the other. As political ideology recedes with the collapse of communism, the politics of identity and community, of religion, ethnicity and gender have begun to occupy the space vacated by political ideology. Directly and indirectly, religion, ethnicity and gender increasingly define what politics is about, from the standing of Muslim personal law and monuments in India to Muslim and Christian Serbs and Croats sharing sovereignty in Bosnia to the Clinton administration's effort to appoint a government that 'looks like America'.

Which identities become relevant for politics is not predetermined by some primordial ancientness. They are crafted in benign and malignant ways in print and electronic media, in textbooks and advertising, in India's T.V. megaseries and America's talk shows, in campaign strategies, in all the places and all the ways that self and other, us and them, are represented in an expanding public culture. The struggle in India between Mandal and *mandir*, between quota government and Hindu nationalism, reminds us that in America too the politics of interest is being overtaken by cultural politics, the politics of gender, family values, race and sexual orientation. When T.V. talking heads and op-ed contributors portray 'mobs' as 'frenzied' and believers as 'fanatic', they have given up the task of discerning the human inducements and political calculations that make politics happen. They have given up making motives visible and showing how they are transformed. 'Ancient hatreds' function like the 'evil empire'. That term too was a projection on a scrim, obscuring the motives and practice that lay behind it. The doctrine of ancient hatreds may become the post-cold war's most robust mystification, a way of having an enemy and knowing evil that deceives as it satisfies. The hatred is modern and may be closer than we think.

Appendix 12

'The Sangh is my soul'

(Atal Bihari Vajpayee, *Organiser*, 7 May 1995)

I came in contact with the RSS in 1939 through Arya Kumar Sabha, a youth branch of Arya Samaj, in Gwalior – then a princely state which was not part of any province. I come from a strong *sanatani* family. But I used to be at the weekly *satsang* of Arya Kumar Sabha. Once Shri Bhoodev Shastri who was a senior worker of Arya Kumar Sabha, and a great thinker and an expert organiser, asked us: 'What do you do in the evening?'

'Nothing', we said, because the Arya Kumar Sabha used to meet in the morning on every Sunday. Then he recommended us to go to the shakha. Thus I started going to the shakha in Gwalior. It was my first association with the RSS. At that time the shakha in Gwalior had just begun. It had mostly Maharashtrian boys and naturally all the swayamsevaks used to speak only Marathi. I started going to the shakha regularly. I liked the games played in the shakha as well as the weekly *bauddhiks* (intellectual discourses).

A pracharak, Shri Narayanrao Tarte had come from Nagpur to start the shakha. He was indeed a superb human being, a very simple man, a thinker and an expert organiser. What I am today is the making of Shri Tarte. Next to him I was inspired by Deendayal Upadhyaya and Bhaurao Deoras. Gwalior was then not within the field of Bhauraoji. But once he had come to Gwalior with Shri Balasaheb Apte who was the then Bauddhik Pramukh. Apteji was very soft-spoken. We were soon drawn towards him. I had talked with him for only a few minutes. But the same year (1940) when I went to see the first year Officers' Training Camp (OTC), I came in close contact with him. I went there just to attend the valedictory function of the camp, not for training. Dr. Hedgewar had also come there for some time. I first saw him there. When Doctorji was ill I went to see him. In 1941 when I was in High School I did my first year OTC. In 1942 when I was in the Intermediate class I did my second year OTC and I did my third year in 1944 when I was doing my B.A.

When I wrote *Hindu Tan-man Hindu Jeevan* I was a student of class X. After completing my graduation from Gwalior I did my MA from the DAV College in Kanpur, because there was no post-graduate college in Gwalior. I then got State Government's scholarship also. Owing to

Partition, I could not complete my law. And then in 1947. We are assertive Hindus. I decided to give up my study to come out as a whole-time worker of RSS. Till 1947 I did the RSS work at the shakha level and carried on my studies. I also participated in the Quit India Movement in 1942 and was jailed. I was then studying for my Intermediate examination. I was arrested from my native village Bhateshwer in Agra district. I was then 16.

My father was not attached to the RSS but my elder brother was. He would go to the shakha. Once he went to a winter camp where he created a problem. He said: 'I cannot take my food with the other swayamsevaks. I shall prepare my food myself.' And see how deftly the RSS handled the situation. The sarvadhikari (superintendent) of the camp complied with his request and provided him all the necessary things for preparing his food. After taking his bath and properly adjusting his sacred thread, etc., he started cooking his food. On the first day he prepared food for himself. The next day, however, he could not prepare it and joined the queue of all swayamsevaks for partaking of the food. Within 44 hours he was changed.

The RSS does not change only individuals. It changes also the collective mind. That is the beauty of the RSS ethos. In our spiritual tradition an individual can attain a great height. Even self-realisation can be possible if one undertakes the right *sadhana* and also attain *nirvana*. But what about the society? Nobody thinks about his obligation to society in general. Now for the first time the RSS thought about it and concluded that by changing individuals we shall change the society. Had the sarvadhikari at the camp scolded him and not allowed him to prepare his food himself his spiritual development would have been thwarted, whereas in the RSS within 44 hours he was a changed boy. This is the 'secret method' of the RSS. That is how society is changed. It is true that it is a long process but then there are no short-cuts, no instant recipes.

Gandhiji had praised the RSS for the absence of untouchability in the organisation. Only the RSS organises the society. Other movements only divide the society by emphasising distinct 'identity', different 'interests', special 'status', etc. They only encourage untouchability by constantly reminding the so-called untouchables of their 'separateness'. 'You are being insulted. You have no place in society.'

The RSS has a two-fold task before it. One is to organise the Hindus. To build a strong Hindu society, well knit and rising above caste and other artificial differences. Some differences will persist but then variety is the spice of life. Like, we have the differences of language. We don't want to destroy this diversity. The other task is to assimilate the non-Hindu like Muslims and Christians in the mainstream. They can follow the faith of their own conviction. No one can object to it. We worship trees, stones, animals and what not. We have hundreds of ways of worshipping God. They can go where they want. But this country must be looked upon as the Motherland for them. They must have a feeling of patriotism for this country. But the Islamic division of the world into *Darul Harab* and *Darul Islam* comes in the way. Islam has yet to learn the art of existing and flourishing in a country where Muslims are in a minority. They cannot convert the whole of India to Islam. After all, they have to live here. So they have to recognise this fact. And today it has become a matter of grave concern and deep thinking in the Muslim countries. Because Qoran offers no guidance in this regard. It only talks of killing *kafirs* or converting them to Islam. But they cannot do it always and everywhere. How can they do it where they are in a minority? If they try to do it, a major clash will take place and only members of the minority will be killed. But Muslims themselves have to change this state of affairs. We cannot change it for them.

Congress has not correctly understood the Muslim problem. They continue to carry on their policy of appeasement. But to what effect? The Muslims of this country can be treated in three ways. One is *tiraskar* which means if they will not themselves change leave them alone, reject them as our compatriots. Second is *puraskar* which is appeasement, i.e., bribe them to behave, which is being done by the Congress and others of their ilk. The third way is *parishkar* meaning to change them, that is, to restore them to the mainstream by providing them *samskaras*. We want to change them by offering them the right *samskaras*. Their religion will not be changed. They can follow their own religion. Mecca can continue to be holy for the Muslims but India should be holier than the holy for them. You can go to a mosque and offer *namaz*, you can keep the *roza*. We have no problem. But if you have to choose between Mecca or Islam and India you must choose India. All the Muslims should have this feeling: we will live and die only for this country.

I wrote *Hindu Tan-man Hindu Jeevan* when I was studying in the tenth class. I had then said, '*Koi batlaye Kabul mein jaakar kitni masjiden todin.*' I still stand by my words. But we (Hindus) did pull down the structure in Ayodhya. It was the first incident in history when the Hindus demolished their worship place themselves. In fact it was a reaction to the Muslim vote-bank. We wanted to solve this problem through negotiation and legislation. But there was no *puraskar* for *burai* (evil act). We change *burai* also with *parishkar*. Now I think, the Hindu society has been regenerated which was the prime task of the RSS. Earlier Hindus used to bend before an invasion but not now. This change in Hindu society is worthy of welcome. So much change must have come with the new-found self-assertion. This is a question of self-preservation. If the Hindu society does not expand itself, it will face the crisis of survival. We have to expand ourselves. We have to take others along with. Now the Yadavs and the so-called Harijans are going with us. After all, we have to live as Hindus. Once a Yadav leader came to me and said: 'Don't condemn all Yadavs. All Yadavs are not with Mulayam Singh and Laloo Prasad. A *samskrit* (cultured) Yadav does not like them. There can be sections of Rajput, Kurmi and Gujjar Muslims but you cannot find any Yadav Muslim anywhere. The Yadavs never accepted Islam. This talk of "Yadav-Muslim" Unity – MY card – is nothing more than an empty slogan for votes.'

The simple reason for my long association with the RSS is that I like the Sangh. I like its ideology, and above all, I like the RSS attitude towards people, towards one another which is found only in the RSS. I remember an incident when I was in Lucknow. The Socialist movement was at its peak. Suddenly a senior Socialist activist fell ill. He was lying alone in his house, and nobody went to enquire after his wellbeing. Then Acharya Narendra Deo came to know and he went to his house to see him.

The Acharya then said, 'What fraternity is this in the Socialist Party? Nobody has come to see you. Look at the RSS. It can never happen in the RSS. If a swayamsevak does not go to the shakha only for one day the same day friends will promptly reach his house to enquire about his wellbeing.' When I was ill and there was an emergency, my family members did not turn up to see me. They were afraid of being arrested for any such action. Only the RSS workers helped me. See, how much living contact and fraternal feeling is in the RSS. Actually the Sangh is our family. We are all one.

In the beginning we could not spread our work in all sections of society because we did not have enough workers. 'Man-making' is the prime job of the RSS. As we now have more workers, we are covering all the sections of society in all fields of life. Changes are taking place in all spheres. But the work of man-making will not be discontinued, it will go on. It must go on. That is what the RSS movement is.

Appendix 13

'A Four-point Appeal to Muslims of India'

(L.K. Advani, *BJP Today*, 16 June 1997)

The BHARATIYA JANATA PARTY has launched the Swarna Jayanti Rath Yatra to commemorate the golden jubilee of India's independence. It is a marathon mass campaign aimed at rekindling the spirit of patriotism and discipline among the people and readying the nation for the arduous task of fulfilling the sacred dreams of our great freedom heroes.

One of the important factors which influenced the course of the freedom movement, and also the complexion of the polity after independence, was the role played by the dominant religio-political leadership of the Muslim community. Before Independence, the fanatical and uncompromising espousal of the two-nation theory by the Muslim League, which sought to keep the Muslim community away from the mainstream nationalist movement, resulted in the tragic Partition of India. After Independence, influential sections of the Muslim religio-political leadership, encouraged by the pseudo-secular practices of the Congress and other parties, have continued to obstruct the community's all-sided integration with the national life. This has created multifarious problems impeding the progress and well-being of both the Muslim community and the nation at large.

The BJP believes that the 50th anniversary of India's freedom is an appropriate occasion to address this issue squarely and sincerely. As President of the Party, I am issuing this statement with the hope of provoking a candid and purposeful national debate.

In doing so, I am aware of the fact that, unfortunately, a significant section of the Indian Muslim community continues to be influenced by our adversaries' vote-bank propaganda about the BJP. This propaganda has often affected the BJP in the electoral arena. But the Muslim community has been the real loser in every sense of the term – politically, economically, socially, educationally and, most important, in terms of earning the goodwill of the majority community.

The BJP is interested in, and will sincerely strive for, a qualitative change in the relationship that now obtains between our party and India's Muslim community. The very thought of excluding such a large section of Indian population from our universe of concerns is repugnant to us. With a view to promoting communal harmony and national unity, I urge my Muslim brethren in India to pay heed following four-point appeal:

(1) **Muslims should purge every trace of the Two-Nation theory from their mindset**: Today the Congress and most other parties have developed a strong reluctance to debate the causes and consequences of Partition. The BJP, however, believes that a sincere debate on the ideological and theological basis of the creation of Pakistan is eminently desirable during the golden jubilee of our independence. This, for two reasons: One, Pakistan continues to be India's foremost problem in the sphere of national security and foreign policy. Secondly, even after 50 years of the creation of a separate Muslim nation, heart-unity, emotional integration, harmony and durable peace between Hindus and Muslims within the truncated India have continued to elude us. Indian Muslims, therefore, have a special obligation to recall this national tragedy and purge from their mindset every trace of the ideological-theological underpinnings of the Two-Nation theory once and for all.

One of the fundamental sources of the Two-Nation theory, and also of the distrust, discord and disunity between Hindus and Muslims in India for the past many centuries has been the Muslim theologians' characterisation of Hindus as 'kafirs'. Over 98% of the Hindus in India are believers in God and practitioners of idol worship. Idol worship is an integral part of the

Hindu spiritual tradition, although both Saguna (God of attributes) and Nirguna (God without attributes) modes of worship are extolled in this tradition. This is the basis of secularism and credal non-discrimination in the Bharatiya culture.

In contrast, Muslim theologians continue to insist that Hindus are kafirs because of their practice of idol worship. It may be recalled that even Mahatma Gandhi, an indefatigable campaigner for Hindu-Muslim harmony, was not spared by the votaries of Pakistan from this arrogant attitude. That is why, Mohammed Ali, who was one of the close associates of Gandhiji in the Khilafat movement, later publicly declared that '**the worst among the Muslims is still a better individual than a kafir Gandhi**'. True communal harmony and national unity cannot be built on the pillars of such credal discrimination and bigotry.

I, therefore appeal to Muslim theologians and intellectuals, in this 50th year of India's freedom, to categorically and irrevocably proclaim that they have stopped considering Hindus as kafirs. They should state that whatever relevance the term 'kafir' may have had in other times and countries, it can have no place in the attitude and behaviour of Indian Muslims towards their Hindu brethren.

No doubt, the process of Muslims' integration with the national mainstream after 1947 is steadily, and happily, gaining momentum. Still, there is a great need for people within the Muslim community to give a firm rebuff to such religio-political leaders among them who wish to halt or reverse this process.

(2) **Bury vote-bank politics and contribute to making democracy healthier**: It is high time our Muslim brethren realised that our adversaries have been raising the bogey of the 'communal threat from the BJP' only for reasons of narrow political gain. Hence their opposition to the enactment of a Common Civil Code and scrapping of Article 370 of the Constitution. They treat you merely as dumb vote banks, whereas we consider you as equal partners in building a New India.

Vote-bank politics has not brought to Indian Muslims security, material well-being of adequate opportunities for playing their legitimate democratic role in the affairs of the nation. On the other hand, the BJP's own track record of governance proves our fidelity to our promise: 'Justice for All, Appeasement of None.' In all those States where the BJP is, or has in the past been, in power, the scourge of communal riots has been eliminated and the administration has guaranteed the security and well-being of all without discrimination. I solemnly assure our Muslim brethren that it will be our firmest resolve to create a riot-free, violence-free and discrimination-free India when the BJP comes to power at the Centre.

(3) **Understand Cultural Nationalism**: Hindutva or Cultural Nationalism is not a narrow, communal, bigoted, exclusivist or theocratic concept. It defines the national identity of India, rooted in her inclusive, assimilative, integrative and secular culture. This is in sharp contrast to the exclusivist, intolerant, communal and coercive nationalism of Pakistan – both Pakistan and Bangladesh, which, even though it seceded from Pakistan with Indian help, lost no time in declaring themselves 'Islamic' states. India, too, could have summarily converted itself into Hindu theocratic state, but it steadfastly remained secular precisely because of her quintessential Hindu ethos of respect for all religions.

The BJP believes India to be **One Country, One People and One Culture**. This does not in any sense erase the identity of Islam or Indian Muslims. For, my Party not only respects but celebrates the multi-religious, multi-lingual and multi-ethnic diversity of Indian society, which is united at its core by Cultural Nationalism.

Since civilisation and culture form the basis of India's national identity, our Muslim brethren should have no hesitation in accepting and respecting the symbols and inspirational sources of our national culture, such as Ram, Krishna, Buddha, Mahavir, Nanak and numerous other personalities. The BJP's support to the campaign for the construction of the Ram Mandir at Ayodhya is born out of our belief that Shri Ram is a symbol of India's culture and civilisation.

The BJP holds that Hindus too should have a similar respectful attitude towards all the positive contributions made by Muslims to India's dynamic national culture in the fields of arts, language, architecture, literature and spirituality. It is this rich, diverse and syncretic national culture of India which Hindus and Muslims must collectively preserve and promote.

(4) **Concentrate on education and economic elevation of poor Muslims**: Lastly, the Muslim community as a whole, and especially its religio-political leadership should focus their efforts on its rapid educational and economic uplift. Promotion of secular education, especially among women, is a need of the hour. It will increase economic and employment opportunities for Muslims. It will also, simultaneously, promote greater interaction and integration between Hindus and Muslims.

Appendix 14

'Nanavati or not, the state apparatus in Gujarat cannot be absolved'

The former chief justice of India excoriates the state's role in and after the 2002 riots
(V.N. Khare, *The Indian Express*, 14 October 2008)

With the kind of evidence that I saw as Chief Justice of India, I would never have exonerated the government of its responsibility during the 2002 riots, if I was responsible for the Commission.

As CJI, I heard a large number of cases from the riot-stricken of Gujarat in 2002. I don't see a case for absolving the state government or of saying that all responsibilities were fulfilled.

There are three primary responsibilities of the state. The first, is the protection of lives of people, all people, and especially the weaker sections, who may not have the necessary voice and strength to look after themselves. Second comes the duty to prosecute those who violate the law. The third is the duty to provide relief to victims of violence. It is important for governments to educate people, build roads etc. but all of that is predicated on their being able to first protect lives.

On the three crucial aspects, the police and the state in Gujarat during the riots was an utter failure. The state, after being unable to protect lives also carried out shoddy investigations. I got the sense that investigations were done to help the accused, rather than the victims.

On February 27, 2002, the terrible incident of the train at Godhra took place. On the 28th, the VHP gave a call against the incident, and on March 1, the riots began. When it was brought to my notice that trial in hundreds of cases was about to begin in Gujarat on this, I stayed the trial.

The Best Bakery case in Baroda is one such case. Tell me, at night, between 8.30 to 10 pm, the Bakery was set on fire, with about 20-22 people inside it. Hundreds, perhaps thousands gathered outside. The police station was very close, about 2-3 kms away. I was told in Court that the PCR stood there, and did nothing. Forget about fire extinguishers, the fire continued to rage all night, till it went out, by itself, at 11.30 am or so the next morning (March 2). Moreover, there were 16 people burnt alive, no effort made to rescue them or take them out, when the police station was so close. Is this the state fulfilling its duty to protect lives? Zahira Sheikh was able to lodge the FIR only by 3.30 pm the next day.

As far as prosecuting wrong-doers, under the criminal penal code, it is the duty of the police to investigate, collect all evidence and then present it before the Court to prosecute offenders. I think the three roles should not be vested in one agency, but as they are, how they perform on that yard-stick will be what we will use to judge them.

Then, not just in the Zahira Sheikh matter, but in most of the hundreds of cases, after the first deposition, several eyewitnesses turned hostile! The job of the prosecution in this case is to argue and cross-examine the hostile witnesses, to ensure that fear or greed are not responsible for making them change their minds. Here, as witnesses turned hostile, the prosecution did not even bother to cross-examine. Is this fulfilment of obligations of the state? I actually had to appoint an amicus (Harish Salve) and send out three or four lawyers to report to me on what the status was.

Therefore, the Supreme Court shifted two cases out of the state, as I felt justice could not be done there. The Supreme Court transferred Best Bakery and Bilkees Bano to Maharashtra. When I found no protection for victims, by my judicial order, I directed the state government to provide protection to the victims, relations and their witness, and in case of violations, report back to the Supreme Court.

If I was on this Commission, I would say that the police had failed to protect the right of people to their life, as no effort was made to stop rioters. What else should a Commission conclude?

The writer was the Chief Justice of India in 2002, when state-wide communal violence erupted there.

Appendix 15

Interview with BJP leader Narendra Modi

(By Ross Colvin and Sruthi Gottipati, Reuters, 12 July 2013)

Narendra Modi is a polarising figure, evoking visceral reactions across the political spectrum. Critics call him a dictator while supporters believe he could make India an Asian superpower.

Reuters spoke to Modi at his official Gandhinagar residence in a rare interview, the first since he was appointed head of the BJP's election campaign in June.

Here are edited excerpts from the interview. The questions are paraphrased and some of Modi's replies have been translated from Hindi.

Is it frustrating that many people still define you by 2002?

People have a right to be critical. We are a democratic country. Everyone has their own view. I would feel guilty if I did something wrong. Frustration comes when you think 'I got caught. I was stealing and I got caught.' That's not my case.

Do you regret what happened?

I'll tell you. India's Supreme Court is considered a good court today in the world. The Supreme Court created a special investigative team (SIT) and top-most, very bright officers who oversee the SIT. That report came. In that report, I was given a thoroughly clean chit, a thoroughly clean chit. Another thing, any person if we are driving a car, we are a driver, and someone else is driving a car and we're sitting behind, even then if a puppy comes under the wheel, will it be painful or not? Of course it is. If I'm a chief minister or not, I'm a human being. If something bad happens anywhere, it is natural to be sad.

Should your government have responded differently?

Up till now, we feel that we used our full strength to set out to do the right thing.

But do you think you did the right thing in 2002?

Absolutely. However much brainpower the Supreme Being has given us, however much experience I've got, and whatever I had available in that situation and this is what the SIT had investigated.

Do you believe India should have a secular leader?

We do believe that . . . But what is the definition of secularism? For me, my secularism is, India first. I say, the philosophy of my party is 'Justice to all. Appeasement to none.' This is our secularism.

Critics say you are an authoritarian, supporters say you are a decisive leader. Who is the real Modi?

If you call yourself a leader, then you have to be decisive. If you're decisive then you have the chance to be a leader. These are two sides to the same coin . . . People want him to make decisions. Only then they accept the person as a leader. That is a quality, it's not a negative. The other thing is, if someone was an authoritarian then how would he be able to run a government for so many years? . . . Without a team effort how can you get success? And that's why I say Gujarat's success is not Modi's success. This is the success of Team Gujarat.

What about the suggestion that you don't take criticism?

I always say the strength of democracy lies in criticism. If there is no criticism that means there is no democracy. And if you want to grow, you must invite criticism. And I want to grow, I want to invite criticism. But I'm against allegations. There is a vast difference between criticism and allegations. For criticism, you have to research, you'll have to compare things, you'll have to come with data, factual information, then you can criticise. Now no one is ready to do the hard work. So the simple way is to make allegations. In a democracy, allegations will never improve situations. So, I'm against allegations but I always welcome criticism.

On his popularity in opinion polls

I can say that since 2003, in however many polls have been done, people have selected me as the best chief minister. And as best chief minister, it wasn't just people from Gujarat who liked me, not like that. People outside of Gujarat have also voted like that for me. One time, I wrote a letter to the India Today Group's Aroon Purie. I requested him – 'Every time I'm a winner, so next time please drop Gujarat, so someone else gets a chance. Or else I'm just winning. Please keep me out of the competition. And besides me, give someone else a shot at it.'

Allies and people within the BJP say you are too polarising a figure

If in America, if there's no polarisation between Democrats and Republicans, then how would democracy work? It's bound (to happen). In a democracy there will be a polarisation between Democrats and Republicans.

This is democracy's basic nature. It's the basic quality of democracy. If everyone moved in one direction, would you call that a democracy?

But allies and partners still find you controversial

Up till now, no one from my party or the people who are allied with us, I've never read nor heard any official statement (about this from them). It might have been written about in the media. They write in a democracy . . . and if you have any name that this person is there in the BJP who said this, then I can respond.

How will you persuade minorities including Muslims to vote for you?

First thing, to Hindustan's citizens, to voters, Hindus and Muslims, I'm not in favour of dividing. I'm not in favour of dividing Hindus and Sikhs. I'm not in favour of dividing Hindus and Christians. All the citizens, all the voters, are my countrymen. So my basic philosophy is, I don't address this issue like this. And that is a danger to democracy also. Religion should not be an instrument in your democratic process.

If you become PM, which leader would you emulate?

The first thing is, my life's philosophy is and what I follow is: I never dream of becoming anything. I dream of doing something. So to be inspired by my role models, I don't need to become anything. If I want to learn something from Vajpayee, then I can just implement that in Gujarat. For that, I don't have to have dreams of (higher office in) Delhi. If I like something about Sardar Patel, then I can implement that in my state. If I like something about Gandhiji, then I can implement that. Without talking about the Prime Minister's seat, we can still discuss, that yes, from each one we have to learn the good things.

On the goals the next government should achieve

Look, whichever new government comes to power, that government's first goal will be to fix the confidence that is broken in people. The government tries to push a policy. Will it continue that policy or not? In two months, if they face pressure, will they change it? Will they do something like – an event happens now and they'll change a decision from 2000? If you change decisions from the past, you will bring the policy back-effects. Who in the world will come here? So whichever government comes to power, it would need to give people confidence, it should build the trust in people, 'yes, in policies there will be consistency', if they promise people something, they will honour that promise, they will fulfil. Then you can position yourself globally.

People say economic development in Gujarat is hyped up

In a democracy, who is the final judge? The final judge is the voter. If this was just hype, if this was all noise, then the public would see it every day. 'Modi said he would deliver water.' But then he would say 'Modi is lying. The water hasn't reached'. Then why would he like Modi? In India's vibrant democracy system, and in the presence of vibrant political parties, if someone chooses him for the third time, and he gets close to a two-third majority then people feel what is being said is true. Yes, the road is being paved, yes, work is being done, children are being educated. There are new things coming for health. 108 (emergency number) service is available. They see it all. So that's why someone might say hype or talk, but the public won't believe them. The public will reject it. And the public has a lot of strength, a lot.

Should you be doing more for inclusive economic growth?

Gujarat is a state that people have a lot of expectations from. We're doing a good job, that's why the expectations are high. As they should be. Nothing is wrong.

On indicators like malnutrition, infant mortality

Infant mortality has improved tremendously in Gujarat, tremendously. Compared to every other state in Hindustan, we are a better performing state. Second thing, malnutrition, in Hindustan today, real-time data is not available. When you don't have real time data, how are you going to analyse?

We do believe in inclusive growth, we do believe that the benefits of this development must reach to the last person and they must be the beneficiary. So this is what we're doing.

People want to know who is the real Modi – Hindu nationalist leader or pro-business chief minister?

I'm nationalist. I'm patriotic. Nothing is wrong. I'm a born Hindu. Nothing is wrong. So, I'm a Hindu nationalist so yes, you can say I'm a Hindu nationalist because I'm a born Hindu. I'm patriotic so nothing is wrong in it. As far as progressive, development-oriented, workaholic, whatever they say, this is what they are saying. So there's no contradiction between the two. It's one and the same image.

On Brand Modi and people behind the PR strategy

The western world and India – there's a huge difference between them. Here, India is such a country that a PR agency will not be able to make a person into anything. Media can't make anything of a person. If someone tries to project a false face in India, then my country reacts badly to it. Here, people's thinking is different. People won't tolerate hypocrisy for very long. If you project yourself the way you actually are, then people will accept even your shortcomings. Man's weaknesses are accepted. And they'll say, yes, okay, he's genuine, he works hard. So our country's thinking is different. As far as a PR agency is concerned, I have never looked at or listened to or met a PR agency. Modi does not have a PR agency. Never have I kept one.

Appendix 16

'Chaining 1,200 Years'

Our PM's recalculation of how long Indians have been 'slaves'

(Hasan Suroor, *Outlook*, 7 July 2014)

Good lawyers and good historians have one thing in common: both are quick to spot the crucial small print that ordinary folk miss the significance of. So, as politicians and the media were concentrating on the big picture of Prime Minister Narendra Modi's maiden Lok Sabha speech, historians were struck by his reference to '1,200 years of slavery', which, he said, had left Indians with a slavish mentality. 'This slave mentality of 1,200 years is troubling us,' he said. 'Often, when we meet a person of high stature, we fail to muster courage to speak up.'

What is troubling historians, though, is his view of India's colonial history, which, according to him, spans 1,200 years. The conventional view is that it lasted 200 years – those of British raj. So where did the remaining 1,000 years come from? Clearly, Modi was propounding what Mridula Mukherjee, former professor of modern Indian history at JNU, described as the 'standard Hindu communal view of history', which regards the period of Muslim rule also as a period of slavery. The problem is that even then the numbers don't add up. Muslim conquest of the subcontinent began around the 12th century and was effectively over by the 18th century, though it lingered on until 1857. Modi's account still leaves us with 400 years to account for, spawning jokes on the internet. On Twitter, someone going by the name 'Angry Brown Man' wrote: 'Narendra Modi claims India has faced 1,200 years of slavery? Is prohibition not on in Gujarat anymore? 'Coz he is obviously high as kite.'

As chief minister of Gujarat, Modi used the same phrase in his independence day speech last year, prompting *Business Standard* columnist Mihir Sharma to note that 'even on Independence Day, he couldn't help saying that India has been "a slave to others for 1,000-1,200 years". I know his maths is bad, but I suspect he's not calculating from the Battle of Plassey.' But forget maths. The bigger question is: what was Modi trying to do raking up ancient/medieval history in a speech about development and building modern India? He's not known to make throwaway comments, so it may be argued he was simply trying to emphasise the need for greater national pride. But surely there are less controversial ways of doing that, say, by highlighting independent India's achievements in science and technology, its robust democracy, the fact that it defied dire western predictions and emerged as a model of democratic stability in the region. Instead, he chose what could be interpreted as equating national pride with Hindu pride, branding Muslim rule as slavery. As Debobrat Ghose, a *Firstpost* commentator, asked: Is prime minister Modi trying to bring about a paradigm change in the way we perceive our history?

Noted historian Mushirul Hasan dismisses Modi's claims as 'falsification of history'. But Modi's supporters say he was stating facts. 'The phrase "1,200 years of slavery" is neither saffronisation nor colourisation of history, but only a reference to the deep conditioning of slave mentality that Indians have undergone over the centuries,' says Prof Makkhan Lal [sic], a pro-RSS historian who was at the centre of a row over rewriting NCERT history books.

I asked Ashok Chowgule, the VHP's working president (external), why Modi chose to hark back to Muslim rule now. He replied by cataloguing the 'brutality' of Muslim conquerors and quoted from American historian Will Durant's book *The Story of Civilisation*, describing the Islamic conquest of India as 'probably the bloodiest story in history'. The VHP's line seems to confirm that Modi's remark was a none-too-subtle attempt to keep old ghosts alive and a nod to the RSS view of Indian history. Significantly, it came on the heels of HRD minister Smriti Irani's reported plans to introduce a 'Hindu perspective' in school textbooks.

Meanwhile, although it is true that many Indians still suffer from a colonial hangover – even the swadeshi Sangh parivar, for example, worries more about what appears in *The Economist* or *Time* magazine than in Indian publications – the tendency is slightly exaggerated. The new generation of Indians has no such complex. If anything, there is now a reverse snobbery, which often manifests itself in the form of a false sense of national pride (especially among BJP supporters) inspired by the hype over India's new status as an emerging superpower. In Britain, Indians are the most cocky lot, and constantly try to distance themselves from their poorer subcontinental cousins.

But coming back to Modi's remark, here's a party which dismisses the 2002 Gujarat riots as old history and tells us to 'move on' and stop obsessing about something that happened 12 years ago. Yet, it itself remains trapped in the past. Hopefully, in future, Modi will talk more about moving forward than looking back. And, yes, get his maths right.

Index of Names of People and Organisations

Abdullah, Sheikh Muhammad 110, 140-5, 148
Adityanath, Yogi 354, 365
Advani, Lal Krishna 25, 42, 52, 107, 120, 131, 156-60, 168, 175, 182, 198-9, 203-5, 209-10, 213, 218-9, 221-5, 228-30, 232, 234, 238-45, 250, 252, 254-8, 264, 267-8, 271, 274-300, 303-4, 307-12, 314-21, 323-6, 341, 352, 364, 370, 391, 402-3, 408-9, 412-4, 516, 522, 524, 528
My Country, My Life 175, 204, 282-3
Advani, Poornima 306
Agarwal, Deoki Nandan 208
Agarwal, P.P. 397
Agarwal, Satya Prakash 184
Ahir, Hansraj 352
Aiyangar, S. Srinivasa 74
Akbar, M.J. 340
Akhandananda, Swami 307
Akhil Bharatiya Vidyarthi Parishad 129-30, 177, 188-9, 215, 223-4, 229, 257, 265, 319-20, 327, 339, 369, 405-9, 411, 414-5, 424, 514
Akhil Bharatiya Itihas Sankalan Yojana. *See* Rashtriya Swayamsevak Sangh
Akhil Bharatiya Karyakari Mandal. *See* Rashtriya Swayamsevak Sangh
Akhil Bharatiya Pratinidhi Sabha. *See* Rashtriya Swayamsevak Sangh
Akhlaq, Mohammed 347, 357
Ali Brothers 99
Aligarh Muslim University 206, 222, 339
Ali, Maulana Mohammed 74, 76
Ali, Mehboob 206
Ali, Qurban 241
All-India Majlis Tameer-e-Millat 396
All-India Sant Samiti 411
All-India Shuddhi Sabha 64, 70
Ambedkar, Dr. B.R. 33, 53, 54, 69, 83, 96, 108, 305, 406, 411
Ambekar, Sunil 405
Andersen, Walter K. 53, 80
Aney, M.S. 100, 382
Ansari, M.A. 75
Apte, Bal 319, 525
Apte, Devdas 306
Apte, Narayan 121-2
Apte, S.S. 407
Archaeological Survey of India 338
Aroda, Darshan Lal 332
Arya Samaj 18, 44, 63-4, 70, 167, 184, 196, 266, 385, 518, 525
Athalye, Balasaheb 58
Avaidyanath, Mahant 249, 411-2
Ayyangar, M. Ananthasayanam 79
Ayyangar, N. Gopalaswamy 147
Azad, Abul Kalam 37-8, 40, 76-7, 112, 332
Azad, Ghulam Nabi 249

Baba Adhav 178-9, 181
Bagrecha, Sankal Chandra 332
Bahadur Shah Zafar 13-7
Bahri, Justice P.K. 244
Bajaj, Ramkrishna 249
Bajrang Dal 42-3, 170, 223, 226, 241-4, 248, 250, 253, 265, 273, 304, 310, 385, 386, 390, 405, 409, 411-5, 424
Bajrang Bhakti Diksha Samaroh 243
Bakht, Sikandar 206
Balakrishnan, S. 255
Balaram, P. 349
Balkrishna, Pandharinath 58
Balwant, Prabhakar 58
Banaras Hindu University 21-2, 307, 361-2, 406
Bande, Raghunath 58
Banerjea, Surendranath 73, 332
Banerjee, Ranendralal 332
Bartwal, Hemendra Singh 294, 302, 314
Basak, Sanjay 306-8, 325, 333
Basu, Kalidas 265
Batra, Dina Nath 338
Beg, Mirza Mohammed Afzal 141, 148
Behere, V.P. 420-1, 500, 512
Berenschot, Ward 389
Bhagaiah, V. 331, 334
Bhagwat, Madhukar 352

INDEX

Bhagwat, Mohan 53, 57, 71-2, 185, 187, 216, 265-6, 276, 287, 289, 292, 294, 298, 305, 311, 316-7, 322, 324, 328, 330, 336, 342-3, 351, 355, 365, 368-70, 372, 376-7
Bhandari, Sunder Singh 151, 203, 224, 253, 257, 286, 408, 411
Bhanot, Harish 185
Bharadwaj, Maharishi 335
Bharat Dharm Mahamandal 21
Bharatiya Jana Sangh 19, 26, 34, 40, 52, 81-3, 87, 114, 129, 131, 133, 135-41, 145-9, 151-62, 165, 168-9, 172-3, 174-5, 177, 179-80, 182-5, 187-90, 195-6, 198-9, 200-1, 203-5, 209-11, 218-9, 221, 230, 238, 247, 259, 264, 266-7, 282, 287, 294, 296-7, 308-9, 332, 342, 363-4, 387-8, 393-7, 399, 403, 405, 514-8
  Allahabad session (1953) 151
  Indore session (1954) 151
  Kanpur session (1952) 141, 165
  Patna session (1969) 165
  Shree Ram Tarun Mandal 396
Bharatiya Janata Party 19, 25-8, 30, 41-3, 45, 48-9, 52-3, 57, 67, 82, 98, 103, 105-6, 114, 123, 131, 139, 157, 159-61, 172, 187, 201, 203-6, 209-11, 213-5, 217-26, 228-32, 234-6, 238-59, 264-5, 267-82, 284-300, 302-4, 306-28, 330-2, 336-40, 342-3, 345, 348-9, 351-5, 357-8, 360-1, 363-70, 372-5, 378, 380, 385-6, 388, 390, 402-3, 405, 408-15, 424, 519, 521-2, 524, 528-33, 535
  1996 manifesto 250
  1998 manifesto 251
  2004 manifesto 251
  Palampur Resolution (1987) 223
  Working Group report (1985) 220
Bharatiya Kisan Sangh. *See* Rashtriya Swayamsevak Sangh
Bharatiya Lok Dal 183-4, 189, 219, 516-8
Bharatiya Mazdoor Sangh. *See* Rashtriya Swayamsevak Sangh
Bharatiya Shikshan Mandal. *See* Rashtriya Swayamsevak Sangh
Bharatram, Sukanya 340
Bhardwaj, Somdev 335
Bhargava, P.N. 348
Bhargava, Usha 387, 392
Bhargav, Vanya Vaidehi 19
Bharti, Uma 249-50, 304, 412
Bharucha, Justice S.P. 27, 29
Bhasin, Prem 218
Bhatia, Rajkumar 405
Bhatkar, Vijay P. 335, 362
Bhattacharya, Neeladri 412
Bhattacharya, Ranjan 278
Bhatt, Ashok 273
Bhatt, Chetan 18, 57-8, 64, 70, 407
Bhave, Vinoba 174-5, 177-82, 488, 496, 498
Bhende, Mangesh 332
Bheri, Ashok 332
Bhide, V.N. 176-7, 180, 488, 494
Bhishikar, C.P. 55-7
  Sangh-Vriksh Ke Beej: Dr. Keshavrao Hedgewar 55
Bhonsala Military School 89, 382
Bhonsle, Raja Laxmanrao 61
Bhonsle, Raja Raghoji Rao 61
Bhopatkar, L.B. 111
Bhushan, Bharat 264, 328
Bhutada, Shweta 359
Birla, B.M. 108
Birla, G.D. 63, 90, 126, 220
Birla, Jugal Kishore 90
Bobde, Justice S.A. 31
Bonnerjee, W.C. 73
Bose, Subhas Chandra 131
Brahmo Samaj 44, 266
Brass, Paul R. 243, 384, 387-8
  Theft of an Idol 384
Burger, American Chief Justice 32

Cardozo, Benjamin N. 33
Casolari, Marzia 21-2, 86-7, 90, 92, 99, 382
Catholic Bishops' Conference of India 346, 372-3
Central Hindu Military Education Society 89, 382
Chaimani, K.H. 420
Chandra, Bipan 81, 86
Chandrachud, Justice D.Y. 32
Chandrachud, Justice Y.V. 153, 156
  Report on Upadhyaya's death 154
Chandra, Lokesh 341
Chand, Sakhal 265
Charan, Judge Atma 120-1
Chari, A.S.R. 393
Chatterjee, Bankim Chandra 64-5, 67-8, 71-2, 167
  Anandamath 65-7
Chatterjee, Manini 223, 279, 288, 291, 294

Chauhan, Gajendra 306
Chavan, S.B. 174-7, 179, 488, 493-4
Chhatra Sangharsh Vahini 191, 513
Chhatra Sangharsh Samiti 177, 405
Chinmayananda, Swami 208, 249, 407, 411-2
Chitnavis, Sir G.R. 61-2
Chopra, B.R. 224
Chouhan, Shivraj Singh 315
Chouthaiwale, M.K. 229
Chowdhury, Neerja 207, 211
Chowgule, Ashok 535
Clinton, Bill 519
Communist Party of India 226, 393
AITUC 320
Communist Party of India (Marxist) 226, 393
Congress (O) 174, 183, 185, 206, 516
Couto, Archbishop Anil 373
Craddock, Sir Reginald 94

Dabholkar, Narendra 321, 356
Dal Khalsa 262
Dalmia, V.H. 211, 250, 253
Dalvi, R.P. 175
Damle, Gajanan Vishnu 122, 123
Damle, Shridhar D. 80
Dani, P.B. 127, 479
Daphtary, C.K. 118, 120
Das, Banarasi 517
Das Gupta, Surendra Nath 87
Das Gupta, Swapan 120
Davis, Richard H. 241, 243, 412
Dayal, Rajeshwar 110, 116-7, 381-2
Debroy, Bibek 337
Deo, Acharya Narendra 527
Deoras, Bhaurao 27, 182, 193, 206, 225, 246, 416, 421, 499, 525
Deoras, Madhukar Dattatraya 100, 127, 170-2, 175-82, 184-8, 192-200, 202, 205-6, 211-7, 224-31, 237-8, 246-7, 252, 288, 369, 392, 398-9, 408, 416, 417, 420-1, 423, 488, 490, 492-6, 498-9, 513-4, 518, 525
Dera Baba Harnam Singh 261
Desai, Morarji 52, 116, 120, 186-7, 193, 200-1, 485, 515
Deshmukh, Nana 151, 154-6, 160, 177, 189, 199, 202, 211, 218-9, 226, 228-9, 294, 310, 337
RSS, Victim of Slander 219
Deshpande, Aniruddha 332, 339
Dev, Arjun 339
Deve Gowda, H.D. 250
Devghar 58
Devi, Madan Das 224, 274, 278-9, 324, 332, 408
Dharma Sansad 208, 223, 409-11
Dharmendra, Acharya 250, 411
Dhawan, Himanshi 359
Dhingra, Madanlal 123
Dhora, P.S. 274
Dixit, Shrish Chandra 248
Dogra, Prem Nath 140, 151
Doniger, Wendy 338, 357
Doval, Ajit 316, 337
Doval, Shaurya 337
Dravida Munnetra Kazhagam 235
Drèze, Jean 340
Drona, Capt. Jagat Vir Singh 248
D'Souza, Victor 245
Dubashi, Jay 358
Dubey, Priyanka 129, 405
Durga Vahini. *See* Vishwa Hindu Parishad
Dutta, Sujan 272
Dutt, Brahm 178, 491, 496
Dwivedi, Chandraprakash 340

East India Company 144
Ekal Vidyalaya. *See* Rashtriya Swayamsevak Sangh
Elst, Koenraad 391

Faiz, Faiz Ahmad 282
Fernandes, George 195, 289
Ferrao, Archbishop Filipe Neri 373
Firaq Gorakhpuri, Raghupati Sahay 37-40
Formichi, Carlo 87
Fullilove, H. Earl 32

Gadkari, Nitin 321, 325-6, 352
Gaikwad, Annaji 58
Gajendragadkar, Justice P.B. 95
Gandhi, Indira 45, 47, 160, 169, 171-2, 175-81, 185, 187, 196, 198, 205-8, 210-1, 215, 217-8, 226, 277, 288, 340, 350, 392, 406, 486-9, 491, 493, 495, 497, 513
Gandhi, M.K. 40, 46, 83, 91, 99, 119, 122-3, 125, 144, 149, 166, 169-70, 173-4, 238, 259, 261, 271, 317, 329, 341-2, 345, 390-1, 440-1, 453, 464, 468, 470, 473, 482, 485, 489, 491, 519, 520, 522, 526, 529, 533

murder of 95, 129, 382, 440, 443-4, 446, 453, 468, 470, 473, 482, 485, 522
The Story of My Experiments with Truth 520
Gandhi, Piyush 274
Gandhi, Rajiv 207, 209, 211, 218, 227-8, 240, 245, 523
Gandhi, Varun 326
Gandi, Sanjay 180, 211, 277
Ganesan, G.A. 73
Ganesh, Anant 58
Garg, Jagmohan 265
Gehlot, Thawar Chand 326
Gentile, Giovanni 87
George, Varghese K. 314
Ghalib, Mirza Asadullah Baig Khan 14, 40, 296
Gharekhan, Chinmaya R. 340, 350
Ghimire, Yubaraj 230, 259, 410-1
Ghose, Aurobindo 65, 71, 94
Ghosh, Surendra Mohan 387
Gill, K.P.S. 271, 316
Godse, Gopal 93, 117, 120
Godse, Nathuram Vinayak 54, 59, 93, 116-7, 120-4, 169, 272, 345, 390-1, 522
Goel, Justice Adarsh Kumar 32
Goel, Sita Ram 45-6
History of Hindu-Christian Encounters 45-6
Jesus Christ: An Artifice for Aggression 45-6
Gokhale, Laloo 89
Gokhale, Namita 340
Golwalkar, Madhav Sadashiv 34, 43, 59, 63, 71, 80, 83-6, 96, 99, 100, 102-3, 105-7, 110, 116-7, 119, 123-8, 131-2, 135-6, 138, 150, 152, 158, 160-4, 169-71, 186, 192, 203, 208, 216, 245, 266, 287-8, 305, 307, 312, 317, 356, 361-2, 377, 379-83, 397, 407, 416-7, 420-1, 423, 431, 434, 440-9, 451, 453-4, 456, 458-9, 463, 465-6, 468-71, 476-8, 480-2, 484, 487-8, 491, 496-7, 500-2, 507-8
Bunch of Thoughts 43, 96, 100, 103, 105, 131, 150, 152, 161, 169, 216, 307, 377, 379, 397, 407, 416, 421, 491, 500, 504, 510-2
Justice on Trial 35, 124, 127, 420, 441-87, 500
We or Our Nationhood Defined 96, 100-1, 152, 162, 169, 307, 416, 421, 491
Gopal, Krishna 331, 339, 350, 363, 369-70
Goswamy, Aseema Kumar 332
Goswamy, Sunilpad 332
Govindacharya, K.N. 129-30, 177, 253, 257, 405-6
Govind, Vitthal 58
Goyal, D.R. 58, 60, 181-2, 426, 430-1, 439-40, 496
Rashtriya Swayamsewak Sangh 58, 60, 181-2, 262, 383, 406, 430-1, 434, 439-40
Gracias, Cardinal Oswald 372
Graham, B.D. 83, 135, 140, 157
Gujral, Feroze 340
Gujral, I.K. 250
Gundevia, Y.D. 49, 51
Gupta, Bajarangalal 332
Gupta, Bharat 340
Gupta, Hans Raj 133, 180, 186, 211, 487
Gupta, Ishwar Chandra 332
Gupta, Partha Sarathi 81, 84
Gupta, Shekhar 278
Guru Gobind Singh 261-2
Gurumurthy, S. 253, 280
Guru Nanak 262
Gusai, Yojna 325

Habib, Irfan 338-9, 349
Haidar, Salman 340
Haq, Maulvi A.K. Fazlul 81, 132, 138
Har Dayal, Lala 69
Hari, Ranga 265
Harvani, Ansar 387
Hasan, Justice S. Shamsul 402
Hastimal 332
Hazare, Anna 322
Hedgewar, Keshav Baliram 35, 54-9, 61-3, 71, 83, 86, 88-9, 100, 132, 170, 193, 307, 309, 379, 382, 391, 416, 417, 421, 424, 431, 434, 447, 467, 485, 499-501, 504, 507, 511, 525
Herbert, Sir John 81
Hindu Dharma Raksha Samiti 393-4
Hindu Ekatmata Yojna 244
Hindu Mahasabha 18, 20, 40, 50, 53-4, 58, 62, 64, 69-71, 78-9, 81-3, 89-91, 93, 95-6, 98-9, 108, 111-4, 118-9, 122-3, 126, 128-9, 132, 138-9, 141, 219, 232, 288-9, 361, 379, 382, 388, 393-4, 482
opposition to the Quit India Resolution 81
Hindu Sahayata Samiti 393
Hindu Swayamsevak Sangh. *See* Rashtriya Swayamsevak Sangh
Hiranand, Swami 40

Hitler, Adolf 46, 87, 89, 138, 247, 382, 405
Hofstadter, Richard 349
Horowitz, Donald L. 388
Hosabale, Dattatreya 324, 329, 331, 341, 367, 369
Hotson, Ernest 93
Hullad Pidit Sahayata Samiti 393
Hyder Ali 15

Inamdar, Laxmanrao 499
Inamdar, P.L. 120-1
India Foundation 340
Indian Council for Cultural Relations 341
Indian Council of Historical Research 330, 337, 339, 341, 362
Indian National Congress 18, 26, 37, 42, 50, 64, 70, 73-4, 103, 126, 149, 152, 160, 166, 198, 211, 213, 220, 227-8, 239-40, 272, 288, 304, 328, 393, 467, 501, 517, 519, 524
  All-India Congress Committee 75-6, 467
  Congress Seva Dal 186, 188
  Indian National Trade Union Congress 320
  Karachi Congress (1931) 76
  Working Committee 67, 467
Indira Gandhi National Centre for the Arts 340, 350
Intelligence Bureau 89
International Monetary Fund 523
Iqbal, Muhammad 15
Irani, Smriti 326, 535
Iyengar, H.V.R. 127, 420, 457, 459-61, 463-5
Iyer, Shekhar 304, 321

Jackson, A.T.M. 93
Jadhav, M.H. 215
Jaffrelot, Christophe 64, 129, 132-4, 151-2, 157, 177, 182, 211, 226, 248, 359-60, 409, 411-2
Jain, Girilal 170, 238, 249
Jain, Meenakshi 338
Jaitley, Arun 254-5, 303, 312, 316, 318-9, 325-6, 405
Jaitley, DIG B.B.L. 116, 381
Jamaat-e-Islami 187
Jamiat Ulema-e-Hind 393
Janata Dal 235, 246
Janata Dal (United) 324
Janata Party 26, 52, 149, 159, 172, 175, 178, 183, 185-6, 188-90, 192-7, 199-206, 209-10, 219-21, 232, 236, 239, 282, 507, 513-6, 519, 521-2
Jatti, B.D. 186
Javadekar, Prakash 339, 352
Jawaharlal Nehru University 337, 376
Jayakar, M.R. 91, 382
Jesus Christ 45-6, 491, 497
Jethmalani, Ram 256
Jha, Prabhat 323
Jinnah, Mohammed Ali 21-2, 26, 37, 40, 74, 82, 138, 149, 283-6, 291-2, 299, 319
Joshi, Ajay 274
Joshi, Appaji 61
Joshi, Jagannath Rao 151
Joshi, Morpant 61
Joshi, Murli Manohar 26, 41, 80, 229, 244, 246-7, 250, 289, 292, 303, 312, 326, 341, 370
Joshi, Prasoon 340
Joshi, Sanjay 203, 275, 285, 287, 292, 296, 303, 308, 312, 322-3
Joshi, S.M. 180, 183
Joshi, Srikant 265
Joshi, Subhadra 496
Joshi, Suresh aka Bhaiyyaji 265, 289, 292, 318, 322, 324-5, 327, 331, 367, 368-71
Joshi, Yadava Rao 198, 224, 408, 499

Kakodkar, Anil 335, 341
Kalaiyarasan A. 359
Kalburgi, M.M. 321, 344, 356
Kale, M.N. 469
Kalhana 23
Kamath, H.V. 78
Kamath, Vasudeo 340
Kamdar, Manoharkant Dayalji 416-7, 420, 424, 499
Kanchi Shankaracharya 279, 305
Kannan, K.C. 331
Kant, Krishna 192
Kanungo, Pralay 54, 61-2, 71, 84, 152, 224, 226, 250, 252, 254, 408
Kapoor, Coomi 219
Kapur, Justice Jeevan Lal 121, 123
  Kapur Commission 121-3
Karkare, Vishnu 122, 123
Kasar, Appa Ramchandra 122-3
Kasuri, Khurshid Mahmud 349
Katiyar, Vinay 223, 243, 250, 304, 409, 411
Katju, Manjari 169, 407
Keer, Dhananjay 96, 123
Kelkar, Rao Bahadur 61

INDEX

Kelkar, Vinayak 58
Kendriya Artha Vibhag. *See* Rashtriya Swayamsevak Sangh
Kendriya Karyakari Mandal. *See* Rashtriya Swayamsevak Sangh
Kesari, Venkatesh 266
Ketkar, G.V. 69
Ketkar, Suresh 265
Ketkar, S.V. 103, 507
Khan, Aamir 347
Khan, Azimullah 16
Khandelwal, Pyarelal 292
Khan, Maulana Wahiduddin 28
Khan, Shah Rukh 347, 354
Khan, Syed Ahmed 14, 20
Khapre, Shubhangi 334
Khare, Justice V.N. 404, 530
Khattar, Manohar Lal 347
Kher, Atma Govind 117, 128-9, 381
Khurana, Madanlal 292-3, 304
Khurshid, Salman 249
Kidwai, Rafi Ahmad 117, 381
Kishore, Giriraj 43, 252-3, 268
Kripalani, J.B. 78, 183, 516
Krishnamurthi, K. Jana 271, 292
Kshirsagar, Pandurang Baliram 417
Kulkarni, Madhubhai 332
Kulkarni, Sudheendra 288-92, 349
Kulkarni, Sunil 331
Kumar, Anand 201
Kumar, Ananth 319, 326
Kumar, Ashwini 292
Kumar, Indresh 286, 315, 363
Kumar, Nitish 324, 344

Lal, Harmohan 214
Lalit, Justice Uday Umesh 32
Lal, Makhan 308, 340, 535
Lal, Ram 203, 312, 326, 355
Lal, Shankar 332
Lankesh, Gauri 320-1, 356
Lastic, Alan de 41
Limaye, Madhu 175, 178, 180, 182, 184, 513
Linlithgow, Viceroy Lord 80, 91
Lipton, Prof. Sara 404
Lohia, Ram Manohar 173, 361
Lok Sangharsh Committee 177
Lokur, Justice B.N. 31

MacKinnon, Catharine A. 384
Madhavan, Sethu 332
Madhav, Ram 203, 277-9, 286, 292, 297, 313, 337, 340
Madhok, Balraj 52, 129, 131-3, 136, 151, 153, 156, 165-9, 219, 259, 297, 310, 393, 405
Madon, Justice D.P. 176, 395, 399
Mahajan, Meher Chand 109
Mahajan, Pramod 250, 256, 286-8, 303
Maheshwari, Srikrishna 332
Mahmud of Ghazni 17, 23-4, 521
Maitra, Pandit Lakshmi Kanta 78
Maitra, Pradip Kumar 228, 322, 330, 351
Majlis-e-Ittehadul Muslimeen 32
Malaviya, Madan Mohan 21-2, 25, 53, 59, 63, 69-71, 74, 106, 220, 222, 379
Malhotra, Inder 160
Malik, Lt. General N.S. 316
Malik, Yogendra K. 243, 412
Malkani, K.R. 228, 380-1, 390
Manakchand, Motilal (Pratap Seth) 382
Mandika, S.M. 423
Mani, A.D. 484
Mani, Buddha Rashmi 338
Mankekar, D.R. 170
Mann, Simranjit Singh 262
Mansingh, Sonal 340
Markham, James M. 211
Masani, M.R. 156
Mathur, J.P. 182, 229, 308-9
Mathur, O.P. 124
Mayaram, Shail 242
Mazumdar, Babu Amvica Charan 74
McNaughton, A.G. 148
Mehrotra, Santosh 361
Mehta, Asoka 14-5, 185
Mehta, Pherozeshah 166
Mill, James 22
Mishra, Brajesh 278
Mishra, Kaushal Kishore 361
Mishra, Lalit Narayan 489, 496
Mishra, Pandit Dwarka Prasad 455
Mishra, Prasanna 279
Mishra, Vandita 407-8
Misra, Lokanath 78
Misra, Nripendra 337
Misra, Prof. Mahesh Dutt 387
Mitra, Chandan 337
Modak, Ashok 229
Modi, Narendra 26, 33-4, 41, 52, 76, 82, 102, 107, 159, 216-7, 222, 226, 255, 268, 269-73, 275, 277-8, 280, 282, 285,

289-90, 295-6, 301, 304, 308, 310-7, 319, 321-8, 330-4, 336-7, 339-54, 356-68, 370, 372, 375, 383, 390, 404-5, 415, 531-5
Modi, Sushil Kumar 405
Mofreel, Krishnaji Neelkanth 58
Mohani, Hasrat 21, 69, 83
Mohan, Surendra 154, 183, 387
Mookerjee, Syama Prasad 56, 80-3, 85, 87, 91, 93, 100, 108, 111-4, 118-9, 126, 129, 131-6, 138-41, 143-9, 151, 158, 160-1, 165, 169, 204
  Indian Nationalism 165
Moonje, B.S. 54, 58, 61-2, 71, 87-9, 91, 382-3
Mukerji, Lt. Colonel U.N. 70
Mukherjee, Mridula 534
Mukherjee, Pranab 375
Mukherjee, Saradindu 337
Mukherji, Anahita 334-6
Muktanand, Swami 41, 411
Mukundan 278
Mukund, Gopal 58
Muley, Madhav Rao 183, 188, 190, 194, 369, 499, 513-4
Munshi, K.M. 41, 219, 407
Musafir, Giani Gurmukh Singh 387
Musharraf, Pervez 272
Muslim League 21, 26, 37, 40, 74, 77-8, 84, 91, 128, 132, 138, 171, 332, 528
Muslim Rashtriya Manch. *See* Rashtriya Swayamsevak Sangh
Mussolini, Benito 86-9, 92, 247, 329, 382

Nagarvala, Jamshed 120, 123
Naidu, Venkaiah 253, 275, 277, 292, 298, 303, 319, 326, 350
Naim, Prof. C.M. 21, 319
Nair, G. Madhavan 335
Nair, N.J. 342
Nair, Ravi 411
Nalanda University 341, 345, 362
Nambath, Suresh 254
Namboodiripad, E.M.S. 234-5
Nandy, Ashis 242
Naoroji, Dadabhai 73, 166, 332
Naqvi, Saeed 196
Narain, Justice Jitendra 397
Narain, Raj 515-6
Narain, Yogendra 316
Narayanan, K.R. 267, 413
Narayan, Badri 376
Narayan, Jayaprakash 172-5, 177-8, 180, 182-3, 186, 188-90, 192-4, 201-2, 204-5, 217, 219, 249, 289, 393, 405, 492, 507, 513-6
Narayan, Shovana 340
Nath, Mahant Digbijoy 119
National Book Trust 108, 337, 341, 345
National Democratic Alliance 226, 285, 298, 316, 324, 355, 357
National Front 234-5, 239-41
Nayar, Kuldip 170, 215
Nayar, Sushila 387
NCERT 338, 535
Neelima, Kota 288
Nehru, Arun 222
Nehru, Jawaharlal 34, 40, 48-50, 63, 73, 78, 91, 108-14, 118, 124-6, 128-9, 131-2, 137-8, 140-1, 143, 145-9, 160-1, 167, 169, 171, 207, 219-20, 233, 238-9, 319, 328, 332-3, 337, 340, 342-3, 345, 349, 362, 364-5, 376, 390, 393, 443-5, 447-9, 451, 461, 468, 477, 486, 491, 500, 502, 519, 520, 523
  The Discovery of India 233
Nehru, Motilal 63, 219-20, 382
Neotia, Harsh 340
Nijalingappa, S. 183
Niranjan Teerth, Swami 410
Nischalananda Saraswati, Swami 362
NITI Aayog 337
Nritya Gopal Das, Mahant 411
Nye, Sir Archibald 381

Oak, Vasant Rao 132
O'Brien, Derek 366
Opera Nazionale Balilla 87-9
Owaisi, Asaduddin 32

Pachauri, Pankaj 235
Padia, Chandrakala 362
Pai, A.V. 125, 447
Palekar, Narhar 58
Panashikar, Mukunda Rao 332
Pandey, Hari Om 353
Pandey, K.M. (Faizabad district judge) 209
Pandey, Ram Pyare 278
Pandey, Umesh Chandra 208
Pandit, Anand 306
Pandit, Uttamrao 183
Pandya, Haren 322-3
Panikkar, K.N. 338

Pani, Subas 340
Pansare, Govind 321, 344
Pant, Govind Ballabh 110, 116-7, 381-2
Paramhans, Ramchandra 411
Paranjape, Purushottham 332
Paranjpe, L.V. 58
Parashar, Sachin 363
Parchure, P.S. 120
Parikh, G.G. 178, 202
Paripoornan, Justice K.S. 27, 29
Parmanand, Bhai 62
Parrikar, Manohar 352
Patel, Arvindbhai 273
Patel, Babubhai 198
Patel, H.M. 183, 393
Patel, Jaidipbhai 273
Patel, Keshubhai 322-3
Patel, Sardar Vallabhbhai 76, 108, 118, 124, 148-9, 166, 332, 416, 420, 440-1, 443, 445, 452, 454-7, 459, 468, 473, 477, 479, 483, 485-6, 491, 500, 502, 504, 533
Pathak, Vikas 322, 337, 371, 414
Patil, U.L. 185
Pavitra Hindustan Kazhagam 256
Pawar, Sharad 32, 358
Pillai, G.K. 340
Pingle, Moropant 237, 265
Powayya, Jiban Singh 253
Prabhu, Suresh 337
Pragya, Sadhvi 320
Praja Parishad (Jammu) 140-7, 151
Praja Socialist Party 218
Prakash, Admiral Arun 316
Prakash, A. Surya 337, 340
Prasad, Jagdish 250, 331
Prophet Muhammad 35, 45-6
Punj, Balbir 326

Radhakrishnan, Sarvepalli 511
Raghavan, R.K. 404
Rai, Lala Lajpat 18-21, 25, 53, 57, 68-71, 93, 97, 106, 219, 222, 379
  The Problem of National Education 20
Rai, Ram Bahadur 350, 406
Rai, Vijay Kumar 362
Rajagopalachari, C. 25
Ramachandran, A. 340
Ramachandran, Raju 404
Ramachandran, Smriti Kak 373
Ramamurthi, M.K. 393
Ramaseshan, Radhika 283, 288, 319, 322, 343
Ramaswamy, Justice K. 27, 29
Ram, Charat 108
Ramdev, Baba 322
Ram, Jagjivan 194-5, 198, 515
Ram, Munshi. *See* Shraddhanand, Swami
Ram, N. 315
Ram Rajya Parishad 141
Ranade, Eknath 126-7, 337, 406, 499
Ranjan, Swata 331
Rao, Aravinda 340
Rao, Justice L. Nageswara 31
Rao, Muralidhar 326
Rao, N.T. Rama 239
Rao, P.V. Narasimha 240, 246-7, 249
Rao, Suryanarayan 265
Rao, Yellapragada Sudarshan 341, 362
Rashid, Engineer 349
Rashtra Seva Dal 188, 513
Rashtriya Janata Dal 324
Rashtriya Seva Bharati. *See* Rashtriya Swayamsevak Sangh
Rashtriya Sevika Samiti. *See* Rashtriya Swayamsevak Sangh
Rashtriya Shaikshik Mahasangh. *See* Rashtriya Swayamsevak Sangh
Rashtriya Sikh Sangat. *See* Rashtriya Swayamsevak Sangh
Rashtriya Swayamsevak Sangh
  Akhil Bharatiya Itihas Sankalan Yojana 264, 339
  Akhil Bharatiya Karyakari Mandal 86, 117, 148-9, 199-200, 308, 408, 433-5, 437, 439, 468, 483, 503
    Karnataka Prantiya Karyakari Mandal 419
    Prantiya Karyakari Mandals 434, 436-7
      Subordinate Karyakari Mandals 437-9
  Akhil Bharatiya Pratinidhi Sabha 86, 161, 187-8, 199-200, 223, 231, 256-7, 259, 265, 269, 276, 308, 317, 330-1, 354, 367-8, 370-1, 434-5, 438-9, 467-8, 503
    Prantiya Pratinidhi Sabha 434, 437-8, 467-8
  as Jagadguru 55, 57, 103, 164, 238, 316, 330, 335, 343
  as Vishwaguru 330, 365
  Bharatiya Kisan Sangh 319-20, 322, 370
  Bharatiya Mazdoor Sangh 183, 188-9, 215, 224, 229, 265, 274, 308, 319-20, 331, 367, 370, 399, 408, 414, 514

Bharatiya Shikshan Mandal 264, 339
Ekal Vidyalaya 329
Hindu Swayamsevak Sangh 215, 265, 301-2, 335, 421
Kendriya Artha Vibhag 419
Kendriya Karyakari Mandal. *See* Akhil Bharatiya Karyakari Mandal
Muslim Rashtriya Manch 315
Rashtriya Seva Bharati 320, 329
Rashtriya Sevika Samiti 265, 343, 514
Rashtriya Shaikshik Mahasangh 264, 339
Rashtriya Sikh Sangat 262, 265
Suruchi Prakashan 55, 72, 150, 264, 307, 343
Swadeshi Jagran Manch 43, 253, 274-5, 308, 331, 370, 378
tabulation of members of Sangh parivar 264-5
Vanavasi Kalyan Ashram 215, 264, 286, 319-20, 329, 414
Vijnana Bharati 265, 335, 339
Vishwa Sangh Shivir (2005) 301
Vivekananda Kendra 215, 265, 329, 337
Vivekananda International Foundation 337
Rashtriya Utsav Mandal 395, 396
Rebello, Mabel 42
Reddy, G.K. 205
Reddy, G. Sanjeeva 320
Reddy, Justice P. Jaganmohan 176, 386, 393
Commission on the Ahmedabad disturbances of 1969 386
Reddy, Venugopal 278
Ribeiro, Julio 269, 348
Rithambara, Sadhvi 250
Rizvi, S.Q. 397
Roy, B.C. 146-7
Roy, Champat 250
Roy, Pran Nath 87
Rudolph, Lloyd I. 48, 225, 519
Rudolph, Susanne Hoeber 48, 519
Rudy, Rajiv Pratap 326

Sachidanand 193
Sagar, Ramanand 224
Sahasrabhojne, Ramchandra 265
Sahasrabudhe, P.C. 86, 91
Sahay, Govind
'Nazi Technique and the RSS' 447
Sahay, Subodh Kant 244
Sakshi Maharaj, Swami 249, 345, 365, 412
Salve, Harish 531
Samajwadi Party 304, 354
Samyukta Socialist Party 393
Samyukta Vidhayak Dal 152, 235
Sanatan Sanstha 345
Sanjevi, D.J. 118
Sanskar Bharati 215
Sapre, Sadanand Damodar 343
Pratyek Rashtrabhakta Ka Sapna: Akhand Bharat 343
Sapru, Tej Bahadur 91
Saraswati, Dayanand 64, 71
Satyartha Prakash 64
Saraswati, Yoganand 249, 412
Sarkar, Sonia 361
Sarkar, Tanika 67-8
Sastry, T.R.V. 127, 442, 480, 484, 502
Satish, V. 278
Savarkar, Babarao G.D. 58, 62, 96, 100
Rashtra Meemansa 96, 100, 307
Savarkar, Vinayak Damodar 15-9, 22, 25, 27-8, 43, 54, 57-8, 61-2, 64, 69-70, 80-2, 87-91, 93-6, 98-102, 104, 106, 113, 116, 118-23, 131-2, 138, 149-50, 152, 165, 169, 186, 192, 198, 203, 245, 247, 307, 361, 382, 386
Hindutva: Who Is a Hindu? 18, 22, 25, 27, 43, 54, 57, 62, 96, 123, 165, 169
mercy petitions 93-5
The Indian War of Independence of 1857 15
Save, Moreshwar 250
Sawhney, Lt. General R.K. 316
Sayani, R.M. 74
Scindia, Vasundhara Raje 315
Scindia, Vijaya Raje 218, 242, 250
Sen, Amartya 340, 345
Sen, Ashoke 348
Seshadri, H.V. 224, 231, 247, 249, 253, 256-7, 259, 265, 369, 408
Seshan, M. 340
Sethumadhavan, A. 341
Seva Bharati 215
Shah, Amit 326, 328, 330, 339, 343, 350, 353-4, 363, 367, 374
Shah Bano 207, 236
Shah, Chetan 274
Shah, Naseeruddin 347
Shah, Prof. K.T. 78
Sharif, Jaffer 249
Sharma, Baldev Bhai 337
Sharma, B.L. 250

Sharma, BSF Director General K.K. 366
Sharma, Din Dayal 139
Sharma, Jyotirmaya 294
Sharma, Mahesh 340
Sharma, Mahesh (Culture Minister) 345
Sharma, Mauli Chandra 52, 131, 135-6, 139, 151, 157, 266, 297, 420, 466
Shastri, Lal Bahadur 112, 160
Shastri, Sripati 265
Shauq, Sumat Prakash 38
Shekhar, Chandra 197, 199-200, 205, 237, 240, 245, 516
Shekhawat, Bhairon Singh 151, 252
Shevgaonkar, Raghunath 341
Shiromani Akali Dal 153, 217
Shiromani Akali Dal (Amritsar) 262
Shiromani Gurdwara Prabandhak Committee 43
Shiv Sena 230, 234, 250, 388, 396, 523
Shourie, Arun 316
Shraddhanand, Swami 70-1
Shukla, Ravi Shankar 266, 454, 471
Simha, Siddhanath 332
Singhal, Ashok 211, 223-4, 228, 244, 247-8, 250, 257, 268, 279-80, 284, 290, 329, 408
Singhal, B.P. 248
Singh, Charan 124, 183-5, 193, 196, 219, 226, 387, 515-7
Singh, Dara alias Rabindra Pal Singh 414
Singh, Digvijaya 350
Singh, Gulab 144
Singh, Hari 109, 147, 261
Singh, Jagmohan 262
Singh, Jaswant 238, 248, 252, 286, 289, 292, 318-9, 333
Jinnah: India, Partition, Independence 319
Singh, Justice N.P. 27
Singh, Kalyan 246, 252, 264
Singh, Kanwarpal 262
Singh, Karan 145, 210-1
Singh, K.P. 316
Singh, Mulayam 527
Singh, Rajendra 41-2, 193-4, 196-7, 199-200, 213-4, 217, 224, 227, 229, 240, 247, 252-3, 256-9, 265, 307, 309, 369-70, 391, 408, 416, 421, 499, 512
Singh, Rajnath 256, 294-5, 300, 302, 304, 306, 309, 312, 314, 316, 318, 321, 325-6, 373
Singh, Raman 315
Singh, Sudan 278
Singh, Surendra 353, 365
Singh, V.B. 208, 243, 405, 412
Singh, Vir Bahadur 208, 243, 405, 412
Singh, V.P. 228, 239, 240-1, 522-4
Sinha, Jayant 337
Sinha, Justice Jagmohan Lal 177
Sinha, Rakesh 307
Sinha, Justice Ram Chandra Prasad 402
Sinha, Shakti 340
Sinha, Yashwant 341-2
Sitaram, Govind 58
Sitharaman, Nirmala 337
Smith, Donald Eugene 34, 43, 232
India as a Secular State 34, 126, 161, 234, 387-8
Smith, Wilfred Cantwell 48
Modernisation of a Traditional Society 48-9
Sofi, Irfan Ahmad 361
Somaya, Kirit 306
Sonarkar, Baburao 58
Soni, Bapusaheb 136, 151
Soni, Suresh 265, 278, 292, 318, 324, 327, 331, 369
Sonwalkar, Prasun 246
Sreekumar, R.B. 404
Sri Ram Sene 344
Srivastava, Jagdish Prasad 250
Staines, Graham Stewart 413
Subramaniam, Gopal 414
Subramaniam, Ramesh 335
Subramaniam, Vidya 313
Sudarshan, Kuppalli Sitaramayya 54-5, 235, 250, 252-4, 258-9, 261-4, 271, 276-80, 285-6, 288, 290, 295, 301, 303, 305-8, 311, 315, 317-8, 324, 333, 342, 356, 362
Sunderlal, Pandit 35
The Gita and the Quran 35
Sureshanand, Swami 249, 412
Suruchi Prakashan. *See* Rashtriya Swayamsevak Sangh
Swadeshi Jagran Manch. *See* Rashtriya Swayamsevak Sangh
Swamy, Subramanian 246, 259
Swaraj, Sushma 25, 254, 286, 292, 303, 318-9, 321, 325-6, 363-4, 390
Swarup, Ram 43-4, 46, 48
Buddhism vis-à-vis Hinduism 46
Hinduism vis-à-vis Christianity and Islam 43, 46

Hindu-Sikh Relationship 44, 46
Hindu View of Christianity and Islam 43, 46
Swatantra Party 156, 219

Tagore, Rabindranath 87
Tambe, S.B. 61
Tarun Hindu Sabha 62
Tata, J.R.D. 219
Telang, Bapurao 58
Telugu Desam Party 235
Thackeray, Bal 238, 396
Thakkar, B.B. 58
Thakre, Kushabhau 203, 253, 257-9
Thakur, Chief Justice T.S. 30-1, 33
Thakur, C.P. 326
Thapar, Romila 22-4, 349, 522
Thengadi, Dattopant 182-3, 224, 378, 408, 499
Tilak, Bal Gangadhar 21, 25-6, 71, 74, 88, 166-7, 222, 421, 501, 507, 520
Tipnis, Air Chief Marshal A.Y. 316
Tipu Sultan 15
Tiwari, Ravish 326, 377
Togadia, Praveen 279-80, 304, 329-30, 346
Tohra, G.S. 43
Tripathi, Balkrishna 332
Tripathi, Girish Chandra 362
Trivedi, Dillip 274
Trivedi, Dr. Sandip 341
Trivedy, Shikha 242
Tucci, Giuseppe 87
Tyabji, Badruddin 26, 73, 332
Tyagi, O.P. 183-5, 193, 211
Tyagi, Yogesh 363

U.N. Commission for India and Pakistan 147
United Christians' Forum for Human Rights 42
United Nations University World Institute for Development Economics Research 351
United Progressive Alliance 316, 325, 339, 360
U.N. Sub-Commission on the Prevention of Discrimination and the Protection of Minorities 26
Upadhyaya, Deen Dayal 55, 135-6, 141, 151-6, 160-1, 173, 203-4, 218-9, 221, 245, 252, 308-9, 342-3, 362-4, 391, 525
death of 153
Integral Humanism 152
U.S. Commission for International Religious Freedom 351

Vaidya, Anna 58
Vaidya, Guru Dutt 139
Vaidya, M.S. 420-1, 499, 505, 507-8, 510-2
Vaidya, Manmohan 331
Vaidya, M.G. aka Baburao 199, 203, 257-8, 265, 286, 293-4, 304, 307, 318, 330-1
Vajpayee, Atal Bihari 25, 52, 151, 195, 230, 282, 284, 298, 322, 326, 340, 515, 525, 533
Hindu Tan-man Hindu Jeevan 525, 527
Vamdeo, Acharya 41, 411
Vanarajan, R. 332
Vanavasi Kalyan Ashram. *See* Rashtriya Swayamsevak Sangh
Varma, Subodh 357
Vatsyayan, Kapila 340
Vedantham, Major T.R. 46
Veer, Peter van der 241-2
Velingkar, Subhash 353
Venkatachaliah, Chief Justice M.N. 248
Venkataswami, Justice K. 27
Venugopal, Justice P. 400
Verma, Justice J.S. 27-8, 31
Verniers, Gilles 360
Vijnana Bharati. *See* Rashtriya Swayamsevak Sangh
Vincent, Sir William 94
Virat Hindu Samaj 210-1
Virat Hindu Sammelan (2014) 329
Vir, Raghavendra 265
Vishwa Hindu Parishad 41-3, 48, 160, 169-70, 207-8, 214-5, 218, 223-6, 229, 231, 237, 240-4, 247-50, 252-3, 256-7, 265, 268-71, 273-6, 279-80, 284-6, 289-90, 298, 307-8, 310, 323, 327, 329, 335, 346, 367-8, 370, 377, 385-6, 389-90, 402, 405, 407-15, 424, 514, 522, 530, 535
Achar Samhita 409
Durga Vahini 414
Kendriya Margdarshak Mandal 286
Vishwanath 265
Vishwanath, Advocate 58
Vishwesha Teerth, Swami 212, 411
Vithayathil, Justice Joseph 396
Vivekananda Kendra. *See* Rashtriya Swayamsevak Sangh
Vivekananda, Swami 71

Vohra, Pankaj 285, 290
Voice of India 48, 391
Vyas, Neena 269, 279, 287, 293, 310, 319

Wadhwa, Justice D.P. 414
Waldron, Jeremy 383-4
Wavell, Viceroy Lord 171
Weiner, Myron 132, 138, 149
World Bank 523
Wylie, Curzon 93

Yadav, J.P. 370
Yadav, Laloo Prasad 240, 253, 306, 324, 411, 527
Yadav, Ram Naresh 517
Yadav, Shyamlal 326, 368
Yagnik, Achyut 242
Yagnik, Viraj 340
Yashwant, Narayan 58
Yoganand Saraswati, Swami 249, 411, 412

Zadaphia, Gordhan 270, 273
Zavos, John 391
Zetland, Secretary of State for India Lord 80